The Collected Papers of

Sherlock

Holmes

Volume I - Tales

The Papers of Sherlock Holmes

and

Sherlock Holmes and

A Quantity of Debt

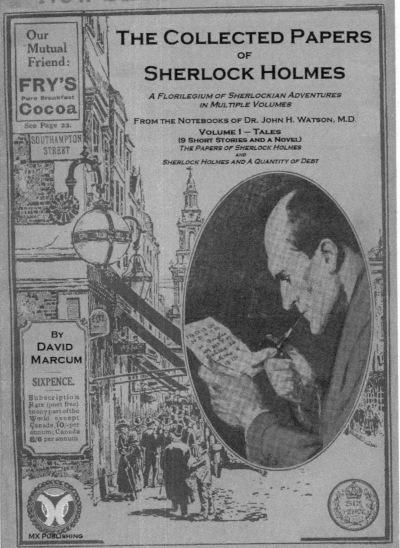

New Sherlock Holmes

SOUTHAMPTON
STREET

THE COLLECTED PAPERS
OF
SHERLOCK HOLMES

*A Florilegium of Sherlockian Adventures
in Multiple Volumes*

From the Notebooks of Dr. John H. Watson, M.D.

Volume I – Tales
(9 Short Stories and a Novel)
The Papers of Sherlock Holmes
and
Sherlock Holmes and a Quantity of Debt

By
DAVID
MARCUM

MX PUBLISHING

Published by MX Publishing, 335 Princess Park Manor, London, England.

"Watson's Descendants" ©2021 by Nicholas Meyer. All Rights Reserved. First publication, original to this collection. Printed by permission of the author.

ISBN Hardback 978-1-78705-899-6
ISBN Paperback 978-1-78705-900-9
AUK ePub ISBN 978-1-78705-901-6
AUK PDF ISBN 978-1-78705-902-3

Published by
MX Publishing
335 Princess Park Manor, Royal Drive,
London, N11 3GX
www.mxpublishing.com

David Marcum can be reached at:
thepapersofsherlockholmes@gmail.com

Cover design by Brian Belanger
www.belangerbooks.com and *www.redbubble.com/people/zhahadun*

Internal illustrations by Sidney Paget

CONTENTS

Foreword

Tales

The Papers of Sherlock Holmes

Sherlock Holmes and A Quantity of Debt

(Continued on the next page . . . .)

Sources

The Papers of Sherlock Holmes was originally published by The Battered Silicon Dispatch Box in 2011, and MX Publishing in 2013 (paperback) and 2014 (paperback).

Sherlock Holmes and A Quantity of Debt was originally published by MX Publishing in 2013 (hardcover) and 2016 (paperback).

These additional adventures are contained in
Volume II – Records
(5 Short Stories and a Novel)
Sherlock Holmes – Tangled Skeins

Volume III – Accounts
(22 Holmes Adventures)

(Continued on the next page . . . .)

Volume IV – Narratives
(19 Holmes Adventures)
The London Wheel
The Two Different Women
The Coffee House Girl
The Affair of the Regressive Man
The Gordon Square Discovery
The Secret in Lowndes Court
The Sunderland Tragedies
No Good Deed
The Dorset Square Business
The Brook Street Mystery
The Colchester Experiment
The Keeper's Tale
The Village on the Cliff
The Tuefel Murders
The Unpleasant Affair in Clipstone Street
The Lincoln Street Minister
The Tea Merchant's Dilemma
The Dowser's Discovery
The Triangle of Death

Volume V – Chronicles
(20 Holmes Adventures)
The Stolen Relic
The Helverton Inheritance
The Carroun Document
The Reappearance of Mr. James Phillimore
The Keadby Cross
The Rhayader Affair
The Cliddesden Questions
The Affair of the Mother's Return
The Painting in the Parlour
The Two Bullets
The Coombs Contrivance
The True Account of the Bushell Street Killing
The Polmayne Puzzles
The Curious Cardboard Boxes
The Bizarre Affair of the Octagon House
The Peculiar Persecution of Mr. Druitt
The Service for the American Colonel
The Rescue at Ypres
The Problem of the Hindhead Minister
The Edinburgh Bankers

As always, this is for Rebecca and Dan, with all my love

"It's all one case."
by David Marcum

It's all about playing The Game.

That's the bottom-line reason behind these stories. And what is The Game? For those who don't know, it's reading the Sherlock Holmes stories with the firm belief that he and Watson were real historical figures. That Dr. Watson wrote the stories, and Sir Arthur Conan Doyle was his Literary Agent. That Our Heroes actually lived in Baker Street (for a couple of decades, off and on, and not forever) and solved real cases for real people, even if names and places and dates were changed and obfuscated to protect the innocent, or maybe because Watson's handwriting was bad, or because of some hidden agenda that the Literary Agent needed to fulfill.

By acknowledging that Holmes and Watson were real, living, breathing, functioning people, then it's a given that were born, lived, and died. (No magic immortal detectives need apply!) And if they were born and lived and died, then these lives occurred across a fixed period. These men aren't Time Lords who can be picked up and dropped into other eras, or supernaturally gifted monster hunters in a world where such things exist, and they cannot be remade into a plethora of completely different people to fit whatever agenda some current reader needs to project upon them.

No, the stories in these books are about the same Sherlock Holmes and Dr. Watson that one finds in the original Canon – those pitifully few sixty stories that were published from 1887 to 1927.

I've enjoyed the notion that Mr. Sherlock Holmes was real from nearly the same time that I discovered him – as a boy of ten in 1975. Before I'd even read many of the Canonical adventures, I found two other books that reinforced this idea: William S. Baring-Gould's biography *Sherlock Holmes of Baker Street* (1962), with its chronology of the events in Holmes's long and amazing life (1854-1957), and also Nicholas Meyer's *The Seven-Per-Cent Solution* (1974), in which Holmes meets historical figures such as Sigmund Freud. How could one read those books, especially at that age, and not be convinced that Holmes was real?

In the decades that have passed since then, my interest in Mr. Holmes has only grown. While I read and collect a great many volumes about my other "book friends", as my son called them when he was small – and there are a great lot of them besides Holmes – I've always had a special interest in the consulting detective in Baker Street and his Boswell. Since obtaining my first Holmes book in 1975, I've managed to collect and read (and create a massively dense chronology for) literally thousands of traditional Canonical adventures. I've worn a deerstalker as my only hat, all year long and everywhere since age nineteen. I've been able to make three extensive Holmes Pilgrimages to England and Scotland (so far), wherein I pretty much visited only Holmes-related sites. So it was probably inevitable that, in 2008, I started writing Holmes adventures.

I'd always wanted to write, all the way back to when I was eight years old and intensely reading about The Three Investigators and The Hardy Boys. Not satisfied with just the official publications, I wanted more new stories too. I spent quite a few Saturdays of my young boyhood tapping away on my dad's typewriter to create new "books".

As I grew, I dabbled with writing little short pieces, mostly humorous, just intended to make family members laugh, because I loved to write, and it always came easily to me. By the late 1980's, I was a U.S. Federal Investigator employed by an obscure government agency, often sent away from home for long periods, conducting investigations that lasted anywhere from five weeks to three months. Once, when I was sent to Albuquerque for several months to conduct extensive field investigations, I impulsively stopped at a local Walmart and bought a hundred-dollar typewriter and a big pack of paper with some of my *per diem* money. (This was the early 1990's – a long time before personal computers or laptops.)

It was there that I sat down for my first real effort at being a writer – and before I departed I'd finished most of a 600-plus page Ludlumesque novel. (One can get a lot of writing done night after night in a bleak hotel room.) The book was coincidentally about a heroic federal investigator – not unlike myself – who stumbled into a vast Russian-led conspiracy in the American southeast where I'm from. I still have that book – *Civil Servants* – stored in my old federal investigator briefcase, pushed underneath my bed. Its plot is mired in the early 1990's when it was written, locked to the aftermath of the Cold War, but it isn't half bad, and it taught me the valuable lesson that other writers also know: *The secret to writing is to put your butt in the chair and do it.*

After that particular trip, I went back home, finished up what was left of my epic adventure novel, and then settled back into writing the occasional short piece for our private amusement – but it was inevitable that at some point I would write a Holmes adventure.

In the mid-1990's, the federal agency where I'd been employed was abruptly eliminated, a victim of the end of the Cold War and a move to reduce the size of government. (After all, the higher-up wise men thought,

2

who needs security now? We won!) Over the next few years, I went back to school and obtained a second degree in Civil Engineering. Then, in 2008 at the start of the Great Recession, I was unexpectedly laid off from my engineering job. With time on my hands, and a desire to try my hand at Sherlockian pastichery, I began writing each morning after the daily job searching was finished.

I ended up with nine of Holmes pastiches, written over several weeks, and then . . . I did nothing with them. That's right. Simply satisfied that I'd written them and that they existed, I put them in a binder labeled *The Papers of Sherlock Holmes* and shelved them with the rest of my Holmes Collection, happy with my secret collector's item.

But eventually I began to wish for other Sherlockians to see them. I shared one with a Sherlockian friend here and another one there, and the response was very positive. Finally I became bolder and wanted more people to see them, asking myself: *Why not put them in a real book of my own?*

I communicated about it with a Sherlockian publisher from whom I'd bought books in the past. He immediately offered to publish *The Papers*, and after a great deal of back-and-forth, my first book eventually appeared. For those who have had that experience – Opening the newly delivered carton to see *your book!* – there is nothing like it. It's a satisfaction that cannot easily be described.

That was in 2011. Over the next couple of years, I became aware of MX Publishing. I saw that an acquaintance of mine who'd also had his first book published with the same original publisher as mine had switched to MX, and I reached out to him. He informed me that he was happy to have switched to MX. With that in mind, I sent an email to Steve Emecz, Sherlockian Publisher Extraordinaire – and that was truly life-changing and improving decision.

In 2013, Steve republished my first book, *The Papers of Sherlock Holmes*, and he made the whole experience so painless that I set about writing a Holmes novel, *Sherlock Holmes and A Quantity of Debt*. That same fall, I was making my long-planned first Holmes Pilgrimage to London, and Steve arranged for me to have a book-signing in The Sherlock Holmes Hotel in Baker Street, where I was staying (when not traveling about to Dartmoor, the Sussex Coast, Edinburgh, and other locations). I was able to meet Steve for the first time on that trip, and found him to be one of the nicest, most supportive, and most thoughtful people around – and that hasn't changed a bit.

Jump ahead a little bit: In early 2015, I woke up early from a dream in which I'd edited a Holmes anthology. Instead of rolling over and forgetting the idea, I arose and started thinking about authors whom I admired and that I might want to invite to write stories. I ran the idea by Steve, and he was willing to publish it, so I began sending invitations. I hoped that I might get a dozen stories (at best) for a modest paperback volume. Fearing a lack of response, I kept sending invitations to everyone that I could think of – and then, amazingly, people started signing up. New Sherlock Holmes stories started to arrive in my email in-box – which quickly becomes addictive. More and more authors heard about it – some that I didn't even know about yet – and before we knew it, the little idea had grown into a three-volume hardcover behemoth of over 60 new Holmes stories – *Parts I, II,* and *III* of *The MX Book of New Sherlock Holmes Stories*, the largest collection of its kind ever produced to that point.

Early on, Steve and I had decided that the royalties from the project would go to support the Stepping Stones School for special needs children, located at Undershaw, one of Sir Arthur Conan Doyle's former homes. The books were a smashing success and received a lot of attention, and I was able to go to London in the fall of 2015 for the release party – what turned out to be Holmes Pilgrimage No. 2. There I was able to meet a number of the contributing authors in person – and to my everlasting regret, I was so thrilled that I barely remembered to take any photos!

After I returned home, I began to receive more emails, now asking when the next book was planned – *Good grief! A next book?!?* – and also stating that many authors (both returning and new) wanted to contribute.

I'd had no plans to do any more books, thinking that the first three were lightning in a bottle that couldn't be recaptured . . . but then I realized that the heavy-lifting in terms of decision-making and set-up and formatting and process-building had already occurred, so Steve and I decided to keep going. (I think I said to him "Let's do one more . . . .")

Part IV came out in the spring of 2016 – and after that, more people kept sending stories for *the next books* and wanting to join the party. We came up with the plan to have yearly books. But we received so many stories that it grew to twice a year. We now have an un-themed spring collection – the yearly *Annual* – and also a fall collection with a specific theme, such as Christmas adventures, seemingly impossible crimes, Untold Cases, etc. As more and more stories kept rolling in, it became necessary for each season's particular set to grow to multiple simultaneously published volumes. That's how, in just a few short years, we're now up to *Parts XXVIII, XXIX,* and *XXX* (to be published in Fall 2021), and as I write this, I'm already receiving stories for the *Spring 2022 Annual, Part XXXI* (and *XXXII* and *XXXIII* too . . . ?)

4

So far the books have raised over $85,000 for the school, and it's my hope and expectation that they'll go over $100,000 within the next few months of writing this foreword.

As part of editing these books, I couldn't let them pass by without adding my own stories – editor's prerogative. Thus, that helped to motivate me to sit my butt in the chair and write more about Mr. Holmes. By way of these books, I've met some really incredible people, including the incomparable Belanger Brothers, Derrick and Brian. Derrick initially contributed short stories, while Brian – a truly gifted artist – became the MX cover artist after the original artist passed away.

At one point, the two Belangers wrote a series of Holmes books for children. Eventually they formed Belanger Books – another amazing Sherlockian publishing venture. Between MX and Belanger Books – both of which cooperate beautifully with one another – the Sherlockian publishing field is amazingly well covered, providing an opportunity for so many people to be Sherlockian pasticheurs when they would otherwise be excluded by those who happily and aggressively seek to squash that aspect of the Sherlockian experience.

In 2016, the Belangers asked me to assemble and edit a Holmes story collection for them. I did, and as it also consisted of traditional and Canonical adventures, and had many of the same authors as in the MX anthologies, I formatted it the same way. After that, I edited another one for them, and another, and those also grew to simultaneously published multiple volumes. This extra editing also served to motivate me to write more Holmes stories for each of those collections as well – because I didn't want those trains leaving without me being on them.

From there, I began to receive invitations to write still more stories for other editors' anthologies and magazines. Along the way I published a couple more of my own books – *Sherlock Holmes – Tangled Skeins* (2015) and *Sherlock Holmes and The Eye of Heka* (2021) – but most of my stories that I wrote over those years remained uncollected within the various anthologies and magazines in which they had originally appeared. All along, I stayed too busy with real life and family and my dream job (as a civil engineer working for my home town's public works department), along with writing more stories and editing various books, to take the time to properly collect them all into my own books.

But within the last few months, I looked up and saw that (as of right now) I've now written 86 Holmes pastiches, (along with 20 pastiches about Solar Pons, "The Sherlock Holmes of Baker Street" – but that's another story and another hero.) Thus, the idea of this collection was born.

5

These initial five books of *The Complete Papers* contain 77 of those 86 stories. The others are still in the pipeline to be published elsewhere. Right now (as of mid-September 2021), I also have five more Holmes stories promised to be written for various editors before the end of the year, and all of these, plus whatever I'm able to write in 2022 – with a plan to reach Pastiche No. 100 – will be published in Volume VI of this set in later 2022 . . . *Fingers crossed!*

Many people have sports figures or musicians or actors or (curiously) politicians as heroes. My heroes have always been my book friends and authors – all the way back to when I was eight or nine and wondering about why I couldn't track down satisfying biographical information concerning the brilliant and prolific and mysterious author Franklin W. Dixon. I've always admired writers for what they accomplish and create while spending great chunks of their lives self-imposed isolation – something which I now understand. And at least if I had to set aside all that time to put my butt in the chair, I've been very fortunate that all of these stories almost told themselves. I almost never outline or plan. Instead, when I write – when I find that it's time for another story – I simply open a blank Word document on the computer and then wait for Watson to begin whispering to me. It's scary, but I trust the process now, and when it works – and it always has so far – there's no feeling quite like it.

Through these stories, I've achieved two important personal goals: In my own small way, I've become a writer, and I've also added to *The Great Holmes Tapestry*, a phrase I coined several years ago to describe the massive collection of narratives about the true Holmes and Watson – novels, short stories, radio and television episodes, movies and scripts, comics and fan-fiction, and unpublished manuscripts – that tell the complete and entire course of their lives from beginning to end. The Canon serves as the supporting structure – the wire core of the rope, the heavy steel girders of the skyscraper – but the thousands of traditional post-Canonical pastiches provide essential depth and color, filling in all the spaces around The Canon, and adding important information about The Whole Lives of Our Heroes.

I've long described myself as a missionary for The Church of the Traditional Canonical Holmes, preaching that the bigger picture of both Canon and the traditional pastiches should be seen and supported. This means giving respect and value to additional Holmes adventures, and not just those original sixty because they were the ones that came across the first Literary Agent's desk.

Ross MacDonald – (Real Name: Kenneth Millar, another of my authorial heroes because of his incredible private eye, Lew Archer) – said

"*It's all one case.*" In other words, a *Great Tapestry*. He meant that even though he'd written eighteen Archer novels and a number of short stories from the 1940's to the 1970's, they were never meant to stand alone. They were all part of one overall arching story – Lew Archer's story – spanning across multiple narratives.

It's the same with the Holmes adventures – *all* of them, Canon and traditional pastiche, mine and everyone else's. They fit together to tell the *entire* story of Sherlock Holmes, and with the stories in this collection, I'm incredibly proud to have added my own contribution.

* * * * *

"Of course, I could only stammer out my thanks."
– The unhappy John Hector McFarlane, "The Norwood Builder"

At some point during the foreword-writing for the various MX anthologies, I began to use the quote shown above from Mr. McFarlane in regard to Thank You's. It's fitting – I can only stammer out thanks, and never adequately express how grateful I am for all the help and encouragement I've received over the years in all aspects of my life – not just the writing and editing of Sherlock Holmes stories.

First and foremost, I am always overwhelmed at how incredibly fortunate I am to have my wife and son in my life. In all aspects, my wife – of 33 years as I write this – is the kindest and wisest and most beautiful person inside and out I know, and she has been there throughout with complete support and encouragement when we went through such things as some terrible jobs and the grind of my returning to school. We have pushed through together, and anything that I can ever accomplish I owe to her. And equally amazing is our son, so incredibly funny and smart, and truly an amazing person in every way. I enjoy every minute spent with him, and it only gets better. I love you both, and you are everything to me!

Then there are my parents and sister, who put up with me during those first couple of decades – I probably don't even realize how bad that was for them. My parents did everything to encourage me – music lessons leading to a piano scholarship in college, all the books that I could read, and generally anything to help me grow as a person, so that it never occurred to me that I couldn't do whatever I wanted. And my sister was my best friend then, patiently listening as I rambled about whatever interested me. Even then, she probably heard more about Sherlock Holmes than she'd ever bargained for!

There is a group that exchanges emails with me when we have the time – and time is a valuable commodity for all of us these days! As the

7

years have gone by, we've gotten busier and busier, and I don't get to write as often as I'd like, but I really enjoy catching up whenever we get the chance. These people are all wonderful writers, and I recommend them highly as both friends and authors: Mark Mower, Denis Smith, Tom Turley, Dan Victor, and Marcia Wilson.

Next, I wish to send several huge Thank You's to the following:

- *Steve Emecz* – When I first emailed Steve from out of the blue back in 2013 – *Only eight years? So much in eight years!* – I was interested in MX re-publishing my first book. Even then, as a guy who works to accumulate *all* traditional Sherlockian pastiches, I could see that MX (under Steve's leadership) was *the* fast-rising superstar of the Sherlockian publishing world.

  The re-publication of my first book with MX was an amazing life-changing event for me, leading to writing many more stories and then editing books, along with unexpected Holmes Pilgrimages to England. By way of that first email with Steve, I've had the chance to make some incredible Sherlockian friends and play in the Holmesian Sandbox in ways that I'd never before dreamed possible.

  Through all of it, Steve has been one of the most positive and supportive people that I've ever known. He works far more than a full-time week at his day job, and he still finds time to take care of all aspects of MX Publishing, with the help of his wife Sharon Emecz, and cousin, Timi Emecz. (That's right – MX is just the three of them who get all of this done!)

  Many who just buy books and have a vague idea of how the publishing industry works now might not realize that MX, a non-profit which supports several important charities, consists of simply these three people. Between them, they take care of running the entire business, including the production, marketing, and shipping – all in their precious spare time, in and around their real lives.

  With incredible hard work, they have made MX into a world-wide Sherlockian publishing phenomenon, providing opportunities for authors who would never have them otherwise. There are some like me who return more than once to Watson's Tin Dispatch Box, and there

8

are others who only find one or two stories there – but they get the chance to publish their books, and then they can point with pride at this accomplishment, and how they too have added to The Great Holmes Tapestry.

From the beginning, Steve has let me explore various Sherlockian projects and open up my own personal possibilities in ways that otherwise would have never happened. Thank you, Steve, for every opportunity!

- *Derrick Belanger* and *Brian Belanger* – I first "met" Derrick Belanger when he graciously reviewed one of my early books, and we quickly became friends. Then he interviewed me several times for his online blog, and when I had the idea for the first MX Holmes anthology in 2015, he quickly joined the party and contributed a fine pastiche. From there he's written a number of others, and then he formed Belanger Books with his brother, Brian. It's turned into a Sherlockian powerhouse, working in tandem with MX Publishing, supporting each other to produce more and more wonderful Holmes adventures. I've very grateful to have had this additional opportunity to further contribute to The Great Holmes Tapestry by editing and writing stories for their different anthologies. Derrick continues to write, but he also stays quite busy as a noted aware-winning teacher, husband, and father, as well as running Belanger Books with Brian.

  Over the last few years, my amazement at Brian Belanger's ever-increasing talent has only grown. I initially became acquainted with him when he took over the duties of creating the covers for MX Books following the untimely death of their previous graphic artist. I found Brian to be a great collaborator, very easy-going and stress-free in his approach and willingness to work with authors, and wonderfully creative too. His skills became most apparent to me when he created the cover for my 2017 book, *The Papers of Solar Pons*, which was one of the most striking covers that I've ever seen. Later, when the Belangers and I began reissuing the original Pons books in new editions, and then new Pons anthologies, Brian's similarly themed covers continued to astound me. He truly deserves an award for these.

9

In the meantime, he has become busier and busier, continuing to provide covers for MX Books, and now for Belanger Books as well, along with editing and occasionally writing.

I finally met both Brian and Derrick in person in early (pre-pandemic) 2020 at the annual Sherlock Holmes Birthday Celebration in New York City, and they're just as great in person as they were by way of email. I immediately felt like I'd known them both forever. I cannot express to either one of you just how grateful I am.

- *Roger Johnson* – I had known of Roger for quite a while, having seen his name connected with the "District Messenger" newsletter of *The Sherlock Holmes Society of London Journal.* I could tell, even then, that he represented the finest kind of Sherlockian. When I wrote my first Holmes book, I sent him a copy – out of the blue, as he had no idea who I was – as a thank you, and with the timid and dim spark of a hope that he would review it, because having him do so would mean (to me) that what I had written was legitimized. He did write a wonderful review, and we began to correspond. When I was able to get to England for my first Holmes Pilgrimage in 2013, I made arrangements to meet with Roger and his wonderful wife, Jean Upton, in person, and I discovered that what I'd already known by email was true: They are both the very best people!

Later, in 2015 on Holmes Pilgrimage No. 2, they invited me to stay with them for several days in their home, and that was one of the best parts of all the trips. They gave me tours, they showed me their incredible collection, they let me see life in a real British household and not just from a hotel room, and we had some wonderful conversations along the way. I was able to see them again in 2016, Holmes Pilgrimage No. 3, when we attended the Grand Opening of the Stepping Stones School at Undershaw.

I'm more grateful than I can say that I know Roger. His Sherlockian knowledge is exceptional, as is the work that he does to further the cause of The Master. But even more than that, both Roger and his wonderful wife, Jean, are simply the finest and best, and I'm very lucky to know both of them – even though I don't get to see them nearly as often as I'd like, and especially in these crazy days! In so many ways, Roger, I can't thank you enough, and I can't imagine these books without you.

• *Nicholas Meyer* – I started reading Nick Meyer's Holmes books before I'd even read all of The Canon, and for that I'm eternally grateful. It was through his first two books, *The Seven-Per-Cent Solution* and *The West End Horror* (the latter of which is still one of my favorite pastiches to this very day) that I firmly understood that The Canon wasn't the be-all end-all of Sherlockian story-telling. I obtained Nick's first book as part of a free book give-away at school, and I found the second not long after when my mother took my sister and me to buy school clothes and I spotted it in the mall bookstore. (I sat cross-legged along an out-of-the-way wall in a Sears while my mother and sister shopped and started reading *The West End Horror* straight out of the bag.)

After those first two books, Nick went on to have a very successful career in film. (More about that in a minute.) But he has continued to dip in an out of Sherlockian pastichery with *The Canary Trainer* (1993), *The Adventure of the Peculiar Protocols* (2019), and *The Return of the Pharaoh* (2021). He is a Sherlockian legend, and it's an indisputable fact that the publication in 1974 of *The Seven-Per-Cent Solution* – a pastiche, mind you! – was the beginning of the Sherlockian Golden Age when has grown and grown, and has never stopped, all the way to today.

If it was just that, Sherlockians – and especially pasticheurs – would owe him an unpayable debt. But then there's *Star Trek*, which he also saved. As mentioned above, I have lots of interests besides Mr. Holmes, although he does demand more and more attention as my years pass. But I've been a Trekkie (or Trekker, or whatever the correct term is) since I was a wee lad in the late 1960's, when my babysitter happened to watch one of the original prime-time episodes. After that, I grew up seeing the original series in re-reruns, and then I was among those who saw the first Star Trek film in 1979 (and truthfully felt mightily disappointed. I do like it better now.) But it was Nick Meyer's *Star Trek:*

11

The Wrath of Khan (1982) which electrified the Trek Universe, jump-starting it into motion in a way that – like the Holmes Golden Age – has only grown. And how it's grown! Hundreds and hundreds of Star Trek novels and comic books, multiple films and television shows, with more in planning and production all the time, and fan interest around the world at an all-time high. As a nearly life-long Star Trek fan, who loves it nearly as much as The World of Sherlock Holmes, I credit the origin of this original escalation entirely to Nick Meyer.

I generally despise social media, but it's a very useful way for Sherlockians to connect. Imagine my thrill when I began to see occasional online posts from Nick Meyer – and when I dared to respond, sometimes he would respond back! I've learned that if you don't ask, you'll never know, so I connected with him a bit more often, and eventually I boldly asked him to write a foreword to one of the MX anthologies that I edit, and he most-generously agreed. After that, we've stayed in touch off-and-on, and that still never ceases to amaze me.

I met him in person at the 2011 *From Gillette to Brett* conference in Bloominton, Indiana, where he was the featured guest. I took my Holmes book, asked him to autograph them, and asked – like everyone does – when he'd write his next Holmes book. He certainly doesn't remember that, but he was the main reason I chose to attend that event.

One of my greatest regrets is that, while attending the 2020 Sherlock Holmes Birthday Celebration in New York, I was almost able to meet him in person again – and this time he'd know who I was – but I didn't get to speak with him, and it was my own fault. We had emailed ahead of time, planning to meet, and that day I entered the famed dealer's room and saw him seated at a table near the door, surrounded by many fans. I wandered away, intending to return in a just a very few minutes and dive into the crowd, hoping that it might have thinned a bit. But when I got back over there, he'd already left! Hopefully I'll get another chance, sooner rather than later, where I can thank him in person for so many things . . .

. . . including generously writing a foreword for these volumes. When I was considering who could write a foreword, I couldn't think of anyone more fitting. Through Nicholas Meyer I found pastiches, which have been so important to me over the years. Nick, thanks from the bottom of my heart for taking the time to be part of these books!

And finally, last but certainly *not* least, thanks to **Sir Arthur Conan Doyle**: Author, doctor, adventurer, and the Founder of the Sherlockian Feast. Honored, and present in spirit.

As I always note when putting together an anthology of Holmes stories, the effort has been a labor of love. This time the labor and love have been mine. These adventures are more tiny threads woven into the ongoing *Great Holmes Tapestry*, continuing to grow and grow, for there can *never* be enough stories about the man whom Watson described as *"the best and wisest . . . whom I have ever known."*

David Marcum
September 8ᵗʰ, 2021
A most important day,
for all kinds of reasons

Questions, comments, or story submissions
may be addressed to David Marcum at

thepapersofsherlockholmes@gmail.com

13

A Note on the
Modern Publishing Paradigm

For the longest time, publishing something was mostly impossible for most people. The Great Publishing Houses – which sounds like something from *Dune* – are giant machines, with carefully calculated formulas to know just how many books they need to sell to make a profit. It's no different than selling cereal: Many of the boxes of cereal on grocery store shelves won't be sold, and they were never meant to be sold, and the manufacturers are okay with that, because they've calculated the amount that they do need to actually sell in order to stay profitable while figuring in just how much can be discarded.

It used to be the same with books. Publishers would create a print run of a certain number of copies, sending out so many of them to bookstores across the country. Some would be sold – enough, hopefully, to cover costs – while many copies would just sit there, unsold, forever. Then, after a certain amount of time, they would be removed – either destroyed, or "remaindered", to be sold at rock-bottom prices in bargain bins.

It's an investment by the publishers to go to the trouble and expense to create all of those physical books, hoping to make their money back on enough of them to justify the waste of the others. That's why they're so restrictive about what they publish: They must meet the razor-thin edge of profit. But that makes the path to being published a very narrow needle's eye.

Several years ago, the paradigm began to shift. Online sales began to disrupt the physical bookstore model. And as people ordered online, some publishers figured out that they didn't have to have back rooms and warehouses jammed full of physical books sitting around waiting for a physical customer to enter a store or a dealer's room, examine it, and possibly buy it. Instead, when an online order arrived, the manufacturing of the book could commence right then, only as needed, and not months or years earlier.

This print-on-demand idea had been around for a while. (When I was going back to school for my second degree in civil engineering, the campus print shop did the same thing for certain locally produced text-books, printing them as they were purchased on fancy copying machines.) Publishers and authors began to take advantage of technological advances to produce their own books – straight from author to reader, happily eliminating the giant publishing middlemen.

Steve Emecz of MX Publishing brilliantly took advantage of this, building his business and allowing authors who would have never had a chance otherwise – like me – to create and connect.

But there are certain legitimate complaints.

In the olden days, the giant publishers slow-walked books through the process, so that it sometimes took literally years for a book to actually be published. Authors could actually die before ever seeing their work excreted at the far end of the giant publisher's process. The print-on-demand process, by comparison, is nearly immediate. As part of the large publishers' slow walk, there were battalions of editors who went through books forwards, backwards, and upside down. With the new technology, where a file can be loaded with the book manufacturer with very little effort and time spent, there is clearly less editing . . . and mistakes slip through.

Some readers continue to expect flawless and perfect works, as if legions of editors were behind the curtain as in days of old, still involved in the process. For this type of reader/consumer, the new format of publishing will always be pain they just can't ease. That's why, with this set of my stories, I want to apologize up front to those who will find typos – *because in spite of every effort, there will be some typos.*

In my own case, I love to write and edit, and I spend a sizeable amount of time doing both, but I also have a very busy and rich life doing other things. I spend time with my family, and I work more-than-full time as a civil engineer, fitting in these Sherlockian writing and editing projects during lunch hours, evenings, and weekends. It's a high wire act with no safety net. I'm the writer and sole editor of the stories in this collection. My wife, with a Bachelor's Degree in Journalism and two Master's Degrees in English Literature and Library Science, and with a first job as a copy editor, used to go through my stories and catch what I missed – because you never *ever* see your own mistakes – but she works way more than full time at her own job, and she just doesn't have any extra time to spare for playing uncredited editor on these projects. So they're all on me.

It's the same with the anthologies that I edit – any mistake that slips through in the end is my fault, because there are no other editors. When assembling a Holmes anthology, I receive the stories, format them to the "house style", print them on 8½ x 11-inch paper, edit and revise, go back and forth with emails to the author – sometimes a lot of emails – and then plug them into a giant Word document for more editing and revision. But from the time I get the story until I send the final file to the publisher, there isn't anyone else to edit, and no time to work one into the process. It's the new publishing paradigm.

As a print-on-demand publisher, MX does not have squadrons of editors. The business consists of three part-time people who also have busy lives elsewhere – so the editing effort largely falls on the contributors. Some readers and consumers out there in the world absolutely despise this – apparently forgetting about all those self-produced Holmes stories and volumes from decades ago with awkward self-published formatting and loads of errors that are now prized as collector's items.

These critics should recall that every one of these new volumes by various authors – even those that have typographic and formatting errors – are the very best efforts that can be produced by very sincere people who don't have professional full-time editors to help, and who would never ever have had the opportunity to publish otherwise, and because of these authors, there is thankfully more Sherlockian content in the world.

I'm personally mortified when errors slip through – ironically, there will probably be errors in this essay – and I apologize now, but without a regiment of editors looking over my shoulder, this is as good as it gets. Real life is more important than writing and editing, and only so much time can be spent preparing these books before they are released into the wild. I hope that you can look past any errors, small or huge, and simply enjoy these stories, and appreciate the effort involved, and the sincere desire to add to The Great Holmes Tapestry.

And in spite of any errors here, there are more Sherlock Holmes stories than there were before, and that's a good thing.

David Marcum

Watson's Descendants
by Nicholas Meyer

It is generally felt that the short story was Sherlock Holmes's best venue. The novellas, by contrast, are judged to be . . . lesser. Even the fabled *The Hound of the Baskervilles* suffers from the detective's absence for many pages. Though *A Study in Scarlet, The Sign of the Four*, and *The Valley of Fear* remain deliciously absorbing, it is in the short stories that Holmes and Watson truly flourish.

As Michael Chabon has observed, all fiction is fan fiction. Almost from the beginning, Sherlock Holmes has prompted imitators of his creator's creation. Arthur Conan Doyle wrote sixty Holmes cases in all – fifty-six short stories and four novellas. When they ended, boys and girls, men and women of all ages mourned Watson's silence and the series' cessation. But it wasn't long before others took up – or attempted to take up – Sir Arthur's pen.

Writing a full-length Holmes novel has always posed a challenge, even for Doyle himself, to say nothing of generations of later writers and filmmakers. Short stories, on the other hand, pose problems of their own. A good short story must compress action and character. It must – obviously – be short. The gift of writing compelling short fiction remains in a class by itself. Poe, Doyle of course, Twain, Saki, and Hawthorne are among the masters of the form from the Victorian and Edwardian eras, but over the years, the short story has produced many masters.

I alas am not among them. Even as a kid in art class, my paintings were so huge the murals I attempted had to be unfurled in the hall, not the studio. And so it comes as no surprise that writing a short Holmes story does not come easily to me. In fact, it does not come at all.

I retain nothing but admiration for those writers who *can* create short fiction, and a special respect for those who can bring off simulacra of Doyle's charming and distinctive Holmes tales. There many practitioners, including some whose efforts, unfortunately, resemble nothing so much as taxidermy. But among the best I must number David Marcum, who, by this point has written more Holmes stories than Doyle himself. Characterized by unflagging imagination and ceaseless ingenuity, along with felicitous prose, these tales continue to provide what we all crave: More Sherlock.

All Sherlock Holmes stories, (except Doyle's), are of course forgeries. And it's the rare forger who can resist signing his own work. See if you can spot David Marcum's fine Italian hand.

Enjoy.

Nicholas Meyer
Los Angeles, 2021

Sherlock Holmes (1854-1957) was born in Yorkshire, England, on 6 January, 1854. In the mid-1870's, he moved to 24 Montague Street, London, where he established himself as the world's first Consulting Detective. After meeting Dr. John H. Watson in early 1881, he and Watson moved to rooms at 221b Baker Street, where his reputation as the world's greatest detective grew for several decades. He was presumed to have died battling noted criminal Professor James Moriarty on 4 May, 1891, but he returned to London on 5 April, 1894, resuming his consulting practice in Baker Street. Retiring to the Sussex coast near Beachy Head in October 1903, he continued to be associated in various private and government investigations while giving the impression of being a reclusive apiarist. He was very involved in the events encompassing World War I, and to a lesser degree those of World War II. He passed away peacefully upon the cliffs above his Sussex home on his 103rd birthday, 6 January, 1957.

Dr. John Hamish Watson (1852-1929) was born in Stranraer, Scotland on 7 August, 1852. In 1878, he took his Doctor of Medicine Degree from the University of London, and later joined the army as a surgeon. Wounded at the Battle of Maiwand in Afghanistan (27 July, 1880), he returned to London late that same year. On New Year's Day, 1881, he was introduced to Sherlock Holmes in the chemical laboratory at Barts. Agreeing to share rooms with Holmes in Baker Street, Watson became invaluable to Holmes's consulting detective practice. Watson was married and widowed three times, and from the late 1880's onward, in addition to his participation in Holmes's investigations and his medical practice, he chronicled Holmes's adventures, with the assistance of his literary agent, Sir Arthur Conan Doyle, in a series of popular narratives, most of which were first published in *The Strand* magazine. Watson's later years were spent preparing a vast number of his notes of Holmes's cases for future publication. Following a final important investigation with Holmes, Watson contracted pneumonia and passed away on 24 July, 1929.

Photos of Sherlock Holmes and Dr. John H. Watson courtesy of Roger Johnson

The
Collected Papers
of
Sherlock

Holmes
Volume I – Tales
The Papers of Sherlock Holmes
and
Sherlock Holmes and
A Quantity of Debt

THE PAPERS *of* SHERLOCK HOLMES

VOLUME ONE & VOLUME TWO

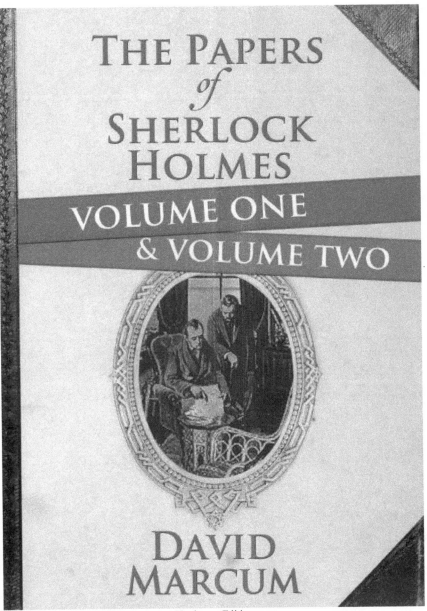

DAVID MARCUM

Hardcover Edition

How This Book Came To Be . . . .

There are two versions of how this book came to be written. The first version is that I, after having spent my thirties going back to school part-time in order to get a second college degree in Civil Engineering, became employed in said field in my early forties, only to be laid off during the recession of 2008. Having a lot of time on my hands, and a list of chores (sweetly labeled "Suggestions" by my wife) hanging over me, I thought "What did Conan Doyle do when he was sitting around waiting for work? Why, he wrote some Sherlock Holmes!" So, after a lifetime of collecting, reading, and studying literally thousands of narratives regarding my heroes, Holmes and Watson, in every conceivable form – novels, short stories, radio and television episodes, movies, comic books, scripts, and fan fiction, as edited by other people – I was able to fulfill a lifelong dream of adding my own efforts to the Great Watsonian Over-Soul. I sat down at the computer and let the stories flow. That's one version of what happened.

The other version is . . . *I found one of Watson's notebooks.*

It happened this way: During the time I was laid off, I went with my father to help clean out my aunt's house. She suffers from Alzheimer's and had been moved to a nursing home several years earlier. The place was a mess, and it had been an ongoing but irregular process to clean it.

On our final trip up there, we loaded the last of what we wanted to save from the nearly empty house. My aunt had always been interested in genealogy and our family tree, and she had accumulated a vast amount of information, none of it too organized. My sister had acquired most of it, since it interested her too, and as far as I was concerned she could have it. As we finished cleaning the house, I saw one old pile of papers, photographs, and notebooks that had been missed during all the other trips. Grabbing them and throwing them into a box, we loaded up and departed. Several weeks later, while sorting through the piles, I happened to go through those papers in order to see if they should be passed on to my sister. One of the items was an old, somewhat stained, school composition book, filled with faded and rather cramped writing. My aunt had been a schoolteacher, and I assumed that this was simply some long-ago assignment from one of her students. I flipped through it quickly, just to make sure it was useless before tossing it.

It was my subconscious that saved the book from the garbage. Years of searching for Sherlock Holmes stories has trained me to observe what others only see. I can scan numerous titles for words beginning with *S* and *H*, and often they seem to jump out at me, occasionally turning out to be something containing the words *Sherlock Holmes*. In this case, I saw on the rapidly flipping pages a few words that would probably not normally be included in an old student essay: "The Adventure of . . . ."

As any Holmes student can tell you, that electrifying combination of words often leads to a Holmes story. But why were they in an old handwritten notebook? Had someone felt the need to copy one of the original stories as an assignment for one of my aunt's classes? That seemed unlikely, and really a waste of time.

I started reading. And then I went cold. I've played The Game for a long time, but I was finally holding the real deal in my hands: *These were original Sherlock Holmes cases, handwritten by Watson.*

Of course, the next question was how did this notebook end up in my Aunt Wilma's papers? Only after reading more of the volume was the question answered, and that answer electrified me even further.

My great-grandmother on my father's side was named Rebecca Watson Marcum, daughter of James Watson. I was amused in my twenties when I finally connected that I had Watson blood in me. Later, in my thirties, I was even more amused when I first heard an episode of the Sherlock Holmes radio show, "The Case of the Very Best Butter" (from *The New Adventures of Sherlock Holmes* Radio Show, April 18, 1948) in which Holmes tells Watson that he is distantly related to the Rathbone family. For you see, my mother's maiden name is Rathbone. At the time I first heard "The Very Best Butter," I just assumed that Holmes's statement about his connection to the Rathbone family was a tip-of-the-hat to Basil Rathbone, who had played Holmes for so long on both radio and in the movies. Little did I know . . . .

Further examination of the notebook from my aunt's house revealed that it contained nine of Holmes's investigations, each from different periods of his career. Six are more traditional narratives. Another of these was quite a bit longer than the others, and seemed to answer several questions about Holmes's family.

The two remaining stories involved a trip by Holmes and Watson to East Tennessee, where my family has lived for generations. It was on this journey that Holmes and Watson met my great-grandmother, Rebecca Watson Marcum, as well as her son (and my grandfather) Willie Marcum, and Willie's small daughter (and my aunt) Wilma, thus setting into motion the circumstances leading to Watson's notebook being found in my aunt's possessions. Also during that time, Holmes and Watson met my maternal grandfather, Ray Rathbone, and became involved in a singular adventure that probably would have gone undetected except for Holmes and Watson's presence.

As I mentioned, Watson's old composition book was stained in places. I have had to make occasional guesses at a few of Watson's intentions and abbreviations, and I have Americanized the British spellings. Anything that appears to diverge from Watson's original narrative is my fault.

I wish to dedicate this volume with love to both my wife Rebecca, who has always been more than patient regarding my fascination with the world of Holmes and Watson, a persistent form of my second – or never-ending first – childhood, and my son Dan, who is the neatest guy that I know, and who always knows a good story. Thank you both for everything!

David Marcum
May 4th, 2013
(The 122nd Anniversary of the Reichenbach Incident)

A Note for the Revised and Combined Hardcover Edition (2014)

Since the publication of the stories in this book, initially separated into two volumes, I have finally been able to travel to England and walk Baker Street, as well visiting countless other Holmes-related sites. My Great Holmes Pilgrimage was something that I had desired for nearly my whole life, and it is something that I highly recommend to every true Sherlockian. You will never read or imagine the Canon the same way again.

I've also had a few other books and essays published in the meantime, with more on the way. The contents of this book have been translated into Russian editions, and have also been made into an audio book, performed by the excellent British actor Simon Shepherd. Additionally, a portion of "The Haunting of Sutton House" was dramatized by Imagination Theater as a syndicated radio broadcast throughout the U.S. in November 2013, and "The Singular Affair at Sissinghurst Castle" is scheduled to be broadcast – hopefully – in late 2014. I cannot express my appreciation and thanks enough to Steve Emecz of MX Publishing for helping to make this amazing ride possible.

I also appreciate all the kind words that I've received related to these stories. Several people kindly pointed out a few errors that had occurred when I attempted to edit Watson's original notes, and hopefully those have been fixed in this edition. Please feel free to let me know of any other instances that may have passed unnoticed, and as always, your comments and thoughts are most welcome.

David Marcum
August 7th, 2014
(The 162nd Anniversary of the Birth of Dr. John H. Watson)

The Adventure of the Least Winning Woman

"Our roles appear to have reversed themselves, old friend," said Sherlock Holmes from his chair at the breakfast table. I continued to look out our window at the tide of human activity surging up Baker Street, one floor below me.

"How do you mean?" I asked, looking to the left toward the Park.

I heard Holmes push back his plate. I knew without looking that he had probably moved his breakfast around without consuming a significant amount. "When we first met," he began, his voice slightly altered and muffled by the pipe hanging from his mouth. I heard a match scrape as he attempted to light it. Removing the pipe, he repeated, "When we first met, I believe you remarked on occasion that I was often impatient while waiting for new clients to bring some sort of distraction."

"It was not just when we first met," I smiled, turning away from the window. "It was that way for years. In fact, it was only after your return to London in '94 that you seemed to have found the ability to enjoy the random quiet moment. Not," I added, "that there have been many of those over the years."

He nodded, the smoke from the fulminating pipe wreathing his smiling face. "Yes, we have been rather busy, have we not? This quiet morning is somewhat unusual. Thus, my comment that our roles had been reversed."

"In what way?" I asked, moving toward my chair by the fire. Laid by Mrs. Hudson shortly before breakfast, it was only now beginning to warm the room.

"I am sitting here, able to appreciate this rare moment of inactivity," Holmes said. "This is exactly the type of morning which would have caused me a certain amount of agitation in my younger days. You, however, are showing significant signs of impatience and dissatisfaction."

"You have deduced this, of course, from the way that I gazed from the window?" I asked.

He stood. "As you know, my conclusions are based on numerous details. But it is my belief that you, Watson, were standing at the window hoping to see a frantic client making his way toward our door."

I had known Holmes too long to respond with surprise at his statement. However, I smiled and nodded to acknowledge that he was correct. I *had* been hoping for someone to arrive with a problem. "So our roles are reversed," I said. "You are able to repose, while it is I that seeks the stimulant of a new investigation."

Holmes didn't respond. He picked up the paper and curled into his chair across from mine by the fire. The morning sunlight was behind him, coming in the window over his chemical table. I saw him frown before I glanced away. "Looking at the war news?"

"Hmm?" he said, glancing up and then returning to the newspaper. He continued to frown, and as my own thoughts turned toward what I had read earlier, I fell into a brown study.

It was late November 1899, the Boer War a little over a month old, and the news from Africa was not good. The Boers had unexpectedly proven to be more effective than the British had first believed. It had been nearly twenty years since I had been wounded in Afghanistan, but I still recalled how I had felt when we, the supposedly superior force, had been routed at Maiwand on the twenty-seventh of July, 1880.

After a few moments, I sighed and stood. Holmes looked up. "Are you going out?" he asked. I realized that I did not have a plan.

"I suppose I will take a walk. The weather, in spite of the cold, is too beautiful to waste by spending the morning sitting huddled around the fire."

"That is unfortunate," said Holmes, pulling a letter from the pocket of his dressing gown. "If you go now, you will miss Mr. Johnson, who proposes to call in – " He glanced at the wall clock. "– twelve minutes."

I stood looking at him for a moment as a small grin formed on his face and his eyes took on a merry glint. Then I snorted. "Role reversal!" I cried. "It is no wonder you were so calm," I said, moving back toward my chair. "When did you receive that letter?"

"By yesterday's last post," he replied. "And a good thing, too. Otherwise, I might have been nearly as unsettled as you have been this morning. It really is quite unnerving, Watson." Then, he laughed. And I joined him.

"What is Mr. Johnson's complaint?" I asked as Holmes dropped the newspaper beside his chair.

"He does not say. He simply requests an appointment. However, as you can see," he said, tossing the note to me, "he is in his mid-thirties, is married, and has one child. He is educated, frugal, works as a professional man, and feels that his family may be in danger as a result of whatever is troubling him." Holmes knew very well that I could not see everything that he had deduced from the letter, but we had known each other for far too long for me to ask him the basis of his conclusions. I knew that when we met Mr. Johnson and heard his story, Holmes's deductions would be verified.

I had just worked out that Mr. Johnson was educated, based on the wording of the note, and also that he was frugal. The paper, which was of

36

good quality, was foxed with age, indicating that it had been saved until needed. I was examining the paper for other clues when I heard Mrs. Hudson's tread on the stairs, along with those of another.

The door opened to reveal our good landlady, followed by a short-bearded man in his mid-thirties, as Holmes had predicted. He was dressed in a dark suit and wore eyeglasses with wire frames. I quickly glanced at his nice but not overly expensive clothing and wedding ring. Beyond that, at this point, I could not confirm more of Holmes's statements.

"Mr. Holmes?" he said, correctly moving toward my friend with outstretched hand. "I am D. Allen Johnson. Very pleased to meet you." He and Holmes shook hands, and then he pivoted toward me. "And Dr. Watson. A pleasure to meet you as well."

Holmes directed Johnson to the basket chair, between us and directly in front of the fire. Johnson sat on the front edge of the chair, hunched forward as if to absorb some of the heat. Holmes usually put clients in that chair, unless they were incapacitated for some reason. He found that he could study their faces in the sunlight shining from the window behind him, while his face remained in shadow. Occasionally he had been foiled, as when the woman from Margate apparently realized his intent and moved so as to avoid that chair. However, that in itself was significant to Holmes, and he realized from her actions that she had no powder on her nose, leading to the correct solution to the case.

"How can we help you, Mr. Johnson?" Holmes asked. "Your note, while somewhat informative, was rather vague on particulars."

Johnson reached and touched his beard as he shifted in his chair. Then, as if realizing what he was doing, he consciously placed his hand on the armrest of the chair, and began to speak. "Mr. Holmes," he said, "I seem to have stumbled into something which has caused me to fear for my family's safety."

"Your family . . . ." Holmes prompted.

"My wife and young son," Johnson answered. Holmes glanced at me. I knew that the rest of Johnson's story would confirm Holmes's deductions. Holmes laid his pipe, which had gone out, on the table beside his chair, closed his eyes and tented his fingers. Johnson did not seem surprised. With a nod, Holmes indicated that Johnson should continue his narrative.

"I have been working as an apprentice with a large engineering firm here in London for the last few months. I realize that I am rather old to be holding such a position, but I was forced to learn a new trade several years ago after my position with Her Majesty's government was eliminated. At that time, I found employment for several years with Lloyd's, but I found the work unsatisfying. I determined through much pondering that I wished

37

to become an engineer, but first I needed to find someone willing to take me on as an apprentice.

"Lloyd's knew of my unhappiness and eventual intention to leave them. Gradually they began to decrease my responsibilities, as I'm sure they felt that it was not worth their time to continue to groom and train me for advancement when I intended to depart. Finally, dissatisfied with my few remaining duties, and convinced that they would be releasing me soon, I resolved to leave on my own terms while I still had a good reference.

"I was not certain when I would obtain an apprenticeship, but I knew that I must support my wife and son. As a way to make ends meet, I took a job as a manager at a messenger service. My background and education were both great assets to the company, and I quickly became an important part of the organization.

"The firm, located near the City, is owned by a Mrs. Trapp. She is a tall, stern woman, with a not-so-hidden pride in herself and her business. I gather that her husband started the firm and then proceeded to die almost immediately. Facing unexpected debts and loss of income, she had no choice but to continue the messenger business, with resulting singular success.

"When I began working there, about a year ago, the business was then nearly fifteen years old. Mrs. Trapp had worked quite hard over the years, and the company had established an excellent reputation. At least, until recently. At the time I started there was only one other similar business in the area which provided any competition.

"As I mentioned, the business was rather prosperous, providing a good income for both Mrs. Trapp and her daughter, Jane, who started working there soon after I did. In fact, the income was so great that Mrs. Trapp began to travel, leaving the office in the care of Jane. However, Jane often left the day-to-day running of the place to me. Initially, Mrs. Trapp journeyed to various locations in England, but that soon palled, and she began to cross the Channel to France. She later started traveling to various casinos up and down the coast. It was at this point that the real problems began."

"I do not want to give the impression that Mrs. Trapp was developing an unhealthy interest in gambling, although she did wager somewhat at some of the tables. I believe that she often simply traveled to these communities in order to see and be seen. She enjoyed the feeling of affluence that she was able to find in her travels. And I also do not want to make it seem that the messenger business was some sort of gold mine. It was not. However, it was a necessary service to many people, and it provided a comfortable income for Mrs. Trapp and her daughter.

"About six months ago, Mrs. Trapp returned from one of her visits, this time to France, I believe. She seemed more cross than usual, but I simply put that down to a less than satisfactory trip. Soon after, she announced that she had hired a new employee. I was not aware that we needed anyone, but we were always willing to take on someone who seemed to have the required skills and work attitude, as our business had a frequent turn-over of employees, and it never hurt to have a good employee trained and ready to work.

"I was greatly surprised when the new employee presented herself a day or two later. I had been expecting a lad or young man to work as a messenger. Instead, the new employee proved to be a woman of about my age, perhaps a little older. Mr. Holmes, Dr. Watson, I always strive to comport myself as a gentleman, and I dislike speaking ill of a lady, but you must understand my shock when I saw that our new employee was a woman of decidedly low character.

"Her name was given simply as 'Margeaux'. She was – to put it rather bluntly – a squat, toad-like creature with tangled black hair and the not-so-subtle hint of a moustache on her lip. She looked and behaved something like gypsies in stories that I have read. She dressed in a shapeless shift, and spoke with some sort of accent, although I'm not exactly sure of what origin."

Holmes opened his eyes and shifted in his chair. "Margeaux, spelled in the French fashion, with an e-a-u-x at the end?" Johnson looked surprised, and then acknowledged the fact. Holmes shut his eyes and waved for our visitor to continue with his narrative.

"My surprise increased when I was told that Margeaux would be working in the office, in a managerial position being created especially for her by Mrs. Trapp. However, it was not my business, and Mrs. Trapp was entitled to run it however she felt. Her daughter, Jane, appeared to be as confused as I, but she offered no initial objections.

"Within a week of her arrival, Margeaux announced that she had hired a half-dozen new messengers. These were lads of obvious ill breeding, little better than the pickpockets and thieves one encounters near the docks. I complained to Mrs. Trapp, telling her that the amount of work we had on hand did not justify hiring new employees, especially this type. I informed her that these associates of Margeaux's were intimidating our regular employees, and that some of them were already threatening to quit. Mrs. Trapp was adamant, however, that the new employees could stay, indicating that Margeaux had arranged for work to be found which would fill the new lads' time.

"Jane was disturbed at Margeaux's arrival and influence as well. The tension in the office quickly built, and finally Jane decided that she must speak to her mother about the situation. I well recall the day when Jane worked up her nerve to enter her mother's office and broach the subject. I continued to work at my desk, curious as to whether Jane's influence with her mother would be enough to cause Margeaux's removal.

"For nearly two hours, I heard nothing but occasional conversation from Mrs. Trapp's office. At the end of that time, the door opened, and Jane exited, her face pale. She did not meet my eyes, and over the next few days she made no reference to the conversation in the office. I did not feel it was my place to ask what had been said, but Margeaux continued to remain employed, and Jane made no more complaints about her.

"Over the next weeks, the situation became more and more intolerable. Margeaux would pick fights with the regular messengers, even on one occasion slapping a fellow in the face. When I attempted to intervene, Margeaux would invoke Mrs. Trapp's name and her own implied authority, and I would be forced to back down. As the situation grew worse, the regular messengers left, each to be replaced with another of Margeaux's crew.

"One afternoon about two months ago, Margeaux walked up to my desk and loudly accused me of falsifying documents. It was completely unexpected, and of course untrue. I looked around and realized that the office was full of Margeaux's new employees. None of the old crew that knew me and my reputation was there to stand for me. As I rose from my seat to respond to the allegation, Margeaux stepped closer and pushed me back into my chair! I have never considered hitting a woman – at least until that moment. All the tension and unhappiness of the past weeks washed over me, and I believe that even Margeaux realized that she might have gone too far.

"Instead of striking back, however, I turned and went to Mrs. Trapp's office. Without knocking, I threw open the door to see the surprised face of Mrs. Trapp, sitting behind the desk, and Jane, standing beside her.

"I explained what had happened, expecting that this would be the event that would finally cause Margeaux's termination. I was stunned when Jane simply looked sorrowful, while Mrs. Trapp explained, 'Mr. Johnson, it is obvious that you and Margeaux cannot work together. While you have been an excellent employee, Margeaux is a *more valuable* employee to the company. If it is to be a choice between you, I am forced to pick Margeaux. Please gather your things and depart.'

"I was shocked, but quickly decided that Mrs. Trapp and Margeaux deserved one another. I was vaguely aware of Margeaux standing near the far wall, her face covered with a gloating expression, while I collected my possessions from my desk. Then I departed without a backward glance.

"Of course, Mr. Holmes, I thought that was the end of it. I was still waiting to find out about my apprenticeship, and I still needed an income. The next day I presented myself at the offices of Mrs. Trapp's competitor, Mr. Appleman. He was glad to take advantage of my experience, and I began working for him right then, with a small raise in pay. It was a similar business, perhaps better and more successfully run. I was glad to think of my experience with Margeaux as a closed book. However, events were to prove that my association with her was not over.

"For several weeks I worked for Mr. Appleman, occasionally suggesting alternative ways to improve his operations based upon what I had learned while at Mrs. Trapp's. Mr. Appleman was always appreciative, and life was going on smoothly, until one evening my wife mentioned a curious incident from earlier in the day.

"She stated that when she and my son had returned from an outing, someone had been loitering outside our home. Although my wife had never met Margeaux, I had given her a complete description of the woman, and my wife was certain that the lounger had been Margeaux herself!

"Apparently the woman had simply stared at my wife and son until they were inside. My wife watched from the window, and the woman stayed for a while in the street, glowering up at the windows, before eventually walking away into the dusk.

"I was outraged that Margeaux should dare to come to my home, and also puzzled. I'd had no dealings with her since the day I left Mrs. Trapp's employment, and although she and I had clearly disliked each other, our association should have been at an end. She had managed to have me removed from Mrs. Trapp's office, and there was no way I could have any influence over activities there any longer.

"Over the weekend, I considered whether or not to speak to Mrs. Trapp about Margeaux's visit, but I decided to let the matter drop. I had no desire to renew any association with Mrs. Trapp or her daughter.

"Several days later, however, my wife reported that she and my son had been followed from the park by the same woman. From her description, I was again certain that it was Margeaux, although I had no idea why she should be following my family. On this instance, she did not follow them all the way to our home, but rather turned off onto a side street about a block away. Again, I was puzzled and outraged, and also uncertain what to do. I finally sent a note to Mrs. Trapp's office, explaining the situation and requesting to see her. I received no response. There was no response to the other notes I sent, as well.

"Over the next few days, my wife told me that she was again followed on several instances, although never all the way to our house. I even missed work one day, discreetly following my family at a distance to see if I could catch Margeaux, but she did not appear that day. Perhaps she saw me first and chose not to reveal herself. I do not know.

"Resolving to make some sense of this situation, I took another half-day from Mr. Appleman's office, to his growing displeasure. I made my way to Mrs. Trapp's place of business and waited outside until I spotted one of the messenger lads, young Jimmy, who had worked for me. I beckoned him over and asked if Mrs. Trapp or Jane was upstairs.

" 'Lor' no, Mr. Johnson,' he replied. 'Mrs. Trapp and Jane haven't been in for weeks. Just that *woman*,' he spat. Further questioning revealed that he was the last original messenger left, and that all the other hard-working lads had been replaced with Margeaux's ilk. He was looking for work, but couldn't afford to leave until he found something equivalent. I told him about Mr. Appleman's establishment, and suggested that he see me the next morning for a job.

"As he happily bounded off, I considered going upstairs to the office and having it out with Margeaux then and there. However, I decided that might be a mistake. I had no business being there, and I knew how her unfounded lies had caused me problems before. For all I knew she might have the law on me this time."

Holmes stirred in his seat. "You were quite right, Mr. Johnson, not to go up. I suspect that there is some devilry going on there. What happened next?"

"Well, nothing for a while. Margeaux continued to show herself to my wife and son, but with no obvious threat. A week after my trip to Mrs. Trapp's office, I was offered the apprenticeship which I had been awaiting for so long. I left Mr. Appleman's employment with his good wishes."

"What finally led you to our door?" Holmes asked.

"Why, I went home two nights ago and heard about Margeaux's latest appearance. This time she was standing on the street outside my son's school when my wife went to pick him up. It was as if she wanted us to know that she knew everything about us and that she could find us whenever she felt like it. Home, school, the park, wherever.

"I don't mind telling you, Mr. Holmes, that this matter has worried me to no end. Margeaux has done nothing explicit. She just appears before my wife, as if sending me a message that business between us is not yet concluded. And I, starting a new position, simply cannot stay home to protect my family, while my wife and son cannot be expected to hide inside.

"That night, after Margeaux's last visitation, I discussed the matter with my wife. It was she that suggested calling on you. She is the youngest daughter of Lewiston, of Scotland, whom you aided so well in the matter of the notorious gravel supplier."

42

"Ah, yes, I seem to recall the facts of the case." Holmes noticed my raised eyebrows and said, "One of those investigations in the eighties, Watson, when you were married and living in Paddington, I believe."

Turning back to Johnson, Holmes said "So, it was your wife who suggested that you consult with me?"

"Exactly, Mr. Holmes. Your name is still spoken of with near reverence in my wife's family."

Holmes waved that away. "How did Mrs. Trapp's business look on the day you visited? Did it still look successful?"

"I suppose so," Johnson replied. "As I said, I didn't go upstairs, but there was no indication of problems from the outside."

"Did Jimmy present himself at Mr. Appleman's establishment to seek employment, as you had suggested? Did he give you any further information about what was happening within Mrs. Trapp's offices?"

"That's a funny thing, now that you mention it, Mr. Holmes," Johnson replied. "He did not show up the next day as I had told him. I have had no further contact with him since that day in the street."

"Did anything else unusual occur around the time of Margeaux's arrival?"

Johnson thought for a moment. "Well, I don't know if it's relevant, but a few days before Margeaux arrived, and not long after Mrs. Trapp had returned from one of her trips, Mrs. Trapp apparently offered to sell the business to her competitor, Mr. Appleman. It was not something that was known to most of the employees, but Jane mentioned it to me in confidence. Mr. Appleman was an occasional visitor to our offices – there was never any unfriendliness in their business competition. I happened to comment on the visit to Jane, and she told me that her mother had offered the business to Appleman. However, nothing came of it. I think he decided not to pursue the matter."

"Did Mrs. Trapp go on any further gambling trips after Margeaux presented herself?"

"No, come to think of it. There were no other trips. Of course, I don't know where she's been since I stopped working there."

"Do you recall which casino she visited on that last trip?"

"No, but she had been to Monte Carlo, if that helps any," Johnson replied.

"Hmm," Holmes said, thinking quietly for a moment. Then he pulled his feet back and stood abruptly. "I think I have a fairly clear picture of the situation, Mr. Johnson," he said. Johnson looked startled, but quickly rose to his feet as well. "I should have some news for you tonight or tomorrow morning."

"That's . . . that's wonderful, Mr. Holmes. And my family? Can you see your way to assure me that this harassment will cease?"

"That is the only feature of this case which provides an element of mystery," Holmes replied. "The rest of the matter is commonplace, and when it is cleared up, the visits by this Margeaux person upon your wife and son should stop."

"Why . . . Mr. Holmes, everything they say about you is true. I realize that this is a small matter, hardly worthy of your time, but in my world it looms large. I have hardly known what to do. To hear that you already understand it . . . I must admit, I am amazed."

Holmes began to move toward the door, holding out his hand to direct Johnson that way, as well. Halfway, Johnson paused, turned, and looked around the room.

"You know, gentlemen," he said, "I have always wanted to visit this room. It is just as I'd imagined it. I must tell you that I was an avid reader of your accounts of Mr. Holmes's cases, Dr. Watson." I smiled and nodded acknowledgement. "I was quite upset when your 'death' was revealed, Mr. Holmes. I must confess that I was unsure at the time whether or not . . . ." He paused, then continued, "Whether or not you were *real*, Mr. Holmes."

Holmes snorted and resumed moving toward the door. Johnson hurried to catch up. "Of course, my wife later told me how you helped her family," Johnson continued, "so I then knew that you actually existed. However, at the time the doctor's stories were appearing in print, I didn't know whether they were true case studies or simply . . . adventure stories."

As Holmes opened the door, he replied, "Dr. Watson's narratives did tend to take on the aspects of romantic fiction, rather than presenting the facts in a clear, scientific manner. It is a complaint the good doctor has heard me make before. There is no wonder that the participants in the events seemed fictional, as well. However, I assure you that both Watson and I are quite real, and we should have some news for you very soon. Good day, sir."

As he shut the door behind Johnson, I remarked, "Your complaints about my small efforts to chronicle your abilities have become somewhat less . . . strident over the years, Holmes. It is almost as if you are now simply repeating your objections and comments out of forced habit rather than deep conviction."

Holmes smiled and moved toward the door to his bedroom. "Perhaps," he said. "I must admit that it was quite a surprise to return to London and find that in my absence my name had become a household word. Although it is still somewhat disconcerting to encounter people on a regular basis who continue to insist that I am a character in *The Strand* magazine."

44

I shook my head as he went into his bedroom. He called, "Of course, I cannot really blame you. You thought me dead, and now I know that my brother, for whatever devious reasons he had at the time, wished to encourage the belief that I was a fictional character. Possibly he thought that my work for the Foreign Office in the Far East would be better served if I was not believed to be real. In any event, I am fortunate that my work will be remembered, and not that character presented in your writings, doctor."

Holmes fell silent, and I heard drawers opening and closing. I believe that he appreciated my writings far more than he would ever care to admit. And although he had prohibited me from any further publication of his cases, I continued to keep extensive notes of his investigations, believing that someday he would relent and allow me to resume placing the narratives before the public.

I heard him rattling around for another moment before he returned to the sitting room, dressed as a lower-class working man. The transformation was so complete that, had I not long ago become accustomed to Holmes's disguises, I would have sworn a stranger had exited the bedroom. He spent a moment filling out a telegram, which he gave to the page boy to be sent. Then he turned to me.

"As I told Mr. Johnson, I have a fairly clear idea of what is happening at Mrs. Trapp's establishment. Deep waters, Watson. Deep waters. There is more here than just an unsavory woman making herself known to Johnson's wife and son. However, I must answer a few specific questions to resolve the matter. I should only be gone a few hours. In the meantime, you might see if there is any reference to 'Margeaux' in my commonplace books. I doubt it, but check and see, nonetheless. If you are free later today, would you perhaps wish to accompany me on a small outing?"

"Certainly," I agreed. "I will take my walk as initially planned, and then I will remain here this afternoon."

"Excellent." He moved to the table, where he spooned some of the cold eggs remaining on his plate onto a folded piece of bread. Taking a large bite, and carrying the remainder of his sandwich with him, he waved and departed.

Stepping to the left of the fireplace, I retrieved the large "M" scrapbook. It was much thicker than the others, and Holmes had once bragged that his collection of M's was a fine one. Moving to the table, I pushed aside my plate and laid the book down, opening it carefully. It was very bulky, a series of wide loose sheets bound with ribbon and stuffed with numerous loose clippings and separating pages. Thumbing through the volume, I glanced at the pages for the three Moriarty brothers and

Colonel Moran, their stories still unfinished. Then there was Mathews, and Mitchell the Taxidermist and his Abominable Collection.

Flipping to the front of the book, I found a single line for Margeaux: *The least-winning woman.*

Not very informative, I thought, smiling at Holmes's laconic style. Returning the book to its shelf, I donned my coat and went for a walk in the cool November sunshine. The sky was a bright blue, and the strong breeze blew away any evidence that a million fires were burning around me. I knew that this month could very easily bring London's evil fogs, which so often combined with the smoke of the giant metropolis to form a crushing and strangling blanket on those unfortunates with breathing problems. I inhaled deeply, decided against lighting my pipe, and walked on, thankful for the beautiful day.

Returning to Baker Street at midday, I read and ate a fine lunch prepared by Mrs. Hudson, while waiting for Holmes's return. When he finally arrived, at nearly four o'clock, he was no longer dressed as the working man. Instead, he was in a suit, although different from the one he had worn that morning.

He stood in the door without removing his coat and said, "If you are ready, we can finish this business tonight."

I put on my heavy coat, as the day had grown noticeably colder. Darkness had fallen, and the air outside was crisp but not entirely unpleasant. As Holmes and I settled into a hansom, he gave an address to the cabbie, somewhere in the City. "Mrs. Trapp's business, I presume?"

"Yes," Holmes replied. " 'London Messenger Service.' I have even used them once or twice in the past, although I fancy I shall be more careful whom I use in the future." The traffic seemed lighter than usual. Holmes appeared to notice as well, for he said, "I believe I will just have time to give you an account of my activities today before we reach our destination.

"After I left Baker Street this morning, I made my way to the City. I located Mrs. Trapp's offices, and proceeded to question individuals at neighboring businesses, on the pretense that I intended to apply for a messenger position, and I wanted to know something about the place beforehand.

"It has been my experience that given a chance, people will take time away from their busy schedules in order to gossip about their neighbors, where they might not be inclined to speak otherwise. The people I questioned were more than happy to speak to me, their stories about Mrs. Trapp being somewhat grim. They stated that for years Mrs. Trapp had run a successful business and had been a valuable member of the local community, that tight-knit group of businesses in the immediate area.

However, recently she seems to have hired a lower class of employee, and her reputation for excellent service had been severely diminished.

"Of course, Watson, you're thinking that this is no more than Mr. Johnson told us this morning. However, in spite of the fact that I had no reason to doubt him, I did feel that it would not hurt to confirm his story. The wire I sent this morning was partially for that purpose. One of the questions that I asked my brother Mycroft was to send me a short précis of Johnson's government career to one of the hidey-holes I keep throughout London."

I was aware of these locations, where Holmes kept clothing and disguises that he might need at a moment's notice. On occasion, he had been forced to hide in these dens as well, playing a waiting game while he was hunted by some criminal. There were at least four of his secret warrens that I knew about scattered on both sides of the Thames, and probably more that I did not.

"Mycroft informed me that Johnson had indeed worked for the government for several years. He was employed in an obscure department, verifying information concerning the backgrounds of other government employees in sensitive positions, such as those we met during the theft of the submarine plans from the Woolwich Arsenal. However, due to the misguided efforts of a crusading and cost-conscious parliament member, the investigatory department was abolished and its employees, including Johnson, released from service. This was no reflection on Johnson, and Mycroft indicated that he had an excellent record.

"Having confirmed Johnson's description of the business, I proceeded upstairs to the offices of the messenger service. It is good that I was in disguise, as I have had a few previous dealings with Margeaux, only in passing mind you, and I would not have had her recognize me before my trap was in place."

"Ah," I said, "I thought you seemed to recognize Margeaux's name when Johnson first mentioned her."

Holmes nodded. "Our paths have crossed before, but she has never fallen into my net. Was there anything in my commonplace book about her?"

"Nothing relevant," I said, shaking my head. "Just a cryptic comment: 'The least-winning woman.' "

Holmes smiled. "Perhaps you'll see why when we meet her." The light from a passing gaslamp highlighted the glint in his eye. This, I was sure, would be an evil night for Margeaux.

"When I entered the office, I was conscious of a number of men, the new messengers I supposed, sitting around the room, smoking and talking in small groups. The shades were drawn, and the room was in shadows.

Thick smoke from their cheap cigarettes filled the air. As I moved into the room, the muted conversations stopped, although there were occasional rustles, as if the room was full of rats and their tails were dragging across old newspaper.

" 'Is Mrs. Trapp in?' I asked.

"Someone snickered, while another said 'She ain't here. Her *managing partner* is, though.'

" 'Partner?' I said. 'Might I speak with him?'

" 'Him's a her,' the man replied, and several in the room laughed. Most didn't, though. At that moment, a door across the smoky room opened, and Margeaux herself stepped in.

" 'What is it?' she said, her voice a shrill rasp, as if she had damaged it somehow. She has a curious accent, which I know to be from one of the smaller French seaports. She is a curious creature, Watson, exuding evil in an ignorant, ineffective, mad-dog way. She has been a useful tool for her masters in the past, but she is too stupid to manage anything effectively for very long on her own.

"I explained that I was seeking a job, and had heard about Mrs. Trapp's fine establishment. There was some more laughter from the group. 'We ain't needing anybody else,' Margeaux replied.

." 'Are you sure?' I asked. 'I have done this sort of work before, and I have excellent references . . . . '

" 'Get rid of him,' Margeaux said, turning and going into the office. She slammed the door. The crowd around me stood as one and shuffled toward me.

" 'Wait,' I said, but they kept moving toward me. I decided there was nothing else to learn, and I wisely departed. I heard their hilarity behind me as I went down the steps.

"After departing from Mrs. Trapp's office," Holmes continued, "I went to the hiding place that I keep near the City, where I changed clothes and read Mycroft's information that had been sent regarding Johnson. Then I went to Mr. Appleman's business, Quick Messenger Service.

"I found him to be a blustery gentleman in his mid-sixties. He had apparently been a sea captain in his early days, and had retired with a desire to stay busy. He had finally decided, for reasons known only to himself, that owning and running a messenger service would fill the bill. Quite a jump from the sea to an office job, but he appears to have made a success of it.

"He's a strange fellow, Watson, but pleasant enough, with a Mediterranean look about him, in spite of having the jolly old name of Appleman. He was dressed in a curious worksuit, with small tools clipped to the numerous pockets. His thin dark hair was combed over his bald head, and a strand or two was always breaking free to fly down and land across his glasses.

"Appleman stated that he and Mrs. Trapp had both started their messenger services at about the same time. Over the years they had helped each other when one or the other had problems. For instance, on one occasion years ago a fire in a nearby building had caused some minor damage to Mrs. Trapp's location. Appleman had allowed her to use part of his facilities until she had things straightened out.

"He confirmed Johnson's statement that he had considered buying Mrs. Trapp's business. He said that she had approached him one day last spring or summer, completely surprising him, and offering to sell it immediately. She said that she needed to raise a large amount of capital in a short amount of time, and was not able to apply for a loan. Appleman said that she was asking too much for what the business was worth, but he took time to seriously consider the offer anyway, based on his long friendship with Mrs. Trapp.

"Appleman said that buying a business like a messenger service is not like buying other businesses. 'It's not like purchasing a factory, with all the actual machines and the building and such,' he said. 'I would have been essentially buying the rights to her clients. I didn't need her office furnishings and such, unless I would have decided to keep her office open as a branch office, which wasn't likely.

" 'I would have been paying her for access to the clients that she had cultivated over the years. And if they didn't like me or the service I provided, they would be free to leave. And I would be out whatever I had paid.

" 'Of course,' he continued, 'I went and examined her books. It seemed like there was far too much money being pulled out of the business lately. I suppose she was paying for those trips. Then there was some talk about Mrs. Trapp staying on as a manager if I kept the place as a branch office, but she wanted too much money for her own wages as well. It wasn't mentioned, but I suspected she also wanted me to hire her daughter. In the end, I had to tell her no. Probably a good thing, though. I hear the place has really gone down since then. I've picked up a lot of her former clients recently that I would have had to pay her for otherwise. I don't know if the decline in business is something she's caused since she and I last talked, or if she saw it coming and that's why she tried to sell out.'

"He ended by telling me that if I heard any way that he, Appleman, could help her, just to let him know. As I started to leave, he called me back. 'Perhaps, Mr. Holmes, you'd like to see the future.'

"I felt that I could spare a minute for something that intriguing. Appleman led me into a side room, containing a long table with several telephones on it. 'A telephonic message service,' he said, gesturing proudly. I must have appeared puzzled, for he explained. 'When I get the whole thing wired up, I intend to have some fellows in here answering these telephones and taking messages. We will rent our telephone numbers to clients.'

"He stepped closer to the table. 'Say there's a fellow, a professional man just starting out, perhaps. He can't afford a big office or staff, but he wants to appear successful. He can rent the use of one of my telephones here, and then he can publish that telephone number in an advertisement, or perhaps some sort of directory, as if it were his own number.

" 'When one of his customers calls, my employee will answer that telephone line as if he is at the client's place of business. My people can take a message, and then get it to the fellow. His caller will be impressed that he has a staff and his own telephone, and also that he's successful enough that he is out working and not sitting around waiting for his telephone to ring.'

"Apparently I did not seem to be impressed, for Mr. Appleman elaborated. 'Say that this young professional man is perhaps an engineer, or a doctor. Now say that engineer needs to visit a work site, or this doctor needs to make rounds, but at the same time he needs to stay in the office to await new patients. He can't afford to pay someone to sit there all day, so he pays a considerably lesser amount to us to give the impression that he has a staff. What do you think?'

"I told him that I was impressed, although, between you and me, Watson, I have my doubts." Holmes turned and looked at me. I shook my head.

"I have mine, as well," I said. "I suppose there might be some sort of need for such a service, but I cannot imagine any true professionals making use of it. I can assure you that doctors would not be a party to such a thing. And," I added, "he seems to assume that everyone has access to a telephone."

"Exactly," Holmes said. "In any case, after leaving Mr. Appleman, I found a few of my informants in the area, who provided me with additional information. Incidentally," Holmes continued, "one of the neighboring business owners told me that Jimmy, the young messenger who never turned up to ask Mr. Johnson for a job, has simply left London for a better opportunity elsewhere. Thus, that mystery is resolved.

"Further questioning of my informants confirmed what I had suspected about the doings at Mrs. Trapp's messenger service. We are fortunate in that some sort of activity is planned for tonight at that location which will allow us to catch Margeaux in the act. Although," he added, "according to my informants, the illegal activities at Mrs. Trapp's have been carried out in so careless and blatant a fashion that we could probably have stopped by nearly any night of the week and caught them."

"So it is a criminal matter, then?" I asked.

Holmes nodded and looked at the passing street. He then knocked his cane against the roof of the cab. "Stop here, cabbie," he said.

We exited and paid the fellow. Holmes gave the man something extra and told him to wait for us on a nearby street. The cabbie seemed to know Holmes, because this did not surprise him. As the man nudged his horse forward, Holmes and I stepped away. "Mrs. Trapp's offices are just around the corner. We will make our way around to the rear entrance."

We turned down an alley, our senses immediately assaulted by the stagnant air, so different from the fresh November breeze in the street. The narrow passage smelled like an animal cage, and I wondered what unseen substances were brushing against the hem of my coat.

We continued past several buildings, each as dark and featureless as the next. However, Holmes appeared to know exactly for which one he was heading. I perceived the gray shadow of a man step from the deeper gloom an instant before the fellow spoke.

"Good evening, Mr. Holmes, Dr. Watson," said the reassuring voice of Inspector Stanley Hopkins.

So it is a Scotland Yard matter, I thought to myself. "Are they in there?" Holmes asked.

Hopkins nodded. "We did as you asked, Mr. Holmes. We have let a few of the smaller fish move in and out unhindered, but Margeaux is still inside. We have ascertained that Mrs. Trapp and her daughter are at their home. Apparently their involvement is passive, at best."

"Yes," said Holmes, "I believe they were victims in this matter, although Mrs. Trapp's gambling problems brought this upon her. My informants have told me that she and her daughter have not been near this place in weeks."

"What exactly is going on, Holmes?" I asked. "We rather ran out of journey before you were able to explain what is happening."

"Smuggling, Watson," Holmes replied. "Margeaux is the local agent for a group of French smugglers. Of course, as soon as I heard her name, I knew what was going on, even if I did not know the specifics. She has long been associated with those groups. My only questions were how Mrs. Trapp had become involved, and why Margeaux had taken it upon herself to begin harassing Mr. Johnson's family.

"When I wired Mycroft, I also asked him to ascertain something about Mrs. Trapp's gambling sojourns. He has a number of agents stationed throughout the Continent, and some of his most valuable men are placed at various watering holes and casinos. Apparently these are excellent locations in which to uncover the kind of information that Mycroft uses on a daily basis. He wired his man in Monte Carlo, and was able to learn within a few hours that Mrs. Trapp had most recently gambled at a location with interests controlled by a French crime syndicate. Interestingly, Watson, one of their primary activities is smuggling into England."

I was beginning to understand. "Hence, the Margeaux connection." I thought for a moment. "I'm willing to wager that Mrs. Trapp lost heavily on her last visit to the casino."

"Very good, Watson," Holmes said. "I should think most of the matter should be clear now."

"Wait, Mr. Holmes," said Hopkins. "You and I talked earlier, and I understand that Mrs. Trapp's business is being used for smuggling, primarily French brandy and other items that are usually heavily taxed with import duties. However, I do not understand why Mrs. Trapp would allow it. Is she being blackmailed by these French criminals for something she did while traveling on the Continent?"

"In the inaccuracy of your statement lies the answer, Hopkins," Holmes said. "It is not correct to call it 'Mrs. Trapp's business' any longer, because in fact, she no longer owns it. Mycroft's agent confirmed that Mrs. Trapp's losses at the baccarat table were excessively large, far more than the woman of a modest messenger service could afford.

"I am fairly certain that Mrs. Trapp's gambling is far more of a problem than Mr. Johnson perceived. I believe that she became overwhelmed while at the tables, and in a moment of foolish desperation, wagered her business. Of course, she lost, and her new French masters were more than happy to have sudden access to and ownership of an existing business in the heart of London. They left Mrs. Trapp in charge as a sort of figurehead manager, but sent their trusted agent, Margeaux, here to manage the day-to-day smuggling activities.

"Mrs. Trapp, of course, tried to find a way out from under her new masters. She felt that if she could come up with money to pay her debts before Margeaux arrived, she might be able to free herself from the French syndicate, even if it meant losing her business. She returned to London and tried to interest Mr. Appleman in purchasing her business, feeling that he would be a better master than the criminals. As Appleman stated, the terms were unacceptable, and he declined. Mrs. Trapp had become greedy, trying to make enough from Appleman to pay off the syndicate and have something extra for herself as well. When Appleman failed to buy, Mrs. Trapp was then forced to accept the new arrangements.

"Margeaux arrived and almost immediately began replacing the existing messengers with her own people. She was probably supposed to keep the messenger service in existence as a legitimate cover for the smuggling operation. However, she is a person of limited intelligence and poor management skills, and she could not resist baiting and offending the regular messengers, until – one by one – they left. She probably enjoyed transforming the respectable business into a low dive that suited her background and natural inclinations and temperament. She made it her mission to force Johnson to leave, as she perceived that he might be a threat if he stayed long enough to see what was going on.

"Of course, Jane had finally been told by her mother what had happened, and why Margeaux was being allowed to ruin the business. However, they had no choice but to go along with Margeaux's plans. It was no longer their business, and they were allowed to stay by their new masters and earn a paltry living only as long as they were useful. Eventually, they stopped coming to the office at all, allowing the firm that they had built up over fifteen years to be ruined in the course of a few months."

"But," I asked, "why did Margeaux begin to follow Johnson's wife and son? She had forced him to leave the messenger service. Why did she need to keep insinuating herself into his life?"

"That is the only point which is still unclear to me. I fancy that because she is simply a low-minded individual, she wanted to harass him as some sort of amusing entertainment for herself. The only way we will know for sure is to ask her. However, it is ironic that by continuing to involve Johnson in the matter, we were eventually asked to investigate, bringing the whole affair to light. Otherwise, in spite of her mismanagement, the smugglers' activities might have gone on indefinitely. After all, who would suspect such a thing being carried out in a City messenger service office? But wait – what's that?"

He pulled us deeper into the shadows as a large dray moved down the alley, coming to a stop behind the messenger business. The heavy old horse sighed, tossed its mane, and hung its head in quiet resignation.

Dark figures of men jumped from the wagon, even as the door of the building was thrown open, spilling light out to create a monochromatic scene that had no doubt played out at this site on numerous occasions.

"I think we should stop them before they unload the cart, don't you, Hopkins?" Holmes whispered. "It will save your men the trouble of reloading it later."

"Well, maybe they should move one or two crates inside so that the men in the building cannot deny their involvement. That way we'll get the whole lot of them." Even as he finished speaking, several of the men carried crates within, prompting Hopkins to raise his police whistle.

With several shrill blasts, constables appeared out of the darkness and converged on the building and wagon. "They are doing the same in the front," Hopkins yelled as we sprinted toward the doorway. "I even have men on the roof. No one will get away."

It was over in moments. The false messengers and those men that came with the wagon were hustled into waiting Black Marias. An inspection of the wagon showed several dozen crates of illegally imported French brandy, as well as lace fabrics and other small but expensive items. An exploration of the building revealed nothing questionable in Mrs. Trapp's offices, and for a moment Holmes seemed puzzled. Soon, however, it was found that hundreds more bottles of brandy were stored in the basement of the building. It was later revealed that the French smuggling syndicate had leased the basement after they took possession of Mrs. Trapp's business.

As we entered the offices, several constables were pulling a spitting and snarling creature from the back room. She was short, not much above five feet in height, and as she twisted and sagged in the constables' grips, she seemed at times to be much shorter. She was dressed all in black, and the front of her blouse was covered in crusted food stains and dandruff. Her tangled black hair had fallen over her pudgy face, but not enough to hide from me the twisted features, the weak chin, and the hint of a moustache mentioned by Johnson.

Margeaux continued to struggle until Holmes stepped in front of her. She stopped suddenly, seemed to go slack as she recognized him, and then lunged at Holmes, nearly catching the constables holding her by surprise before they yanked her back.

"Ah," said Holmes, "I see you recognize me, Margeaux. I, of course, recognized you when I visited your office earlier today seeking employment." Understanding crossed her low features, and she began to curse in French. Holmes waved her away. Or possibly he was fanning away the smell of stale garlic that rose around her. "Take her out of here." She hadn't been taken through the door, however, before Holmes called after her. "Wait. I have one question." The constables turned her around, and Holmes said, "Why did you feel the need to follow Mr. Johnson's wife and son?"

She appeared puzzled, as if he were speaking a language she didn't understand. "Johnson," Holmes said, "the former office manager."

"Ah," she replied, "that pig. Just having a bit of fun. He was always acting so superior, letting it be known that he was only working here until he began his *profession*." She spat the word. "As if this place wasn't good enough for him." She spoke strangely, as if she had some personal pride in Mrs. Trapp's business. "I had nothing better to do. I decided to make him suffer a bit. It was a game. A good game!"

"It is as I thought," said Holmes, flicking his hand to send her away. Hopkins began to give orders to his men, making sure that all the brandy was properly cataloged and accounted for. In a moment, he was interrupted by Holmes.

"Hopkins, my friend, it has just occurred to me that perhaps Watson and I should accompany Margeaux to the station. I assume she will be searched when she gets there."

"I should think so, Mr. Holmes," Hopkins replied. "We keep a matron on duty for just such a job."

Holmes smiled at some inner joke, seemed to hesitate for a moment, and then declared, "No, Watson and I really should be there. I will leave the aftermath and the clean-up in your able hands, Hopkins."

"Of course, Mr. Holmes. And thank you again. Perhaps this will put a dent into the French smuggling efforts."

"Well, a small dent at least. The French syndicate will quickly set something else up, but no doubt we have inconvenienced them for a bit. Drop by tomorrow, if you have any further questions. Good night, Hopkins."

Outside, we walked through several connecting alleys before emerging into the open street. The fresh air was a relief, although I noted that the sky was clouding, obscuring the stars. I suspected the weather was turning.

We found our waiting cabbie, and Holmes gave him instructions to make for the nearby police station, where Margeaux was being taken.

"Of course," Holmes said, "all the new messengers hired by Margeaux were actually delivering the smuggled brandy, lace, and so on, to their customers around the city, a bottle or two at a time. At that rate, it would not have been noticed for quite a while. It is due to the French smugglers' mistake in entrusting Margeaux with any responsibility that their plans failed. She was unable to stop herself from mismanaging the messenger service, which would have been a perfect cover. Also, she was unable to stay away from Mr. Johnson's family, simply because she needed some sort of cruel amusement."

We arrived at the police station and paid our cabbie. As he drove away, we stepped inside, only to hear a woman's screams, followed by Margeaux's guttural shouts. Holmes smiled. "We are too late, I fear."

We stepped down the hall, past the empty front desk, and into a rear office crowded with constables. Sitting on a chair in the center of the room, receiving the sympathy of a few nearby officers, was the matron assigned to the station. She appeared to be on the verge of hysteria.

Across the room, standing near a screened area, was Margeaux, struggling in the grip of two burly constables who held her onto a chair.

"I had hoped," Holmes began, "to get here in time to avoid this. No doubt I should have said something to Hopkins sooner. My apologies to

55

you, madame," he said, addressing the matron. She ceased her weeping for a moment to look at him as if he were mad.

"Perhaps, Watson, you would be willing, in your capacity as a doctor, of course, to examine Margeaux, making sure that there are no concealed weapons."

"Surely, Holmes, an officer would be better . . . " I began, before Holmes stopped me. He stepped close and whispered, while staring at Margeaux. I heard his words, and my head whipped around to stare at her as well.

"Really, Holmes," I said, "You should have told someone. Your perverse sense of humor will cause serious problems someday. You really should apologize again to the matron." I stepped across the room, indicating to the constables that they should bring Margeaux behind the screen. They appeared reluctant, but I softly repeated what Holmes had told me. They appeared shocked, and then angry, while Margeaux renewed her struggles.

After a few moments, the examination was concluded. I returned to Holmes. "You were right," I said. "Margeaux is a man."

"Truly," he replied, "the 'least-winning woman.'"

The next day, Holmes and I visited Johnson at his new place of employment, informing him of the previous night's events, and that Margeaux would cease bothering his family. After a period of imprisonment, the smuggler would be deported. Holmes had already sent a cryptic anonymous wire to Margeaux's French masters ensuring that she – that is, *he* – would stay out of England forever.

Holmes also chose to tell Johnson about Margeaux's true gender. After a moment's thought, Johnson declared that he was not surprised. Holmes related that Margeaux's choice of women's clothing was a longstanding habit, and it was no secret in France. However, it was obvious that none of the men smuggling from Mrs. Trapp's office were aware of it. Later, when Holmes and I visited Mrs. Trapp and her daughter, he chose not to reveal Margeaux's secret. He did provide them with details regarding what they did not know about the smuggling plot.

He assured Mrs. Trapp that there would be no charges filed against her, as she had been coerced into helping the smuggling ring. Finding that she was free from the French criminals, she seemed to be somewhat relieved, but also vaguely hostile and embarrassed about the whole matter. Although Holmes and I encouraged her to set about rebuilding her business, she appeared uncertain and noncommittal. I later learned that she and her daughter had moved away from London without restarting the business. I do not know where they finally ended up.

Stepping out of Mrs. Trapp's residence, Holmes and I paused on the stoop to raise our umbrellas. I had been right the night before: The weather had changed.

"I was serious last night, you know," I said. "Sometimes your sense of humor is perverse."

"Yes, Watson, perverse. But somewhat accurate as well?"

Thinking of Margeaux as she – *he* had been led to the men's cells the night before, cursing and writhing, I had to agree.

"The least-winning woman, indeed."

The Adventure of the Treacherous Tea

I had not realized that I was asleep until the clattering noise from the stairs jarred me awake. The warm fire, probably too warm for such a fine spring day, had conspired with a large lunch to leave me drowsy and useless for much of the afternoon. I straightened myself in my chair, pain shooting up my injured leg, twisting as the door to the stairway landing flew open.

I heard Mrs. Hudson's angry protests, but it did nothing to distract me from the great bear of a man standing in the doorway. As he stepped in, the door flew back. It surely would have hit the wall behind it, the knob possibly cracking the already-dimpled plaster, if the man's large right hand had not shot out at unbelievable speed and grabbed it, arresting its motion.

"Where is Holmes?" he demanded. Mrs. Hudson shifted and sputtered behind him. He paid her no mind, as if she were a yapping pup dancing around the legs of an ox.

"Sir," I said, pulling myself to my feet. I was certainly no longer drowsy. "You cannot simply barge in here – "

"No time for that!" he cried. "They're after me. Be here any second. I need Holmes. I've got to tell him – "

While he had been speaking, I had heard the front door open, none too gently. A rush of feet on the stairs, and then the entrance to our rooms was boiling with constables subduing the invader. Mrs. Hudson disappeared in a tangle of uniforms and arms. I stepped quickly across the room and retrieved her, pulling her from the throng in the nick of time.

In just a moment, the large man was subdued, his arms and hands pulled behind him, bound by shackles. Seeing that struggle was useless, the man immediately ceased all resistance. Thankfully, the room and Mrs. Hudson appeared to be undamaged.

As the man was led out, he looked back over his shoulder and sought me with his eyes. "Ericson. Billy Ericson. Tell Holmes. Tell him I didn't do it. Get him to help me – Tell him!"

The entire group made its way down the steps. Thankfully, when they reached the turn at the landing, there was no sound of breakage from the table or vase standing there.

The sudden quiet was overwhelming. My heart was still pounding, half from the excitement, and half from suddenly being pulled from sleep. "Well," I said.

Mrs. Hudson looked back at me. "Well, indeed," she agreed.

I heard footsteps climbing the seventeen stairs to the sitting room. These were quieter and lighter than those of the burly constables and their prisoner. As the figure rose up the steps and into the light spilling from the sitting room, I saw that it was Inspector Lestrade of Scotland Yard.

In later years, I was proud to call Lestrade a friend. On many occasions he felt that he was in some sort of competition with Holmes, but he was always a dogged and honorable man, interested in doing the right thing. We went through many adventures with Lestrade, including hiding together on an eerie, foggy night in Dartmoor while waiting for a particularly evil murder to be attempted.

At the time of this case, however, I did not know Lestrade nearly as well as I would in later years. This was in the spring of 1882, a little over a year after I had been introduced to the Inspector, and my impression of him then was not as fond as it would become. I believed him to be simply using Holmes's skills without giving Holmes any credit. Holmes had been slightly more charitable, calling Lestrade and fellow inspector, Gregson, "the pick of a bad lot."

"Sorry about the fuss," Lestrade said, puffing slightly from climbing the stairs. "That fellow got away from us," he wheezed.

"He said his name was Billy Ericson," I said. "What had he done?"

Mrs. Hudson moved toward the door, stepping around Lestrade, who moved deeper into the room. She paused before leaving, waiting for Lestrade's answer.

"Poisoned a man," the inspector replied. "Slipped something into a co-worker's tea, can you believe it?"

Mrs. Hudson shook her head and turned to go. She made the same disgusted noise, as only a good Scots woman can, that she often produced when Holmes was at his most vexing.

As the door shut, I waved Lestrade toward the basket chair. I asked if he wanted a drink. "It's a bit early, doctor. But perhaps just a small one. To recover from the chase, you know."

He took the drink and swallowed it in two gulps. As he set down the glass, I asked "More?" He shook his head. "Where is he employed?" I queried.

"Gilder and Sons. Builders located over near Paddington Station. Less than a mile from here, actually." He settled back, in his chair. "The owner's wife works there, says that the dead man had words with Ericson a few hours ago. She's the one who accused Ericson. He heard her and denied it, of course. He was sitting quietly, being detained before we finished the investigation and took him to the station. He got away from us as we were leaving, and set off running. It's lucky we kept him in sight, although it's no great credit to our men that it took a mile to run him down."

"Especially so large a man," I agreed. "It is a wonder he could outrun so many officers."

"He always was a quick one," Lestrade said. I raised a questioning eyebrow, and he replied, "Used to be on the force. Got let go earlier this year. You remember some of those troubles?"

I nodded. Several inspectors had been released after they were implicated in various schemes involving pay-offs from known criminals. A few constables had been caught in the housecleaning as well.

"Was he one of the constables?" I asked.

Lestrade shook his head. "An inspector. Of course, he claimed he was innocent, that he didn't do anything wrong. And I was inclined to believe him. Seemed to be just a man in the wrong place at the wrong time. But he appeared to land on his feet. He's held several jobs since then, but always of a respectable nature. He'd been at this builder's for two or three months now, most of the time since he left the force, studying the building trade."

"What happened this morning?" I asked. Lestrade started to protest about the confidentiality of Yard business, but I told him, "Holmes is going to be involved, one way or another. Ericson was asking for him as they took him away. You may as well tell me. It may save having to repeat it for Holmes later, although he will probably want to get the facts first hand in any event."

Lestrade sighed and relented. "This business where the murder took place, Gilder and Sons, has about eight or nine employees, involved in various aspects of the building trade. There is the owner, Charles, and his wife. Although the name of the business is 'and Sons,' I saw no signs of them.

"Ericson was working there to learn the trade. Apparently he got along well with everyone except the murdered man. Fellow name of Cheltenham. Ernest Cheltenham. He was on Ericson's level, both apprentices learning the business. He was a little younger than Ericson, but had worked at Gilder for a longer period of time. To hear them tell it, Cheltenham had taken it in his head to try to exert authority over Ericson, authority that he didn't actually have.

"Ericson had apparently put up with Cheltenham for a while, but people could see he was getting a little weary of it. The owner's wife, who appears to run the place, stated that on several recent occasions, Cheltenham had brought in plans that Ericson had worked on in order to point out mistakes. Ericson had started talking back to Cheltenham, pointing out that there

60

was nothing wrong with the plans or his work, and that it wasn't Cheltenham's place to correct him.

"This morning, they had some sort of blow-up, and Ericson ended up walking outside, he said to cool off. Later, he came in and fixed a cup of tea. There is a set of plain, heavy, white mugs used by everyone in the office. That's important, doctor.

"After Ericson was back at his desk, Cheltenham had walked up. He, too, was carrying a cup of tea in the same type of mug. It seems that the two of them were constantly sipping tea, and that was the only point of friendliness and agreement between them.

"Anyway, Cheltenham comes up and sits down beside Ericson's desk. From what people nearby overheard, Cheltenham was apologizing, and seemed to have realized that he was pushing Ericson too far. Ericson appeared to accept it. They talked quietly for a few minutes, seemingly about nothing important. Ericson said they were just discussing the weather and such, trying to find some point of friendly common ground.

"At that point, there was a call from the back of the building, where some heavy furniture was being delivered. Cheltenham stood and went to help move it, and in just a moment Ericson followed. Everyone agrees that Ericson stayed behind for just a moment before following Cheltenham.

"After the furniture was brought into the building, Ericson and Cheltenham returned to Ericson's desk, where Cheltenham retrieved his teacup and returned to his own desk. The office worked quietly for about half an hour, maybe less, with Cheltenham sipping his tea.

"Suddenly, with a croak, Cheltenham threw up his hands, slid from his chair, and collapsed on the floor. Those sitting around him recalled later that he seemed to look ill for a few moments before the attack. He was sweating and fidgeting in his chair.

"Of course, he was dying. The co-workers crowded around him, and they tried to prop him up and give him sips of water, which was just silly. Someone thought to send for a doctor, but a passing constable was found instead. By the time he got there, Cheltenham was certainly dead.

"It was not long before I arrived. It was obvious that he had been poisoned. You know the rest. Questioning revealed the disagreements between Cheltenham and Ericson. No one else was anywhere near the teacups, or has any motive against Cheltenham. The owner's wife told us about the tea. She implied that somehow Ericson poisoned it, maybe slipping something into Cheltenham's mug when Cheltenham went to move the furniture, or possibly putting it into his own mug, and then switching it with Cheltenham's. It would have been easy, since the mugs are identical. Also, Mrs. Gilder knew that Ericson had been with the police in the past, and stated that he would know how to obtain poison.

61

"In any event, it's open and shut, although I do hate a poisoning case. I suppose Ericson wanted to find Holmes and have him clutter things up with a lot of theories. But between you and me, doctor, it's cut and dried."

I could see that he had nothing further to add, so I did not question him. We sat companionably before the fire for a few more minutes. Lestrade again refused my offer for another drink, and pulled himself to his feet. "Well, doctor, I must get on to the station. Reports to be written, witnesses to be interviewed. The work of a theorist is fine if you can get it, but nothing can take the place of good old-fashioned police work."

I did not comment on this statement. Instead, I said, "I'm sure Holmes will be in contact with you soon." He nodded, and then, wishing me a good afternoon, he departed.

I resumed my seat by the fire, wondering when Holmes would arrive. He had left the evening before, intending to spend the entire night watching a certain public house in the East End. At that time, I did not accompany Holmes on nearly as many investigations as I would in later years. I was still somewhat lame from the injuries I had sustained in Afghanistan. Holmes, knowing this, only occasionally asked me to join him.

It was not too long before I heard the front door open. It closed, and I could hear the familiar sounds of Holmes pausing to remove his coat and the ear-flapped traveling cap that he insisted on wearing, even in town, both in cool and warm weather. In a moment he climbed the seventeen steps to the sitting room with his peculiar cat-like bound.

"Ah, Watson," he said, entering the room, hanging the hat and coat on a hook. "I am glad you're here. I need your professional services."

He held out his right hand, which had a bloody rag tied around the knuckles.

I retrieved my medical bag. "This is becoming a regular event," I said, motioning him toward the better light from the bow-like window near our dining table. "However, I should add that I am glad that you sought treatment rather than ignoring your wounds, as you have done before."

"I assure you, my friend, that you are my physician of choice. Besides," he added, wincing as I applied an alcohol press to the scrapes along his puffy knuckles, "you are one of the very few doctors that I have encountered that I have not had to turn over to the police for some crime."

As I tied a fresh bandage around his hand, I told him that when the bleeding and oozing had stopped, he should uncover the wounds and allow them to dry. "And how, may I ask, did you come by these bloody decorations?"

"That, Watson, is another of the sordid little tales that occur when several million people collect in one area, and the worst of them drain into that few square miles known as the East End.

"As you know, I have had my eye on Ratchett's Tavern for some time now. It is no wonder that the people there refer to it as 'Wretched's' Tavern, for there is nowhere more bleak or evil. There is no good cheer to be found there, no singing or fraternizing. The women of the street stay away, for they know that the only reason men go there is to drink. Drink and forget.

"In spite of the fact that the men who frequent the place are the forgotten dregs of society, there are a few, a very few, who still have someone in this world to love them. One of these men disappeared recently, and his daughter, who was trying to find him, was sent to me by a friendly inspector at the Yard.

"I might not have become involved, but at nearly the same time, an acquaintance within the government informed me of another situation of which he had recently become aware. I am sorry that I cannot reveal his identity to you at this time, Watson, but he wishes to remain anonymous, due to the nature of the work that he performs."

Although I did not realize it at the time, in later years I came to understand that Holmes was referring to his brother Mycroft, whose identity was revealed to me in the fall of 1888. Up until that time, I had believed that Holmes had as little family in England as I.

"I cannot give you specific details, Watson, for I have given my word to keep this matter quiet, lest the public panic. Suffice it to say, my government source informed me that men were being taken throughout the lowest quarters of London and killed, their bodies being sold to several of our better known hospitals for scientific classroom dissection. It is as if Burke and Hare have returned, but instead of digging up fresh corpses from the local graveyards, the criminals are creating their own corpses.

"Of course, the public might not care if forgotten members of the lowest classes from the East End are being systematically murdered. But they might. There might be a panic that would spread in ways the government would like to avoid. Hence the involvement of my source. And the public would surely be outraged that several of our respected hospitals are participating in this evil scheme. In any case, the murders must stop.

"I divined a connection between the missing man and what my source had told me. I determined, no matter how," he said, holding up his bandaged hand, "that the man had in fact been taken by the killers from Ratchett's Tavern. The men taken from there had nothing left to live for, and most would probably never be missed. Further questions confirmed

63

that other men had vanished from the same location. None, however, with concerned daughters who wished to find them. I set out to watch the tavern, with the aid of some of the Irregulars."

"Holmes," I asked, "Was it wise to involve children in such a matter?" The Irregulars were Holmes's band of street children, able to go anywhere and see everything while remaining ignored and unnoticed. They were fiercely loyal to him, due to his trust in them and his willingness to value them when no one else ever had.

His face turned grim. "Probably not," he replied. "These are evil men, Watson. Killers with a total disregard for the value of another human life, no matter how wasted and pathetic that life is. However, I only used the boys as watchers along side streets, quite far from the tavern. They were simply there to identify which vehicles went in and out of the vile alley where Ratchett's is located.

"Suffice it to say, we caught the killers in the act. Sadly, the man I initially sought was one of the victims, and we were unable to prevent the final murder. However, my government friend has assured me that all of those involved, from Ratchett himself, to the lurkers and killers, and also the doctors at the hospitals who received the bodies, will all be punished to the full extent of the law. And in this case, Watson, I do not refer to the law of courtrooms and speeches and musty law books and negligible punishment for those who can buy it, but rather to that shadowy but very effective law used by the government when justice must be served decidedly but quietly."

I considered this firm, grim form of justice of which he spoke. I had always known, I suppose, that the government could take that kind of action if necessary, but I had never dwelled too much upon it. I knew it was useless to ask Holmes further details. His word was inviolate, and if he had promised not to say anything more specific on the matter, he would not. However, I wondered if St. Bart's, the hospital where I had received my training and where I had met Holmes on New Year's Day 1881, was one of the organizations guilty of participation in the crimes.

As a young student, I had never given much thought to the cadavers from which we learned. One managed quite early to create a distance in the mind between living, breathing people and the cold, broken machines laid open on the tables before us. In this case, some people, including doctors whom I possibly knew and respected, had hardened their feelings concerning the distance which separated life and death to the point where they had no emotions or compassion whatsoever for the living or the dead.

I had been involved with Holmes in the past on a few cases that had led to my awareness of the certainty regarding that secret justice of which Holmes spoke. I suspected that in the near future several noted physicians would retire, or in some extreme cases, possibly die or simply disappear. And I would never know which ones had done so naturally, and which others had brought punishment upon themselves.

After a few moments of silence, I said "By the way, we had a visitor today. A man named Billy Ericson. He was arrested soon after his arrival."

"Ericson," he replied. "A good fellow, who has had some bad luck. I determined for myself at the time of the great scandal at the Yard that he was in no way implicated. However, my assurances were not enough to save his job. I understand he is doing fairly well for himself now as some sort of apprentice."

He glanced toward the door and smiled. "I perceived when I returned that a group of men had been scuffling near the door, but I did not wish to pry, fearing that it was due to a celebration by you and some of your cronies." I scowled as he continued, "What did Ericson want?"

I recounted Ericson's dramatic entrance and subsequent arrest, followed by Lestrade's short sketch of the events leading to Ericson's pursuit and capture in our sitting room. In the middle of my narrative, Mrs. Hudson arrived with hot tea, and it is to her credit that she did not attempt to stay and overhear our conversation, although surely she was curious regarding the afternoon's events.

Holmes stood, his tea half finished, and walked behind me to the wall shelves holding his scrapbooks. I heard him flipping pages and muttering for several moments before he slid the last book back into place and returned to his chair. "Nothing on Gilder and Sons," he said. "And my notes simply confirm what I said about Ericson. An honest man with a turn for bad luck." He stood again and looked pointedly at my tea cup, raised halfway to my lips. "If you're quite finished, Watson," he said, "we can be on our way to the police station to speak to our client."

Less than thirty minutes later, we were in a room awaiting Lestrade to bring in the prisoner. When Ericson was led in, still shackled, Lestrade indicated that our time would be limited. "And a constable will be right outside if you need him, gentlemen," he said pointedly.

The room was dim, except for the sunlight from a high barred window and the low gaslight burning on the wall. Holmes and Ericson stared at one another for just a moment, before Holmes finally said, "Well, Billy, how did you find yourself in this dilemma?"

"I don't know, Mr. Holmes. All I know is that Cheltenham died, right there in front of me. I thought he was having some sort of fit. Even when the police were called in, I believed it was just a matter of routine. I used to be on the force, Mr. Holmes. If I'd known there was anything wrong, I would have certainly paid more attention.

65

"It was only when I became dimly aware through all the noise that Mrs. Gilder was accusing me of a crime that I realized what was happening. Suddenly, I was surrounded by constables, told that I was under arrest for the murder. It was all dark at that point. It was like I was in a tunnel, and could only see straight ahead of me. My blood was roaring in my ears, and I couldn't believe my ill luck. Then I thought of you. I was still on the force when you solved that difficult murder out in Norwood. You know, the one where the man was found dead on the parlor rug, with five women's wedding bands laid around his head?"

Holmes nodded, but I had no knowledge of the case. Ericson mentioned. "I've never forgotten how you lectured us that day, Mr. Holmes, on the importance of trifles. All I could think was I needed to get you on my side, Mr. Holmes. Before I really knew what I was doing, I had broken free of the guards and was running down Praed Street toward your house. Of course they were following me, but I wasn't even aware of it. I know that it makes things look worse for me, running like that, but I just wasn't thinking. I just ducked and dodged around the traffic and people until I saw your door. Your landlady happened to be standing in the open doorway, checking the post I suppose, and I moved around her and inside. Then I ducked up the stairs, where I managed to speak to this gentleman," he said, indicating me, "before Lestrade and his boys nipped me."

"All right, Billy," Holmes said. "What happened this morning at Gilder's, before the man died?" Ericson proceeded to give us a summary of the events, which was surprisingly close to what Lestrade had related to me earlier in the day. "I don't know how he got poisoned, Mr. Holmes," Ericson concluded. "For all I know, it might have been meant for me."

"A possibility that had already occurred to me as well," Holmes replied. He stood. "Well, Billy, I shall ask around some and see if we can get to the bottom of this. We will be back if I need any further information."

Ericson thrust out his shackled hand. "That's good enough for me, Mr. Holmes. I know I didn't do it, and with you working to find the truth I am certain that I shall soon be freed." He shook my hand as well, and turned toward the door. It opened before he reached it, revealing the constable waiting to return him to his cell. After they had passed down the hall, Lestrade slipped into the room.

"Well, Mr. Holmes? Do you agree that we've got the right man?"

Holmes didn't answer for a moment, and then said "We'll see, Lestrade, we'll see." He left without further comment. I met Lestrade's amused glance, shook his hand with murmured thanks, and followed Holmes.

Outside, Holmes hailed a cab. "Dear me, Watson," he said. "What if Lestrade actually turns out to be right some day?" He laughed in that odd silent way that he had. "It is not far to Gilder's, but I have noticed that your leg is causing you some pain. Let us forego a walk, although the day is certainly pleasant enough, and take a cab."

We rattled west in a hansom, traveling for short distances on several busy thoroughfares mixed with less crowded side streets. Turning onto Praed Street, I gave no notice whatsoever to No.7, little realizing at the time that in a few years it would be the site of my home with my second wife, Mary, and my small but growing medical practice. Many years after that, it would become the lodgings of one of Holmes's relatives. However, that was in the future. On the day of Cheltenham's murder, I had no idea that I would live on Praed Street near Paddington.

Gilder and Sons was located in an old, short building, with only two floors and a partial basement. The ground floor front had originally been some sort of shop, but it had been recently walled off to make a small reception area. The rest of the ground floor was filled with drafting tables and conference rooms. At the back was a large doorway which opened onto a storage room. I could see a sliding door leading to the loading dock in the rear alley. Upstairs, the first floor was divided into offices, while the basement was given over to storage. The building was freshly painted, and obvious construction work had taken place inside, as evidenced by new decorative moldings and trim work.

No one was in the reception area when we entered, although a small bell over the door rang. We waited a moment, but no one came from the back to greet us. The building was filled with an unidentifiable musty smell, although it appeared to be orderly and clean. We could hear muted conversation through the door at the back of the reception lobby. With unspoken agreement, we went into the next part of the building.

A number of employees were standing in two or three small groups, clustered in several parts of the large room. The drafting tables stood empty, the cluttered sheets on top of each table ignored. Gradually the room fell silent as, one by one, the small groups noticed us. The last to stop talking was a heavy-set woman with her back to us. Perceiving the silence, she turned and saw us.

As she walked across the room, I had a chance to observe her. She was in her early forties, and moved with a peculiar and heavy rolling flat-footed gait. Her clothes were obviously ten pounds too tight for her, and her thick, blonde, curly hair had come loose from its severe bun in several places, waving around her head like coiled springs. She had some sort of rouge on her face, but it did nothing to cover the coarseness of her skin, as well as several pock marks. The color of the make-up sharply contrasted with her

67

wan coloring and yellow hair, making her face look as if it were bruised. Her eyes were bright and clear, set unusually close together, and there was no sign of grief there.

"What do you want? Are you with the police? Are you reporters?" she asked.

"Neither," replied my friend.

Before he could continue, the woman stated "Then you will have to leave. We have work to do here." Then, as if realizing that she had to establish her authority, she added, "I am Mrs. Gilder."

"How do you do," said my friend. "I am Sherlock Holmes, and this is my associate, Dr. John Watson."

Mrs. Gilder did not bother to glance in my direction. Her eyes remained locked on Holmes's face, although they did narrow, seemingly with irritation and a trace of suspicion.

"I know of you, Mr. Holmes," she said, stopping within a few feet of us, close enough that she had to look up sharply to see into Holmes's eyes. "I've heard of you. I'm sure you're here about today's ugly business. But there can be nothing for you to detect, can there? The matter has been settled, and the killer taken by the police."

"I would like to ask you a few questions," Holmes stated. "And perhaps if Mr. Gilder is available as well?"

"Mr. Gilder is ill. After the events of the last few months, it is no wonder."

She turned away, looking for someone. "Robbins," she said, spotting a thin gray fellow standing near one of the drafting tables. "Show these men out." She walked away and through a door at the rear of the room. We were clearly dismissed.

Robbins stepped forward in an odd, stooping way. "This way, gentlemen," he said quietly, gesturing toward the door to the reception area. As there was nothing else for us to do, we followed him. I was aware of the silence in the room as the remaining employees mutely watched our progress. As we passed out of the room, subdued conversations resumed behind us. Robbins held open the outer door, and then followed us out onto the sidewalk, pulling the door to in a smooth silent motion. "I must apologize for Mrs. Gilder's shortness with you, gentlemen. She is usually most gracious, but today's events . . . " His voice faded as he recalled what had happened that morning.

"We understand," Holmes said. "What exactly has happened to Mr. Gilder? My friend here is a doctor. Perhaps he can help."

"Oh, Mr. Gilder has his own doctor, sir. Dr. Rossman. A good old man. He has been the physician to Mr. Gilder's family since long before Mr.

Gilder was born. I'm sure he will be fine, sir. He's strong, Mr. Gilder is. It's just his spirit that needs mending after the last few months."

"Yes," said Holmes. "Mrs. Gilder said something along the same lines. Have there been other incidents before today's murder?"

"Well, not like today, sir. Nothing like that, thank the Lord. I wouldn't want to have to see something like that again. No, a few months ago, both Mr. Gilder's sons died from some sort of food poisoning. And a few months before that, back around Christmas, Mr. Gilder's first wife died as well. She had been quite ill for some time, so that was no surprise to any of us."

"His first wife?" Holmes asked. "So the current Mrs. Gilder is a recent arrival?"

"Well sir, only somewhat recent. She had been the Gilders' housekeeper for some months before Mrs. Gilder died. Since last fall, I believe. After that, she stepped in, helping Mr. Gilder through his grief. It wasn't long before she was accompanying him to the business, offering suggestions about how he might improve things here and there. Before we knew it, they were married."

I could see Holmes was ready to ask another question, but suddenly Robbins became aware that he was perhaps spending longer than he should have talking to us. He stated that he needed to return to his tasks. Holmes asked if we might meet with Robbins later to speak more of the matter, but Robbins did not answer, simply telling us goodbye and stepping back into the building.

We began to walk slowly east along Praed Street, Holmes deep in thought. After a few moments, he asked if I wished to get a cab.

However, my leg showed no signs of discomfort, and I indicated that we should continue walking.

Allowing Holmes to lead, I was unsurprised after a few minutes to see that we had returned to the police station. Inside, we asked after Lestrade, who soon appeared from a back office.

"Autopsy report?" he replied to Holmes's initial question. "I was just reading it when you came in. Strychnine poisoning. Really not a surprise, considering the symptoms and the rapid effects. There was residue in Cheltenham's teacup, and it was all through his system." He paused to glance at a sheaf of papers in his hand. "*Strychnine nux vomica.* Almost half a grain – you know that's more than lethal, Mr. Holmes."

He handed the papers to Holmes, who glanced through them quickly. "This saves us a trip to the morgue, Watson," he said. "Strychnine is extremely bitter, Lestrade. Did Cheltenham give no indication that he tasted it in the tea?"

"Apparently not. Drank it right down, he did." Lestrade replied. "Several people stated that Cheltenham liked his tea very strong. Brewed it as black as he could get it, much like strong coffee, no sugar or cream. It was common knowledge around the office. Ericson confirmed this. He said that he likes it the same way himself. Drinking tea was about the only thing he and Cheltenham had in common."

"Is Ericson still here? Has he been moved yet?" Holmes asked. "I would like to speak to him again."

"He is here, Mr. Holmes. Follow me, gentlemen."

Lestrade took us back through the building, into a locked narrow hallway passing along a series of cell doors. At the fourth on the right, he stopped, looked through the Judas Hole, and signaled to a nearby constable to unlock the door. "Let us know when you want out," Lestrade replied before departing.

Ericson was stretched out on a cot, but not asleep. He pivoted and sat up as we entered. He did not appear to be stressed or upset. "Any luck, gentlemen?" he asked. I could tell that he had been serious when he placed his unwavering confidence in Holmes.

"Not yet," Holmes replied. "But I did want to ask a few more questions. We have been to Gilder's, but information was not very forthcoming."

"Not surprising," Ericson said as he offered us a seat on the cot. We both declined. "I had only worked there a few months, but during that time I had noticed a certain atmosphere there. Kind of 'Don't ask any questions, just do your work.' I always put it down to the recent deaths in Gilder's family."

"Yes, we heard about that from a man named Robbins. What do you know about him?"

"Ah, Robbins," Ericson stated. "He started there as an apprentice, probably twenty years ago. He knows all there is to know about the trade, but he was never encouraged to rise any further in the business. I suppose it has served the Gilders well. Another man might have wanted a partnership, or would have left long ago for something better. Robbins just keeps on coming to work each day. He's really the backbone of the place."

"I understand the original Mrs. Gilder died around Christmas, and the sons somewhat later," Holmes said. "Were you working there at that time?"

"No, sir. I actually obtained my position a couple of weeks after the death of the sons. They died in mid-March, and I started in early April."

"Death certainly seems to be lurking around Mr. Gilder," said Holmes. "How did he happen to lose his whole family in so short a time?"

70

"I don't rightly know the exact details," replied Ericson. "The first Mrs. Gilder had apparently suffered from a weak heart. She had taken to her bed, and was found one day while Mr. Gilder and his sons were at work."

"What about the sons?" Holmes asked. "Some sort of accident?"

"Well, not quite, not in the sense you mean, Mr. Holmes," said Ericson. "There was apparently a type of food poisoning at work. A lot of the employees came down with it. Stomach distress, I heard. They had to close up shop for a few days. Most everyone got well, and I heard the sons had started to, as well, but then they took a turn for the worse and both died suddenly. There was talk of cholera, or some such. The authorities didn't want to start a panic, and they tested to see if there was a problem at Gilder's with the water, but nothing ever came of it. It was finally decided that it was food poisoning. There had been an office gathering soon before the illnesses began, and it's probable that there was something wrong with a portion of the food."

Holmes thought for a moment, rubbing his finger along his lower lip. "And was the current Mrs. Gilder helping at the office by the time you started?"

"Yes, sir, she was. Mr. Gilder was pretty much useless by that time, overwhelmed by grief, you understand, and it seemed he had nothing left to live for but the business. Mrs. Gilder – she wasn't Mrs. Gilder then, but Miss Wickett – was coming in with him, acting as a go-between for him, passing on instructions to Robbins and the others while he stayed shut up in his office. It was just a few weeks before they announced that they were going to be married. Gilder explained that he realized that it was a short time since the deaths of his family, but he needed her and did not want to wait. Some people whispered and were scandalized, of course, but I was a new employee and hardly knew any of 'em, so I didn't care." He stopped to rub his nose. "Lately, Mr. Gilder just stays at home, and Mrs. Gilder handles the day-to-day running of the office."

"Did you get along well there? What was your relation with Cheltenham?"

"It was just fine, Mr. Holmes. Just fine," Erickson replied. "I don't care what has been said, I'm old enough to know how to get along with people, and Cheltenham had certainly never done anything to cause me to murder him. He got on my nerves because he spent a lot of time trying to correct my work, when in fact what I had produced was just fine. It just didn't match the way he did it. Two different ways of getting to the same answer, if you get my meaning."

"What about everyone else?" Holmes queried. "If you didn't murder Cheltenham, someone else did. Strychnine doesn't just happen to be lying around, and it doesn't get into someone's tea by accident. If you didn't

71

murder Cheltenham, someone else did," he repeated. "or for some reason someone was trying to murder you."

"I have been trying to puzzle it out myself, sir, and I just cannot picture it, Mr. Holmes," Ericson replied. "I got along well with everyone there. Robbins was teaching me a lot, and people were always friendly. I never saw any of them away from work. Well, except for the one time I saw Mrs. Gilder."

"Oh?" said Holmes. "When was that?"

"Let me see. I guess it was probably around last Christmas. I remember I was still on the force then, and questioning some people in Mr. Gilder's neighborhood about whether they had seen anything suspicious in the area. There had been a few burglaries at some houses on a nearby street.

"As I recall, Gilder's was one of the houses I went to. Mrs. Gilder answered the door – she was the housekeeper then, and was still Miss Wickett. In fact, I believe it must have been right after the first Mrs. Gilder died, because there was a black wreath on the door.

"Of course, I remembered her. Have you met her? She is rather unique looking, as you will have seen, with that curly blonde hair. But when I went to the house, I simply explained what I was doing and asked if there had been any questionable people in the neighborhood. She said no, and when I asked who had died, she explained that the lady of the house had just passed away. I expressed my condolences and left."

"And you had no further contact with her?"

"None. Soon after, I left the force, and after a few odd jobs, I obtained the position at Gilder's. In fact, my meeting in December had made no impression on Mrs. Gilder at all. Just a couple of weeks ago we were talking, and I mentioned that she had been gracious to me when I called on the house at Christmas. She didn't remember the incident at all until I recalled it for her. She seemed surprised that I had once been on the Force, and that I was working at Gilder's now. We talked about what a small world it was."

Holmes was silent for a moment. Then he looked up. "I believe that is all for today, Billy," he said. He turned toward the door. "I hope to have some news for you soon."

As Holmes knocked to be let out, Ericson said, "Do you have any hope, Mr. Holmes?"

"I see a thread," Holmes replied, as the door opened and he and I moved through it. "A small thread," he repeated. "I will pull it and see what unravels."

Back in Baker Street, Holmes stopped long enough to remove his coat before walking to his commonplace books on a shelf by the fireplace. Apparently he did not find what he was searching for, as he went out to the landing and on upstairs to our lumber room. He did not come down when Mrs. Hudson brought up tea, and when I checked on him later, I found him sitting cross-legged on the floor, looking through the piles of newspapers that he saved, according to his own eccentric organizational system.

Holmes came down an hour later, covered in dust. He summoned the page boy and sent several telegrams. He was mostly silent during dinner, absently pushing his food around before moving to his chair and lighting his briar pipe.

I read most of the evening, and when I became impatient with the story I began to consider going to bed. Holmes looked up. "There is nothing to do for Ericson but wait on replies to my wires," he said. "In the meantime, I shall spend tomorrow finishing up some of the loose ends related to the events at Ratchett's Tavern."

I stood and stretched. I could see that Holmes showed every sign of sitting in his chair all night, smoking and thinking, as he wrestled the problem from every angle until he thought he understood what was going on. "What do you expect to hear from the wires you sent?" I asked.

"Whether or not the Gilder family can be exhumed," he replied.

On that note, I climbed the stairs to my room and went to bed.

I did not see much of Holmes the next day. I myself had some personal errands to run in the morning, and he was gone until evening. Holmes returned just before dinner, and did not seem surprised when I told him that no replies had come to the previous day's wires.

"I expected as much. I had some time to devote to the matter, so I made several calls related to Ericson's problem while I was out today.

"Early this afternoon, I met shortly with Dr. Rossman, the Gilder family physician. He was Gilder's mother's doctor, and has been taking care of Mr. Gilder since the man was born. As Mr. Gilder is in his early sixties, you can imagine that Dr. Rossman is getting rather long in the tooth.

"The good doctor was not able to add any further details to what we have already heard. He examined both the first Mrs. Gilder at the time of her death and the sons a few months ago. He is certain that the wife died of a weak heart, and the sons both had a relapse from the food poisoning that swept through Gilder's business. He attributes both sons' deaths to the effects of food poisoning on possibly weakened constitutions that the boys had inherited from their mother.

"Incidentally, the Gilder sons, Stuart and Henry, were both only in their early twenties. Apparently the Gilders had been married for some years and had been unsuccessful at starting a family. Suddenly, when both parents least suspected it, Mrs. Gilder became pregnant with the boys,

73

almost back to back. Rossman attributes the unexpected pregnancies as a factor contributing to her weakened heart.

"Later, I managed to have a note sent in to Robbins at Gilder's, arranging for him to step out and meet with me for five minutes. He was late, and I initially did not think he would show up. However, he did, and we spoke for nearer a quarter of an hour. He did not add any substantial information to what we already know, other than some facts about the current Mrs. Gilder, *née* Wickett.

"According to Robbins, she started to work as a housekeeper for the Gilders in the fall of last year. However, she soon began spending an unusual amount of time at the business. She started by delivering baskets of food to Mr. Gilder and his sons. She would often stay, appearing interested in the workings of the business. By this spring, she was a regular fixture at the place, and during the affair which led to the company food poisoning incident, a birthday celebration for Mr. Gilder, she actually cooked most of the dishes which were fed to the employees.

"I tried to see Mr. Gilder at his home, but his current housekeeper said that he was in bed under doctor's orders, and he was not able to see visitors. She referred me to Mrs. Gilder, at the place of business, but I chose not to go back there and speak to her.

"I also visited with Cheltenham's wife. She could not offer any theory as to why her husband was killed, and stated that he really had no relations with anyone at Gilder's except in the workplace.

"I met with Lestrade today," Holmes continued. "I explained my theories to him, and somehow managed to convince him of their validity, at least somewhat, so the exhumation may proceed without our involvement. However, I believe that Lestrade will include us at the end, if my suppositions are correct."

I asked him to elaborate on his theories, but he just smiled and said, "I fancy you can reason it out from here, doctor. I noticed a look of enlightenment cross your face during my short summary of today's events." I did not take offense at his secrecy. I knew it was part of his personality to preserve the solution so that it could be dramatically revealed.

I stood up as his eyes followed me and walked to my desk between the two windows. I wrote two words on a sheet of paper and sealed it in an envelope, which I then stood on the mantle. "This is my solution," I said. "We shall see."

He smiled. "Yes, we shall."

I asked him if there was any further word on the Ratchett's Tavern business. He replied cryptically, "It is being taking care of. I am really sorry that I cannot tell you more, Watson. It is truly a singular business."

I knew that I would not get anything further out of him on the matter.

The following morning, while we were eating breakfast, Holmes received a wire. Tearing it open, he read it, said "Ha!" and tossed it to me as he stood and walked toward his bedroom, removing his dressing gown.

The wire simply said 'Strychnine present. Meet at Gilder's all possible speed to participate in arrest. Lestrade.' "

We were able to hail a cab almost immediately, and mere moments later we were deposited in front of the Gilder building. The police were already there, and as we walked up, two constables hauled a subdued and defeated Mrs. Gilder through the front door. Lestrade followed behind her. Inside, I could see Robbins, wringing his hands and speaking over his shoulder to a cluster of employees remaining in the shadows.

When Mrs. Gilder saw Holmes she stood taller and began to hurl a series of vile epithets his way that seemed especially shocking, coming from a woman of her supposed standing. However, her whole manner had changed from the day when we first met her. Now she seemed much more coarse and offensive. She did not stop her rants, even as she was loaded into the waiting carriage for transport to the police station.

Lestrade stood beside us as we watched the carriage move down Praed Street. "Mr. Holmes, Doctor," he said. "Well, the strychnine was there, just like you said. I must say, I was really going out on a limb this time, Mr. Holmes. But as they say, the proof was in the pudding. I must be going, but I will expect you down at the station later for your statement, please."

Lestrade turned and walked back into Gilder's. "Another triumph for Inspector Lestrade," Holmes said softly under his breath.

"I assume you will be explaining this to me," I said.

"Of course, my dear Watson," he replied. "But let us return to Baker Street. We can discuss it as well in front of our fire as we can here in the street."

In just a few minutes, we were back home, relaxing in front of the fire, drinking coffee still warm from breakfast. Holmes gestured toward the mantle. "May I see what you wrote?" he asked.

I stood and handed it to him, a smile dancing around my lips. He tore open the envelope and pulled out the slip of paper.

" 'Mrs. Gilder'," he read. "Very good, Watson. Very good. And tell me, how did you arrive at your conclusion?"

"Nothing specific, I'm afraid. Death simply seemed to surround her."

"Ah, but the same could be said for Mr. Gilder, as well," Holmes said.

"True," I said. "You remarked on that fact the other day. However, I could see no benefit in it for him. He might have killed his wife in order to marry his housekeeper, Miss Wickett, but he would have no need to kill his own sons. And I can see no reason for him to murder Cheltenham or

Ericson, whichever was the intended victim. In fact, I cannot see a reason for Mrs. Gilder to murder Cheltenham or Ericson, either, unless she thought that one of them had discovered information implicating her in the previous deaths.

"I suppose Robbins, or even some other employee we have not met, could have been involved, but again I did not see how or why. Robbins has shown no interest in rising in the company, and apparently has no ambition strong enough to commit murder. It just made sense to choose Mrs. Gilder. She has certainly benefited. She is now the wife of the company owner. And after all, you did tell me once that poison was a woman's weapon."

"Often true, Watson, but not always. I also arrived at Mrs. Gilder as an early suspect, for exactly the same reasons that you did. After hearing some of the family's sad history, I realized that she was the most logical person to have benefited from the death of the first wife. It did not take her very long at all to move in and marry the widower. The death of the sons only made things easier. Mr. Gilder was at a very low point following the deaths of his family. All of this seemed to indicate that she was, at least, the person who needed to be examined the most.

"Of course, the deaths could have been exactly what they seemed to be – a middle-aged woman's heart problems, and later, food poisoning that affected everyone at the business, and simply took the sons by some random chance because they were somewhat weakened. And Cheltenham's death could have been an entirely separate incident, related to something in Cheltenham's life, unconnected with the business, or even a misplaced attempt to kill Billy Ericson.

"After we returned to Baker Street the other afternoon, I went through the old newspapers in the lumber room, searching out the original accounts of the Gilder family deaths. There was no additional information to be found that substantially added to what we had already learned. I then spent the rest of the evening building and tearing down theories. Time after time I would construct a tenuous framework that might explain a connection between the earlier deaths and Cheltenham's murder. And each time I would tear it down, until I built one that seemed to be better than the others.

"My idea was that the first Mrs. Gilder could have been killed somehow by Miss Wickett, who was in the house with her each day as the family housekeeper. The death from heart problems could have been legitimate, or it could have been caused in some way. In any event, it was unlikely to be investigated, as the first Mrs. Gilder had been in ill health for some time.

"I have no doubt that the housekeeper had her eye on Mr. Gilder. Whether she helped the first wife shuffle off this mortal coil, or whether the death was accidental, did not affect my theory. For I felt that the subsequent deaths of the two sons had to be examined in light of Cheltenham's murder.

"As you know, Watson, some of the symptoms of strychnine poisoning are similar to the results of food poisoning. Now suppose, as I did the other night, that the housekeeper managed to poison some of the food to be taken to the office gathering by the Gilders in order to cause a widespread illness in which to hide her actual scheme. You know that there are ways to do such a thing if a person is diabolically clever."

I nodded. "She would simply have had to mix in some spoiled ingredients into her food. Possibly tainted fish . . . . "

"Exactly," Holmes agreed. "Ingestion would cause violent illness. No doubt she picked a dish to alter that the sons favored. Perhaps she even poisoned some of their food at home, as well, in order to particularly weaken them. Poisoning the food taken to the gathering would have the added result of sickening anyone else who ate it as well. If someone else died, it would simply lend credibility to the events. A round of apparent food poisoning would then sweep the office, disguising what the housekeeper intended to do.

"As the sons tried to get better, they would of course recuperate at home. The housekeeper would then be right there in the house, giving them broth and whatever else they could tolerate in order to build up their strength. She would then be able to re-poison them as necessary, causing relapses and further weakening their systems. Eventually, she would be able to slip them some of the strychnine that she may or may not have used on their mother a few months earlier. Both young men would die, and who would question it? Certainly not the rather ancient Doctor Rossman, who accepted the deaths due to food poisoning with no questions. The young men would simply be tragic victims of the same food poisoning epidemic that had so recently swept their workplace."

"Leaving the housekeeper to step in and marry Mr. Gilder," I added.

"But why did Cheltenham have to die? Or Ericson?"

"Oh, Ericson was always the intended victim," Holmes replied. "Of course, Lestrade will have to confirm my supposition, but I theorized that Mrs. Gilder believed that Ericson was in some way suspicious of her, and she decided to kill him. She slipped the strychnine into his teacup during the time Cheltenham and Ericson were at the back of the building bringing in the new furniture. Ericson's disagreements with Cheltenham were common knowledge, and she intended that Cheltenham should be blamed for the death. Somehow, the identical mugs were reversed, and Cheltenham drank the poisoned tea, thus resulting in his death."

Lestrade dropped by a few hours later, accompanied by a grateful Billy Ericson. As they sat near us by the fire, Lestrade confirmed the essentials of Holmes's theory.

"She seemed almost proud, once she started talking," he said. "She confirmed that she had been giving the first wife an overdose of digitalis, interfering with her heart rate. Finally the poor woman had taken to her bed. After a few weeks, the housekeeper had simply helped matters along by holding a pillow over the poor woman's face.

"Of course, she and Gilder had been having an affair for several months before that, almost since she had been employed at the house. After his wife's death, Gilder was overwhelmed with guilt, but she simply used that to manipulate him. She kept talking about how easy he was to fool.

"She said she didn't originally intend to kill the sons as well. At first, she simply planned to marry Gilder. However, as time went on, she realized that she didn't want to share any of the man's fortune. She had worked as a nurse at some time in the past, and knew something about illnesses and poisons. She poisoned some of the food at the birthday celebration, just like we thought, Mr. Holmes," – Holmes smiled at Lestrade's use of "we" – "and after it was common knowledge that the boys were weak from food poisoning, she killed them with strychnine.

"Soon after, she married Gilder, and she thought everything was working out perfectly. Then our friend Billy, here," he said, nodding at Ericson, who smiled, "got a job there. A week or so ago, they were talking and it was mentioned about his previous visit to the Gilder house last year. She remembered when he'd talked to her there last Christmas. She began to worry that he was actually still employed with the Yard as a detective, and that he was only working at Gilder's in order to obtain evidence against her. As she worried about it more and more, she began to plan how she could kill him and make it look like Cheltenham's fault.

"It's a good thing we got her when we did," added Lestrade. "She hasn't been spending all these months learning the business just because it interested her. Once she felt that she had a grasp of how to run the place, she planned to get rid of Mr. Gilder as well.

"Even after we had her down at the station, she wouldn't believe that Ericson hadn't been working there as an undercover officer. She was trying to get her solicitor to say that she had been coerced into accidentally killing Cheltenham by the pressure and worry that Ericson's presence had created for her. The solicitor kept trying to make her be quiet. I wouldn't be surprised if he doesn't try to beat the hangman with an insanity plea."

"They let me see her before we came here," Ericson said. "She was calm at first, and seemed almost proud of what she'd done, until she couldn't get me to admit that I was still on the Force. At that point she started to rage and had to be restrained."

"So it was all resolved due to a mistake," I said. "If she had left well enough alone, and stopped with the deaths of Gilder's sons, none of the murders would have ever been suspected or detected."

"Exactly," said Lestrade. "I must admit, when I took Mr. Holmes's request for an exhumation to my superiors, I thought I would soon be looking for another position, much like friend Ericson here. Thankfully, they were willing to listen. Lethal amounts of strychnine were found in the bodies of the two Gilder sons. Of course, nothing questionable was found in the first wife's body, but after today's confession, that doesn't really matter."

Later that night, I questioned Holmes about the matter. "It seems to me," I said, "that you were willing to base your solution on somewhat more guesswork than is usual."

He did not speak for a moment. Then he rose, knocked out his pipe into the grate, and placed it on the mantle. "Perhaps you're right, Watson," he said. "The chain of events that I hypothesized was somewhat unsupported. However, all I can claim is that it held together better than the other theories that I examined, and that, along with my experience, seemed to be enough to suggest additional action. I decided in this case to go ahead and proceed with confidence in my interpretation of the facts, thus eliminating some unnecessary steps. I was aware that if Lestrade followed through on my request for exhumations, and that there was no evidence of previous poisonings, my credibility would be seriously damaged.

"However, it did seem worth the gamble. I gambled and won. Mrs. Gilder gambled and lost. All one can do in life is take a chance. And now, Watson, I wish you good night."

Mrs. Gilder was convicted, but her death sentence was later commuted. I believe that she has remained in an asylum ever since. Ericson was offered a new position with the police force, but chose to continue his apprenticeship with another company. Robbins bought Gilder and Sons, retaining the name of the company due to its long reputation. However, he soon mismanaged it, showing that while he had excellent building skills, he did not have a gift for running a business, and it closed for good. Mr. Gilder moved to the north of England, and I have heard no more of him. Within days of these events, Ratchett's Tavern in the East End mysteriously burned to the ground, and around that time, a number of noted doctors connected with London's teaching hospitals either retired, or in the case of two notable men, committed suicide.

The Singular Affair at Sissinghurst Castle

"What do you say to a day in Kent, Watson?" Sherlock Holmes asked me with a smile.

I folded my newspaper and laid it in my lap. "No doubt you simply want to get out in this fine spring sunshine and look at the plants and flowers."

"Something of the sort," Holmes replied.

"And that wire?" I asked, glancing at the telegram he held in his hand. "Would that perhaps be the motivating factor behind your suggestion?"

"Perhaps, Watson. Perhaps."

I looked past him at the warm sunshine pouring in the window above his chemical table. The angle of the morning light prevented me from seeing the house across the street. However, I could imagine the bright reflection on the bricks and pavement outside, washed by the previous day's rain. It would surely be a wonderful day to be out of London, and in the beautiful countryside.

I stood up. "Kent sounds wonderful. When do we leave?"

Forty-five minutes later we were on a train meandering through South London, heading toward Tunbridge Wells. I shifted impatiently in my seat, waiting to break free of the city and start seeing the natural unspoiled beauty of the English villages and farmlands.

That spring of 1888 had been a difficult one for me. The past December, I had lost my first wife, Constance, to a sudden illness. Holmes had immediately invited me back to my old rooms in Baker Street. I had sold my medical practice in Kensington, which had never been very interesting or involving at the best of times. New participation in his investigations had served as a useful distraction from my loss. Already that year we had been involved in the Birlstone tragedy, as well as the singular matter of the misplaced ruler. The previous week Holmes had identified the mysterious neighbor of Mr. Grant Munro. It will be recalled, however, that Holmes's prediction of the neighbor's identity was far more grim than the happy truth that was actually revealed.

Holmes interrupted my thoughts. "Work truly is the best antidote, my friend," he said quietly. I looked up and smiled. I had been rubbing my finger where I used to wear my wedding ring. It had not taken Holmes's great powers of deduction to understand about what I had been thinking. My late wife had been in my thoughts a great deal this spring.

80

"So," I asked, looking around as we began to move into more rural areas. "Where in Kent are we going?"

"Sissinghurst. Do you know of it?"

"Not at all, I'm afraid."

"It is a small village south of Maidstone and east of Tunbridge Wells. I am not aware of anything remarkable about the village itself. However, we are specifically traveling to the manor house there, which I understand is the most memorable structure in the area.

"I received a letter several days ago from the owner of the house and surrounding farm, a Mr. Stanley Cornwallis. I then researched the area, endeavoring to find something to help Mr. Cornwallis with his problem."

The train was picking up speed, heading to the southeast. The sun was now higher in the sky, as it was getting on toward late morning. Everywhere I looked seemed fresh and green. The previous day's rain and the recent warm weather had combined to give extra beauty to the spring-time growth. In the distant lowlands toward the south, I saw occasional pockets of mist as the sun evaporated the residual moisture.

"What does Mr. Cornwallis require from Mr. Sherlock Holmes," I asked.

"He is being bothered by a treasure hunter," said Holmes.

I cocked my head and smiled. "Treasure? In Kent? I might believe that about some of the areas along the coast, with their centuries of smuggling and the occasional shipwreck. But deep in the heart of the county? Not likely."

"There is more than one kind of treasure, Watson," Holmes replied. "It was only a few months ago that I told you about Reginald Musgrave at Hurlstone, and the recovery there of the lost crown of the former King of England."

I nodded. The odd tale of the ritual, repeated by the members of the Musgrave family for centuries, and Holmes's subsequent solution, was only one of many of the cases related to me by Holmes during the past January. Always very private in the past, Holmes had become more open recently, talking about his earlier cases as a way of distracting me from my recent bereavement.

"As I recall, King Charles's crown was hidden at Hurlstone during the reign of Cromwell and the Commonwealth. Does Cornwallis suspect something similar is hidden at Sissinghurst?"

"No, he believes exactly the opposite. He is certain that there is nothing hidden at the house. The estate apparently has some connection with events relating to those muddled times of transition between Queen Mary and Elizabeth. It is a common story in that area, but there has never been any hint of treasure. However, several weeks ago, an American arrived in

Sissinghurst, repeatedly insisting on searching the buildings and grounds for something of value. So far, Mr. Cornwallis has denied him any access, apparently because he simply does not wish to be annoyed.

"However, it seems that in spite of his initial disbelief, Mr. Cornwallis did become more interested in whether there is any truth to the American's claims," Holmes continued. "Cornwallis's first letter to me simply related the basic facts of the situation, and asked if I would be interested in doing some research to determine if there was any possibility of truth in the matter. I replied, writing to him that I would do some small investigation in London, but that I did not expect to find anything too interesting, and that I did not propose to spend a great deal of time on the matter.

"I devoted part of a day earlier in the week in the reading room at the British Museum, where I spent so many hours early in my career during those long days when clients were few and far between. Although there is some local historical significance to Mr. Cornwallis's farm, I found no evidence of anything relevant to a treasure at Sissinghurst.

"I was ready to relay my results to Mr. Cornwallis when this morning's wire arrived. Something seems to have happened that made our presence necessary. As you can see," Holmes said, fishing the folded sheet from his waistcoat pocket, "the message is rather vague as to details."

I unfolded it and read, "Come at once. Situation becoming intolerable. Please wire details of arrival. Cornwallis." I handed the wire back to Holmes. "Vague, indeed. It could be anything from an unpleasant encounter with the American, to murder."

"Well, perhaps not murder," Holmes smiled. "If it was murder, Cornwallis might have used stronger language than to simply call the situation 'intolerable.' "

"Could you tell anything about him from his initial letter?" I asked.

"Nothing substantial. Mid-twenties, well-to-do, well educated. Nervous disposition, somewhat careless. Possibly asthmatic. Surely some sort of breathing problem. And he has traveled extensively on the continent."

"Of course, you can tell this from his handwriting, choice of wording, phrasing, writing numbers in the continental fashion, etcetera?"

"Of course."

"And the breathing problem?"

"The odor of camphor hung about the letter, and especially the glue used to seal the envelope."

I nodded. All of this would have been instantly apparent to Holmes as he read the letter, as clear as if the young man were standing in front of him. By this time, having known Holmes for over seven years, I was not surprised when he was able to deduce so much from so little. I did not take it for granted, and I did not demean it, but I was no longer surprised.

We rode in silence for a while, carrying on desultory conversation when the mood struck us. This was one of the rare occasions when Holmes did not bury himself in a stack of newspapers obtained at the station before our departure. The land gradually became flatter, and large agricultural fields spread around us. We began to pass the odd looking oast houses, those cone-shaped buildings so common to Kent. They had always reminded me in some strange way of the Netherlands, looking as they did like windmills without wheels. I observed Holmes looking at them as well. "We are truly a diverse country, Watson," he said. I nodded in agreement.

Arriving in Tunbridge Wells, we waited for nearly half an hour before catching a local train, heading in the general direction of Sissinghurst. I had eaten a sandwich at the station while waiting for the local, although Holmes had nothing. Instead, he spent his time verifying train times in our Bradshaw.

The local arrived on time, and we boarded. The combination of warm weather and the rocking of the carriage caused me to take a short nap. However, I quickly awoke when we reached the next station. After traveling as far as we could by rail, we had arrived in a small village whose name I have long since forgotten. Holmes had wired ahead the time of our arrival. However, it soon became apparent that Cornwallis had not sent transportation to pick us up. We hired a carriage to take us east for the remaining distance to Sissinghurst. Our driver was a heavy-set fellow of the same coloring, build, and temperament as the burly horse pulling our conveyance. We drove some miles through the pleasant sunshine in silence. At one point, Holmes asked the man if he could tell us anything about Sissinghurst.

"Not much to tell," the man replied. "There's the village, and the main farm. It's well run, it is. The farmhouse is very nice. And then there's the old house. Hundreds of years old, it is, but it's mostly fallen down now. Some calls it a castle, maybe because it has something of a tower, but it's really naught but an old house."

"Anything interesting ever happen there?" Holmes said. I knew he was avoiding the use of the word "treasure."

"Not much. Of course there was 'Bloody Baker'."

Holmes glanced at me. "A fellow with the appellation 'Bloody' certainly sounds somewhat interesting, eh, Watson? What can you tell us of this man?"

"Not much," the driver replied, flicking the reins. The horse did not change speed. "Baker were a Catholic man, back during the reign of Mary. He was the owner of Sissinghurst, and he made it his business to make life hell for the Protestants living around here. That's about all I know for sure, but I've heard about him all my life."

The man settled back into a slumped silence, occasionally clicking his tongue at the horse, who turned an ear but made no other acknowledgement. After several more miles, we crossed a low rise, and the driver indicated with his whip a structure in the far distance.

"There's Sissinghurst."

Across the well-tended fields we could see the manor house, as well as the ruins of a far older structure spread nearby. As we drove closer, farm hands looked up from their varied tasks to examine us. Soon the carriage had wound through the fields and meadows to the house, where a young man in his mid-twenties had appeared and was waiting for us.

"Mr. Holmes?" the young man said, approaching us as we stepped from the carriage. "I am Stanley Cornwallis. Thank you for coming. I apologize for not sending transportation from the station. I have been too distracted by today's events."

"It is quite all right, Mr. Cornwallis," Holmes said. Indicating me, he said, "I have brought Dr. John Watson with me. He is an experienced investigator as well, and often accompanies me."

I shook hands with Cornwallis, feeling no small amount of pride at Holmes's words of praise. As Cornwallis and I murmured greetings, Holmes asked, "What are the events today to which you referred?"

"Come this way, gentlemen." He turned and began to walk around the side of the house. Over his shoulder, he asked, "Is Dr. Watson aware of the reason I originally wrote to you?"

"Somewhat," Holmes replied. "However, I have not revealed to him as yet the little bit of information that my researches revealed."

"I have not received a report from you, either, Mr. Holmes," Cornwallis said, somewhat archly. "Did you find any indication whatsoever that there might be some sort of treasure at Sissinghurst?"

"None whatsoever," Holmes replied. "While there appears to be a long history to the place, there is nothing monumentally outstanding, and certainly nothing that makes this small byway any more interesting than countless other villages across Britain."

"Then why," Cornwallis asked, leading us around the back corner of the house, "would that insane American do *that*?"

Stopping, Cornwallis gestured toward the grounds along the rear of the house to a wide flagstone terrace. At various places, with no apparent pattern, a substantial number of the large flat stones had been pulled up, some dropped back crookedly onto their original location, while others lay on their backs by adjacent stones. The stones that were turned over were discolored, their long-buried undersides covered with mud and stains, exposed to the bright spring sunlight for the first time since the terrace had been constructed.

Occasionally, where the earth had been exposed by an overturned stone, someone had used a pick or spade to dig into the raw earth, creating small holes only one or two feet in depth and diameter. One such hole, near the edge of the terrace, had a long thin tree root sticking from the hole up into the air, its newly cut end looking bone-white in the sunshine. As I watched, a bird landed on it, but immediately took off when the root sagged under the bird's weight. The root continued to wave as the bird flew up into a nearby tree.

Holmes and I stepped closer. The terrace was probably once quite beautiful, but at present it was simply a wreck. I began to notice other details as the initial shock of the destruction wore off. Set off to the side, on the lawn running beside the stonework, was a collection of immaculate outdoor furniture. It was arranged in a haphazard way, and had obviously been moved off of the terrace before the vandalism began.

I also became aware of chunks of loose mortar lying around the turned stones. In some cases, strips of the mortar were still clinging to the irregular edges. On stones that had, for whatever reason, remained undisturbed, the mortar lay between them, surprisingly clean and free of grass or moss.

In spite of the random and disturbing destructive scene before us, I could see the hint of a smile playing about Holmes's lips. "Is this what you meant, Mr. Cornwallis, when you wired that the situation was becoming 'intolerable'?"

"Of course that's what I meant," Cornwallis replied, his voice becoming rather strident. "This situation! That American! It's all intolerable. And I want you to gather evidence to stop it. I will prosecute him, sir. I will! I wired for you as soon as we found this, and I have sent for the law as well. The man will pay!"

Holmes asked, "What indication do you have that the American is responsible for this? Did you perhaps catch him in the act?"

"No, no. It was this way when we came out this morning. He did it during the night. I'm sure he did it. He has been pestering me for weeks to dig on the grounds for his ridiculous treasure. When I said no, he obviously came back on his own and did this."

"And you say that you have called for the police?" I asked.

"Actually, I did not notify them immediately," Cornwallis said, calming himself somewhat. He continued, rather sheepishly, "My first thought was to send for you, Mr. Holmes. I sent one of the farm hands into the village to send a wire. He waited for your reply, and then returned here. It was only several hours later that I realized that I had not told him to send for a representative of the law as well. By the time I did send someone back, my man was told that the local constable was already involved in another matter in the village, and would be out here as soon as he was able. I expect him at any moment."

"Perhaps," Holmes said, "we could go inside while we wait, and you can tell us about this American, and we can discuss the history of this estate and why there might or might not be any treasure here."

We passed into the building, which appeared to be a solid, comfortable house thirty or forty years old. It was much cooler inside than out, and I shivered unexpectedly as our host led us deeper into the building before reaching what was obviously his study. It was a low, snug room, lined with books and paintings along three walls. The fourth wall looked out on the lawn through a series of shadowed windows. The center of the room contained a heavy desk, covered with ledgers. A small settee was under the windows, and two chairs were in front of the desk. Cornwallis motioned us toward these while he stepped into the hallway and called for tea. Then he moved behind the desk.

After we were seated, Cornwallis began to lecture us about the history of the estate. "There has probably been some sort of dwelling here," he began, "since the twelfth century. The first reference to 'Sissinghurst' for this area is recorded in a local charter, which mentions a 'Stephen de Saxingherste.' There are no certain dates for when the various houses on this site have been built, torn down, rebuilt, and so on.

"Over the course of the centuries, various wings were added onto original houses before falling into disrepair. At some point the tower, which you will have noticed on your arrival, was built. During Elizabethan times, this tower was at the center of a large house which spread out on either side of it. However, the entire structure fell into neglect over the years. In about 1800, despite the fact that the house was still in reasonable shape, everything but the tower was pulled down, and a new house was built around it."

"In my researches," Holmes said, "I saw reference to Sissinghurst as a 'castle.' However, it seems that the tower was the only large and permanent part of the building, and even in olden times, it was not enough to earn the title of castle."

"You are correct, Mr. Holmes," Cornwallis replied. "Actually, in the 1760's, the entire estate was used as a prison to house French soldiers captured during the Seven Years War. It was during that time that house was first referred to as a castle. The name has stuck ever since with the locals, even though the modest tower is all that has remained.

"The house was greatly damaged during the time it was used as a prison. Following the war, the owner at that time could not meet the

86

mortgage, and the house was purchased by a distant ancestor of mine, Edward Louisa Mann. It has been in the family since that time."

I shifted in my seat. "Have you ever seen any indication of anything that might be considered treasure here?" I asked.

"No, Dr. Watson," Cornwallis replied. "The property has been in my family for many generations, and there has never been anything like that here. This estate is simply one of a series of farms owned by my family. No doubt it is the best and most important of them, but that is its true value.

"My great aunt Julia, Lady Holmesdale, inherited the house in 1853, I believe, and the current house we are sitting in now was built and finished a couple of years later. Five years ago, in 1883, she died childless and left her estate to me. And we have made do quite peacefully, until this recent foolishness began."

"Was there ever any evidence of visits here by royalty?" I asked. "Did anyone in your family ever travel or have adventures in foreign lands which might have given them an opportunity to obtain a treasure?"

"There is a rumor that Edward I stayed here in the village in the early 1300's, but if so, he would certainly not have hidden a treasure here. And of course, there was Sir John Baker, who owned the house in the early 1500's, and was left two-hundred pounds by Henry VIII, in spite of Baker's noted pro-Catholic beliefs."

"Ah, yes," said Holmes. "Sir John Baker. 'Bloody Baker,' I believe he was called. He is the center of your American's treasure theories. What can you tell us of him?"

I glanced at Holmes, realizing that he must have already learned something of Baker before the carriage driver mentioned him to us while traveling to Sissinghurst. It was characteristic of Holmes that he had not indicated then that he already had knowledge of the man, knowing that revealing it might have made the carriage driver less likely to share what he knew.

"That is Sir John, over there," Cornwallis said, gesturing to a dim portrait hanging on the study wall, opposite the windows. Holmes and I stood, walking closer to examine it. Baker was shown as a man who appeared to be in his mid-forties, dark-haired, bearded, and expressionless. He was wearing dark, high-collared robes and one of the peculiar round puffed hats so common to men of that time. Behind him, the portrait artist had left the background dark, with no attempt to paint in a landscape or other scene. Overall, the man did not seem threatening, certainly not worthy of the name "Bloody Baker," but at the same time, there was nothing friendly or cheering in the portrait. On a small brass label tacked to the bottom of the frame were the words "Sir John Baker (c.1488-1558)."

"Long lived for his time," Holmes said, returning to his seat. "As I understand it, he was quite a successful man in this region."

"Yes, he was. He was fiercely pro-Catholic, and there is actually a priest's house built nearby on this property that is still standing. Quite a contrast to other locations where Catholics were forced to hide their beliefs to avoid persecution from Henry. So many Catholic houses of the time were forced to construct secret 'priest-holes' in which to hide the priests visiting the houses to perform various religious rites."

I was aware of these hiding places of which he spoke. On several occasions, Holmes and I had been called in to investigate the various and sometimes criminal ways these long forgotten places had been used by the modern inhabitants.

"Sir John enjoyed an excellent relationship with King Henry VIII," Cornwallis continued, "in spite of Henry's fierce anti-Catholic beliefs. In fact, during the time Henry was taking so many estates, churches, and monasteries from pro-Catholic citizens and redistributing them to his friends and cronies, he actually gave many properties to Sir John Baker, who ended up owning a number of manors and farms scattered around this area of Kent.

"As I said, when Henry died, he left two-hundred pounds in his will to Sir John. When Henry was succeeded by the fiercely Catholic Queen Mary, Sir John became even more successful, becoming her agent and actively seeking out and persecuting local Protestants.

"One story is often told by a local family, the Wellers. It is said that at the time, when Sir John was serving as a representative of Mary's government, he was prosecuting against an Alexander Weller for his Protestant beliefs. Weller was forced to flee his home to a neighboring town and seek the protection of a powerful friend there. While there, Weller learned that Mary had died and her Protestant sister Elizabeth was now the queen. When Mary died, the pro-Catholic power in the country went with her. Weller returned to his home. Soon after, Sir John became aware of Weller's reappearance, and he prepared to move against him. However, before he could do so, he also learned of Queen Mary's death, and he realized that his authority was gone. It is chiefly from this incident, retold for generations in the Weller family, that Sir John has been given the name of 'Bloody Baker'."

"But there was nothing bloody about that story," I said. "Was there ever any indication of Baker showing excessive violence toward the local Protestants?"

"None, doctor," said Cornwallis. "He questioned them, and often they had their property taken from them, but I have never heard anything that would lead to the name 'Bloody Baker.' Apparently the Weller family was especially bitter, and they have darkened his memory because they felt their grievances stronger than most."

"As I understand it from your original letter," Holmes said, "it is the claim of the American treasure hunter . . . I'm sorry, what was his name again, Mr. Cornwallis?"

"Burke. Philo T. Burke."

"Ah, yes. Peculiar name, isn't it, Watson?" said Holmes. "It is the claim of Mr. Burke that during this time Sir John took something of great value from the Weller family and hid it at his Sissinghurst home. During the confusion following the Queen's death and Weller's return, the item was never recovered. And soon after Sir John died, and his secret with him."

"That is Burke's assertion, yes. However, there is no basis for such a fabrication of lies. The Weller family has long told the tale of Sir John's actions against them, and it is through their family legends that the details of Alexander Weller's return to the area have been handed down, but they themselves have never mentioned any lost treasure, or have they ever listed the theft of a treasure amongst their grievances against Sir John."

"There is even more reason to doubt Burke's claims," said Holmes. "My researches in London have proved that Sir John Baker was not even in this area of the country at the time of Queen Mary's death. Sir John was in London at the time, and he too was dying. It was not possible for him to have been here and to have planned a move against the return of Alexander Weller because he was on his own death bed. The entire story of Sir John's plans against Alexander Weller being frustrated by the death of the Queen is false."

Cornwallis appeared to ponder this for a moment. "Well, that is interesting, Mr. Holmes. Kind of takes the wind out of the Wellers' sails, doesn't it? And it leaves Burke's claims completely groundless as well. I suppose all this is easily proven."

"Oh, yes," Holmes replied. "The documents are easily found at the British Museum. While there, I extended the field of my research in attempts to locate other possible connections between this area and treasure, but as you have said, there simply are none. This area has spent the better part of the last thousand years in relative ease and peace. Even the tensions between Catholics and Protestants in the area never achieved any great level of bloodshed."

"Would you be willing to present your evidence to Burke?" asked Cornwallis. Holmes nodded. "Excellent."

At that moment we heard the sound of an approaching carriage. Cornwallis stood up. "That will be the constable. Will you relate to him as well what you have told me?"

"Of course," said Holmes, as we moved out of the study and toward the front door.

Cornwallis walked ahead of us into the sunlight, where he stopped abruptly. I could see a carriage full of a group of men stopping in front of the house. In the distance were two other carriages, also full of men, being drawn by tired horses into the yard.

A stocky man jumped lightly to ground from the lead carriage. He landed as if he had springs in his legs, and immediately began to walk quickly toward us. He was in a plain brown suit, obviously made in America. In the carriage, the rest of the men slowly stood and began to descend more carefully. It seemed as if all of them were smoking cigars, cigarettes, or pipes, and the entire carriage was clouded in a haze. Cornwallis stepped forward toward the stocky man. "Burke!" he cried. "What is the meaning of this? I have told you that you are not allowed on my property!"

Burke gave a meaningful glance back over his shoulder at the men clustered around the wagon. The other wagons pulled up, and they too were filled with smoking men in rumpled suits. They soon joined the original group, all standing silently watching. Some pulled small notebooks from their pockets and began to write.

"Good morning to you, Mr. Cornwallis," said Burke, stopping before us. "I realize that we have had some disagreements in the past, but we cannot let something like that stand in the way of the historical find of the century. Just think, sir, when the truth is revealed, your little castle here will be the destination point of visitors from both Europe and America!"

"Leave!" yelled Cornwallis. "Leave now! The law will be here soon, and then I will have you arrested! Do you think you can get away with vandalizing my property and trespassing? I will have you arrested, and I will file suit against you for repairs on my property, and I will have you deported from this country! Or jailed!"

Burke ignored Cornwallis, turning his gaze at Holmes and me. "I don't think we've had the pleasure, gentleman. My name is Philo Burke, of Cleveland, Ohio." He smiled ruefully. "I'm sure Mr. Cornwallis has told you about me."

"Yes, I have," said Cornwallis. "They are here because of you. They can debunk your whole treasure theory. This is – "

"We have been doing been doing some research for Mr. Cornwallis in London," Holmes interrupted, sticking out his hand, which Burke shook. I did the same, while Holmes continued. "Mr. Cornwallis is right. There is no evidence of any historical event here that would indicate the presence of treasure. Specifically, your assertion that Sir John Baker obtained something from the Weller family is groundless, as my research has shown that Sir John was dying in London at the time his supposed confrontation with Alexander Weller was supposed to be taking place here."

The group of men huddled by the lead wagon had spread out some while we were talking, and now they were shuffling forward, making notes and listening intently, looking from Burke to Holmes and back again. I realized after a closer look at them that they were reporters, obviously lured down to Sissinghurst for the day by Burke's claims, looking for a story about lost riches and intrigue.

"Of course that is what the official records would say," replied Burke. "If there was a conspiracy to hide the fact that Baker had hidden a treasure here, he would have covered his tracks well." He turned to the reporters. "Boys, I've looked at the same papers that this gentleman is referring to, and I can tell you that there is more to it than the simple claim that Baker was dying at the time. In fact," he lowered his voice, "I was even able to find a coded message contained in the papers, which is what led me to search under the flagstone terrace behind the house!"

"You destroyed that terrace!" shouted Cornwallis. "It has only been there for thirty years, since the current house was built. It wasn't even there when Sir John lived here!"

Burke straightened himself. "Mr. Cornwallis, I do not know if you are truly ignorant of the historical nature of what is hidden here, or if you yourself are part of the conspiracy to keep the truth hidden. I will not take the time to reveal exactly how I uncovered evidence that the treasure is here, or that I knew it was under the flagstone terrace. That will all be revealed at the proper time. But I will tell you that the truth must come out, and you cannot stop it! I have brought these fine men of the press," he said, gesturing to his left and right, "to assure that the truth will be told today. For too long the secret has been kept!" he concluded, his fist held in the air in a dark, dramatic way. "Come along, boys," he said to the reporters. "Whatever it is, it's been buried for over three hundred years. It's time to bring it out into the sunshine!"

Several of the reporters reached into the carriages to retrieve long crow bars. Cornwallis ran into the house, muttering that he would have the servants summon the field hands to stop the invaders. Holmes and I looked at each other. A smile danced around Holmes's lips. "What do you say to a day in Kent, Watson?"

"Kent sounds wonderful," I replied. "If we don't get killed in the crossfire."

By this time the three carriage drivers had dropped to the ground and were curiously making their way around the house to the terrace, following Burke and the reporters. Holmes and I trailed along with them.

"I assume you didn't want Burke to know you are a detective," I said, referring to Holmes's interruption of Cornwallis's introduction.

"Exactly. Burke may or may not have heard of me, but I want to see what his game is for a while, and the best way to do that is to let him play it out. The terrace is already damaged. A little more destruction cannot hurt it too badly. Let us see what Mr. Burke has planned for us."

We rounded the back corner of the house. Most of the reporters were standing along the perimeter of the tumbled terrace stones, while several were working with crowbars, turning over stones that had not been moved the previous night. We stood with the quiet carriage drivers, while Cornwallis danced around, threatening all the men with legal action and promises of violence once his field hands arrived.

Burke was lecturing the writing reporters. "As you can see, I was unable to finish my search last night. I was forced to flee when I thought I was about to be discovered. Of course, I will recompense Mr. Cornwallis for the cost of repairs to his terrace," he added, looking with pity at the raging property owner. "However, I feel that once the treasure is recovered, he will be so grateful that he will understand why this was necessary, and he may not even ask for any compensation."

The reporters were writing busily. One looked up. "And what is your deal in all this, Mr. Burke?" he asked. "If they find a treasure, you don't get to keep it."

"Certainly not," replied Burke. "My only interest is in the advancement of historical knowledge. It boggles the mind, gentlemen, to think how many artifacts there probably are, hidden all over your fine country. Each one that could be found would add so much to the understanding of history. Possibly what we find here may even help to rewrite history."

"How did you get onto it?" asked another reporter. "Being from Ohio and all?"

"I came across some old documents, which made references to other documents," Burke replied vaguely. "I followed the trail, using the specialized knowledge I have acquired from a lifetime of study, until I found conclusive proof of the Sissinghurst Treasure."

He was interrupted by one of the reporters, who had pried up one of the larger stones. "Oi! What's this?" he cried.

Holmes stepped forward. "I believe we are about to see Mr. Burke's surprise, Watson," he said softly. I tore my gaze from the worker, who was looking into a hole underneath the overturned slab to Holmes's face. He was expressionless, but a merry glint was in his eyes.

Stepping closer, we could see into the hole. It appeared to be about one foot deep, and about four feet long by two feet wide, slightly smaller than the circumference of the slab. The sides were of dark reddish clay, and there was loose dirt crumbled along the sides and bottom of the hole. However, that was not what immediately grabbed my attention.

Lying on its side in the hole, its legs pulled up in a fetal position, was a skeleton. The white bones were shining in the sunlight, in stark contrast to the surrounding reddish soil. The figure was lying on its left side, and clutched in the loose bones of the upper right hand was some sort of necklace, made of discolored metal discs connected by small chain links. On the upper right side of the back of the skull, visible to all of us, was a hole, the mark of some strong violent blow.

Everyone, including Cornwallis, had grown silent. After his initial penetrating look at the dead bones, Holmes had kept his gaze on Burke.

Soon, Burke drew himself up dramatically and said, "Well, I had not expected this. No sir. Had you, Mr. Cornwallis? Did you perhaps know what we would find?"

Cornwallis simply stared into the hole for a moment, before returning to himself, saying, "No. No, of course not."

"And what did you expect, Mr. Burke," asked Holmes.

"Well, sir, to be honest, I did not rightly know. Treasure of some sort, of course, perhaps a chest, but I never expected to find a murder."

"Murder?" said a voice behind us. "What's this about a murder?"

I glanced around to see a constable approaching us, followed by a number of farmhands, each grasping various farm tools in assorted threatening manners.

The constable pushed his way through the reporters and stared into the hole. After a silent moment, he stepped back and looked for Mr. Cornwallis.

"How was this found, sir?"

Cornwallis related to him how he had discovered the terrace vandalized that morning, and about the subsequent arrival of Burke and the reporters, who had continued what Burke had started in the middle of the previous night. Burke stayed a step back, looking with interest at the reporters who were writing frantically in their notebooks.

"Any idea who this might be?" asked the constable, gesturing toward the skeleton.

"None," said Cornwallis. "This terrace is only thirty or so years old. There is no indication that there has ever been a treasure here, contrary to Mr. Burke's wild claims. He will tell you. He has researched the matter." Cornwallis gestured toward Holmes.

The constable walked a few steps to us. "And your name sir?" he said to Holmes, with a look of recognition on his face.

Holmes nodded to the side. "Might I speak with you in private for a moment?"

"Certainly," the constable replied. They moved away ten or so paces and spoke in low tones for several minutes before returning to the group.

"You people," the constable said, gesturing to the reporters. "I want your names and which paper you are with. Then I want you to clear out of here. Return to the village, and don't leave until I tell you so." He walked over to one of the reporters, requested and got a sheet of paper, and recorded the men's names. Then, despite their mutterings of protest, he herded them around the house with the carriage drivers and farmhands. He dispersed the hands and sent the reporters back to the village.

While the constable was at the front of the house, Cornwallis and Burke stood silently on each side of the make-shift grave, each looking into the hole silently. Cornwallis stood with a tense attitude, and his breathing was becoming ragged, reminding me of Holmes's speculation about the man's breathing problems. I kept him under close observation in case he began to have an asthmatic attack.

Meanwhile, Burke was relaxed, his arms crossed, and a satisfied look on his face as he appeared to enjoy the sunshine. Holmes and I stood together silently on the third side of the grave.

The constable returned. "My name is Constable Wagner," he said. "Mr. Cornwallis, I am going to leave the remains here under your responsibility until I can return. I must go speak to my superiors. Mr. Burke, you will return to the village with me."

Burke appeared to be suddenly angry. "You cannot simply go off and leave this find unprotected. We don't know how it got here. His family," he said, gesturing at Cornwallis, "may have had something to do with it. You may get back and the treasure may be gone! Or the bones!"

"Sir," explained Wagner, as Cornwallis started to bristle with anger, "there are a number of witnesses regarding both the skeleton and the necklace that it is holding. Most of those witnesses are reporters that you brought here yourself. Too many people have seen this. It won't matter if someone tries to hide it, and I know Mr. Cornwallis won't try. I don't think that anything will happen while I am gone, and I trust these men to watch over things until I return."

After promising Cornwallis that he would return soon, Wagner nodded toward the front of the house, and he and Burke departed, with Burke still complaining loudly to the indifferent constable.

After they had gone, Cornwallis looked at us with despair. "Mr. Holmes, what does it all mean? Is it possible that Bloody Baker was not the innocent man your researches showed?"

Holmes ignored his question. "Perhaps you should go inside and rest, Mr. Cornwallis. Dr. Watson and I will be responsible for the body and its effects until the return of Constable Wagner."

"Yes, of course. Thank you, Mr. Holmes." He turned and left. After he was out of earshot, Holmes gestured toward the skeleton and asked me, "What do you make of it, Watson?"

I squatted by the side of the hole. It only took me a moment to draw my conclusions. "This is certainly no murder, is it?"

Holmes shook his head. "As I'm sure you can see, the bones are clean and white. More importantly, they were obviously once *wired together.* What does this suggest?"

"This fellow has, until recently, been the resident of some sort of teaching facility, perhaps a hospital. He is from a body that has been prepared after death so that the skeleton could be used as a display, probably in a classroom. I imagine, from his excellent condition, that he has not been dead and preserved for too many years, and that he certainly has not been in this hole for very long."

"No," said Holmes, "not for more than twelve hours or so, I would say. The bones are extremely clean, and there is no sign of discoloration from exposure to the soil or the groundwater. In addition, the sides of the hole are still quite vertical, and there has been no creep or collapse of the hole walls. The little bit of dirt that is lying on the bones was obviously scattered there on purpose when he was buried."

"But why was he placed here? I assume that Burke is behind this."

"Oh, of course he is. Obviously, he came out here last night and buried the fellow under a flagstone large enough to cover a skeleton. Then he replaced that stone and proceeded to disrupt a number of others. Then, as we saw a few minutes ago, he arrived and claimed that he was interrupted last night before he could finish looking under all the stones. He let someone else discover these bones, creating the shocking effect that he was attempting to create."

"But surely he realizes that a cursory examination would show that this skeleton is of very recent origin?"

"Possibly. It may be that he has such a low opinion of the country constabulary that he believes the skeleton's condition would not be noticed. Or more probably, he does not care. He intentionally made sure there were reporters here, and he seemed pleased that they were writing down everything they saw and heard. Perhaps he only cares about the first impression made for the reporters, and he is not worried about the illusion of a long buried body standing up under scrutiny for very long."

"When you referred to this as Burke's surprise, did you know exactly what was going to be found?"

"Not quite. When Burke arrived with the reporters to continue the vandalism he had begun last night, I realized that he had probably hidden something that he wanted to be found in front of witnesses. However, I did not know what form the item would take. In addition, I had noticed on our first inspection that the stone which covered the skeleton had been previously disrupted, but I never thought to look under it earlier today to see if something had been hidden there before replacing the stone. I simply thought that during the night's activities, that particular stone had happened to fall back in nearly its original location, not realizing that it had been carefully replaced to cover its secret."

"But what about the treasure? This necklace?" I asked, squatting again by the hole to get a better look. "And the hole in the skull?"

"They simply add to the effect," Holmes replied. "The necklace appears to be constructed from some sort of metal discs, beaten flat to give them an old look. The discs have been connected with chain links, but you will see that the links themselves are rather shiny and new looking. No doubt analysis will reveal that the metals involved are modern alloys, and certainly not anything available three hundred years ago.

"I'm sure the hole in the skull was knocked there by Burke to give the initial impression that the fellow had been murdered. If you look, you can see that the exposed cracked edges around the hole in the skull are clean and white, even cleaner than the surface of the skull, indicating that the wound is of recent origin."

"So all this," I gestured around me, standing up as my knees cracked, "all this has been arranged for some reason as a show for those reporters brought down by Burke."

"Exactly. Although I am not quite certain of his motive at this point. I believe that we shall have to give Mr. Burke a little more line in order to set the hook before we can reel him in."

"And the constable? Did you make him aware of all this?"

"I did. He appeared to recognize me, and was in fact about to identify me when I stopped him. I quickly explained to him what we have seen about the age and provenance of the skeleton, as well as Burke's apparent actions in the matter. He immediately picked up on what I was telling him, and he agreed that we should allow Mr. Burke to act out his little drama for a while, in order that we might have something more against him than a simple charge of terrace vandalism. As it stands now, Burke could simply claim it was a joke, pay a small fine, and disappear without the real reasons behind this ever becoming known."

Constable Wagner arrived back an hour or so later with a village doctor and several laborers. The doctor confirmed that the skeleton was simply a medical exhibit and not a murder victim. The laborers placed the bones into a coffin that had been brought with them and loaded it into a wagon. They and the doctor waited to one side while Holmes and I conferred with the constable.

"I've sworn these men to secrecy," Wagner said. "Burke is being watched by one of my men at the local inn. He's been holding court with those reporters, spinning one wild theory after another. By the time I left, he had one going where Bloody Baker had kidnapped half the countryside at one time or another during Queen Mary's reign, holding them for ransoms until the families gave him their valuables. He's even saying that Mr. Cornwallis will be putting this place up for sale soon in order to get away from the horrible reputation that this place has acquired. He's hinting darkly that the place is haunted. The reporters are eating it up. They're already clogging up the local post office, passing on these stories to their newspapers."

Holmes thought for a moment. "I am sorry that we must let Burke continue to play out this nonsense until we can discover his true motives. It is going to cause a certain amount of distress for Mr. Cornwallis before it is all over. However, as I told Watson, it will be better if we can arrest Burke for more than simple vandalism."

"Perhaps I can charge Burke with being a bad influence in the community," said Wagner. "It is his fault that the village is full of those reporters. They are certainly a disruptive bunch. They are the reason that it took me so long to get out here this morning. Two of them started a fight with each other as soon as they arrived. A shop window was broken. I had to stay in town and get statements, and deal with an irate shop owner, before I could get away. Then I arrive here and meet up with a mob of angry farm hands carrying picks and scythes, marching from the fields toward the house. I had no idea what I had pushed myself into."

We all laughed. Then Holmes asked, "Do you suppose that you could get a few wires off for me without alerting the reporters?"

Wagner grinned. "Of course. The telegraph agent is my brother-in-law."

Holmes took a moment to write out the messages before handing them to Wagner. "Stress the urgency of these," he said. "The longer this goes on, the more mess Mr. Cornwallis will have to deal with."

"Certainly, sir. I'll let you know if I hear anything. Will you be staying here with Mr. Cornwallis?"

"I believe so. It would be better if I do not give Mr. Burke too much opportunity to realize who I am. I am already uneasy that one of the London reporters may have recognized me and passed on the information to him."

"I hadn't heard anything of that sort before I came back out here," Wagner said. "Mr. Burke certainly seemed to be confident, as if whatever he's doing is going according to plan. Anyway, it's probably good that you're staying out here, as the inn is full of reporters. I turned them loose and said they could go back to London, but they refused. On the scent of a story, I suppose."

"Yes," Holmes agreed. "As I said, it is unfortunate for Mr. Cornwallis, but perhaps we can pull something positive out of the situation."

We went inside, where the housekeeper informed us that Mr. Cornwallis was lying down. She added quietly that he sometimes had breathing problems following stressful situations. I informed her that I was a doctor, and offered to examine him, but she said it would not be necessary, as rest and relaxation had always been the best cure.

She offered us lunch, which we gladly accepted. We were led to the dining room, where we were served a huge meal consisting of farm-fresh vegetables and cured ham. Even Holmes, not usually noted for his appetite, managed to put away a substantial portion. Afterwards, we retreated to Cornwallis's study, where Holmes lit his pipe, and we awaited word from Constable Wagner.

Cornwallis appeared, much refreshed, later in the afternoon. Holmes explained to him all that had happened, including the facts regarding the skeleton, and Burke's obvious machinations. Cornwallis was perplexed as to Burke's reasons, but seemed willing to wait until such time as they were revealed.

We were offered a tour of the grounds of the estate, but Holmes declined, preferring to wait on replies to his telegrams. I accepted Cornwallis's offer, however, and he showed me around the farm. His pride was evident, and I could see why this was considered the best of his family's estates. We went into the ruins of the old building, and up into the tall tower, from which we could see far over the Kent landscape.

Cornwallis explained that the tower had been altered and added onto several times since its original construction. He hoped that someday the old building would be completely restored. Later, we quickly looked into the nearby priest's house, which was in surprisingly good condition considering that it was several hundred years old.

That night, there had still been no response to Holmes's wires, and Constable Wagner had not been back with any further news. Holmes was clearly impatient, and was almost curt when accepting Cornwallis's offer to stay the night at Sissinghurst. As I said goodnight to Holmes and pulled his door shut, I knew that he would not sleep, but instead would sit up all night, smoking his pipe and constructing alternate theories to explain Burke's motivations.

The following morning I was up early, but Holmes was up even earlier. I saw him from my window, pacing around the terrace. I met Cornwallis at the top of the stairs, and we went outside together, where we greeted Holmes. He told us that there was still no news from Constable Wagner. I could tell that he was irritated. "The man seemed quite intelligent, Watson," he said. "I cannot understand why we have heard nothing."

"Perhaps he has nothing yet to tell," I said. "And if the gaggle of reporters are still in the village, he has no doubt had other matters to deal with."

"Possibly, possibly."

At that point, Cornwallis, who had wandered to the far side of the terrace, returned and asked if Holmes thought it would be all right to begin repairs. Holmes stated that he did not know of any reason not to. Cornwallis said that he would see his farm manager immediately, and then join us momentarily inside for breakfast.

In the dining room, Cornwallis and I ate the hearty country breakfast, while Holmes made do with coffee as he stared impatiently out the window. I was nearly finished when I heard the sound of a carriage arriving at the front of the house. Holmes stood and dashed out of the room. Cornwallis and I looked at one another, and then followed more slowly.

As we stepped outside, I saw Holmes reach the carriage, where Constable Wagner was stepping down. Without a word, he handed a sheaf of cables to Holmes. With his other hand, he handed a stack of newspapers to Cornwallis. "This story is in all the papers, I'm afraid, sir," he said. Cornwallis handed half the stack to me, and then began to look through his own. In a moment he leaned against the carriage and placed a hand to his head with a groan.

"Treasure!" he cried. "They all have stories about the estate being filled with buried treasures. We shall be overrun!"

The papers in my stack confirmed what Cornwallis had said. Each story that I quickly examined showed references to secreted fortunes, bloody murders, and speculations enough to fire any boy's wildest dreams. One paper even hinted that there were lost entrances to a vast underground cavern on the estate, filled with hoards of gold and jewels.

Another spoke of the tower, which was said to be designed with hidden passages and booby traps for the unwary. Several speculated that the current owner, Mr. Sidney Cornwallis, intended to sell the estate and leave the country, due to the fact that the "foully murdered victim" found under the "ancient flagstone terrace" was such an embarrassment to the family that he could no longer stand to remain in England. One paper said that Cornwallis was aware of the murdered victim, as well as many others hidden around the estate, and that he would flee from the authorities before he could be questioned or jailed.

"Mr. Burke has spread it around that he will be exposing another surprise here today at eleven a.m.," said Wagner. "Mr. Cornwallis, the reporters will be coming back here then. It appears that half the village will be joining them. My men and I will be here, but I'm afraid there aren't enough of us to stop them. We will arrest as many as we can, if you'd like, but I cannot do anything until they actually trespass on the property."

"Of course. Thank you," said Cornwallis.

"You can arrest Burke, however," said Holmes, waving the telegrams.

"Yes sir. Anytime you say. And a good thing, too. I simply wanted to speak with you about it first."

"Excellent," Holmes said. Turning to me, he added, "Watson, do you have your Bradshaw with you? May I examine it for a moment?"

When I returned, Holmes handed me the telegrams, while I handed him the railway guide. Holmes quickly determined what time the local train left from the village station. "Eleven a.m.," he said. "An amazing coincidence, wouldn't you say? Exactly the time everyone will be gathering here at the manor house."

I glanced up from the telegrams. "Perhaps we should be at the station then."

Holmes nodded. Cornwallis asked, with a strident tone in his voice, "What? Won't you be here at eleven when Burke and the reporters come back?"

"I believe that the reporters will be here without Mr. Burke," Holmes said, "and without him to provide any entertainment, I feel that they will soon become disinterested and leave. In the meantime, Mr. Burke will probably be attempting to slip out of town on the first train of the morning."

"What?" said Cornwallis, clearly confused.

"I am still not entirely certain as to Mr. Burke's reasons for creating this entire production," said Holmes, "although certain aspects of the matter are becoming clear. However, yesterday I cabled several acquaintances of mine in the United States, particularly a police officer in Cleveland, Ohio. What he replied about Mr. Philo T. Burke was of some interest indeed."

I glanced down at the telegrams. Confidence man. Thief. Forger. Murderer. All these words had been used to describe Burke, who was a very wanted man in America. Holmes caught my eye. "Rather careless of Mr. Burke to reveal his true name and place of origin, wasn't it?"

Wagner interrupted to explain a few of the charges against Burke to Cornwallis. "Once they found out where he was, the Americans then wired me as well as Mr. Holmes here to hold Burke until they can send someone after him. Should be here in about a week." He turned to Holmes. "As soon as I got this information, I quietly sent to surrounding areas, requesting some additional constables. I'm sorry I was not able to get out here sooner,

Mr. Holmes. Of course, Burke's under observation in the village by my men, but right now it's not a problem. He's still sitting around, feeding whatever crazy stories that he can think of to those reporters."

"However," said Holmes, "when the time comes to travel out here from the village, he will arrange for the reporters to go on ahead of him. Then he will quietly slip away to the train station and head back to London."

"That's the way I see it," said Wagner. "Of course, we will stop him."

Holmes and I left Cornwallis in a nervous state, as he prepared to meet the reporters. He said he would attempt to create some sort of prepared statement for the reporters to negate all of the fabulous and ridiculous damage done by Burke. Wagner promised Cornwallis that as soon as we had taken over surveillance of Burke in the village, he would send back another constable to stay at the farm with Cornwallis while the reporters were there.

In the village, we were careful to avoid being seen by either Burke or the reporters. Taking up positions near the small station, we waited in the shadows as the morning crept on toward eleven o'clock.

Soon after ten, a great mass of reporters disgorged from the local public house and moved toward several waiting carts. Burke, who had exited with the men, hung back, waving to them, and yelling that he would be along in just a few moments. He waited until they had departed, and then made his way toward the inn. Mere moments after entering, he came back out, carrying his bag.

We let him get to the station, where he bought a ticket and seated himself to wait upon a bench. As we stepped into his field of vision, he stood but made no move to flee. As we approached him, other constables began to show themselves behind him and to the sides. He glanced at them, and then faced us with a smile.

"Is there a problem, gentlemen?"

"There doesn't need to be," said Wagner. "Mr. Philo T. Burke, of Cleveland, Ohio, I place you under arrest."

A wild look came into Burke's eyes, and he looked as if he might bolt and run. However, his arms were grasped by two burly officers, and he relaxed. Looking at Holmes, he said, "What are you? One of those Scotland Yarders?"

"I am Sherlock Holmes."

Burke's eyes widened, and then he shook his head. "Heard about you," he said. "In fact, someone I met over here, never mind who, warned me not to get tangled up with you. I thought this far out in the country I would be safe." He shook his head again. "Never had a chance, did I?"

He was taken to the small police station. We followed, Holmes, Wagner, and I, with Holmes carrying Burke's bag. At the station, Burke was seated in a wooden chair, while Holmes opened the bag. Inside was a small pile of clothing. More of interest to us, however, was a substantial stack of the same newspapers that Cornwallis and I had examined at the Sissinghurst estate. In many cases there were multiple copies. Obviously Holmes had been correct in stating that Burke wished for the incident with the skeleton to be widely reported in the press.

"But why, Holmes," I asked. "Why come all the way out here to carry out such a plan?"

Holmes, who had been reading a stack of handwritten documents found at the bottom of the bag, said, "This is why, Watson."

He handed me the papers, which had been the only other items of interest in the bag. On them I saw numerous handwritten paragraphs, each describing the upcoming sale of the Sissinghurst farm and castle.

Many of the paragraphs were similar, having only slight variations with those that preceded them. Obviously the sheets were rough drafts of some sort of prospectus. In many cases, there were numerous scratched out words, as if the author had tried differing combinations before settling on phrasing that pleased him.

Holmes tapped the newspapers. "I am not completely certain, but I believe that I have a reasonable understanding of Burke's plan. It fits his background as a confidence man and trickster. Correct me if I'm wrong, Mr. Burke." Burke simply stared, expressionless.

"Burke had researched and found a likely spot in Sissinghurst. The place was old, but there never was any reason to think that treasure had been hidden there. However, there was enough history to the place that stories of treasure could be fabricated, at least long enough to serve Burke's purpose. And of course, there was the association with the fascinating 'Bloody Baker.'

"After picking Sissinghurst, Burke showed up and began to make himself a nuisance to Mr. Cornwallis. His plan was to continue that for a few weeks until he could stage the incident with the reporters, the skeleton, and the terrace." Holmes turned toward Burke. "I expect that when you got here, you did not know exactly where or how the incident would take place, but I'm sure you had the skeleton with you, as you looked for a likely spot. Did you buy the skeleton, Mr. Burke, or did you steal it from a medical school or hospital?"

Burke did not answer. He simply raised an eyebrow, as if indicating that Holmes should continue.

"It was his intent all along to create a story that would grab the imaginations of the reporters. He made it seem as mysterious and exciting as possible, throwing in hidden treasure, an unexpected dead man, and hints of hauntings and conspiracy. What he was after, of course, was numerous stories about the incident in as many different newspapers as he could find.

"He never intended that the story should hold up to any kind of close scrutiny. He planned to be gone as soon as possible. He didn't care if the exact origins of the skeleton or the cheap trinkets supposed to be treasure were quickly discovered. As long as he had the newspapers containing the stories of treasure and a possible sale of the estate, he would be able to carry out the rest of his plan.

"He intended to leave for London on this morning's train. He would wait there for a few days, seeing if any other useful newspaper articles were printed that might add to the recently fabricated treasure legends of Sissinghurst Castle. He would buy up as many old copies of today's newspapers as he could reasonably carry, for future use. Then he would return to America.

"Once there, he would have printed a series of brochures, false deeds, and other bogus documents, each implying that he was the agent responsible for selling the Sissinghurst estate. He would let on that people in England were reluctant to buy the estate, possibly afraid of ghosts. By showing a number of legitimate British newspapers, each with stories verifying Burke's claim that the estate was for sale and why, he could sell the estate over and over again to gullible American investors. Each would think they were getting the place at a bargain, and not only acquiring an actual English estate with a castle, but also a property fairly loaded with hidden treasure and an interesting ghostly history.

"Of course, after each false sale, he would simply move on and try the same thing in a different town. I have no doubt that he planned to use a variety of names, and did not intend to remain Philo T. Burke after his return to the United States. That is why he did not mind using his real name here in Sissinghurst. Is that correct, Mr. Burke?"

Burke simply smiled. "You're the one telling it, Mr. Holmes. I'm just listening. So far, all you can charge me with is vandalism of Cornwallis's terrace, and you'd have to prove that. What difference does it make if I decided to leave town? And maybe I just bought all those newspapers because I thought it was an interesting story." He stood up. "So unless you can do better than that, gentleman, I am going to depart."

"I don't think so," said Holmes as Wagner pushed Burke back into his chair. "You were a little careless in telling me that you were from Cleveland, Ohio. I wired to some professional acquaintances there about you. Your history is an interesting one. Apparently your violent attack on one of the city's most prominent citizens, which caused you to flee America late last year, is still the subject of much discussion there. The man later died. The Cleveland police were quite pleased to know that you are here, and they are sending someone to retrieve you, even as we speak."

Burke lunged out of the chair, trying to make his way to the door.

With the aid of both Holmes and myself, as well as one of the constables, Wagner was able to drag him down a short hall and place him in a cell. As we walked back into the outer room we could hear Burke cursing and throwing himself against the bars.

Later, on the train back to London, Holmes settled back against the seat and said, "An interesting case, Watson."

"Yes," I replied. "But poor Mr. Cornwallis. I fear that he will be bothered by the aftermath for years to come."

We had reached the Sissinghurst estate early that afternoon, after the reporters had come and gone. Cornwallis listened half-heartedly as we explained Burke's plot and subsequent capture. He seemed more preoccupied with the future consequences of Burke's actions than Burke's impending punishment.

"I suppose there will be people trespassing here for years, digging and looking for treasure, and then bringing suit against me if they somehow fall and hurt themselves in the process."

"Perhaps not," I said. "You were able to give the reporters some of the facts, and Constable Wagner will be telling them the rest of the story when they return to the village to catch the train to London. I think the whole matter will die a quick death."

That proved to be the case. In later days, the newspapers printed quick retractions, followed by more extensive stories on the questionable life and career of Philo T. Burke. His trial and subsequent execution in Ohio were closely followed by the reading public throughout that spring and summer.

In later years, Mr. Cornwallis continued to manage Sissinghurst quite successfully. Holmes and I visited there during the course of another investigation several years later. At that point, Mr. Cornwallis was somewhat older and more settled. However, I was never able to completely forget the agitated and possibly asthmatic young man who was so upset over the destruction of his terrace.

It was early afternoon when the train arrived in London. As our hansom cab left the station for Baker Street, Holmes asked me, "Would you enjoy attending a concert tonight? They are playing German music, which I find especially appealing."

"Certainly," I replied.

"Good," said Holmes. "Then I believe we shall just have time for me to tell you of an investigation I conducted not long after I entered private practice in London. It was on an estate similar to Sissinghurst, in central Norfolk. Unlike Sissinghurst, however, this estate did indeed reveal a singular treasure, which we might, if you are not too busy, go to see tomorrow at the British Museum, if you are interested."

EDITOR'S NOTE: For further information regarding the history of Sissinghurst Castle, the reader should examine the highly informative booklet *Sissinghurst Castle: An Illustrated History* by Nigel Nicolson, F.S.A. (Privately printed)

The Adventure of the
Second Chance

"I am afraid, Watson, that I shall have to go," said Mr. Sherlock Holmes.

I glanced up from my breakfast, raising my eyebrows. Swallowing my bite of egg, I managed to ask, "Go? Where to?"

"To Dartmoor. To King's Pyland."

And so later that morning, I found myself accompanying Holmes as we crossed the platform at Paddington toward our train, which was unexpectedly running a few minutes late. This delay, while unusual, was no less strange than the fact that Holmes and I were slightly early. Holmes had the irritating habit of arriving for trains at the very last second. This trait was balanced, however, by his uncanny ability never to arrive too late.

Holmes stopped to buy a stack of the latest papers. I knew that he would want to read about the disappearance of Silver Blaze and the death of the famous racehorse's trainer, John Straker. As he rejoined me, I was consulting my watch.

"We appear to have a few minutes," he said. "I shall be watching the speed of the train during our journey. I am curious as to whether the driver will be able to make up the delay en route."

As we began to move toward our carriage, a man sidled up to us and quietly whispered Holmes's name. We paused, but the man kept moving, saying out of the corner of his mouth, "Keep walking with me."

Without any awkwardness, Holmes resumed walking. I was less adept, but managed to lurch into motion again, hoping that my pause had not been noticed.

The man led us to the side of the platform, behind a luggage cart, piled over our head with trunks and bags. Once out of sight, the man turned to us. "Do you know who I am, Mr. Holmes?"

Holmes adjusted the ear-flapped traveling cap he often wore, pushing the brim slightly higher on his forehead, allowing more light to reach his eyes. "You are Mr. Tom Morgan," he said. The man nodded and smiled slightly. The smile went away when Holmes continued, "Tom Morgan, Watson, is what is known as a runner, working in the employee of the infamous Professor Moriarty. Tom here is somewhat more respectable than some of the Professor's creatures, especially the ones he recruits from the East End, and Wapping and Limehouse. Tom lives somewhere near here, don't you, Tom? You and your family, I believe. This allows Tom to have a higher level of respectability than some of the Professor's tools, and thus Tom is able to move unmolested in a different level of society."

Morgan showed a level of rising irritation as Holmes spoke of him and his history. However, he consciously made an effort to control himself, and by the time Holmes finished speaking, he had returned to the same lack of emotion shown when he first spoke to us.

"That's right, Mr. Holmes, I work for the Professor." His voice lowered by the end of the sentence, speaking Moriarty's title in almost a whispered, fearful reverence. "It's no secret that you have been on to us for a long time. We have been warned to keep an eye out for you and the doctor, here. Oh, nothing has been said about threatening you, sirs. Just to be aware if you were around, so we could be somewhere else, if you get my meaning."

He glanced around to make sure we were still unobserved. "I saw you, though, this morning, and it came upon me that I should speak to you while I had the chance. Although it might have been better if we had stayed out in the open. Then I could say that *you* had wanted to speak to *me*, and even if it had meant a few hard minutes before the Professor or that Chief of Staff of his, I could have claimed ignorance." He looked around again. "Although speaking with you behind this cart, in secret, it might be much harder to explain away if I'm caught . . . ."

"Well, no matter. But I would ask that we leave separately when we are done." Holmes and I nodded, and Morgan continued. "I . . . I just wanted to ask your advice on something, Mr. Holmes."

There was still no sound of impending departure from the train. Holmes was listening for it, as was I. Holmes said, "Go ahead." I knew he was hoping for some sort of information from Morgan that would give him one more advantage against Professor Moriarty and his organization.

"It's my son, sir," said Morgan. "Young James. Jamie, we call him. I don't want him to end up like I've done, wondering what blood was spilled for every shilling that I've earned, always living in a kind of uncertain fear when there's a knock on the door, or when I walk down the street and see a constable heading toward me from the far end of the block."

"How can I help?" asked Holmes.

"Jamie is sixteen now," replied Morgan. "He's old enough to start thinking about what he wants to do with his life. I've already been hearing some suggestions from the Professor's lieutenants that I should be involving Jamie more in the business. 'Time to make him a part of the family,' they say. They want to include him in some of the easy things at first, carrying money or papers, or watching when they have someone they are observing.

"I don't want that for Jamie. He's too talented for that. I want to help him find a different path. If he can do something else, I can let him go and keep him from following in my footsteps."

"Talented, you say?" Holmes asked. "What sort of talent?"

Morgan reached into his coat and removed a sheaf of folded papers. "Why, this, sir." He unfolded the sheets, revealing a small stack of sketches, done in ink.

Holmes shuffled through them and then passed them to me, one by one. Though somewhat amateurish, the drawings showed incredible skill and mastery of the art form. There were drawings of everyday street scenes, a horse with a carriage, a newsboy, a vegetable man selling from his cart. There was a sketch of a hand holding a flower that was as good as anything I had seen by Duhrer.

The papers were frayed around the edges, and showed evidence of much handling and examination. Morgan said, "That's just the ones that I've carried with me. He has many more, and he can draw them out in no time at all. It's as if what he is seeing flows directly out of his hand. And he can do the same with pencil and charcoal and paint, as well. We keep the really beautiful things at home."

Holmes restacked the drawings and handed them back to Morgan, who replaced them in his inner coat pocket. "If these are only the average drawings, and you keep the 'really beautiful' ones at home, your son has an exceptional talent indeed," he said. "What can I do for you?"

Morgan stepped a little closer, his voice taking on an urgent tone. "I don't know anyone who would be able help Jamie. I don't even know who to ask. You're right about my job, sir. The Professor uses me to carry out his business with the shop owners and such who wouldn't want to deal with the people that he gets out of the East End. But I have no idea who to see about getting Jamie the training and attention he deserves.

"It's really getting pressing, sir, the way they're asking me to put Jamie to work for the Professor. He can do better than that. I know it. I know how I started, doing just the things they are wanting Jamie to do, and before you know it, you're doing worse, and then you start to believe that you are that kind of person, and there's no going back. I don't know how I'll end up, but I know it will be no good end. It's too late for me. If I'm lucky, it will just be some jail time, but by the time it's all over, they may have had me do something that is a hanging matter. But not Jamie! I won't have that!"

We heard the movement of the crowd change on the other side of the luggage carriage. Doors on the train carriages began to open and shut, indicating the imminent departure. Holmes rummaged in his waistcoat and

108

retrieved one of his cards. On the back he wrote a name and address, and handed it to Morgan.

"This is how to reach Sir William deVille. If you get a message to him, mentioning my name, and show him some of Jamie's works, I assure you that he will take great interest in the matter. He has taken several other young artists under his wing, from all walks of life, and his only interest is in the encouragement of the arts. I once did him a small favor regarding the retrieval of some stolen masters, and he is in my debt."

Holmes started to walk away, but he was stopped when Morgan grabbed his hand and pumped it. "Thank you, sir. Thank you so much!"

He dropped Holmes's hand, and grabbed mine, firmly shaking it as well.

Holmes glanced toward the card in Morgan's fingers. "I would hide that, if I were you. Memorize the name and address, and destroy the card. It would not do you much good at all for it to be found on your person by Moriarty or his men."

"Right, sir. I'll do that immediately."

"Watson and I must step out first or we are in danger of missing our train," stated Holmes. "Good luck, Morgan. And it's not too late for you, either, if you really want to get away from Moriarty. Come talk to me some time."

We left him in the shadows of the carriage, and made it to our reserved compartment just seconds before the train began to move.

"That's more like it," I said. "It wouldn't feel right to climb onto the train and just sit for a few minutes, arranging myself on the seat, leisurely removing my hat and coat. When traveling with Sherlock Holmes, one should always feel the carriage start to move as you try to make it to your seat before doing yourself an injury."

Holmes, already unfolding the first of his many newspapers, glanced up under the brim of his ear-flapped cap and snorted before returning to his reading.

That took place on the morning of 25 September, 1890. I have recounted elsewhere how Holmes and I traveled on to Dartmoor that day to investigate the strange death of John Straker, killed by a blow to the head during a rainswept night on the moor. Holmes's subsequent discovery of the murderer, as well as the recovery of the missing racehorse, Silver Blaze, was but one of many of his successes during those years.

The following spring, Holmes's efforts to destroy Professor Moriarty's organization had reached their culmination. Nearly all of the Professor's criminal minions were arrested, leaving only the Professor and few of his lieutenants free. Holmes and I traveled to the Continent, luring Moriarty away from England toward a final showdown with Holmes. It was after their meeting at the Reichenbach Falls in Switzerland that I came to believe, along with the rest of the world, that Holmes, as well as Moriarty, had perished. For three long years, until the spring of 1894, it was believed that Holmes was dead.

Back in London, I followed the crime news, occasionally being called as a witness in some of the trials for Moriarty's men, which were being conducted in the aftermath of the destruction of his criminal web. I recall at some point during those years reading that Tom Morgan, a member of Moriarty's gang, had died in prison while awaiting trial. I idly thought of Holmes's offer to meet with Morgan, and how Morgan had never taken him up on it, as far as I knew. I considered Morgan's son, Jamie, and wondered if Morgan had taken Holmes's advice and contacted the wealthy art patron who offered a way out for the young prodigy. However, I was involved in my own problems at the time, as my wife Mary was suffering from the combination of illnesses that would eventually take her life, and I did not have the energy or ambition to follow up on Jamie Morgan's progress.

I had no further thought of the Morgans for many years, until early in the spring of 1901, when Holmes received a letter with the morning post. "Pentonville Prison," he remarked before opening it.

"Hmm?" I responded, looking up from my newspaper.

"A letter from Pentonville Prison."

"Deduced from the high percentage of wood pulp contained in the paper of the envelope, no doubt."

"No doubt," replied Holmes. "That, coupled with the return address from the prison on the envelope, makes it almost certain."

He opened the letter with an Italian dagger he had kept as a souvenir following its use in the murder of a lecherous count by his not-so-tolerant wife. He walked across the room before settling into his chair by the fireplace. He examined both the envelope inside and out, as well as the front and back of the single enclosed sheet before reading the short message.

"Do you remember," he asked after a moment, "our short, singular meeting with Tom Morgan on the platform at Paddington some years ago?" I thought for a moment, my mind running over various past incidents as I tried to place the fellow. Finally, an image of the man, leading us behind the luggage carriage, and showing us his son's beautiful drawings, fixed itself in my mind. "Yes," I said. "Yes, now I do. But surely he has not written to you. I had heard that he died in prison during the early nineties, while you were missing."

"This is not from Tom, but rather from his son, Jamie. Or as he signs his name now, Jim."

"What does he want," I asked, and then realization dawned on me. "Oh, no," I said. "He is writing from Pentonville. Did his father's hopes for him fail? Is he in prison?"

"Worse," said Holmes. "He is sentenced to death, due to hang within days from now." Holmes passed me the letter. "And he has requested to see us."

The day was lovely and bright, with the promise of renewal that always accompanies spring. However, as we walked from our hansom up to Pentonville Prison, the gray buildings seemed to absorb the seasonal goodness from the very air. The closer we stepped, the more our view was filled with the grim structure. Even the plants growing in the shadow of the place seemed to have missed spring, still drooping with brown despair. Holmes and I had been to Pentonville on several occasions, and would be there again several years in the future to attend an execution. I have never visited the place without believing that a physical location can absorb the pain and suffering that occur within it. Long after men are gone, I believe that the location of that prison shall remain a haunted and forbidding place.

We were expected, and met at the door by the warden, who welcomed us with a stern expression, informing us that the execution of Jim Morgan was to take place on the dawn of the following day. After letting us know that he was available to us if needed, he turned us over to a guard and returned to his office.

We followed our guide through the twisting passages. At one point we passed an open door, revealing a courtyard deep within the prison walls. I only saw a glimpse as we passed, but it was enough to recognize the gallows built in the center. Men moved on the sturdy wooden structure like ants on a carcass, testing the mechanism so that the upcoming event would proceed without complications. Eventually, after what was probably only minutes but seemed much longer, we reached a closed cell door with a guard standing outside. The man who had led us through the maze-like prison stated softly, "We keep a fellow outside the cells of those who are about to be executed. In case the prisoner becomes agitated, or tries to do himself an injury, you understand."

We nodded, and I wondered about the oddity of keeping the condemned man whole and healthy long enough to kill him. I began to regret agreeing to accompany Holmes on this errand.

The guard looked for a moment through the small Judas Hole in the door. Then he pulled a ring of keys from a deep pocket on his uniform and unlocked the stiff mechanism. With a loud snick, the lock turned and the door opened. The guard stepped aside and motioned us in. "Stay as long as you like."

As the door shut behind us, the darkness of the cell seemed absolute for a moment before my eyes adjusted to the dim light coming from a high opening on the rear wall. The cell contained a table with a weak candle burning on it, a chair, and a cot under the window. As we stepped forward, the man on the cot rose and moved into the dim light. He was tall and thin, much taller than his father, who I had only seen on that one occasion. Apparently he took after his mother. His prison garb did not fit well, and hung awkwardly in spots, while too short in others. He started to speak, but his voice just made a scratching sound. He cleared it, and tried again. "Mr. Holmes? Dr. Watson? Thank you for coming." Gesturing toward the cot, he asked if we would like to sit. We declined, but Holmes indicated that Jamie should use the chair. Jamie sat down on the edge, his feet pulled under him as if he might spring up at any moment.

"Thank you for coming," he repeated. "I truly appreciate it."

"What can we do for you," Holmes asked. "Your letter was rather vague, simply stating where you were, and reminding me of the previous encounter I had with your father that day at Paddington. I believe he said at the time you were sixteen years old then."

"Probably," Jamie agreed. "I don't know exactly when you met with him, but I was around that age when my feet were set on the path that has led me to this cell. I know that you tried to help my father that day, but as you can see, my life did not turn out the way my father planned and hoped.

"As you may know, my father died in prison, and so it appears will I. But this awful pattern must stop, Mr. Holmes. I, too, have a son, and he must not follow this path. I must prevail on you, in the name of the help you once gave my father, and ask for the same help."

"I had assumed," said Holmes, "that you wanted some sort of aid in overturning your death sentence conviction. I only know what I have read in the newspapers, but I am willing to listen. I cannot deny that to a man hours before his execution."

"No, no, Mr. Holmes. I did what they say. I deserve to be here. But I must break this . . . this curse that hangs over our family. My son must not end up as I and my father have done, our lives poisoned by Professor Moriarty's plans, even years after his death. Please promise me that you will help."

Holmes moved around the table and sat on the edge of the cot. Jamie shifted in the chair, turning to follow Holmes as he moved around the room. When seated, Holmes leaned forward and said, "Tell me."

Jamie Morgan spent a silent moment looking at his hands. As he leaned forward, I could see the back of his thin neck, showing under his ragged

112

hair and looking yellow and ill in the candlelight. Shadows danced on the bumps of his spine. I shifted around him in order to see his face. My movement seemed to bring him back to the room, and he began to speak.

"It will not take long, and it will explain what I need you to do for my son.

"My father told me what he had asked you that day on the platform, Mr. Holmes. About how you took time to help him and give him a name, even though my father was working for your enemy. He told me later on, of course, several months later. By that time I was working for the Professor, too. I know that you saw my drawings, and how you gave my father the name of that man who would have taken me under his wing and given me training and a better chance. But it didn't work out that way.

"After you talked with my father, he kept your card with the rich man's name written on it. He knew you had said to get rid of it, and he meant to, but he didn't. He only held on to it for a day or so, but that was all it took. My mother found it, and started asking him about it. He couldn't tell her that he had asked you for help, so he made up a story about how you had somehow heard about my drawings, and had taken it upon yourself to see that I got a better education. He told my mother that *you* had approached *him* at the train station, and had given him the card on your own.

"My mother was angry, and started to rant about how we didn't need any help from a rich man, and certainly not from you. She said it was dangerous for him to talk to you, and what if he had been seen? Our family had the Professor to take care of us. I was listening to all of this, of course. Where we lived was never too big, and there was nowhere they could go to have a private conversation. That's why for a while I believed what my father had said, that it was your idea, Mr. Holmes. I agreed with my mother, that we didn't need you interfering with our lives, although I was intrigued by the idea of receiving additional training.

"By this point, my father was trapped in the lie. My mother was afraid that he might have been seen talking to you, and she was worried that word would get back to the Professor. If so, he would punish us all with no mercy, if for no other reason than as an example to his other people. It was because of this that my mother decided to tell the Professor's people on her own about the card, hoping that if we admitted to it first, it wouldn't seem so bad.

"My father tried to talk her out of it, but not too strongly, as he was always somewhat weak, especially where she was concerned. She took the card and managed to get the word up the line to the Professor. That was how he came to learn of my drawing abilities.

"The result was probably not what my mother hoped for or expected. In no time at all, I was taken from home and told that I would be entering

113

the Professor's service. However, first I would receive a great deal of specialized training, to go along with my existing abilities. I was taken away from London, as well as from my mother and father, and sent to an old house in Reading, where I lived for several months with an old man and several of Moriarty's staff. The old man was someone you've probably heard of, Mr. Holmes. Old Penrod, the forger."

Holmes nodded. "He's dead now, I believe."

Jamie Morgan nodded. "A few years back. He died in prison, as well. He was caught with most of Moriarty's other people in ninety-one. He passed away from some sort of blood disease. He thought maybe it was due to something that had accumulated in him from all the odd dyes and metals he had used over the years. Who knows? Anyway, I lived with him for a number of months in that house while he studied how much I already knew, and began to teach me everything he could. It wasn't long, I must frankly admit, before he told me that my skill was extraordinary, and that soon the student would surpass the master.

"I learned of inks and dyes, and special tools known and used only by forgers. He taught me about different kinds of papers and parchments, and the use of palimpsests. In addition to the technical side of the trade, I learned about the great frauds and forgeries of the past, and how the con is as important in passing the document as the actual look of the document itself.

"In the spring of the next year, 1891, I had absorbed everything practical that he could teach me, although I had years of work still ahead of me, practicing and refining what I had learned. I returned to London, with the idea that I would be creating items for use by the Professor. I was proud of my abilities, and ready to use them, no matter that I was on the wrong side of the law.

"It was back in London that I saw my father again, at the Professor's headquarters, where he was receiving some message or other to deliver. He was glad to see me, of course. It was then that I learned that my mother had died the previous winter. The Professor had ordered that the knowledge be kept from me, so that I might not be distracted from my lessons.

"My father seemed to be a changed man, much older and withdrawn. He seemed resigned to his future, or whatever was left of it. I guess the burden of what had happened with me as well had been upon him, because it was then that he pulled me aside and told me the truth about his meeting with you. I think he hoped that if I knew the truth, and that there was another opportunity for me, I might still take advantage of it and get out while I could. I knew, however, that once I was in the Professor's organization, there was no leaving. And I didn't really want to leave,

114

anyway. In spite of my anger at not being told of my mother's death, I was proud of my abilities, and of surpassing Penrod, my teacher.

"Within weeks of my return, I had been set up in Birmingham, well away from London, working on the forging of a series of stock certificates. I finished those, and sent them off to the Professor. Within days I had a new assignment. I didn't think about whether what I was doing was right or wrong. I was simply amazed at my own skills and what I was able to create. To start with nothing, just blank paper or parchment, and end up with a veritable masterpiece . . . I never ceased to be amazed. I was still there in Birmingham several months later, working on something or other, when word came that the Professor's entire organization had been destroyed, and everyone in London arrested, including my father.

"Days later, we learned of the Professor's death at that waterfall in Switzerland, along with yours, Mr. Holmes. I was in a right panic, I can tell you. I spent days, and then weeks, expecting the coppers to show up at any minute, busting down my door and dragging me to jail.

"But as the weeks went on, no one came, and I began to realize that somehow, there must have been no trace between Moriarty's London operation and what I was doing in Birmingham. Miraculously, I had escaped. By this time I was running out of money, and I had no choice but to continue with my forgeries, this time producing just enough five pound notes to spend on food. They were of really good quality, and I was careful to use them well away from where I was living.

"You can guess some of the rest, I suppose. Time went by, and no one seemed suspicious of me. I began to produce more fraudulent stock certificates, and cautiously asked around until I managed to find someone who could help pass them. I was always careful, and never tried anything too long in one area or too much of the same thing. It became almost a steady business. I eventually set up a print shop as a legitimate cover. The shop soon gained a reputation for quality work, and to my surprise I began to be a successful business man.

"In just a few years, I had reached the point where I was able to stop forging documents completely. My printing business was going well, and I married and soon had a young son. I named him Thomas, after my father. He is about six years old, now, and shows every indication of having the same skills that I possess, possibly greater.

"My life couldn't seem to be any more perfect, and every night I thanked the Lord for my blessings. It seems, however, that life waits for such moments to step in and remind you how unfair it all really can be.

"I had not done anything illegal for several years, and was concentrating on my family and my growing business. Then, about a year ago, into my shop walks a man I hoped I would never see again.

"I was in the back, in my office, when one of the assistants in my shop came in and announced that I had a visitor. Thinking it was one of the tradesmen I regularly deal with, I said to bring the fellow back, not asking who it was. If I had known, perhaps I would have fled out the back door, and never ended up here. But I suppose it was always destined to turn out this way, and if I had run away that day, my stepping on the path to this cell would have only been delayed by a few hours.

"Into my office stepped a man named Albert Giddry. If you read of my trial, you may recall the name. I had known him from the old days, when I was building up my business with the funds I made from my illegal activities. At that time, he had served as a courier, delivering my finished products to whichever fence or distributor I was using at the time. Occasionally, when I was pressed for time, I had actually put him to work during parts of the printing process.

"I had never worried about any of my former contacts revealing what I used to do. Most didn't have actual dealings with me, instead meeting with go-betweens such as Giddry. Others would never let on what I had done without revealing their own involvement. We had all been small-timers, just interested in making enough to get by. When the supply of my forged documents had dried up, no one had complained or asked for more.

"Even as Giddry entered my office that day, however, I realized that he was dangerous to me, because someone such as him knew everything that I had done, and had nothing to lose by ratting me out. I knew what he was going to say before he said it.

"You have already guessed, I suppose, that Giddry was there to blackmail me. Standing there in his worn, run-down clothes, he looked around at the office, my large desk and comfortable furniture. 'It's a lot different from where we used to meet, isn't it?' he asked. 'You've done right well for yourself.'

" 'What do you want?' I countered, well aware that he would only come to see me for one reason.

"He looked around another moment before stepping closer to my desk. 'Some of us haven't been as fortunate for the last few years,' he said. 'I've just spent a spell in jail. I could have probably made a deal with them, and been released sooner, if I'd told them everything I knew. I knew some interesting things, as you are aware. But I didn't tell. And I think you owe me for that.' "

" 'What's to tell?' I asked. 'You have no proof of anything.' "

" 'Can you be sure?' he asked. 'Can you afford to take that chance? I'll wager you never got rid of the plates and engravings for the certificates and pound notes. I'll bet you had them hidden somewhere around here.

116

You wouldn't have been rid of them. Just finding them in your possession would be enough to convict you.'"

" 'You're mad!' I cried. 'There is no evidence against me!' "

" 'Maybe I came by here one night last week, right after I was released. Maybe I've already found the plates where you put them, and maybe I've re-hidden them. I can tell the police exactly where to search, and they'll believe me when I say it was *your* hiding place.' He stepped back and looked out into the workroom. 'Maybe I put them out there, or maybe even somewhere in your fine house.'

" 'What do you know of my house?' I asked, stepping around the desk. 'You must go nowhere near my house!'

"He grinned and proceeded to recite my home address, along with a description of its appearance. Realizing how much he knew about me, and how I was in his power, I rushed him before he could finish, attempting to get my hands around his throat. He broke away and pushed the office door shut.

" 'Now, now, Jim, we wouldn't want the employees to get involved, would we?' He coughed and rubbed the marks left by my fingers on his neck. Then he reached into his coat pocket and pulled out a heavy object. I recognized it immediately. It was one of the zinc plates that I had used to print five pound notes.

" 'As you can see,' he said, 'I did find your secret hiding place. It was very informative. All I ever knew about was some of the certificates I helped print and delivered for you. You printed a lot more items than I was aware of during the time I helped you. Printing money, Jim. That's really a serious crime, isn't it?'

"I was thinking quickly. I knew he must have been in my shop at night, when it was deserted, and had searched very carefully and diligently to have been able to find the plates. They had been well hidden, or so I had thought, so that none of my employees might casually run across them. I had not checked them in a while, believing them to be completely safe. He must have been quite thorough, and there had never been any sign or indication that an intruder was entering the business after hours.

"Finally, I asked, 'What do you want?'

"His demands were simple. He wanted to be placed on the payroll and given a comfortable living. He wanted an office and no responsibilities. 'After that,' he concluded, 'after that, we'll see what else I need.'

"Well, needless to say, I announced to the employees that Mr. Giddry would be starting as an advisor. The staff was surprised, and none more so than Nate Jones, my manager, who had to be turned out of his own office in order that a place might be found for Giddry. It wasn't long before Nate left for other employment.

"It only took a matter of weeks before Giddry began to make other demands. I had thought it would be bad enough for him to force himself onto the payroll, but I knew I could make up the difference by being as frugal as possible and working my shop that much harder. Things would have been fine if they had remained as they started. Giddry, who now had an office for himself, never showed up except to collect his weekly pay. I knew the employees were talking and speculating about Giddry's function and his power over me, but it was none of their affair.

"Things would have gone on that way, but Giddry began to assert himself, showing up more often, sitting in his office and yelling out demands, and generally making a nuisance of himself. He began to go into the work area, asking questions and making ridiculous suggestions about ways to improve the business that took on the tone of commands. I attempted for a while to stop him, but he would make veiled comments or give me knowing looks, and I would defer to him, further weakening me in the eyes of the employees. It was during this time that Nate left in disgust, and I did not replace him, instead taking on his duties myself as a way to save money. However, Giddry continued to move among the employees, as did the serpent in Eden, sowing dissention, whispering and causing no end of trouble.

"Several more employees left, and it was becoming difficult to keep the place running as it should. We began to lose orders because we could not complete them on time or because of slipping quality. The whole process seemed to feed on itself, one disaster contributing to the next. Meanwhile, Giddry continued to poison my business and expect his pay.

"It was only a matter of time before Giddry came to me and said he knew what was going on with the business, about how it was starting to fail, and that the only choice we had left to make up the lost revenue was to pull out the hidden plates and use them illegally once again. Of course, I had spent countless hours searching both the business and my home, looking for the plates that Giddry had re-hidden, but with no success. I had looked in my original hiding place on the first day, just to make sure Giddry had really found it, but it was empty, as I had truly expected all along.

"For months I had been in his power, afraid of losing all that I had built. My wife had noticed my tension, which I had tried to pass off as simple worry about the business. However, as time went on, the matter grew between us, causing a coldness to exist where none had before. This only added to my despair and unhappiness.

"I resisted Giddry's cajolings for several weeks before finally giving in. One night, after everyone else had gone home, Giddry and I stayed late and affixed the plates to the printing press, where we began to print batches of five pound notes.

"I tried to instruct Giddry to handle this intelligently. He should go far away to pass them, leaving no trail behind him that would lead to me or the print shop. If he did this correctly, the scheme should work to both our advantages. I tried to remember what I had learned from the Professor's system when it had been in operation, and to incorporate it into what I told Giddry. However, he had no use for the finesse of the system, and insisted on passing the money as blatantly and carelessly as possible.

"In spite of Giddry's lack of caution, the scheme went on for a number of months without detection. He had showed up at one point with some of the old stock certificate plates, and I gave in and printed some of those as well. He stated that he knew someone in the City who had agreed to sell them. The sale went well, raising much needed money for both the shop and myself, as well as Giddry and his unknown partner. Apparently the sale caught the attention of some other criminal element, and they decided they wanted a piece of the pie, as well. A representative of that criminal organization visited my shop and told me and Giddry that we would start using them as our distribution point for the forged documents. He then outlined how many documents we were expected to produce. It was a huge number, and seemingly impossible for just Giddry and myself, working at night when the regular employees were gone. In addition, he listed a number of future stock certificate plates that I would be expected to produce in the coming months. He seemed to mistakenly believe that I could create these works of art in a matter of days. Of course Giddry and I protested, but we were not given a choice, or an opportunity to say no.

"I believe that at this point, Giddry was getting as fearful as I about what we were into. We were simply small expendable pieces of this vast criminal machine. I had the most to lose, in terms of my family and business, but at least I had some value as the creator of the plates. Giddry himself had outlived his usefulness. He and I both knew that after he had connected the criminal organization to me and my plates, there was no further use for him. He certainly knew that I would not go out of my way to defend or save him.

"As part of my sudden involuntary servitude, I was finding it necessary to use my evening hours printing more and more documents for my new masters. Of course, Mr. Holmes, I knew who they were. I had met with them by this time, and had come to understand what was expected of me and how I would be compensated. However, I will not tell you who they were, just as I would not reveal it to the police or at my trial. It is part of the bargain I made with them. If I keep my knowledge to myself, my wife and son will remain safe. If I reveal what I know, their lives are forfeit."

Holmes, who had been watching Jamie Morgan intently throughout the entire narrative, interrupted. "Of course, you refer to the new organization founded by the late Professor's brothers, the Colonel, and the other brother, the former station master. They wasted no time in attempting to rebuild the organization that was smashed with the death of Professor Moriarty. I have been aware of it for quite a while. Their time is coming, Mr. Morgan, I assure you.

Morgan did not speak for a second, and then said, "I'm not going to say yes or no, Mr. Holmes. But I do hope, for my family's sake, that no one questions why I wanted to speak with you today, and that this organization you spoke of is destroyed as soon as possible."

Morgan shifted on his cot and continued his narrative. "Giddry, hoping to bargain for his life, knew that all he had to trade were the rest of the counterfeit plates that he had stolen from my hiding place. He had apparently gone into hiding, as he had not been to the shop in several days. Finally, he contacted me and indicated a night when he would be willing to come to the shop and sell me the rest of the plates. He intended to take the money and flee the country, starting over again somewhere in the United States or Canada.

"He arrived that night, carrying the heavy metal plates awkwardly in a cloth bag. As they rattled and banged together, the craftsman in me could not help but wince when I thought how they had been treated by him, and the possible damage that they were suffering due to being improperly wrapped and stored.

"As he set them down, I prepared to pay him the money he had requested. He stopped me. 'There has been a change of plan, Jim,' he said. 'I'm going to need much more than that to set myself up the way I want in my new home.'

"I told him that would be impossible. 'This is all the money I have brought,' I said. 'Besides, I am doing you a service simply by meeting with you at all. We both know that if you are found you will die. You are too much of a risk to their operation.'

" 'Let me tell you about risk, Jim,' he said. 'You are the one who is at risk if anything should happen to me. I know that you have been plotting with them against me.'

"Of course, I had been doing no such thing. I wanted no more contact with them than I had to have. I certainly wouldn't be involving myself in some plot to murder Giddry. I told him so, but in his growing paranoia, he refused to believe me. And then he made the statement which led to the end of his life.

120

" 'You'd better hope nothing happens to me, Jim. For I've written it all down, everything you did, and it's set to go to the police. You'll lose it all. The money, the business, that fine house with your wife and son . . . .'

"A reddish haze seemed to bleed into my vision as he spoke. I knew that the chances of his survival were not good. The organization which had enslaved us was looking for him, and it was very effective at finding and eliminating threats against it. I believed that he was probably going to be killed, and if that happened there would no way to stop the police from receiving his document implicating me. I could not understand why he had chosen to do this to me, when I had, however unwillingly, helped him, from the time he showed up at my shop to this very night, when I was buying my own stolen plates from him, rather than turning him over to the organization which would have killed him and retrieved the plates for free.

"He kept talking, but the words stopped making sense. The room appeared to grow darker, all except in the center of my vision, where he stood proudly declaiming his plans to destroy me and my family. At that point, something snapped. The years of hiding, the blackmail, the hopelessness. I leapt forward and grabbed one of the heavy plates lying beside him on the press. He was too surprised to move. Raising my arm, I swung down on his head.

"It didn't kill him, not that blow. He cried like a wounded animal, rolled away, and moved toward the door. I moved after him, still carrying the blood-slicked plate as I saw the red stain running down the side of his head and onto his coat.

"He was still screaming and crying. It was all happening so fast. I grabbed the back of his collar with my left hand and yanked him away from the door. His feet went out from under him and he sagged backwards toward me. I stepped back, avoiding him as he fell. He landed on his back, his head near my feet, his own legs curling up to kick at my head as I bent over.

"I pivoted on one foot, so I was beside his legs, looking down on his face. He tried to shift and kick me again, but his awkward position prevented any contact. I raised my hand and hit down at his head. The first blow was deflected by his hands, but I must have hit a finger or two, possibly breaking them, because he cried out again and pulled his hands down, curling them to his chest. His head was clear then, and I began to rain blow after blow on it, the sharp corner of the metal plate doing ungodly damage. Soon, he had stopped making any noise at all.

"I don't know how long I stood there, wheezing as I bent over him, but somehow forgetting to stand up. Even when someone knocked the plate out of my hand and pulled me back away from him, my gaze remained fixed on the body on the floor. 'For God's sake,' a voice rasped, 'you've killed him!'

"Unknown to me, Giddry's cries had been heard by a passing constable, doing his nightly rounds. He had managed to find his way in just in time to witness my leap for Giddry, followed by the repeated blows to Giddry's head. I seemed to be floating for the longest time. I recall being taken to my own office and forced to sit in the visitor's chair for quite a while, under the stern gaze of another constable. Later, in that same office, I was questioned by an inspector, and then a hazy series of strangers. I told them the whole basic story, how I had been trained by the Professor, my subsequent forging career and transition into successful businessman, and the reappearance of Giddry, who had blackmailed me back into a life of crime. I did not make any mention of the organization which had recently been controlling us. Even during that time of despair, when I seemed to have no sense of self-preservation. I was doing what I could to protect the rest of my family.

"And so here I am," he said, looking up at us for the first time since he had began his curious narrative. "My solicitors believe that I should have appealed my verdict, on the grounds that my initial confession was under some sort of duress because of my mental condition immediately following the murder. However, it cannot be denied that I killed a man. I know how I felt when the rage was coming over me. There was murder in my heart. Evil. It was meant to be that the constable was passing by right at that moment in order to discover me. My path had led to that moment, and there was no avoiding it."

"And your son?" Holmes asked. "What does this have to do with your son?"

"The curse, Mr. Holmes," Morgan replied. "The curse must be broken. My father, then me. My father killed someone before the end of his time with the Professor, and now I have killed as well. I don't want that for my son. I never want him to see the red rage that I did. He cannot end up here, waiting through the passage of every final minute, trying as I do to imagine what kind of man I'll show myself to be on the last walk. He deserves a normal life.

"My wife came to see me once, before the trial. She offered no comfort, nor did I expect any. I want her to raise Thomas, my son, so that a life such as mine is never a consideration. So that it never has to be. You tried to help my father, once, Mr. Holmes. Can you do the same for me? It is the final request of a dead man."

Holmes looked at him for a moment, until finally Morgan dropped his eyes. "To be clear, you are asking me to find some way for your son to receive the training that you never received?" Morgan nodded. "And your son has the same talent that you showed?" Holmes continued.

"Yes, yes, he does, Mr. Holmes," Morgan said, urgently.

Holmes was silent, thinking to himself. Then he said, "Sir William is still taking an active interest in encouraging young artists." He paused for another moment, and said, more softly, "And he still owes me. I will do what I can."

Morgan grabbed his hand, pumping it in an eerie replay of that day so many years ago on the Paddington platform when his father had shaken Holmes's hand for the same reason. "Thank you! Thank you, Mr. Holmes. That is all I needed to know."

"How shall this be handled?" Holmes asked. "Should I present myself to your wife? Will she have any interest in this plan? Will she give her approval?"

"I believe she will," Morgan replied. "When she came to visit me, after my arrest, I told her some of my unhappy history, including the missed opportunity you had once arranged for me when I was a boy. She and I both know that my son has extraordinary talent, and we have always been in agreement that it should be shaped and encouraged. She will be willing to listen to you. Your association with the plan will assure her that there is nothing underhanded, nothing questionable from my past, involved."

Morgan went on to tell us where his wife and son lived. Holmes stood and agreed to see them as soon as possible. Morgan seemed to accept this with a new peace in his eyes.

As we turned to go, I found myself anxious to leave the tiny cell, with its occupant counting out his final hours. Whatever his crimes, I was glad that we would be able to help him, making the man's final passing somewhat easier.

"There is just one more thing, Mr. Holmes," said Morgan, stopping us before we could knock on the door, signaling our intended departure.

"Yes?" asked Holmes, as we turned back into the cell.

"Someday, perhaps," said Morgan, who then swallowed and started again, "someday, could you perhaps check on my son, and if possible, convey to him how much he means to me?"

Before Holmes could answer, Morgan continued. "And could you . . . could you tell him about your visit today, in such a way as to let him believe that you were here to investigate the circumstances of my conviction? Could you perhaps leave him with the impression that there was some doubt as to my guilt? Don't lie to him, but perhaps leave it so that he could have one little bit of his heart that might still believe that his father was a good man? So that he might hold just a little love for me there through the years?"

Holmes said nothing. He stood there for a minute, looking at the supplicating attitude of the condemned prisoner, leaning forward in the candlelight. Finally, he spoke.

"Yes," he said softly. "Yes, I can do that."

I nodded as well. Morgan nodded back at me, a peaceful smile on his face. Holmes left the room, and I followed. Morgan was executed the next morning.

"It is a harsh existence, Watson," said Holmes as we drove away from Pentonville Prison. Soon we would be back in Baker Street, warm and safe, with the illusion that the evils of the world were shut outside the door. It would be a long time, however, before the feelings of today's visit and the stark images within the prison would be less sharply etched in my mind.

"Life dangles by such a precarious thread," Holmes continued. "A puff of breeze, and it is blown in one direction. Another, and it changes course, never knowing when it will tangle and be irretrievably changed, tied to an unexpected fate."

In my agreement, I could offer nothing but silence. "What if," Holmes said. "What if Tom Morgan had destroyed my card as I told him to? What if his wife had not felt the need to notify the Professor's men? How might Jamie Morgan's life have been different? What suffering could have been avoided?"

There was silence for a while. Then, I said, "I believe that one must actively seek the positive. The winds will push us where they want, of course, but one must also make the correct choices in life to somewhat negate or change the effects of the winds. Jamie Morgan had the chance to do the right thing on several occasions. Unfortunately, he chose incorrectly. However, his final choice was to seek your help, as his father had done.

"You made a choice today, as well, Holmes," I continued. "You chose to honor that man's request to help his son. Not just using your influence with Sir William, but in a way that might give that boy a little less hopelessness and anger than he would have if he had only hate for his father. I believe that it is choices such as these which make the world, little by little, a better place."

We rode in silence for a few minutes. Finally, Holmes said, "Perhaps, Watson. Perhaps."

We did not speak again until we were back home.

The Haunting of Sutton House

I was greatly surprised that morning to find that Mr. Sherlock Holmes had preceded me to the breakfast table. As a rule, he tended to sleep late on mornings when no investigation was occupying his time. As often as not, he would stay up late the night before, playing his violin or immersing himself in some abstruse chemical experiment. On those occasions when an inquiry had presented itself to him, he would curl himself into his chair by the fire and smoke the night away, alternately building and destroying various theoretical edifices until a solution revealed itself to him.

On this morning, I knew that Holmes had stayed up late the night before, only because I myself had been unable to find the deep sleep which I sought. At various times throughout the night, I had risen to consciousness from my shallow slumbers to hear Holmes alternately playing his Stradivarius, or perhaps pacing the floor of the sitting room.

I did not begrudge Holmes his wakefulness, and I did not resent the sounds of music wafting up the stairway to my bedroom, one floor above. I knew that he was wrestling with the events of the previous day.

Holmes and I had just completed a particularly nasty investigation in Surrey, initially involving a robbery, and eventually ending in the discovery of something much worse. The circumstances had been unusually ugly.

I went downstairs and entered the sitting room. Holmes was already sitting at the table in front of his breakfast, pouring himself a cup of coffee. After filling his cup, he reached over and repeated the process with mine. "Good morning, Watson," he said, attempting to sound cheerful. "And how did you sleep?"

"Not very well, I'm afraid," I said, truthfully. "And not," I said, interrupting him before he could apologize, "because of your violin playing. That caused me no distress at all. I could not get that girl's face out of my dreams," I added.

He glanced at the window. I could see the rain running down the glass. "This day will not help us forget our recent business in Surrey, I'm afraid," he said.

I nodded. "Perhaps I shall write the matter up for my notes. It is certainly a day to stay in out of the rain."

"Indeed," replied Holmes. "I, however, may pursue a different activity today. On a day such as this, the London criminal prefers to stay inside just as much as the consulting detective and the semi-retired medical doctor. One can usually find this fellow ensconced amongst his peers around the fire or leaning against a bar in various locations all over the city. I propose to spend the day huddled with him and his friends, listening to their conversations, and trying to pick up the vibrations of whatever plans are currently afoot."

"In disguise, of course," I said.

"Of course. Now, let me see. Should I go as a dock worker, or perhaps as a groom? No, I believe that today I shall appear as Lancing, a mobsman who occasionally shows himself around the watering holes of the East End."

"Lancing?" I asked. "Is there a real Lancing out there, or is he one of your creations?"

"Oh, Lancing is completely mine," replied Holmes. "I first created him in the late seventies, when for several weeks I worked my way into the good graces of the Binner Mob. Fortunately, Lancing was not at their hide-out when Sherlock Holmes and the police broke in and arrested Binner and his men as they were examining their collected spoils. Later, I have found it useful for Lancing to make an appearance here and there every few weeks, giving the impression that he is involved in planning his latest crime. The Professor's men think he is a member of the Willett gang, and the Willetts think that he is under the protection of the Professor. I never let Lancing seem important enough to be a threat to either."

By this time, I had seated myself at the table and begun to load my plate. I rang for more hot coffee, which was soon brought by Mrs. Hudson, along with a note. "This just arrived, Mr. Holmes," she said, handing it to him before departing.

"Thank you, Mrs. Hudson," replied Holmes over his shoulder, pushing back his plate, which was filled with uneaten food. Opening the letter, he quickly scanned it, then threw it on the table in my direction. "So much for Lancing," he stated.

Assuming that he meant for me to read the letter as well, I picked it up. It was on common, cheap stationery, somewhat thin, and written with a wide-nibbed pen using blue ink. The ink had not been thoroughly blotted, resulting in one or two smudges.

"Good, Watson," said Holmes. I looked up with an enquiring expression on my face. "In the early days, you would have immediately jumped to reading the contents of the letter. But now I observed that you first examined the paper, the ink, and the writing style. Do you have any conclusions?"

"Written by a man of limited means, careless, and in a hurry." I reached to pick up the envelope. It was of the same quality, and written with the same ink. The handwriting was the same as that of the letter writer.

"I can see nothing else."

"Watson, you see . . . . "

126

" . . . but you do not observe," I finished, impatiently. "What else is there?"

"The man chews tobacco, as seen from the grains protruding under the envelope flap where he has licked it. He had some sort of cut on his finger, as shown by the small blood stain making a streak on the paper near his signature. He is left-handed, from the direction of the text, and finally he is somewhat gloomy, as seen from the downward direction of each line of the letter as read from left to right."

"Yes, I see all of that, now that you mention it," I said. "And now I shall read the letter."

It was a short missive, only a few lines, reading:

Dear Mr. Holmes,

I called upon you on Sunday without an appointment, and was told by your landlady that you would probably be returning to London Sunday evening.

I need to discuss with you an urgent matter regarding the purchase of some haunted property. With your permission, I will call upon you at eleven o'clock this morning.

Sincerely,
Raymond Thorne

I raised an eyebrow and looked up at Holmes. "Haunted property?"

Holmes snorted. "Normally I would complain about the type of cases that my little practice was reduced to receiving. However, after the recent events in Surrey, perhaps something like this will prove strangely refreshing."

I nodded my head toward the windows, where the rain appeared to be falling even harder. "Perhaps Lancing can wait a day or so to visit his friends."

"I believe you are right," Holmes agreed, standing up and turning toward his bedroom.

I finished my meal and retreated to my chair by the fire, carrying the morning newspapers with me. The details of our recent visit to Lord Bretton's home in Surrey were on one of the inner pages, the story not meriting more extensive treatment. I read the small article twice before my thoughts drifted off to the previous weekend's events.

Two days before, on Saturday, Holmes had been called in by Inspector Youghal to offer his opinion on a theft at Lytton House, the large country place in Surrey of Lord Bretton and his family. Normally, the house stood empty for most of the year, except for a caretaker named Jonas who lived on the grounds. However, that spring, following some financial reversals,

Lord Bretton had been forced to sell his London home, and the Surrey place was opened when the family moved down permanently from London. Lord Bretton and his wife had seven children, from the oldest, Emily, to the youngest, Patrick, who was nine years old, and the only boy.

Emily, at age sixteen, was a pale and quiet girl who had become something of a second mother to the younger children. This was necessary, due to the fact that Lady Bretton was often in ill health, resulting in extended periods where she could not leave her bed.

A few days earlier, the housekeeper that had accompanied the family from London noticed that a painting was missing from the large formal dining room. The canvas was rather large and unwieldy, and it had always been left in the Surrey house when the family returned to London, as it was too awkward to move back and forth. It was the only thing of value that was usually in the house.

The painting was one of Constable's lesser-known works. Although the existence of the painting was not common knowledge, it was considered valuable, especially due to some reawakened interest in the work of that artist. The scene was quite large, approximately three by four feet, and contained in an ornate and heavy wooden frame, itself something of a minor work of art.

Prior to the discovery of the missing painting, it had been several days since anyone had entered the dining room, so the exact time the painting was stolen was uncertain. The previous Saturday had been the last time the room was used, when of Lord Bretton's former business partner, Sir Sheffield Frye, had visited the family and stayed for dinner. Although Sir Sheffield was a regular visitor at the family's town home, it was the first time that he had journeyed to the Surrey residence. It was on the following Wednesday morning that the picture was found to be missing. The police were called in, but no evidence was found. On Thursday, young Patrick disappeared. By Friday, Inspector Youghal was involved, and he sent for Holmes and me on Saturday, one week after the last time the painting had been seen . . . .

I was roused from my contemplations by Holmes, who returned at that moment to the sitting room. I looked at my watch, observing that it was almost eleven. At that moment, the front bell rang. I folded the newspapers on my lap, and laid them aside. I stood as the door opened, revealing Mrs. Hudson and our visitor.

Raymond Thorne was a tall, sallow fellow with thinning brown hair combed across his head in a sad attempt to cover his balding scalp. The hair was cut rather longish, and the strands traversing horizontally across his forehead tended to slip frequently down over his right eye, forcing him to jerk his head in a peculiar sideways motion, tossing the hair back up for a few moments until it dropped again. Over the course of our interview with him that morning, I became concerned for his neck, afraid that the constant motion of his head would cause some sort of permanent injury.

His plain brown suit was somewhat worn, but presentable. I observed the package of chewing tobacco rolled and placed in his waistcoat pocket, as well as a small red cut on the side of one of his left fingers, the wound that had left the small bloodmark on his note to Holmes. Holmes ushered Mr. Thorne to the basket chair after asking the man if he would like any tea or coffee. Thorne declined, and Mrs. Hudson backed out of the room, closing the door behind her. Holmes seated himself in his chair and turned to face Thorne. "So," he began, "you wish to consult me regarding some haunted property?"

"Yes, sir, that is correct," said Thorne. His voice was somewhat thin, and rather querulous. With a toss of his head, he continued. "There is an old house on the eastern side of the city that has been offered to me by my cousin. I can get the money together, but first I want to find out exactly what kind of property I would be buying. There is a rumor that the place is haunted, and although I'm not sure that I believe in that sort of thing, I want to know what I'm getting myself into."

"Who is your cousin?" asked Holmes.

"Walter Mason," replied Thorne.

"The banker?" I interrupted. Holmes glanced at me, and then returned his attention to Thorne.

"That's right," said Thorne. "I guess you've read about him recently. I understand he's on the short list for the Queen's Birthday Honors. He's something of a hero, the way he sorted out that French credit mess last year. I'm very proud of him. Sadly, I don't get to see him as often as I used to, now that he's so busy. It's really a shame, seeing as how we are the last two left in our family. Our parents have all died, and neither of us have any brothers or sisters. His wife died a couple of years ago, leaving him childless, and I've never married.

"He has been so involved in the French affair that I haven't had any contact with him for months. Therefore, I was quite surprised when he wrote to me late last week and asked me to visit him at his home. After we reminisced for a few minutes, he asked me if I would be interested in purchasing the house."

"Yes, the house," replied Holmes. "What can you tell me about it?"

"I'm sure you've heard of the place," Thorne said. "It's somewhat famous in London, simply due to the fact that it is so much older than most of the other houses here. Sutton House, in Hackney."

"Of course," I said. "In Homerton High Street. I've been by it several times."

"I know of the place, as well," said Holmes. "It was built in Tudor times, as I recall, and is one of the oldest houses in East London."

"That's correct, Mr. Holmes," said Thorne. "It was built in the 1530's by one of the officials in Henry VIII's court, I don't remember exactly who. It has been sold to many different owners through the following years, and earlier this century it served as a boys' school, only to be reopened at some later date as a girls' school."

"How did your cousin acquire it?" Holmes asked.

"I believe it had something to do with the house serving as collateral on a loan that went bad. Now my cousin is stuck with the house, which he has no desire to keep. As I said, he approached me last week, after no contact between us for months, and asked me if I would be interested in purchasing the property. You see, gentlemen, I have always had a desire to open a school of my own, of which my cousin has been aware for years. Knowing something of the past history of the building, and the former schools which were housed there, he thought of me.

"I researched the building and found a little of its history, but what concerned me was the reputation of the place. Apparently, it has become labeled as a haunted house, due to the various manifestations of spirits that have appeared within it. I personally have some qualms about purchasing a haunted building, and I certainly would not want to open a school in one." Thorne jerked his head, and looked at me, and then back to Holmes.

"I must tell you," interrupted Holmes, "that I do not believe in ghosts, and that this agency stands flat-footed on the ground in that regard. I'm not sure what you want me to do. I am not interested in either setting out to prove the existence of these ghosts, or conversely spend time disproving them. By making any effort to disprove the existence of ghosts in the building, I would actually be conceding the point that there might be ghosts somewhere else, if not specifically within Sutton House."

"No, no, Mr. Holmes," said Thorne. "I am not asking you to prove or disprove anything. I am simply asking for your presence when I myself examine the place. I am ashamed to admit it, but I am somewhat nervous about the whole idea of spirits, and I do not trust myself to examine the place impartially. If I were to go there, I am certain that I would talk myself into hearing things that were not there, and seeing evidence of phantoms that did not exist, manufactured out of my imagination. I simply wish for you, and Dr. Watson as well if he will join us, to be there while I make up my own mind about the place. Your logical and scientific skepticism is exactly what is needed to balance my possible inclination to panic."

"When do you want to examine the house? Now?" Holmes asked, glancing at the rain running down the window panes, perhaps even heavier than before.

130

"No, tonight if that is agreeable to you. I have arranged to meet my cousin Walter at the house at ten o'clock. We can then spend several hours in the place, exploring it and seeing if anything unusual manifests itself." He looked down, and continued with a softer voice. "I understand that it is more likely that, should they actually exist, the spirits will become more active during the hours of darkness." He looked back up and glanced at Holmes and then me through his fallen hair, before twitching it back into place across his high forehead.

Holmes looked at me. There was a sparkle of amusement in his eyes, but only someone who knew him well would spot it. "Well, Watson?" he asked. "Will you accompany us tonight?"

I sighed, thinking of the previous night, when I had slept so poorly. "Of course," I answered.

"Splendid," said Holmes, rising to his feet. "Shall we meet at Sutton House, Mr. Thorne?"

"Yes, Mr. Holmes. At ten o'clock."

Holmes ushered Thorne to the door, letting him out and shutting it. He then leaned against it for a moment, listening as Thorne made his way down the stairs. In a moment we heard the front door close.

Holmes walked across the room, rubbing his hands. "I apologize for planning an activity that will deprive you of another night of sleep, Watson," he said. "Perhaps you can catch a nap this afternoon."

"And what will you be doing during that time?" I asked.

"Making a few enquiries," he said. "As you know, I make it a habit never to accept anyone's story at face value without independent confirmation. Now, let's see what my scrapbooks say about Sutton House." He reached for one of the thicker books on the shelf by the fireplace.

I stood and crossed the room, looking out the rain-streaked window at the street below. As soon as I glanced down, I saw Thorne step away from our front door, where he had been sheltering himself from the rain. He did not have an umbrella, and he lunged out into the deluge, heading south toward Oxford Street. There were several empty cabs driving past him on the street, but he made no effort to hail one of them.

"Perhaps you should have discussed your fee with Thorne," I remarked. "I deduce that he is unable to afford a cab on such a day as this."

"Hmm?" responded Holmes, reading the scrapbook. "I am not surprised. The state of his shoes indicated as much. One must wonder where he intends to obtain the funds to purchase the house from his cousin."

He stepped around to his chair and sat, laying the scrapbook across his knees. "Sutton House was built in 1535 by Sir Ralph Sadlier. Sir Ralph was the principal secretary of state to Henry VIII. In subsequent years, the house has been owned by a number of people, including weavers, schoolmasters and mistresses, clergymen, wool and cotton merchants, and sea captains. I do not show any recent information regarding the place, however."

He snapped the book shut, rose, and returned it to its shelf. "I must ask some further questions," he said, stepping to the door, where he wrapped himself in his coat. Lifting his ear-flapped traveling cap from its hook, he turned to me. "I should be back by dinnertime. In the meantime, I suggest you get some sleep. I don't know how long tonight's excursion is likely to take." Pulling on his cap, he departed.

Left alone in the room, I returned to my chair. Picking up the morning newspapers from the floor where I had previously placed them, I again turned to the headlines concerning the main events of the day. I tried to lose myself in the intrigues of government, but my mind quickly wandered to the tale of our new client and the haunted house. However, without any further information, my speculations soon ended, and my thoughts drifted. I suppose it was inevitable that again I considered the recent tragic events in Surrey.

On Saturday morning, Holmes and I had been summoned to Lord Bretton's home by Inspector Youghal. The incident of the missing painting in itself was not serious enough for Youghal to request Holmes's presence. However, the added matter of the missing boy, Patrick, had changed the nature of the investigation. Lord Bretton had remembered hearing of Holmes in regard to other investigations, and he had insisted that Holmes be called. Holmes had worked with Youghal before on several small matters, and Youghal had no objection whatsoever at asking Holmes to come down.

Youghal met us at the train station and took us to the house, explaining the situation as we drove through the sunny countryside. We reached Lytton House, an old picturesque pile, surrounded on all sides by wide fields and gently flowing hills. The occasional old farm building was scattered here and there across the landscape, adding to the beauty of the scene. However, the fact that a child was missing seemed to chill the setting, as if one were seeing it while suffering from an illness or fever.

Inside, we met Lord Bretton and his family. After expressing our concern, we excused ourselves so that Holmes could begin his investigation. Holmes examined the dining room, lamenting that it had been disrupted by so many people in the last week. He did find that the dining room window had been opened recently, which appeared to have some significance, as Lord Bretton maintained that the window was never usually opened, even in summer, due to the fact that it faced in the direction of the prevailing winds, and the currents played havoc with the dining room linens and draperies, not to mention the valuable painting hung there.

As to young Patrick, there was still no sign. He had last been seen by one of the house staff on Thursday morning, and had not been missed until that evening's meal. However, it was only when dark approached that the family began to really fear for the young boy. Holmes questioned the family and staff, but no one could offer any further information on the boy's whereabouts. Inspector Youghal had alerted the police in nearby towns to be on the lookout for anyone matching Patrick's description, but no word of him had arrived.

Holmes and I discussed the case on Saturday afternoon, and it was then that I learned some of the questionable history of Sir Sheffield Frye. Lord Bretton regarded the man as simply a friend whom he had first met at his London club, the Nonpareil. Later, they had become partners in a matter of business. However, Holmes was aware of numerous questionable activities involving Sir Sheffield, including several instances of theft, cheating, and an incident on the continent where one of his detractors had ended up crippled for life, and his face ruined by acid.

The previous year, Sir Sheffield and Lord Bretton had both faced near financial ruin while partnering in their business venture. Sir Sheffield had seemingly recovered, and had actually just purchased Lord Bretton's London house, as a way for the family to have enough funds to live in the Surrey home.

Holmes noted with interest a curious clause in the contract, stating that Sir Sheffield was to take possession of the London home in its entirety, including all contents therein, lock, stock and barrel. Sir Sheffield's journey to Surrey the previous weekend had been for the purpose of bringing the payment to Lord Bretton for the house, thus sealing the deal.

Meanwhile, I was interested to observe the family firsthand, dealing with the situation as best they could. Holmes had felt that Patrick's disappearance had something to do with the missing painting, but he could not say why, and he couldn't prove it with any certainty whatsoever. Patrick had clearly disappeared after it was discovered on Wednesday that the painting was missing. By that point, the police had already visited the house, and it seemed unlikely that a kidnapper could have entered the property and taken him.

Lord Bretton tried to be strong for his family, and frequently stated aloud that he did not care at all about the painting, as long as he could have his boy back. His wife had been sedated and kept to her room by the family doctor. The five younger girls were all cared for by the oldest, Emily, who stoically went about her business with her eyes downcast and *distant. However, on one or two occasions when I did catch her gaze, her lashes were rimmed in tears and she revealed that she was suffering like the others.*

With questions about Sir Sheffield at the top of his mind, Holmes, Youghal, and I had returned to London that Saturday night . . . .

I must have dozed during my recollection of the events of the previous Saturday, because I was startled awake by Mrs. Hudson, asking me if I was ready for lunch. I stated that I was, noticing that the rain outside had stopped, and now the light outside was bright an pleasant.

Holmes returned, as expected, before dinnertime. His mood was quite cheerful, but he did not volunteer any information, and I knew better than to ask. He changed into his dressing gown, and then busied himself at his chemical table, in the corner between the fireplace and the window.

Later, as we ate, there was no mention of Thorne's problem, or our upcoming expedition to Sutton House. As I recall, Holmes spent the meal expounding on the relationship between a person with an unhealthy interest in abstruse and theoretical mathematics and the contempt such a person would develop for the average flawed human being. Recognizing that he was speaking obliquely about Professor Moriarty, I joined the conversation with a few examples of my own, mostly involving medical professors I had known who were so interested in cold facts regarding the functions of the human body that they had ceased to see individuals as people, but rather as machines to be tinkered with before discarding them.

At nine o'clock, Holmes gathered a few dark lanterns and placed them near the door. Then he entered his bedroom, only to return in a moment fully dressed and ready to depart. I was ready, as well. Holmes noticed as I placed my service revolver into my pocket. He made no comment as we put on our coats and hats.

The cab ride across London was chill and damp. The heavy rains of the previous night and morning had left a great deal of humidity in the air, which had condensed into a thick fog as the night temperature dropped. It was nothing like one of the deadly London particulars, which rolled in with great regularity, their choking fumes quite deadly to the elderly and those with respiration problems. This fog was much cleaner, although it was quite unpleasant in its own way simply due to the wet chill it presented.

We reached Hackney a little before ten. The cab had been forced to travel slowly due to the fog, but we had proceeded without incident, as there was very little traffic out that night. We pulled up in front of the house, and the cab stopped. We stepped down and Holmes paid the driver, who then clicked to his horse. As they departed, we looked up at the building, and then stepped backward into the empty street, in order to get a better view. There was no sign of our client or his cousin.

The house was three stories high, and faced with red brick. An oddly shaped cupola rose among the rooftop chimneys, and all along the front of the building were numerous windows of varying sizes and elevations. The effect was one of jumbled asymmetry, as well as a massive and brooding bulk. All of the windows were dark, but I seemed to feel as if something were watching me from inside the structure, and I involuntarily shivered. Setting down the dark lanterns on the street beside his feet, Holmes glanced at me, and then back to the house.

"I spoke to Alton Peake today," he said. "This house actually does have quite a reputation."

I had met Peake several times during the course of Holmes's investigations. He was a sort of consulting spiritualist, maintaining the paranormal equivalent to Holmes's practice. He specialized in investigations of haunted locales, bringing the vast knowledge of many years of study to his work. By his own lights, he tried to be fair, and he actually debunked many more ghostly legends than he substantiated.

Although both Holmes and I had no use for ghost stories, I knew that we both respected Peake, even if we did not agree with him. If Holmes had consulted with him, and Peake had confirmed something of the history of Sutton House's nature, then perhaps my apprehension before the dark building was not entirely unfounded.

I asked Holmes if he had learned any of the details regarding the spirits said to inhabit the house, but before he could answer, we were interrupted by the sound of hurrying footsteps coming up the street. In a moment, our client stepped out of the fog and into the pool of light beneath the gas lamp under which we stood.

"Mr. Holmes, Dr. Watson. I'm glad to see you." Thorne glanced at the imposing old house. "It's easy to believe what they say about the place, isn't it. Especially on a night such as this."

"Indeed," replied Holmes. "In fact, I posed some questions about the house earlier today, and it appears that your concerns are not completely without merit."

Thorne turned his gaze back from the house to Holmes. The sudden movement of his head caused his hair to slide down toward his eyes. I idly wondered why Thorne was not wearing a hat. With a twist of his head, Thorne threw his hair up and off his face. "What did you learn, Mr. Holmes?"

"Let us discuss it inside," Holmes said. "Unless you would prefer to wait out here for the arrival of your cousin."

135

"Oh, Walter will not be able to join us tonight," Thorne replied. "I received a message from him an hour or so ago. Some unexpected business came up, and he sent his apologies. He did indicate that he wished he could be with us, however, and that we should feel free to explore the building without him." Jerking his head, he added, "He really wanted to meet you, Mr. Holmes."

Thorne led us up onto the low stoop, where he fumbled in his pocket for a moment before producing a large old-fashioned key. He awkwardly placed it into the lock, which was in deep shadow on the right side of the door. After a moment, the mechanism turned, and the door slowly opened.

A cold, dank puff of air flowed out of the place, past us into the street, where it dissipated. Thorne looked back over his shoulder at us, took a deep breath, and said, "Well," before stepping inside. Holmes and I followed, the dark lanterns in Holmes hand knocking softly together.

We found ourselves inside an entrance room, containing a few odd sticks of furniture more fitting to a parlor. We turned slowly, looking about the room. I pulled my coat tighter. The room was cool, but it was a welcome relief to get out of the pervasive wet fog. Now that we were inside, the place did not seem as threatening. It was merely a very old building, abandoned and neglected. Still, there was no smell of damp or rot inside, and the flooring appeared very solid and sound as I stepped across it.

"I'm glad you thought to bring the lanterns," said Thorne. "I did not have any myself that I could bring. I forgot to mention it this morning, and I'm afraid the house is not laid on for gas. I suppose we can find some candles."

"I'm sure it will not be necessary," said Holmes. "It will probably be best if we conduct our investigation in as much darkness as possible." He turned toward a doorway leading to the rear of the building. "What can you tell us of the layout of the place?"

"It is a rather curious place, gentlemen," said Thorne, twitching his head. He was speaking in a low tone, as were we all, and I stepped closer to hear him better. "The original building also included that house next door, but at some time in the past the two were separated, and each has taken on a very individual appearance. The exterior of this house was bricked up at some point, giving it a markedly different look from its neighbor.

"The house is three stories, and there is also a small basement chapel, accessed from the adjacent room. All three stories surround an inner courtyard. The oddest fact about the house is that it is not squared. Rather, the entire footprint of the building is a strange mixture of odd angles and rooms that jut out in haphazard ways, rather like a trapezoid made out of randomly arranged boxes. The ground floor is a mixture of about six or so rooms, all of varying sizes and shapes. They are clustered together in a loose arrangement around the courtyard.

"The two floors above are mirror images of the ground floor. One would be tempted, I suppose, to blame the mad shape of the place to the poor building practices of our ancestors, as if they were adding on a piece at a time as needed. However, other buildings of the same period do not have such strange geometry, and whatever can be said about the unique shape of the building, it is quite solid."

Holmes paced the floor for a moment. "It is indeed," he finally agreed. "It is quite amazing for a building to be this old and still be so well put together." He motioned toward the door leading out of the room. "Perhaps we can see the rest of the building?"

"Wait," said Thorne. "You said that you had asked about this house today, and that you had discovered some information regarding my concerns. Pray, tell me what you learned."

Holmes walked back to the center of the room. He set down the lanterns and fished out his matches. Then picking up one of the lanterns, he proceeded to light it while he spoke.

"I met with an acquaintance of mine and Dr. Watson's today. Alton Peake." Holmes waited to see if Thorne showed any recognition, but he did not.

"Peake is something of an expert in the matter of hauntings and such," said Holmes, who then gave Thorne a short sketch of some of Peake's investigations, including the matter of the Barton Hill Riddle, in which Holmes and I had aided in the examination of the sinister stairway. "Perhaps," continued Holmes, "Peake would have been better suited for the type of examination you proposed tonight."

"No," replied Thorne. "I need someone to be an objective witness. Mr. Peake sounds as if his mind might be *too* open, if you get my meaning. His presence here might have goaded me into a panic."

"Nevertheless," began Holmes, and then he paused to set down the first lantern and begin lighting the second. "The house has gained a reputation in the last fifty years or so for being haunted. Apparently, according to Peake, this is common knowledge among the people with whom he has regular contact."

He retrieved the third lantern and began to light it. Thorne tossed his head and said, "Go on."

"The supposed hauntings manifest themselves in several ways," said Holmes. "There is apparently some tapping on the walls which occurs in the dining room, which I believe is on this floor, but on the opposite side of the building. Upstairs, on the first floor, there have been reports of the sounds of a woman crying, as well as areas of sudden cold on the staircase, and moving furniture in one of the bedrooms. The legend is that a woman died in childbirth in one of the rooms on that floor. Also on that floor is a great chamber and a smaller adjacent room, both with numerous curious incidents taking place within. More about those in a moment.

"On the second floor is a large room, where a woman has also been spotted. Peake did not know if it was the same woman from the floor below, or perhaps a different woman. Also, throughout the house, there have been other reports of 'blue ladies' and 'white ladies' moving about, and of opening and closing doors and moving objects."

I glanced around me, but the items in this room remained static. The place was silent, with no sounds whatsoever, not even from the street outside. However, this was not surprising, I supposed, since very few people would be about on such a foggy night. "On the first floor is a great chamber, as I mentioned. The walls are covered with wooden panels featuring a great number of engravings of dogs."

"Yes, I have seen those panels during my initial tour of the house," said Thorne. "In daylight," he added. "They are quite lovely, and in excellent condition, as is the rest of the house."

Holmes nodded. "According to Peake, they were placed there in the mid-1500's, sometime after the house had passed from its original builder to a wool and cotton merchant named John Matchell, or Mitchell. Supposedly he was a great dog lover, and he even had dogs incorporated into his coat of arms. It is commonly believed by Peake and his acquaintances that one can still hear dogs in the room, as well as scratching noises coming from within the walls. There is supposed to be whispering in the room, and also from the small room off the great chamber. At times visitors to the rooms have been pelted with small stones, which seem to appear out of thin air."

I felt an involuntary shiver coming over me, and fought it so that it would not be observed by Holmes, who stood motionless, staring at us while he held the third lit lantern.

After a moment, Thorne spoke. "Well," he said, "It seems that there is no floor of the building which does not have some story connected with it. But what about the basement chapel, Mr. Holmes? Is it haunted as well?"

"I stress that I do not believe in hauntings, Mr. Thorne," replied Holmes. "I am simply relating to you the stories about the place, as collected by Mr. Peake. And yes, there is a story connected with the basement chapel as well.

"It is said that the chapel contains the spirits of two men, enemies, locked in eternal combat. Their anger and animosity appear to pervade the whole room, and sometimes their struggles spill over into this world." He paused, and then added with a small smile, "At least they do, according to Alton Peake." He turned toward the doorway, framing an impenetrable darkness. "Shall we explore the house?"

Thorne and I each bent and picked up a lantern. Adjusting the light to its maximum brightness, I followed Holmes into the darkened room.

Once inside, I perceived that it was not as dark as I had thought. On the right were windows, opening onto the central courtyard, about which Thorne had told us. On the left was a passage leading down some stairs into a deeper darkness. "The stairs to the chapel," said Thorne. He started to move that way, but Holmes stopped him.

"Let us see the rest of the house first," he said.

"That suits me, Mr. Holmes," said Thorne. "The violent history of the room makes it seem the most likely one in which to see some manifestation, should there be one. Perhaps we can spend some time there after we have examined the rest of the building."

We proceeded through the back of the room into a long passage along the rear of the house. In the lantern light, the windows appeared completely black. Holmes suggested we decrease the lantern light, in order to allow our eyes to adjust to the darkness. We did so, and soon I was able to see some of the ambient light outside through the windows on both sides of the room, looking out into the back garden on one side, and into the internal courtyard on the other.

At the far end of this passage was another room. The sparse furniture there indicated that it was the dining room of which Holmes had spoken. He raised his hand for a moment, and we paused listening intently. I heard nothing, and after several minutes, I was ready to move when suddenly Thorne hissed, "Did you hear it?"

There was a frightened thread running through his voice, and for a second a thrill of fear ran along my spine as I strained to hear whatever it was. He was leaned forward, and as I watched he twitched his head. In the silence, the rustle of his coat as he did so seemed particularly loud.

"What was it?" asked Holmes, turning his head slowing from side to side, attempting to hear as he unconsciously mimicked Professor Moriarty's odd and sinister reptilian head movements.

"A tapping," said Thorne. "I heard a tapping. Did you not hear it?"

"No," said Holmes. I shook my head when Thorne turned his questioning gaze my way. Thorne straightened and attempted to relax.

Holmes led us across the room toward the next, always keeping the courtyard windows to our right as we moved through the building in a counter-clockwise motion. Suddenly, Thorne cried out again.

"There!" he cried. "I heard it again."

We again paused for a long moment before Holmes started forward. "If something is here, and trying to get our attention," he said, "perhaps it will try harder as we move further into the building."

We passed through another couple of empty rooms before returning to the entrance where we had begun. Without pause, Holmes mounted the stairs to the next floor.

On the stairs, I recalled what Holmes had said about areas of cold on this staircase. I was already cold, and my imagination tried to make me feel the touch of a passing spirit, but there was nothing there. It was simply a narrow and rather steep stairway. In a moment, we were on the first floor. I could see what Thorne had meant about the upper floors being mirror images of the ground floor. As we passed through the room, I could see that the layout and oddly shaped chambers were exactly like those below, although they were not decorated in the same way, and there was a great deal less abandoned furniture. We traversed the rooms, again in a counterclockwise fashion, first beginning in some sort of study, located immediately above the entrance hall.

"This would be the room where Peake believed a woman died in childbirth," Holmes said, looking around. "There are supposed to be areas of cold within this room, as well as voices and moving objects. We will wait here for a few moments to see if we observe anything. Please close your lanterns."

We stood in the dark for several minutes. This room was in complete darkness, as there were heavy drapes over the windows. After a moment, I sensed Holmes walking about the room, taking careful steps. "Have you felt anything, Mr. Thorne? Watson?"

I started to answer when there was a great noise. Thorne cried out, and I heard a thump. I hurried to open my lantern to find Thorne sprawled on the floor, with Holmes leaning over him, gripping his arm.

"I apologize, Mr. Thorne!" he cried. "I tripped as I was crossing the room and fell right into you. Are you all right?"

Thorne rolled over and got to his knees. Holmes gripped his arm and helped him stand, brushing him off as he did so. "Watson," said Holmes, "please find our lanterns before we start a fire."

I turned hurriedly from side to side, spotting both lanterns lying nearby. As I moved toward them, the light from my lantern veered crazily, throwing shafts of light around the room. As I bent to pick up the two fallen lanterns, Holmes appeared to lose his balance again and fell back into Thorne, who sagged for a moment, then regained his footing, supporting Holmes and helping him remain upright.

140

Holmes laughed, sounding unnaturally loud in the dark curtained room. "I am so very sorry, Mr. Thorne. I fear that if there are any spirits here, they have been mightily entertained by my clumsiness!"

Thorne adjusted his overcoat, patting it into place with an annoyed look. Apparently satisfied that it was adjusted properly, he ran his fingers through his hair, which had completely collapsed and dropped in thin strands over his face. "It is all right, Mr. Holmes," he replied. "Perhaps, however, we should leave the lanterns on, at least whenever you intend to be moving about."

"Agreed," said Holmes. "And since the spell of this room has been broken tonight, shall we move on to the other rooms on this floor?"

We walked through the various rooms, listening quietly in each but hearing nothing. The light through the outside windows was diffused by the fog, giving the feeling that the house was cut off from the rest of the world. On the inner side of the house, the windows overlooking the courtyard were much darker. The fog had not penetrated the courtyard.

We ended our tour of the first floor in the great chamber. By lantern light, we examined the wooden panels and their curious dog carvings. This had been the room of the wool and cotton merchant, but that was over three hundred years earlier, and except for the carvings, there was no evidence to mark his previous tenancy.

Holmes walked into the adjacent smaller room as well. I stood in the doorway and looked in, but there was nothing to see. Suddenly, I heard Thorne hiss with surprise in the great room behind me. Turning, I saw him looking at me with great fear in his eyes. Holmes stepped out of the small room to my side, asking "What is it?"

"I heard them!" he whispered. "I heard the dogs! They were in the walls. They scratched, and then one of them whined. I heard it!" Holmes and I glanced at each other, and then back at Thorne. "We heard nothing, Mr. Thorne."

"Perhaps the wind," I began, but Holmes shook his head and nodded toward the outside window. "There is no wind, Watson. Observe the fog. It is not moving or blowing away."

"I heard it!" Thorne repeated. "I swear to . . . " He paused, and then said, "There it was again! You heard it, too. You must have!" He stepped closer, tossing his head. "Tell me that you heard it!"

I crossed to him and placed a hand on his shoulder. "You must calm yourself, Mr. Thorne," I said. He was trembling like a nervous horse.

"You think I'm mad," he said, "but I did hear them."

"Ahh," said Holmes, suddenly, as he quickly raised his hand to his cheek. A second or two later, I heard the sound of several small objects striking the floor behind him.

141

"What is it?" I asked.

"Something hit me in the face," he said, lowering his hand. I stepped closer, and saw a red welt on his cheek, below his right eye. Thorne moved past him, holding out the lantern. He bent down, and then stood and turned, looking at us with an odd expression on his face.

"There are stones here," he said, "several small stones. Gravels."

"This is the room," I said, "where it was reported that stones appeared out of the ether." I walked over and examined the floor. After a moment I reached out and picked up the stones. There were three of them, small, discolored and irregularly shaped gravels, such as might be found in any street in the city.

"Actually," said Holmes, "stones were reported to appear in the small room next door. However, I was facing in that direction, so I suppose they could have been thrown from in there and through the door." He walked quickly to the doorway leading into the smaller chamber. "Empty," he called.

Thorne looked from one to the other of us, and then turned toward the door. "I must get out of this room," he said. I offered the stones to Holmes, but he simply shook his head quickly and turned away. I slipped them into my pocket, and we followed Thorne, finding him waiting for us at the stairway to the top floor.

Upstairs, we circled the floor as before, but saw no signs of any supernatural activity. However, Thorne seemed to become more agitated with each passing moment. He moved his lantern back and forth erratically, as if trying to catch something in the light before it could hide itself. As we passed through one of the rooms, Holmes commented that it was supposed to be the site of one of the appearances of the ghostly women. Thorne made no comment, simply moving from one end of the room and out the other without pause. In fact, we traversed the entire floor without stopping in any of the rooms to see if anything unusual might occur.

At the stairs, Thorne looked back to see if we were behind him, and then he started down. He reached the landing on the first floor and turned, continuing downward. Halfway down the stairs to the ground floor, he suddenly cried out and fell backwards, landing in a sitting position on the stairs at Holmes's feet, who had been behind him. Luckily Holmes was able to stop in time. Otherwise, he might have tripped over Thorne, and pitched over him to the floor below.

"It was cold," Thorne moaned, wrapping his arms around his thin chest. "Did you feel it? It was suddenly so cold, as if an icy wind were blowing right through me!"

Holmes reached down to help Thorne to his feet. "We felt nothing," he said. "However, perhaps you are more sensitive to these things than we are."

Thorne turned and looked up at Holmes, squinting in the light coming from our lanterns. "Then do you believe, Mr. Holmes?" He shifted his glance to me. "And Dr. Watson? Do you believe as well?"

"Let us just say that my conclusions are still . . . pending at this point," replied Holmes. "Let us wait and see what else happens tonight." He pulled out his watch. "It is now a little after eleven. I suggest we wait somewhere and see if anything else happens."

Thorne nodded and straightened himself, jerking his head to the side. "Yes, yes. Of course. At least until midnight. That is the hour when spirits are said to be most active." He sighed deeply, and then added, "Perhaps we should wait in the chapel. After all, Mr. Holmes, you did say that the spirits there have the most . . . violent stories associated with them. An eternal struggle, you said. Perhaps that is where we shall see enough for you to make a conclusion. Although I must tell you," he continued, "that what I have felt has nearly convinced me that I do not want to purchase this property."

We crossed the entrance parlor and on into the adjacent room, where we again reached the stairs to the basement chapel. Holmes offered to go first, widening the aperture on his lantern to its widest. The bright light revealed rough whitewashed walls on either side of the steep narrow staircase. Thorne followed Holmes, while I brought up the rear.

The room we stepped into was about fifteen feet square, with a surprisingly low and oppressive ceiling crossed by thick wooden beams, supporting the floor of the room above us. The walls and ceiling were whitewashed the same as the stairwell, and had the same rough texture.

On the wall opposite the stairs were several barred windows, placed high in the wall immediately next to the ceiling. Around the floor were several rude wooden benches, seats without backs, obviously very old and used to fulfill the room's purpose as a chapel. We stood in silence for a moment before Holmes asked, "Do you feel anything, Mr. Thorne?"

"No, nothing yet," replied Thorne hesitantly. "I'm cold, but not like the cold I felt on the stairwell. But there is something. Something here. An anger . . . . " he trailed off.

Holmes pulled one of the benches over toward the wall, out of sight of the stairwell. He sat, leaning back against the wall, and shut his lantern, plunging the area around him into darkness. "I suggest," he said, "that we wait here for a while. It is not long until midnight. Perhaps we will observe something at that time."

I joined Holmes at the other end of his bench and shut my lantern as well. Thorne looked at both of us, and then back toward the stairs, as if considering whether to bolt up them and out into the night. Eventually he pulled another bench to the wall beside the stairs, opposite the windows, and sat down as well, closing his lantern.

The initial darkness seemed overwhelming, but gradually my eyes adjusted to the light coming in from the high windows. These were set on one of the outer side walls of the building. There were shadows across parts of the windows, thrown there by trees growing at the side of the house between the windows and the street lights. I could tell by the light diffusion that the fog was still there, possibly even thicker than when we had arrived.

While we waited, I pondered the actions of Sherlock Holmes. He sat silently beside me, unmoving as always in this type of situation. I knew that he had made his own investigations earlier in the day, and I felt certain that Alton Peake was not the only person he had consulted. In the house, he had seemed to show an increasing belief in the minute possibility that something supernatural might be occurring. I knew this to be completely false, and that there was no way he would be convinced that the house was haunted, especially based on the slight evidence shown by Mr. Thorne's reactions to the phenomena that Thorne had experienced.

My final indication that Holmes was playing some deeper game occurred when he had declined to examine the stones that had landed on the floor of the upstairs room. He had obviously been much more interested in Thorne's reaction to the incident than the items supposedly hurled from some other-worldly region. I resolved to remain alert as to whatever might happen. I suspected that midnight would bring the matter to a crisis.

Meanwhile, on the bench beside us, Thorne was becoming more and more agitated. I could hear him shift frequently from side to side, and his breathing was increasing in both rapidity and audibility. I could not see his face in the darkness, but I could make out his dark shadowed form, and it was easy to see him tossing his head with mounting agitation.

As this situation continued, I found my mind wandering, even though I remained fully aware of what was happening around me, ready to move in an instant if necessary. I thought back to the Sunday morning in Surrey, a little more than thirty-six hours earlier, when Holmes, Inspector Youghal, and I had returned to Lord Bretton's home.

We had returned late Sunday morning, with Holmes looking as pale and grim as I have ever seen him. Beside him was Inspector Youghal, his mouth drawn into a tight, thin line. We were in the drawing room, waiting with Lord Bretton and his daughter, Emily.

144

As Youghal moved around the perimeter of the room, Holmes said, "Lord Bretton, I am afraid that I have some terrible news."

Youghal came to a stop beside Emily, who looked up at him, before wildly turning her gaze toward Holmes. Lord Bretton half rose from his seat, and then sank back down, his hand moving uncertainly toward his brow. "Patrick?" he said.

"I am sorry, sir," Holmes said. "Your son is dead."

With a sob, Lord Bretton sank back onto the settee and pressed his hands to his eyes. He began to cry, and then looked from side to side with a shocked expression. Emily continued to look at Holmes, not seeming to notice that Youghal's hand was now firmly grasping her upper arm. I walked over to Holmes. He nervously fumbled and lit a cigarette. I could tell that he was more shaken than he would have wanted to admit.

"We located Sir Sheffield last night," Holmes replied. "He was at his club, the Nonpareil. By speaking in a rather vague way, implying that we knew more than we really did, it was a quick matter to get the story out of him. During his visits to your London home, he had been secretly romancing Emily." He turned his head, meeting Emily's eyes as she listened to every word he was saying. "Not because he cared anything about her, of course. He was simply dallying with her, always on the lookout for an opportunity if one should present itself." His tone became somewhat harsher, and Emily physically flinched at his words.

"Sir Sheffield blames you for the financial disaster that nearly ruined you both last year. When you asked him to buy your London home to provide you with funds to live here in the Surrey house, he saw a way to take even more from you. He wrote the contract so that when you sold the house, you sold all of the contents contained in it, as is.

"Over the course of his past visits, he had learned of the Constable painting, here at the Surrey house. He arranged to visit here last Saturday to get a look at it. It was everything he thought it would be, and as he had some pressing gambling debts to cover within the next fortnight, it appeared to be a heaven-sent opportunity. He would arrange with Emily to remove the painting to the London house, and he would then maintain that it had been located there all along. Emily would back his story, and he would claim it as part of the complete contents of the house that he had just purchased. He thought that he could keep Emily on his side with further empty promises of love, and that the thief's identity might never be discovered. And if it was, the threat of scandal might silence the family if necessary.

"He managed to arrange with Emily for the painting's theft. She passed it out of the dining room window on Tuesday night, setting it on the stony ground outside the window. She closed the window, and then left the

145

house, carrying the canvas to a long-abandoned barn quite a distance to the south of the house.

"There, she hid the painting in a root cellar under the barn flooring. Apparently she had discovered the cellar during some of her solitary explorations of the property. On Thursday, she slipped away, intending to meet Sir Sheffield at the barn and give him the painting. However, she did not realize that she had been observed by young Patrick, who followed her."

By this time, the room had quieted, and Lord Bretton was listening with growing horror to Holmes's narrative. Emily had sunk into the chair behind her, but Youghal still stood by her, his hand resting lightly on her arm.

"This much we from Sir Sheffield last night," said Holmes. *"He showed up on Thursday to receive the painting. Of course, it had not been discovered the previous day by the police during their searches. They had paid scant attention to the abandoned building, and they had not even realized that there was a root cellar, as the trapdoor had been concealed with straw by Emily when she first hid the painting.*

"Sir Sheffield met Emily at the shed as arranged, where she was waiting with the painting, next to the open chamber. As he took possession of the canvas, he was dismayed to hear Patrick's voice coming through a crack in the building's wall, where the boy had been watching. The boy apparently realized what was happening, and said that he was going to tell where the painting was. Emily urged Sir Sheffield to flee, saying that she would take care of her brother. He and Emily then left the building, he to run with the painting to a nearby copse where he had left his horse and trap, and she to catch the boy, who was still leaning against the wall.

"Sir Sheffield stated that he does not know what happened after that, as he turned away from the scene to drive toward the road. He took the painting to the London house, where we found it last night, and where it hangs now. Under the contract, he intended to keep it, and claim that it had been hanging there all along. Emily's false testimony would be used to confirm that. He claims to have no knowledge of the final fate of the boy."

Emily leaned forward, her hands pressed to her face. Then she sat up straight, her eyes wet, tears standing on her lashes as I had seen several times on the previous day. She had been weeping for her missing brother then, I realized, although not in the way I had believed.

"We went to the abandoned barn a few minutes ago, as soon as we arrived on the property. The trapdoor to the root cellar was closed, and again covered by straw so that it would not be found by anyone except

those who knew it was there. Were you aware that there was a root cellar in that building, Lord Bretton?"

"No," the man whispered, and then cleared his throat. "No, I had no idea," he rasped, his eyes locked on Holmes, as if he were afraid to look to his left at Emily.

"We spoke to Jonas the caretaker, and he was unaware of it, as well," said Holmes. "It is not much of a chamber, a mere five feet or so deep, and about the same area square. Unless you had plans to remove the building anytime soon, it is likely that the whole thing would have continued its slow collapse on top of the chamber, and no one would have realized for many years, if ever, that it was there.

"When we found it, we were dismayed to discover the body of young Patrick inside." Lord Bretton sobbed again, and continued to weep. However, Emily's expression did not change in the least. She continued to stare at Holmes, eyes tearful and unblinking.

"The boy had been wounded gravely on the head. A piece of bloodstained wood, cut for stove length, was lying beside the body. There were numerous similar pieces in the building, and Emily must have grabbed one when she went out to stop Patrick."

"She had thrown lime over the boy," Youghal rasped, speaking for the first time. "She didn't want the body to be found. She covered up the trapdoor." His fingers tightened on her shoulder, but she did not change her expression.

For the first time, Lord Bretton turned toward Emily, trying to ask why, but unable to overcome the sobs trapped in his throat. After a moment, when Emily made no comment, Holmes continued.

"Sir Sheffield said that she believed he was going to run away with her someday. Of course, he never had any intention of staying with her," he added, an edge to his voice. "No doubt she felt that if her perfidy were discovered, her plans to be with Sir Sheffield would fall through. Perhaps she did not mean to kill Patrick, and only lashed out unthinkingly to stop him. However, once the deed was done, she deliberately hid the body, fixing it so that it would not be found. She threw lime liberally into the hole, in order to minimize the problems associated with decomposition. There was no lime in the abandoned building, so she would have had to get it from elsewhere on the grounds. This took intentional effort and planning. Then she covered the trapdoor with straw to make certain that the boy would not be found during the subsequent search which was sure to be made over the entire estate."

"Why did Sheff tell?" Emily said, speaking for the first time. Her voice was strangely childlike and confused. "No one would have ever known," she said. "He could have sold the painting, and then he would have come

147

for me. Then I wouldn't have had to take care of the children any more. I've never liked children."

Lord Bretton stared at her in horror, tears running down his cheeks.

Youghal motioned to a constable standing in the door, telling him to remove the girl. "And make sure no one tells their mother what's happened yet," he said. "She's in poor health, and I want to make sure she finds out as easily as possible."

Holmes and I had stayed until the family doctor arrived. We were in the downstairs hall as Lord Bretton and the doctor climbed the steps, going to tell Lady Bretton the terrible news of Patrick's death. Youghal and Emily had already departed with the police for the local station. We had declined to ride with them, preferring to find our own way back to the village, thus avoiding any more of the mad, reddish wet gaze of that deluded young woman.

We had arrived back in London that Sunday night, strangely unnerved at the unexpected violence we had discovered at the lovely Surrey country house. Although warmly congratulated by Inspector Youghal as he departed, Holmes had clearly wanted none of it. He felt, as did I, somewhat unclean by the association with the crime. We were both quiet that night, eating little, and speaking less to one another. I had gone up to bed early, but had slept poorly, while Holmes, as I previously mentioned, spent a sleepless night pacing and attempting to find comfort in the music pulled from his violin . . . .

I shook myself back to the present when a thump sounded through the ceiling of the chapel, caused by something striking the floor of the room above. Thorne gave a small whimper and pulled his legs back underneath the bench, creating a small scuffing sound across the floor.

I sat up, my senses highly alert. Holmes put a hand on my arm, signaling to wait. I could tell he wanted to let this thing play out.

Another sound moved across the floor above us. Thorne made a small animal sound in his throat, and half raised himself from the bench, facing the stairs and supporting himself with his hand on the wall behind him. A third thump sounded, this time heard both through the ceiling and echoing down the stairwell at the same time. Thorne rose fully to his feet, whispering harshly, "Do you hear it? Do you both hear it now?" He glanced wildly toward us, and back to the stairs, where whatever it was had started down.

Thorne crossed in front of us, away from the stairs, to stand underneath the windows. He began to fumble with his left coat pocket, trying to extract something. Whatever was on the stairs was closer now, halfway, shuffling and wheezing. "It's coming," moaned Thorne softly.

Under the windows, Thorne had pulled out a revolver. He backed up against the wall and raised the gun, holding it with both hands as he aimed toward the stairway. I moved to stop him, but Holmes kept his hand on my arm, pulling me back.

From the darkness of the stairwell a form appeared. It resolved out of the darkness into a massive man-like creature. It was still too much in darkness to perceive its face. It lifted an arm, revealing in the light from the windows a wide hand, raised in greeting.

With a guttural cry, Thorne stepped forward and began pulling the trigger of his revolver. Over and over he pulled, each try clicking as the firing pin apparently fell on an empty chamber. Beside me, Holmes opened his lantern, throwing the chapel into stark yellow light.

"It won't do, Mr. Thorne," he said. "I have taken all of your bullets."

Thorne looked at us, and then back at the shadowy figure stepping from the stairwell. In Holmes's light, he was revealed to be a gentleman in his mid-forties. He was a bulky man, obviously overweight from years of high living. He was clearly out of breath from simply descending the steep stairs, and listening to his wheezing was quite painful.

Holmes raised his hand to his lips and blew a police whistle, which he had been concealing. Thorne started to run toward the stairwell, but his way was immediately blocked by a group of constables who boiled down the stairs, blocking his way. His useless gun was taken from him, and he was quickly handcuffed and held against the opposite wall.

A small man separated himself from the mass of constables and moved out of the stairwell. He looked at Thorne in the custody of two large bobbies, and then turned to the large man. "Are you all right, Mr. Mason?"

The fat man tried to catch his breath and nodded. "Never better," he finally responded. He looked at Thorne. "Although I cannot quite believe this is all true."

"I'm afraid it is, Mr. Mason," said Holmes, stepping away from me to the center of the room. "Until earlier tonight, the gun which Mr. Thorne just tried to use was loaded, and I have no doubt that it was his intention to fire every bullet that it held in order to guarantee your death."

"When you told me your theories this afternoon, Mr. Holmes, I admit that I couldn't believe you. I thought Raymond had simply arranged this as a joke on some of his friends. I willingly went along, since he was my only relative and I was anxious to reestablish the ties between us that had lapsed over the last few years. However, it happened just as you predicted."

He turned to Thorne. "Why, Raymond? Why?" However, Thorne refused to meet his gaze, and did not say another word before he was eventually taken out by the constables.

149

"Well, Lestrade," I said to the small man, "I suppose congratulations are in order. At least, I think they are. I might be able to say for certain if I was told exactly what was going on."

Holmes laughed and patted my shoulder. "My apologies, Watson. Once again, I could not resist the urge to provide a dramatic solution, and as always, you are my best audience." Turning to the large man, he said, "Watson, may I introduce – "

"Mr. Walter Mason, I presume," I interrupted. "Banker, and cousin to our recent client, Raymond Thorne."

"Exactly, sir. Exactly," said Mason, extending a great paw of a hand. "And of course, you are Dr. Watson. Mr. Holmes told me today that you would be on hand to help guarantee my protection in this matter."

I glanced sideways. "Perhaps I might have been of more use if I had known what was going on."

"There was never any real danger," said Holmes. "We simply had to give Thorne some rope to see if he would actually hang himself. There was always a chance, even up to the end, that he would choose not to go through with his scheme."

"Which was?" I asked.

"Why, the murder of his cousin, Walter Mason, and the subsequent inheritance of all of Mason's assets."

"I begin to understand his plan," I said. Turning to Mason, I said, "I take it that Thorne, as your only surviving relation, is your only heir."

"Correct," said Mason. "However, I am planning to be married in a few months, and that would have changed the picture completely. Perhaps that is what inspired Raymond to attempt this horrible plan to kill me."

"And what was the plan?" I asked. "Did he pretend to work himself into a panic, before Holmes and myself as witnesses, and then try to shoot you as if he believed you were some sort of ghost or monster, later to claim that it was simply a tragic accident?"

"That was it, Watson," said Holmes. "As I said this morning, I do not accept anyone's story at face value. Besides checking on the history of the house with Alton Peake, I decided to stop in and visit one of my oldest clients, Mr. Walter Mason here."

"That's right," said Mason, with a fond smile. "It was in the early seventies, and my bank had been the victim of a particularly clever swindle. We didn't want word to get out, as it might shake the public's confidence in our institution. One day, however, I was surprised with a visit from Mr. Holmes here, who was much younger than he is now. He had learned about the swindle from sources of his own, and had taken it upon himself to retrieve our stolen property. He marched into my office that day, introduced himself, and laid the missing bonds on my desk. My first thought was to have him arrested, thinking he was working somehow with the thieves. I even had my guards summon the police. However, I was quickly told that the true criminals were in custody, and that Mr. Holmes had been responsible. After that, I've always held him in the highest esteem.

"Then of course, last year Mr. Holmes was instrumental in helping me sort out that French credit mess."

I turned my head toward Holmes. "You never mentioned that."

Holmes simply shrugged. "Thorne did not realize when he came to us this morning that I was an old acquaintance of his cousin," said Holmes. "Of course I did not tell him, and after I went out today, I first visited Mr. Mason at his bank. I asked him if he could tell me about the property that he was planning to sell to his cousin.

"Mr. Mason was quite puzzled, as he did not own this property, and was not intending to sell Thorne anything. In fact, his version of the events was completely opposite from what had been told to us by Thorne this morning.

"Thorne had approached him last week, after having no contact for several years, and asked Mr. Mason to help him in carrying out a little joke he was going to be playing soon on some friends. Thorne told Mason that he had rented a house in East London with a reputation for being haunted. Thorne was going to lead these friends through the house on the following Monday night, trying to scare them and set the mood by acting as if he were becoming progressively more aware of various ghostly presences. He would then end up in the downstairs chapel, where we are now, and would wait until midnight. At that time, Mason would slip into the house and make frightening noises while coming down into the chamber. Thorne would then whip his friends into a final fearful panic while Mason entered the room, before all would be revealed."

"He made me promise not to tell anyone, lest some word get back to his friends," Mason said. "He stopped by earlier today to confirm that the affair would take place tonight, and that he would leave the front door unlocked."

"When I heard Mr. Mason's version of the events," said Holmes, "I knew that Thorne was obviously lying to us, but I was not sure why, although a vague outline of his plan was starting to take shape in my mind. I spent the afternoon checking on Mr. Thorne's personal situation. He is nearly destitute, overdue on his rent, and in arrears on a number of accounts. He has accrued a number of gambling debts as well.

"I had confirmed that Thorne was Mr. Mason's only heir. I began to see that Thorne's plan was to invite us to the house in order to serve as independent and unbiased witnesses as he killed his cousin, later claiming that it was simply a terrible accident. He would lead us through the house, pretending to hear and see supernatural incidents along the way that would provoke him to act in an increasingly panicky manner. Of course, we would not hear the sounds or believe in the spirits, but that would not matter as we would be able to testify about Thorne's increasing fears. By the time midnight approached, he would present a completely irrational façade to us, and when Mr. Mason entered the chapel, he would be so fearful that he would shoot the man in supposed blind terror, only to pretend to realize later that he had killed his poor cousin, who had decided to come to the house after all."

"What about later," I asked, "when it would be learned that Mr. Mason had not even owned the house that he was supposedly trying to sell to Thorne?"

"I'm sure he would have turned it around, and claimed that the entire tragic incident was the result of some trick that Mr. Mason was trying to play on Thorne."

"And this house?" I added. "Is he actually renting it?"

"No," interrupted Lestrade. "After Mr. Holmes came and told me what he suspected, he and I went around together to the leasing agent, where we learned that the place has stood empty for some months now. Apparently it has the reputation of being haunted." He laughed. "In any event, Thorne must have heard about the place, and seen that it was empty. He probably kept an eye on it for several days to make sure that no one was coming in or out, especially at night, before he decided that he would use it for his plan.

"The leasing agent checked for us and determined that one of the front door keys he kept for the place was gone. We think that somehow Thorne got in and stole it. That's how he was able to open the place up tonight when you and Mr. Holmes arrived."

I thought for a moment about the events of the night. "When you stumbled over Thorne in the dark," I said to Holmes. His eyes lit up, and he smiled. "That's when you removed the bullets from his gun!"

"Close, Watson," Holmes agreed. "I had managed to brush up against him as we initially came into the building, ascertaining that he was armed, and that the gun was in his left coat pocket. He is left-handed, you know. Later, as we passed through the downstairs rooms, I managed to remove the gun from his pocket, using some pick-pocketing skills that I have acquired over the years." He glanced at Lestrade, who pretended to look the other way.

"As the two of you went on ahead, I opened the gun and dumped the bullets into my own coat pocket, where I had placed a handkerchief to muffle the sound. Later, I tried to replace the gun in his coat, but I was unable to position myself in the correct way. Eventually I had to resort to the clumsy stratagem of pretending to fall on the fellow, whereupon I was able to slip the gun back into his pocket."

"I recall now that when he stood up, he seemed to be adjusting his coat. He was probably making sure that the gun was still there."

"Correct," said Holmes.

"But the stones?" I asked. "What was their purpose? Surely they weren't really thrown by the long-ago wool merchant? And I was watching Thorne. He didn't throw them." I took a moment to explain to Lestrade and Mr. Mason the incident of the small gravels which had hit Holmes's face in the upstairs room.

"I simply tossed those myself," said Holmes. "When I learned earlier today that there was a room in which the supernatural energy manifested itself as thrown gravel, I took the time to gather a few gravels from the street, in case they were needed later. While you and Thorne were talking, I slipped them into my hand, gouged my face slightly with one of them, and then lowered my hand. A moment later, I cried out. As I raised my hand to my face, I tossed the gravels back over my shoulder, where they landed seconds later. I'm sure it looked to you and Thorne as if the sequence were slightly altered – the gravels were thrown, hitting my face, and *then* landed on the floor."

"But why?" asked Mason. "If you were letting Raymond appear to work himself into a fearful panic, why did you do something that might make him think there actually *was* something supernatural going on in the house?"

"I'm really not sure," said Holmes. "Perhaps I just wanted to see his reaction. In the end, it was instructive. Instead of immediately escalating his panic, it actually seemed to stop him in his tracks for a moment. He simply stared at Watson and myself as if anything supernatural actually taking place was something totally unexpected. His reaction served as something of an additional confirmation of my theory, although it already seemed completely certain at that point."

Later, we stood outside the front door while Lestrade used Thorne's stolen key to relock the building. Mason heaped praise onto Holmes until we were able to slip away, walking down the empty street toward a busier thoroughfare, where we hoped to catch a cab.

"I know you don't believe in ghosts, Holmes," I said, "but . . . there was something about that place. I realize that Thorne's manufactured reactions helped fuel the mood, but Peake did tell you that the house had a reputation."

Holmes was silent for several minutes. Then he took a deep breath, and said, "I suppose I must admit that the place had a certain atmosphere about it. It has had a varied history, and in over three hundred years, I am sure it has acquired something of the energy of the people who lived there."

He was quiet for another moment, and then he spoke again. "Who knows what has happened there, or what types of incidents might lend themselves to these things that people call 'hauntings.' You and I have both seen many horrible things, Watson. Surely if there was ever such a thing as a ghost, it would be created by the horrible incident of a murder within a family. If there are no ghosts there now, perhaps there would have been one if Thorne had actually been able to murder his cousin. Family member killing family member."

We continued walking down the street for some minutes. I thought back to our recent trip to Surrey. "A sister murdering a brother . . . " I began.

"I believe that they will find her to be quite mad," said Holmes. "I am afraid that Lord Bretton's family is only at the beginning of their pain. Not only is their only son and brother dead, but they have to live for years with the constant reminder of what happened in the form of Emily, who will no doubt be hospitalized for quite a long time. I do not see her condition improving."

"And Sir Sheffield Frye?" I asked.

Holmes shook his head. "He will get a few years for the theft of the painting, but he was clearly not involved in the murder. I hope this will serve to break him, but a rogue like that will no doubt rise from all of this like a phoenix."

"And what about Raymond Thorne," I asked.

"A few years in prison. Perhaps he will learn his lesson, but probably not. I suspect he will rise from crime to crime until he comes to a just end."

After a moment, Holmes said, "What is it about families, Watson? How can such violent actions arise out of such a supposedly nurturing structure?"

"I do not know," I said. "This morning you said that after the recent events in Surrey, this case would prove to be 'strangely refreshing.' It turned out to be just another sordid case of family ugliness and greed."

Holmes didn't respond. After a few more moments, we turned onto the main road, where we spotted a waiting cab. I moved toward it, only to pause after a few steps, realizing that Holmes was not with me.

Looking back, I saw that he had stopped.

"I think that I would rather walk, if you have no objections, Watson," he said.

"No, none at all." I glanced back toward the cab, whose driver had now looked up and noticed us. Turning back toward Holmes, I said, "If my leg will stand the effort, would you mind some company?"

154

He smiled. "Not at all." He resumed his pace, and as he reached me I set out as well. The cabbie looked at us curiously as we walked past him. Up ahead, the streetlights thinned and disappeared in the rolling fog. Holmes and I continued our walk into the darkness.

The Adventure of the
Missing Missing Link

From his seat across from me in the small Sussex cottage where he had now lived for a number of years, Sherlock Holmes asked, "What do you know of Sir William Osler?"

I made no move to reach for the telegram that I had first seen only moments before. Holmes would hand it to me when or if he wanted me to read it. "An American doctor and teacher," I replied. "Probably in his early sixties, I suppose, perhaps a little older than I. He came to England six or seven years ago to teach at Oxford. He has previously taught medicine in the United States for a number of years, and was one of the major proponents of a system where medical students make up a substantial part of a hospital's staff, learning by doing, so to speak."

Holmes nodded. "A fairly succinct account of the man's life. However," he said, gesturing toward one of his scrapbooks, open on the table near me, "some of your facts are incorrect, as well as somewhat incomplete. He is Canadian by birth, and not American, for example. I had occasion to examine my clippings earlier this afternoon, when I received this telegram."

I glanced over at the rows of scrapbooks, carefully maintained for more years than I could remember. Even now, in June 1912 when Holmes was spending most of his time roaming the United States in the guise of an Irish-American criminal, he made the effort to update his files on the rare occasions when he was able to return home as himself.

If I have given the impression to my readers over the years that Mr. Sherlock Holmes had faded into some hazy agricultural oblivion following his unexpected retirement, then I was completely successful in my endeavors, for that was my intention. In the fall of 1903, when he was only forty-nine years old, Holmes suddenly announced his plan to withdraw from London and to move Sussex, where he intended to keep bees. My initial surprise was complete, but I soon understood his reasoning. I was tasked with placing this information before the public in the form of a newly published *Strand* magazine story, in which I stated that Holmes's previous prohibition against making his investigations available in a common forum had been lifted. Mycroft Holmes helped to spread the news throughout England, and even abroad, that Sherlock Holmes had retired.

Needless to say, Holmes did not go quietly, although he wished people to think that he had. For several years at the turn of the century, his practice

156

had turned more and more toward investigations dealing with matters of national security, usually at the request of his brother, Mycroft. With each success, rising from triumph to triumph, Holmes was pressured more and more by his brother to abandon the private consulting practice which he had labored to build, in order to turn his attentions to those little jobs that Mycroft was anxious to provide.

Finally, in October 1903, events which need not be discussed here had conspired to convince Holmes that the change that he had avoided for so long must be accepted at last. Within a very few days, to my great surprise, he had ensconced himself in a small cottage near the sea on the Sussex Downs. He convinced Mrs. Hudson to go with him, a move which she was more than willing to undertake, having spent the greater part of her life in the toxic fumes of London.

Contrary to popular belief, however, Holmes did not entirely give up the Baker Street rooms. Mrs. Hudson retained the lease of the building, then nearing its ninetieth year of solid existence, and Holmes continued to pay rent for the sitting room and bedroom on the first floor, as well as my old bedroom and the box room on the second floor. I have no doubt that Holmes could have purchased the building outright for all the rent money that he paid to Mrs. Hudson over the years. However, the arrangement as it stood was agreeable to both of them, and so it remained. Mrs. Hudson benefited from the extra income, and Holmes was able to have a base of operations when his investigations took him back to London.

I had remarried by that time, of course, and I remained in town with my wife and my growing practice in Queen Anne Street. However, I did not lose touch with Holmes following his change of location, as has been commonly believed. The idea that Holmes and I had very little contact with one another after his retirement was somewhat encouraged as a part of the effort to make people believe that he had completely abandoned his earlier life for that of a reclusive apiarist.

Certainly, many of the aspects and activities of Holmes's life during this time must remain secret, even now. Some of the things that he did during that time are completely unknown, even to me, while others are so entwined with the shadowy interests of the government that the truth can never be publicly recorded. Other events during this time relate to Holmes's own personal life and the sad occurrence of October 1903, and these must remain hidden at his own request.

As the years passed, I continued to publish accounts of some of Holmes's cases on an irregular basis in *The Strand*. Occasionally, readers complained that Holmes did not quite seem to be the same fellow as before, and they questioned whether these were actual accounts of his investigations, or simply made-up stories about a fictional character that many people had come to accept as Conan Doyle's creation. I can assure the readers that each case was real, and if Holmes seemed somehow different from the way he was remembered when the first narratives were published in the late eighties and early nineties, then I can only agree, and ask if those dissatisfied readers are still the same people that *they* were ten or fifteen years earlier. All of us, even Sherlock Holmes and myself, change over the years. Holmes and I are certainly not fixed in some never-changing imaginary world where it is always 1895. If Holmes seems different in the later published cases, it is simply because he has evolved, as have my observations of him over the many years that we have been friends.

My friend Conan Doyle, now Sir Arthur, once remarked to me that old men have approached him, fondly reminiscing about how they enjoyed the Holmes stories when they were schoolboys, and then they are puzzled when this compliment does not receive the reaction that was expected. As Sir Arthur said to me, these fellows do not understand that their backhanded compliments about the efforts of one's youth cause mixed feelings as one's personal dates are handled so roughly.

As I watched Holmes puff his pipe in contemplation, I settled back more comfortably in my chair. In the kitchen, down the dark hall, heard Mrs. Hudson finishing her chores for the day, leaving her counters and stove as clean as possible for the resumption of her labors the next morning. Shifting my gaze to the pleasant fire, I fought drowsiness as I continued to think of Holmes's career over the past few months.

Through the early years of the century, Holmes had continued to involve me in those cases that he could, when it did not interfere with national security. We traveled extensively during those years throughout England and the Continent, as well as making trips to the United States, Canada, and even India, Africa, and Japan.

In late 1911, Holmes departed on one of the greatest endeavors of his career, assuming a role that would take up much of his life for over two-and-a-half years. Of course I refer to his infiltration of the vast global German organization, which was at that time creating mischief all over the world as the German government prepared for the war which we had labored for so long to avoid. Holmes literally became a disaffected Irish-American trouble-maker named Altamont, and worked his way slowly into the German confidence.

Buried deep in this personality, Holmes traveled throughout America and Europe from late 1911 until August 1914, becoming well known in various criminal organizations, and making sure that he came to the attention of the watchful German agents. Of course, his efforts were more than successful, culminating in the arrest of the German master spy, von

Bork, in August 1914. Holmes had managed to gain the trust of the Germans in such a way that he had been able to pass false information to them for several years. This information had been completely believed by the Germans, thus insuring that many of their command decisions, especially at the beginning of the war, were completely wrong, allowing Great Britain the time to bring itself to a better war footing.

Holmes had initially been reluctant to commit so much of his life to this massive undertaking. It was only due to the repeated urgings of the Prime Minister himself that Holmes was eventually convinced. Fortunately, he had spent the time leading up to his long-term impersonation, as I have stated, giving the impression that he was an eccentric recluse, keeping to himself on the Downs and nursing a recurring but persistent case of rheumatism. I do not want to give the impression that he spent the entire two-and-a-half years of his impersonation of Altamont in character. There were many times that he actually returned to his home, or to London, in the guise of Sherlock Holmes, so that there would never be any suspicion that Holmes and Altamont were the same man. On these occasions we would meet, and I would receive any necessary instructions for tasks that I could perform in order to help his labors.

One of the first times Holmes returned to Sussex was in May 1912. At that point, he had only been traveling as Altamont for about five or six months, and then not continuously. He had been arranging contacts and hidey holes in various locations in both Europe and America, aware that his impersonation was a long-term commitment, and he had only allowed Altamont to show himself when it would do the most good before temporarily and mysteriously retiring him again.

I had seen him several times over the last few months, most recently that May, a few weeks before, soon after his most recent return. He had made an appearance in Sussex before going up to London, where he stayed in the Baker Street rooms for a few days. He maintained a Spartan existence there, using the rooms as a staging area, in the same way that he had kept hiding places throughout London when he needed a place to disappear, or simply to change his costume. I visited him in the old sitting room on several occasions before he returned to his country cottage.

It was not long before I saw him again. In mid-June, I traveled for a few days to Sussex, to stay with him and Mrs. Hudson while my wife cared for a sick relative. Life with Holmes was never boring, and even as we spent time catching up on the recent events in his life, he and I found time to become involved in several short investigations, the details of which I have recorded in separate journals.

I had spent that particular day pestering Holmes for information relating to some of his earlier cases that he had solved during times when

I did not accompany him. He had spent much of his afternoon telling me of his activities in Paris in the late spring of 1891, after his supposed death at the Reichenbach Falls, but before he had left on his extended journey to Tibet and points beyond. It was the evening of that day, as we sat in front of the fire in companionable silence, that Holmes had roused himself, pulled a telegram from the table beside his chair, and asked me about Sir William Osler.

Holmes stirred himself from his thoughts, and said, "I believe I have remarked in the past, Watson, that you have the supreme gift of silence."

He leaned forward, handing me the flimsy telegram which had been resting on his bony knee for several minutes. I saw that it was from Osler himself, in Oxford. "Urgent," it read, "Reputation in danger due to theft of artifact. Require your assistance all due haste. Cable arrival times, tomorrow morning if possible."

"Is that all you know?" I asked, looking up with raised eyebrows.

"Yes," said Holmes, "but based on what I have read about the man, I feel that I must honor his request for our presence."

"He only requested you," I noted. "There is nothing here about needing my assistance as well."

"My dear Watson," Holmes said, "need I even ask, at this late date in our association, whether or not you would be willing to assist me in this matter?"

"Of course I will help, Holmes," I said. "But perhaps Osler wanted the matter kept in confidence. He may only desire *your* presence in Oxford."

"Nevertheless, you and I will go together. After I meet him, I will judge what type of man he is. And then, if he does want to exclude you from the matter, I will decide then whether or not to take his case." Holmes then fell silent again, busying himself with his pipe, which had gone out. I turned and pulled the open scrapbook onto my lap, leaning forward in the dim light to read the various clippings glued there relating to Osler.

He had been born in 1849, three years before me, in Ontario to an Anglican minister. He had intended to follow his father into the ministry, but after entering college, he discovered an interest in medicine. Following completion of his medical degree in 1872, he studied for a few years in Europe before returning to Montreal. There he became a professor at McGill University.

Even then, he began to formalize a method of teaching that would soon come to revolutionize the way that doctors are trained. Instead of subjecting medical students to years of stultifying lectures, he tried to get students involved as early as possible with actual patients, allowing them to take case histories, as well as collect samples and conduct laboratory experiments. Medical students learning in this manner seemed to become

160

much better doctors at a faster rate than the old teaching methods allowed, and Osler's way soon caught on. He moved to the United States in 1884, becoming the Chair of Clinical Medicine at the University of Pennsylvania in Philadelphia. In 1889, he moved to Baltimore to serve as the first Chief of Staff at Johns Hopkins Hospital. While there, the size and abilities of the hospital increased dramatically, principally due to Osler's influence. In addition, he also spent much of his time in Baltimore teaching at the School of Medicine.

In 1905, he came to Oxford, where he was appointed the Regius Chair of Medicine, a position he had held to the present. His teaching methods were being adopted by Oxford, and as near as I could tell, he was still highly respected and revered in every way. The previous year, he was knighted in acknowledgement of his many contributions to the field of medicine. I skimmed the rest of Holmes's clippings, but saw nothing else relevant to the matter at hand.

Seeing that I had finished, Holmes stood and knocked out his pipe on the grate. "We must make an early start tomorrow, Watson, if we want to catch the milk train. I no longer keep those late city hours of old. Here in the country it is early to bed, early to rise. I will see you in the morning. Good night!"

"Good night, Holmes," I said, but he had already gone, and I am not sure if he heard me.

The following morning we were up early. I had time to quickly partake of Mrs. Hudson's small but delicious breakfast before Holmes hurried me out the door. He drank only coffee, and not even a full cup at that. Mrs. Hudson murmured her long-standing exasperation, but Holmes ignored it, as he had, off and on, for over thirty years.

The train made its way into London without incident. I gazed at the capital as we approached it, lit from the east by the rising sun, and thought about the many times Holmes and I had returned to the great city after journeying out on some case or another. From a distance, in the half-light, the place looked timeless, as if frozen in some mid-world between reality and fantasy. The illusion was shattered, however, as we made our way deeper into the metropolis, where the everyday gritty details of people living their lives intruded on the dream. I roused myself from my reverie, and joined Holmes, who was gathering his things as we prepared to change trains for Oxford.

Leaving the city, Holmes and I fell into a discussion of his recent travels as the disaffected Altamont. I was not surprised to learn that he had based some of his plan on the experiences of our long-ago acquaintance, John Douglas, also known as Birdy Edwards, and his infiltration into that infamous criminal gang which had held a Pennsylvania valley in the grip of fear. "Someday," I promised Holmes, "perhaps in a year or so when you have completed this Altamont business, I will publish an account of your investigation of the Birlstone murder in '88."

"As you like," replied Holmes. "I would be curious to see how you can condense the matter into a few pages of prose. The explanation of John Douglas's previous life in America would make an entire book, all on its own."

"Perhaps," I replied. "Doyle has been after me to publish something again. The last thing that was in *The Strand* was last Christmas, when we submitted that business relating to the rescue of Lady Frances Carfax. Possibly I could write the part of the Birlstone narrative which relates our investigation in Sussex, and Doyle could novelize the events of Douglas's story. Rather like he and I did in *A Study In Scarlet*, when he composed the central Mormon section while I recounted our part in the matter."

Holmes muttered something that sounded like "romantic drivel," but it was nothing that he had not stated before, and I chose to ignore him.

It seemed very soon indeed that we spotted the towering spires of Oxford in the distance. The train began to slow, and within moments we were standing on the platform. A small man stepped forward, inquiring,

"Mr. Holmes? Dr. Watson? I am Sir William's driver, Byrd. This way, please."

He led us out of the station to a smart-looking brougham. The horse waited patiently, even as several automobiles growled and shook nearby, as their owners suited up for their journey, adjusting the mufflers and goggles of their driving costumes. "It is not far," said Byrd, making sure we were seated, before urging the horse into motion.

It had been several years since I had been to Oxford, that great center of learning and thought, and the place seemed busier than before, although the architecture and general feeling of the town had not otherwise changed. I glanced at Holmes and saw him looking eagerly to his left and right. I knew that he had started his days at university here, in the early seventies, and I wondered what memories the sights around him evoked. His father had originally insisted that he go to Oxford in order to study engineering. Holmes had been at the great center of learning for at least two years, I knew, before deciding to pursue his unique goal of becoming the world's first and only (at that time) consulting detective. However, I was certain that Holmes, being the man that he is, found adventures even during those days, even before he knew what path his life would take. I was only sorry that I had never heard all of the details of what I was sure must have happened during those long-ago days.

The horse stepped smartly, with minimal encouragement from Byrd, and it did not take long at all before we pulled up to a rather fine house, not large but obviously well maintained and appointed. "Sir William is not teaching this morning, then?" asked Holmes.

"No, sir," said Byrd. "He will be meeting with you here." He turned the horse down the short circular drive that passed by the front steps of the house. Stopping, he allowed us to get down before telling us that he would no doubt see us later, when we were ready to leave, and to have a good morning. We returned the wish, and climbed the steps. We had not fully crossed the porch when the door was opened by Sir William Osler himself.

He was in his early sixties, and I could immediately sense his vitality and intelligence. He stood with barely suppressed energy, nearly bouncing on his toes as he greeted first Holmes, and then myself. He stepped back quickly, gesturing for us to come inside. After helping the maid to take our coats, he led us toward the back of the house and into a comfortable, well-apportioned study.

"Gentlemen," he began, after determining that we did not require refreshments, "I thank you for coming, although I must admit that I have had some misgivings this morning, and in hindsight, I would not have asked you to make this long journey. For that I apologize."

I was relieved that Osler did not seem to have any objections to my presence there, seemingly accepting me without question. I glanced at Holmes, who said, "What misgivings would those be, Sir William?"

Osler shook his head with a small grin. "Still can't get used to that 'Sir William'," he said. Then his face turned serious once more, and he sat up straighter. "After I wired you yesterday, Mr. Holmes, additional events have taken place. I began to turn the matter over in my mind, and I became aware that I did not need to involve you. I have recently been assured that the object that I thought was missing is in safe keeping. This morning, I was certain that I should have done what I could to stop you both from making a journey up here, but by then it was too late – you were already traveling."

Holmes crossed his thin legs and settled deeper into his chair. He was obviously not going anywhere soon. "You are telling the story back-end first, Sir William," he said, "and you must realize that you have only increased our curiosity. Surely you can tell us what has happened, and perhaps there is some way that we can still help, even if you believe the matter has been resolved."

Osler thought for a moment, and then nodded. "I suppose you are right," he said. "There is no mystery for you to solve at this point, but it cannot do any harm to tell you what I thought had happened, even though subsequent events have proven me to be wrong. I owe you both that much, for traveling all this way at my request."

Holmes gestured for him to continue, and then he closed his eyes, preparing to devote his full concentration to Osler's narrative.

"What do you both know," Osler asked, "about the recent discovery of the fossilized bones found at Piltdown?"

Holmes opened his eyes with a puzzled look and said, "I know nothing of it, I'm afraid. I have been somewhat . . . out of touch with certain events during the last few months. Watson?"

"I only know what was vaguely reported in the press earlier this year," I said. "Somewhere in Sussex, archeological diggers working in the gravel pits uncovered the remains of some sort of ancient man. There was very little mention of it made at the time, as I recall. It was just by chance that I happened to notice the story at all in a local Sussex newspaper, and I don't believe that anything has been mentioned about it since then. I can really add nothing else."

"It is quite understandable that you don't have any more specific information than that, Dr. Watson," Osler said. "Very little attention has been given to the find, outside certain scientific circles. This is intentional, I believe, and nothing else will be published until a scientific presentation can be prepared for the leading thinkers in that field. Within those realms, however, a great deal of excitement has arisen. Some experts feel that the remains that have been found are actual physical evidence of the missing evolutionary link that has been theorized between apes and man!"

Holmes glanced at me, and said, "That truly would be of great scientific importance, indeed, if something like that has actually been unearthed. Tell us more, Sir William."

"Of course," Osler continued. "When I say that remains have been found, I do not want to give the impression that a complete mummified corpse has been uncovered. Actually, diggers in the gravel pits of Piltdown, a small village near Uckfield in East Sussex, have simply unearthed a number of random bone fragments and pieces, including several which have been fitted together, rather like pieces of a puzzle, to form a complete skull. It is this skull which has excited such comment.

"The skull itself is very much like that of modern man, with a similarly shaped cranium, although the brain case size is somewhat smaller than ours. The occipital region is structured quite differently, however, and the jaw bone seems almost ape-like in its construction. This tends to favor the current way of thinking that human evolution was led by increased brain size first, allowing for evolutionary changes in other parts of the body, such as the jaw, to follow."

"What led the archeologists to explore the Piltdown gravel pits in the first place?" asked Holmes.

164

"I'm not entirely sure," replied Osler. "I believe that the man who has collected the current fragments, Charles Dawson, first learned about some remains found at that site as early as 1908. I do not know if that is what led him to dig there now. I do know that Dawson has been digging there off and on for several years, even before the discovery of the first skull pieces this past February. Dawson took the skull to Arthur Smith Woodward, the keeper of the geological department at the British Museum. He and Dawson have gathered a few additional pieces since then, including part of a lower jawbone and a few teeth, and have assembled them to reveal the pre-human form that we have been discussing. Woodward and I have been somewhat acquainted for several years, and it was he that asked me to examine and evaluate the skull, with the idea that I might be willing to write a paper on it at some point.

"The box containing the object had only arrived day before yesterday, brought by a messenger from Woodward late in the afternoon, and I had been unable to do more than have a cursory look at it, in a completely unscientific way. Then, yesterday morning, I came in here to the study to discover the skull and the cardboard box that contained it were gone. I was initially consumed with panic, as you might imagine, extremely worried that something so rare and entrusted into my safekeeping had vanished.

"I questioned my staff, but none could offer any explanation. An examination revealed no signs of forced entry, and while I had not made any real effort to hide the box with the skull inside it, there was nothing that made it seem outwardly valuable in any way. Nothing else from the house was taken. I was quite upset, as I'm sure you can imagine, but I was unwilling to involve the police at that point, not wanting to cause a scandal. After several hours of uncertainty, I wired you, Mr. Holmes, requesting your assistance. And yours too, of course, Dr. Watson," he added, including me with a gracious glance.

"And at what point were you told that the skull had not, in fact, been stolen, but had been retrieved by someone with the authority and guile to do so?" asked Holmes.

"Why, early this morning," replied Osler. "Of course, you have deduced correctly what happened, Mr. Holmes. After avoiding my responsibility for several hours yesterday, I finally wired Woodward late last night and informed him of the skull's disappearance. This morning I was visited by . . . someone who must remain nameless, I'm afraid. And he explained that the skull had been removed with great care from my house due to legitimate concerns, and that I was not to worry over it any longer. He implied that I should not have been sent the item to begin with, and he apologized that I had not been informed at the time it was removed from my home. Apparently some sort of misunderstanding, and the agent sent to retrieve the skull believed he should do so in secret."

"Did you inform this mystery individual that you had requested our assistance?" asked Holmes.

"Why, yes I did, Mr. Holmes."

"And his response?"

"Well, there was none. At least not initially. Later this morning, an hour or so after I had tried to decide if there was any way to stop you from coming up here on such a wild goose chase, I received another visit from the man who talked to me this morning, indicating that I should tell you both to proceed to Piltdown in order to speak with Charles Dawson. I was not told why you should go there, but possibly Dawson can provide you with further information."

"I don't suppose you could provide any more information about this morning's visitor?"

"I'm afraid not," replied Osler. "I was told to keep the other details of his visit, including information regarding his appearance, in confidence. The information I have revealed to you already is only that which he did not specifically prohibit."

"I expected as much." Holmes tapped his finger to his chin several times. I could tell that he dearly wished to pull out his pipe and ponder these recent events. "Does it not strike you as rather strange," he asked Osler, "that this skull seems to have caused such a remarkable effort to retrieve it? Were you not offended that your house was skillfully burgled in order to retrieve the skull?"

"Oh, not at all, Mr. Holmes," replied Osler. "Once the nature of the whole business was explained to me, I had no objections at all. And," he added, "I was given to understand that if you both journey to Piltdown, your questions will be answered as well." Holmes seemed to look inward for a moment, and then he stood. "It seems, Watson, that our next stop is Uckfield. Back to Sussex, old friend."

Osler led us to the door, where he gratefully shook hands with us both, apologizing continuously for the wasted trip and the fact that he could not reveal any further information. "I do hope Mr. Dawson will be able to explain more to you," he said.

Holmes paused in the doorway. "Sir William, you said that you had been unable to give the skull more than a cursory examination. Can you reveal what your first impressions were?"

Osler thought a moment. Finally, he said, "I can see no objections in that, I suppose. It seemed to me that the bones, while initially assembled to look like a primitive human ancestor, could have been assembled a variety of other ways as well, so that completely different characteristics might be shown. The brain case fragments, for instance, could have been arranged to mimic that of modern man's, with a much greater cranial capacity. And the jaw and teeth were very similar to those of a chimpanzee. This does not necessarily discount the veracity of Dawson's claims, however, since it is believed that the chimpanzee, at least evolution-wise, is our closest cousin."

"Did your visitor this morning indicate that you should keep any of these specific conclusions to yourself when you spoke to us?"

"Why, no, he didn't," replied Osler. "Actually, he didn't ask if I had made any conclusions at all. I simply told him that I had initially been unable to do more than glance into the box at the skull fragments. He did not ask me to elaborate on that statement."

"Thank you," said Holmes, turning to go. "I hope that we shall meet again some day, at which point I will be able to give you further information about the skull and your brief stewardship of it."

I shook Osler's hand and followed Holmes to the waiting carriage, which, under Byrd's skillful driving, quickly returned us to the train station. Later, after we had studied the various train connections and were seated in the proper carriage to take us to London, and then on to Sussex, I asked Holmes what it could all mean.

"We are being manipulated, Watson. I believe it is all harmless, but it is manipulation, nevertheless. However, if you have nothing better to do, I would enjoy your company as we continue to play out this silly little farce."

With my full agreement, we continued to London, where we obtained something to eat in the station before continuing on to Uckfield. There, we hired a dogcart to take us out to the tiny village of Piltdown. The rolling Sussex hills, with their lovely farms and mysterious copses randomly scattered about on hills and low spots, captured for me the very heart and soul of the southern English countryside.

In past years, I had questioned Holmes's decision to retire to the country, knowing as I did his intense love for the fogs and mysterious byways of the city. However, as I saw him beside me, glancing hungrily from side to side, smelling the fresh spring grass, I knew that he was now a countryman through and through. It was perhaps at this moment that I truly realized what a sacrifice he was making every time he left the tranquility of this place to return to the dark and anxious world of Altamont.

We came over the last rise before Piltdown, and followed the road's fork toward the diggings, as we had been instructed back in Uckfield.

There, near a long row of trees, were the gravel pits, tended by three men moving in a slow, lethargic way back and forth, bent over and staring at the ground in the afternoon heat.

Holmes pulled up the horse near the diggings, and as we hopped down, one of the three men, a small but solid chap, walked toward us, a spring in his step. He was browned by long hours in the sun, and dusty from his work, especially about the knees of his pants. His sleeves were rolled up, but strangely he, as well as the other two men, was wearing a waistcoat, which could only have made him feel hotter.

"Mr. Charles Dawson?" asked Holmes as the man reached us. The fellow stuck out his hand, which was exceptionally wide, dirty, and calloused.

"That I am," he replied. "And you must be Sherlock Holmes."

Glancing my way, he added, "And of course, Dr. Watson. Pleased to meet you both."

Holmes did not appear surprised to hear our names mentioned. "You expected us?" he asked.

"I was informed that you might be along," he said. "You made good time. I have a message for you. But first, since you're here, would you like to take a moment or two to inspect our site?"

We agreed that we would like to see the gravel pits where the contentious bones had been found, and Dawson gestured for us to precede him, only a short distance from the road. As we approached, the other two men, dressed similarly to Dawson, stood from where they had been bent over, turning the gravel with short trowels. "Give us a few minutes, gents," Dawson said. Both men nodded and walked over to the road. One proceeded to make friends with our horse, while the other leaned against the dogcart and rolled a cigarette. Both watched us with fixed intensity, each strangely similar to the other, with their dark sunburned complexions and military moustaches.

The gravel pits peeked through the grass at several random locations across the better part of an acre. There seemed to be very little system to the excavation. I had read of various other archeological explorations, and along with Holmes I have visited one or two during the course of our investigations, but this site did not contain any of the order or method present at any of the others I had seen. Instead of well-defined and marked digging areas, there were areas of freshly overturned gravel scattered throughout the pits, surrounded by other zones of completely undisturbed stone.

Dawson scuffed from one digging to the next, pit to pit, pointing out sites where this or that skull fragment had been unearthed. "And just last week," he said, stopping beside a slightly deeper hole, "we found some of the teeth and part of the jawbone right here."

Holmes nodded, but seemed to be glancing around in a vague way without paying too much attention to where Dawson pointed. Returning his gaze to Dawson, he asked, "Are you the same Charles Dawson who found the Roman cast-iron figurine several years ago?"

"Why, yes," said Dawson, somewhat surprised at the abrupt change of subject. "Back in ninety-five. You've heard of me, then?"

"Yes," said Holmes, shortly. "I take it that you were unaware that Woodward was going to ask Sir William Osler to examine the skull fragments that you had assembled. If he had discussed it with you, no doubt you would have stopped it. After all, Osler is a noted anatomist."

Dawson glanced toward the two men standing at our carriage. The one by the horse noticed and began to walk our way, tossing his cigarette into the grass. "I don't believe I will be answering any more questions about that subject, gentlemen."

The other man had joined us, and was reaching inside his waistcoat. It occurred to me that we were all alone, out in this field between the trees and the empty road. I was aware of the sudden tension between us and the men at the gravel pit, and I prepared myself in case the man was retrieving a weapon. However, his hand reappeared holding a small note, which he held out to Holmes.

Holmes took the envelope and lifted the glued flap with his thumb. He pulled from within a folded sheet of creamy stationery, which he opened and read. He frowned for a moment, and then his visage cleared.

With a loud "Hah!" he lowered his hand and turned toward Dawson.

"Thank you so much for your hospitality, Mr. Dawson," he said, with just a trace of irony in his voice. He glanced around the sloppy excavation. "We shall leave you to carry on with your business." He turned toward the cart. I nodded at the two men and followed him.

The other man was waiting there, holding the horse's tackle until we were both seated. Then with a slight wave he stepped back and moved to rejoin his companions. Holmes gigged the horse and we moved off down the country lane. I looked over my shoulder to see the three men, looking alike in the distance with their dusty clothes and waistcoats, watching us as we drove out of sight.

"Where are we going now, Holmes?" I asked.

He handed me the folded note. "We have been invited to visit an old friend," he said.

I opened the small sheet and was surprised to see the sender's identity. "My dear Holmes and Watson," it read. "I would be most honored if you would join me for afternoon tea. I believe you know the way, and I shall be looking forward to seeing you again." The signature was the strong and confident fist of someone I had known for nearly thirty years, Conan Doyle.

"What does it mean?" I asked, completely bewildered as to the nature of the day's events.

"I must admit it is not entirely clear to me, as yet," said Holmes. "However, I think that we have simply stumbled into some ridiculous little scheme, and we must play it out to the other end. It seems obvious that whatever was supposed to initially happen did not involve Osler's participation, or his asking us to journey to Oxford."

"That much I can see," I said. "Do you think Osler is in any kind of danger?"

"No, no," said Holmes. "Whatever this is, it is not a dangerous game. No doubt things started to go wrong when Woodward took it upon himself to ask Osler to examine the skull fragments. Up until that time, whatever is going on with the relics had been kept within a tight circle. Woodward let the fragments get out of his hands when he sent them to Osler.

"When it was found what had happened, someone went to get the skull back. Obviously, it was a person of specialized skills that was able to retrieve the skull, entering Osler's house in such a way that he could not even find any evidence of illicit entry."

"I noticed that you made no offer to examine the locks, or the carpets or grounds outside, to look for any clues."

"It would have been pointless," replied Holmes. "The person who was sent to retrieve the skull was a professional, and would have been most careful not to leave any traces of his presence. Besides, whoever he was, the later explanation of what happened to the skull was enough to convince Osler that nothing was wrong.

"I fancy that there was no misunderstanding about the way that the skull was retrieved, as Osler was led to believe. Probably it was intentionally taken in a mysterious way to rattle Osler, so that he would be suitably impressed soon after when he was approached and convinced that he should not mention the matter any further. It was only then, when Osler told what he had done, that the agent learned of our involvement, and realized that the small scheme was spinning out of control."

"But what is Doyle's involvement in this? I confess that I am somewhat concerned that he seems to be connected with something that has rather sinister overtones to it."

"Strangely, it was the note from Doyle that convinced me that there is no danger whatsoever connected with this little drama."

"Speaking of danger, I did sense something of that sort when we were talking to Dawson."

"You refer to the threatening nature of his two assistants? Their backgrounds were readily apparent to me. No doubt they are dangerous men, but not to us."

"I could see nothing about them, except for the fact that they had spent a great deal of time in the sun, and they both wore military moustaches."

"Exactly," replied Holmes, who did not elaborate. I could tell that he wished for me to solve for myself the truth about the two dangerous men.

"From your memory of Dawson's previous find," I said, "I understand that you have heard of him before."

"Yes, I have some notes about him in my scrapbooks, although I cannot recall their exact nature. I do remember that he claimed to have found the first Roman-made cast iron figurine discovered in Britain, nearly twenty years ago."

"You say 'claimed.' Is there some doubt as to the object's authenticity?"

"Some doubt, yes, although it is hard to find many experts who will go on record and completely denounce the findings of a colleague, no matter how much they quietly express their disbelief. Dawson has been involved in several other minor discoveries that have always been rather questionable. That is why his mere association with the skull fragments from Piltdown immediately place their authenticity into question."

"So you think the skull is a fake, then?"

"I do not know," Holmes replied. "I have never seen it, and would not presume to place my opinion equal to that of a true expert, although I do have some knowledge of anatomy that I could bring to bear on the subject. However, the fact that Dawson happens to be the discoverer of the skull pieces, and also the fact that they were never meant to be examined by Osler, who saw some doubtful characteristics after only a short initial glance at them, leads me to believe that the items are not as genuine as some might wish."

During this time, our dogcart had been winding up the roads, initially back through Uckfield, and on to the northeast, towards Crowborough. The land began to look familiar as we neared Doyle's fine home, where I had visited several times since he moved there three or four years earlier. As we turned down the drive toward the house, Doyle himself was standing out front, examining some flowering bushes and watching us approach while several comfortable dogs lounged on the grass. As we stopped, he called for the boy to take our cart, and moved to help us alight.

"Watson!" he cried. "And Holmes! So glad you could make it! We've been waiting for you. Do you need to freshen up after your drive? Then come around the house to the back. We've waited tea for you."

"And will your wife be joining us and my brother?" Holmes asked.

171

Doyle glanced at him for a moment, and then burst into a hearty laugh. "You can't surprise me anymore," he said. "Mycroft said you would know he was here. I don't even ask anymore how you both can know these things. Well, come along." He started to walk away, and then spoke over his shoulder. "And no, I'm afraid that Jean won't be joining us today for tea."

We rounded the corner to find Holmes's brother, Mycroft, sitting uncomfortably in a chair that was far too small for him, placed in the shade of both a tall shrub and a large umbrella. Mycroft lifted his great flipper-like hand in our general direction, and said peevishly, "It is about time. What took you so long?"

"Well, well," Holmes responded, "Jupiter leaves its orbit. Perhaps if you had simply had Osler send us here, instead of that pointless detour to Piltdown, we wouldn't have delayed your meal." Holmes dropped into a chair next to Mycroft's. "Or better still, you could have simply sent a message to us on the train, aborting the whole trip. I cannot speak for Watson, but I would have preferred to stay in Sussex today."

I started to speak, saying something about my enjoyment of the journey to Oxford and back, but Mycroft interrupted me. "You were already involved, thanks to Osler's wire yesterday. Somehow that slipped past us. If you had been ordered to end your trip to Osler's home based on a message you received on the train, it is unlikely, knowing your persistence, that you would have simply walked away from the matter. You might have gone off on your own, in a direction that would have been entirely unwelcome. It was decided to let you continue on to Oxford, as it might be useful to have you be seen moving around."

Holmes glanced at him shrewdly. "I see," he said. "In the end, this was nothing more than a chance to make sure that Sherlock Holmes was observed to be chasing about on his latest investigation."

"Exactly," replied Mycroft. "You can be sure that we will manage to get the word out that you have been involved in something important. If it becomes known that it was related to the Piltdown relics, so much the better, as long as you do nothing to denounce the items as fakes."

Doyle was watching me, and he must have seen something in my patient but confused expression that caused him to feel some pity. "Perhaps we should explain the matter, for the benefit of poor Watson, here."

"Yes, yes," said Mycroft, "but after we eat, if you please."

"Certainly," said Doyle, rising and moving toward the house. Within moments, his staff was bringing a wonderful early summer feast to the table. I tried not to eat too much, as I did not want to find myself too sleepy throughout the rest of the afternoon to understand what was being said.

Finally, after the uneaten food and dirty dishes had been cleared, we all sat back and prepared to talk. Holmes worked over his pipe and looked at his brother, waiting for him to begin.

"What do you know?" asked Mycroft. "Or rather, what do you think you know?"

"I know that Dawson, working under your orders, has fabricated some sort of cobbled-together spurious Neolithic skull, using bone fragments from other human skulls, and possibly pieces of ape skulls as well. I do not know if he originated the scheme on his own, or if you devised it and recruited him to help you. In any case, the entire matter somehow now falls under your purview. Dawson continues to putter about in Piltdown under the mindful gaze of two of your steely-eyed agents."

I realized as soon as he said it that Holmes was correct about the two men. Their dangerous air, dark complexions, and military moustaches all helped to point out their true nature. No doubt Holmes had seen a dozen other things about them that confirmed his statement.

"I do not know," continued Holmes, "whether Woodward at the British Museum is aware of the true nature of the Piltdown skull, and if he is in the affair because of you or in spite of you."

"Because of me," interjected Mycroft. "And Doyle here, of course. Go on."

"In any event, Woodward overstepped his instructions when he sent the skull to Osler so that it might be examined. Perhaps Woodward believed that the fake was better than it actually is, and that it might fool Osler. If Osler was persuaded to write a monograph on the skull, touting its authenticity, the document would be of use later in whatever scheme you have devised.

"Based on the notes in my scrapbooks, as Watson no doubt read last night, Osler has the reputation for being a masterful practical joker." I remained silent, having skimmed the scrapbook the night before without noticing any mention of the fact just stated by Holmes. "I might have thought that his whole participation in the matter, including involving Watson and myself with a trip to Oxford, was a part of some elaborate joke of which he was a part, if he had not genuinely showed his puzzlement and unease at the whole affair.

"Perhaps, with his reputation as a trickster, Osler would have gladly participated in whatever it is you are doing with the skull, Mycroft, but instead he was recruited without permission by Woodward, and so he had to be disengaged as skillfully and quickly as possible.

"The skull, sent to his house on the day before yesterday by Woodward, was quietly removed by one of your professional agents later that night, leaving no other sign of forced entry or disturbance. The plan was for Osler to worry about the matter for a day before a suitable warning arrived from His Majesty's government, advising Osler to forget the whole matter. The government agent would identify himself, and explain how the parcel had been taken, in order to give the whole matter the air of something mysterious that had been managed with great skill and omniscience.

"Unknown to you, Osler did not behave as expected, but instead wired to me for help yesterday without your knowledge. When your agent went to his home this morning to provide the dramatic warning to forget the whole matter, he was dismayed to learn that I had been already been invited to Oxford, and was scheduled to arrive in a few hours. Your agent left and reached you, asking for further instructions. You decided that my peripheral involvement in the matter might somehow be useful, so you allowed me to continue on to Oxford.

"Your agent went back and warned Osler not to say anything about the matter, and to direct me back to Sussex and Dawson at the Piltdown site. In the meantime, you reached Dawson, telling him to deliver the note which was sent from Doyle. And then you made the incredible step of journeying down here yourself in order to meet us and enjoy the fine meal of which we just partook.

"And so," Holmes concluded, "the only question left to ask, is why you are carrying out such a bizarre scheme with a collection of mismatched bones, and what do you hope to accomplish?" Mycroft shifted himself and folded his fingers across his middle.

"The answer, Sherlock, must by necessity remain somewhat vague, as there actually is no definite purpose in mind, as of yet."

Holmes puffed silently on his pipe, while I glanced back from one man to another. Mycroft and Holmes were each evaluating their thoughts, while Doyle sat patiently, with a good-humored smile on his face. Finally, Holmes spoke.

"So this matter of constructing the skull of the missing link is nothing more than some sort of potential plan that may or may not ever be used?"

"Exactly," replied Mycroft. "My department has literally dozens of similar schemes at various stages of preparation, all waiting to be pulled off the shelf at a moment's notice and refined for some specific occurrence, should they be needed.

"For example, we keep a ship moored at Portsmouth. It has a somewhat sinister reputation, with a glowering and ill-tempered captain and a larcenous-looking crew. We encourage all sorts of rumors to swirl about the ship, and every once in awhile, we send it off for a journey before it returns with more stories to add to its sinister reputation. What is not known to the general public is that captain and the crew, to a man, are working for my department. This ship, whose name is certainly not important right now – "

"It is the cutter, *Alicia*," interrupted Holmes, to Mycroft's irritation. "I have encountered it before. Please continue."

"As I was saying, this ship is always ready if it is needed in some part of the Empire, either as a distraction away from some other event, or to participate in something more directly, such as, let us say, the rescue of a friendly leader whose country has temporarily decided that he isn't fit to live."

"And you say that there are dozens of these theoretical contingency plans, just waiting until you need them?" I asked.

"Yes," said Mycroft. "Some plans, such as that involving the ship, are ongoing concerns, involving the continuing participation of actual agents, while others are simply schemes that can be enacted if needed. As you both know, war in Europe is coming, soon. It will be in a matter of just a few years now, not decades, in spite of all our efforts to delay or prevent it. I don't have to tell the three of you what that will mean, as all of us here have spent a great deal of energy ourselves over the last few years trying to stop a war from coming. In order to prepare, my department has been brainstorming, attempting to develop as many various operations as possible, so that when the time comes, we will be ready.

"We have involved a number of our best thinkers in this process, men of imagination who are able to create something unique and unusual, or who are able to see an existing event and are able to build upon it in some way in order to devise a future plan.

"Doyle, here, is one of our imagination men." He waved a languid hand in Doyle's direction. Doyle grinned, and ducked his head slightly. "He gets the credit for seeing the potential involved in the Piltdown findings. Initially, Charles Dawson came up with the skull fragments on his own. It is not the first of his questionable archeological findings, as I am sure you are already aware."

Holmes nodded, and Mycroft continued. "Since Doyle lives just up the road from Piltdown, it came to his attention fairly quickly earlier this year, when Dawson made his initial announcement. Doyle has been working with me for several years, and he immediately saw the possibilities that might present themselves in connection with the fraudulent skull."

"But what possibilities could there be?" I asked. "Obviously, this skull cannot stand even the slightest examination by an expert. Osler recognized its questionable aspects after a single glance into the box. What can you hope to accomplish?"

"It is too soon to tell," replied Mycroft. "Perhaps the skull might be sent somewhere someday, and something important, such as another item or message, could be smuggled in the box with it, the skull serving as a decoy. Possibly it could be used to discredit some academic who provided a strong opinion on it one way or another, whereupon we would produce opposing proof. It has even been speculated that, in this time of impending war, it could be used as a rallying symbol for British pride, in that one of man's earliest intelligent ancestors came from right here in England. I can assure you that the Kaiser would be quite upset if something like that were thrown in his face."

"But," I asked, "what about scientific reputations? Is Woodward at the British Museum in on this plan, or has he been duped?"

"He is a willing participant," replied Mycroft. "We are not sure yet how we wish to proceed with this matter, but we have recruited several top individuals to help us. Woodward took it upon himself to call in Osler, which was a mistake, as in our opinion Osler would not wish to participate. In any case, Dawson continues to muck about in Piltdown, now on the British payroll, as he and his minders prepare to find any other bone fragments that we think are required."

"And what of our trip to Oxford?" asked Holmes. "Was that really necessary? I have been working under your direct orders for several months now. If you had contacted me on the train and warned me off, I can assure you that I would have obeyed."

"Yes, but I decided that your involvement today couldn't hurt," said Mycroft. "It has always been part of the plan that you would divide your time between your real life and that of Altamont."

Holmes glanced at Doyle, and Mycroft continued. "Do not worry. Doyle is privy to your ongoing brief."

"I've been working with your brother off and on since the early nineties," Doyle interjected. "As you no doubt know, Watson was initially asked by Mycroft to start writing shorter narratives of your investigations that appeared in *The Strand*. Mycroft occasionally used the published versions of the narratives as tools to send messages to his agents. At times, inaccuracies regarding dates or names in the stories were intentionally placed there as coded messages.

"When Watson and I were publishing those stories during your supposed death, Mycroft got the idea that it would help you to accomplish your mission in the Far East, whatever it was, if people became convinced that you were a fictional character. Of course, I didn't know what his thinking was at the time, as I was not told that you were still alive.

"However, I did my part to give the impression that I was simply a former doctor turned writer, presenting a series of tales about a fictional detective in *The Strand*." Doyle glanced my way. I knew what he was thinking. He and I had gone through a falling out for several years after

176

that, as I had believed that he was trying to take credit for inventing the character of Sherlock Holmes. It had seemed to me that he was enjoying the fame associated with Holmes, while in fact he was actually somewhat resentful of the fact that the Holmes stories were eclipsing his other writings.

It was actually Doyle who had pushed for the publication of "The Final Problem," relating the details of Holmes's supposed death at Reichenbach Falls and ending the run of the popular *Strand* narratives. At the time, I had been willing to continue publication of Holmes's cases indefinitely, but Doyle had wearied of his participation in the affair. In later years, I had learned the truth, and of Mycroft's involvement in the plan. Doyle and I had patched things up in the late nineties, and we had gone on to publish a new set of stories, beginning with *The Hound of the Baskervilles* in 1901-02.

"In any event," Doyle concluded, "I am aware of your current mission for the government, and I wish you the best of luck."

"Thank you," said Holmes. Turning back to Mycroft, he said, "So this was simply a way to get me moving about the countryside so that I would be visible as Sherlock Holmes, the somewhat retired and reclusive detective?"

"Exactly," said Mycroft. Holmes glanced at me, reminding me that he had deduced something of the sort already. "Today, you have been rather like the cutter *Alicia*, figuratively sailing out of Portsmouth harbor, and giving certain people with an interest in that sort of thing a topic to discuss for a few days."

Holmes looked at the three of us, and then knocked his pipe out on his boot. "Well," he said, "I cannot say that I minded too much. It has been a fine day to travel, I met some new and interesting people, and I am able to spend the afternoon with a few good friends. Speaking to you as a man who has recently returned home from a far shore, I can assure you that there are few things better in life."

"Hear, hear!" cried Doyle, rising to his feet, and indicating that he was going to the house to request more refreshments.

Holmes settled back in his chair and began to refill his pipe. "I would be very interested to hear about some of your other theoretical contingency plans," he said to his brother.

"No doubt," replied Mycroft. "The inner machinations that governments put themselves through at times in order to fool their enemies, as well as their friends, is an incredibly interesting and instructive thing indeed. Sadly, the afternoon is waning, and there just is not time to tell you everything that is going on. However, when Doyle gets back, I will relate some interesting facts we have manufactured regarding

177

Stonehenge and the bluestone quarries. Or perhaps I will tell you of an idea I have involving the fabrication of photographs of children and fairies. Possibly you can help me convince Doyle that his participation is essential. I'm not entirely certain at this point what intelligence operation will necessitate the use of these photographs, or what set of circumstances would call for such a thing, but I can assure you that when they are used, it will be for a most important purpose.

"That is the beauty of the world, however. There are infinite possibilities, and one is always capable of being surprised. Ah, there is Doyle with the drinks. Might I trouble you, doctor, to pour me a whisky and soda? I find that all this talk has made me thirsty."

We talked into the twilight, and I like to think that moments like this were of comfort to Holmes when he departed again a few weeks later, to return to that netherworld of intrigue and betrayal, where he fought alone as Altamont for the benefit of his country.

The Affair of the
Brother's Request
Holmes and Watson in Tennessee (Part I)

I have related elsewhere how Sherlock Holmes and I visited the United States in May and June of 1921, as we traveled from New York City to Johnson City, Tennessee, and over the Blue Ridge Mountains to Linville, North Carolina. There, Holmes and I found ourselves involved in a complicated affair relating to his long-standing feud with the Moriarty family.*

By the fourth of June, the matter had not been completely resolved. However, there was nothing we could do for several weeks but wait for events to unfold. Holmes and I spent a few additional days exploring the beautiful areas around Linville, including nearby Grandfather Mountain, and the picturesque towns of Blowing Rock and Boone. My third wife had passed away several months earlier, and I was in no hurry to return to England. I sensed that Holmes felt no pressing need to return, as well.

At some point during our explorations, I mentioned to Holmes a few of the details of a visit that I had made to America the previous December with my wife. At that time, I had followed up on some of the research I had been making into my own family tree, and had managed to trace a branch that had emigrated to the United States many years before, traveling down through Virginia and into the wilderness of northern Tennessee. Although I tried to be subtle about my wishes, in case Holmes did not wish to fall in with my plans, he immediately perceived what I hoped to do.

"I certainly have no objection whatsoever to returning over the mountains and visiting for awhile in Tennessee," he said. "In fact, I was going to suggest something along those lines myself in the next day or so, as I have some business there that I have put off for far too long."

* EDITOR'S NOTE: The exact details of Holmes and Watson's journey through Johnson City, Tennessee and Linville, North Carolina can be found in "Sherlock Holmes and the Brown Mountain Lights", edited by James McKay Morton. The narrative was originally published *Mountain Living* magazine in 1977-78, and subsequently on the internet in a slightly revised form at *www.carolina.cc/sherlock.html*. It was this narrative that provided additional proof of Holmes and Watson's travels in the southeastern United States during the lifetimes of my grandparents.

Holmes asked me where my relatives lived. "I suppose one can use the term relatives only in the loosest sense," I replied. "Their branch of the Watson family left Scotland so long ago that one would have to examine many generations to determine the exact connection between myself and my American cousins. However, the branch of the line in question appears to have ended in a small town on the northern Tennessee border known as Oneida. I have not communicated with anyone there, and I have only one specific individual to try to contact. I'm not sure if she has married with some other family, or if the name has been absorbed or lost."

At the time of this conversation, Holmes and I were sitting on the porch of the Green Park Inn in Blowing Rock, which had been our base of operations during the past few days as we explored the local countryside. As I rocked in my chair, Holmes leaned forward and checked his handy United States atlas, laid open on his bony knees. He ran his finger along the page, tracing a route and murmuring to himself. Finally, he sat back in the chair and said "This is more than satisfactory, Watson," he said. "My business is not too far from your Oneida. Train travel to the place may be a nightmare, but if you are game, we shall leave tomorrow."

"Where is your destination, Holmes," I asked. "And what longstanding business could you possibly have in the wilds of Tennessee?"

"Ah, Watson, I'm sure you've never heard of where I need to go. It is a curious little village known as Rugby, located some miles southwest of Oneida. I fear a long carriage ride that day. And as for my business . . . I am going to fulfill a promise from long ago, made if I should ever find myself back in that part of the United States."

"Back in that part?" I asked. "You have been there before?"

"Yes, Watson, many years ago. But I will tell you the tale in a few days, after I have had a chance to refresh my mind on the circumstances, and when we are closer to Rugby. It was long ago, and I must confess that the details have become somewhat hazy."

We continued to sit on the porch as I thought about Holmes and his previous trip, unknown to me, to the American Southeast. I had known him for over forty years, and although we were both in our late sixties at this point, he still had the power to surprise me. There were so many parts of his past that I would probably never be told, in spite of the fact that in many ways we were as close as brothers. He was naturally secretive, he liked to withhold other facts just in case he could reveal them dramatically someday, and the nature of his work required that some things could never be told. I was simply grateful that, even after so many years, I would soon be finding out additional information about something that had taken place during Sherlock Holmes's travels.

The next morning, shown in my journal as the seventh of June, 1921, Holmes and I departed quite early to make certain that we did not miss our train. Slowly we wound our way over the mountains. The scenery was amazing, like nothing I had observed anywhere else in the world. I had seen the mountains of the Indian highlands and Afghanistan, as well as the Swiss Alps and other wonders of six continents. However, nothing could compare with the wildness around us. The ancient forests spilled down the mountains to shallow, fast streams and rivers. Occasionally a tiny hamlet or grouping of cabins or farm buildings might appear, on a small plot cut back into the forest, but they were nothing compared to the thousands of square miles of old-growth forest and wildlife.

At times the train seemed to struggle as it pulled its tired way up along steep mountainside drop-offs. I questioned the wisdom of building a railroad in some of the locations where we traveled, and then realized that the builders had probably picked the easiest way, indicating that other routes would have been even worse. I simply tried to have faith in the railway and hope for the best.

The view never palled, in spite of hours of being surrounded by tall dark trees, so thick that one could not see much past those growing beside the tracks. We saw deer, too many to count, eating in the shade along the tracks. Most were visible in the morning, but the observations decreased dramatically toward the middle of the day. We saw a fair number of black bears, however, throughout the day. Both the deer and the bears appeared to have no fear of the train, simply pausing in whatever activity in which they were engaged as we passed, staring at us as we stared at them.

I have since read that the Appalachian Mountains are among the oldest in the world, and that their rounded heights are due to many more millennia of weathering than the younger Alps or the American Rockies. I know that the mountains over which we traveled contained some of the last remnants of the old forest that at one time covered a great deal of the entire North American continent, and that they were not as deserted or wild as they appeared to me that day. Settlers had moved all through those mountains, creating little communities and pockets of civilization connected throughout the wilderness. On that day, however, I found it easy to believe that, except for the train in which we rode, there were no other people within hundreds of miles. The mountains seemed to be saying that they were here before us, and they would be here long after we were gone.

The landscape gradually began to change as we descended on the Tennessee side of the slopes. Farms and towns became much more apparent, and the illusion I had felt while riding through the forest faded somewhat. By mid-afternoon, our train arrived back in Johnson City, where we had departed for Linville just days before.

As I waited on the bustling platform, looking at the nearby hills and breathing the clear air, Holmes arranged to find seats on the train bound south for Knoxville. I eavesdropped on several nearby conversations, enjoying the various local dialects in the same way that I did when traveling through different parts of the British Isles.

Holmes gestured toward me. As I joined him, he began quickly walking down the platform. "We are just in time to catch the Knoxville train," he said. "I was afraid that we were moving so slowly through the mountains that we would miss it, and have to stay here tonight."

Like all the trains I had seen in this part of the United States, the carriage did not have separate compartments, so we found seats within one that was only two-thirds full. After several minutes of maneuvering through the busy train yard, we reached an open landscape and picked up speed, heading south.

I was fascinated with the surroundings, but Holmes appeared lost in thought. Finally, he sank lower in his seat, made himself more comfortable, and began to doze. I, on the other hand, continued to look around me at the passing countryside. We were traveling south down a long, wide valley, with mountains in the far distance on both the east and west. Although we passed some wooded areas, none were as thick or old as those we had been through that morning in the mountains.

Most areas seemed to be devoted to agriculture, with many lonely houses perched in the middle of vast fields, within sight of the train tracks, but miles from their nearest neighbors.

I recalled Holmes once commenting on lonely country houses, and the horror that they gave him. "You look at these scattered houses, and you are impressed by their beauty," he had said. "I look at them, and the only thought which comes to me is a feeling of their isolation, and of the impunity with which crime may be committed there."

I had questioned how he could feel that way. He replied, "They always fill me with a certain horror. It is my belief, Watson, founded upon my experience, that the lowest and vilest alleys in London do not present a more dreadful record of sin than does the smiling and beautiful countryside."

"You horrify me!" I had cried.

He had explained that in town, everyone lived so closely that no vile deed could go unknown or unpunished. In the country, however, there were no nearby neighbors to know the crimes that happened there.

"Think of the deeds of hellish cruelty," he had said, "the hidden wickedness which may go on, year in, year out, in such places, and none the wiser."

Looking at the lonely houses, now in shadows from the setting sun, I was glad that Holmes was asleep. Although I knew that he was probably right, I preferred to look at them with optimism, and try to see their beauty, rather than their potential for evil.

We arrived in Knoxville late that evening. As we stepped out of the ornate station, we could smell the nearby stockyards and meat processing plants, along with a smell that I later identified as roasting coffee. On the horizon was a glow which resembled a fire, but I knew that it was simply electric lighting, shining from the businesses along the city's main thoroughfare. We engaged a cab, who drove us several blocks before depositing us at a small hotel, located beside the bluffs dropping to the nearby Tennessee River.

We checked into the hotel, and after freshening ourselves, went out onto the street, where we walked for an hour or so before finding a restaurant. We ate a quiet meal, and then set off to the west, where we found the sprawling grounds of the University of Tennessee. Compared to the ancient buildings of Oxford and Cambridge, the school appeared to be an upstart child. We entered some of the buildings, including Estabrook Hall, which were left open for late studies by the students. After an hour or so we returned to our hotel rooms, planning to make an early start in the morning.

The next day, Holmes and I were at the train station with time to spare, making sure we understood the convoluted route we would need to take to reach Oneida. After hearing the details of our journey, I began to question why I had not simply opted for a return to England by way of New York. Perhaps a few days in America's most successful city would have been more enjoyable than moving west into the remote and rugged poverty-stricken areas of the country. However, I recalled that Holmes had business there as well, and if I had not initially suggested a trip to Tennessee, he probably would have.

Our train left promptly, an odd mixture of passenger and freight cars. I had not thought of Knoxville as a particularly prosperous city, although I knew it was probably the largest metropolis in that part of the world. However, its citizens had looked considerably wealthy in retrospect as compared to the individuals currently sharing our carriage. Although a few of the men, such as Holmes and myself, were dressed in suits, most were dressed in work clothes, clean but much worn and well used. The few women traveling on the train wore plain dresses, augmented by bonnets, often the only color shown in their outfits.

As I pondered our fellow traveling companions, I thought of what I knew about the area to which we traveled. Based on my researches of the previous year, I had learned that the area was still considered somewhat wild, lying toward the middle of the state along the Tennessee-Kentucky border. It was a land of harsh, dramatic wilderness, but in a different sense from that which we had crossed in the mountains the previous day. The geographic feature to which we journeyed was on the edge of Tennessee's central Plateau region, a vast area which straddles the center of the state like a table. The western side of the state drops from the plateau toward the rich fertile lands along the Mississippi River. On the eastern side was the wide Tennessee River valley, down which we had partially traveled the previous day from Johnson City to Knoxville. Of course, other smaller mountain ranges bounded different portions of this valley as well, but essentially the valley lay between the plateau and the Appalachian Mountains on the state's far eastern border.

The plateau itself existed due to a variety of geologic causes. I had learned that the area near Oneida was quite unique in terms of its various natural wonders, such as stone arches and towering sandstone bluffs. In some way they reminded one of America's southwest, except that there the natural wonders were exposed in a desert-like setting, while I had read that the eastern Tennessee Plateau was still covered in old forest, hiding the geologic formations from view until one was almost on top of them and only if one knew where to look.

The state's capital, Nashville, lay to the southwest of our destination, far beyond the initial rise onto the plateau that we were now traversing.

As we traveled northwest, the land became more mountainous, folding on itself. We rode along the low-lands, beside streams and rivers and through dry valleys, our view of the sky limited to the open space between the tops of tall peaks.

After several hours, the people in the carriage began to shift restlessly and rearrange their belongings. I deduced that they were aware of our impending arrival. Holmes, who had been silent through the entire journey, seemed to notice as well, and sat higher in his seat. I wondered at his silence. I considered that perhaps he was still thinking of our unfinished business in Linville, or more probably that he was considering his task in the mysterious Rugby, where we would visit after finding my distant relations. I could tell that something about the idea of going to Rugby saddened him, but I knew better than to ask, and that he would tell me only when or if he was ready.

The train pulled into a station which lay next to a wide tangle of tracks, far more than I would have suspected for a remote town such as Oneida. Many of the tracks had rows of rail cars sitting idly, being connected in some random manner in order that they might be taken elsewhere. Our train seemed to be pulling the only passenger cars in sight, as all the others

184

were loaded with heaping mounds of black coal or long trees, stripped of their branches, bound for the lumber mills.

As we stood next to the station, the conductor yelled, "All aboard! All aboard for Jamestown!" The last of the passengers not already loaded scurried to the train, and within moments, the great mechanical beast had gone, continuing down the tracks away from the direction of Knoxville.

There were no cabs outside the station, but as the town did not seem to be very large at all, we asked a man at the ticket window for directions to a hotel. He looked at us for a long silent moment, no doubt considering our British accents, before directing us down a dirt street and around the corner of some buildings in the distance.

Holmes and I picked up our meager bags and started down the dusty lane. Luckily we had always traveled light, and carrying the bags was no great burden. As we moved closer to the cluster of buildings, I could see that they were actually the back of a row of structures that stood side-by-side up a paved roadway. A similar group of buildings was facing them across the street. In the distance were some houses, located on dirt side roads, each standing under large shade trees.

As we stepped onto the main street, and apparently the only paved street, of Oneida, we were watched by the natives with expressionless faces. All were dressed as the people on the train, the women in plain dresses, the men in worn work clothes. Some of the men were obviously coal miners, while others were farmers. Only the business owners and shop keepers were dressed in suits, although these were quite worn as well.

I was struck by the obvious poverty of the area. I knew that the town subsisted on the local coal mines and timber industry, as evidenced by the products loaded on the train cars in the rail yard. I was greatly reminded of towns in Scotland and Wales, where Holmes and I had traveled during several of his investigations. The people there had the same look, a lean pride and suspicion of outsiders. It was no surprise that I was reminded of those British towns and villages, as most of the people in this area were descended from Scottish, Irish, and Welsh immigrants. That, combined with the fact that coal mining towns have the same look and feel to them, whether in Wales or eastern Tennessee, and it was no wonder that it felt familiar.

We found a small hotel where we were able to obtain two rooms. I sensed that the rate charged to us was perhaps more than the manager usually asked, because we were obviously from somewhere else, but it was still cheaper than our rooms had been in Knoxville, so we made no complaint. After getting settled, we made our way to a nearby restaurant, where we ordered a late lunch.

I was intrigued by an item on the menu which I had seen elsewhere during a previous trip to the United States. It was identified as country ham, I suppose in contrast to city ham, which uses a different curing process. The country ham was very salty, thinly sliced, and fried tough in its own grease. However, the flavor was wonderful, and went very nicely with the local vegetables, green beans, potatoes, and turnip greens, as well as homemade bread. Holmes made do with a bowl of hearty stew, and bread as well.

Following a dessert of some sort of apple and dough confection, I leaned back quite satisfied, while Holmes glanced idly about the room. "Well, Watson," he said, "how do you wish to proceed in finding your distant relations?"

I glanced at the waiter, heading toward our table. "I suppose the best way to start is simply to ask." As the waiter arrived, I said, "We are looking for a lady that I believe lives here in town or somewhere nearby, and I wonder if you might know her. Rebecca Watson?"

The waiter said nothing for a moment, and then replied, "Why do you want to talk to her?"

"I am a distant relative," I said. "A very distant relative, and while I am passing through this area, I thought I would like to introduce myself to her."

The waiter thought for a moment, and finally seemed to decide that I passed some sort of test. "She lives here in town at times, and out at their home place at No Business on the Big South Fork at others. And she isn't a Watson anymore, either. She's been married for years to a man named John Sherman Marcum."

Before I could ask where the picturesque area known as "No Business" was located, the waiter added, "But some of her sons live here in town. One of them works at the lumber mill, just on the other side of the train yard, not far from here. Willie Marcum. He should be there now."

Thanking the waiter, we paid our bill and departed. As we walked back down the humble street toward the train tracks, I thanked Holmes again for accompanying me on this journey.

"It is no bother, Watson. It is always a pleasure to see new parts of the world, and to observe that no matter how differently people live, in what circumstances or locations or state of wealth or poverty, they are still essentially the same, wherever one looks. And in any event," he continued, "I am still expecting your company when I complete my errand in this part of the world, at nearby Rugby."

After crossing through the rail yard, stepping gingerly over each parallel track, we reached the far side, where we found ourselves at the lumber mill. The whine of saws became louder with each approaching step, and the smell of freshly cut wood filled the air. We began to walk through small drifts of sawdust and strings of sawn bark.

Identifying the office, we entered and asked to speak to Willie Marcum. The man there did not question our business, but simply told us to wait a minute while he stepped outside. In no time, he returned with a tall man in his late twenties, his thin hair cut rather short but unkempt and waving in the slight breeze. He was wearing overalls, and sawdust was sticking to his clothing up and down his body.

In appearance, he somewhat physically resembled a younger version of Holmes. However, his facial expression was one of open friendliness, whereas Holmes, in contrast, had always maintained the watchful look of a predatory bird.

"Mr. Marcum," I said, "My name is Dr. John H. Watson, and this is my friend, Sherlock Holmes."

Mr. Marcum stuck out his hand in my direction, but his glance turned sharply toward Holmes at the mention of my friend's name. After shaking my hand, he shook Holmes's, whereupon he said, "You're kidding, right? Sherlock Holmes? I read about you in some books. I thought you were a made-up story."

Through the years, as my writings had become increasingly well known, this experience had happened more and more often. Holmes had managed to learn to respond politely when this type of thing occurred, but I knew that he had never come to appreciate the attention he had received from my published narratives.

"It is nice to meet you, Mr. Marcum," he said. "I am afraid that Dr. Watson's stories have given many people the impression that I am a 'made-up story.' However, I assure you that I am, in fact, a real person."

Mr. Marcum grinned and looked at the two of us. "I can see that. And call me Willie. It's short for William. What can I do for you two?"

I explained that I had been to the United States the previous year, and during that time I had researched some of my own family background, tracing various offshoots of the Watson family that had come to America from Scotland. "One linear relationship seems to have passed through Virginia and Kentucky into this area. Your mother is the most direct descendent of that branch that I can identify, and as Holmes and I were journeying through this part of the country, I wished to make a detour and possibly meet her."

"Well, I think she'd enjoy that very much," said Willie. "But she doesn't live here in town right now. The family has land here in Oneida, quite a bit of it actually, due to my father's foresight. My brothers and I have divided it and are farming it, but my parents spend time here and also a ways out in the woods, where all of us boys and my sisters were raised.

Right now the family is out there, getting some things cleaned up after the place sat empty last winter."

"The waiter in town who told us how to find you said it was a place called 'No Business'."

"That's right," Willie replied. "I've been planning to go out there soon myself to help out. What I can do is leave today, if that's agreeable with you, and take you both with me."

"Why, certainly," I replied.

"Well, let me just tell my boss that I'm going, and we'll be on our way."

He was back in a moment, and said he was ready to go. "I hope you don't mind walking some, but I live a mile or two away, and we'll need to go by my house to get my truck. The saw mill is so close that I usually just walk back and forth every day."

Holmes and I assured him that it would not be a problem, and we headed back across the tracks and into town. On several occasions we stepped to the side of the road as horse-drawn vehicles went by. Much more rarely, we were passed by automobiles, or occasionally trucks, as the Americans called them, carrying lumber.

As we neared the hotel, Willie asked if our things were there. When we said yes, he replied, "You might as well check out and bring it all with you. By the time we get to my parents' place, it will be too late to come back tonight, and anyway, mother will insist that you stay overnight. It won't be as nice as the hotel, though. I hope you won't mind."

We assured him that we did not, and we entered the hotel. We were soon checked out, to the relative displeasure of the man behind the desk, and resumed our walk down the street. Within the lengths of a few buildings we had left the main part of town behind. We continued on out the dirt road, passing several nice homes, before bearing left onto a smaller lane. Around us were tilled fields, crossed by small brooks, and bordered by distant woods. "Almost there," Willie said, smiling.

We could see a white frame two-story house, wrapped on two sides by a wide porch, in our path. Behind it was a large barn. Near the barn was parked an old truck and a hay rake. Before we got too close to the house, the door opened and a woman stepped out and watched us approach. She was very pregnant, and I could see that she would deliver within just a few weeks. A young boy, six or seven years old, stood beside her, while a girl of about three years stood behind her, peeking from behind the woman's skirts.

As we reached the porch, the woman looked at us, and then said to Willie, rather sternly, "You're home early."

Willie nodded and said, "Ola, I want you to meet some people. These men are Mr. Sherlock Holmes, and Dr. John Watson, all the way from

188

England. Gentlemen, this is my wife, Ola, my son Howard, and my daughter, Wilma. The doctor is distant kin to my mother, and I am going to take them out to the home place tonight to meet her."

Willie's wife greeted us politely, but I could see that she was not pleased that he was going to be leaving. "Will you be staying out there tonight as well?" Willie said yes, and she turned to us. "Could I fix you something to eat before you go? I've got some dinner left on the stove."

Holmes and I politely declined, explaining that we had only recently had lunch. Willie left us and walked to a nearby barn, where he was soon involved in starting the balky truck. Holmes glanced around the farm, his gaze lingering on a large walnut tree in the front yard. "You have a lovely place here," he said. "Are you from this area as well?"

"Yes," replied Ola. "I grew up right over the hill there. I was a Smith, and my father owns a small store."

The girl, Wilma, had sat on the porch floor and begun to play with some small broken bits of toys. Holmes gestured to the road near the house, which at that point was somewhat sunken between two high banks on either side. "That road must have been here quite a while to have been worn down so," he said. "I had not realized that Oneida had been settled for so long."

Ola glanced at the road. "I don't know how long that road has been there, but they say that General Burnside and his army marched on it during the Civil War. In fact, the troops camped right here on this land during the march. Although they were from the North, they were welcomed here, you know. When Tennessee seceded from the Union to join the South, the town of Oneida and Scott County, where we are located, remained loyal to the North and seceded from Tennessee. As far as I know, we've never officially been put back into Tennessee, although it doesn't seem to matter to anyone now.

"This area was settled for who knows how much earlier, though, by Indians, although there's none left around here now. There are many places around here where you can find Indian bones and pieces of pots and arrowheads. There's a great rock sticking out of the ground within walking distance of here that has something of a cave beneath it. Everyone knows you can find old bones under the Indian Rock.

"And that field right over there," she said, pointing behind us. "We plow it every spring, and I can't tell you the number of arrowheads that turn up in the dirt. We have buckets full of them. I don't know what happened, whether there was a village there or a great battle, but somehow all those things were left behind in that field."

189

At that point, Willie drove up with the truck, and we took our leave from his wife. "Is it all right to leave your wife so close to her term?" I asked.

Willie nodded. "She's got kin staying with us. I'm just in the way. In any case, I'll be back before anything happens." He turned the vehicle, and started out in a westerly direction. "Sorry the truck's not more comfortable," he said. "But if we went by wagon it would take until tomorrow to get there. I actually had one of those new automobiles, once. Ola and I managed to get it right after we got married. We drove it into town, the first one that was ever driven into Oneida. It was a rainy day, and the thing sank into the mud on Main Street, up past the tires. It was very embarrassing, but pretty funny, too."

We drove on past some farms before entering the woods again. "All this belongs to my family," he gestured, pointing left and right. "We used to have much more. My grandfather owned most of the land where the town is, but we've been selling it off over the years." The creaking of the truck's springs and the occasional grind of gears or a racing motor could not hide the sounds of the numerous birds in the trees surrounding us. Holmes spent some of the time questioning Willie about the Indian artifacts and settlements mentioned by Willie's wife, but Willie had nothing further to add.

Suddenly, I interrupted when a question occurred to me. "What can you tell me about Rugby?" I said. "Are we close to it?"

"Rugby is about ten or fifteen miles on the far side of No Business, through some fairly rugged woods. It's a pretty rough ride. Why do you want to know about Rugby?"

I looked at Holmes, to see if he had any objection to my revealing the reason behind my question, or if the matter was some sort of secret. He showed no reaction. "After we meet your mother," I said, "Holmes has said he would like to go to Rugby. However, I've never heard of the place, and did not know exactly what it was. The name sounds British," I added. "There is a town in England of that name."

"I suppose I can take you there tomorrow," Willie said, "after we leave my parents' place. Then I can bring you back to Oneida, or take you on down to Rockwood, where you can catch a train to wherever you want to go. But as to Rugby, well, there isn't much there anymore. Although I hear that it was something special, once."

"You said you'd been there before, Holmes," I said. "Do you know anything of the place?"

Holmes's gaze, which had seemed distant and unfocused, sharpened, and he said, "Yes, I know some of the history of Rugby. Please feel free, Willie, to add in anything you might recall."

Holmes took another moment to focus his thoughts, and then began.

"Rugby was a community founded in about 1880 by Thomas Hughes, the British author – "

"– of *Tom Brown's Schooldays*," I interrupted. "I enjoyed it when I was much younger."

"As you say," agreed Holmes. "He named the town after Rugby in Warwickshire, where he had attended school, and which I believe served as the setting for his book.

"Hughes developed the idea that he wanted to build a perfect community, an experiment in cooperative effort with a strongly agricultural atmosphere. He recruited the younger sons of the English gentry, who had rather limited prospects if they chose to remain in England."

"Why limited?" asked Willie.

"In England," I answered, "there is an accepted system among the rich and noble classes known as *primogeniture*. Under this arrangement, the eldest son in a family inherits the property, the wealth, and the title should there be one. Often properties and estates are entailed, so that the eldest male heir has use of them through his lifetime, but he cannot sell them or pass them on as he might like. After his death, the next eldest male heir inherits the entailment.

"For younger sons in this system, there is usually very little money or property left over. They can live off their elder's charity, for as long as that lasts, and if anyone is willing to provide it. Or they can seek employment. There are very few socially acceptable jobs for younger sons. In many cases, it is assumed that younger sons will enter the military or government service, or will undertake a diplomatic post at some location in the Empire."

"I see," said Willie. "And these younger sons were the men that Mr. Hughes recruited to come live and work in Rugby?"

"Yes," said Holmes. "The idea of traveling to an area far from England and creating something of a 'New Jerusalem' in the wilderness was very appealing to these young men, the ones who did not want to or who were not suited to enter the military or government employ.

"Hughes and his new disciples came to Rugby, which had been purchased earlier by Hughes due to its proximity to a newly-built rail line nearby. They set to work, many of the young men doing that type of labor for the first time. They worked hard, and learned from their many mistakes. Soon a number of buildings were constructed on the site. From my research at the time, I believe that in the first few years, the early 1880's, there were over seventy structures built, and over three hundred residents in the growing community.

191

"The young men, all of whom had been well-educated while growing up in England, attempted to bring their culture and society with them. By day they would work in the fields, tending their crops, and making repairs to their houses and community buildings. At night, they would have meetings of drama clubs and literary societies and numerous sporting teams. Within a few years, a fine inn had sprung up, a large well-stocked library had been built, and regular train service was connecting the town to the outside world, providing a means of obtaining other valuable goods and services.

"Of course, trying to build a paradise on earth is always doomed to failure. In the early years of the colony, a typhoid epidemic swept through the citizens. Word of this reached England, causing a decrease in confidence in Hughes's planned community. Later, in the mid-1880's, the inn, which had been the center of the community's activities and cultural efforts, burned to the ground. As time went on, Hughes himself began to spend less and less time in Rugby, possibly due to the fact that his family, which had initially lived there with him, began to absent itself more and more, eventually staying there only one month out of each year.

"Hughes continued to pour much of his own money into the colony, but it continued its downward slide into failure. Hughes died in the mid-1890's, a few years after I visited. By about 1900, the official colony was at an end, although I understand some people, descendents of the original settlers, continue to live there."

Holmes looked at Willie. "Is that essentially correct?"

Willie replied, "I suppose so, Mr. Holmes, but actually you know more about the place than I ever did, and I grew up near it. There are some people still living there, but they have always tended to keep to themselves, and now I guess I understand why a little better.

"I guess we will go over there tomorrow," he continued. "I would have liked to have seen the place in its heyday. You say you were there in the nineties?"

"In 1893," Holmes replied.

"The year I was born," interjected Willie.

Holmes nodded. "I was presumed dead for several years during that time, as you may have read."

"I read how you came back, too," said Willie with a grin. "Back when I thought you weren't real."

"Yes," said Holmes. "During those three years, I carried out a number of activities for my brother, working for the British government, in various locations in Asia, Europe, and North America. I traveled under a variety of aliases, and for a time, I lived in New York City. I think I may have referred to those times in the past, haven't I, Watson?"

192

I nodded, and he continued. "During the time I was in New York, I was notified that one of my great enemies, Colonel Sebastian Moran, might possibly be in that city as well, hunting me. In order to verify or disprove this, I surfaced and traveled quite openly from New York to Florida, taking care of several small matters of business along the way. Of course, I was constantly on the alert to see if I was being stalked.

"As my business in Florida neared completion, I notified Mycroft, who said he had a task for me in New Orleans. I went west for a short period of time. While still traveling there, Mycroft arranged for information to be sent ahead of me to New Orleans about Rugby and a small task he needed for me to accomplish there. I then passed through this part of Tennessee on my way back to New York."

"But what was the task?" I asked. "Why would your brother, whom you have said sometimes *was* the British government, need you to travel to this remote location?"

"Ah, Watson, that is a part of the story that I will tell you tomorrow, when we are on our way to Rugby."

The sun was setting as we finally reached the Marcum cabin. We had journeyed through the ancient forests, occasionally lurching as the truck was driven through narrow rock-choked streams, and once across a shallow riverbed. The muddy water came rather high on the wheels, and seemed as if it were threatening to overtop the sides of the vehicle as well on one or two occasions. However, it probably looked much worse to me than it actually was. "This is the Big South Fork," Willie said, calmly turning the wheel as the truck pulled us onward, seemingly oblivious to the water surging around its wheels and the uncertain footing in the hidden rocky river bottom. "The Big South Fork of the Cumberland River. We're lucky it's low right now. I would have had to go the long way around otherwise."

"Lucky indeed," I muttered, as water splashed over the side of the door, drenching my face.

We had no other mishaps on the river, however, and we were soon at the cabin, located in the bottom of a gorge along the river bank. As we neared our destination, I saw countless other homes nearby, and realized with surprise that this area was much more heavily populated area than I had expected. "Welcome to 'No Business,' " said Willie. "I guess they call it that because nobody has any business living way out here."

I had smelled wood smoke hanging in the air for quite a while before we arrived. Finally we rounded a bend and saw the Marcum cabin in the distance. At the side of the river nearby was a great round rock, probably twelve to fifteen feet around, squatting along the shore. Tied beside it was a small boat. My attention was drawn back to the cabin as a series of barks arose, coming from a group of lean-looking dogs rising to their feet near the door.

An older man and woman stepped from out of the cabin. In a moment they were joined by several young men and women, Willie's younger brothers and sisters, I assumed, from their similar physical features. The entire family had the look I had seen on a variety of people since arriving in this area. Obviously most of the people in these parts were of Scots-Irish descent. They were so similar to those that I had met in the small towns and villages of England. As I watched, more of the family appeared from various buildings around the main house. They waited silently as we arrived.

Willie hopped down lightly, while Holmes and I descended more cautiously. "Mother? Father?" Willie said. "I have brought someone who would like to meet you." Willie then introduced us, again explaining that we were from England. His father, a tall older man, stooped and wearing a large mustache, stepped up and gravely shook our hands, while his wife and children simply nodded. "Dr. Watson here has been tracing his family tree, and he has found that we are distant relations, Mother."

I had noticed an added interest when my name was mentioned. When Willie finished explaining my purpose, the small woman stepped forward, smiling for the first time. She was wearing a plain cotton dress, covered with a flour-specked apron. Her graying hair was pulled back in a bun, and her finely drawn features showed a beauty and grace that was unexpected to me in that wilderness. However, she reflected the hard life where she had lived, and looked older than she probably was.

"Welcome to our home, cousin," said Rebecca Watson Marcum. She took my hand, smiled also at Holmes, and pulled me toward the door. "You're just in time to eat."

We went into the log and plank building, very clean and tidy, and surprisingly well lit considering the small windows. The odor of kerosene was immediately noticeable from the numerous lanterns hung about the room, but it was not unpleasant. Mixed with it was the smell of vegetables and heat from the stove.

We crowded around the table, and the room began to fill with good-natured conversation as the brothers and sisters started to ask Willie of news from town and the farther world. We began to pass the dishes around, and both Holmes and I took generous helpings of the pork loin, green beans, potatoes, and the corn meal bread with fresh butter. Soon both Holmes and I were answering questions about life in England and our visit to the United States.

Willie explained that Holmes was a famous detective, and he told one of his brothers to go upstairs to retrieve a book, apparently originally

194

owned by Willie and now left for the younger men. In a moment, everyone was eagerly passing around one of the published collections of Holmes's cases, amazed that we were actually visiting in their home, and commenting that the illustrations did not much look like Holmes. I pointed out that the American illustrator had unfortunately based his drawings of Holmes on the likeness of a popular actor, while the British illustrator had been much more accurate in his portrayal of his subject.

Holmes took all of the attention in stride, responding good-naturedly to questions, and making a few simple deductions about the brothers and sisters, to the delight of all at the table. The meal passed far too quickly, and I tried to treasure every minute of it.

Later, Holmes and I sat with Mr. and Mrs. Marcum, and Willie, while the others went about their business. Mrs. Marcum and I spent a while looking through her old and fragile family Bible, tracing dates and relationships back to our common ancestor. I had brought some of my own documents with me, and we compared our information. Mine was surprisingly consistent with what was written in the Bible, and I could tell that Mrs. Marcum was glad to learn some about her family's earlier history in Scotland and England before her branch had emigrated to America.

I was aware that Holmes was talking with Willie and Mr. Marcum about various matters, including the description of the geology of the local area, with its dramatic bluffs, caves, and sandstone arches towering over the ground below. Willie offered to take us by one or two of the sites on the way to Rugby the next day, saying that it would not be too far out of the way. I heard Holmes asking a few questions about Rugby, but neither Willie nor Mr. Marcum had any additional information to offer.

That night, we were offered Mr. and Mrs. Marcum's bed, and when we wouldn't hear of it, they tried to turn out their children and give us their upstairs loft. Finally we convinced them that sleeping in the clean straw in the barn loft would suit us down to the ground, and, wrapped in warm blankets, we fell asleep to the sound of a soft wind and the distant chuckling of the river.

We were up early the next morning, finding that Mrs. Marcum had been up even earlier, making biscuits, which we ate with more of the fine country ham, preserves, and local honey. After saying our goodbyes, Willie drove us away in his truck. I turned and waved until a bend in the dirt road put them out of sight. Settling back in my seat, I was very glad that we had come here. My new world relatives, however distant, were fine people, and I would not have missed this for the world. I was saddened when I realized that I would not be able to share my experiences with my recently deceased wife, who had participated so often in the research into my family's history.

Willie drove through a meandering series of narrow roadways, up and down hills, along ridges, and down in small valleys opening onto flat lands before rising again. He seemed to know exactly where he was going. Occasionally through the trees, I could see distant cliffs, rising far over the valley, their vertical walls worn smooth by countless eons of wind and rain. Sometimes caves seemed to be visible high on the inaccessible cliff faces, but it may have been a trick of the shadows.

Once we stopped at a cabin so Willie could pass on a message from town to the occupants. It was a rude little place, with low ceilings and small rooms that could only be reached from the outside, with no internal access between rooms. It seemed as if the place were more of a barn than a home for the poor little family that lived there. Nearby was a small stream that Willie identified as Charit Creek. I knew that if the creek flooded, portions of the home would be underwater.

Eventually we departed, the children staring at us in silence until we were out of sight. I realized that our visit was probably the most exciting thing that had happened there in weeks. Gradually we were pulled higher until we seemed to be out of the valleys and onto a small plateau. A short distance away, suddenly visible, was a pair of twin arches, giant stone behemoths carved by uncountable years of water and wind.

Willie stopped beside them and we all stiffly climbed down, sore from sitting for so long, and also from constantly moving to retain our balance in the ever-shifting truck. We walked up to the arches, dwarfed by their size. Standing under the larger arch, I looked up, realizing that the inner roof was so far above me that I could not make out any details in the stone. The floor of the arch was shaded and sandy, and filled with large boulders, some as big as a room. I assumed that they had fallen from the arch ceiling in generations past.

I was content to walk under that arch, and a few minutes later to make my way through tangled shrubs to the smaller arch as well, before returning to the vast room under the larger one. Holmes, however, was like a child, dashing back and forth, leaping like a goat from rock to rock, never betraying that he was in his late sixties. He found a narrow cave leading out of the base of the larger arch, disappeared into it, and soon reappeared in a completely different place, explaining that the passage had exited somewhere on the far side of the great rock. Then he was gone again, and when he returned a quarter of an hour later, he revealed that he had been to the top of the arch, climbing a ladder that had been built for that purpose by the locals who obviously used this place as an occasional picnic spot. Although I'm sure we could have spent longer there, we eventually returned to the truck and resumed our progress toward Rugby. We drove in silence for a while, until Holmes asked, "How close are we?"

"Not far now," said Willie.

"Then perhaps it is time to tell you why we have come here," Holmes replied. "I hope you don't mind having to listen to me reminisce, Willie."

"Not at all, Mr. Holmes," said Willie. "It is an honor, sir."

"Well, I don't know about that," he said. "In any case . . . As I said yesterday, I was asked to stop by here years ago by my brother, Mycroft. I was traveling from New Orleans to New York in 1893, and I assure you that before I had received information from my brother I had never heard of the Rugby colony.

"Mycroft had sent a package to me in New Orleans, delivered by a fast steamship of the British Navy. It contained several sets of instructions for upcoming tasks he wished for me to carry out. None of those are relevant to this tale. But included in the packet was the request to stop in Rugby, as a personal favor to Mycroft. He wished for me to deliver a message.

"The message was from the Earl of Nash and his older son, William Sexton, to their son and younger brother, respectively, Thomas Sexton, asking him to please come home to England. Thomas was one of those men who had come out to Rugby to participate in Hughes's dream of a perfect society. In addition to the message, Mycroft had sent the history of the whole unhappy family, which I read before I arrived.

"It seems that the family had estates in Somerset, near Frome. In years past the family's wealth had drained away, leaving them with a title and a great run-down house, but not much else. William and Thomas's father, the Earl, had made a new fortune in textiles, and with his increased wealth, had refurbished the family estates to their original condition. In the eighteen-eighties, the family lived there, with the Earl making regular trips to London and other cities to keep track of his interests.

"The family consisted of the Earl, whose name was Joseph Sexton, his wife, and his two sons, William, the eldest, and Thomas. There were no other children living. The sons were close in age, and had always spent much time together, although they were vastly different in temperament. William was somewhat studious, while Thomas was wilder, preferring to spend his time roaming outdoors. As they grew older, Thomas seemed to tease and bait his older brother, sometimes excessively, although William took it all good-naturedly.

"By the mid-eighties, both boys were in their early twenties, and William was obviously being groomed by his father to assume the duties of running the business, as well as someday becoming the next Earl. Although Mycroft made it clear that younger Thomas always knew that there would be a place for him in managing the textile mills, he seemed to resent it, as well as the fact that simply because he was younger, he was not able to inherit the title or much of the estate.

197

"As the young men grew older, Thomas's anger at his long-suffering and patient older brother continued to grow. On many occasions, Thomas picked fights with William, seemingly for no reason at all. During one of these, Thomas worked himself into such a rage that he grabbed a nearby pair of scissors and stabbed William in the arm. The family was shocked, but William kept insisting that it was an accident, and nothing further came of the matter.

"Throughout this time, William continued to be shaped for his future position, learning both the business and his responsibilities as a future earl. By the late eighties, William became engaged to be married to the younger daughter of a minor nobleman from Surrey.

"Unknown to anyone else at the time, including the young lady, Thomas himself had been interested for a while in William's new fiancée, although there was never any sort of real contact between the two. However, William's announced engagement was enough to inflame Thomas's jealousy even more. While William continued to prepare for his future, Thomas brooded about the house, sometimes disappearing for days at a time before returning smelling of drink. His parents, who loved him greatly, did not know what to do, and could not understand his growing rage at what he felt was an unfair arrangement. In particular, his mother seemed to suffer more and more as Thomas became increasingly wild and angry.

"These matters had continued for a number of years, until one night, not long after the engagement was announced, William became violently ill. His parents feared for his life for several days before he eventually recovered. As he rested weakly in his bed, the doctor spoke to the Earl and his wife, informing them that he believed that William had been poisoned. This was later confirmed through a privately hired chemist. The doctor did not know what circumstances might have led to this poisoning, but he felt that it must have been intentional due to the substance used, arsenic. However, he agreed not to call the police, and to let the Earl handle the matter.

"The Earl thought for several days, watching Thomas's behavior throughout that time. It soon became obvious to him that Thomas knew something about the poisoning. Finally he could avoid it no longer, and the Earl asked Thomas if he could offer any information about the matter. To his surprise, Thomas readily confirmed that he had poisoned William, although he said it was not his intention to kill him. Rather, it was just to scare William, and that it had all been a brotherly joke. However, the longer Thomas talked, the more he worked himself into a rage, and the Earl was soon convinced that the poisoning had indeed been a murder attempt.

"When William was better, the Earl called in his wife and sons, and explained that he had given the matter a great deal of thought. It was with a heavy heart that he had decided that he had no choice but to send Thomas away. He could not have his own younger son arrested and prosecuted, but he also could not let the younger son try to kill the older.

"The family was shocked and dismayed, especially the boy's mother, who sobbed with grief. William himself argued to let Thomas stay. Thomas simply sat, stunned and feeling betrayed, in spite of the fact that he himself had tried to kill his own brother. When his father announced that he had arranged for Thomas to move to America, and to join the Rugby colony, Thomas simply stood, bowed, and left the room. He packed and moved out that night.

"It was several days, however, before Thomas was scheduled to depart. He seemed to be in perfect agreement with the plan, and was visited several times by both his father and William. The meetings seemed to be cordial, but strained. On the night before his departure, Thomas attended a dinner at the family home, where the participants were civil, if somewhat saddened and subdued by events. Thomas said goodbye to his father and weeping mother, and reluctantly shook hands with his brother before departing.

"The next morning, a pair of prostitutes presented themselves at the home of William's fiancée. They proceeded to relate a vile – and totally spurious – tale about their supposed long-standing relationship with William. One claimed to have married William the previous year in Penzance, while the other said she had proof that she had borne William a child. The women stated that unless they received one thousand pounds, they would relate their story to the press.

"Of course, no blackmail was paid. The fiancée's father contacted the Earl, who quickly showed that the rumor was an ugly lie. Further investigation, in the form of arresting the prostitutes and learning their story, revealed that they had been hired by Thomas several days before his departure, and coached specifically in whom to approach and what to say in order to ruin William's reputation.

"William was absolved of the lies, but it came out what his own brother had tried to do to him. William attempted to reconcile with his fiancée. However, the young woman was shocked and scandalized, nonetheless. Within days, the engagement was called off.

"At the same time the prostitutes were relating their fabricated story, Thomas was boarding a train to the coast, where he would catch a ship to America."

The trees had begun to thin as we listened to Holmes's story. The ground around us flattened into fields, many overgrown, but some with occasional early summer crops reaching toward the sunshine. I thought of the happy family with whom we had stayed the night before, and felt all the more the sadness of the Earl's family, and how it had been hurt by one young man's jealousy and anger.

"My brother, Mycroft, was a longtime friend of the Earl, and during this time he learned some of the Earl's difficulties," Holmes continued. "The next time the Earl was in London, Mycroft made a point of inviting him to dinner, where the whole story came out.

"Thomas arrived in America, and proceeded to Rugby as planned. I suppose one might expect that a person of Thomas's nature would have done something else instead, possibly falling into hard times, and certainly not followed through on his father's plan to join a rural agricultural colony. But Thomas appeared to be willing to give his new future a chance. The distance between himself and England, and his family, appeared to calm him. He arrived at Rugby, and was soon a hard-working and respected member of the community.

"Not much is known specifically of Thomas over the next few years. He seems to have fit in well with his peers, been active in the community events and opportunities, and generally managed to make a new home here. In the meantime, the Earl's family was devastated. William was heartbroken, both at the loss of his future wife, as well as by the treacherous actions of his brother. He was a good man, and could not understand why his brother, whom he unconditionally loved so much, hated him so, for no comprehensible reason. Thomas's mother seemed to age overnight, and she became ever-more weaker. Her health had never been good during the best of times, and Thomas's actions and subsequent departure had accelerated her declining condition. The Earl was in a similar plight, as worry for both his wife and William wore him down as well.

"In the meantime, Thomas built a home in Rugby, married, and had a child. His new wife was the daughter of one of the other colonists, who had brought his family here in the early days. Finally, Thomas seemed to have found a place to be happy. However, by this time, the early nineties, the colony itself was somewhat in decline, and Thomas's luck was about to change. In late ninety-two, his wife took a sudden fever and died. He was alone after only a year of marriage, and forced to raise his very young child by himself. The community attempted to step in and help, but the death of his wife seems to have reawakened the old Thomas. He became bitter and withdrew from the community. His house fell into disrepair, and as time went on, it became obvious that his child suffered from some sort of long-term, debilitating illness. Thomas began to feel cursed, and he would often tell whomever would listen that it was the fault of his family, back in England. His rants soon made him so unpopular that the rest of the residents began to avoid him whenever possible.

"The Earl had managed, with Mycroft's help, to keep track of Thomas in the colony, and he was initially cheered that Thomas was living a successful life. When he became aware of the death of Thomas's wife, as well as the poor health of the grandchild that he had never seen, he resolved to do something to help his estranged son.

"He discussed the matter with Mycroft for some time, and it was finally decided to offer passage to Thomas and his child back to England, with the promise of forgiveness and a fresh start. Should Thomas not wish to leave his new life in America, the Earl was prepared to send him a small fortune in order to improve his circumstances. This was in the spring of 1893, and Mycroft explained to the Earl, in confidence of course, that I was not actually dead. In fact, I was working on something for Mycroft in the southeastern United States at that moment, and Mycroft would be happy to divert my path in the direction of Rugby if the Earl wished me to relay the message.

"The Earl graciously accepted the offer, and Mycroft then sent a message to me. He included a narrative of the family history with the packet he dispatched to me in New Orleans. And that is how I ended up in Rugby the first time.

"I do not recall exactly how I reached Rugby that day. It may have been by way of that town you mentioned yesterday, Willie. Rockwood, I believe you said. In any case, I did not approach from the direction we are traveling this morning. My route was much more genteel, arriving by rail in the small town, and then riding in a well-kept carriage down a tree-lined road, passing the occasional fine home.

"In those days, Rugby had somewhat passed its glory days, but it was still a showplace, with several hundred fine houses of varying architectural styles. I took a few minutes to walk around the streets, admiring this plucky British colony. I examined the library and its proud collection of over seven thousand volumes. I was quite amused to see several periodicals with your stories in them, Watson.

"Eventually I asked my way to Thomas Sexton's residence. Even without directions I fancy that I could have identified it. It was much more rundown than the neighboring houses, with weeds growing in the yard, pickets missing from the fence, and peeling paint and bare patches on the house boards.

"I had knocked several times with no response before I finally heard the sound of movement deep within the house. The door flew open to reveal a man who appeared to be in his forties, although I knew that he was only in his early thirties. A stale sour smell rolled out of the house, and behind the man I could see that all the curtains and blinds had been drawn, leaving this house in a depressing midday darkness.

"I introduced myself, and asked if I was speaking to Thomas Sexton.

" 'Yes,' he replied, 'and if it's about the bill for the medication, I'll tell you the same thing I told your employer. You'll get paid when I get the money, and if you do anything to withhold the medicines in the meantime, I'll see you are all held responsible for what happens!'

"I quickly explained that his assumption was mistaken, and that I was not there about payment for medication. Rather, I had been sent by his father, the Earl, to ask if he would not consider returning home. Failing that, I let him know that his father was prepared to offer him a substantial amount of money to ease his current conditions.

"He was silent for several moments, staring past me. Finally, he said softly, 'Does my brother still live?'

" 'Yes,' I replied. 'He has never married, and spends his time alternately between helping with your father's affairs and doing good works.'

" 'Then,' he said, taking a step back, 'You can tell them both to go to hell.' With that he shut the door. As I heard him turn to walk away, his muffled voice came through the door. 'And you, too!'

"I knocked several times more on the door, and walked around the house, pounding on the back door as well, but there was never any answer. I went back several times that same afternoon and evening, again with no response. I spoke to several people in town, and they confirmed that Thomas's condition was becoming somewhat strained, and that his baby son appeared to be suffering from some sort of wasting illness. I wrote a letter to Thomas, explaining again his father's offer and urging him to accept it. I then took some of the money I had with me and spoke to the chemist, paying the outstanding debt for the child's medicines, as well as arranging the purchase of additional medication for several months into the future. I also let him know the address in England of Thomas's father, and told him that all debts would be taken care of if only the Earl were notified.

"There was nothing else that I could do. My schedule required that I return to New York as soon as possible, and I could not force Thomas Sexton to accept his father's charity. I continued on the next day, pursuing Mycroft's errands. At a later date, I was able to wire Mycroft my singular lack of success during the visit to Rugby.

"The next year, some months after my 'resurrection' and return to England, I happened to call on my brother at the Diogenes Club, only to find that he already had a visitor in the Stranger's Room, the only place in the entire club where conversation can occur. The visitor was William

202

Sexton, who was now the Earl of Nash following the death of his father a month or so before. Mycroft introduced me to the Earl as the man who had visited his brother in 1893. William was a pale, gray fellow, quite thin in a stooped, scholarly way. When he learned who I was, his face lit up with sudden color, and he grasped my hand, asking for every detail I could remember about his brother, Thomas.

"It saddened me to have to relate the circumstances in which I had found his brother, as well as the reception that I had received when relaying the Earl's offer. I considered withholding part of the story, but I was uncertain how much had already been told to him by Mycroft, and so I told him everything. He did not seem surprised, and the initial joy at meeting me faded into the persistent chronic sadness that hovered about the man.

"Later, after William had departed, Mycroft told me that William and Thomas's parents had died not long after I had visited Thomas in Rugby. Mycroft had not doubted that the sadness resulting Thomas's final rejection of them had led indirectly to their deaths. Over the next several years, after that meeting in the Stranger's Room, I heard of William, the current Earl, as he continued to perform the good charitable works that he had begun as a young man. He never married.

"I saw him again, one last time, not long after the end of the War. I was traveling near Frome, and my name appeared in the newspaper, against my express wishes, in connection with a trifling matter there. The next day, I received a small note at the inn where I was staying, from William. He stated that he had seen my name in the paper, and asked me to visit him."

By this time, we had arrived in Rugby. It had been over forty years since the optimistic little community had been founded. After the death of the founder in the mid-nineties, a slow malaise and decline had obviously settled on the area. Now, there were only a few dozen standing houses. There was no inn, and no one building that seemed to serve as a center of the community. Holmes paused in his story for a moment, and we all took a few moments to look around. None of the residents seemed to be outside, and we felt the illusion that we had the place to ourselves. Holmes looked into the distance, toward a church steeple rising above trees in the early afternoon haze. "Drive that way," he said.

We rode in silence for a few minutes, before Holmes resumed speaking. "At my last meeting with William, he informed me that he was dying. His life, he felt, had been a good one, but it had been full of regret at the pain caused by the separation from his brother, whom he loved but could not understand. He did not know why Thomas had hated him so, and he knew that now he never would know, at least not in this world. In spite of his brother's rejection, William had continued to keep track of Thomas since that day we spoke at the Diogenes Club in 1894. He told me some of what had happened since, and that Thomas had remained in Rugby. It was William's wish that I would pass on a message to his brother, should I ever find myself in this part of the world again.

"I let him know that it was highly unlikely I would ever be returning to Rugby. He said he understood that, but just in case, he wished me to promise him that I would relay the message. 'Promise me, Mr. Holmes,' he whispered, a man wasted by illness, lying alone in a large bed on bright, sunlit sheets. 'I don't know whom else that I could ask.' He fumbled on the bedside table and gave me an object, folding my fingers around it with his own. 'Take that to him. So he will know what you say is true.'

"I promised him. I told him that if it were ever possible I would relay the message, never believing that I would ever be back here to do so."

Willie pulled the truck to a stop beside the old church. Opening the door and dropping to the ground, Holmes said, "When I knew that we were coming to North Carolina, I brought the object with me, thinking we might have an opportunity to travel here as well."

Willie and I were standing on the ground beside him, as he turned to walk away. For one shocked instant, I thought I might understand. What if Thomas had redeemed himself, and found some worth in his life? What if he was the minister at this little church? What if he had made up for the pain he had caused for his family, doing good works in this small forgotten village?

I began to see that my hope was wrong when Holmes made no effort to enter the church. Instead, he walked along the side of the building, and I began to feel a little cold inside, in spite of the sunshine.

"William had kept track of Thomas," Holmes said, over his shoulder as we followed. "He sent money here, but there was never any acknowledgement. None of the local creditors ever sent any bills to London, as I had instructed them to do during my original visit."

We had reached the back of the church, and Holmes led us through a small iron gate into a fenced, poorly tended cemetery. The decline of the community was painfully obvious when observing the leaning, overgrown tombstones and shabbily painted church. Holmes began to move systematically among the graves, stepping respectfully over them when necessary, intently reading the carvings on the markers. Some took longer to decipher than others. Finally, on the far side near the rear fence, in a somewhat sunken area below a ragged pine tree, he stopped in front of three stones. "Here," he said softly.

Although I did not want to go over there, I joined him. Willie was silent at my side. We stood on either side of Holmes, staring down at the three

204

lonely graves and their cheap stones. That area of the cemetery was in a low spot, and the rainwater runoff from the church and the rest of the cemetery had carved an eroded path across these graves. There was no grass here, simply exposed reddish earth, pebbled with countless bits of protruding gravel and mica.

The gravestone on the left was smaller and somewhat older, reading simply, "Jane Powell Sexton 1870-1892." In the center was a smaller stone, topped by a worn and moss-encrusted carving of a lamb. On it were the words "Joseph William Sexton, b.1892 d.1894 Beloved Son." To the right, a slightly larger stone read "Thomas Sexton, b.1863, d.1896 Far From Home."

Holmes fished in his pocket and produced a heavy gold ring, bearing some sort of family crest. He wiped it on his waistcoat, and turned it in the sun as he examined the results. Apparently satisfied that it was clean, he knelt down and pushed the ring into the loose soil of Thomas's ill-kept grave. Then he rose and stood silently for some minutes, his arms hanging and his hands folded together while he looked at the stone. Overhead, a mockingbird sang with uncontrolled joy in the June sunshine.

"Your brother sent you a message, Thomas," Holmes finally said, speaking softly but clearly. "He loves you. He always did." After another minute, he added, "And he forgives you."

Holmes turned and walked away. Willie soon followed, but it was several minutes before I joined them. We climbed in the truck and drove away.

The Adventure of the
Madman's Ceremony
HOLMES AND WATSON IN TENNESSEE (PART II)

"We really are quite unaware of so much that happens around us," stated Mr. Sherlock Holmes, as we sat in a lurching truck moving through the surrounding forest. We had been discussing the unseen events that were occurring in the all-encompassing woods during every minute, as animals, insects, water creatures, and microscopic beasts struggled, lived and died in their own epic dramas that would never be known or recorded by man.

Although I understood that Holmes's statement referred to the conversation we were having then, his words could well have applied to the small town we would soon visit. There, the residents were completely unaware of the sinister events threatening to take place within days, or that evil itself was about to be revealed in their midst.

As I have related elsewhere, Holmes and I traveled to the United States in May and June of 1921*. While waiting for events to conclude during our initial investigation in Linville, North Carolina, Holmes and I spent nearly two weeks traveling in eastern Tennessee. It was during the first part of this visit that I was able to become acquainted with a distant relative, Rebecca Watson Marcum, and her family, living in one of the northern Tennessee border counties.

After meeting with my distant American cousins, Holmes and I had been taken through the nearly untouched wilderness by Rebecca's son, Willie, to a wayside train station in the small town of Rockwood, Tennessee. Along the way, we had made a short stop in Rugby so that Holmes could fulfill an old promise.

Rugby was started in the eighteen-eighties as a social experiment, where younger sons of the British upper classes could come and work and live in an agrarian community while retaining the civilization and culture of their forebears in England. The effort was failing by the mid-eighteen-nineties, and at the time we passed through, only a few houses were left of the once-thriving colony

EDITOR'S NOTE: See "Sherlock Holmes and the Brown Mountain Lights", edited by James McKay Morton (Mountain Living Magazine,1977-78), and *www.carolina.cc/sherlock.html*. See also "The Affair of the Brother's Request" in this volume.

The day was turning toward a pleasant afternoon as we passed through Harriman, having wandered through more of the same rugged and dramatic landscape that we had traversed that morning. Willie explained that Harriman had originally been founded as a temperance community. It was another attempt at a wilderness Utopia, much like Rugby, where we had been visiting just a few hours before. The original inhabitants of Harriman had soon failed in their purpose, but the town remained, apparently surviving due to its proximity to the coal trains that regularly passed through.

Willie indicated that it might interest us to visit in Harriman for a day, after having seen Rugby, but I could tell that Holmes was ready to return to Knoxville. Soon we reached the train station in nearby Rockwood.

We stopped on the main road by the station, seeing more cars than we had the previous day in Oneida, where we had arrived to meet Willie and his family. The town was laid out alongside the railroad tracks, which traversed from east to west at the base of a great mountain that loomed over the northern horizon. At the top were numerous rocky crags, hardly covered by the scrub trees that managed to root there. I was certain that the view from those heights would be wonderful, but at my age, I would never think of attempting the climb. Unless there was an unseen, easier way to the top, I doubt if many of the residents ever did.

We were in time to catch the last train of the day back to Knoxville. I tried to give Willie money in order to stay at some local lodgings for the night, as I felt that it was too late for him to return through the woods to his parents' home. He did agree that he would stay in town, but he refused to take any of the money both Holmes and I urged upon him. Finally, we said our goodbyes as the train seemed ready for imminent departure.

"A fine young man," said Holmes as we found our seats in the half-filled carriage. "You can be proud of your relations in the colonies, doctor." I agreed, and we did not speak again for several hours, as we each settled in for the long journey and prepared to read the newspapers purchased before boarding the train.

We reached Knoxville after dark, and again stayed at the small hotel near the river, as we had done several nights earlier. After finding something to eat, I returned to my room, while Holmes decided to explore the small city by night. After urging him to be careful, we separated. I went to bed early, somewhat sore from the past two days of riding in a truck over very uneven terrain.

A knock on my door the next morning revealed Holmes, as neat as ever, and apparently completely unscathed by his explorations of the previous evening. "Good morning, Watson," he cried. "Ready for breakfast?"

"An old military man never turns down the chance for a meal," I replied. "A soldier never knows when the next one might be."

"Oh, I venture to say that we shall safely remain in civilized territory for a day or so," he replied.

After breakfast, we strolled up the street for several blocks, and down a side street toward what sounded like a great deal of activity. Rounding a corner, we saw the city's market house, doing only moderate business on this mid-week morning. Various vendors were set up throughout the site, dealing in vegetables, poultry and meat, and other farm products.

"Not quite Covent Garden Market, is it?" I asked with a smile.

"Indeed," replied Holmes, before stepping away for a moment to speak with a heavy-set and jolly man selling honey. While he and Holmes had a short and esoteric discussion of joys and sorrows of keeping an apiary, I explored the adjacent stalls. I discovered a little old woman selling a confection called a fried pie. It appeared to be some sort of bread-like crust, folded over a mashed fruit filling. The edges were pressed closed, and the entire thing was fried in oil and then covered with a sprinkling of sugar. In spite of the fact that I had just eaten breakfast, I purchased one of the apple pies. While the woman watched, I devoured it in three bites. I smiled my pleasure, and she simply nodded.

"You have pie filling on your mouth," said Holmes, joining me.

Wiping my lips with my handkerchief, I urged him to try one of the pies, as well. He selected a peach pie, which I had not noticed. As he finished his pie and announced that it was delicious, I purchased another peach pie for myself.

"For later," I said. Then I noticed that Holmes had made a purchase as well.

"For comparative purposes?" I asked, nodding toward the small bottle of honey that he held.

"I am curious," he replied, "about the taste of honey gathered from American clover by American bees. As you know," he continued, as we walked out of the market, "the flavor of honey is affected by the flowers from which the bees gather nectar. You may also recall the matter several years ago when I discovered that Jonas Finley had been poisoned with honey made by bees that collected solely from poisonous plants."

As we walked, Holmes asked if I had any objections to remaining in the local area for a few days. "We are not due back in Linville for a while, and I have some research that I can do here, if it suits you."

"By all means," I answered. "I will visit the local college again, and perhaps see some of the other sites in and around the area."

For several days I did just that. Holmes spent his days at the University of Tennessee, located less than a mile west of Knoxville, while I looked at some of the downtown buildings. On one afternoon, I hired an automobile and traveled west out of town, along an excellently engineered rural road, admiring the well-tended farms and occasional larger houses. On the second afternoon I stopped at a fine old brick house, ten or eleven miles from town, with the intention of asking for some water. I ended up visiting for several hours with the gracious hosts, learning some of the more interesting details of Knoxville's history, as well as that of the house where I was visiting. It was reputedly haunted by the ghost of a man killed it he Civil War. I saw no signs of him, however, and when I mentioned it to Holmes that night, he simply scoffed.

On the morning of the fourteenth of June, a Tuesday as I recall, Holmes asked if I had any objections to moving our base of operations slightly south. "None at all," I replied, setting my coffee cup down on the breakfast table. "May I ask why?"

"Just a little more research," he replied. "I have spent the past several days examining some of the American newspapers for the last few years. The University library has an excellent selection, and my researches were as easily carried out here in this picturesque little town as they would have been elsewhere.

"Yesterday I received a message, forwarded from England, from an old acquaintance, Mrs. Mary Thaw, widow of the famed Pittsburgh railroad mogul and philanthropist."

"The wife of William Thaw?" I asked. "Wait," I said. "Surely she is not the mother of the infamous Harry K. Thaw?"

"One and the same," Holmes replied. "You know of the case?"

"I followed the news reports of the murder and subsequent trial with some interest. It was in 1906, I believe. You were living in Sussex by then. Isn't Thaw still in a hospital for the insane?"

"Yes, for at least the past five years."

"Don't tell me that you know Mrs. Thaw due to some sort of involvement in the murder of Stanford White?"

"Thankfully, I had no involvement in that seamy affair," Holmes said.

I recalled the details of the case quite clearly, in spite of the fact that they had taken place a number of years before. Mrs. Thaw's son, Harry K. Thaw, had grown up a troubled and sometimes violent young man. In his early thirties, he had become increasingly unstable, and he irrationally blamed more and more of his problems on a young architect, Stanford White. His paranoia increased, as did his anger toward White, although as I understood it at the time, White was probably innocent of any questionable actions toward Thaw. At some point in the early 1900's, Thaw fell in love with a chorus girl named Evelyn Nesbit, who had been romanced in the past by White.

Thaw began to pay frequent visits to the girl, spending a great deal of money on her, and taking her to Europe on several occasions. Over several years he begged her repeatedly to marry him, but she always refused. Eventually, however, he overcame her resistance and they were wed. In part, this occurred because Harry Thaw's mother begged Evelyn to marry her son, as she hoped it would be some sort of stabilizing influence on him.

Harry Thaw continued to show the same instability that he had displayed his whole life. After marriage, he appeared to lose interest in Evelyn, often traveling for long periods without her. Finally, in early 1906, Harry and Evelyn went together to Europe. On their return to New York, they happened to see Stanford White at a restaurant. This seemed to reawaken Harry's jealousy. Harry learned that White would be attending a show that evening, a performance that the Thaws were already planning to see. That night, Harry wore a heavy black overcoat to the theatre, and refused to take it off, in spite of the evening's heat.

He wandered erratically through the audience during the performance, approaching White several times before veering off. Eventually, at the end of the show, he approached White and shot him three times in the face. White was killed instantly.

The crowd had initially believed the entire incident to be a joke, or part of the show. Harry Thaw walked through the crowd with the gun held high above him, collected Evelyn, and departed. Soon Thaw was arrested. His first trial ended in a jury deadlock. Mrs. Thaw, Harry's mother, urged Evelyn to testify at the second trial that Stanford White had abused her, and that Harry had killed White in an effort to protect her. Evelyn was promised a great deal of money and a divorce from Harry if she so testified. Evelyn did so, and Harry was found not guilty by reason of insanity. He was placed in a mental hospital for the criminally insane, where he resided for several years before his release. In the meantime, Evelyn was granted her divorce.

I recalled that the events of the White murder had been heavily reported in the British press at the time. Seamy murders amongst the American rich were always of great interest to the masses, on both sides of the Atlantic. The later details of Thaw's life were less clear, but I thought I recalled one further fact.

"Wasn't Thaw arrested a year or so after his release for some other violent act?" I asked.

"Yes," replied Holmes, "He was convicted of assaulting and horsewhipping a teen-aged boy. He was again judged insane and returned to an asylum, as you mentioned, where he currently resides."

"Surely Mrs. Thaw does not want you to look into the matter of her son's current conviction?" I asked.

"Luckily, no," said Holmes, "and I would not do so if she did ask. I have no interest in becoming involved in the lifelong madness of Harry K. Thaw. People will be discussing him for years, and I do not wish to have my name associated with him.

"Mrs. Thaw has something much more sedate in mind for me. It seems that she has pledged a large amount of money to a local college near here, in order that they might construct a new building. However, some whispers of possible corruption at the institution have reached her ears in Pennsylvania, and after learning that I was nearby, she asked if I would discreetly look into the matter."

"How did she know that we were here?" I asked.

"It seems that we were observed by someone a few days ago when we were in Blowing Rock, at the Green Park Inn. This person, a crony of Mrs. Thaw's, recognized us, and happened to mention that we were in North Carolina. Mrs. Thaw, using those speedy and efficient resources available to the very rich, verified the fact by cabling England. She determined that a message sent there could be forwarded to us here in America. She then sent a wire, which followed until it found us. I sent a return message, informing her that we were indeed in the United States, although we had now moved from North Carolina to Knoxville, Tennessee. She replied that it was very fortunate that we were here, as the college she wishes me to investigate is located only fifteen or twenty miles south of where we are seated now."

"How could a small college in this area have attracted the charity of a rich Pennsylvania family?" I asked.

"According to Mrs. Thaw," Holmes said, "one of the former presidents of the school approached Mr. Thaw in the 1860's. At that time, the school had been closed due to the Civil War, and the president was trying to raise funds to reopen it. Thaw sent a check for $1,000, which was used to buy the land where the current college is located. Thaw became very interested in helping the school, and gave a number of donations over the years, until his death in 1889. After that, his widow has continued to contribute, most recently giving a substantial amount of money to construct the large building on campus as a tribute to her late husband."

Pushing back from the table, I said, "That sounds like a pleasant way to spend a few days. Do you wish to leave this morning?"

Holmes was indeed ready to depart. Within a few minutes we had packed and checked out, and were on the local train headed south for the short journey.

"How did you initially come to know Mrs. Thaw," I asked, looking nervously down at the river as the train crossed over the narrow trestle bridge from the city side on the north bank to the rugged bluff on the south side.

"In 1913, when I was traveling in the United States under the name Altamont, I spent some time in various cities, cementing my reputation as an Irish radical. Starting in Chicago, I traveled through numerous towns, including Pittsburgh, Pennsylvania. While there, I happened to come across a plot to sabotage some of the mining facilities and related railway connections. These happened to be owned by the Thaw family. I could not warn anyone as Altamont without taking the chance that my disguise would be penetrated. In the end, I slipped into the Thaw home, where I revealed my true identity to Mrs. Thaw. I can tell you that I had a few tense moments as that feisty woman held me at gunpoint while I urgently tried to explain why I was there.

"Once she understood what I was telling her, and more importantly, believed me, she wasted no time. She set her own forces in motion, quickly ending the plot, and all without ever revealing my own involvement. Over the years, we have corresponded sporadically, but she has never asked me to help her professionally until now. Thankfully, she did not seek to involve me in any of her son's defenses. I would have refused, and her goodwill toward me would have evaporated."

The train had picked up speed, and the cars settled down to a steady rocking as we left the points and junctions of the city behind us. The morning was beautiful, somewhat windy, but with skies as blue as I had ever seen them. It seemed no time at all that we were slowing. I expected to reach the station momentarily, but our fellow passengers showed no signs of preparing to disembark. I soon realized that the train had slowed to navigate a complicated series of parallel and intersecting tracks. In the distance I could see some of these running toward a large factory made of brick, belching smoke into the air from its tall stacks.

"What is that?" I wondered.

"I have no idea," replied Holmes. "I really do not know anything about this town we are visiting, although it has a pleasant enough name: Maryville."

The town, with its inclusion of my dear deceased wife Mary's name in it, saddened me for just a moment. Although Mary, my second wife, had been gone since 1893, I still missed her. My pain was increased by the recent passing of my third wife earlier in the current year. This entire trip to America had been partially due to Holmes's efforts to distract me in order to help me move past my mourning.

Eventually we traversed the crazed pattern of tracks and pulled into a small station. It was a fairly new building, set between two lines of rails, with platforms constructed all around the building to provide access to the trains on either side. On one side of the building were several warehouses, surrounded by horse-drawn wagons, automobiles, and trucks.

As our group disembarked, I noticed an equal number of people on the opposite platform, apparently waiting to depart on the return train to Knoxville. Everyone on our train had departed at the station, and I watched as it left, the empty carriages rocking as they were pulled away.

"This would seem to be the last stop on the line," I deduced. As Holmes nodded, a young energetic man stepped up to us.

"Right you are," he said. "The engine goes right up the line there to a turntable, where it will be reversed, re-attached to the cars, and returned to Knoxville." He stuck out his hand to me, shaking vigorously before moving on to Holmes. "Ray Rathbone," he said. "I'm pleased to meet you." He stepped back and looked at us. "You sound like you're from England," he said. We confirmed it, stating our names. He appeared to have no recognition of us, replying, "If you need anything here in town, I'm your man. I drive a taxicab," he said, jerking his thumb over his shoulder at one of the automobiles parked beside the station, "and I'd be happy to take you wherever you want to go."

We stepped to the side as a group of passengers moved past us to the stairs down from the platform. They walked together in a strange shuffling manner, their eyes all downcast. Holmes appeared to study them as they descended from the platform and walked away, and then he looked at Rathbone for a moment before stating, "We are going to be in town for a few days, while I do some research at Maryville College. Are we close? Can you recommend somewhere to stay near the college?"

Rathbone nodded. He was a stocky man, about twenty years of age. He was dressed in a worn white shirt and work pants, faded as well, but clean. His high hairline was damp in the morning heat, and he pulled out a handkerchief, running it across his brow, carefully avoiding the glasses with small, round, rimless lenses perched upon his nose.

"It's an easy walk from here to the college," he said. "Right up that hill, in fact. Usually it's only the students in the spring and fall, with their big trunks, that need any help getting there. As for a place to stay, well . . . " he said, and then faded into thought for a moment. "I know just the place," he exclaimed. Replacing the handkerchief in his pocket, he said, "I'll be happy to drive you there. It's about a mile past the college. I was just speaking to the woman who owns it this morning, and she said that she was thinking of renting out the little outbuilding behind her house. I'm sure she won't mind letting you use it for a few days. Right this way, gentlemen!"

We were led to an old Model T Ford, well on in years, but clean and excellently maintained. Rathbone stowed our few bags and held the doors as we entered. Within moments, we were bouncing across the tracks by the station and turning left onto the dirt street.

"You were right about this being the end of the rail line," Rathbone said. "We've only had an L&N spur from Knoxville to here for a few years. It's already changing things, though. The town is growing like crazy. Just two years ago, we got our first library, and an airplane even landed on a farm near here! We've started changing some of the street names to sound more like a city, and we even have a five-story building, which is more than you can say for most of the towns around here. Why, last year, our population grew to over thirty-seven hundred people."

As the vehicle bounced through several water-filled holes in the dirt street, Rathbone twisted the steering wheel from left to right, maneuvering his way out of town. "We just got a second fire truck," he said proudly. "In fact, Mayor Cox has even started talking about some sort of permanent road being built to Knoxville. I think it's a good idea, but a lot of people think it's a mistake. They say that ever since the railroad arrived here, we've started to grow too fast, and the whole nature of the area has changed."

On the left, fields stretched for a distance before revealing small residential neighborhoods in the distance. A group of buildings was prominent on our right as we motored past.

"There it is," said Rathbone, pointing to the buildings. Holmes, in the front seat, leaned his head, while I shifted in the rear seat to look out the right window. Almost immediately, we saw a tall white tower, topped with a flagpole flying the American flag. The tower was twenty or thirty feet tall, and rested centrally on a three-story red brick building. The bottom of the building was not visible, as our view was blocked by trees and bushes. On either side of the building were several wooden frame buildings, as well as a few brick structures of varying sizes. "That's Anderson Hall," said Rathbone. "That's the main building at the college. Those wooden buildings are dormitories for the students. There's a gymnasium, and a library, and some other buildings as well. In a minute you can see part of the college farm."

The road continued to climb slightly as we headed east, and in a moment we topped a low rise. In the distance, fifteen or twenty miles away, we could see the Smoky Mountains, as this part of the Appalachian range was named. The morning sun was over them, so they simply appeared to be one long, flowing, blue shape, where individual peaks seemed to blend together. In front of us, and quite a number of miles away, stood a mountain that looked to have three distinct and equal summits, sitting side by side. Rathbone noticed where I was looking and said, "Those are called 'The Three Sisters.' They're actually three separate mountains, well separated from each other, but the way they are lined up from this view, it appears that they are one mountain. And that," he said, gesturing to the right, "is the College Dairy Farm. The male students work there to earn money. Best milk and butter around."

"Male students?" Holmes said. "So the college is co-educational."

"That's right. The women work in the sewing shop. It just opened last year." He braked the car as we started down a shallowly-sloped hill.

"We're almost there now."

He negotiated a narrow one-lane bridge across a small stream that was joined on the south by a wide mere, filled with cattails and bobbing dragonflies. The bridge itself was about fifty feet in length. Holmes saw me notice it and smiled.

"It is rather like the bridge where Mrs. Gibson killed herself, is it not?"

"Indeed," I replied, recalling those events from so many years earlier.

Rathbone applied more power to the engine of his automobile, and we started up the slight hill on the other side of the stream. After another few hundred feet, we rounded a corner and saw a white two-story house, set back fifty feet or so from the road. Around it stretched several fields containing various crops, including young corn plants already standing a foot or so high. The fields extended behind the house for several hundred feet before joining a stand of trees that appeared to rise out of a lowland.

Parking the automobile in the drive, Rathbone opened our doors and led us onto the porch of the house. Before he could knock, the screened door was pushed open and a small woman stepped out with a welcoming smile. Rathbone introduced us, explaining that Holmes and I were from England, "to do some important research," he added mysteriously, and asked if the rooms that she had mentioned to him earlier in the day were available.

The woman, Mrs. Jones, stated that the rooms were available, and that they were located in the small building immediately behind her house and next to the barn. "If that's acceptable," she added. We readily agreed, and went with her to inspect the rooms.

I should add at this point that the woman's name was not actually Mrs. Jones. However, after the subsequent events that took place in Maryville, our temporary landlady recognized who we were, and she asked me to keep her name out of any future narrative that I might record of the matter. Honoring her wishes, I have changed her name to Jones. However, I must state that during the few days we stayed on her property, she was a most gracious hostess, and that we were fortunate to meet her.

About one hundred feet behind her house stood a large barn, with a small whitewashed cottage located to its right. The farm smell was strong here, both from the tilled soil of the nearby fields and from the livestock.

However, it was pleasant and clean, and Holmes seemed happy that he was within walking distance of the college. Mrs. Jones pointed out that her fields and those of the college farm joined one another, and Holmes would be able to walk to the school either by the main road, or on the trails that crossed the properties.

Arrangements were made with Mrs. Jones regarding the short rental of the cottage. No meals were included, although she would supply us with linens. We settled our debt with Rathbone and retrieved our things from his cab. Holmes stopped Rathbone before he could climb back into his automobile. "Are you aware of any distant relatives you might have in England?" he asked.

"Possibly," Rathbone said. "How come?"

"Simply curiosity," Holmes replied. "Several days ago, Watson and I stayed with some of *his* distant relations, and this morning after hearing your name, I recalled that I am somewhat distantly related myself to the Rathbone family*. I did not know if you might have some information relating to your family history."

"As a matter of fact, I do," replied Rathbone. "Or at least, my sister does. I'll speak to her tonight, and let you know what I find out. You'll be here a few days, you say?"

"Yes," said Holmes. "I look forward to seeing you again."

As we unpacked our few belongings, I asked Holmes his plans. "I will go over to the college this afternoon, in the guise of a researcher. Actually, meeting Rathbone was fortuitous. I will use our possible family connection as a reason to examine local genealogy records, while also checking to see if anything appears to substantiate Mrs. Thaw's suspicions of possible corruption at the school. And what are your plans, Watson?"

I pointed to a small table beneath the rear window, facing a southern view across the fields filled with verdant growth. Some of the distant mountains could be seen over the tops of the trees rising from the lowland. "I will sit there for a while, catching up on my journals. Then perhaps a walk."

"Excellent," said Holmes. "Then we shall meet tonight for dinner."

And with that, he turned and left.

---

* EDITOR'S NOTE: See "The Case of the Very Best Butter" *The New Adventures of Sherlock Holmes* Radio Show (April 18, 1948) in which Holmes tells Watson that he is distantly related to the Rathbones.

I stood for a moment before settling at the table. I spent a few minutes describing the events of the last few days within my journal. Soon, however, my memory returned to the small bridge we had recently crossed in order to reach this house. The bridge was very similar to the one where Mrs. Neil Gibson had died, back in early October 1900. The initial antagonism between Holmes and Gibson had dissolved following Holmes's brilliant solution of the case, and a warm friendship had developed between the two. Holmes and I admired the humanitarian impulses shown by Gibson after his marriage to his second wife. It had been several years since I had visited Gibson's estate, but as I sat at the small table, all the details of those days investigating the mystery of Thor Bridge came flooding back to me.

Recently I had published an account of "The Mazarin Stone" in *The Strand* magazine, and I resolved that the next manuscript to be submitted would be the account of Mrs. Gibson's death. I had no doubt that the public would be gratified to learn of the strange events on that peaceful country bridge.

I wrote for an hour or so, I suppose, before I recalled that Holmes and I had never eaten lunch. Wishing that Rathbone and his cab had not departed, I left and began to walk back toward town to begin my explorations with a midday meal.

We arrived in Maryville on a Tuesday. I spent the rest of the week leisurely exploring the town, while Holmes used his days at the college. On occasion he visited with several local civic leaders, bankers, and such, couching his relevant questions within innocent ones. Once he visited the new town library, but found it decidedly lacking in the materials he required. On Wednesday afternoon, I ended my day's rambles at the college library, a small, attractive brick building with a large stained-glass window.

Holmes was finishing up his research, and I spoke for a few minutes with the college minister, Reverend Stevenson. He pointed out a few of the campus buildings, including the site where initial construction had begun on Mrs. Thaw's donated building, which would be the largest on the college campus. Some of the walls were beginning to rise from the foundations, surrounded by scaffolding. As Holmes prepared to leave, Stevenson invited us to tea on Friday afternoon, at a small home that had been built in the woods adjacent to the college dairy farm.

Holmes and I walked by the half-completed building, making our way down the trail that passed through the college farm, going towards Mrs. Jones's house. I started to take the wrong trail before Holmes corrected me. "I have already explored this area," he said, pointing toward the direction I had initially chosen. "That trail goes to a spring house, not far

217

from the house where we are taking tea on Friday." He gestured to the numerous saplings growing within the fields around us.

"The college farm has only been in existence for two or three years, and it is already something of a failure," he said. "There are less than two dozen young men enrolled here who are involved in agricultural studies. There is talk at the college that within a year or so, the program will be discontinued, and this entire area will probably be allowed to return to woodland."

My own explorations had been pleasant, but rather without purpose. I spent several hours the first day walking along the main street, placed along a ridge-top, circled on three sides by the wide stream that seemed to be the initial reason for the town's location. I strolled through the nearby residential neighborhoods, before moving on to the college grounds, where I examined more closely the large, partially finished building being funded by Mrs. Thaw. I walked around the site, and then spoke for a moment with the construction supervisor, asking him about some strange openings in the ground next to the building's proposed foundation.

"Oh, it's one of them sinkholes, doctor," he said. "It happens a lot around here. There's limestone rock under this whole part of the county, and wherever you find limestone you'll find sinkholes." He gestured toward the low areas of the college farm behind us. "Down there you'll find lots of rocks sticking out of the ground, and some springs as well. There are numerous springs all along the bottom of the ridge where Main Street is built. This whole area is probably riddled with caves."

During my time walking about the town, I had noticed a number of small groups of people walking together, all displaying the same downcast mien that I had observed from the group at the train station the day we arrived. Talking with Rathbone one afternoon, I asked him if he knew anything about these people.

"Not really, doc," he said. "They've been showing up for a week or so. They get off the train and head out of town. I heard they're camping somewhere north of here. I suppose if they get to be any trouble they'll be asked to leave, but so far they're laying low."

On Thursday night, Mrs. Jones invited us to eat with her and her sons, a quiet group of young men who listened politely to our conversation with their mother before solemnly turning their attention to the food.

Later that evening, as Holmes and I strolled through the empty main street, I asked him if he was having any luck at finding indications of corruption.

"None, Watson. I suspect that Mrs. Thaw has simply become suspicious for no reason. Perhaps it is a function of her age. She is quite elderly now, you know." We stopped by an old brick church building, looking at the streetlights from the nearby main thoroughfare as they reflected off the building's windows. The structure was very much like other churches I had seen in England, and could have been picked up from any number of small British villages and placed here. The wind sighed through the tall trees growing within the adjacent cemetery.

"All has not been wasted, however," Holmes continued. "Rathbone stopped by yesterday with some of his sister's family papers. The connection between his family and mine is there, although somewhat convoluted. He did not seem to be as impressed with his English ties, however, as with those to a German family, which he can trace back much further."

Friday evening was spent at the small house on the college farm, inhabited by Reverend Stevenson and his wife. It was a pleasant brick building, with a high sloping roof, and much larger inside than it had seemed from without. I had an enjoyable time, and even Holmes appeared to be relaxed and in a good mood. The following day, I accepted an invitation from Stevenson to take a drive around the area, in order to see some of the more distant sites that I had missed during my strolls in town. Holmes chose to continue his research.

Stevenson showed me the locations of some of the original forts, or stations as they were called, that had been built by the first settlers to the area. Originally, the Cherokee had used this area, and in fact the great north-south Indian Warpath, stretching all the way from the northeastern United States to the far south, had passed through Maryville.

"A number of Indian attacks occurred at these forts. None matched the massacre of the British soldiers, however, in the mid-1700's."

Stevenson went on to explain that twenty or so miles south was an abandoned fort, Fort Loudoun, constructed well before the American Revolution, and manned for several years by British troops. The Cherokee Indians had held it under siege for a number of months before allowing the inhabitants to depart in safety, as long as they promised to return to England.

The troops, along with their families, had departed from the fort and traveled several miles before the Indians broke the agreement and massacred the entire British contingent. I was surprised to learn of this event, as I had always been under the impression that the American settlers' problems with Indians had taken place in the northeast, or later out west. I had grown up reading the works of Cooper, and later the stories of cowboys and Indians. When I had visited my relatives northwest of here several days earlier, the only mention of Indians had been the implication that they were ancient inhabitants, long gone by the arrival of the settlers.

219

Later in the afternoon, we motored north in his automobile, with the intention of seeing some of the marble quarries that lay along the Tennessee River. These had supplied some of the stone for several of the national buildings in Washington, D.C.. Off to the right I could see the large factory that I had observed on the day we arrived in town.

"That's the Aluminum Company," Stevenson said, pronouncing *aluminium* in the American fashion. "That is the largest factory building in the world. They manufactured their first aluminum last year." He explained that after the invention several years earlier of a process to produce relatively cheap aluminum from bauxite ore, a factory site was sought that would provide access to the abundant electricity necessary for the procedure.

The area north of Maryville was chosen due to its proximity to railways for transportation of the finished product. A hydroelectric dam was built many miles away, and electric lines were run across the countryside to the factory building. My minister friend showed his disgust as he related the story. "The dam was built in the mountains, making a mountain river into a lake, and using the water to power the electric generators. The community around the dam is known as Calderwood.

"When the Aluminum Company approached the state legislature for permission to incorporate a town, they provided a series of map coordinates where this town would be located. Everyone assumed that they would be incorporating the area around Calderwood. The new town was to be called 'Alcoa,' which stands for 'Aluminum Company of America.'

"What no one realized was that the map coordinates were not for Calderwood, the mountain town near the dam, but instead for a sizeable chunk of what we called 'North Maryville,' right over there around that factory," said Stevenson. "No one thought to actually look at a map to see where the new town would be, and the legislature approved it. Suddenly, the town of Maryville lost a third of its area, and had another town growing out of the top of it. This was all done, of course, so that any tax revenue generated by the place would go to the new company-owned town, and not to Maryville.

"I must admit," my new friend continued, "they are trying to make the place nice, for a company town. They've laid down streets, and built a number of houses, although many of them are completely identical to one another. There is talk of building parks there, as well. I suppose it will turn out all right. It's not as if anything would have been built there otherwise. The place was unofficially known as the 'Maryville Swamp.' Lots of groundwater there, poorly drained. I've even heard rumors of a cave or two."

The following Monday, Holmes continued his researches while I decided to visit Alcoa, and look more closely at the largest factory in the world. Little did I realize how the day would end. I walked into town, where I contracted with Rathbone to drive me to the factory in his cab.

He dropped me off and offered to wait, but I declined, wanting to explore for a while. I visited the main office of the great factory, and was given some slight information regarding the history of the aluminum separation process invented by Charles Hall, the company itself, and the decision to build a town here. However, I was soon given to understand that idle tourists were not encouraged, and I departed, intending to walk some among the nearby residential streets before returning to Mrs. Jones's farm.

As my new friend the minister had told me, many of the houses were identical to one another. They were all of wood frame construction, most only one story high. The entire area was clouded with the smoke from a hundred cook stoves and fireplaces. I noticed that several of the street names, Dalton, Maury, and so on, were named for famous scientists, while the significance of others, such as Vose, completely escaped me.

While strolling down Maury Street, I observed a young man standing in front of one of the rarer two-story houses, watering a young tree. All along both sides of the street, oak trees had been set out in rows several feet back from the roadway. In later years, I was certain that the tree-lined avenue would be quite beautiful as one traversed it. Now, however, the trees were little more than saplings.

The young man, probably in his early teens, spoke to me as I passed. I stopped and answered, complimenting him on the neighborhood and his house, which was well-kept. He informed me that his father was one of the company managers, and as such, was entitled to one of the larger two-story houses. At that moment a woman, obviously his mother, stepped out onto the porch. I introduced myself, and explained that I was exploring the neighborhood. "My name is Mrs. Wade," she said, "and this is my son, James." She graciously invited me in for some lemonade.

While Mrs. Wade stepped through the swinging door to the left of the fireplace, into the kitchen, I looked at the pleasant room. Stretching along the left side of the house, it had tall windows at the sides and rear. While somewhat dim this morning, I was sure it would be bright and cheerful in the afternoon. The house itself, a great square box, seemed to have only three rooms on the ground floor. The long formal parlor in which I sat took up the left half of the ground floor, while the other half contained the kitchen at the rear and a small dining room at the front of the house. The stairs must have been located somewhere behind the fireplace, between the kitchen and dining room.

The woman returned with the lemonade, and as we sat and talked, she asked polite questions about England. At some point during the conversation, I became aware that her son was becoming somewhat agitated. Finally, his mother could not ignore it any longer, and asked, "What *is* the matter, James."

He started to whisper, but she asked him to repeat it aloud. "He's Dr. Watson!" said the boy.

"Yes, that is his name."

"No, *the* Dr. Watson. Like in Sherlock Holmes!"

She looked at me anew, and raised an eyebrow, as if asking me to confirm or deny her son's statement. I acknowledged that I was that Dr. Watson, and stated that Holmes and I were visiting in town for a few days, but that we did not want knowledge of our stay to become widespread.

She thought for a moment, nodding to herself, and then stated, "Perhaps, since you are here, you and Mr. Holmes can offer an opinion on something that has been bothering me."

She proceeded to relate a tale so strange that I agreed to seek Holmes's help. She let me use her telephone. I managed to be connected to Maryville College, where I found someone willing to relay a message to Holmes, if he was still in the college library. In a while, Mrs. Wade's telephone rang. It was Holmes, to whom I repeated the basics of her story. Within twenty minutes, he was stepping to the curb in front of her house from Rathbone's cab. He indicated that Rathbone should wait.

Young James appeared to be stunned as he watched Holmes energetically walk up the front walk to the house. Mrs. Wade gave no such impression, ushering Holmes in and offering him lemonade and refreshments. When he had his glass in hand, I had her repeat for him what she had told me.

Essentially, her story concerned recent goings-on in a nearby clearing. "It has become something of a neighborhood park," she said, explaining that the aluminum company, which owned all the houses and property in the town, intended to improve the location eventually, "building recreational areas, and schools." In the meantime, however, the vast fields had remained a wide open space, cleared and mowed, but with numerous old-growth trees allowed to remain, shading the various havens created by the meandering brook that wandered through the tract.

"The small stream is formed from several springs that rise near a hillside in the center of the parkland. The hill is more of a small cliff, really. The largest of the springs, a rather wide sandy pool, is near this small cliff, which is something of a rocky outcropping exposed in the hillside.

"At the base of these rocks is a wide crack in the earth, extending back at a downward angle, out of sight and into the darkness. The crack extends thirty feet or more from left to right, and is only one or two feet in height at the entrance. A cold breeze blows from it, and animals shy away from the place. In fact, during the times I have walked there, I do not recall birds even sitting in the nearby trees to sing.

"As James can tell you, I often take strolls in the mornings, and I frequently go by the place of the springs and the cliff, to look at the wildflowers growing among the rocks. In spite of its eeriness, I have never felt any fear or nervousness about the place. I believe that a cavern of some sort begins there, and that would probably explain the excessive number of springs around this area. I have read something of geology, and I understand that areas such as this, with a large number of rocky outcroppings sticking up out of the ground, are indicators of high groundwater, as well as caves and sinkholes."

Holmes nodded. "It is known as a *karst* area."

"Exactly," said Mrs. Wade, nodding. "In any case, we have lived here for a couple of years now, and nothing has changed until just recently. In the last week or so, a great number of people have been arriving in town and making their way to that park, setting up campsites throughout the fields. They are quiet enough, I suppose, but they do not belong here. They have even taken to walking through our neighborhood, sometimes knocking on doors and asking if they can buy eggs or bread. I thought that Dr. Watson was one of them when I saw him talking to James earlier. I rushed out to send him away, and I was so relieved to learn that the doctor was not one of the strangers that I invited him in for lemonade.

"Several of the residents have complained to the company, which owns the land, but we were put off by Mr. Timmons, one of the managers who seems to have given them permission to camp there. He stated that they are part of a religious group, here to celebrate one of their holy days, and that once they are done they will go. Mr. Timmons's wife is said to be a member of that faith, and possibly Mr. Timmons is as well. It was because of this relationship that the strangers knew to come here in the first place, and why he gave them permission to stay here."

Holmes and I looked at one another. We had both seen some of the people to whom she referred over the last few days, as the groups were arriving in town. We had discussed them on several occasions, and one evening as we smoked our pipes I had told Holmes what Rathbone had said about the group camping somewhere north of town.

"I went walking there this morning, as I usually do," continued Mrs. Wade, "making my way around the edge of their camp. The people were somewhat standoffish, but friendly enough, and I spoke to one of the group's women. She said that the festival they are celebrating will culminate tomorrow morning at sunrise. She implied there is something special about this particular gathering, and that they do not assemble this way every year.

"As I was leaving, I saw some of her laundry, a pile of folded white robes. A closer look showed that the robes were hooded, and embroidered on the shoulder was this emblem."

She leaned forward and picked up a piece of paper, turned face down until now on a side table. "I tried to draw it when I returned home." She held it up, showing Holmes the sketch of a symbol that I had instantly recognized when viewing it a few minutes earlier. Seeing it had been enough to make me reach Holmes immediately.

Holmes's eyes widened minutely, but he made no other movement or comment. Mrs. Wade leaned forward and handed him the paper, which he brought closer to his eyes. I knew what he was seeing.

Drawn on the paper was an egg-shaped circle, surrounded by the squeezing coils of a snake. The wide part of the egg was at the top, and hovering over it was the serpent's head. His tail jutted from the smaller end at the bottom. Shaded onto the oval behind the body of the snake were a pair of large dark spots, giving the impression of eye sockets, and making the egg into the death-head of a human skull. Around the outside edge of the oval were a series of small faint crosses.

Pointing to them, Holmes asked, "What do these small x's represent?"

"The stitching on the white robes was in much greater detail than I was able to draw," said Mrs. Wade. "I am not much of an artist, I'm afraid. There were actual diamond-like patterns on the snake's body, and its face wore an expression of crafty evil, almost gleeful and proud. Around the edge of the skull were a series of smaller symbols, rather like letters, but nothing like the alphabet that I know."

Holmes pulled a pencil from his pocket and wrote for a moment at the bottom of the page. "Did these markings resemble the embroidered writing you saw?" he asked, holding up what he had produced.

Mrs. Wade leaned closer and examined the sheet. "That looks quite similar to what I saw. Of course, I cannot say for sure."

Holmes nodded. "I am fairly certain that what I have written is correct, combined as it is with the skull and serpent design which you copied. I have made a small study of these symbols in connection with a past case. The writing is Ogham, an ancient Celtic script sometimes used by the Druids."

I had also learned something of the symbols on Mrs. Wade's paper years before, during an investigation in which Holmes and I were called to Stonehenge in order to determine who had chalked the serpent drawing

224

on various menhirs in the ancient ruins. At the time, Holmes had taught me that the representation of a snake coiled around an egg was one of the ancient symbols of the creation of the universe, used variously by Egyptians, Indians, Druids, and even Freemasons. However, sometimes the symbol was polluted, changing the egg to a skull. I had no doubt that the text written by Holmes said exactly what had been written years before on the great monoliths at Stonehenge. Loosely translated, "For new life, first death."

Holmes looked at it for another moment. We both knew that the symbol, combined with the writing, was the ceremonial badge of death. I saw that he wished to pull out his pipe and smoke, but he would not ask to do so here in the Wade's home. Finally he looked up at me.

"Tomorrow is June twenty-first," he said.

I nodded. "At sunrise?" I asked.

"Most likely." Turning to Mrs. Wade, he asked, "Do you know of anyone that has gone missing in the last day or so? Any children? Any animals or pets?"

Mrs. Wade said, slowly, "No, no, I'm not aware of anything like that."

James interrupted, "What about Tyler?"

"Oh, well, there is Tyler," Mrs. Wade replied, with a small laugh. "Tyler Roberts. He's a young boy, several years younger than James. He lives a few doors up the street. He often disappears overnight. He likes to camp and hike. He's a very self-sufficient boy, and his mother has learned to stop worrying when he is gone. He wanders off all the time. I was not aware that he was away right now, but it is not unusual."

"He is gone," James said. "His mother asked me this morning if I had seen him. Usually he only stays away overnight, but he has been gone for two nights now. I think she is starting to get a little worried. And also, Mrs. Floyd up the street said that their dog is missing. Maybe it just ran away, but Mr. Holmes did ask about any missing pets."

"How old is Tyler," asked Holmes. "Please describe him."

"He is about twelve," said Mrs. Wade. "Small for his age, but very strong and scrappy. His skin is quite tanned and dark, but his hair is blonde, almost white. His skin is often covered in one place or another with scrapes and scratches from whatever outdoor mischief he is into."

Holmes checked his watch, and then stood. "Mrs. Wade, I believe that what you have described in the nearby park is a gathering of individuals who are up to no good. I regret that I have to ask this, but I would like you to keep secret the fact that Dr. Watson and I have visited you this morning, and also what you have told us. Please do not discuss with anyone what you have seen in the park. I'm afraid that I must ask you and your son not to tell even your husband."

225

"That would be fine," said Mrs. Wade. "When I tried to talk to him about it before, he gave me to understand that I was simply being a busybody, and that in any case the people would soon be gone."

"Thank you," said Holmes. "Dr. Watson and I are going to discuss this matter with the local police. I think it is quite serious. I would like your permission to take James with us. In case we have any further questions, he will be at hand to answer them. He may be with us until tomorrow, if that is all right."

James immediately showed his eager agreement, and Mrs. Wade had no objection, although she did seem somewhat worried, and repeatedly made James promise to stay out of the way and to stay out of trouble. Thanking her again, and reminding her not to mention our visit, we departed in Rathbone's waiting cab.

When we directed Rathbone to take us to the police, he explained that the new city of Alcoa only had the beginnings of a police department, and that the city of Maryville had just appointed a police chief for the first time that year. "N.L. Brewer," he said. "Seems like a good man. Before we had a police chief, we made do with a town marshal."

At the courthouse in the center of town, we introduced ourselves to the chief, a seasoned man who carried himself with a military bearing, no doubt earned in the recent European war. Brewer listened with patience as Holmes explained his suspicions about the group camping near the Aluminum Company neighborhood. Holmes drew the symbol that Mrs. Wade had seen on the hooded white robes. James nervously told of the missing boy and dog. Finally, Holmes outlined what he believed was about to happen, and the significance of tomorrow's date.

Brewer listened with intelligent gravity, understanding exactly what Holmes was telling him. He did not seem to question either Holmes or the story, replying, "You were right to come to me, Mr. Holmes. I have also been noticing these people arriving in town for a week or so, and wondered what they were about. If someone at the Aluminum Company invited them, it is probably better not to involve the company. I have some men that I trust completely. We can use them. When do you want to begin?"

Holmes indicated that immediately would suit him. The chief set about finding his men, while Holmes and I explained the situation to Rathbone, whom Holmes had instructed to wait. Rathbone was eager to join us, and showed no surprise that Holmes and I had turned out to be more than simple visitors doing research.

By late afternoon, Brewer's men had gathered. They were carefully briefed on what to expect. A number of them were veterans of the War, and they all appeared to be exactly the type of men we would require that night. Weapons were issued to some of the men, while others made do

226

with clubs fashioned from new axe handles purchased at a nearby hardware store. Now we simply had to wait until sundown.

Holmes had explained that the group we would be facing no doubt intended to have an initial bonfire ceremony after the sun had gone down. The revels would certainly last for hours, and to a casual observer it would seem curious but harmless. The ritual would likely turn sinister with the approach of sunrise on the next morning. The plan was to sneak into the Druids' camp after dark, when they were gathered at the bonfire. Holmes explained that we would still need to be quite cautious, as guards would likely be placed around the gathering. "Remember," Holmes said, "most Druids are harmless. It is the inclusion of this death symbol that makes these people more dangerous. All of them may be involved, or it may just be a few of the leaders. In any case, stay alert."

As the sun finally dimmed over the western horizon, we departed in a collection of automobiles, driving in a roundabout way to the far side of the parkland, so that we would not be observed by anyone in the houses that surrounded the park or the factory. Holmes, James, and I rode in Rathbone's cab. James had been allowed to accompany us, on the condition that he stay in the cab while we carried out our invasion.

Holmes had privately told me earlier that he wished to keep James close so the boy would not return home and be tempted to reveal our plans to his mother and father.

It was full dark when we and the other vehicles arrived. We were nearly half a mile north of the park, in an abandoned pasture on the far side from the company houses. The men around us formed up. With Holmes and the chief in the lead, we set out across the choked fields.

Our progress was slow due to the necessity of finding a path through brush and brambles in the dark, as well as the need to cross the occasional small brook or rill, produced by some nearby spring. If there was any moon, it was hiding behind the clouds. Several times I tripped over some of the karst stone showing above the plants. However, it was all small and insignificant compared with the great rocky tors that I had seen on Dartmoor many years before.

As we progressed, I began to be aware of the light of a great bonfire in the distance. It flickered and waved, and in front of it were countless black shapes, dancing and swaying as they rotated around it in some trancelike orbit. The wind was light, and blowing from the direction of the fire. I could sometimes smell smoke, and once or twice heard the eerie songs of the revelers as their monotonic chants were carried by the breeze.

The chief had known exactly which spot we meant when describing the great horizontal crack below the rocky cliff. It was only a hundred feet or so from where the bonfire was located. The fire burned on the top of a nearby cone-shaped hillside, its very brightness helping to make the surrounding areas seem much darker. Even though we were in shadows, the light from the fire reflected on the rock face of the stones above the cavern entrance. Suspecting that there might be guards, Holmes and the chief had arranged for two of the more stealthy men accompanying us, both big silent fellows, to move ahead and clear the way.

Our group paused in deep shadows as the two men, both stepping soundlessly, crept toward the open space before the rock. In a moment I heard the peculiar ringing sound of an axe handle striking another object, followed by a soft dusty thud as something sank to the ground. In a few seconds, one of the men returned, gesturing us forward.

The other man was tying a robed figure, lying unconscious on the ground. I knelt and examined him briefly. He would be out for quite a while, but his breathing was sound, and he would recover. In the meantime, Holmes was directing the men toward the crack. Only inside would they be allowed to use their electric torches. Initially, they must all crawl into the black passage in blind darkness.

I myself felt some trepidation, but none of the men showed anything of the sort. The chief went first, followed by Holmes. Then it was my turn, aided by a dark figure whose face I could not see. Only when he said, "Easy, doc," did I recognize that it was Rathbone, now dressed in dark clothing like the rest of us. It was the first time I had not seen him in his white shirt and light faded pants.

The crack dropped into the earth at a fairly steep angle. The floor entrance was dirt, pebbled with gravel, and the feeble light from the bonfire only revealed the first few feet. As I slid in feet first, I initially moved on my back. As the overhead rock loomed closer, I tried to turn so that I would be sliding on my stomach. I discovered that the awkwardness of turning while dropping only made me slide faster, and I experienced a second of blind panic as I pictured myself dropping ever faster before sliding off the edge of the entrance, shooting over a final lip of rock and falling into eternal darkness.

Almost immediately, however, hands grabbed me and helped me stand upright on the floor of the inner cave. I was pulled back as other men slid down into the spot where I had just stood. As my eyes adjusted, I could see that we were in a small chamber, approximately fifteen feet square, with the floor about four feet lower than the sloped entrance rock above me. The floor itself was stone, and dropped gradually toward the rear of the room, where an opening in the rock seemed to lead deeper into the earth.

The last men to enter brought the bound guard with them. He could not be left outside where his discovery would signal our presence. Holmes stepped over to the rear passage out of the room and snapped on his torch, shielding it with his hand. A path led down into the darkness. I joined him, followed by Chief Brewer and Rathbone. In the distance we could hear the sound of rushing water. With the others following, we moved deeper into the cave.

The passage only lasted a hundred feet or so before opening into a much wider room. While traversing the connecting corridor, I observed the walls and floor, which appeared to have been widened and formed at some point by tools. However, the marks and grooves on the walls and floor appeared to be ancient, and I idly wondered how long this site had been in use by men before tonight.

The large room we entered was about fifty feet across, and nearly twenty feet high. The ceiling was rounded, and there did not appear to be any stalactites or stalagmites whatsoever, as if they had been cleared out at some point to preserve the openness of the chamber. Numerous large boulders stood around the perimeter of the room, where the roof sloped down sharply to join the floor. Along the far side of the chamber, running from left to right, was an underground stream, only three or four feet across, its depth unknown in the near darkness. The surface of the water was a black mirror in the torch light, and it could have been six inches or six feet deep. I could see from the sides of the room that in times of great rains the water level would rise and fill the entire volume of the place.

Holmes walked around the room, examining foot scuffs in the mud on the floor. He gestured me to his side, and indicated a curious stone located centrally in front of the stream. It was carved out of the very floor of the room, left in place by the ancients, rising in one solid piece out of the ground. It was about six feet long and three feet high. Flat on top, it resembled a narrow table. Placed in the center of it, apparently there for future use, was a dagger. It was not beautiful craftsmanship. Rather, it had a homemade look, as if the metal had been shaped and sharpened by pounding it with a stone. It looked very old, and in that setting, very evil. Holmes and I looked at one another. Our interpretation of the embroidered symbol had been correct.

Holmes called our group together and explained that we were not certain when the people at the bonfire would shift their location to this cavern. Therefore, the men would need to hide behind the rocks around the walls and wait, hidden, possibly for many long and miserable hours.

They were all hardened men, and they did not need to have any explanation about what was to come. Silently, each man took a position, two slinging the bound and gagged guard between them, and we all settled into our places of concealment. Holmes was the last, remaining in the center of the room with his torch until we were all in place. The other torches went out, leaving Holmes holding the single source of light. Then, he found a place near me, sank to the ground, and turned off the torch, plunging the cavern into darkness.

How to describe those hellish hours of waiting? The cool damp air of the room quickly permeated our clothing. The constant sound of the tumbling water in the stream, moving from God knows where to God knows where, soon became a maddening drone in my ears. Within minutes or hours, I could not tell, I was hearing what I thought to be voices murmuring in the dark. I knew that it was my imagination, but at times I was tempted to stand and remind everyone to be quiet, so certain did I almost become that people were carrying on conversations.

The worst, of course, was the darkness itself. It was absolute, and my eyes would not adjust. Countless instances I held my hand in front of my face, but I could see nothing. I am not a fanciful man, but there were times when I had to remind myself that I was sitting behind a solid rock on a solid floor, and that the darkness was not closing in on me. On another occasion, I became obsessed with the idea that the clouds I had observed earlier had thickened, and it had started raining outside. We would never know it, in this room under the earth, until the underground stream began to rise. Soon we would drown, trapped in the rock chamber, unable to ever find the exit before it was too late.

The only awareness I had of anything other than myself was the occasional movement beside me of Holmes as he shifted to a more comfortable position. I was certain that his disciplined mind was not misbehaving like mine, and that his hand knew exactly where the electric torch was, ready to turn it on at a moment's notice.

My watch would later reveal that it was somewhere after four in the morning, a half hour or so before sunrise, when we first became aware that someone was entering the cave. At first, I heard chanting, weaving its way into the eternal song of the underground stream. I believed that it was my imagination, but gradually the terrible music became louder, and I knew that it was real. Then my eyes, in the dark for hours, began to perceive the glow of light as it increased from the direction of the opening. The walls around it seemed blacker as the rude stone doorway grew brighter, illuminated by the first robed people entering the room, carrying smoking torches.

I shifted on the ground, keeping behind the rocks as I carefully observed the newcomers. They continued to enter, their feet scuffing through the dried mud, filling the center of the room, swaying and singing. Only a few held burning wood torches, so the light never became very bright. As the majority of the group finished entering the place, they started to shuffle, splitting into two groups and leaving a pathway between them leading from the entrance to the stone table on the far side by the stream.

A group of three men appeared in the door, taking solemn steps as if they were university dons participating in a convocation ceremony. The first man was tall and thin, and his white robes were decorated with numerous embroidered designs, leaf-like patterns winding about his shoulders and arms. He was obviously the leader, and a shudder passed through the crowd with his appearance. The droning of their chant never faltered.

Following him were two men, each in plain robes like those worn by the general followers. They were large men with stern expressions, and they each had their hands on the shoulders of two boys being pushed in front of them. From where I hid, I could tell that the boys' hands were bound behind their backs, and their mouths were covered with gags. The first was a small boy with very light hair. He was struggling as he was pushed forward with each step. The second prisoner did not fight his captor, and looked both right and left with terror in his eyes. He was James Wade, who was supposed to have waited for us with the automobiles.

As the boys were stopped in front of the raised platform, the chanting changed from a monotonous drone to some sort of words, in a tongue that I could not understand. It was full of sibilant hisses and odd tonal changes. In that setting it seemed extremely evil, as malignant as something uttered by the tempting serpent in the Garden. The pitch seemed to rise as the first boy, obviously the missing Tyler Roberts, was lifted onto the table and placed on his back, held down as he kicked and fought.

James watched from the side, terrified and still. I glanced at my watch in the dim flickering light. Outside, the sun would be rising on the morning of June twenty-first, the solstice, the first day of summer, the day of rebirth. The leader, from his place behind the sacrificial table, raised the ancient dagger and began to shriek in the vile language of the chanters.

"Stop!" shouted Holmes, standing beside me. The mass of robed figures paused, fell silent, and stared at him, but the leader continued his sing-song call as Tyler renewed his bound struggles. As the knife began to descend, I heard an explosive report beside me. The leader's hand snapped back, and the dagger flew away from him into the rushing stream.

At my side, Rathbone stepped around the boulder behind which he had hidden, a smoking pistol thrust in front of him. All around the room, other men were appearing, holding guns, rifles, and axe handles. One robed man bolted toward the cavern entrance, only to be stopped as an axe handle met his skull, dropping him instantly to the muddy floor.

The leader stood motionless, holding his bleeding hand above Tyler, who was staring up in fascination. The hand was now nothing more than

231

a thumb jutting out from a ragged mess that was the remaining bottom half of the man's palm. Blood ran down his wrist, staining the sleeve of the white robe. Rathbone later explained that he had chosen to use expanding bullets in his revolver, which had caused the extreme damage to the leader's hand. Rathbone did not appear to regret his decision.

The boys were quickly freed, while I tended to the leader's shattered hand. As I bound it with strips torn from his decorated robe, I examined the man's face. He was expressionless, and appeared to be in shock. He gave no indication that the pain affected him at all. When he had entered the cavern he had seemed to be one of the most sinister and fearful figures I had ever seen. Now, up close and defeated, he was simply a middle-aged man, his face covered with the broken veins of the chronic alcoholic, and his shoulders and thinning hair flaked with dandruff.

It would later be revealed that his name was Lloyd Duff, and that he had founded this branch of Druid revivalists in England several years before. When that country became too hot for him, he had relocated to America, where he had continued his nefarious activities. Initially, he had been nothing more than a con man, playing on the weakness of those who sought false comfort in the rituals of ancient religions that they did not understand. Gradually, Duff began to believe in the hokum that he was peddling. He had sought out the darker side of the religion.

It was then that he became acquainted with the two men who had been herding the boys, Luther Simmons and Matthew Boyd. They were criminals from their early years, also originally from England, and they had exploited Duff for their own gain. Using Duff's corrupted knowledge of ancient Druid practices, they fashioned a new cult, which progressed from simply bilking the money of the worshipers to the occasional sacrifice.

It was discovered that Duff, Simmons, and Boyd were linked to several murders in England, related to their activities there before they fled to America. Eventually, they were extradited back to England, where Duff was tried and placed in a hospital for the insane, while Simmons and Boyd finally received their long overdue punishments in the form of poorly attended and barely reported executions.

The robed revelers, now with broken spirits, were herded from the room to the open ground outside. They huddled like sheep by the spring near the rock face. Vehicles were summoned to transport them in groups back to the county jail. As the sun continued to rise, Holmes and I verified that both boys were all right before they were sent home. A quick check revealed that Mrs. Floyd's dog, as well as several other pets, were all right, and were tied up in the Druid camps.

Holmes walked over to the man who had been knocked unconscious while attempting to flee the underground chamber. He was now awake and being questioned by Chief Brewer, who explained to us that the fellow was Mr. Timmons, the Aluminum Company official who had allowed the group to camp in the park.

"He says that he and his wife are long-time Druids, and that today is one of their holy days," said the chief. "He first discovered the cave a few years ago when he first moved to this area, and he could tell that it had been used in the past for ancient ceremonies. When Duff communicated with him about plans to pass through this area, Timmons suggested using the cave. Duff then finalized plans for his followers and recruits to meet here for this special day. Only after they had arrived did Timmons realize that Duff and some of the others were not harmless worshipers. It became obvious to him that some sort of sacrifice was planned, and he did not know how to stop it.

"He was afraid to go against Duff, and so he and his wife just let it go on. Apparently they had originally planned something else, possibly just the sacrifice of some of the local pets that have been missing, but when that Tyler boy showed up in their camp the other day, and they caught him exploring the cave, it was decided that he would be offered instead. Timmons said he only found out a few minutes before the ceremony that the sacrifice was to be human. Before then, Tyler Roberts had been kept in the Duff's tent and Timmons never saw him.

"It was only when things were happening in the cave, and Timmons finally understood what was going to happen, that he realized that he had to do something to stop it. That's his story, anyway. He claims that he was trying to run out of the cave to get help. Funny that he didn't run for help until Rathbone shot Duff, though."

"How did they find James Wade?" I asked.

"James came following after us last night," said the chief. "He didn't stay with the automobiles like he was supposed to. The guards caught him when he got too close to the bonfire. Luckily, they all just assumed he was a curious boy from the neighborhood, and never thought to ask him if anyone else was with him. I'd hate to think what would have happened if they had known we were in that cave and came in after us."

Holmes theorized that after the sacrifices, Duff, Simmons, and Boyd had intended to flee the area, leaving the other worshipers to be questioned later by the locals regarding the missing boys. This was later confirmed by Boyd, who seemed to have no feeling one way or another about the deaths in which he had been involved, and those which had just been prevented.

Later in the morning, Holmes, Rathbone, Brewer, and I reentered the cavern. Holmes agreed with me that the walls appeared to have been shaped and augmented by man at some distant point in the past. Even with the faint daylight penetrating through the outer entrance into the chamber, and with the light of our torches, the place held an evil aura.

Back in the sunshine, we held a discussion. The chief stated that he could vouch for his men, and that this matter would be kept in strict confidence. "It wouldn't do for the folks around here to realize what has just happened," he said. He indicated that most of the people arrested had probably not realized what they were getting into until the boys were actually brought forward to the sacrificial table. Then, they had been too caught up in the religious frenzy to try and stop it.

Holmes stated, "I suppose that is possible, and there is really no way to prove otherwise. However, for so many Druids to have willingly agreed to greet the sunrise on one of their most important days while deep in a cavern, with no possible view of the sun, indicates to me that they were quite aware of what was going on. As soon as Watson and I saw the Druid death symbol, and learned of the proximity of an underground opening, we both knew that we were dealing with a dark mirror of true Druidism. Surely these people knew it as well, or they would never have agreed to miss the rising of the sun."

Brewer explained that the participants would simply be charged with vagrancy and thrown out of the county. He was certain that none of them would ever return. Duff and his cronies would be charged with attempted murder, but he would work to keep the graphic details of the events from becoming common knowledge.

"I think that it would be best if this place were filled up," said Holmes, gesturing toward the entrance to the chamber. "Locations like this are magnets of evil. You need to prevent something like this from happening again."

The chief agreed, and stated that some of his men would begin immediately to fill the chamber with stone and then blast the entrance, making it impossible to enter. "And I'm sure I can get Mr. Timmons to arrange things so that the aluminum company will pay for any expense, in the name of making this park safer. After all, Timmons probably won't be charged in the matter, either, and he is going to owe me."

Rathbone drove us back to our lodgings at Mrs. Jones's farm. We retired to change out of our dirty clothing, and then returned to the main house to find that Rathbone was engaged in relating our night's adventures to the lady. It was at that moment that Mrs. Jones recognized us, and it was then that she made me promise not to use her actual name, should I ever write a narrative of what had taken place. We agreed, as long as she promised not to reveal what Rathbone had told her.

234

Later in the day, we checked on Mrs. Wade and James, where we found that he had completely recovered from the incident. In his mind it had already become somewhat dreamlike, and the horror was starting to blur. We told Mrs. Wade some of the less graphic details of the previous night's events, and assured her that the Druids were gone and that the cavern was to be destroyed.

James went to Tyler's house, returning with the small boy in a few minutes. He confirmed that he had been captured by Duff and his men while trying to explore the cavern. He had been aware of the passageway and buried chamber for months, and he wondered what the visiting Druids were doing in it. He thought of the whole thing as a great adventure, and was not traumatized in the least. His parents were not concerned at all for the simple reason that he had not told them of it, and had no intention of doing so.

Back in town, we met with Chief Brewer once again, who informed us that work was already underway to close the ancient underground room. We gave him information on how to reach us with future details regarding the disposition of the case. He looked at our addresses, mine in London and Holmes's in Sussex. "Not 221b Baker Street?" he asked with a grin.

"No," replied Holmes, "not anymore."

The next day, Rathbone delivered us to the train station, where we intended to travel to Knoxville, and from there back to Linville, where we would conclude our business before returning to England.

As we shook his hand, Holmes thanked Rathbone for his assistance. "Think nothing of it, gentleman," he said. "Most fun I've had in years. Too bad that you had that hole filled in, though, Mr. Holmes. I would have liked to have set up a stand and given paid tours through the place. Just think, 'Ladies and gentleman, this way to the amazing Druid Death Cave!'"

We laughed, and Rathbone waved and walked to his cab. Later, as we adjusted to our seats for the short ride to Knoxville, Holmes remarked, "I have enjoyed this little side trip, Watson."

"As did I. By the way, did you ever find any evidence of corruption at the college?"

"None whatsoever. I have been in touch with Mrs. Thaw several times by wire, and I learned that her suspicions arose out of a comment relating to the construction of the new building. Apparently there are some sinkholes beside the proposed location, and the builder indicated that those would have to be 'covered up.' Word reached her, and in her confused elderly state, she misunderstood and believed that the college was involved in a different kind of 'cover-up' relating to the building. From that, she extrapolated the notion that there was some sort of plot afoot to misuse her funds."

I laughed, and said, "Perhaps if we let him know, Rathbone can persuade the college to leave the sinkholes open. It's not quite a Druid horror chamber, but he could still sell admission."

Holmes shook his head with a smile. "An enterprising young fellow, this American cousin of mine. As was your relative, Willie Marcum."

"Yes," I agreed. "We have no reason to worry about our American relations."

"What if, Watson," said Holmes, "what if, someday, Willie were to have a son or daughter, and that person were to marry Rathbone's son or daughter. Then our families, however distant, would be linked."

"I think I would like that, Holmes," I replied. "That would be a fine thing to happen."

The train picked up speed, our first step on the return home. Holmes and I fell into a comfortable silence, each gazing out the window at the beautiful passing landscape.

The Adventure of the Other Brother

With many thanks to Sir Arthur Conan Doyle,
August Derleth, and Rex Stout (the Literary Agents),
and William S. Baring-Gould (a Perceptive Biographer)

Part I: The Other Brother

In late October 1896, I had been involved in a series of personal matters that caused me no little distress, as well as the inconvenient requirement that I temporarily move out of our Baker Street lodgings for nearly a week. During that time, I had seen Mr. Sherlock Holmes on a daily basis, as I stopped in to get fresh clothing and linens, as well as to retrieve my mail. As my presence was not always required elsewhere during the daytime hours, I had also accompanied Holmes on several investigations during that time.

On the last day of the month, I had returned to Baker Street for good, my business completed. Although the specific details of the matter have no relation to the present narrative, they did contribute to my mood that day. I was quite grim following a long week of struggles with a patient whose identity must remain anonymous. It was in such a dark attitude that I dropped into my chair in front of the sitting room fire.

Holmes was moving around in his bedroom. I could hear his occasional murmurs as he opened and closed drawers in the bedroom behind me. Soon he came in, and as if noticing the darkness of the room for the first time that afternoon, he stepped to the windows and threw back the drapes.

The weak additional light barely improved the condition of the dark room. Holmes sat in his chair across from me and glanced at my bag standing near the landing door. "It is finished, then?" he asked.

I nodded. "For better or worse."

"I, too, have received word today of some business relating to a painful matter from the past." He tossed me a telegram that had been hidden in his dressing gown pocket.

As I scanned the message, the events of the previous summer came flooding back to me, temporarily pushing aside my despondency over the day's conclusion.

"So he has escaped," I said softly.

"And apparently with no great difficulty. He must have been biding his time. The local constabulary waited far too long before notifying any other

237

authorities. By the time Mycroft became aware of the matter, and was able to bring more skilled forces to bear, it had become apparent that the fugitive had fled across the German sea. . . ."

We were silent for a moment. "Do you think we shall meet him again?" I finally asked.

Holmes reached for his pipe. He did not answer as he went through the process of packing it with the dry shag tobacco from the Persian slipper. Finally, he replied, "Yes, Watson. I do not know how or when, but I very much fear that we shall meet him again."

As we continued to sit in the growing darkness, I recalled the events of half a year earlier. I had been amazed at the time, as well as angry with Holmes for his infernal habit of keeping secrets from me. However, at the conclusion of the case, I had believed that a great wrong had been righted. Now I knew that we would always be waiting to learn when this evil would reappear.

It was on a morning in early June of that same year that we became involved in the affair that I have always called "The Other Brother." I had been in the process of writing up several matters relating to Holmes's activities, including some incidents that took place during his travels for the Foreign Office from 1891-94, when everyone but his brother Mycroft believed him to be dead. Unfortunately, except for certain members of Her Majesty's government, the exact details of these events must remain secret until late into the next century.

Holmes had been involved for several days in a number of cases, including most recently the singularly unrewarding matter of Mr. Josiah Uppenham's tedious financial miscalculations. He was sitting at our dining table, surrounded by numerous stacks of documents, each threatening to slide and spill into its neighbor. At times Holmes would mutter, and lean forward with his head on his hand, squinting at the minuscule purple entries and jottings. Sometimes he would make a note, and other times he would lean back, sigh, and reshuffle and stack the papers a different way, occasionally making a note on a document as some sort of cross-referencing.

I did not know how long this would go on, but I suspected that Holmes would stop soon, if only to relieve the pain he must be feeling in his stooped back. It was into this setting that Mrs. Hudson arrived with a telegram.

Holmes stood, sighed, and stretched with an audible crack from his back. "Watson, I am tempted to let Mr. Uppenham suffer the consequences of his foolishness," he said, opening the wire. "He needs a team of sharp solicitors, not a lone consulting detective with a leery respect at best for mathematics. Luckily I am being generously compensated, in this instance for my reputation, I believe, more than my skills. . . ."

His voice trailed off as he read the telegram. The fatigue seemed to slough from him as he stood taller. He finished reading, looked toward the door for a short moment, and then moved toward his bedroom. Over his shoulder, he stated, "Can you come to Yorkshire today, Watson? Are you available for several days?"

I turned in my desk chair. "Of course," I replied.

He returned to the door, carrying some folded clothing. "Bring your service revolver."

I stood up as he turned back into the bedroom. "What is it, Holmes?"

He called from the other room, "My brother has been arrested for murder."

"What?" I cried. "Mycroft arrested? In Yorkshire?"

"Not Mycroft," he said, reappearing around the doorway. "My older brother, Sherrinford."

Later, as we sat in our compartment on the northbound train, I caught Holmes's eye and asked the obvious question. "You have another brother?"

He looked at me for another moment, and then out the window at the landscape, which began to pass more quickly as we left the sprawl surrounding London.

Earlier, I had grabbed my bag and gun, meeting Holmes on the landing within minutes of his request for my company on the trip. I am an old campaigner, and after years attending Holmes on his investigations, I had learned to always keep a bag ready for immediate departure. We had been silent in the hansom ride to King's Cross, and I could tell that Holmes was in deep thought and would not appreciate being disturbed.

He had, however, at one point silently handed me the telegram that had precipitated this journey. It simply said, "Sherrinford arrested for murder. Compartment booked for you on special train, King's Cross. Information to follow upon your arrival. Mycroft."

Now, in the train, I wanted answers, and knew that we had several hours for Holmes to provide them. "Perhaps," he said, "I should give you a little background information about my family, so that you will know something about them when we arrive." I nodded, and he continued.

"In the fall of 1888," he began, "I believe you were surprised to learn that I had an older brother, Mycroft."

"Surprised is hardly the word," I replied. I still remembered that evening vividly. Holmes and I had been sitting before our fireplace, long periods of companionable silence mixed with random conversation.

239

Holmes had begun to explain that he believed traits and abilities often ran in families. He had sought to prove this point by saying that his older brother Mycroft possessed even greater deductive skills than did Holmes himself. My amazement at learning of a brother, after having known Holmes for over seven years, had led to our visiting Mycroft at the Diogenes Club, that odd gathering place for the most unclubbable men in London. Before the evening was over we were involved in the strange matter of Mr. Melas, the Greek Interpreter.

"At the time, I had come to believe that you had as little family in England as I," I said.

"I had kept Mycroft's existence a secret for several reasons, not the least of which is my own natural tendency towards a certain reluctance for sharing information unnecessarily. It was not that I did not trust you, Watson. I simply had felt no need up to that point in time to mention Mycroft.

"As I said at the time, Mycroft was employed within the British government. I recall mentioning to you last year, during the matter of the stolen submarine plans, that on occasion Mycroft *is* the British government. Again, I did not distrust you by not mentioning this sooner. It was simply not relevant in 1888 to let you know how important Mycroft's position was and continues to be.

"In 1868, Mycroft graduated from Oxford and obtained a government position through the influence of a family friend. He moved to London, and found lodgings in Montague Street near the British Museum. The building was owned by a distant family relation, and it would in fact be these rooms in which I would reside when I came down to London several years later.

"Of course, given Mycroft's incredible skills at sorting information and perceiving various relationships between facts unnoticed by others, he was soon being consulted by all sorts of departments within the government. It was a natural progression that he would find himself offering opinions on the mysterious activities and motivations of foreign countries and their leaders. During that time, Mycroft was not nearly as sedate as he would later become, and on several occasions he traveled abroad on a number of secret missions, the nature of which he has never revealed, not even to me.

"During this time, I was a young fellow, spending my time alternately between my family's home in Yorkshire and several schools in different parts of England. My family consisted of my father Siger, my mother Violet, my older brother Sherrinford, and his growing family.

"My father was the second son of a country squire, and had spent time serving as an officer in the military in India before being invalided home due to an injury. His older brother lived in Yorkshire as the squire of the

240

estate. During the time my father was traveling home, his older brother had died, and my father arrived on Portsmouth jetty to learn that he had inherited the estate.

"Not long after taking up his position as a country squire, my father met and married my mother, Violet Sherrinford, the daughter of Sir Edward Sherrinford, a not too distant neighbor. My brother Sherrinford was born about a year later, in 1845. Mycroft followed in 1847. I was born in 1854.

"My father was a great bear of a man, loud and with a full black beard. He was strong-willed and highly opinionated, and he knew exactly what he wanted for each of his three sons. Sherrinford, the oldest, was to be educated and then take over the family estate, continuing the line of country squires that had run the place for ages. Mycroft was to attend university as well and then obtain a position within the government.

"Each of my brothers followed my father's plan and ended up where they were supposed to be. For myself, my father had decided that I was to be an engineer. It was with this in mind that he hired a mathematics tutor to get me ready during the summer of 1872. As I have related before, Watson, this tutor was none other than Professor James Moriarty.

"The Professor and I did not get along at all during that time, but I had no idea then how our differences would grow. In later years, as I became aware of a criminal network forming in England, I still had difficulty believing for sure that my former mathematics tutor had become the leader of the vast underworld machine that he himself created. During that long summer before I went away to university, the house was filled with tension as I fought with Moriarty over the need to learn mathematical theorems, which I felt to be irrelevant, and I questioned my father endlessly about whether I really had to become an engineer.

"The only enjoyment that I had during that summer was playing with my young nephew, William, who had been born the previous year. He is a fine lad, much like his father Sherrinford, and even at that young age his intelligence seemed remarkable. He has also always been a wonderfully even-tempered boy, considering that for a portion of his early years he grew up in the same house as my tempestuous father.

"I credit William's wonderful nature to his mother, Roberta, formerly Roberta MacIvor, who had married Sherrinford in 1868. She became like a second mother to me, especially as my own mother was already in failing health at that time.

"In the fall of 1872, I left Yorkshire to attend Oxford. I was not at home during early 1873 when Sherrinford's second son, Bancroft, was born. I did try to stay in contact with the family as often as I could. On several occasions, however, I accepted invitations to visit other homes with friends I had made while away at school. It was during one of these trips with Victor Trevor to Norfolk in the summer of 1874 that I finally realized my future lay not in the field of engineering, but rather in defining and creating the profession of consulting detective." I recalled the matter of which he spoke. I had learned of it in early 1888, following the death of my first wife. I had moved back to Baker Street, and Holmes had begun to tell me some about his past and a few earlier cases as a way to help me forget my grief. I had later chronicled the matter under the title "The *Gloria Scott.*"

"As you might expect, my father was not pleased when I informed him of my decision," Holmes continued, "and he quickly wrote to me, explaining that he would continue to provide funding for me, but that he never wanted to see me again. Thus released from my duties as a student engineer, I traveled to London, moved into the rooms in Montague Street, and promptly enrolled in Cambridge for the fall, feeling that its scientific emphasis might be better suited in order to prepare me for my new calling.

"For several years I alternated between classes at Cambridge and the Montague Street rooms, learning what I could in the classroom, and more practical lessons on the streets of London at other times. During this period, I found what cases that I could, always trying to use each as a way to extrapolate knowledge for my future profession.

"Over the next few years, I attended classes less and less and worked much more often. I began to build a fairly steady practice, and started to believe that I could make a true profession out of my work. I had also managed to arrange an uneasy truce with my father, and I was able to visit my family as frequently as I could get away, which sadly, was not very often. In 1880, as you know, I traveled with a Shakespearean acting company for a good part of the year to various parts of the United States, and so had no contact with them at all for several months.

"It was during this time that Sherrinford's youngest and last son was born. Coincidentally, Watson, he arrived on the twenty-seventh of July, 1880, the same day that you were fighting for your life at Maiwand. After my return to England in August, I traveled briefly to Yorkshire, where I met this nephew for the first time.

"I must say that of Sherrinford's three children, it is this fellow to whom I feel closest. His name is Siger, after his grandfather, and physically he is very much like me. Although all of my brothers and nephews are quite adept in the art of deduction, which does seem to run in the family as I have previously stated, Siger seems to approach the matter more like me than the others. Interestingly, my oldest nephew, William, is much like Sherrinford, warm and intelligent and suited for country life, while the middle son, Bancroft, is in many ways like his uncle Mycroft.

He and Mycroft both have that coldly analytical trait that works so well for those involved in government intrigues.

"In fact, Bancroft has been working for several years in Mycroft's department in London, although in a rather strange way. When he completed his studies at university in 1892, Bancroft expressed a desire to follow in Mycroft's footsteps. However, he wanted it made very clear that anything that he accomplished would be on his own merits, and not due to the influence of his uncle Mycroft or the Holmes name. Therefore, when he went to work, he fashioned a different last name for himself, and has used it ever since, preferring that no one there know that he and Mycroft are related.

"Bancroft based his name on a variation of his father's name, Sherrinford, which comes from the old name for a local spot in a stream used for shearing sheep. The area was known as the *shearing ford,* which was later simply pronounced *sherrinford.* Likewise, the name *Mycroft* comes from a similar local derivation, based on an ancestor exclaiming '*My croft!*' Thankfully, I am not aware of any local words or phrases that have been derived or corrupted into *Sherlock.*

"Since his father's name was based on a ford across a stream, Bancroft decided that he would figuratively build a bridge across that stream, instead of using the ford. He initially took the last name *Bridge*, but he decided that he did not like the alliteration of *Bancroft Bridge*, and subsequently changed his pseudonym to the Latin for bridge, *pons.* Bancroft's choice to change his last name and the way he created it are typical of the crafty and, if I may say it, rather twisted way that his and my brother Mycroft's minds work. No doubt this is why they get along so well together, and also the reason for the great success of the department that Mycroft has created.

"As I said, Bancroft went to work in Mycroft's department in 1892, and he was soon placed in charge of managing my activities as I traveled throughout Asia and the Middle East, as well as various locations in Europe and the United States. It was good practice for him, as I understand that he is now fairly in charge of most of Mycroft's field agents, as a good part of Mycroft's time is still spent collecting and arranging data from all departments of the government, not just for the Foreign Office, as well as dealing with politicians and military leaders."

By now, we were quite a distance from London, and the train was moving at a good pace. I could not believe how much information about his past that Holmes had just related to me. I had understood for years that he had no family, and had been amazed years before when I learned about Mycroft. To learn that there were others, parents, a brother and sister-in-law, and three nephews who each strangely mimicked the three older

243

Holmes brothers, was almost too amazing. I did my best not to interrupt, as I did not want Holmes to realize just how much he was revealing and suddenly decide to stop. However, I had to ask one question.

"I still do not understand," I said, "why these people had to remain a secret."

"Ah," said Holmes. "Normally they would not. However, there was an incident which threatened them, and it was felt that a certain . . . separation between the Yorkshire family and their wayward London relations was necessary.

"As I said, Mycroft began to be noticed by the government early on, and his position advanced at a very quick rate. Soon he was helping to evaluate and decide policy for many departments. It was also not long before agents of foreign governments began to hear of this wonderful man whose brain was being used as some sort of human calculating machine.

"To this day, I do not know all the details of what happened. Likewise, Sherrinford's family does not know exactly what threat faced them, only that they were in danger, and Mycroft will not disclose what happened, or what action was taken against the aggressors. All I do know is that in September 1880, just a month after I visited my new nephew Siger, something happened to threaten the family at the Yorkshire home, and it was clearly related somehow to Mycroft's position with the government. Even then, Mycroft's incredible value to the Crown was recognized, and it was decided at the highest levels to prevent anything like that from happening again, so that nothing of the sort could be used against him or to bring pressure on him.

"Members of the village around the family estate were contacted by agents of Her Majesty's government and asked to help give the impression that the Holmes family of North Riding had nothing to do with Mycroft, and me as well. I suppose that even then, I had been of some use on a few matters, and Mycroft included me in the plan, as he knew I would be staying in London and continuing to get into all sorts of trouble with the more questionable elements of society.

"After making sure that the local individuals understood what was required and were willing to cooperate, references to Mycroft, myself, and various other family members were quietly removed from the official records. That is why you will not find a record of me at Oxford, or Cambridge, or at Bart's Hospital. And none of that branch of the Holmes family will be recorded in the local Parish book near our family home.

"It was not a perfect plan, but it was hoped that it would be enough to confuse or stop the actions of an enemy agent trying to use threats against Sherrinford's family to coerce Mycroft or myself. Over the years, neighbors have reported occasional attempts to find out something about our family, sometimes by reporters, at other times by mysterious individuals whom we can only assume have been agents of criminal or foreign organizations.

"Our biggest fear was always some sort of threat from Professor Moriarty or his organization. The man had actually stayed in our house for most of a summer, and he certainly knew where and who we were. However, he never made a move against my family, and I can only assume he had some sort of odd code of honor that prevented him from doing so. Perhaps he felt a sense of obligation due to the fact that he was well treated while he was there. Possibly he thought that I knew something about his own family as well, and he mistakenly believed that I would make a move against them in retaliation. Perhaps I would have. Luckily, he appears to have kept all information about us and the summer that he stayed there to himself, because there has never been any indication that the subsequent individuals who tried to resurrect his criminal web have any clue of our existence."

We pondered these thoughts in silence for a moment, before I said, "You have described your family in Yorkshire as Sherrinford's family. Does this imply that your parents are no longer living?"

"My mother passed away in April 1888. I did not mention the fact to you then, although you were living in Baker Street. In retrospect, the event left me far more shaken than I acknowledged at the time. My father had died much earlier, in the summer of 1877, before he ever had a chance to see that I had managed to make a real success of the career that I had chosen, and that he had ridiculed."

I recalled that spring of 1888. Holmes had never given any indication to me at the time of the death of his mother. Perhaps the only sign of a problem at all was a stumble during a few of his cases, most noticeably the investigation into the mysterious tenant living in the house adjacent to Mr. Grant Munro. It will be recalled that Holmes had theorized a completely incorrect and rather grim solution, and upon learning that the truth was far more pleasant, he had asked me to whisper "Norbury" in his ear if he ever again seemed to be becoming over-confident in his powers, or not taking the proper amount of interest or care in a case.

The train sped on, and we sat in silence for a number of miles, each lost in our own memories. I understood how Holmes felt. My father had died of alcohol poisoning following a wasted life that had spiraled down from success, solidity, and respectability to unbeatable failure. The death of my mother, which occurred much sooner than it should have due to anguish over my father's abandonment, had left me unsettled and grief-stricken. When I was older, after becoming a doctor, I had traveled for a number of years, as well as spent time in the army, coming to grips with the bitter feelings I had retained following my parents' deaths.

I gradually became aware of the train compartment, and Holmes watching me from his seat on the other side. Clearing my throat, I asked, "So now who resides at the family home?"

"Sherrinford and Roberta, their oldest son William, who has not yet married, and Siger, who is about to turn sixteen. I confess I am looking forward to seeing Siger again. It has been a year or so since I visited. The last time was just prior to my return to London in April '94, a day or so after I arrived back on English soil. When I saw him then he was already using the methods of ratiocination in a way far more advanced of my skills when I was at that age."

I laughed. Most people would have commented that the boy was taller than expected, or some such observation. Only Holmes would think in terms of deductive skills. "You still thought that you were going to be an engineer at that age," I said. "An engineer, indeed."

He laughed as well, but just for a moment before the seriousness returned to his expression.

"Do you know anything of Sherrinford's arrest?" I asked.

He shook his head. "Nothing more than what is in that telegram. I assume we will be able to begin our investigation as soon as we arrive. No doubt Mycroft will manage to reach us with any information that he believes we will need."

We continued on northward, each lost in our private thoughts. As for myself, I was still thinking of the wealth of information that I had just received regarding Holmes's background and family life. Holmes's frowning face was pinched in concentration, his pipe – which had long since gone out – clamped in his teeth. Although he made it a practice never to theorize in advance of data, I did not see how he would be able to refrain from some sort of speculation regarding his brother Sherrinford's dilemma. However, I knew he would be unwilling to discuss the matter, and I left him to his thoughts.

Part II: Home

We changed trains in York for the line to Thirsk. After arriving in that picturesque town, we found seats on a smaller branch line, and I must have slept at some point. When I awoke we were pulling into a tiny village station. Following Holmes's lead, I began to gather my things for departure. We had no sooner stepped onto the platform than a neatly dressed man stepped forward to intercept us.

"Mr. Holmes," he said. "Dr. Watson? I am Inspector Tenley. I have been briefed on the matter, and I will be accompanying you to your family home."

In actuality, Tenley did not say "your family home." Rather, he named the community which was our destination. However, in spite of the passage of years since these events took place, I will not name or identify the location any more specifically than I have already done so. Even though this narrative will be placed in my tin dispatch box following its completion, where it is intended to remain for at least seventy-five years after my death, I am not willing to compromise the security of the Holmes family, or to negate the incredible efforts already made over the years by the British government to shield and protect them.

Tenley led us to a connecting train for the remaining journey to the village in question. The trip was tedious, as we were in a compartment with a stranger, requiring that we make no discussion of the case to pass the time.

Arriving at the village station, Tenley gestured toward the adjacent roadway. "This way, gentlemen," he said. "I have transportation waiting."

Outside, a rugged four-wheeler stood, pulled by a stout and patient horse. Holding the reins was a small, wiry man who looked once at us, then faced forward again without comment. As we found our seats, Tenley said, "This is Griffin. He can be trusted."

Griffin softly snapped the reins and the four-wheeler lurched into motion. "I believe we have time to discuss the details of the case now, Mr. Holmes, if you prefer."

"That will be fine," Holmes said. "We know virtually nothing, as we left London immediately after being notified of the arrest. The charge is murder, then?"

"Yes, sir. No possibility of an accidental death or suicide. Your brother has been very cooperative, but professes to have total ignorance on the matter."

"Pray give me the facts," said Holmes, shifting in his seat toward Tenley.

Tenley watched for a moment as Holmes closed his eyes, so that he might better concentrate on the narrative. "Yesterday morning," Tenley began, "your nephew William arrived at the local police station, quite agitated, requesting that the constable accompany him back to the Holmes farm, where the body of a middle-aged man had just been discovered, brutally murdered.

"The officer, Constable Worth, quickly joined William, who drove them in a carriage the five miles or so out to the house. Upon entering the estate, they bypassed the house and adjacent farm buildings, driving out into a pasture several hundred feet away. The area is rock-bound, and has many low and hidden areas created by the steeply rolling hills."

"The north pasture," Holmes said, without opening his eyes. "Go on."

"The entire area has been used for sheep grazing, as I'm sure you know," continued Tenley. "William drove the carriage around a number of rocky areas until they reached a low spot, surrounded by several farm hands and your brother Sherrinford.

"Upon reaching their destination, Worth jumped down and advanced through the ring of silent men, all staring at something below them. The location is a natural pit in the earth, an inverted cone some eight or ten feet deep, and whatever is in it would be quite hidden below the view of anyone on the surrounding pasture. I was told that during times of heavy rain, the pit fills with water before it gradually seeps away into the ground. We have had no rain, however, for several weeks, and at the time of the murder, it was dry. Although," he said, glancing at the sky, "I suspect we are due for some rain shortly."

"I know of the place you speak," said Holmes. "I used to camp there as a small boy."

Tenley nodded, unnoticed by Holmes. "At the bottom of the pit was the body of the victim, a fellow in his early fifties. He was lying on his back, and had apparently only been there a few hours, as there was no sign of disturbance of the corpse by birds or animals.

"Constable Worth questioned your brother, Sherrinford, who told him that William discovered the body that morning. While walking toward a distant field, he had happened to glance into the pit as he skirted its edge. Upon seeing the body, he rushed down and ascertained that the man was dead. He then returned to the house, where he informed his father. By that time, a number of farmhands had gathered around them. Sherrinford sent William for the police, saying that he and the hands would guard the body until William returned. Sherrinford then walked to the body's location with the other men. He made sure that no one approached the body while they awaited the constable's arrival. He stated that he was aware, Mr. Holmes, of the need to preserve the area around the body.

248

"Constable Worth is a capable man, a typical rural official and quite observant in his own way. He made a cursory examination of the area. He did not see any signs of footprints or disturbances around the body, although as I have said, we have had no rain for several weeks, and it is unlikely that anything would show on the ground. Worth was unable to even see any of William's footprints at the immediate site, or any of his own, for that matter.

"The body had a great torn cut on the throat, but strangely there was very little blood around that wound or on the collar of the man's suit. There was more blood on the man's back that had soaked through the coat, but a quick examination by Worth did not reveal the nature of that wound. Also, Worth reported that there was very little blood on the ground below the body. I have since verified this, as well as Worth's conclusion that no footprints were detectable in the hollow. It seems, based on the evidence of the blood, that the fellow was murdered elsewhere and the body was placed there after the fact.

"Worth immediately recognized the murdered man, and asked Sherrinford if he knew who it was, as well. 'Of course,' replied Sherrinford. 'We all know him. It is Davison Wilkies. I have given him and his people permission to camp on my land. They have been here for a week or so.'

"This agreed with Worth's knowledge of the situation. Wilkies was the leader of a group of a dozen or so odd folk, apparently part of some self-styled religious cult. They had arrived in the area about ten days ago, like a band of gypsies, all traveling in six or eight large wagons pulled by heavy teams of horses. Your brother had given them permission to stay on the Holmes land, although he directed them to the southern side, where the fields are much flatter and more hospitable, and there is access to water from the stream.

"It was common knowledge that Sherrinford had visited with Wilkies at the campsite on a number of occasions, usually in the evening. Your brother stated that he was curious about the group's beliefs, and that he was simply going to see Wilkies in order to ask questions. We learned this from both Sherrinford, as well as from Wilkies's daughter, Sophia.

"Sophia indicated that on the night of the murder, Wednesday night, your brother visited Wilkies's wagon, as usual. She states that while she did not hear the exact conversation, the tone between the two men became tense, and then somewhat hostile. They appeared to be arguing regarding the nature and validity of Wilkies's beliefs. Sophia indicated that Sherrinford appeared to be of the opinion that Wilkies had turned away from the 'true path,' whatever that means. Sherrinford denies that this conversation ever took place, and states that his visit that night was cordial, and no different than those of other nights. He also does not even know what was meant by the phrase 'true path,' since he was only a curious and casual visitor with little knowledge of Wilkies's beliefs.

"No one else in the campsite can be found to verify or disprove either of their statements. However, Sophia said that she doubted if anyone else would have overhead the conversation. Although she says that the two men were disagreeing quite strongly, they were quiet about it, and even though Sophia overheard some of the conversation from her location immediately outside the wagon, she does not believe the voices would have carried any farther.

"Sophia initially related this information to Constable Worth, when he questioned her yesterday morning following the notification of her father's death. When asked who might have had a reason to kill her father, she could think of no one, with the exception of your brother, whom she stated had argued with her father the night before. She indicated that the group did not know anyone else in the area, and that no one within her group would have had any reason for murdering her father.

"She also did not know how her father's body could have come to be located so far away from the campsite. Wilkies's party is quite a distance to the south of the house, while the rocky area where he was discovered is to the north. Constable Worth's investigations did not show any signs of blood in the campsite, indicating that he was not murdered there, and my subsequent examination confirmed this.

"Based on Sophia's statement, Worth returned to the Holmes farm, where he made a surreptitious examination of the grounds and outbuildings. In one of the barns, he thought that he found something of interest, a bundle of old clothing, consisting of an old shirt, the sleeves covered in blood and gore. However, subsequent investigation revealed this to be simply an old shirt belonging to one of the farm workers, used in the past during butchering time. However, based on the evidence of Sophia's story, Worth felt that he had no choice but to arrest Sherrinford.

"It is Worth's belief that Wilkies and Sherrinford must have known each other at some time in the past, although Sherrinford denies it. Worth feels that Wilkies did not just come to this area by chance, and that he was actually invited here by Sherrinford, who let him stay on the Holmes property because of their past relation. They must have both been members of the same religious belief at some point in the past, but Wilkies has changed or modified his beliefs. Sherrinford was dismayed upon learning that Wilkies no longer followed the 'true path,' and this turned to anger, which led to Wilkies's murder.

"Worth believes that Sherrinford lured Wilkies to some spot Wednesday night, where he killed him, before concealing the body in the hollow. He intended to return and bury it the next night, but it was discovered by William before he was able do so. He then had to play along. Worth has not yet found where Wilkies was killed, but he is still looking. Obviously, wherever the murder took place, a great deal of blood will have been spilled, and there is no sign of this in any of the farm buildings or on locations immediately near them. It is Worth's contention that Sherrinford hid his own bloody clothing and knife, having changed following the murder. He meant to bury them with the body, but he never got the chance. He hid the body in the dark following the murder, not realizing that it would be visible when that area was in daylight.

"As I said, Mr. Holmes, this is Constable Worth's contention. He did investigate the likelihood of any other possibility all yesterday, but by late evening he had no choice but to arrest your brother. As of right now, we have found no evidence to the contrary, so I have allowed Worth's arrest of your brother to stand. However, I am interested in finding all the facts in order to get at the truth.

"Following Sherrinford's arrest, his family, of course, wasted no time in contacting London. Within hours, I was assigned to the case. I came out with Worth this morning, and we reexamined the hollow where the body was found, and spoke with both your brother and Sophia. I reported directly to your brother, Mycroft, in London. He informed me that you would be arriving soon to investigate as well."

Holmes opened his eyes. "Is Sherrinford being held in the village, or in the facilities of some larger town?"

"In the village," Tenley replied. "Worth is rather ambitious, and he seemed to want to keep the matter within his own sphere of influence. He had made no effort on his own to call for any assistance, believing that he was handling the case sufficiently by himself. He was in fact somewhat resentful when your family arranged for my participation."

Tenley added, "As I said, Mr. Holmes, Worth is quite competent and observant, but also ambitious. I will be watching to make sure that his ambition does not cloud his judgment."

"Quite," replied Holmes. "And the body? Is it also still in the village?"

"Yes," replied Tenley. "Worth requested an autopsy this morning, but I stopped it until you could be here to examine the body first."

"Excellent," said Holmes. "Who will be doing the autopsy?"

"Dr. Dalton," said Tenley.

Holmes smiled tightly. "As I supposed."

"Do you wish to see the body first, or go on to the site of its discovery?" Tenley asked.

Holmes glanced at the low clouds. The wind had picked up somewhat since we had left the train station, and the air was noticeably cooler. I agreed with Tenley's earlier observation about the imminent arrival of rain.

"I suppose we should see the hollow first," said Holmes, "although I am sure that you are correct and that very little will be discovered."

Tenley instructed Griffin to continue on to the farm. We rode in silence, Tenley and Holmes both wrapped in their own thoughts, while I looked from side to side at the surrounding fields and copses, examining with interest that area from which Holmes had sprung. I tried to imagine him as a boy, with his great and curious intellect, roaming and exploring this countryside. It was difficult, to say the least. Holmes had always been comfortable and competent in all situations, but I generally thought of him as a man of the city. However, I also knew that he had showed a familiarity with country life, including knowledgeable experience with horses, and that living once in a rude stone hut on the wilds of Dartmoor had not seemed to cause him any serious distress. Obviously, he had gathered these and other skills here, as a boy.

We topped a low rise, and spread out before us was a tidy manor house, surrounded by a cluster of barns and smaller farm buildings. The house was unostentatious but well kept. On several sides were fenced paddocks, and the fence rails were brightly whitewashed. The ground around the buildings was flat and trim, and stretched away smoothly to the south. Behind the house, beyond the trees obviously planted as windbreaks, the land changed, turning rocky and rippled toward the north. I knew that this was the area where the body was found. "What is in that direction?" I asked, gesturing toward the rocky piles.

"Nothing," said Holmes. "Eventually one would run into the German Sea. The ground stays jumbled that way for a number of miles before flattening out on a high, rough tableland. There are a few shepherd cottages scattered out there. I suppose that is where William was going yesterday morning when he discovered the body."

"That is correct, Mr. Holmes," said Tenley. "He was going to take a message to one of the men out there, asking him to drive the sheep back toward the main house. Your brother says he wanted to examine them to make sure there were no signs of any infectious disease in the flock. There had been reports of something going through farms in nearby towns."

As we approached the house, the front door opened, and two men and a woman stepped out. Two or three farmhands also moved into the darkening daylight from a nearby barn. They stayed there, in the doorway, while the people from the house moved closer to us. The four-wheeler stopped, and the woman walked to the side.

"Sherlock," she said. "Thank you for coming." Holmes stepped down, and the woman reached and drew him into a hug. Holmes looked mildly uncomfortable for a moment, and then relented to the woman, hugging her back.

I looked at the woman, assuming that this was Roberta, whom Holmes had said was like a second mother to him. She was short, not much over five feet in height, with thick brown hair pulled back into a loose bun. The hair was somewhat shot with gray, but it only added to her commanding and confident presence. "Why have you waited so long to visit?" she asked. "It shouldn't have taken something like this to get you up here."

She turned to me. "And you must be Dr. Watson," she said, shaking my hand with a firm and warm two-handed grip. There was no pretense of delicate lady-like behavior here. She was a woman of the country, strong and not uncomfortable about showing it. "I am Roberta Holmes. I'm so happy to finally meet you, and sorry that it has taken this long to do so," she said, glancing at Holmes with scolding eyes. "You have no idea how many times I have told Sherlock to invite you. It has been nearly impossible, however, to even get *him* to visit . . . . "

While she had been speaking, the older of the two young men behind her stepped forward, his hand outstretched toward Holmes. "Uncle," he said. "I'm very glad that you're here."

Holmes returned his handshake. "William," he said. "It has been too long."

William was a tall, solid fellow in his mid-twenties. He was more heavily built than Holmes had been at that age, although not nearly as portly as his uncle Mycroft. His face clearly showed the Holmes family features, including a high hairline, aquiline nose, and piercing gray eyes. He was dressed in work clothes, and when he turned and shook my hand, I could feel the rough calluses on his palms.

Holmes turned to face the second young man, a thin fellow who was the spitting image of a young Sherlock Holmes. Tall, perhaps an inch taller even than Holmes, with Holmes's same sharp gaze and precise movements. I knew that he was nearly sixteen, but he seemed much older. He was not dressed for farm work. Rather, he was in more casual clothing, as if our arrival had interrupted his studies. He stuck out his hand, which Holmes grasped and shook.

"Siger," he cried. "Your mother wrote that you had grown, but I did not realize how much so. How have you been?"

"Tolerable," Siger replied. "I will be better when I can get down to London."

"Siger," his mother interrupted, with a warning tone. "This is not the time to start that, with our visitors just setting foot on the place." She turned to us. "You'll hear all about it before you go, but life on the farm is not going to satisfy Siger, here. He has heard too much of London from

253

his brother Bancroft, as well as what he has gleaned over the years from you, Sherlock, and Mycroft, and your writings, Dr. Watson."

Siger turned in my direction. "Ah, Dr. Watson, we finally meet." He shook my hand, and then said, "You have been in Thirsk, I perceive."

Then he laughed in a peculiar silent way. I had only ever heard one other person laugh that way: Sherlock Holmes.

I smiled, recognizing the source of Siger's joke, but Roberta said, sternly, "None of that smart tongue of yours, Siger." Turning to me, she apologized. "He reads too much, I think, doctor."

"Not at all, mother," said Siger. "Of course he's been in Thirsk. They just arrived here on the train. But I didn't just assume it and accept it. I *verified* it." He pointed to my shoes, which had a grayish mud clinging to the instep. "That mud is only at one location around here. It is from the side yard at the Thirsk station, where the coal dust and crushed clinker mixes with the local soil to form this distinctive gray material. There has been no rain for several days, so obviously the doctor walked through a damp spot of that particular mud while getting to their vehicle. There is some of it on the floor of the four-wheeler there, where the doctor was sitting. It has obviously fallen off of his shoes.

"It isn't enough to assume that they came from Thirsk simply because we knew their approximate arrival time and also that Thirsk has the closest major train station. I was able to verify it by observing the mud and relating it to the assumption. Isn't that the correct way to do it, Uncle?" Siger concluded, turning to Holmes.

"Exactly right," answered Holmes. "You are learning. Keep it up. There will be a place for you in London if you do."

"Don't go filling his head full of *that*," said Roberta. "He's going to university in a year or so, and that's that."

"Be careful of whom you hire as a math tutor," Holmes muttered softly, so that only I could hear.

Roberta turned toward the house. "Now come inside and have something to eat or drink, and let's talk about why you're here. I'm sure you'll want to examine things, and I know Sherrinford is looking forward to speaking with you."

"I'm afraid we cannot join you inside just yet," said Holmes. "We must get out to the pit where the body was found before the rains come."

All eyes glanced skyward. The wind was picking up, and sighing through the nearby windbreak. Hanging from one of the eaves of the house was a set of wind chimes, tolling anxiously.

"Of course," said Roberta. "We will be here when you return."

"May I go with them, mother?" asked Siger eagerly, seeing that William had moved to join us.

254

Roberta smiled with tolerant affection. "Yes, but try to leave something for your uncle to solve, won't you?"

As she returned to the house, we climbed back into the four-wheeler with Griffin, who turned the horse and drove us out of the yard. Passing several of the outbuildings, we were observed by the farmhands who had come out to watch our arrival. They nodded in our direction, and then returned inside to their tasks.

As we passed the trees, the wind hit us full on, carrying with it a strong indication of impending rain. Siger shifted in his seat to face me.

"When will you be publishing some more narratives of my uncle's cases, Dr. Watson?" he asked.

I glanced at Holmes, whose mouth tightened in irritation, although conversely his eyes crinkled in suppressed humor. "I am currently . . . prohibited from making public any of the records of Holmes's investigations."

"And it shall remain that way," added Holmes. "Perhaps someday, when I am retired, I will write an extended monograph detailing my methods and how they were applied in specific instances. However, they will be published in a single volume encompassing the whole art of detection, and not as romanticized segments in a throw-away magazine."

Inspector Tenley caught my eye with an amused smile. I shrugged.

Siger, however, did not appear to notice, as he was looking at his uncle with some shock. "I am sure that I cannot wait until you have retired to hear more of your adventures," he said. "I have attempted to make use of Dr. Watson's narratives as something of a guide for my own studies, and frankly I need more information. Two dozen narratives do not provide enough data for well-rounded instruction. And besides," he added, with a grin, "I don't even know the real story of why you allowed us to believe you were dead for three years, what you were doing while you were gone, and how you managed to come back. When I have asked Bancroft, he simply informs me that I am too young. Typical Bancroft bluster."

"Most people do not know the story of Holmes's journey and subsequent return," I said. "He has refused to allow me to publish it. In the meantime, his practice has increased substantially over what it was before his hiatus, and many of the clients indicate that it is because they became aware of Holmes through my writings."

"And how many of them express surprise that I am a real person, and not some fictional creation in a storyteller's tale?" asked Holmes acidly.

"You cannot blame me for that," I said. "It was your brother, Mycroft, who managed to spread the word during your supposed 'death' that you were a fictional character, no doubt in order to aid some scheme of his while you carried out his tasks during your disappearance."

Siger leaned forward intently, and I realized that I might possibly be on the verge of revealing too much of Holmes's activities during his travels. Holmes, seeing that I needed a way to escape from this path of the conversation, said, "Siger, if you are serious about following in my footsteps, take my advice. Do not let the facts of your cases be placed into narrative form, giving the majority of the public the impression that you were created by a doctor with too much time on his hands." Seeing the somewhat hurt expression on my face, he added, "However, if you are able to find a doctor who is of invaluable assistance both in your work and as a friend, I highly recommend it."

Feeling somewhat mollified, I looked around me as the four-wheeler slowed to a halt. We were near a rocky outcropping, sprawled around a hollow in the ground before it. We climbed down and walked to it. Only when we were at the edge were we able to see into the bottom of the pit.

It was about fifteen feet across and eight feet deep, with steeply sloping sides. The bottom was irregular, pierced in several areas by boulders sticking up out of the ground. At the top, there was a path running along the front side, opposite the rocky outcropping. It lay quite close to the edge of the pit, so that someone walking on it would have no trouble seeing what lay at the bottom. Even from a few feet further away, however, the contents of the pit would be hidden.

"Where was the body?" asked Holmes, looking about on the path.

"On the front side of the pit," said Tenley, "directly below the trail. Still, it might have remained unseen if William here hadn't looked in while he was walking by."

"It is a regular thing when I pass this way, to make sure that no sheep have fallen in," added William.

Holmes moved several feet up and down the trail. "Nothing left here," he said. "Too many people have passed this way, beginning with William, and then Sherrinford and the farm hands standing here to guard the body." He moved along the edge of the pit, back to where the rocky outcropping behind it began to rise. Then he climbed down, choosing that spot to enter so that he would not disturb where the body had rested.

William watched the darkening clouds, while Siger followed his uncle's actions with a hawk-like intensity. He stepped to rim of the pit, but away from where the body would have been placed, somehow instinctively knowing where he should stand so as not to impede his uncle's investigation.

In the hole, Holmes moved back and forth across the bottom, bent nearly double so that his eyes were close to the ground. In a moment he called, "How did the body lie?"

Tenley replied, "He was sitting up with his back against the wall of the pit, right under the trail side so that he wouldn't be seen unless you were standing right on the edge, looking down. The arms were tucked in around him. He was obviously placed in that way intentionally after he was rolled in."

Holmes's examination of the bottom only lasted a further few minutes. As he climbed back out, the first drops of heavy rain began to fall around us. "You were correct, Inspector. There is no blood here. The man was killed elsewhere and brought later." He looked up at the sky, they pulled his cap tighter. "We can learn nothing else here. We'd better get back to the house."

We climbed into the four-wheeler, which Griffin immediately set into motion, moving at a faster pace than when we had traveled out to the pit.

The rain began to fall harder, and we huddled into our coats. Siger had not brought a coat or hat, and was somewhat more miserable than the rest of us. Looking at Holmes's fore-and-aft cap, he stated, "That hat would surely be useful right about now. I'm going to get one of those."

Holmes smiled. "I can tell you, it is a fine item for the country, but I often get odd looks in the city." He gestured over his shoulder. "It is not much further to the house." Soon, we arrived, and the lights of the building and smell of wood smoke made the place seem very inviting indeed.

Inside, the house was warm and pleasant, with the lingering smell of a baked dessert. Roberta asked if we wanted a full meal, but we declined. Roberta insisted that we partake of something. Soon we were seated around a large table as she cut a large iced cake, which had been made that morning. "You seem to be holding up very well," said Holmes, his voice cutting across the muted conversations, "considering the fact that a little over a day ago, a murdered man was found nearby, and your husband arrested."

The people in the room fell silent, and Roberta paused for an almost unnoticed second before she resumed cutting the cake. Passing a filled plate around the table, she answered, "Of course I'm calm. This is all a terrible mistake, and it will soon be sorted out."

We ate for a moment, although none of the conversation resumed.

Suddenly, a knock at the front door made us all look at one another. We heard the front door open, followed by quiet conversation. Then an elderly woman, a member of the household staff, stepped into the room.

"Mr. Augustus Morland is here, ma'am," she said.

Before Roberta could reply, a man appeared in the doorway behind the old woman, who looked back and forth between him and her mistress in a flustered way. The man handed his rain-soaked outer garment to the woman, who took it automatically. "That's all right, Hilda," said Roberta, moving across the room and patting the woman on the shoulder. "Go on back to the kitchen." Turning to the man, her voice grew flat and less friendly, as she said, "What can we do for you, Mr. Morland?"

The man was in his late forties or early fifties, well dressed, and with somewhat long hair combed down beside his thin face. He stood there with a posed arrogance, looking around the room and examining each of us quickly but dismissively. When he looked at me, I could see that his eyes were an odd light brown, and the whites around the pupils were discolored and bloodshot, giving the impression that each entire eyeball was one solid muddy marble. His nose was large and red, covered with tiny broken capillaries that extended out onto his lined red cheeks. In a few seconds, his expressionless gaze at me moved on, but in that short space of time, I felt that he had judged me and found me to be useless.

"I'm sorry to disturb you," he said, his voice strangely high-pitched and staccato. "I simply wanted to stop by and see if there was any help that I could provide."

"Thank you, no," replied Roberta. "We appreciate the gesture. I would offer you some cake, but as you can see, we are having a family meeting with Inspector Tenley here," she said, gesturing toward the inspector, who nodded, "and our discussions are confidential."

"Of course, of course," Morland said. "But before I go, I would like to take a moment to introduce myself to Mr. Holmes." He turned to Holmes. "I was speaking to Constable Worth earlier, and he told me that you were expected in today to look into the matter." He stepped forward, his hand outstretched. "Augustus Morland. Pleased to meet you."

Holmes rose and returned the handshake. Nodding toward me, he said, "This is my associate, Dr. John Watson."

I rose as well, extending my hand, but Morland barely glanced my way. "Yes, of course. I assumed he would be here as well." He moved back toward the door. "Well, I will be going, but as I said, if there is anything that I can do to help during this time, do not hesitate to let me know."

With that, he stepped out of the room, followed by Roberta, who led him to the front door. As she shut it behind him, Tenley said, "Well, what do you suppose was the purpose of that?"

"Not actually an offer to help, I'll wager," said William.

Roberta returned to the room, scowling. "That man!" She said. "You can bet that he is probably enjoying this."

"How do you mean?" asked Holmes.

"Because he's been pressuring father to sell the place," said Siger, sitting forward on his chair.

"Now, Siger," began his mother, but he interrupted her.

258

"It's true. Just because you haven't chosen to tell me about it, doesn't mean that I didn't know. He's some rich man from Manchester who moved here last year, bought up several of the old farms, and keeps trying to acquire more. He has talked to father several times about buying this place, but father has always turned him down." Roberta shook her head and sat down. "I can see that you've been eavesdropping when we thought you were studying, young man."

"That's not all," continued Siger, without any sign of contrition. "Like William said, he didn't come here to offer help. He wanted to let us know that he knew about our affairs, and that he was receiving information from Constable Worth. I'll bet that Uncle Sherlock's arrival this morning and involvement in the investigation was supposed to remain confidential, was it not, Inspector Tenley?"

Tenley nodded. "It was. You can be certain that I will be speaking to Worth about this."

Holmes spoke to Roberta. "Tell me more about Morland's offers for the property."

"As Siger said," she replied, "the man moved here late last year. His agents had already purchased a couple of adjacent farms before his arrival, and he moved into the larger of the farmhouses when he got here. He is supposedly very wealthy, and there's talk that he may be knighted soon. Within weeks of his arrival, he had purchased several additional holdings, some that had been in families for countless generations, by making huge offers that they couldn't refuse. He's bought one or two more since then, but he has slowed down somewhat. His time has been taken up with other activities, as he has begun building a huge house, a mile or so from the one where he currently resides.

"Not long after arriving here, he visited Sherrinford one day, arriving in the late afternoon. He introduced himself out in the yard, by the big barn, and declined an offer to come inside. Instead, he jumped right to the point, saying he had decided to buy this farm. Sherrinford said that Morland put it as if the place had already been for sale and he was doing us some kind of favor by taking it off our hands. He then named a ridiculously high sum and asked when the matter could be settled legally.

"Sherrinford simply laughed, and explained that the place wasn't for sale. Sherrinford told me that Morland looked at him for a minute, in that curious way you just saw, and then said, 'Everything is for sale. If money doesn't interest you, perhaps you can be persuaded another way.'

"He turned and left that day, but he has been back several times since, increasing his original offer, and becoming more and more frustrated when we kept turning him down."

"And you say he's from Manchester?" Holmes asked Siger.

Siger nodded. "I haven't been able to determine yet how he made his money."

" 'Determine yet'?" his mother said. "Have you been investigating the man?"

"Of course," replied Siger. "As much as I could, anyway. I've asked around the village, and in Thirsk as well, when I've gone there. He has had a number of visitors at his home, all passing through the village. None have Manchester accents. He also receives a lot of telegrams from Manchester and London."

"And how do you know that?" asked Roberta.

"I questioned people," Siger replied. "I considered contacting Bancroft in London, but I decided that he would simply have turned around and let you and father know what I was doing. I would have been able to find out more," he added, "if I had access to better sources of information, and if I was not trapped out here in the middle of nowhere."

William laughed at this statement, and Holmes looked proudly at his young nephew. Roberta threw up her hands in mock despair, before laughing herself, although rather ruefully.

Part III: Gathering Information

After another twenty minutes or so, I could see that Holmes was getting restless. Finally he announced that it was time to return to the village, where the autopsy was being delayed until Holmes could examine the body. "Dr. Dalton will not appreciate it if we wait any longer."

We stood and went to the front door, where we began to put on our damp coats. Only after a moment did I realize that Siger had prepared for departure as well. I caught his mother's eye. She smiled and turned her head, as if to accept what she could not change.

Outside, the rain had slackened, and Griffin drove out of the barn, where he had been watching for us.

The drive back into the village passed without conversation. We were soon at a tidy stone house, well kept, with a small sign informing us that we were at Dr. Dalton's surgery. We were arriving well past consulting hours, but in this case it did not matter.

A knock on the door was followed by footsteps echoing across the floorboards inside, and in a moment the door flew open to reveal a man in his early forties, lit from behind by several bright lanterns. He was in his shirtsleeves and waistcoat, and his hair was somewhat long and curly, dancing in the light.

"Come in, come in," he said, moving aside and gesturing for us to enter. "I saw you go by hours ago, thought you might stop then, certainly expected you back before now."

We entered the waiting room, which had apparently once been the front parlor of the house, and removed our coats and hats, which our host set about hanging up. I was able to observe him better, and I could see that he was well built and over six feet in height. He had a weathered face, most notably marked by a strong square chin. There were lines around his eyes, but they seemed more likely to have been formed by years of squinting in the outdoor sunshine rather than from laughter. He shook Tenley's hand, and then mine after Tenley's mumbled introduction. He nodded at Siger and William, and then turned to Holmes.

"Well, well," he said. "The prodigal returns."

Holmes returned his gaze for a silent moment, before remarking, "Wesley. It has been too long."

"Yes, it has. Long enough for you to have died, and then returned."

He gave a short bark of a laugh and stuck out his hand. "Welcome back, Sherlock."

They shook hands, and the tension which I had felt since we entered the home seemed to change somewhat, although it did not entirely abate.

261

Dalton stepped back, and his face took on a peevish air. "I have really delayed my duties long enough. Are you here to make your examination of the body so that I may proceed with the official one?"

"Certainly," said Holmes. "Please lead the way."

Dr. Dalton took us back through a short hallway, into an examining room. Over his shoulder, he remarked to me, "I live upstairs, and the housekeeper has the run of the kitchen at the back of the house. The rest of the ground floor is given over to my practice. We are going to my laboratory, which is set up along one side of the building.

As he finished speaking, we entered a small room, obviously at some time in the past designed to be a ground floor bedroom. Now its walls were covered with shelves containing books, chemicals, and scientific apparatus. In the center of the room was an examination table, upon which lay the body of the dead man, unclothed except for a sheet draped across it.

"As the local coroner," Dalton said, "I am occasionally called upon to conduct autopsies on unfortunate individuals."

Holmes ignored him, stepping closer to the body. I followed, while Siger moved along the other side of the table, showing no signs whatsoever of squeamishness or timidity in the presence of violent death.

The victim was a heavy-set man in his fifties, his head covered in a still-thick toss of grey hair. His face was covered with a thick beard and mustache, both quite unkempt, with the untrimmed beard climbing his cheeks halfway to his eyes. His nose was broad, and appeared to have been broken at some point in the distant past. His eyebrows were a tangled thicket, jutting up from the broad shelf of his forehead like a hedge across his face, running unbroken from side to side.

All of this, however, was secondary to the most noticeable characteristic of the man; namely, a wide puckered gash running across his throat.

"You say that there was very little bleeding from the throat wound?" asked Holmes.

"That is right," said Tenley. "The man's collar and clothing were hardly stained. The wound must have occurred after death."

"The killer was right-handed," interrupted Siger, leaning closely over the gaping opening.

"Correct," said Holmes. "And his throat was cut by someone standing in front of him."

I leaned in and confirmed their conclusions, noticing where the initial tear on the right side of the man's throat was hesitant and somewhat ripped before becoming a clean slice that moved slightly upward toward his left.

262

"How can you tell that it wasn't caused by a left-handed man standing behind him and reaching across before drawing the weapon back?" asked William.

"The direction of the slash, upward as the blade moved from Wilkies's right to his left, indicates that the killer was moving his arm in that direction while standing in front of him, and that it would have been in the killer's right hand. A man cutting from behind would have most likely pulled the blade in a downward path. Here," said Holmes, moving behind Dalton, "let me show you."

He stepped behind the doctor, and then placed his left arm around the doctor's chest, so that his left hand rested on Dalton's right shoulder.

"Now," he said, "the blade makes initial contact with the throat on the victim's right side, causing a rip before the actual clean slice begins."

He began to pull his hand slowly from his right to left, across Dalton's upper chest. "As you can see, my hand, which would have been holding the blade, drops as it moves across your throat. It would be awkward to pull the blade in an upward direction as it crosses."

"And," said Siger, stepping up to Dalton from the front, "if I were to slash you from the front," he said, crossing his arm so that his right hand was over Dalton's right shoulder, "my hand makes the initial cut in the same place, but as my knife hand, the right hand, moves across your throat, it tends to swing up, as so." And he proceeded to demonstrate, to Dalton's discomfort.

"Yes, yes, thank you very much," he said, pulling himself loose from Holmes and out from underneath Siger's imaginary knife. "However, I'm not sure what difference it makes. Most people are right-handed, you know."

"Yes, but if we encounter a left-handed suspect, it will be something else to weigh in the balance while we consider him," replied Holmes. "Or her." He turned, and resumed his examination of the body. He muttered to himself as he turned the sheet down, peering at the corpse through his lens. Then, with the help of Siger and myself, he rolled the body, and examined the massive wound in the fellow's back.

"Most of the blood on his clothing was from the back wound, you say?" Holmes asked.

"That's right," Dalton confirmed.

"May I see the clothing?"

"Certainly, although I examined it myself. There is nothing in the pockets to give any indication of the murderer's identity. In fact, the pockets were completely empty."

"Nevertheless," said Holmes, taking the bloody bundle from Dalton.

263

In spite of Dalton's statement, Holmes proceeded to examine the clothing carefully, beginning first with a minute examination of the pockets. As expected, there was nothing in them, not even any lint.

Finally, Holmes shook out the clothes and laid them across the body. Turning them this way and that, he finally said, "Hello, what's this?"

"What?" asked Dalton, although Holmes ignored him.

"Siger," said Holmes, "see if you notice anything."

Siger examined the clothing for less than a minute before announcing, "Wilkies was not wearing these clothes when he was killed."

"*What!*" exclaimed Dalton. Tenley and I were silent. Tenley was watching intently, and I had been around Holmes for too long to be surprised. Holmes nodded for Siger to continue.

"It is obvious that the throat wound was committed sometime after death, due to the lack of bleeding from that site, and that death would have been immediate from the large stab wound in the back, correct?"

"Correct," said Dalton. "The back wound went straight through the heart, and in fact it appears that the knife was rotated and twisted within the body, as if to cause the maximum amount of immediate damage."

"This would appear to be confirmed by the vast amounts of blood on the back of the man's shirt and coat?" continued Siger.

"Yes," said Dalton, with a wary tone. "A wound of that sort would produce copious amounts of blood."

"Then we must ask ourselves," said Siger, warming to his speech, "why the man's shirt and coat, which are both soaked in blood, have no rip or tear in them whatsoever which would have allowed passage of the knife through them and into Wilkies's back?"

"Let me see that!" Dalton said, stepping forward. He leaned in, and then began lifting the clothing to the light. It was obvious that the shirt and coat were whole, and even though the backs of both garments were crusted with blood, there were no holes in the fabrics.

"What does it mean?" asked Dalton.

"Simply that, for reasons unknown to us at this time, Wilkies was killed by a vicious blow to the back. He was either wearing something else at the time, or perhaps entirely unclothed, although this seems less likely to me. Soon after death, the clothes were changed. The wound was still fresh, and so large that a great deal of blood continued to spill from it, staining the clothing. Some time later, after the bleeding had completely stopped, the throat was cut, possibly after Wilkies was propped at the side of the pit."

"But doesn't that invalidate all your evidence about a right-handed man standing in front of him?" asked Dalton.

"Exactly the opposite," replied Holmes. "If the body was propped up and then the killer slashed it, probably to add further evidence of violence, or to complete some ritual, the cut would travel up and to Wilkies's left, as I have theorized. If the killer then stood in the pit, held Wilkies's head back by the hair, and slashed up and to the right, it would be exactly as I have surmised."

Dalton looked irritated. Refolding the clothing, he said, "I would have noticed the lack of cuts in the garments myself, eventually." Placing them on a shelf, he turned back to us. "After all, I have been prevented from carrying out the full autopsy as I have been waiting for your arrival."

Holmes smiled. "Then by all means, Wesley, let us not delay you for another moment. Please let me know of any other information you discover." Then he turned to go. Tenley and I stayed to shake hands with Dalton, although Siger had already departed with his uncle.

Outside in the four-wheeler, Holmes shook his head. "I had forgotten how sensitive and proud Wesley can sometimes be," he stated. "He and I were always competitors as boys. I think that he was rather gratified when he learned that I did not finish my degrees at either Oxford or Cambridge, while he went on to become a doctor. Upon the completion of his medical degree, he returned here and has become an important man in the area. It cannot sit well for him to have me return and intrude on what he thinks of as his own personal bailiwick."

Tenley asked where Holmes wished to go next. "To visit my brother, Sherrinford," replied Holmes.

Part IV: The Prisoner

It was only a matter of minutes to wind through the village to an odd building, standing alone from its neighbors and quite tall for the area, reaching three stories above the ground. On the top floor I could see barred windows.

"This is new," said Holmes, looking at the building.

"Yes sir," said Tenley. "It was constructed a year or so ago. A man in York, Sir Clive Owenby, put up the money. He made some talk about providing proper facilities for the local law enforcement authorities. I believe that he is a close acquaintance of your brother Mycroft."

We entered the building and began to divest ourselves of our wet outer garments. From a side office emerged a short, powerfully built man in a spotless uniform. I was not surprised when he introduced himself as Constable Worth.

"It is a pleasure to meet you, gentlemen," he said, shaking our hands. "Unpleasant business all around, I'm afraid."

"Have you learned anything further since we last spoke?" asked Tenley, cutting through the introductions.

"Not a thing, sir. The prisoner has not made any further statements."

"I meant from anyone else, such as members of Wilkies's campsite."

"No, sir. Haven't been back out there."

Tenley gestured to us. "These men will be going up to visit Mr. Holmes. May I have the key to the cell?"

Worth looked surprised. "Sir, these cells are my responsibility . . . ."

"The keys, Constable," said Tenley, holding out his hand. Worth reluctantly produced the keys, laying them in Tenley's palm.

Tenley immediately handed them to Holmes. "Top of the stairs, sir," he said. "I will stay down here with Constable Worth and discuss today's visit by Mr. Morland."

"But sir," said Worth. "The prisoner . . . These men are not authorized to just go up and open the door. They are members of his family, sir . . . ."

Tenley waved his hand. "These people are entirely trustworthy, and I vouch for them completely. Mr. Holmes and Dr. Watson have performed countless services for the government of this country. And young Siger, here, is training as well to continue his uncle's work."

Siger widened his eyes and pulled himself straighter, adding to the already existing impression of great height and leanness. Holmes caught my eye, his lips turned up in a minuscule smile. As one, we turned from Tenley and Worth.

We started upstairs, leaving Worth looking uncomfortable in the feeble light of the entrance hall. We reached a landing on the stairs, and then climbed to the first floor, which seemed to consist of a series of closed rooms all opening from the small landing by the stairs. Only a single gaslight burned on that floor to illuminate our progress. We turned toward the next set of stairs, moving past the final landing before reaching the top floor. I arrived first, and waited for my friends, all of whom were more out of breath than I.

Holmes stepped in front of me to a closed door. Turning the knob revealed a short hallway, with metal-barred cells on each side. The room was lit by a single lamp hanging in the hall from the ceiling between the cells. Siger stepped through the door and stopped at the first cell on the left. Taking the keys from Holmes, he opened the door.

A man was sitting in the shadows at the back of the cell. He stirred, rose, and stepped forward into the light. He was several inches over six feet, and looked much like his brothers, but mostly like his son William.

He thrust his arms out when he saw Sherlock Holmes and smiled. The expression lit his face with kindness and good-hearted joy, and in spite of the grimness of the location, with the rain pounding on the roof above us, I grinned myself.

Sherrinford Holmes hugged his younger brother and laughed. I glanced at Siger and William and saw that they were smiling as well. I knew immediately that Sherrinford was a good man, and could not be in any way responsible for that of which he was accused. There was an air of kindness about him that was I unable to define, but it existed nonetheless. It was as if someone had managed to combine Sherlock Holmes and Father Christmas.

I missed whatever Sherrinford mumbled to Holmes. Then he released his brother and reached for his sons, who also received great hugs. Then he turned to me. I feared that I would be clasped to the big man, but instead he thrust out a great paw of a hand and grasped mine, shaking it and introducing himself.

"I am so sorry it has taken us so long to meet, Dr. Watson," he cried. "It is as much my fault as my brother's, I'm afraid. I'll wager he never even told you that he had people up here in Yorkshire, did he?" Without waiting for an answer, he continued. "It has always been his way. However, I have not made my way down to London to see him, either. Not in all the years that he has been down there. Unforgivable, doctor, simply unforgivable on my part."

He stepped back, and looked at Holmes in mock sternness. "I understand that Dr. Watson was wounded in Afghanistan, Sherlock, shortly before the two of you met." Holmes nodded, and Sherrinford continued. "I now perceive that the wound was in his leg. Tell me, why on earth did you make him take the room upstairs from your sitting room at your lodgings? Shouldn't you have offered to let the wounded war veteran have the more easily accessible bedroom on the first floor near the sitting room, while you took the one upstairs on the second?"

He moved back into the cell, gesturing for us to enter. I had known Sherlock Holmes at that time for over fifteen years, counting the years when he had disappeared. I had seen his brother, Mycroft, on numerous occasions since meeting him in the fall of 1888. By now I should have been used to the deductions of the Holmes brothers, and if I could not immediately follow their logic to understand how their conclusions were reached, I should have at least learned to keep my mouth shut. However, as was usually the case, I had to know.

"How did you know that my bedroom is upstairs and your brother's bedroom on the first floor?" I asked.

Sherrinford smiled. "Siger?" he asked, "will you explain it to the doctor?"

Siger stepped forward, his hands clasped in front of him, as if he were reciting his multiplication tables at school. "Was it Dr. Watson's breathing?" he asked.

Sherrinford nodded. "Exactly. Go ahead."

Holmes moved into the cell, leaning against one of the walls. Sherrinford gestured toward his cot, offering me a place to sit. I shook my head, and Sherrinford seated himself in the middle of the rickety structure.

Siger took a deep breath. "When we reached this floor, Dr. Watson arrived first, while Uncle Sherlock, William, and I arrived seconds later. No doubt you had been expecting us, and you were listening for our footsteps. You heard Dr. Watson first, during the several seconds he was alone at the top of the steps, and you realized from his limp who he was. You also could tell that he was not out of breath. Then you heard the rest of us arrive, and we paused to catch our wind for a few seconds, before entering the cells.

"You already knew about Dr. Watson's war service from his narrative, *A Study In Scarlet*, as well as other published accounts. You were able to determine that his wound was in the leg, both from the limp, and also from the fact that he is quite comfortable with it at this point, sixteen years later, so much so that he was able to climb the steps better than his companions.

"The evenness of the doctor's breathing indicated that he is used to climbing to the second floor on a regular basis, while Uncle Sherlock is not. Obviously both men are conditioned to climb to the first floor, where their sitting room is located, but since Uncle Sherlock has not had to get used to climbing any higher on a regular basis, his bedroom is obviously on the same floor as the sitting room at their lodgings, while the doctor's room is one floor higher."

"Absolutely right," said Sherrinford. "And of course, Siger, as active as you are, there are not many steps for you to climb at our house, either, so you were as out of breath as your uncle."

"But why couldn't I be used to climbing to the second story somewhere else," I asked. "Why do you assume I have only conditioned myself to climb that many steps to my rooms at our lodgings? Couldn't I have done so at my practice, or at a hospital?"

"I knew from Sherlock's letters that you had sold your practice and had placed your self back in harness with my brother," stated Sherrinford. "It seemed logical that the only place you were regularly climbing that many stairs would be at your home." He looked at Holmes. "However, Sherlock, you didn't answer my question. Why did you make Dr. Watson take the higher room all those years ago when he was a recently invalided soldier?"

Holmes looked slightly uncomfortable, and even, perhaps, guilty. "When I found the rooms in Baker Street, I knew that I could not afford them by myself. When I mentioned the need to find a fellow lodger to my friend Stamford, at Bart's, I did not seriously believe that anything would come of it, and I never really thought that I would be able to obtain the rooms. When Stamford introduced me to Watson, I immediately saw that he had been wounded in Afghanistan, but in all honesty, it simply never occurred to me to offer him the bedroom adjacent to the sitting room on the first floor.

"I suppose that I rationalized that since I had been the one to find the rooms I should take the more accessible one. Also, to be honest, I was not certain that Watson would be residing there for any length of time"

He smiled in my direction. "I believed that a combination of my increased professional success, allowing me to afford the rooms by myself, as well as my generally poor attractiveness as a fellow lodger, would soon encourage you to move on to something better. And I must admit, that until now, I have selfishly never thought of the added discomfort climbing those extra steps must have caused you, my dear Watson."

Holmes lifted his hand. "It is far too late to ask, but would you like to trade rooms?"

I laughed, and everyone joined in. "Of course not," I said. "Climbing up and down those steps was probably excellent therapy for me. Besides," I added, "I was so lazy in those early days that climbing to my room every time you needed the sitting room to meet with one of your clients was the only exercise I took."

Sherrinford nodded. "Excellent job of reasoning, Siger," he said to his son.

Siger looked surprised. "But I was just explaining what *you* had determined," he said.

Sherrinford waved this away, and turned to Holmes. "I don't have to reason anything out to determine why you are here," he said. "Roberta must have contacted you."

"Actually, she contacted Mycroft, who in turn enlisted the efforts of Inspector Tenley, followed by Watson and myself."

Sherrinford nodded. "What do you need to ask me?"

"Simply begin at the beginning, and I will ask questions as needed."

"Well," said Sherrinford, rubbing his hands together and settling on the cot, "about two weeks ago, in the morning, a group of wagons arrived at the farm. The lead wagon pulled a little closer to the house, and a man hopped down. I was in the barn and went out to meet him.

"Of course, it was Wilkies. He introduced himself, and pointed to his daughter, who had remained on the seat of the wagon. He said that he and his group were heading into the north for the summer, and they wondered if they could stop on our land for a week or so before moving on. They seemed respectable enough, and I agreed. I directed them to the southern fields, where I knew the conditions would be pleasant, with shade trees, and there would be plenty of water from the stream.

"That night, after they had set up camp, I walked over to see how they were doing. Wilkies invited me into his tent, a large, spacious affair that was obviously military surplus. There were nearly a dozen other tents, spread around a central area, and each with its own campfire. A rope paddock had been set up somewhat downstream for the livestock.

"Wilkies instructed his daughter to prepare tea. She did so without comment, moving silently about the tent, and, if I may speculate, somewhat resentfully of my presence. While she worked, I questioned Wilkies about the nature of his group. His description led me to believe that they are some sort of offshoot of Druidism, with an eccentric mixture of Christianity, Egyptian pantheism, and some Germanic mythology as well. He had apparently been a Church of England theology student in his early twenties, before developing his own unique beliefs. He published some tracts ten or fifteen years ago explaining his theology, and at one point had started his own church, where he attracted a few loyal followers. At some time, he was forced to leave his church building, and he and his congregation took to the road, traveling throughout the countryside, much like gypsies from north to south, and back again.

"I visited his tent every two or three days, questioning him about his beliefs. In the second week, I was becoming somewhat curious as to when he intended to depart, as his people had shown no signs of preparing to

270

leave. However, I never came right out and asked him, and he never volunteered the information on his own.

"The night of the murder was simply another visit, and there was no anger between us. In fact, there was not much conversation at all. He and I sat on camp stools in front of his tent, facing the fire, in companionable silence. I saw no signs of his daughter, Sophia, although it is possible she may have been in the tent. As to what she claims to have heard, I can only say that if she believes that conversation to have taken place between me and her father, she is completely mistaken. Perhaps she heard him arguing later, with someone else. I do not know what the phrase 'the true path,' which was attributed to me, refers to."

"Did you ever have any conversations with any of the other followers, either at the camp or elsewhere?" Holmes asked.

"Never," replied his brother. "As far as I know, none of them ever ventured away from camp, and they kept to themselves when I was there. For that matter, Sophia never spoke to me either. She would simply meet my eyes with a somewhat reserved expression before looking away, or gesturing me toward the tent where her father and I would talk."

Holmes was silent for several minutes, before asking, "What can you tell me of Augustus Morland?"

Sherrinford cleared his throat and looked at Siger. "Have you been telling Sherlock of your suspicions of Morland?"

"He came to the house today," said Siger. "He claimed that he wanted to offer his help, after he had been told of your arrest by Constable Worth." Then he added, "How did you know of my suspicions about him?"

Sherrinford waved a hand. "Fathers know everything, son." He turned back to his brother. "I have met Morland half-a-dozen times or so in the last few months. He has been trying to buy up all the land in this area, including ours." He went on to relate the same narrative of events that had earlier been provided to us by Roberta. "He appears to be trying to create an unbroken estate stretching from here all the way to the sea. And he seems to have the money and resources to do so, eventually. If he doesn't get our land, he will simply buy some around it until he gets the contiguous layout that he desires."

Holmes shifted away from the wall. "Have you conferred with legal counsel?"

"Not yet," replied Sherrinford. "I believe that Worth has forgotten about it. Tenley and I talked earlier today, and we both felt that at this point it was not necessary. I am willing to wait here for a little while longer while the investigation progresses. Hopefully, this will lull the real murderer into a false sense of security, if he believes that his plan to frame

271

me has been completely accepted." Sherrinford stood. "Can I tell you anything else?"

"I think that I have heard enough for tonight," he said. "Is there anything we can do for you? Can we bring you anything?"

"No, no, I am quite all right," Sherrinford replied. "Worth is basically a good fellow, for all his pretensions. I am quite sure that you will have me out of here in a day or so."

"I am confident of that as well," said Holmes. "I begin to see where to pull the red thread running through this tangled skein."

Sherrinford stepped forward, and Holmes shook his hand. Then Sherrinford shook mine as well, before drawing his sons into another hug. "Give my love to your mother," he said.

"We will," replied Siger, quietly. We left the cell, and Siger solemnly relocked the door.

Downstairs, he handed the keys to Tenley, who was standing near the front door. In a side room we could see Worth, sitting at his desk, looking chastened and somewhat embarrassed. I nodded to the man, and we left the building. Tenley followed in a moment, after returning the keys to Worth.

In the four-wheeler, Tenley said, "What next, gentlemen?"

"I need to send some wires, and then back to the farm for the night, I suppose," replied Holmes. The ever-patient Griffin turned the horse, and then drove the four-wheeler for a few short minutes to the office where Holmes jumped down, going in to send his telegrams. Siger, William, Tenley, and I waited in the four-wheeler, grateful that the rain had stopped, although a cold damp wind still blew.

Holmes returned in a minute, climbed in, and we set off for the Holmes farm. It was not long before we arrived. Tenley asked, "What do you have planned for tomorrow, Mr. Holmes?"

"If you and Griffin could be back here by about nine o'clock, I believe that we will interview Miss Sophia at the campsite."

"Very good," said Tenley, as we climbed down. "See you in the morning, then."

As they drove away, the door opened, spilling light into the damp yard. We went inside to find that Roberta had prepared something of a feast. Siger passed on the good wishes of his father, and we sat down to eat. Over the years I had often thought of Sherlock Holmes as a lonely man, buried in his studies and thoughts. That night, I was able to see a new side of him, as part of a family that treasured and cherished him. As Holmes's friend, I was given some of that affection as well. The entire evening was somewhat muted, due to the absence of Sherrinford and the awful events that had led to his arrest. However, in spite of that, there was an optimism that the incarceration was only temporary, and the warm feelings of that house could not be quelled.

As we climbed the stairs to our rooms later that night, I told Holmes, "I am honored to meet your family. They are fine people, indeed."

"Yes, they are," he replied. "I must never take them for granted. Perhaps I should try to visit here more often."

"I agree, Holmes. I heartily agree." We reached the door of my room.

"Good night, Holmes."

He continued down the hallway. Over his shoulder, he said "And good night to you as well, Watson."

Part V: The Camp

We arose early next morning to find that Roberta had prepared a large farm breakfast, which I greeted with enthusiasm. I was unsurprised to see that Holmes picked at his food, and seemed content to consume several cups of strong black coffee. William kept pace with my appetite, but Siger seemed to eat even less than his uncle. He looked tired, and acted rather nervous, glancing at Holmes often before directing his eyes elsewhere around the room.

After William and I had eaten as much as we could, William pushed back from the table and stood, announcing that he wished us good luck, and that he would like to accompany us but someone must continue to direct the daily activities of the farm. With a wave he departed. Siger, who had grown more and more nervous, finally blurted out,

"Uncle, may I have a word with you and Dr. Watson? Outside," he added, cutting his eyes toward his mother. Roberta smiled, but did not say anything. Thanking her for a wonderful meal, we stepped out of the house and into the yard. Siger was carrying a worn knapsack, which he had kept beside him throughout breakfast.

Holmes pulled out his watch. "Tenley should be here in ten minutes or so. What is it, Siger?"

His nephew appeared uncertain, now that he had his uncle's attention. After a few awkward seconds of silence, he said, "I have discovered something important, uncle, but in doing so I may have jeopardized your case."

Holmes indicated that he should continue. "Last night," said Siger, "I could not sleep. Without taking time to explain all my reasoning and the various dead ends I let my mind travel, I finally came to the conclusion that Mr. Morland must somehow be involved in this matter. So I arose and slipped out of the house. I then made my way over the fields to Morland's."

Holmes looked quickly at me, and then back to his nephew. A glint had caught fire in Holmes's hooded eyes. "And what did you find?" he asked.

"What I expected to find," Siger said, opening the knapsack. "And more that I did not expect." He reached in, and pulled out a rolled bundle of white bloodstained cloth. Glancing toward the house to make sure he was unobserved, Siger dropped the knapsack and began to unroll his discovery. His hands revealed some sort of religious robe, almost completely soaked in dried blood. As the bundle was nearly unrolled, he stopped and carefully extricated two items which had been tucked in the center.

The first was a dagger, its thin narrow blade about six inches long. It seemed quite old, and the handle appeared to be made of iron, with blunt

274

and clumsy runes engraved in it. The blade was covered with dried blood. The second item from the bundle was something far more sinister.

I had seen a thing like it once before, years earlier, although I never expected see one again, and surely not in the heart of beautiful Yorkshire. It was a Hand of Glory, the foul device used by witches' covens while practicing their hated black magic. In the early eighties, Holmes and I had been involved in the destruction of a nest of the evil practitioners. At the time, I had been shocked to my core by the evil to which the human heart was capable of sinking, in spite of my experiences on many continents and the horrors I had seen in war.

I must have gasped, because both Holmes and Siger looked away from the bundle and toward me. I swallowed and said, "Holmes, what can it mean?"

He did not reply. Instead, he reached for the white robe. Taking it from Siger, he finished unfolding it. He searched for a moment with his long thin fingers before finding what he sought. On the back of the robe, centered in the place equivalent to where Wilkies's fatal wound had been on his body, was a long ragged slit. This part of the robe was the most blood-soaked portion of the whole garment.

"This is what Wilkies was wearing when he was murdered," said Holmes, pushing his finger through the hole. "It is some sort of ceremonial robe. For some reason, he was changed into conventional clothing after death." He rotated the robe to examine the clean neck line. "And his throat was not slit while he was wearing this. As we believed, it took place post-mortem."

He then held up the knife, turning it from side to side in the morning sunlight. "I think it is safe to say that this is the murder weapon," he said. "The width of the blade corresponds to some of the marks on the body." Turning to Siger, he asked, "Where did you find this?"

"It was in one of Morland's stable buildings, an unused one, in an empty stall under some straw."

"How did you know to look there?"

"It wasn't the first place that I looked," replied Siger. "Of course, I couldn't get in the house, but I did think that I would be able to search most of the out-buildings."

"Weren't you afraid of being caught?" I asked.

Siger replied, with a look that must have made his uncle proud, "When I search, I do not get caught."

"Why did you decide to search Morland's premises?" asked Holmes.

"I simply reasoned that he, of all the people currently around here, would have the most reason to frame my father, simply because Father will not sell him our farm. If someone in the religious camp wanted to murder Wilkies, they would have done so without involving my father."

"That is not necessarily so," said Holmes, "but no matter, right now. Did you expect to find this?" he asked, holding up the robe and the items that had been hidden within it.

"Not exactly," said Siger. "I knew that Wilkies had not been murdered in the clothing in which he was found. I decided to look for the actual murder clothing, which must have been taken away by the murderer. If my assumption was correct, and Morland was involved, then logically he would have taken the clothing.

"Of course, there was every reason to think that it could have been already destroyed, or hidden somewhere in the fields, or even buried or burned. However, if I spent the night exploring Mr. Morland's barns, all I could lose would be a night's sleep, and look what I found." He gestured at the robe, and added, "Of course, I did not expect to find this, exactly. I thought I would possibly just discover another suit similar to the one that Wilkies was wearing when his body was found."

Holmes was silent for a moment, and then he began to re-roll the bundle, making sure that the dagger and the Hand of Glory were concealed within. "It is very important," he said, "when gathering information in a criminal case, to protect the chain of evidence. By that, I mean that one must be able to demonstrate in a court of law that the evidence has been untainted and unaltered before it is discovered by a legitimate and verifiable source." He pushed the bundle into Siger's knapsack. "I realize that you took this in order to show it to me, and also to make sure that it was not removed and destroyed in the meantime. However, the authenticity of the evidence is now somewhat compromised."

Siger lowered his head. "I am sorry, uncle."

"I agree with you that somehow, Morland is involved in this matter. I had decided that yesterday, before your important discovery. However, if the matter came to court as it stands now, Morland's attorneys could argue that he was an innocent victim of a plot, or that one of his own employees had hidden the items without his knowledge. In fact, they could even argue that you, Siger, had been involved in the murder yourself and that you had pretended to find the items at Morland's farm in order to frame *him*."

Siger looked up with an apprehensive expression. "Inspector Tenley would tell you the same thing," continued Holmes. "By removing this evidence, its effectiveness is decreased or eliminated altogether." Holmes handed the knapsack to Siger, who widened his eyes in surprise. "Inspector Tenley would tell you that, I suppose, if he knew about it."

Holmes turned and glanced down the lane, toward the approaching four-wheeler containing Tenley and Griffin. "We are going to Morland's house later this morning," said Holmes. "Would you be so kind, Siger, to slip away from us at some point so that you can replace the items in question where you found them? Without being observed, of course. We are taking a chance that they will not be destroyed in the meantime, until we are ready to find them legitimately. Also, we can only hope that their absence has not already been discovered, causing the murderer to move before we are ready to outflank him."

Holmes continued to stare at the approaching vehicle, while Siger shouldered the knapsack. He turned to me with a relieved smile on his face. I reached out and gripped his shoulder.

The four-wheeler had barely stopped before Tenley jumped down, reaching us in a few steps. "These arrived this morning, Mr. Holmes, from Mycroft," he said, holding a stack of telegrams out in front of him.

"They were addressed to both of us, so I've already read them. I think you will find them interesting."

Holmes took the forms and quickly studied them, one after another, before passing them to me. As I finished them, I handed them on to Siger.

"Will we be going to Mr. Morland's, then?" asked Tenley.

"Not yet," replied Holmes. "First I want to go to Wilkies's camp, and to meet his daughter."

In the four-wheeler, I pondered the astounding information I had read in the long telegraph forms. Obviously Mycroft, working for the government, had no hesitation at sending extensively long wires when the mood suited him.

The telegram forms consisted of one long message, relating the curious and sinister history of Augustus Morland. It seemed that Morland had moved to Yorkshire from Manchester, as we had already heard. However, his background was slightly more convoluted than the story of his origin in Manchester had led us to believe. He had graduated from university nearly twenty-five years earlier, and had immediately left on a year-long tour of the continent. While this was not unusual, the subsequent events were. Soon after his arrival in one of the smaller German spa towns, he had disappeared. The local police were unable to find him, and for over a year there was no sign of him whatsoever. During that time, his mother in Manchester had sickened with despair and died.

At that time, in the early 1870's, Germany had still been a patchwork of small kingdoms, duchies, and petty fiefdoms, with little cooperation or communication between them. It had proved nearly impossible to discover anything about the disappearance and whereabouts of young Morland. Then, over a year after he had gone missing, Morland had resurfaced, claiming that he had been kidnapped by anarchists who had argued amongst themselves the entire time about whether to kill him outright or request a ransom. Finally he had managed to escape and make his way to safety. However, he had refused to return home to England, instead stating that he preferred to remain in Germany.

His father had begged him to come home, sending urgent letters and telegrams, but young Morland refused. The father, already sickened by the death of his wife and the extended mystery of his missing son, was too weak to travel to Germany in order to try in person to convince the young man that he should return to England. The father soon died, and Morland inherited the estates.

Morland remained ensconced in Germany for nearly a quarter of a century, maintaining his business interests from there, and increasing his wealth many times over. It was only in the last year or so that he had returned to his family home in Manchester, where he had lived for a few months before moving again, this time to Yorkshire, where he began his bullying acquisitions of the surrounding farm lands.

The final sheets of the telegram revealed that Mycroft Holmes, as well as his nephew Bancroft, had become interested in Morland several months earlier. A closer investigation was made into the man's past, and Mycroft's agents had recently determined that the man was not actually Morland at all, but rather an imposter who had been set in place years earlier, following the original abduction and murder of the actual young man.

"I knew it!" stated Siger, as we discussed the matter in the rocking four-wheeler. "I knew that there was something wrong about the man."

"Is the telegraph agent who took this information completely reliable?" Holmes asked Tenley. "Can he keep the information confidential?"

"He is one of my men," Tenley replied. "He can be trusted."

Holmes eyed Tenley speculatively. "You do not seem surprised by what is in these messages," he said.

"Your brother, Mycroft, keeps a pretty close eye on things," he said. "Especially around here. Apparently, when Morland started buying up vast amounts of land, it came to Mycroft's attention pretty quickly."

"I would wager that you knew about it as well," said Holmes. "Probably for quite a while before this murder actually took place." He shifted in his seat. "Why wasn't I told about this aspect of the case to begin with?"

"Your brother felt that you would benefit by beginning your investigation with an open mind. He was not necessarily convinced that Morland's background and activities were directly related to the murder. Mycroft decided to reveal Morland's background to you after you had seen the initial lay of the land. At that point, you could determine Morland's relevance to the investigation. However, your wires to London last night

278

indicated that you had already decided that Morland is somehow involved."

Holmes asked, "Are you actually an inspector with the Yard, or do your responsibilities require you to pursue different activities?"

Tenley smiled. "They know me at the Yard. However, much of my work is carried out more in your brother's purview."

"I thought as much," Holmes said, nodding. "You are one of my brother's agents." Holmes folded the telegraph forms and put them in his pocket. "Were you assigned to this area as part of your responsibilities to my brother's department?"

Tenley nodded. "Keeping an eye on Morland is just part of my job up here."

Holmes gestured around him. "Just how much land has this German agent actually bought?"

"Enough," Tenley replied. "Too much. We think that he hopes to obtain even more, so that he can create some sort of vast staging area, with buffer zones on either side so that no one will be able to notice or tell."

"Tell what?" asked Siger. "That there are German soldiers surreptitiously landing in England?"

"Soldiers?" I asked. "Is it to be war, then?"

"Eventually," said Tenley, without emotion. "Not this year, maybe not through the rest of this century, or even into the first part of the next, but it is coming. The Kaiser is interested in creating his own global empire, and he is too resentful of the British Empire, as well as the restraining influence of his grandmother, Queen Victoria. Eventually the Germans will lash out."

"Mycroft and I have been predicting as much for years," said Holmes. "However, as respected as Mycroft is, he has had the devil of a time convincing his superiors of the obvious facts."

" 'A prophet hath no honor in his own country.' Eh, Mr. Holmes?" asked Tenley with a smile.

"John 4:44," replied both Holmes and Siger at the same time. They looked at each other with surprise, and then they began to laugh. Tenley and I joined in. Griffin, as emotionless as ever, continued to guide the horses. We were soon within sight of Wilkies's camp.

As we had been told the day before, the campsite consisted of a loose grouping of tents. These were clustered underneath the trees that grew beside the stream watering the south side of the Holmes land. From my military days, I was able to quickly confirm that the tents were military castoffs of a style that had gone out of date at least twenty years before.

Each of the tents was a dull brown color, the original dyes having long been faded and replaced by weathering and mildew of too many years of use. Each tent's ugly hue, however, was tempered somewhat by the canvas patches of varying shades that were randomly sewn along their sides, giving them something of a gypsy air.

Tenley led us to the larger and more central tent, in front of which sat a young woman on a camp stool. Before her were the smoking remains of a fire, apparently left to die following the completion of her breakfast preparations. As we approached, the woman stood to face us, dropping her arms and holding her fisted hands at her sides.

"Sophia," said Tenley, "these are the men from London who are here to investigate your father's death. This is Mr. Sherlock Holmes, and Dr. Watson. And this young man is Siger Holmes, the son of Sherrinford Holmes."

"The son of a murderer, you mean!" she hissed, turning quickly in Siger's direction. He was surprised, and took a startled step backward before remembering himself and holding his ground.

Sophie Wilkies was a sallow young woman in her early twenties, not much over five feet in height. Her hair was loose, with shading somewhere between black and dark brown. Her hair was actually her most attractive feature, and it shone in the morning sunlight, obviously freshly brushed. She was somewhat unfortunate in her facial features, as she had bushy eyebrows similar to her late father's, on a prominent ridge shading her dark eyes. Also, her lower lip was heavy and pendulous, and tended to sag toward her rather weak chin, revealing white but quite crooked lower teeth. When she spoke, her lip would tighten, giving her whole face a look of determination, As she completed her thought, however, her face would relax and her lip would droop back down, again revealing her unfortunate and rather distracting mouth.

"Miss Wilkies," said Holmes, "I was wondering whether you could repeat for us the conversation that you said that you heard the night your father was murdered."

"I didn't *say* I heard it. I *did* hear it! That man had come around here again, that *murderer*, and started in browbeating my father about how he had abandoned 'the true path,' whatever that means. They had discussed it every single night that the man visited, but the night when he killed my father, he was much more angry about it. He even threatened my father. He said that anyone who turned away from the 'true path' would not have long in this world to reconsider his mistake."

"You say he threatened your father?" asked Tenley. "You did not mention that when we spoke of this matter before."

"I just remembered it," said the girl, crossing her arms defiantly.

"What is the 'true path'?" asked Holmes.

"I do not know," said the girl. "My father has been the shepherd of this flock since before I was born. When I was a little girl, we had a church building, but my father decided that his calling was to lead the faithful to sojourn at the holy sites of Britain, reawakening the lost beliefs. In the last few years, we have occasionally traveled to the continent as well, visiting holy sites in France, Germany, and even Belgium."

"How does your congregation finance itself?" asked Holmes. I had wondered the same thing myself. The condition of the campsite did not indicate that funds were immediately available for pilgrimages across the Channel.

"My father inherited some money as a young man," Sophia answered. "And members of our congregation have funds of their own that they provide for us all when they join our group. They contribute as needed. As you can see, our wants are simple." She gestured toward the other tents, where several members of the group were going about their own business, mending clothing, or tending to pots suspended over small fires.

"Who will lead your group, now that your father is gone?" I asked.

"I will," the girl said simply. "My father would have wanted it that way."

"Did your father have any enemies?" asked Holmes.

"I see what you are doing!" cried the girl. "You want me to say that maybe someone else could have killed my father. Well, no one else did. It was this boy's father who did it! I will swear to it!"

Holmes and Tenley continued to ask questions for a few more minutes, but the girl provided no additional information, and could not be swayed in her single-minded belief that the murderer of her father was Sherrinford Holmes. Her dogmatic assertions tended to reveal her somewhat limited intellectual gifts. Siger stood to the side, watching uncomfortably as the girl's story remained unshaken. His knuckles, gripping the straps of his knapsack, were white.

Finally we thanked the girl and left. She flounced into her tent and pulled the flap down, shutting herself inside. We started to walk toward the four-wheeler, where patient Griffin sat hunched in the warming morning sunshine. We were thirty or forty feet from the girl's tent when an old man, sitting on a stool in front of a much smaller tent, hailed us.

"Her father never talked any about 'the true path' with anyone," he said. "The only people who ever discussed that around here was Sophia herself, and that rich man who has been coming around here to see her."

We crowded closer, keeping our voices low so that no one would overhear us. "What rich man?" Holmes asked.

"That Morland fellow," the old man replied. "He has been here several times since we made camp. He and Sophia huddle and whisper to each

281

other, usually near my tent. They don't pay me any attention, and they don't seem to mind talking in front of me."

"What have they said?" asked Tenley.

"Sophia talks about how she is the one that's going to lead everyone back to the 'true path,' and that what her father has always believed is simply a weak and watered-down reflection of the truth. Morland whispers to her, telling her how right she is, dear, and they will lead the people together, dear. It right makes me sick."

"What is the 'true path,' then?" asked Holmes.

"I don't really know," said the old man. "From what I could hear, Sophia believes that her father was right to visit the old places, the great stones and ruins and such, but that when we were there, he was wasting his time trying to get in touch with the wrong kind of spirits. It sounds to me as if the spirits Sophia wants to reach are quite a bit more grim than what her father believed in."

"And what exactly did her father believe in?"

"Well, I don't know exactly," said the old man.

"What?" I said, reflecting the astonishment of my friends.

"Well, I don't. I don't believe in all this stuff. Don't pay any attention to it, really. My wife did, though, and when she wanted to travel with these people, I didn't really object to it. I had roamed some in my younger days, and always found it agreeable. When my wife wanted to go a-traveling I didn't mind at all, even though it meant going about with these folks, but I never was really a part of this group. I just enjoyed the journey, you see, and got to visit some places I might not have seen otherwise.

"I had inherited a little money, and once long ago I had a store that I later sold for enough of a profit to pay for my daily bread, so I can afford to play at this game with these people. They all seem nice enough, and harmless, too, I suppose. All except for Sophia. After my wife died a year or so ago, I decided to just keep going about with them. No one has said anything against it, and I guess I've been a part of the group for so long that no one questions it anymore, even though my wife was the real believer."

"How often has Mr. Morland been here?" asked Holmes.

"Usually every day, since we started camping here a couple of weeks ago. At first he spoke to both Wilkies and Sophia, but later he just came by to see Sophia by herself. I don't even know if her father realized it, because he was usually in his tent at the time, praying, or taking a nap."

The old man shifted in his seat and leaned forward, lowering his voice somewhat. "Morland hasn't been back here since Wilkies was murdered, though." He glanced at Sophia's tent. "I'll tell you something else, as well. This wasn't the first time we had met this Mr. Morland. He first showed up a couple of years ago, when we were traveling through Germany. He looked a lot different then, wasn't dressed nearly so fine, but it was him.

"Depending on where we camp, we sometimes get visitors from the nearby towns who are curious about whatever it is that Wilkies was teaching. In some German town, I forget which, Morland showed up one day with a group of those people. It wasn't long before he and Sophia met each other. Even then, the two of them would find time to walk apart from everyone else and whisper to one another. I first thought it was something romantic, but all Sophia seems to be interested in is reforming her father's religion, and Morland seems happy to encourage it."

"You said he looked different," asked Holmes. "In what way?"

"He looked more . . . German when we met him in Germany," replied the old man. "His beard and mustache were cut in a different way, and he walked stiffer, somehow. He didn't wear fancy clothes like he does now, but what he did wear still seemed . . . expensive, if you know what I mean. And of course he spoke German. Sophia speaks some German too, you know, although they've been speaking in English whenever Morland visits this camp. I heard that Sophia's mother was originally from Germany. Maybe that's how she learned it."

Despite further questioning, the old man could provide no additional information, and he assured us that he would not be telling anyone else about our conversation, especially Sophia. We thanked him, and Holmes stated that he appreciated the old man's observations. "That's *my* religion," the fellow replied. "Watching people. There isn't any better entertainment than to sit back, smoke a pipe or two, and watch folks going about their daily business. Sometimes it gets a little tedious, I will admit, but generally after a while someone will do something worth watching."

We stepped away from him, to the center of the camp, and Holmes thought for a moment. Then he led us closer to Sophia's tent, while telling me, "Watson, I need you to feign an illness. Just for a moment or two, that's a good chap."

Without giving me time to protest or prepare myself, he signaled that I was to begin. I froze for just a moment, before letting out a feeble moan. Holmes's brows contracted in irritation, and I could tell that he expected a better effort from me. With a sigh, I began to stagger while braying like some farm animal that has found its way into fermented feed. As I began to sag, lowering myself to a less dusty part of the clearing, I could see that Holmes was running to Sophia's tent, calling her forth for help.

In a moment, Sophia was kneeling beside me as I groaned and attempted to keep her attention. Over her shoulder, I could see other members of the community gathering around us while Holmes slipped unseen into Sophia's tent. Sophia kept asking me where it was hurting and what the matter was, but I pretended not to understand her, repeating this process until I saw Holmes exiting the tent and walking toward us.

Holmes nodded, and my illness miraculously healed itself. Within moments I was able to rise to my feet, thanking Sophia for her help, and assuring her that I had simply had an attack related to a fever picked up during my war service overseas, and that there was no need to be concerned. She seemed puzzled, but then with a gesture that she was washing her hands of me, she turned and went back into her tent.

As we walked to four-wheeler, Holmes said, "Excellent, Watson. I almost believed it myself."

"I hope you got what you came for," I whispered with irritation.

"What were you looking for?" asked Siger as our four-wheeler rolled away from the camp.

"This," replied Holmes, fishing a pair of folded notes from his waistcoat pocket. "Finding them was a long shot, but it will save us some trouble, I think."

He handed the papers to Siger, who unfolded them and spread them on his knee, where Tenley and I could see them. The first was simply a scrap of paper with a supply list scribbled on it. It was on poor quality paper, and the handwriting was poorly formed and uneducated. "That is a sample of Sophia's handwriting," said Holmes. "I thought it might come in handy later for a little idea that I have."

The second sheet of paper was about five inches square, and of exceptional thickness and good quality. The top edge was somewhat ragged, as if it had been torn, while the sides and bottom were straight and clean.

"It is a sheet of expensive stationery," said Holmes. "It was originally an inch or two longer."

"The portion with the monogram at the top has been torn off," said Siger, "in order to disguise the identity of the sender."

"It isn't disguised very well," said Tenley. "This paper is still somewhat unique. I'll bet we won't have to look too hard to find a matching sheet."

"Indeed," said Holmes. "That reminds me. Griffin, would you take us to Mr. Morland's house next, please?"

Griffin did not respond, but nudged his horses into a slightly faster gait.

"What do you make of the message?" asked Holmes.

It was handwritten, and quite short. In bold pen strokes, someone had written:

Nyy vf jryy. Frr lbh fbba. Z

"It is code," I said, causing everyone's eyes to raise and look toward me. Holmes's expression seemed somewhat irritated, while Siger and Tenley looked amused. I hastened to add, "Written by a man with a good quality pen and expensive black ink."

"Much better, Watson," said Holmes. "Does anyone want to take a try at decoding it?"

Tenley and I looked at one another, and then by tacit agreement, deferred to Siger, who was bent over the paper, his brows bunched in concentration.

"The letter *e* is the most common letter, and is likely to occur in double letters," he said softly. "However, there are several sets of double letters in this message, any of which could be *e*. If this were a simple substitution code . . . ."

He fell silent for a few moments, but his concentration never abated. The four-wheeler rocked down the road, and I glanced over at Holmes, who was looking fondly at his nephew. He turned his head to me, saw that I was watching him, and nodded in reply.

After a few moments, Siger's expression cleared, and he looked up with a joyous expression. "That wasn't so difficult," he said.

"It would have to be a simple code, so that Sophia could remember it," replied Holmes.

Tenley and I looked at one another, before I stated, "But what does it say?"

"Oh, that," said Siger. "It simply says '*All is well. See you soon. M.*'"

"M.," I said. "Morland!"

"Of course," said Holmes.

"Tell us about the code, Siger," said Tenley.

"Luckily, it was not too difficult," replied the young man. "The letter *e* is the most common letter used in the English language and can present itself as a double letter, such as in the word *seek*. This short message, however, had three sets of double letters, *yy*, which was used twice, *rr*, and *bb*. The simplest code is a substitution code, where one letter of the alphabet is substituted for another. If one wanted to make this code even simpler, the letters are not substituted at random, but are simply shifted, so that *a* can equal *b*, *b* equals *c*, and so on.

"Sometimes the coded alphabet will be reversed, so that *a* equals *z*, and *b* equals *y*. I quickly ran through a few of these combinations in my head, but none seemed to make sense. Then I thought that perhaps the coded alphabet had shifted more than just a letter or two. I started trying the message as if each double letter combination was *ee*. None of them worked until I tried *rr* as *ee*.

"This combination did produce an actual message, and I was able to see that the code simply shifted the alphabet so that *a* equaled *n*, *m* equaled *z*, and *n* equaled *a*. By shifting the alphabet exactly halfway, by thirteen of the twenty-six letters, perception of the more obvious substitutions would be avoided, but there was no need to have a key for the code lying around, which would have been the case if the letters were random substitutions.

"Excellent, Siger," said Tenley. "You have quite a gift for cryptography."

Siger looked somewhat bashful. "I simply read my Uncle Sherlock's monograph on the subject," he said, causing a momentary flash of pride of pass through Holmes's eyes. I was certain that he had already decoded the message before he ever revealed it to us. However, he had allowed his nephew the pleasure of solving the small mystery. I knew Sherlock Holmes was a wise man, but he continued to surprise me by revealing that wisdom in new and unexpected ways.

Griffin chose that moment to gesture ahead of us, muttering in his gruff and efficient manner, "Morland's."

It was time for the next act of our drama to begin.

Part VI: Setting the Trap

We had been told by Roberta the day before that Augustus Morland was constructing a new, large home a few miles from where he currently lived. It seemed rather foolish to me, considering that the old manor house where he was currently living was very large on its own. I asked myself what use a single man could have for occupying such a large house while building an even bigger one. Then I remembered Tenley's description of a staging area, with hidden German troops quartered in secret until they could be turned loose on an unsuspecting nation.

Suddenly, the idea of huge houses standing throughout the largely empty Yorkshire countryside, each filled with smuggled arms and men over a long period of time and waiting until needed, made more sense.

We stopped at the front door and climbed down to the ground. There were several outbuildings scattered in the distance, but there did not seem to be any people working or carrying out the day-to-day tasks of running an estate. I wondered which of the buildings had been the location of Siger's grisly discovery.

As if reading my mind, Holmes said, "Siger, I would like for you to make a small reconnaissance of the outbuildings. See how many people are about. Afterwards, join us in the house, but as soon as it is convenient, try to wander off and obtain a sheet or two of Mr. Morland's stationery. You will know the type I mean. Some of it was used to write that coded message to Sophia."

Siger nodded and slipped away, as the rest of us turned to the front door, upon which Holmes knocked with authority. Tenley watched Siger disappear around the corner of the house in a speculative manner. In a moment, the door opened to reveal an old man, wearing ill-fitting and faded clothing. Holmes presented his card to the man. We were ushered in and asked to wait in the drawing room while the old fellow checked to see if Morland was available.

While Tenley perched himself in a chair, Holmes and I wandered about the room, looking at the artworks hanging from the walls and resting on table-tops. The items were obviously quite expensive, and showed good taste, but they were layered with accumulated dust. "These came with the house," said Holmes. "Morland cannot take credit for originally acquiring them."

Our inspection was interrupted by the arrival of Augustus Morland, who strode into the room looking somewhat peeved. However, he made an effort to sound gracious, welcoming us and offering us refreshments, which we refused. He motioned for us to be seated, then lowered himself into a chair with the window at his back, haloing his figure against the morning sun.

"What can I do for you gentlemen today?" he asked. I tried to perceive any hint of his hidden German ancestry, but he revealed no sign whatsoever, from his appearance to his perfect Manchester accent.

"We are simply speaking to some of the people in the area, and wanted to see if you had any relevant information to add to our investigation," said Holmes.

"Such as?" asked Morland, in his odd high-pitched voice.

"Oh, the usual type of thing. Are you aware of any problems Wilkies had with the neighbors? Have you heard of anyone speaking out against him, or possibly resenting that he and his congregation have been staying in the area?"

"No, no, nothing like that. In fact, I'm afraid the only stories I've heard about anyone having ill feelings toward Wilkies came from the testimony of his daughter, Sophia." He shook his head with a smile. "Such as it is."

Holmes raised an eyebrow. "What do you mean?"

"Oh, nothing, I suppose. From the few times I have seen her, she seems somewhat . . . limited in her thought processes. You may have met her yourself?" We nodded. "Then I think you must agree that she did not inherit her father's intellect."

"I had not heard it established that her father was an intellectual," said Holmes. "Am I to understand that you met him?"

"I visited their camp a few times, to introduce myself, and to see what type of people your brother was allowing to stay in our area."

"You were making rather free with Sherrinford Holmes's borders, weren't you, Mr. Morland?" asked Tenley. "After all, they were camped on his land. Wouldn't your visits be something of a trespass?"

"I, um, I didn't see it as a problem," said Morland. "We are all quite friendly here in the country. I meant no harm, I assure you. In any event, the important fact is that I was able to meet both Wilkies and his daughter, and it allowed me to form my opinions of Sophia, with which I'm sure you must agree. I would think that her limited intellectual powers would actually tend to support the veracity of her claim that your brother, Mr. Holmes, had serious words with Wilkies. Someone like Sophia, someone who is rather simple like that, would not be distracted by uncertainties. If she heard your brother arguing with Wilkies, and saying the things that he said to Wilkies, it would be definite."

"As you might imagine," replied Holmes, "my efforts are directed toward discovering a somewhat different interpretation of events."

"And Inspector Tenley here?" asked Morland. "Is he with you because he agrees that there is a different interpretation, or is it simply professional courtesy that causes him to accompany you? Do you believe, Inspector, that you have placed the correct man in your cells?"

"I believe that based on the evidence initially presented, Constable Worth was correct in placing Mr. Sherrinford Holmes in custody," replied Tenley. "However, Mr. Sherlock Holmes here has a lot of clout, especially with my superiors, and it does not do any harm for me to accompany him during his further explorations of the case."

Morland nodded, then looked over us toward the entrance to the room. I turned to see Siger standing there, his knapsack held in front of him, looking much emptier than when we had arrived. I had not heard him come in. He nodded at his uncle, and then at Morland.

"Sorry, sir," he said, "I was just admiring your house a little bit."

Morland waved his hand. "Ah, boys must be boys. The temptation to explore is great, no doubt." He stood, as if indicating the interview was at an end. "But temptation must always be tempered with good manners, as well. Remember that, my boy."

Ringing for the servant, Morland said, "I'm sorry that I cannot help you in your quest to save your brother, Mr. Holmes. Even to me, it seems that the case against your brother is too strong to tear apart. As a famed criminologist, you must confess that the evidence is only open to one interpretation."

"I have found," said Holmes, "that interpretations can change with just a slight shift of perspective. An illusion, painstakingly created, can be revealed to be nothing more than canvas and wires if one simply walks a little to one side or the other and sees exactly how the construct is propped up. Good day to you, sir."

We followed the old man to the door. Outside, we climbed into the four-wheeler, where Holmes asked Siger, "Was your mission successful?"

"In all aspects, sir," he replied. "Even better than expected, if I may say so."

"Excellent."

"Did you get some of Morland's stationery?" asked Tenley, unaware that part of Siger's tasks included returning the bloody items to the empty outbuilding.

"Not only that," said Siger, glancing to make sure that we were far enough from Morland's house, "I found this on his desk."

He opened the knapsack, pulling out several sheets of new stationery and a soiled plain piece of cheap paper, containing a short written message. The stationery was the same as the torn and coded square that Holmes had found in Sophia's tent. The plain piece of paper, matching Sophia's supply list taken from the tent, had another similar coded message on it:

" 'When can I see you? S.' " said Holmes, almost instantly.

Siger nodded. " 'S' for Sophia. She even capitalized the *V* for the word *I*. To make the code less clear, they should probably only use lower-case letters, and run the words together. However, that might be a little too complicated for Sophia to manage."

"Where was this?" asked Holmes, holding up the coded sheet.

"On Morland's desk, upstairs. It was lying in a pile of other papers, bills and receipts. He had made no effort to hide it, but it wasn't lying out in an obvious way, either. I think he had simply tossed it there, and I don't think he will miss it."

"Were you seen?" asked Tenley.

"Not at all," said Siger. "Not anywhere that I went," he added, for Holmes and my benefit, I was sure, in order to let us know that he had not been observed while replacing the items in the empty outbuilding.

"The place is nearly deserted. After looking around the outbuildings, I came in through the garden. No one was around, so I went up the back stairs and searched until I located Mr. Morland's office. Finding the stationery was simple, and the message from Sophia was easily seen. After that, I came back downstairs."

Holmes held up the papers. "This is really excellent, Siger. This makes my little plan even easier to accomplish than I had originally imagined it to be."

"And what plan would that be, Mr. Holmes?" Tenley asked.

"If you would have Griffin take us back to the family home, I will give my nephew a little lesson in forgery. In the meantime, let me explain what I have in mind."

And he did. It would be something of a gamble, but it also seemed the simplest shortcut to bring this whole business to a close. I sighed, imagining yet another night, like so many before, squatting outdoors in the darkness waiting for a criminal to fall into one of Holmes's traps. At least, I thought, this time there will be no Hell Hound to deal with.

Back at the Holmes farm, Tenley asked what time he should return.

"Around ten, I expect," replied Holmes. "That will be after dark, but will still give us a couple of hours to get into position."

"I'll have my men watching earlier than that," said Tenley. "The outbuildings, you say?"

"Yes," replied Holmes. "To see if Morland visits any of them."

Tenley turned to Siger with a wry smile. "Any particular outbuilding, Siger?" he asked.

Siger looked startled. Tenley reached out and tapped the limp knapsack hanging from Siger's hand. "I won't ask what was in here," he said. "I'm not sure that I want to know at this point, and I trust Mr. Holmes. If I was really a Scotland Yard Inspector I might worry a little more about what is going on, but I'm not.

"Whatever was in this bag is not there now, and it disappeared sometime while you were searching around Morland's property. Now, you may have hidden it in the house, but since Mr. Holmes wants me to have the outbuildings watched, I'm betting it's hidden in one of them. So I ask again, just so we won't take a chance on missing it, is there any particular outbuilding that we should watch?"

Siger looked at his uncle, who appeared both pleased and amused.

Holmes nodded, and Siger replied, "The empty stable, to the west of the house." He looked down at the knapsack, and back to Tenley. "Your men should be especially aware if they see Morland go there, and then leave the building carrying something. Perhaps a white bundle, for example."

"Very good," said Tenley, with a smile.

"Tenley," said Holmes.

"Yes, sir?"

"Do not let my brother waste your talents," said Holmes.

"Oh, he doesn't, sir. I can assure you of that. He never has." He touched the brim of his hat and turned to go.

After Tenley and Griffin departed, Holmes, Siger, and I looked at one another with expressions of amusement and relief. Then Holmes and I moved to return to the house. Siger stopped us with a question.

"What exactly was that . . . that mummified and pickled hand that was wrapped in the murdered man's robes?" he asked.

Holmes glanced at me, as if to ask how much to tell the boy. My look must have indicated to be perfectly frank, because Holmes answered with complete candor. "It is called a 'Hand of Glory.' It is an item used in the practice of black magic."

"I suspected as much," said Siger. "I knew that something like that must be used for an evil purpose. But why is such a thing in the heart of Yorkshire? What can these people believe such a thing is for?"

"No doubt it is used in dark rituals, probably the 'true path' that seems to interest Sophia so much. I suspect that it was used in the murder, giving it some sort of ceremonial flavor. Somehow, Wilkies was convinced to wear his robe and was taken to some obscure place we may not find. There, he was murdered by both Sophia and Morland, although I do not yet know if anyone else was involved, although I doubt it. Then he was placed in the pit.

"After Wilkies died and his clothing was changed to hide the ritual nature of the murder, the body was propped up in the pit, and a ceremonial slash was made across his throat, resulting in very little blood on the man's regular collar, as he was already dead at the time, and had bled out through the great wound in his back."

Siger was silent for a moment, before asking, "Where does such an item as the dead hand come from? I don't imagine one could buy something like that at just any shop in London."

Holmes replied, "These items are usually made from the dried and preserved hand of a man who has been executed, most often for murder. Usually the left, or *sinister*, hand is taken, although sometimes, if the hand is removed from a murderer, the . . . believers will try to obtain the hand that actually committed the murder.

"Occasionally the hand will be used to hold a candle, with the belief being that only the user can see the light. More extreme practitioners of the dark arts may try to make the candle from actual fat rendered from the dead man who supplied the hand. It is also believed that the possessor of such a talisman can unlock any door.

"Watson and I stumbled across a group of practitioners making use of a Hand of Glory back in the early eighties."

"What happened?" asked Siger, with wide eyes.

"They were convinced to stop using it," said Holmes, with characteristic understatement. He managed to give no indication of the danger we had both faced, and the terror and pain that we had managed to bring to an end by the violent destruction of the Black Coven. I would never forget the escape we both made though the burning house, which stood over the entrance to the coven's underground catacombs, and how we had nearly lost our lives, as well as that of the small child that I had carried up from the smoke-filled tunnels.

"That Hand of Glory is now in a museum in Walsall," Holmes added, turning toward the door. With a pat on Siger's shoulder, I followed Holmes into the house.

Inside, Holmes announced to Roberta that we would have need of the dining room for a little while. She acquiesced with a silent smile, and Holmes sent Siger off to search the house for whatever types of inks and pens he could find.

When Siger returned, he laid all the items on the table before Holmes, who had taken off his coat and rolled up his sleeves. Siger observed but did not comment on the various scars and acid marks dotting his uncle's forearms. Holmes laid out the coded messages, samples of handwriting, and blank stationery. Then, he searched among the pens and ink until he found those that most suited his purpose.

"Forgery," he said, "is an art, not a science. I can, and probably will at some point, teach you the specifics of ink types, paper qualities and manufacture, pen nibs, and so on. However, at the end of the day, the only real way to produce a forged document is to have practiced interminably beforehand, so that one knows exactly what task one's hand will be expected to perform. But also, you will need to have some sort of inborn skill, and that can never be taught, simply refined and improved. I have no doubts that you can learn the intellectual basics of the forger's business, Siger. It remains to be seen whether you have the artistic ability.

"However," he added, "we are descended from Vernet, both you and I, and that must count for something."

"Art in the blood," I muttered. Holmes thought for a moment, and then, with a sure hand, began to write a coded message on some of Morland's blank stationery. He did not write it out beforehand in order to check that he had used the correct substituted letters. Rather, he produced the final message with surety and confidence. As the letters appeared on the paper, I glanced at Morland's original message to Sophia. The writing between the two was indistinguishable.

" 'Must see you, midnight tonight, Great Rock at edge of valley forest. Urgent. M.' " Siger read, translating over his uncle's shoulder. "Do you think she will know where that is?" he asked.

"Probably," said Holmes. "It is one of the landmarks of the area, and not too far from either the campsite or Morland's house. If she does not know, she has time to find out." He blotted the paper carefully, and then said to Siger, "Can you find me a sheet of cheap paper, such as Sophia uses, so that I can construct a similar message for Mr. Morland?"

"Certainly," said Siger, dashing from the room with the enthusiasm that only a sixteen year old can produce.

I smiled at Holmes. "You are going to teach him to be a forger?" I asked. Holmes raised an eyebrow, and I said, "His mother will never forgive you."

Siger returned with several sheets of cheap paper, nearly identical to that used by Sophia. Holmes took one, thought for a moment, and then composed a similar message to Morland, signed S. After blotting it, he reached for the forged message to Morland and began to tear off the monogram at the top. Then, he stopped for a moment and handed one of the duplicate cheap sheets to Siger. "See what you can do," he said.

Siger's face took on a frown of concentration, but he showed no hesitation. He picked up the pen previously used by Holmes, pulled over the correct ink bottle, and thought for a moment, observing both the sheets with Sophia's original handwriting, and Holmes's more recent forgery.

His hand moved over the blank sheet, but he did not write, not yet, as his fingers made practice swoops and lines, over and over.

Finally, he dipped his pen into the ink, lowered his hand to the paper, and wrote the coded message with confidence.

After he was done, he pushed it back, and then remembered to blot it. Then he handed it to his uncle.

Holmes examined it critically for a moment before stating, "Not bad. Not bad at all. You have captured her vowels correctly, and the narrowness of her capitals, and the down-slope of her line. However, there is too much confidence in the k's and h's, and the loops of your t's are too narrow." He dropped in onto the table. "Try again."

Siger took another blank sheet of paper, and this time, with only a moment of thought, again wrote quickly and without seeming hesitation. Blotting the message, he handed it to Holmes, who studied it intently before looking up at his anxiously watching nephew.

"Very good," he declared. "We shall send yours to Mr. Morland."

Siger nodded, and did not show much expression, but I could not miss the excitement and pride which flared just for a moment like twin lanterns deep within his gray eyes. His enthusiasm was interrupted, however, when Holmes said to him, "Go get into your oldest clothes."

"Why?" Siger asked.

"Because," said Holmes, "after a suitable amount of disguise, you are going to deliver these messages to Mr. Morland and Sophia."

As Siger bounded out of the room, I shook my head, considering what Roberta's reaction would be if she discovered what Holmes had in mind for her youngest son. I decided that I would not be the one to tell her. Siger returned within moments, wearing a set of very old and tattered clothes, somewhat too small for him, with the bottom hem of his pants legs showing several inches of shin above old boots, with noticeable holes worn in the sides. Holmes stood and led Siger outside, where he proceeded to brush the lad's face and hair with dirt from the yard.

Arranging Siger's hair down over his eyes, he instructed him in the proper way to carry himself with a different posture, taking several inches off his height, and how to maintain a subservient attitude that would cause him to be ignored by most of the people that he would encounter.

"It is important," said Holmes, "for Morland to think that you have come from Wilkies's camp, while Sophia must think that you are one of Morland's stable boys. Both have met you, so it will be a challenge to make them see you as someone else. Perhaps, although I am loathe to suggest it, you might smear a little horse manure on your boots or your cuffs. That way they will be anxious for you to depart, and will pay even less attention to you."

Without hesitation, Siger stepped out, away from the house, to a mound of horse manure, in which he proceeded to muck about for a moment or two. With a grin, he returned to us, noting our involuntary expressions of distaste.

"Exactly," said Holmes. "Now let us see you walk."

Siger settled into a slouch and began to make his way back and forth across the yard. The transformation was incredible. He appeared to be nothing like the young man who had sat across from us at the dining table just a few minutes earlier. Instead, he looked like any one of the anonymous stable lads one sees and ignores everyday throughout the length of the countryside. Clearly, this boy had inherited more than just his family's deductive abilities and resemblance to his uncle. He had inborn acting talent, as well.

"Excellent," said Holmes. "Remember to seem somewhat more . . . penitent when you visit Mr. Morland. After all, you are supposed to be religious. And appear more horsey when you are at Sophia's camp. Report to us when you get back."

With that, Holmes turned and went back in. Siger, amazed that he was being trusted to do something so important with no further warnings or instructions, stood for just a moment before turning toward Morland's house.

Siger had only been gone for a few moments when a man on horseback rode up to the house. "I work with Inspector Tenley," he said. "Another cable has arrived for you, sir." Handing them to Holmes, he touched his fingers to his brow, wheeled the horse, and without a further word, turned back toward the village.

Opening the flimsy sheet, Holmes read it and then passed it to me. It simply contained more about Augustus Morland's true German background, and the name of his actual identity. "I can't see that this adds anything to helping us solve our immediate problem," I said.

"All information is useful," said Holmes.

As we walked toward the house, I said, "Didn't you once tell me that the brain is like a lumber room with limited space, and one must be careful what one takes in, so that it remains organized and does not become littered with unnecessary items, in order that something new does not crowd out something older and more useful?"

He waved his hand languidly. "I was younger then. Times and beliefs change. One must adapt or die."

Inside, Holmes seemed indisposed to talk, indicating that he wished to be alone for a while, to smoke and order his thoughts. I settled myself in a chair in the sitting room, intending to rest and think about the case. I had no sooner arranged myself, however, than I stood again, walking across the room to examine several photographs that I had not previously noticed, perched on a cabinet near the window.

They were obviously old, done in the antique style used during the middle of the century. I observed one stiffly posed formal shot of a gruff man of early middle age, with a wild black beard, and the petite blonde woman beside him. Presumably these were Holmes's parents. Beside it was a small oval-shaped frame, containing a photograph of three boys.

Certainly this was of Holmes and his two older brothers. Holmes was no doubt the small fellow, only around one year of age, dressed in some sort of gown. Beside him was an already pudgy boy with extremely intelligent eyes, around eight years of age. Mycroft, I was sure. And at the right of the picture was Sherrinford, slightly older and taller, but already looking like the man he would grow to become.

There were a few other photographs of more recent origin scattered along the cabinet, all of Sherrinford, Roberta, and their three sons. I was interested to see Bancroft, the nephew that I had not yet met, and had never heard of until yesterday. He was posed in an academic gown, looking extremely intelligent, but rather haughty and proud, and already somewhat heavyset. I could see a strong resemblance to his uncle Mycroft, for whom he worked in London. "So this is the young man," I thought, "who wants to make his future without relying on the Holmes name. Bancroft Pons, indeed."

I returned to my chair, wondering when I might find something for lunch, and intending to think about the day's events and what was planned for that night. It was not long, however, before I fell asleep, that heavy afternoon sleep when the dream world and the waking world appear to merge. When the front door slammed several hours later, announcing Siger's return, I had a difficult time separating its actuality from dreamlike fantasy as I struggled to awaken.

As I rose from my chair, I heard Holmes meet Siger in the entrance hall. "How did it go?" he asked.

"Without any problems whatsoever," said Siger, with barely suppressed excitement. "They took the notes without even glancing at me, and when I mumbled about a reply, they both dismissed me. Morland either decoded his message immediately, or decided to wait until later, because he dropped the hand holding the message almost as soon as he looked at it. Sophia was hunched over when I left, puzzling through it."

"And there seemed to be no suspicion about the paper or the writing? Or about the method of delivery?"

"None at all," replied Siger. "This must have been similar to how they communicated in the past." Siger began to remove his dusty jacket.

"What do we do now?"

296

"We wait," said Holmes. "And hope that they simply plan to meet each other at the Great Rock tonight, without sending each other additional clarifying messages, leading to the unfortunate unraveling of our scheme."

"There is one thing that you can do, Siger," I added. Siger turned to me with an inquiring glance.

"You can take off those manure-covered boots outside before your mother sees you tracking them further into the house."

At a little before ten o'clock, Tenley and Griffin arrived, pulling up to the front of the house in Griffin's four-wheeler. I realized that I had never seen the man when he wasn't sitting on the driver's bench, his hands loosely holding the reins. We stepped outside and met Tenley, who had hopped down from his seat.

With us was Siger, who had informed his mother in no uncertain terms that he was coming too. We were all armed, and I could see the protests forming on Roberta's lips. However, she had held her tongue, although right before we stepped outside, she had made Siger and William promise to be careful, all the while looking at Holmes as if to make him understand that he was responsible for her sons' safety.

"Are your men in place?" Holmes asked.

Tenley nodded. "I sent some people that I trust, all with no love for Morland. They were in place soon after dark. They reported that he never went near that outbuilding. They did see him ride away for a time this afternoon, but they had no orders to follow him, so we do not know where he went." Tenley coughed, looked at the ground, and then looked back up at Holmes. "I took it upon myself to sneak into the empty stable after dark. You'll never guess what I found, Mr. Holmes. Why, it was the murdered man's robes, with the murder weapon, and something far more sinister."

"Really," said Holmes. "Well, it is fortunate indeed that it was discovered by a representative of the law, so that it can be properly taken into evidence."

"No curiosity about what else I found wrapped in the robes, Mr. Holmes?" Tenley asked with a smile.

Holmes gestured with his hand. "Time is wasting, Tenley. Perhaps we should start making our way to the Great Rock," he said, "so that we can be well concealed before our visitors arrive." We began to stroll away from the light spilling into the yard from the house windows, and into the darkened fields.

"Finding that dead hand," said Tenley, abandoning the pretense that we didn't know what he had found wrapped in the bloody robe, "puts this whole matter into a different light. It's not just a murder now, but rather some sort of diabolical execution."

"I'm sure that was how Sophia perceived it," said Holmes. "She sincerely believes that her father's form of religion was too tame, and needs to be replaced with something more evil. As for Mr. Morland, I'm not so sure. I believe that he simply used Sophia, convincing her to murder her father as a means of implicating Sherrinford so that his land grab could continue. If he hadn't found Sophia to manipulate, he would have arranged for something else to remove Sherrinford from the board."

Tenley nodded. "When he met her in Germany, back before his move to England and when he took on the Morland identity, he must have learned from her then that she disagreed with her father's teachings. At that time, he might have just spoken with her, or possibly even encouraged her, with no idea that she would be useful in the future."

"Exactly," said Holmes. "Later, when Morland was here, he decided that he needed to get rid of Sherrinford, who was an important holdout in his land purchases. Murdering him outright would cause too many problems, so he decided to have Sherrinford framed for murder instead. Having stayed in touch with Sophia, he realized that he could use her. He sent her a message and no doubt suggested that she arrange for Wilkies's group to camp here. There are certainly no old ruins or ancient sites here that would have attracted them otherwise.

"After they arrived, Morland no doubt began convincing Sophia that her father would need to be killed as a sacrifice to the 'true path,' and that Sherrinford would be the perfect man to take the blame. Sophia is obviously easily influenced, and Morland is certainly a master of manipulation. Morland has probably told Sophia that he believes the same things that she does. Possibly, he has even romanced the poor deluded girl, and she believes that he will marry her. Who knows?"

By this point, we were well away from the house, and our eyes had adjusted to the bright starlight. The fields flowed gently over rolling hillsides, and in the distance I could just make out a darkness crawling along the bottom of a low spot. This must be the valley forest, in which we planned to hide. Standing some feet out from it, shining bright in the reflected light, was a tall thin stone, fifteen to twenty feet in height. This, I was certain, was the Great Rock.

"In any event," continued Holmes, "Wilkies was ritually murdered. The weak link, of course, is Sophia, although her dogmatic stubbornness may actually keep her quiet about what was done. However, I have no doubt that at some point in the future, Morland plans to have Sophia eliminated, so that the only person who can tell the truth about what they did will be gone."

As we approached the stone, I glanced at William and Siger. William, who had been briefed by his brother earlier in the afternoon, walked forward and looked straight ahead, seemingly intent on his task. His brother, Siger, was much more alert, and his eyes darted between his forward path and Holmes. The boy listened intently to everything his uncle said, almost physically leaning toward Holmes as he walked.

"This is it," said Holmes, stopping before the tall stone. "The Great Rock. Perhaps it is not one of the old places that Wilkies traveled about to visit, but it is the closest thing that we have to it around here. Possibly Sophia will feel some sort of energy here that will make her feel like talking." Holmes glanced about. "We already have enough information on Morland to have him arrested as a spy. Now we need to get him and Sophia talking in order to have them discuss what was done to Wilkies, and so clear Sherrinford."

"Aren't you taking something of a chance with Sophia's life," I asked Holmes. "As you said, at some point Morland would probably need to eliminate her, as she is the weak link in his plan."

"I am, Watson, but I have to make that gamble. I must confess, I do not like the idea that Morland rode away this afternoon and no one knows where he went."

A figure stepped out of the nearby trees. "Everyone is hidden, sir," said Constable Worth to Tenley. "As you ordered."

"Very good," said Tenley. "I suggest that we get ourselves under cover as well." He pulled out his watch. "Ten-thirty," he said. "We must be well hidden before they arrive, especially if anyone makes early appearance to see if the place is safely deserted."

We entered the darkness of the trees, and each settled to wait in his own way. Holmes and I sat with our backs to a large tree trunk, patient as the old hunters that we were, while Siger crouched easily several feet away. William spread his coat and sat upon it cross-legged, and Tenley moved off to confer with his men.

The time passed more swiftly than it sometimes did when Holmes and I had waited in the past. The night temperature was not uncomfortable, and it was too early in the season for insects to be a problem. I could see where this low-lying growth of forest might be somewhat damp at other times of the year. A few night birds called, from one part of the forest and then another. A breeze rustled the leaves overhead, but did not make enough noise to impede our attempts to hear anyone that might be approaching.

Siger occasionally shifted from side to side, but never lost the hawk-like focus that had settled on his face from the very beginning of our vigil. William, on the other hand, appeared introspective, always looking alert, but generally watching his hands, folded on the rifle lying across his knees.

As midnight approached, we all became more alert, expecting the momentary arrival of our targets. I knew that Holmes hoped that Morland and Sophia would say something incriminating to one another, especially when they realized that each had not written and sent the coded messages to the other. Hopefully, in their momentary confusion, they would make admissions that could be used against them, in order to open them up during interrogation.

I looked at my watch as midnight came, and checked it many times again over the next quarter hour, when there was no sign of any approaching visitors. Beside me, I could sense Holmes's frustration and disappointment that his stratagem had apparently failed. Finally, he signaled Tenley to draw closer, and in a whispered conference, they conceded that Morland and Sophia probably weren't coming. Siger, William, and Constable Worth joined us. After listening for a few minutes to Holmes and Tenley discuss possible options, Worth interrupted. "I think that you've been mistaken about Mr. Morland all along."

Holmes turned to him with raised eyebrows. "I concede that you have known him longer than we have," Holmes said. "What makes you think that he is not involved in this crime?"

"What would he have to gain?" asked Worth. "An important man like that, with big plans for this whole area, would not involve himself in the murder of some itinerant preacher."

"What big plans are you talking about?" asked Holmes.

"Why, the man means to bring prosperity to this corner of England," said Worth. He added, somewhat proudly, "He has discussed it with me on several occasions. It is only a matter of time until he owns all the land, creating a vast estate that he can develop into an industrial area to rival the Midlands."

"And does he have a place for you in all this?"

"Well, of course he has mentioned something of it," replied Worth. "He recognizes real talent when he sees it, and he knows the value of using a local man to police a local area."

Something in Worth's tone must have alerted Holmes. With a sharp change in his voice, Holmes asked, "How many pieces of silver did it take for you to betray us to Morland? When did you tell him that tonight was a trap?"

Worth seemed to be puzzled for a moment, as if he did not understand the question. Then he took a step back, shaking his head. "No, Mr. Holmes, you've got it all wrong. I didn't take any money."

"So you just told him as a favor between a friend to a friend?"

"No, it wasn't like that. We're not friends. He's too important to be friends with a man like me. But he respects me, and he's got important plans for this whole area. He visited me this afternoon, and he asked me how the investigation was going. I know the Inspector told me not to discuss it with Mr. Morland, so I just let him know that you and the Inspector were on the wrong track. He asked me if you were involved in a message to lure him out to the Great Rock tonight. I told him I didn't know anything about a message, but there was something being planned tonight, and that he need not inconvenience himself by coming out here at midnight."

Holmes looked at Tenley. "Inspector?"

Tenley looked into the darkness. "Holder! Jacobs! Come here!"

Two burly men appeared beside us. I hadn't heard them coming, and never saw them until they were standing there. Tenley gestured toward Worth. "Take him into custody." As the men grabbed Worth, he gave one sob and momentarily sagged toward the ground, before scrabbling his feet and trying to stand again. Tenley turned toward Holmes. "Holder and Jacobs are men that I can trust." He pulled Holmes and me aside. Siger and William followed.

"What do we do now, Mr. Holmes?" Tenley asked. "Morland is bound to be onto us."

Holmes turned back to Worth. "Constable!" he said sharply. "When you told Mr. Morland about tonight's trap, did he ask any other questions about the message used to lure him here?"

Worth ignored him, and Holmes stepped closer, raising his voice and asking the question again. One of the big men holding Worth shook him, and he finally seemed to comprehend what was being asked. "No, no he didn't. But he . . . He just said something about how the girl must have sold him out."

Holmes turned back to us. "We must get to Morland's house as quickly as possible. Tenley, how many men do you have here tonight?"

"Ten," said Tenley. "Holder and Jacobs, and eight more still out there in the dark."

"Can you trust them all?"

"Yes. I recruited them myself. They have nothing to do with Worth."

"Good. William," he said, turning to his oldest nephew. "Take four men and go to Wilkies's camp. Take Sophia into custody. Keep her there, but allow no one in to speak to her, either members of the camp, or anyone from the outside. Wait until we arrive."

William nodded, and Tenley called for the additional men still hiding in the trees to come forth. Picking four of them, William turned without a word and headed for the campsite.

Holmes said, "Holder and Jacobs. Constable Worth is under arrest. Please accompany him to the village, where he should be locked into a cell. Do not let him speak to anyone along the way. And," he added, "tell my brother that he will soon be free."

"Right, sir," said the taller of the two big men.

"Wait," said Tenley. He stepped to Worth and fished in the man's pockets, coming up with the keys to the cells. "Use these to lock up Worth,

302

and to release Mr. Sherrinford Holmes." The big men nodded, and with little effort on their part, they began to walk the little constable between them across the fields, back toward the village.

"Right, then," said Holmes. "The rest of us, on to Morland's."

We set out at a quick pace, the eight of us, and made good time across the fields until we reached the road, where we began to increase our speed even more. There was no conversation between us, each concentrating on keeping up with Holmes, who had set a fast pace with himself out in front. Siger's long legs matched his uncle's strides. The countryside was fairly well lit by stars, in that way that is possible only in the country, where the light from the cities does not occlude the sky's visibility. Eventually, however, I began to notice a glow bleeding from behind a distant hillside. This would be Morland's house, well-lit, although it was now quite past midnight.

Reaching the house, Tenley dispersed his four men to various sides of the building, setting them in place to watch all the exits. Then we remaining four approached the front door, whereupon Holmes tried the knob, only to reveal that the door had been unlocked all along. Glancing at Tenley, who nodded to go ahead, Holmes opened the door, and we silently advanced inside.

We quickly moved from room to room, finding the ground floor abandoned. Meeting at the base of the stairs, Holmes whispered, "Siger, where is Morland's office?"

"Just upstairs, to the right," the young man replied.

"Lead on, then."

We climbed the stairs, and it did not go unnoticed by me that as we ascended, Tenley placed himself in front, taking the lead from Siger. I do not think that Siger realized what Tenley had done, so intent was he on glancing from left to right and back again, his sharp eyes missing nothing.

At the top of the stairs, Siger gestured toward a nearby doorway, lit from within and spilling light into the dark hallway. Holmes nodded and stepped to the door. I reached him as he said, "Going somewhere, Mr. Morland?"

Inside, a single desk lamp burned, revealing the thin man packing papers into a dispatch case. He looked up, more with irritation than surprise or guilt. "As a matter of fact, I have been called back to Manchester. I must leave immediately. Family business, you know."

"I don't think so," said Holmes. "You see, Sophia Wilkies has told us everything."

Siger glanced at his uncle, but showed no surprise in his face, and nothing to give away his uncle's lie. "Everything?" Morland asked. "Everything about what?"

303

"About the murder of her father. About how you planned it, and helped her to do it. About how you both lured him to some obscure spot in his robes, telling him it was some sort of ceremony relating to his own beliefs, and then ritually executed him. About how you changed him back to his regular clothing, propped him up in the pit, and then cut his throat."

" 'Ritually executed him' ?" repeated Morland. "Are you quite mad? I have no doubt that the girl is insane, but anything she has said that involves me is untrue. I shall have her prosecuted for slander. And you as well, I believe."

"She didn't tell us everything, of course," continued Holmes. "Not quite everything. Yet. For example, we do not know yet whether the Hand of Glory belonged to her, or if it was originally yours."

Hearing about the evil talisman used during the murder seemed to shake Morland. He did not realize that we had found it, and as far as he knew, it was still wrapped in his empty stable.

"Hand of Glory?" he said. "Don't know what you mean." He reached back toward the desk for more papers. Holmes and Siger both raised their guns higher. Seeing that, I raised mine also. "You need to step back from the desk," said Holmes. "Now," in a stronger, more commanding tone.

With a smile, Morland raised his hands and took a step backward.

"Watson?" asked Holmes. I stepped forward, taking care to stay out of my friends' line of fire, and pulled open the desk drawer for which Morland had been reaching. Inside, lying on a stack of papers, was a small, but deadly and efficient, pistol. It was obviously freshly cleaned, as gun oil had soaked and spread through the papers on which it rested.

Picking it up, I placed it in my pocket and stepped back.

"Did you wonder about the coded message from Sophia?" asked Holmes. "Would she have written it and helped to lure you into a trap if she hadn't already revealed everything to us?" he bluffed.

"Message?" asked Morland. "Do you mean that scrap of gibberish that was brought to me this afternoon by that filthy gypsy boy? Are you saying that it was a coded message from Sophia, luring me into a trap? This is quite ridiculous, Mr. Holmes. Surely if I could have understood that message, I would have gone to this meeting, thus confirming your suspicions. But since I didn't go to see her, obviously it was because I could not understand the code, which therefore confirms my innocence."

"You didn't go because Constable Worth warned you," said Holmes, noting the narrowing of Morland's eyes. "We have Worth's testimony as well. You really are caught, you know," he added. "We have even retrieved the dead man's robes and what was contained within them from where you hid them in your stalls." Morland said nothing for a moment. He did not even allow any expression to pass across his face. Finally, he said, with just a possibility of tentativeness in his voice, "Robes? In my stalls? I don't know what you're talking about. If you found anything in my out-buildings, it must have been placed there by someone else. Possibly this mad Sophia put it there, or one of her people. Maybe that filthy boy that delivered the message did it."

"This is the 'filthy boy,' " said Tenley, nodding his head toward Siger. "He brought the message to you. You're not as smart as you think. You didn't even take a good look at who he was."

"You are the one who is not very smart, Inspector," said Morland. "You have burst into my house, held me at gunpoint, and detained me from my lawful activities, based on the ridiculous story of some crazy girl who apparently murdered her father, and has since tried to mask her own guilt by spreading it around onto her betters! I'm soon to be a peer of the realm. I cannot be treated this way!"

"Peer of the realm?" said Holmes. "It won't do, *Mr.* Morland. It really won't. Or perhaps I should address you as *Baron Ennesfred Kroll!*" Morland stepped back, and seemed to sag for just a moment before pulling himself back up. His eyes widened, and he moved his mouth as if to speak, but nothing came forth.

"We really do know it all, Baron Kroll," said Holmes. "We know about your true identity, and how you assumed that of the real Morland more than twenty years ago, following his death in Germany. We know how you took over the family fortune, estates, and title following the death of Morland's father, and how you ran the Morland business from Germany.

"We know about how you met Sophia when she was in Germany, and learned of her fascination with the Satanic religions, something her father never would have tolerated. We know how you finally returned to this country, and began buying lands to create a vast unobserved area on the northeast coast of England, which could be used at some point in the future as a sort of secret German colony, for troops and supplies to be assembled and organized under cover, should an invasion ever occur.

"Finally, we know how my brother was a hold-out to your plan, refusing to sell his large and centrally located estate. It wasn't supposed to happen that way, was it, Baron Kroll? All of the land owners were supposed to be easily swayed by your offers and your seeming infinite financial resources, backed by the very German treasury itself. We know how you manipulated Sophia into convincing her father to come to this area, and finally how you helped her to murder him, using the iron dagger, with its oddly Germanic markings, and the hideous dead man's Hand of Glory.

"As you can see, Baron Kroll, we know it all. And we have known it for quite a while. There is an old saying about giving a man enough rope

305

to hang himself. Do you have such a saying in Germany? Well, you were being given rope, and far earlier than was expected, you hung yourself by becoming involved in a murder."

The sound of footsteps came up the stairs and then down the short hallway. William stepped into the room, breathing hard. I knew that he was supposed to stay with Sophia, and wondered what could have happened to make him come here instead.

"Well?" asked Holmes.

"She was dead," replied William. "In her tent. Throat cut. None of those people heard or saw anything. Or so they say."

Holmes cursed and met my eyes. We both knew where Morland had gone this afternoon when no one followed him. I was aware that Holmes would hold himself responsible for allowing the girl's death to occur. Morland, or Baron Kroll, as I would have to think of him now, smiled and said, "I believe that without a witness, any attempt to link me to this murder will be doomed to failure." He stepped forward. "Now, as I said, Inspector, I must be leaving on family business. I do not know what this foolishness is about me being a German citizen, but I can assure you that if you do not stand aside, I will make sure that you yourself are brought up on charges. Do I make myself clear?"

Tenley smiled. "You don't seriously think I'm going to let you walk out of here, do you, Baron Kroll? Because I – "

Before he could finish, Kroll had pivoted and dropped, reaching for a lower drawer on his desk. Pulling it open, he rose in one fluid movement, holding another pistol, and swinging it up. From my position, I could not tell where he intended to aim it, and I could not see whether his finger was tightening as he prepared to fire. In any case, I considered the man to be as dangerous as a mad dog, and I had no hesitation whatsoever.

I fired twice. The first bullet passed through Kroll's upraised wrist, causing the gun to spin and sag on his forefinger before dropping to the floor. The sound of it hitting the wood was unheard as it was drowned out by my second shot, the bullet flying true into Baron Kroll's knee. As he turned to me in shock, and started to sag to the ground, I stepped forward, kicking him to one side as I knocked his fallen gun to the other.

"Well done, Dr. Watson!" cried Siger. "Oh, well done!"

I cleared my throat. "Holmes usually prefers to avoid this type of conclusion to his cases," I said. "However, I suspect that if I had allowed this madman to shoot either of her children, or even her brother-in-law, Roberta Holmes would have shot me as well, and I did not travel all the way to Yorkshire in order to make such fine new friends, only to have to turn around and bury some of them."

When we arrived at the village cells, Holmes paused for a moment in front, staring up at the tall structure. "You say this oversized building was financed and built by Sir Clive Owenby?" he asked.

Tenley regarded him with a smile. "Yes," he replied. "Sir Clive lives in York."

"I believe that you stated that he is a crony of my brother Mycroft's," said Holmes.

"They are somewhat acquainted," confirmed Tenley. "Is it important?"

"I theorize," said Holmes, "that the idea behind this building's construction lies along the same lines of thinking as Baron Kroll's attempts to create a pocket German fiefdom here in Yorkshire. This building is intended to remain here, looking simply like the location of an oversize village constabulary, until such time as it might be needed. Sir Clive, at my brother's urging, has financed this inconspicuous fortress. No doubt there are some interesting secrets inside, possibly an unknown cellar, or cellars. And perhaps some of the Queen's weapons stored in them as well, in case the citizens might someday need to be armed at short notice against German invaders?"

Tenley looked to make sure that Kroll was a considerable distance away. "I won't confirm anything specific, Mr. Holmes, but I will say that whatever secrets that building does contain, they are well hidden and there is no way Constable Worth of any of his ilk ever suspected anything, and certainly no way that the Germans could know about it."

Upstairs, we found Sherrinford talking with Holder and Jacobs, while Constable Worth sat on the cot in his locked cell, his head resting in his hands. Outside in the hall, Baron Kroll was surrounded by all of Tenley's remaining men and Dr. Dalton, who had been summoned to treat Kroll's wounds. Kroll was nearly completely hidden within the cluster of angry Yorkshiremen and one grim doctor. Sherrinford stepped forward, embracing his two sons, and then grabbing Holmes in a bear hug, before releasing him and shaking his hand. Then he turned toward me. I stepped forward, my hand outstretched, but he bypassed it, hugging me as well. After releasing me, he turned back to Tenley. "Worth hasn't said a word since he got here," he said. "Holder and Jacobs let me know what he did. What has happened since they brought him here?"

We related to Sherrinford the confrontation at the Morland house, and William's subsequent revelation that Sophia had been murdered. Worth moaned to himself. Upon hearing of the girl's violent death, Sherrinford leaned to one side, looking into the hall as if to get a glimpse of Kroll. He

307

was unable to see him, however, due to the fact that the German was blocked by the big country men surrounding him.

"I think that we shall have to release Worth on his own recognizance," said Holmes, to our surprise.

"Why, Mr. Holmes?" asked Tenley. "If we leave them together, we might overhear some incriminating conversation."

"True," replied Holmes. "However, Baron Kroll is going to be a very different kind of prisoner, and we would do well to keep him entirely separated from Worth. The murders of Wilkies and his daughter are simply a small part of the bigger picture. This man is a German agent. Mycroft may or may not decide that it is more effective for Kroll to disappear into a prison somewhere, leaving the Germans in disarray and confusion regarding their land-grab plan and the disappearance of their man. Or it may be decided to try Kroll as Augustus Morland for the murders, but limit information from the trial that is released to the public. In any case, we need to keep Kroll separate from everyone that we can from this moment on.

"I'm sure," he added, glancing at Worth, "that this man can be released without any risk of flight. After all, only a few of us here know about his involvement. He is a ruined and broken man, and I'm certain that he knows what's good for him. He will not be the type to talk about these events, which put him in such a bad light. I'm certain that we can count on his discretion."

Worth, who had apparently been listening despite his attitude of despair, jumped up. "Oh, I promise, sirs!" he cried. "I won't say anything. I have learned my lesson."

"Of course," Holmes went on, conversationally, "you have resigned your position as constable, effective immediately, and you will be observed closely for a long time to come." Worth stared at him, seeing that his freedom was not going to come without some cost, after all. He swallowed once or twice, and then said, in a much quieter and emotionless voice, "Yes, sir. Of course. I understand."

Worth's cell was soon unlocked, and he was led by one of his big guards – I never did know which was Holder and which was Jacobs – out past the group of men in the hall, making sure that he was allowed no contact whatsoever with Kroll. After he had gone, Kroll was placed in a center cell. Holmes remained behind for a moment, staring wordlessly at the prisoner, who returned his gaze with venomous hate.

Then Holmes joined us in the hall, leaving the German under guard by several of our night's companions. Downstairs, Tenley emphasized to the remaining men the need to keep the entire affair secret, no matter what

308

version of events that they might hear in the next few days. The men, all good British citizens, agreed and departed.

"I will cable London and your brother with the details," said Tenley. "You get Mr. Sherrinford Holmes here back to his family."

He shook hands with all of us, and went back inside. I looked around, and saw, sitting off to the side of the building, Griffin. He was on the driver's seat, as usual, with no indication that he wanted to be anywhere else, in spite of the fact that it was after three in the morning. Stepping over to him, I asked whether he could take us back to the Holmes farm. Without a word, he nodded. In a moment, the five of us were on board and the short trip began.

Roberta was still up when we arrived. Her joy at seeing the safe return of her husband and two sons was palpable. She would not rest until she heard the whole story. We had to repeatedly decline her offer to make a full meal right then instead of waiting for breakfast. Finally, as the sky began to lighten with the coming dawn, we made our way to bed in order to catch a few hours of sleep. All of us, that is, except Holmes and Siger.

If Siger was like his uncle, he did not need much sleep in any case, so I doubt if staying up the rest of the night seriously tired either of them. To this day, I do not know what they talked about, although I am fairly certain that the discussion probably included an examination of the minute details of the recent events. I also believe that they discussed Siger's chosen future.

I do know that later that year, Siger entered Oxford at the young age of sixteen. His intellect was a deciding factor, but possibly the influence of his uncles helped as well. A few years later, in 1899, Siger graduated and immediately approached his uncle, asking Holmes to allow Siger to become something of an apprentice, learning the varied skills needed by a consulting detective. At that time, I was still living in Baker Street, and I had been prohibited by Holmes from publishing any more of his cases. Holmes knew that I still kept extensive notes on his investigations, however, and he instructed me that I was never to mention Siger in any of them, most likely because he wanted to spare Siger from gaining a reputation based upon appearances in a popular publication.

In October 1903, Holmes was faced with an unexpected crisis in the form of the sudden death of Irene Adler. I have never mentioned in any published accounts the regard Holmes had always felt for Irene, who had been widowed by Godfrey Norton in late 1890. The following year she had given birth to Godfrey's daughter, and had resumed her career on the operatic stage. Holmes had become reacquainted with her soon after his supposed disappearance at the Reichenbach Falls. In 1892, she gave birth to a son, Scott. After Holmes's return to England in 1894, we had infrequent contact with her. Her fortunes went into decline, and in the late 1890's she married a wealthy man who subsequently died.

Several more meetings between Irene, Holmes, and myself took place over the next few years. Eventually Irene moved with her family to Montenegro, a location that seemed to hold some sentimental attachment for her. In 1901, she married her third husband, a man named Vukcic, which loosely translates to "little wolf." Vukcic had a son of his own. Irene remained in Montenegro until her untimely death.

I had initially believed Irene Adler was something of an adventuress, based upon the original description of her by the King of Bohemia, but as I came to know her in later years, I realized that she was a lady of high morals who had been much maligned by the king. As this document which I am preparing will be placed with my other records at the Cox and Company Bank for at least seventy-five years after my death, I feel that I can elaborate on what happened after Irene's death, and how those events relate to Siger, without bringing any negative reflection on the lady.

I will never forget that October 1903, when I received Holmes's request to visit his rooms in Baker Street. I had remarried by then, and was living several streets away in Queen Anne Street, where I had resumed my private medical practice. I found Holmes smoking in his chair before his fire. Littering the floor of the sitting room were several packing boxes. "Going somewhere?" I asked Holmes.

"I have decided to retire."

Before I could process this odd and unexpected statement, for Holmes was only forty-nine years old at the time, Holmes handed me the telegram, containing the details of Irene's death in a railway accident. The implications washed over me. Some were obvious, and some I was not supposed to know but had figured out for myself.

"What about her son and daughter?" I asked.

"They are all right," said Holmes. "Her daughter wishes to remain in Montenegro. Her son . . . . He will be here in a few days." He paused for a second, and said, "Watson, there is something that I must tell you about the boy." He shifted in his seat, looking uncomfortable, one of the few times I have ever seen him so. The time he had apologized to me after making me believe that he had been poisoned by Culverton Smith. The time that he had returned from a three-year absence, leaving me to believe that he was dead, while only his brother Mycroft had known the truth. A few others as well. I saw no reason to extend his discomfort.

"I already know, Holmes." He didn't look up. "I know that he is your son."

We were silent for a moment, and he did not ask how that I knew. We never discussed it again, and to this day I do not know the details. Nor do

I want to. After a moment, he began to speak. He told me how he had been spending more and more time of late working on matters for his brother Mycroft, especially relating to Britain's relations with the rest of the world, and specifically Germany. For a year or more, Mycroft had been pressuring him to become something of a full-time agent for the shadowy secret department that Mycroft controlled, as the certainty of war with Germany loomed ever closer. The arrival of the boy would allow Holmes to do as Mycroft wished, in a limited way.

He intended to announce his retirement immediately, and depart to live near Beachy Head in Sussex, in a small coastal cottage that he had acquired several years earlier, during the course of an investigation. He intended to maintain the Baker Street rooms, however, as a retreat while in London. Mrs. Hudson had agreed to move to Sussex with him, to help care for the boy. And he was going to keep bees.

In order to complete the illusion of Holmes's retirement, I would begin to publish accounts of his cases once again in *The Strand* magazine, which had been approached by the government and was more than willing to help, considering the financial windfall they would be reaping. My old friend and literary agent, Conan Doyle, had already been briefed and was willing to help. The first published case would be *The Empty House*, relating Holmes's return to life in 1894. And I must specifically include a statement that Holmes had retired, and that it was only due to that reason that I was allowed to resume publication of the stories.

And so, within a day or so, Holmes had ensconced himself in Sussex. Soon after that, Scott Adler Holmes arrived at his father's new home.

I was there when the precocious eleven-year-old greeted his father.

They had met several times over the years, but I never knew if Scott realized before his mother's death and the subsequent reading of her will that Holmes was his father. Mrs. Hudson bustled around and made the boy feel at home, and I did my best to welcome him as well. However, I do not think that anyone comforted him more during that time than did his cousin, Siger Holmes.

At that time, Siger had trained with Holmes for several years, one of several apprentices that Holmes had taken on during the early years of the century. Siger's activities had transitioned gradually from those of a consulting detective to that of an agent, working for his uncle Mycroft and brother Bancroft, now himself quite a rising figure within the British government. Siger had been on hand during Holmes's move to Sussex.

At that time, he was twenty-three years of age, tall and lean, and looked almost exactly like his uncle Sherlock. He still retained much of his boyish enthusiasm, however, and I believe that was what bonded him to Scott Holmes.

The young boy adapted well. He met Mycroft and Bancroft a few days after his arrival, and I went with them all to Yorkshire in November, where Scott was welcomed by the rest of his new family. It warmed my heart to see how Roberta mothered the boy, immediately surrounding him with the unconditional love with which she had filled her home and had raised three fine sons. In later years, while Holmes was off continuing his investigations, Scott would spend a great deal of time in Yorkshire, and Roberta would become like a second mother to him, as she had been to his father as well.

That November was the last time that the Holmes family, with myself included as a sort of adopted uncle and brother, would all be together in one place. In later years, with the War approaching, the family would be scattered, and there was never a chance to assemble the entire group again.

As Scott grew, his friendship with Siger grew as well. Siger nicknamed the boy "Caesar" due to Scott's assured bearing and attitude.

By this point, Scott was showing the same deductive skills as evidenced by the rest of his family. In 1907, Siger opened his own practice as a consulting detective, finding increasing success over the course of several years. However, he was dismayed that many people came to him expecting the services of his uncle Sherlock, based upon the name Holmes. He began to see why his brother Bancroft had taken a different last name.

In 1911, Scott inadvertently became involved in a series of events that resulted in the defeat of a group that would have prevented the crowning of King George V. By that time, the nineteen-year-old young man had eschewed college, preferring to educate himself, learning more that way than he probably could have by attending any university. As a result of Scott's service to the Crown, he was officially recruited into Mycroft Holmes's organization, where he and Siger became a team that was unparalleled for its masterful successes in discovering information to aid the British government as the threat of war rolled ever closer.

Working together, the two young men criss-crossed Europe. Siger often used the name "Mr. Bridges," an Anglicization of his brother's assumed last name, *Pons*. Scott would usually go by his nickname, Caesar, or other names of Roman leaders, combined with variants of the word *wolf* as a surname. Their exploits and antics during this time became something of a legend, and although they frequently vexed Mycroft Holmes and Bancroft Pons to no end, no one could argue with their results.

This continued, of course, until the Great War began. I was staying with Holmes in Sussex in late August of that year, 1914, when Siger came to see his uncle. Both realized that their conversation might be the last quiet visit they would have for some time. Holmes had recently returned from a two-and-a-half-year absence, traveling the United States and Great Britain

312

as "Altamont," the renegade Irishman and German agent. His masterful impersonation had ended only a few weeks before, with the arrest of the sinister von Bork.

Siger stated that after the war, he wished to resume his private practice, but he would like to make his own name, and not rest on his uncle's reputation, as had been the earlier problem. He seemed to be asking for some sort of permission from Holmes to step away from the family name. Holmes suggested that Siger use an alias, based on Siger's previous preference for "Mr. Bridges" and also his brother Bancroft's changed surname at the Foreign Office. They experimented with several variations before Holmes suggested something appealing, recalling a comment made by Holmes at the end of the Yorkshire investigation in June 1896. Siger decided that he would adopt the name suggested to him by Sherlock Holmes: *Solar Pons*.

Of course, that was years in the future. Little did Holmes and Siger know, during that early morning conversation in Yorkshire while the rest of the family slept, what was ahead of all of us on our long road. The successes and tragedies were all hidden from us then, as well as the fact that Baron Ennesfred Kroll would escape from British custody in October of that same year, only to resume his true identity and vex Siger in later years, much as Professor Moriarty had plagued Holmes.

I arose late that morning, and was dismayed and embarrassed to see my watch indicating that the morning was nearly gone. I dressed hurriedly and went downstairs, where Roberta did her best to make me feel as if my long slumber was the most natural thing in the world. She and Sherrinford, along with William, had been up since daybreak, taking care of the daily work, while Holmes and Siger had gone back to the village to check on the prisoner.

Later that morning, I was just finishing my belated breakfast when a commotion arose out in the yard. Roberta leaned in and said, "You'd better come out, Dr. Watson."

Stepping into the sunshine, I saw several men descending from Griffin's sturdy four-wheeler. As my eyes adjusted to the light, I saw Holmes and Siger, followed by the heavier and more awkward figures of Mycroft Holmes and a similar looking younger fellow who could only be Bancroft.

Sherrinford and Roberta greeted their prodigal son, while William and Siger grinned. Mycroft nodded in my direction, and when Bancroft was free, he stepped over and introduced himself.

"Bancroft Pons, doctor. A pleasure to meet you."

"The pleasure is all mine," I said, shaking his hand.

313

"Bancroft *Holmes*," said his mother. "You are home now. That other silly name can remain in London."

"As you like," replied Bancroft.

We went inside, where Roberta bustled about, serving refreshments. I was not very hungry, having just eaten, but I did manage to put away at least one serving of a delicious yellow cake. As I was eating, discussions moved quickly around the table, as everyone was caught up on the events of the last few days. Mycroft and Bancroft explained that they had arranged a special train to leave London as soon as they had received Tenley's wire, explaining the details of Baron Kroll's arrest.

"I understand you were quite helpful, brother," said Bancroft to Siger.

"He was truly a bridge of sunlight throughout the whole affair," said Holmes, causing his youngest nephew to puff up in a most comical way with pride.

Bancroft snorted. "A bridge of sunlight, indeed! If only you could approach your studies with the same solar intensity that you have shown relating to your desire to become a detective."

"By the way, Watson," Holmes said, changing the subject, "Baron Kroll tried to kill himself last night."

I raised my eyebrows. "Really? How?"

"His guards thought he was asleep, and he tried to fashion a noose from a bed sheet. He was caught, however, and his attempt was prevented."

"Just as well, I suppose," said Mycroft. "We will have to let him go, eventually, but not before we get all the use out of him that we can."

Baron Kroll ended up staying in the village lock-up for several months, during which time he was closely interrogated by Tenley and other individuals sent up from London. He was not moved to a larger prison in order to preserve the security of his arrest. Before he could be officially sent back to Germany, he escaped.

Mycroft shifted his big frame in the small chair. "Baron Kroll does seem to have conceived an intense dislike for the Holmes name."

"And the Pons name, as well," added Bancroft. "After we identified ourselves, I could see him committing it to memory with the same hatred that he was showing towards you, uncle."

"Pons, Pons," cried Roberta. "I wish you'd never decided to use that name."

"Actually, the boy comes by it honestly," said Sherrinford, speaking for the first time. He had been looking with quiet fondness from one member of his family to another since we had come inside.

"How do you mean?" asked Siger.

"He is not the first to use that alias," replied Sherrinford. "I myself used it, a few years back."

Roberta and Mycroft both looked at him suddenly, their glances filled with similar warnings. Sherrinford continued as if he did not notice.

"William probably remembers some of this, and I know Bancroft is aware of the details, but you have never heard this story, Siger. Back in 1880, just before you were born, I did a little favor for your uncle Mycroft."

Siger sat up straight, eyes alert. I glanced at Holmes, and could tell that he had never heard this tale, either. "Without getting into many specifics," Sherrinford continued, "I was asked to travel to Prague, where I carried out a mission for Her Majesty's government, delivering a message to the Bohemian royal family. In order to hide my activities, I traveled with my family. William was only nine, and Bancroft was about seven. And your mother was very much burdened with you at that point Siger, since this was right before the time of your birth."

"A mad time to make me travel," muttered Roberta. "Although I will admit that Prague was a lovely city . . . ."

"In any case," said Sherrinford, "I carried out my mission, although I must say that sort of intrigue is not to my liking. I am happy to leave it to those who enjoy it. While we were there in Prague, Siger, you were born."

"I did not know that," said Siger softly.

"Neither did I," said Holmes. "As I recall, I visited Yorkshire a month or so after Siger's birth, and you were all here at home as if you had never left, and no one mentioned a thing to me at all about a trip to Prague."

"I'm sure you understand the nature of security, Sherlock," interrupted Mycroft, "As do you, Sherrinford. I think that this discussion should be concluded."

"Strange," continued Holmes, ignoring Mycroft, "when I met the King of Bohemia, he never mentioned having previously met my brother."

"He didn't know me as your brother, you see," replied Sherrinford. "Hence my previous use of the name *Pons*. When I traveled there, I went under the identity of Asenath Pons, a visiting consular official. Years later, when Bancroft went to work for Mycroft, he must have read the file and taken the name Pons as well, for his own reasons."

"And I always thought you came up with it on your own," said Siger to his brother, who did not comment.

"As did I, said Holmes. "I understand the derivation of the name Pons from your name, Sherrinford, but I wonder if mad old cousin Asenath would appreciate that you appropriated *his* name for your role?"

"He will never hear about it," grinned Sherrinford. "Security, you know."

Mycroft interrupted at that point, urging that all discussion of the matter be dropped. Siger and Bancroft joined in as well, with Holmes and

315

Sherrinford offering their opinions, and in a moment, even William was participating. I watched them, two generations of Holmes brothers, the air in the room nearly popping with the electricity being generated by their combined personalities and intellects. I became aware of Roberta, sitting beside me and watching them as well, her lovely face beaming with pride.

"They are something wonderful, are they not, doctor?" she said, very softly.

"Indeed," I replied. "And you have made a wonderful home for them here."

"Thank you," she said. Then turning slightly toward me, she said, "You must consider this your home, and yourself a part of this family, as well."

Her earnest gaze stopped any polite refusal that might have initially risen to my lips. I glanced back at the group of men, all arguing and teasing each other in a good-natured way. I realized that I would be very happy, indeed, to be included in such a group.

"Thank you," I said to her. "It pleases me very much to be a part of your family."

She patted my arm and turned back to look at the men surrounding the table. I realized that I was hungrier than I thought, and reached to cut another piece of cake.

Postscript: Two Letters*

9 July, 1929

Dear Willie,

I hope that this letter finds you and your family in excellent health, and that you are doing well. I apologize for not having written in so long, and can only beg your forgiveness and understanding. I could plead that the long intervals between letters is due to my age, but I must confess that I have been writing, working on more records of Holmes's cases, so I really have no good excuse at all.

I was sorry to hear of your mother's passing, as well as the tragic death of your young son Howard from rabies. I realize that it has been two years since they both passed, but I know that you must still think of them every day. I am greatly saddened that in this modern world in which we live, a treatable disease such as rabies was still able to take your son from you.

As I mentioned, I have been working to complete a number of my records of Holmes's cases, and recently I came across the notes I made during our visit to your part of the world in 1921. Although it was just a few short years ago, I must confess that it seems like much longer, as my age has really caught up with me in the intervening years. Upon completion of the manuscript, I propose to send you a copy, with the fond hope that you and your family might enjoy a record of those two days.

Holmes and I have stayed busy since that time, although I must admit that Holmes has been more active than I. He has still engaged himself in the occasional investigation, while I am more content to remain in England. However, he and I both traveled to your country in the fall of 1927, where we were involved in one of the most trying matters of our careers.

Before the case was over, we had asked several people to come over from London to help us, including Holmes's nephew and a former Belgian policeman, both of whom have set up private consulting detective practices in London. Joining Holmes's nephew was his good friend, Dr. Parker. In New York, we were assisted by Holmes's son – now there's a fellow you didn't know about, I'll wager! – as well as his assistant, a Mr. Goodwin, and also the unlikely team of one of the New York Police inspectors and his brilliant son, Ellery, who shows every sign of being Holmes's deductive rival.In spite of the fact that we had all of that deductive brain power working on the case, I don't think that the matter could have been satisfactorily concluded without the last minute arrival of

317

a young law student from California named Mason, who provided the last bit of missing and vital information to our case.

After the matter concluded, we had a wonderful celebration at the Hotel Algonquin, before those of us returning to England all set sail together. (Of course, I know that I don't have to ask you to keep this information to yourself, as the identity of both Holmes's son and his nephew are both rather closely guarded secrets.)

Since that time, I have lived a relatively peaceful life, working, as I said, on putting my notes in order. However, I was excited to hear from Holmes just the other day. He needs my help on another case! It seems that his son, who has been living in New York for several years and working as a private detective under some outlandish assumed name, has traveled to Zagreb to track down the whereabouts of a girl, Anna, that he adopted in 1921, during the time he wandered Europe after the War. Now he has been thrown into jail there, and we are off to rescue him! Joining us will be Holmes's nephew and Dr. Parker.

While I am traveling, I will continue to work on the manuscript of our Tennessee visit, along with a few others, and will forward to you a completed version when I return to England. In the meantime, I hope that everything is going well for you and yours, and that I will be able to visit the United States again at some point in the future, where we will be able to renew our friendship in person.

Until that time, remember that I am,

Always your friend (and distant cousin!),

John H. Watson

* * * * * *

8 August, 1929

Dear Mr. Marcum,

I am very sad to inform you that Watson passed away on 24 July of pneumonia, which he acquired while traveling with me and some associates to Zagreb on something of a rescue mission. I knew that Watson's health had been failing for some time, but against my better judgment, I allowed him to accompany us. It thrilled him, I believe, to be asked to go along on one more investigation.

He became ill on the way back from our journey, which I can tell you was a complete success. I insisted that he return with me to my Sussex home to recuperate, but after we had settled in there, his condition worsened, and he died peacefully a few days later.

As the enclosed letter from Watson mentions, he had worked for the past several years on the monumental task of wrestling his voluminous notes into some sort of readable shape. He had completed a number of manuscripts, some of which have been place in safe-keeping, while others he generously gave to the individuals involved in the events that he had recorded.

He had finished preparing the narrative of our trip to your part of the world, as well as a few other stories contained in the same copy book, when he died. I have kept his final versions of the events, but I thought, as it was his intention to send you a copy of the narrative, that you might like to have the original copy book, containing a few other matters as well.

It may interest you to read that after we left you in Rockwood that day, we journeyed back to Knoxville, and then on to Maryville, where we were able to stop a rather diabolical assembly. During that time, we had a chance to spend several days in and around Maryville College. I believe that Watson has mentioned to me how you attended this college for a few years in 1911 or 1912. Possibly you will recognize some place where you walked there as you read Watson's narrative.

Watson and I both enjoyed meeting you, and Watson was very proud of his American cousins. If there is ever anything that I can do for you, do not hesitate to let me know.

With all best wishes,

Sherlock Holmes

NOTE

*   These are the letters that were folded in the back of the composition book found in my aunt's belongings. – DM

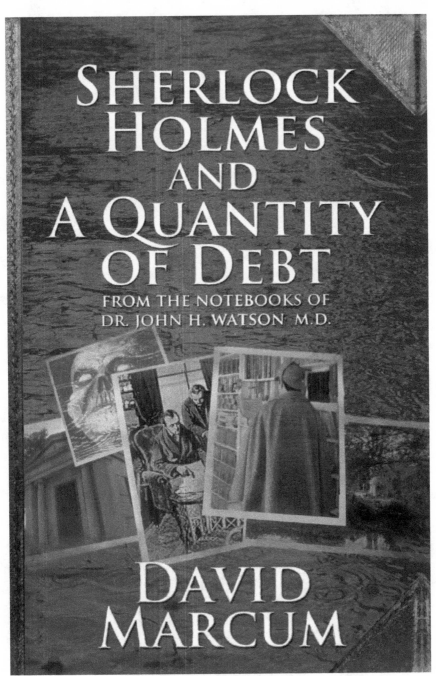

SHERLOCK HOLMES
AND
A QUANTITY
OF DEBT

FROM THE NOTEBOOKS OF
DR. JOHN H. WATSON M.D.

DAVID
MARCUM

2016 Paperback Edition

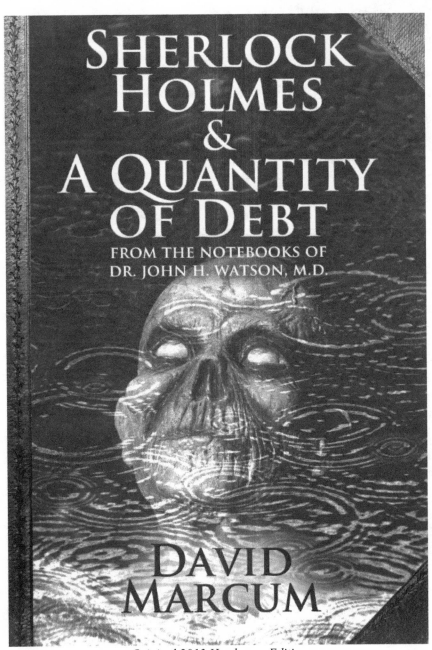

SHERLOCK
HOLMES
&
A QUANTITY
OF DEBT

FROM THE NOTEBOOKS OF
DR. JOHN H. WATSON, M.D.

DAVID
MARCUM

Original 2013 Hardcover Edition

Editor's Introdction
(From the 2013 Hardcover Edition)

I t was a dark and stormy afternoon . . . .

I recall it vividly, that afternoon when I really first encountered Mr. Sherlock Holmes of Baker Street. It was in the summer of 1975, I was ten years old, and some weeks (or months – who knows at this point?) earlier, I had acquired my first Holmes volume. I hadn't really wanted it at the time, so it had been put on a shelf for unloved books.

On that particular and wonderful afternoon, a very rainy and dark Saturday, we were sitting around the house, my mother, my sister, and myself. I'm not sure where my dad was at the time, so he wasn't present at my epiphany. (I recently asked my sister, and she doesn't remember the event, but I do.) The room was dark, with the only glow coming from the television. That was unusual, because we usually had the lights on. The darkness reflected the grim boredom of the whole day.

Back then, there were only three channels on the television. I stood up and walked across the room in order to try to find something better than whatever we were watching – there were no remote controls in our house in those days – and came across *A Study in Terror* (1965), starring John Neville as Holmes, and Donald Houston as Watson.

Of course, I didn't know what movie it was then, or who the actors were. It would be years before I would find the film again and be able to watch it in its entirety. But somehow, even in my ignorance on that day, I knew that this was Holmes. Don't ask me how. I had never read a Holmes story or seen a Holmes movie at that point. Maybe it was just an awareness of who Holmes was, the same amazing thing that makes him one of the most recognizable figures in the world. More likely, it was simply that fact that the speakers referred to the main character as *Sherlock* and *Holmes.*

In any case, it was the scene where Mycroft, played by Robert Morley, comes to call and squabble with our hero. The quick dialogue, and possibly even the bright colors of the 1960's film, somehow appealed to me. During a commercial, I ran back to my room and found the then-single Holmes volume – I still have it – in my eventually massive collection and brought it back with me for further study. It didn't take long to read the nine stories in that book.

It all tumbled after that. I sought out more tales of the Canon. I borrowed ahead on my allowance and purchased the complete Doubleday edition. At Christmas, my parents presented me with Baring-Gould's

Sherlock Holmes of Baker Street, and I had really found the door into Holmes's world.

Not long after that, Nicholas Meyer, who had started the great 1970's Holmes resurgence with his novel *The Seven-Per-Cent Solution*, published the follow-up, *The West End Horror* (1976). This was the first truly great non-Canon tale that I had ever read. (Strangely, it is often mistakenly referred to as a Holmes-versus-The Ripper tale. However, it is set in 1895, not 1888, and involves the murder of actors and critics in the West End, and not the poor Whitechapel victims. I highly recommend it, nearly forty years after I first read it, and I was fortunate enough to say the same thing to Mr. Meyer in late 2011, when I got to meet him at a Sherlockian gathering in Bloomington, IN.)

In Meyer's introduction, he relates how, after the publication of *The Seven-Per-Cent Solution*, he received a number of newly discovered Watson manuscripts from various sources. Some were obvious forgeries, but not all of them.

I had a similar experience after the publication of my recent books, *The Papers of Sherlock Holmes* Volumes I and II. After many kind comments, (and a few wondering why the books weren't about Cumberbatch and Freeman's "Sherlock" and "John"), I received a cryptic email with a single PDF image of a handwritten page containing Watson's handwriting.

I can't tell you much more than that. After some back-and-forth communications, it was arranged that the following narrative from Watson's journals could be published. I had been prepared to beg and plead, and perhaps take a second mortgage on my house, in order to obtain the manuscript, but the mysterious owner, who insists on anonymity, had wanted all along to make sure that the story was told. I have the impression that there are personal motivations and perhaps some old grudges involved, but I have no knowledge of any specifics.

I was glad to see that the manuscript seemed to confirm some of the information about Watson's *first* wife, as detailed in Baring-Gould's *Sherlock Holmes of Baker Street*, which has meant so much to me over the years. As was the case with *The Papers of Sherlock Holmes*, any misunderstandings of the contents of Watson's smudged journal and rather cramped handwriting must be blamed on my editing and not on the good Doctor.

And also, as I did with the previous volumes, I wish to dedicate the effort involved in preparing this manuscript to both my wife Rebecca, with much love for her patience and support regarding my fascination with the world of Holmes and Watson, and my also my son Dan, best friend and patient listener to my wound-up ramblings. Thank you both for everything!

David Marcum
August 7th, 2013

The 161st Anniversary of the Birth of Dr. John H. Watson

A Word for the 2016 Edition

What an amazing journey so far!

Back in 2013, when this book first appeared, I was just venturing out into the wider Sherlockian world after most of a lifetime of solitary enjoyment and study of the lives of Our Heroes, Sherlock Holmes and Dr. Watson. I had found one of Watson's notebooks several years before, leading to their eventual publication as *The Papers of Sherlock Holmes*. As described in the earlier 2013 introduction to this volume, the appearance of those adventures connected me with the person who wished for *Sherlock Holmes and A Quantity of Debt* to be made public.

At that time, it was still my fondest wish to be able to visit England, and specifically Baker Street and London, the locations which I had imagined for so long. I was finally able to do so in September 2013, completing my first extensive Holmes Pilgrimage. That trip allowed me to stumble into a new cache of Watsonian manuscripts, thus leading to the publication of the three-volume *Sherlock Holmes in Montague Street* (2014) and *Sherlock Holmes – Tangled Skeins* (2015).

In early 2015, I had the idea of gathering together the top "editors" of additional Watson-related adventures, producing what would eventually become the largest collection of new Sherlock Holmes stories ever assembled in one place, *The MX Book of New Sherlock Holmes Stories*. The author royalties for this project are being donated to the Stepping Stones School for special needs children at Undershaw, one of Sir Arthur Conan Doyle's former homes. The initial idea for the anthology, containing possibly a couple-of-dozen stories in a paperback edition, grew and grew to finally include sixty-three adventures in three massive hardcover volumes, *Part I: 1881-1889*, *Part II – 1890-1895*, and *Part III – 1896-1929*. And it turned out that the idea was so popular that it's become an ongoing treat, with *Part IV – 2016 Annual* appearing in May 2016, *Part V – Christmas Adventures* in Fall 2016, and *Part VI – 2017* to be available in Fall 2017. And these collections will keep going as long as there is interest, because the school can always use the funds, and there are never enough stories about the True Sherlock Holmes!

As a result of the publication of those first three Anthology volumes, I was able to return to London in September and October 2015 for my second extensive Holmes Pilgrimage, whereupon I found a new collection of Watson manuscripts, which – with any luck – should keep appearing regularly for the foreseeable future.

While I was growing up, my interest and study into the life of Mr. Sherlock Holmes was accomplished in isolation. There are no Sherlockian societies or Scions where I live. With the publication of these stories, I've been able to venture out and meet (either in person or electronically) some really great people along the way. Thus, with them in mind, I'd like to especially thank, in alphabetical order: Derrick Belanger, Bob Byrne, Steve Emecz, Roger Johnson, Denis Smith, Dan Victor, and Marcia Wilson. I must also express my gratitude to Dr. John H. Watson, Sir Arthur Conan Doyle, and William S. Baring-Gould.

And of course, as always, I wish to thank both my wife Rebecca and my son Dan for all their support and tolerance for this fascination with the world of the Detective and the Doctor. My wife knew what she was getting into, coming up on thirty years ago now, when she started dating and then married this guy who wears a deerstalker as his only hat, fall-to-spring, everywhere and for all occasions. But my son was born into all of this Sherlockiana, and he has stood up to it very well. I love you both!

David Marcum
May 4th, 2016
The 125th Anniversary of the events at Reichenbach Falls

Inspector MacDonald nodded. "It is a case of murder. But," he added, dramatically lowering his voice, "it seems to be a murder from the days of our grandparents!"

"So now, as an infallible way of making little ease great ease, I began to contract a quantity of debt."

— Pip in *Great Expectations*
by Charles Dickens

Chapter I
A Baker Street Visitor

"I should not be so inclined," stated Mr. Sherlock Holmes, from his stool at the chemical table in the corner.

I roused myself from the brown study into which I had fallen as the morning progressed. With a sigh, I pulled my gaze from the rain-streaked windows and back to Holmes. "And to what would you be referring?" I asked.

Holmes did not speak for a moment, as he leaned closer to the elaborate glass apparatus before him, titrating some violet-colored liquid between the interconnected pieces of narrow tubing. He placed his eyes level with the thin vertical structures, clamped in place above the blue gas flame that flickered across his sharp features. I started to utter a warning, afraid the collar of his dressing gown would touch the flame, but it proved to be unnecessary. Then, satisfied with the results, Holmes leaned back, stretching like a cat, and shifted to face me.

"I would not be inclined to record the events of the last couple of days in your journals. Our recent trip to Kent* is hardly worth preserving for posterity. The matter was simple child's play, and was quickly resolved by means of a single telegram to my professional contacts in Ohio. It really is not worth the effort that would be expended in adding it to your notes."

I straightened in my chair. "I must disagree, Holmes. Your analysis of the matter was masterful, you brought peace of mind to that unhappy young man, and – incidentally – you did capture a murderer."

Holmes turned back toward his research, leaned toward the deal table, and reached for his pen. With his left hand, he pulled a sheet of paper toward him, already half-covered with cryptic notes. "Nevertheless . . . ."

My thoughts that morning had indeed touched upon the events of the previous day in Kent, and the audacious scheme the wily American had planned there. If Holmes and I had not been summoned, doubtless the fellow would have accomplished his goals and escaped unscathed.

But I had been having other thoughts as well, more personal and grim than just the facts relating to our recent investigation. Perhaps Holmes

* See "The Singular Affair at Sissinghurst Castle" in *The Papers of Sherlock Holmes*

335

realized that, and had chosen to direct the conversation toward my literary efforts, rather than let me brood, as had been my habit the last few months. Or possibly he did not realize the true path of my thoughts at all. But knowing Holmes, that was unlikely indeed.

I shook my head and tried to turn my thinking to other matters, but as I glanced around the sitting room, so filled with souvenirs and relics from Holmes's past investigations, I realized that very little of my own possessions were in evidence. It had only been a little over one hundred days since I had returned to Baker Street, and I wondered if it was time for me to think about getting back into harness and finding a new practice. How different were those one hundred days from what I had planned for the rest of my life! And how different would the next hundred be, and the hundred after that?

I decided to respond to Holmes's query, out of politeness, if for no other reason. If he had actually made an effort to distract me, as he had done so often since the events of last December, I was obliged to return his volley, if only out of friendly gratitude for the trouble that he was taking, such as it was. I looked back at the pile of newspapers littering our dining table, souvenirs of our most recent investigation. They had drawn my attention all morning. "And how," I asked, "did you know that I was thinking of our recent trip to Sissinghurst?"

Holmes patiently stilled the pen for just a moment, but did not turn to face me. "It took no deduction, I assure you," he replied, and then recommenced writing in his careful precise way. "After you finished your breakfast, you carried the mementos of our investigation to the table, and then you moved to your desk, where you stood for some three-and-a-half minutes, running your fingers over your journals while eventually declining to actually pick one up."

"You could tell that from just listening?" I interrupted.

"You were, after all, right behind me. And I've heard the sound before. You then paced back to the table, opened some of the newspapers related to the Sissinghurst matter before laying them back down. Then, returning to your chair, empty-handed I might add, you have spent the rest of the time sighing at regular intervals as you attempted to find the will to start recording the matter. Finally, I decided to assist you in your decision by offering my opinion."

"I did not realize that even the sounds I make are so predictable, or distracting – "

"Do not trouble yourself, Watson. Luckily, my research here requires no great amount of concentration, and I was in no way distracted from reaching the correct conclusion."

"And you do not think that recording yesterday's events is a worthwhile activity on this rainy morning?" I asked.

"It is of no concern to me," Holmes replied, only to immediately contradict himself by stating, "However, if your narrative is to be presented in any way similar to that melodrama that was foisted upon the unsuspecting public last Christmas – " His voice trailed off, as everything that he had to say had already crossed my mind, and my answer had crossed his.

We had been down this road before. I was weary of trying to convince Holmes that, while his accounts should be shared with the public, they must be presented in such a way that the public would actually *want* to read them. If Holmes had his way, my recently published narrative, constructed with all the respect and admiration that I could put into it, would have appeared in some scholarly journal, perhaps *The Lancet*, detailing in a detached and clinical fashion the procedure for determining which of two identical water-soluble pellets contained a fast-acting poison, while never mentioning the dramatic events stretching across two continents that would lead one to the manufacture of those deadly objects in the first place.

"I see," I replied, refusing to rise to the occasion, and glancing once more at the papers littering our dining table. I did not feel like fighting that battle yet again, on that dark morning, and I did not say anything else as he adjusted the sheet of paper on the scarred tabletop and continued to write.

A particularly strong gust of wind threw the leaden rain against our window, pulling my mind away from the disagreement. The past couple of days had been beautiful, with the promise of spring showing strongly. But as we were returning from Kent the previous evening, the skies had opened and poured forth a veritable deluge that seemed to have settled in for the duration. It had rained throughout the night, and the morning skies had revealed themselves to be filled with heavy, ominous clouds. Even with the currently torrential rain, there was a sense of impending tension, as if the next wave of something worse might begin at any moment.

There had been some talk the previous day, as we set out for our return to London, of the two of us going to the British Museum in the morning, in order to view a singular treasure that had ended up there many years ago, following one of Holmes's early investigations in central Norfolk. Holmes had told me the matter had some similarities to the events just resolved at Sissinghurst. However, when I had descended from my room that day, Holmes had been busy at the chemical table, and no further mention was made of the outing. I found I rather felt like a petulant child, deprived of a trip to the zoo because his papa unexpectedly has chosen to work instead.

Holmes continued to scribble for another moment before flinging down his pen and then springing to his feet, bellowing for Mrs. Hudson as he moved across the sitting room, the paper waving in his hand.

Throwing open the door to the landing, he again cried, "Mrs. Hudson!"

I heard the footsteps of our long-suffering landlady start up the steps. At exactly that moment, the front doorbell rang. She paused for an instant, as if undecided which way to turn, and then I heard her move off the steps and down the hall in order to answer the door. Holmes snorted impatiently from the open doorway and then walked to the fireplace, side-stepping the sturdy basket chair in his path that was usually reserved for visitors. He reached to the mantel for his cherry pipe, which he smoked when in a disputatious mood, and began to pack it with his strong shag tobacco, kept in a Persian slipper tacked to the side of the mantelpiece.

He had successfully lit the pipe, and was smoking and drumming his fingers on the mantel when Mrs. Hudson appeared in the sitting room doorway. Holmes looked over at her, stated "Ah!" and crossed the room with his quick decisive footsteps. "No need to wait in the hall, Mr. Mac," he said. "Come in! Come in!"

Mrs. Hudson moved aside, allowing the tall figure of Inspector Alec MacDonald to enter the room. He nodded, first to me, and then to Holmes. I was surprised, as I had only heard Mrs. Hudson coming up the steps, but then the Inspector was always a canny fellow, and I'm sure he had matched his steps to those of our landlady, perhaps seeing if he could get one over on Holmes.

When I first came to live in Baker Street, initially as a wounded war veteran without friend or kin in England, and began sharing rooms with the strange young man recently introduced to me as Sherlock Holmes, I had no idea what his chosen place in life actually was. Over the course of those first few months, I knew that Holmes was often consulted by a number of unusual individuals, including many I later learned were Scotland Yard Inspectors. Initially, they seemed embarrassed to seek out Holmes's services, or even resentful. They certainly attempted either to claim credit outright for Holmes's efforts in providing them with a solution, or more often, deluded themselves into thinking that they had actually figured things out on their own, with some small assistance from the unofficial consulting detective.

But as time moved on, I began to see a change in the way that Holmes was treated by the official force, subtle at first, but later quite obvious. Holmes's opinion was respected without reservation, and many was the time that a Yarder beat a path to our door with something unusual, because they had come to learn that Holmes craved the *outré* in the same way a prisoner craves freedom. As the respect, and I will have to say the friendship as well, grew between Holmes and the Inspectors of the Yard, one could see that they too enjoyed being able to bring something unique to offer to the Master. Inspectors Gregson and Lestrade, of course, had finally come around, along with Lanner, Youghal, and Bradshaw soon after. Peter Jones was much quicker to offer overtures of actual friendship and respect toward Holmes than was his brother and fellow Inspector, Athelney. But the first Inspector that truly seemed to appreciate Holmes, not just as a useful tool toward clearing his caseload, but rather as a friend as well, was Alec MacDonald. And I, who had watched this process for a number of years, was glad to see it.

"Gentleman," MacDonald said, with his soft Scots burr, "'tis not a fit day to be out, I know, but I'm afraid that I'm requesting your company."

Holmes cocked his head and raised a questioning eyebrow. He took a deep pull on his pipe, as he seemed to ask without words, "Well?"

Inspector MacDonald nodded. "It is a case of murder. But," he added, dramatically lowering his voice, "it seems to be a murder from the days of our grandparents!"

"Excellent," replied Holmes, with a nod. "Just the thing."

Holmes glanced to the left, toward Mrs. Hudson, who was gathering up the cold coffee pot and cups from breakfast. He stepped in her direction, the paper he had been holding thrust out toward her. "Mrs. Hudson, please have the boy dispatch this telegram immediately."

With a tolerant smile, and a glance toward me as well, she took the paper, laid it among the coffee detritus, and said, "Will you have time for some more coffee, or tea, before you have to leave?"

Holmes looked toward MacDonald, who answered, with his accent suddenly thicker than I had ever heard it, "Ah believe 'at we hae th' time. An' frae a body Scot tae anither, Mrs. Hudson, Ah cannae hink ay anythin' 'at Ah woods loch better."

Hearing him speak in such a thick dialect, I was reminded of my own father, and my childhood in Stranraer. I suddenly realized that Holmes was greatly outnumbered by Scots, and I whimsically considered having a go at saying something in my boyhood accent as well. Mrs. Hudson simply smiled and nodded, and then turned to go, carefully pulling the door shut behind her. I wondered if it did her good to hear the sounds of her homeland as well.

MacDonald moved into the room, heading toward the basket chair centered before the warm fire. He had been there many times before when seeking Holmes's counsel. "Such a spring," he muttered, sounding again

339

like the more familiar Alec MacDonald. He sat down and simultaneously leaned forward, large hands outstretched. His damp boots matted the bear skin rug underneath his feet. "Beautiful weather we've had for the last two days, and now this," he muttered. "Such a spring," he repeated.

Holmes had moved to his chair as well. Seating himself, he arranged his dressing gown around him and asked, "And where will you be requiring us today, MacDonald?"

"Three miles back this side of Woburn," MacDonald replied, "out in Bedfordshire." Then something seemed to occur to him. "That is, unless you're already involved in something else? I apologize. I hope – "

"As a matter of fact, we did just return from Kent, where our most recent investigation – " I said, observing with a sour eye that the rain running down the window glass, looking out onto Baker Street, now seemed to be heavier than before.

Holmes interrupted me. " – But we are currently free at the moment to assist you, Mr. Mac. And in any event, our journey to Kent *wasn't* technically my most recent investigation," he said. "I've since been consulted on another matter following our return to London yesterday, and having just concluded that case as well – "

"Concluded it?" I asked. "When? Did it involve the chemical experiment that you just completed?"

"As I was saying," Holmes continued, "having just concluded that matter as well, I believe a trip to the countryside around Woburn will satisfactorily fill our day."

"But what of the chemical experiment?" I asked. "I had believed you were simply carrying out some test or other as a way to pass your time on such a rainy day."

"Not at all, Watson," Holmes replied. "I received information for which I had been waiting just this morning, before you arose. It came in the form of a wire from Lestrade, concerning the little matter of the fourth clerk, as was described to us so vividly last week."

"Ah," said MacDonald. "The Titian Oils?"

"Quite." Holmes glanced at the mantel clock. "Tell me, do we have time for this discussion, or should we be making preparations for departure?"

MacDonald also looked at the clock, and then pulled out his watch for comparison. Apparently satisfied, he returned the watch to its pocket and stated, "We have enough time, and to spare. You will both be able to make ready, and I will be able to enjoy some of Mrs. Hudson's fine coffee. Then we will set out on our expedition to reach Euston. And," he said, with a rueful grin in my direction, "perhaps – although I don't really

340

believe it – *perhaps* the rains will have departed by the time we are ready to go."

"Not likely," I said, grimly. Sitting up straighter in my comfortable chair, I asked, "What is this about, MacDonald? Murder, I believe you said?"

"Ah, there's plenty of time to discuss it on the train," he said, the grin sliding off his face. "I will tell you, however, that it involves the Briley family of Bedfordshire, and the discovery of an old corpse, more of a mummy really, in a most unusual place. And Mr. Holmes, the dead man has *a missing little finger on his right hand!*"

MacDonald made his final statement with lowered voice and an ominous overtone, but the significance of the statement completely escaped me. Of what importance was a missing finger on a desiccated corpse?

In contrast to my confusion, Holmes's eyes seemed to focus more sharply for just an instant with understanding, and then he slightly relaxed, although only in a way that someone who had known him for so long would recognize. "This does seem to promise to be of some interest," he said. I started to ask in what way, but MacDonald interrupted me.

"Right now, however, I'd dearly love to hear about Mr. Holmes's discovery related to Mr. Lestrade's investigation. Am I to understand that you have solved it, then?"

Holmes had been working to relight his pipe, which, in this damp weather, was resisting him. Seemingly frustrated for the moment, he paused and stated, "That particular storm seems to have broken, so to speak, last night, when the villain in question finally lost his patience and acted indiscriminately. Lestrade's men were watching as I'd advised, and they were able to take the samples as I had requested. Lestrade arrived before daybreak this morning, knocking Mrs. Hudson up. She proceeded to do the same to me. After studying the samples that Lestrade had obtained, I compared one in particular to the different fluids previously found at the scene, and determined through my analysis that the poison could only have been placed there by Brooks. That was what was written in the wire I just sent out with Mrs. Hudson. As you can see, there was really no taxing effort involved at all, and I am now quite fully rested. As I hoped you were, as well, Watson."

He finally gave up trying to light his pipe and laid it aside. "Will we be traveling to Leighton, then?"

MacDonald nodded. "And then on by carriage, I'm afraid. Four miles. But it's just as bad to go past and work our way back and around from Stratford."

341

Mrs. Hudson chose that moment to enter with the coffee and fresh cups. MacDonald stepped up to help her, and I stood as well, as I wished to fortify myself before beginning our journey.

"As I recall," said Holmes, clearly indifferent to the call of the hot, dark brew, "the Euston train to Leighton leaves within the hour. I suggest that we depart on time, in case the weather conspires to delay us."

He stood, and started to walk toward his room, shedding his dressing gown as he went. "Should we plan for an overnight sojourn, MacDonald?"

MacDonald, trying to blow on the coffee in order to cool it, stopped long enough to reply, "It probably couldn't hurt, Mr. Holmes. I'm not sure to what extent this affair will stretch. They have certainly uncovered a mess out there. Literally uncovered, as you shall see."

Seeing that I held a cup of coffee as well, and was returning to my chair by the fire, Holmes paused on the way to his room and asked, "Am I to understand, then, that you do not wish to accompany us, Watson, and rusticate in Bedfordshire, in order to recover from our outing yesterday to the Kent countryside?

With a snort, I stopped before pausing beside my chair and raised the coffee to my lips. Forgetting MacDonald's example, I nearly touched my lips to it before remembering its scalding power. Placing it on the small table by my chair, I said, "Never fear, Holmes, I will answer the call."

I started for the sitting room door, intending to go upstairs to my bedroom. I kept a traveling kit there, ready for just such excursions as these. With an abrupt and knowing "Ha!" Holmes continued into his room.

Within just a few minutes, my preparations were complete. Placing my bag by the sitting room door, I crossed to my chair and picked up the cup. The coffee was now at just the right temperature, and in a few sips it was gone. MacDonald was finishing his as well, and he looked longingly at the pot on the table. But he reluctantly set his cup aside, and we made to leave, moving around one another near the door as we retrieved coats and hats.

As we started down the steps, MacDonald in front of us, Holmes gripped my shoulder and murmured, "After all, Watson, work *is* the best antidote." With an additional squeeze, he released me and moved downstairs behind the Inspector. I shifted my bag from my right hand to my left, gripped the rail, and realized that Holmes had probably divined the nature of my thinking while he conducted his chemical analysis.

I found that I had to agree with him. I had discovered during the early part of that year, and on into the spring, that assisting in Holmes's investigations had indeed helped to heal me from my grief during the previous Christmas season. I only hoped that the matter which had now

342

captured our attention would also prove to distract me from my sad thoughts earlier that morning.

Chapter II
Out To Bedfordshire

Fifteen minutes later, we were in a four-wheeler, flying toward Euston Station. I realized that Holmes was displaying extraordinary patience as he waited to hear the details of the murder near Woburn. I wished to know more about the cryptic statement concerning the Briley family and the corpse's missing little finger. Before we had departed the sitting room, Holmes had briefly examined the "B" volume of his massive index before closing it with a resounding snap and dropping it on the settee. He had then seemed more eager than ever to begin our next investigation.

I was looking forward to hearing about it as well, and I knew we would have plenty of time on the journey to sort out the reasons behind our summons. I shifted in my seat, and felt the comfortable lump of my old service revolver in my topcoat pocket. In the early days, Holmes would often have needed to specifically remind me to bring it. I had long since learned not to leave home without it. Beside me, Holmes focused off into the distance, his nostrils twitching as if he were already catching the scent of whatever trail was waiting for us.

He remained silent but tense, like a coiled spring, until the four-wheeler turned in to the bustle and noise of Euston Station. With a bound, Holmes leapt to the ground, tossing some coins to the driver, while I made to follow as best as I could.

We made our way into the station and through the crowds to the correct train. MacDonald had anticipated our agreement to his request and had already arranged for a First Class Smoker. After we were settled in and the train began its first lurchings toward departure, Holmes, who had possessed himself in a patient state for long enough, said, "And now, Mr. Mac, tell us more about the mysterious corpse and the Briley family."

MacDonald, in the process of lighting his pipe, was not to be rushed. Seeing this, Holmes decided to join him, pulling out his old oily, black clay pipe, which he often used while traveling. After they had both gone through the comforting rituals of preparation, and after I had declined both their offers to join them, MacDonald was finally ready to speak.

"I could see," he began, "that my mention of the Briley family and the missing little finger seemed familiar to you, Mr. Holmes."

"Indeed," replied Holmes. "I recalled something of the family characteristic, and a review of my index confirmed it."

"Well, I don't know anything about it," I interrupted, finding I was still in a somewhat surly mood, "so please enlighten me." Hearing how my voice had sounded, I resolved to moderate it in the future.

"Certainly," said Holmes. "Living in Bedfordshire, nearer Woburn than Leighton for more years than I know, has been the Briley family. The family's great wealth has been matched only by their odd stand-offishness. They have always maintained a successful estate, but have never shown interest in journeying to London for the season, or currying favor with the Royal Court. In short, they have maintained their affairs for several generations, conserving their resources, and generally staying out of the public eye."

"And the intriguing business of the missing finger?" I asked.

"There is a Briley family trait," said MacDonald, "that generally manifests itself, for generation after generation in the male line of the family. Briley boys are always born with a missing little finger on their right hand."

"What?" I said. "Surely such things would occur on both hands, and not just one. And it would have been bred out of the family by now."

"Not necessarily, Watson," said Holmes. "Consider some of the other unique traits that run through different families. Royal families, for instance, often display characteristics that become well-known. Our own Queen's children and grandchildren have had to face the possibility of hemophilia with each new generation of births. And of course, there is the unfortunate Hapsburg Lip or Jaw. I'm afraid the idea of a congenital missing finger is not at all inconceivable."

He looked back at MacDonald. "And in what way is a missing little finger related to a corpse? Is it somehow connected to Martin Briley, the current head of the family, who, if I am correct, is in his sixties and in poor health?"

"You are certainly correct about Mr. Briley," replied MacDonald. "But it is not his missing finger to which I refer. When I left there late last night, Mr. Briley was still alive, and he is certainly not the dead man in question. No, the corpse to which I refer was uncovered in a workman's trench on the property, and appears to have been buried there for nearly fifty years!"

"And it is missing a finger? The little finger on its right hand?" said Holmes. "Are you implying that it is a family member whose body has been concealed for nearly half a century?"

"I am, Mr. Holmes. That's what makes it a delicate situation, and that's the truth. You can see why I asked for your help, and that of the doctor."

"I begin to perceive your dilemma," said Holmes.

345

"And that dilemma would be?" I asked.

Holmes shifted his pipe, and said, "In a case such as this, one must be careful about ruffling the feathers of someone as wealthy as Martin Briley. He has a reputation of being a good man, although he tends to keep strictly to himself. He has spent a lifetime making the area around his estate a better place for all who work and live there, at no little expense to himself. In some ways, he has lived his life as something of a benevolent king of his own little fiefdom. But," he added, "it is always a treacherous path when someone in the Inspector's position has to rake up old family skeletons. In this case, literally."

"You're right, Mr. Holmes. The local constable instantly saw the implications of finding a long-buried and possibly unknown Briley, and called me in. Now it's become my problem, and I'm hoping you will see a way to a solution that might be outside of my means."

Holmes took a deep draw on his pipe and said, "Begin at the beginning." And he closed his eyes to listen.

MacDonald took a deep breath and spoke.

"Several months ago, the estate agent, George Burton, began a series of long-overdue repairs. Burton, a man of about thirty years, grew up on the estate, and had an eye for what needed to be done. He said that Mr. Martin Briley was more than willing to fund the work, and left the matter completely in Burton's hands as to what would and would not be fixed.

"Many of the repairs were routine, including painting the buildings where needed, reclaiming the old family mausoleum from the vegetation that was overtaking it, reworking some of the drainage around a mere on the property, and so on. One of the jobs involved replacement of the drain tile that leads away from a series of cottages that had been built for the estate workers back in the 1820's. The pipe to be replaced leads from these buildings down a long hill, where it empties into the mere. Burton told me the cottages are on a part of the estate that retained water in times past, apparently due to the rocky geology at the top of the hill where they were built. Several people had gotten sick in the old days, before the drains were installed. Or at least Burton says they had. He couldn't know himself for certain, as he is far too young. Burton says the old estate records show that the pipes were first installed in 1840. In recent years, the drains have started to clog, and Burton finally instituted repairs before things could get any worse.

"Two days ago, on the fourteenth, workmen were digging down to replace the line from the cottages to the mere. They had been working on that particular job for several weeks, starting at the top of the hill near the cottages, and moving downhill. On that day, they routinely uncovered a section of clay pipe that had been buried there since the drains were installed, much like all the other pieces of pipe they saw as the repairs progressed. The ground around the excavation appears to be acidic it approaches the mere, and the ground has a certain peat-like quality to it, especially as it gets near to the water. That is important, as you shall see.

"As the workmen were digging around the existing pipe, they saw what appeared to be a leg sticking out from under it. Burton was called, and not long after, the local constable and a doctor. For several hours, the workmen slowly exposed the pipe, until they were able to carefully free the body.

"It was that of what seems to have been a young man, amazingly preserved, probably due to resting in the peat soil. He was wearing clothing from several generations back, matching the period when the pipe would have first been installed there."

"What was the condition of the ground at that location before any of the repairs began?" asked Holmes.

"You will be able to see for yourself," replied MacDonald, "but the foreman and the workers assure me that it was untouched. Nearby was a tree stump and roots that had been growing at that site up to the time the repairs had started there. I counted the tree's rings, and there were almost fifty clear ones, which means it probably started growing soon after the pipe was installed, forty-eight years ago. Part of the reason repairs were needed in that area was that some of the roots from the tree had worked their way into the clay pipe. If you're thinking that the body was placed there more recently, the evidence argues against it."

"Evidence can argue several ways, depending on the angle from which it is perceived," replied Holmes. "However, for the time being, I am willing to provisionally accept your theory that the body has been buried there since the installation of the pipe in 1840, pending the revelation of additional facts."

Settling back slightly, Holmes added, "To leap to the dramatic conclusion of your story, the body of the young man was missing the small finger of his right hand."

"Correct, Mr. Holmes," said MacDonald. "The body was incredibly well preserved, although there has obviously been some collapse of tissues, and the skin has browned from leaching fluids out of the peat soil. The hands were clenched, but were found to be still flexible, and they readily opened upon examination. The constable and the doctor immediately noticed the missing finger, but rightly did not announce the fact to the foreman or the workers. Recognizing the relationship between the missing finger and the Briley family, the constable wisely sent word to his superiors. Thus, my eventual involvement in the matter, and now yours.

"I traveled to Bedfordshire yesterday, in much better weather than we're seeing now, and on out to the estate, where I examined the excavation for myself. I'm convinced the location of the body has not been disturbed in the past half-century. I examined the hand with the missing finger with great care, and the deformity appears to be naturally occurring. There is no sign of a scar or past injury that would have accounted for the finger being lost after birth."

"But who could it be?" I interjected. "Is there some member of the Briley family that is unaccounted for?"

"I believe I can anticipate the Inspector's answer," stated Holmes. "From the notes in my index, I saw that the current Briley, Martin, is the last of the family, and was an only child. His father before him was also an only child. Therefore, there were no brothers or cousins extant from either Martin's or his father's generation."

"That we know of," I said.

"True," said MacDonald. "There could have been an illegitimate child with Briley blood that would have been the appropriate age in the late 1830's or early 1840's."

"Curious," said Holmes. "The body seems to have been hidden there from the time the pipe was first installed, in a location that has remained undisturbed since then. The apparent dating of the clothing would tend to confirm this. The tree must have started growing around the late 1830's or early 1840's, if your count of nearly fifty rings is correct. And my research showed that the current head of the family, Martin Briley, came into his inheritance in 1840 as well, upon the death of his father, Galton Briley."

"Martin is still the head of the family, and the *last* head of the family," added MacDonald. "He has no children, and as far as I can determine, he has no heirs whatsoever. The estate is not entailed, and Briley has not publicly named who will succeed him when he dies. As his health is poor right now, and he is in his late sixties, the question is of some concern to the locals, who depend on the running and upkeep of the estate for their own livelihoods."

"What did Mr. Briley say when you questioned him about the corpse?" asked Holmes.

"Very little indeed," said MacDonald. "At first I had to pass the gauntlet of the man's harridan of a housekeeper, Mrs. Lynch. She gave me to understand in every possible way that the old man was too sick to receive visitors. The doctor was there, along with the local constable, and they were forced to concede that there was merit to the old woman's arguments.

"Finally, I was allowed to see him for ten minutes. He was in a corner of the library, in some sort of elaborate bath chair, bundled in blankets and placed near a roaring fire, as if he were unable to warm himself. I became quite uncomfortable in the short time I was there.

"He offered no information, except to say he hadn't any idea who it was that had been found, and there was no one at all that he could remember who might possibly be the body with the missing finger. Eventually he seemed to stop hearing me altogether and didn't respond any further to my questions.

"It was at that time, gentlemen, that Mrs. Lynch, who had hovered nearby throughout the entire interview, stepped in and informed me that I should leave. I did not feel I would make any further progress with the old man in any case, since he had stopped answering my questions, so I departed.

"I spent the rest of the day speaking with the various laborers who had helped uncover the corpse, and so on. You'll meet them yourselves." Holmes nodded, and MacDonald continued. "At some point I realized I had already decided to seek your help, Mr. Holmes. And now, here we are, halfway to Bedfordshire."

"And that is probably a good place to stop," said Holmes. "Unless you have any additional pertinent information, we will be tempted to start speculating, and by the time we arrive at the estate, we will each have formed some theory or other in our minds that we will start trying to prove, bending what facts we find to fit our construct, instead of weighing each new revelation on its own merit.

"As you say," Holmes added, "I will wish to meet with these people myself when we arrive. Until that time, I beg of you not to speak until I've smoked a pipe or two while I arrange my thoughts."

As Holmes settled back to ponder what we had heard, I turned my attention from my companions inside of carriage and focused on the rainy, wet English countryside, visible through the window. The rain was streaking the glass, and I could only see bits and pieces of the passing landscape as we sped north toward Leighton, and then our ultimate destination, a few miles this side of Woburn. As the minutes moved by, I found myself settling back into the brown study of earlier that morning.

That spring of 1888 had been a difficult one for me, to say the least. I was not quite thirty-six years old, and I was at loose ends yet again. My original path, that of a military surgeon, had come to an abrupt end in 1880 on a hot Afghan battlefield. I had been fortunate enough to find a new purpose when I met my friend Sherlock Holmes half-a-year later. And then, after several years, I had perceived a new direction for my life, one I thought would last for the rest of my days. I had married and bought a practice, believing that I would live out my life as a husband, physician, and most certainly a father. But it was not to be.

The previous December, I had lost my wife, Constance, to a sudden illness. Tragically, we had only been married a little over a year at the time. I had met her in March 1885, during a period when I was living in San Francisco, attempting to rescue my brother from one of his spells of chronic drunkenness. I had gone to the western United States when my brother summoned me, in spite of the years of distance and disagreement between us. Holmes had advanced the funds for the journey without question, reaffirming to me – yet again – that he was more of a true brother than the actual one of my blood had ever been, or ever would be.

Arriving in San Francisco, I set out to make money in order to repay my brother's debts, as well as what I now owed to Holmes, doing the only thing for which I was qualified. Establishing a small medical practice on Post Street, I was fortunate enough to receive as my first patient the lovely Miss Constance Adams.

Through a series of events that do not need to be recounted here, including a return to England later that year, and a subsequent visit back to the United States in early 1886, I realized that I wished to make Constance my own. In the spring of 1886, I returned to England, and Baker Street, for good, where I began to make plans to find a practice and a life I could share with my future wife.

As I recalled the promise of a life with my new bride, my thoughts were pulled for the moment back into the carriage, as Holmes was preparing to attempt to light his pipe. He was knocking the ash from the bowl against the window sill onto the floor below. After several sharp thuds, which did not seem to disturb the now-napping MacDonald in the least, Holmes was satisfied with his efforts, and he began to pack the bowl with the filthy shag that he favored. I smiled to myself and turned back toward the rain-streaked glass, letting my ruminations return to my dear departed wife.

Constance and I were married in late 1886, and we set up housekeeping in Kensington. My days were full and rewarding as we built the practice together. Like any newly married man, my interests turned inward toward hearth and home. And yet, I still found time to assist my best friend, Sherlock Holmes, on many of his investigations.

This arrangement seemed as if it would last indefinitely. However, I could not ignore the signs, as Constance appeared to weaken as 1887 progressed. She and her mother, who had journeyed to England with Constance before our marriage, tried traveling to various spas both around England and on the Continent in order to improve her condition, but all to no avail. I was forced to remain in London as I continued to attempt to build up my practice by day, while by night I turned to writing to fill the empty hours.

Some time before, I had become acquainted with a fellow physician and aspiring writer named Conan Doyle. He had often tried to convince me to put some of Holmes's adventures down on paper, with an eye toward publication. I must confess that he did not have to urge me too strongly, since I already had the desire to do that very thing, and had felt that way since first observing Holmes in action in the Jefferson Hope matter, in 1881.

Doyle had long felt that I should either recount some of Holmes's cases, or perhaps even the events of my time in San Francisco. In fact, Doyle himself had tried to write his own version of some of the incidents from my California days, but when I saw what he had written, an awkward play entitled *Angels of Darkness,* I forbade him to continue, as some of the changes he made to the actual events were simply ludicrous.

During Constance's illness, Doyle's efforts began to wear me down, so that I finally agreed to write my own account of the Hope case, which was the first investigation that I ever shared with Holmes. Doyle himself wanted to write a portion of the narrative providing background information relating to the events that led to the crime. When he was finished, I saw that he had incorporated portions of his aborted play, recounting some of my San Francisco days. After much disagreement, we agreed that his contribution could be included as written, in spite of several historical inaccuracies.

The narrative was finally published toward the end of 1887 in a cheap journal. I must admit that I was somewhat secretly disappointed, having pictured my hours of hard work appearing in something more substantial and permanent. Oddly, although my portion of the work clearly credited me with the segments that I had written, it was Doyle's name that appeared alone on the cover. However, I had no wish to seek literary fame, having only pursued the matter to make sure that Holmes's methods were brought to the attention of the public, and I did not seek to make any correction.

Two days after Christmas of 1887, I had stopped by Baker Street to present Holmes with a copy of the publication. His reaction, as might be expected, was – at best – not enthusiastic. I believe that he thought both Doyle and I had been preparing something that would be placed in a scientific journal.

Two days after my visit with Holmes, Constance unexpectedly died.

For a time, I was a man in a daze. Holmes took charge of everything, having served as best man at my wedding, and now as my best friend in my time of greatest need. He immediately invited me back to my old rooms in Baker Street. Within days, I agreed, having realized that I did not want to continue pursuing the practice I had been working so hard to build. It had never been very interesting or involving at the best of times, and I quickly sold it to escape from the unpleasant memories there. I was back in my old chair, before the fire in the sitting room, by the New Year.

New participation in Holmes's investigations had served as a useful distraction from my staggering loss. Already that year, both Holmes and I had been involved in numerous cases, including that of the Birlstone tragedy and puzzling brand discovered on the dead man's arm. Then there was the terrible affair of The Eye of Heka, in which an international crisis had been narrowly averted. The previous week Holmes and I had been down to Norbury, where he had identified the mysterious neighbor of Mr. Grant Munro, with whom I felt a special kinship, since both his wife and my deceased Constance were from America. It will be recalled that Holmes's prediction regarding the identity of Munro's neighbor was far more grim than the happy truth that was actually revealed.

As I had pondered over my journals that morning before MacDonald's arrival, I had considered adding the events of yesterday's journey to Kent. It would just fill the remaining space in the book, following the narrative concerning Munro, and Holmes's subsequent instructions to whisper "Norbury" into his ear if it should ever strike me that he was getting a little over-confident in his powers, or giving less pains to a case than it deserved.

My collection of notes regarding Holmes's adventures was growing impressively, and I considered whether I should eventually publish something else. If so, I did not know if I would involve Doyle in the process the next time. I felt I could do an adequate job on my own, both in terms of writing the pieces and having them published. And I had a wealth of information to choose from, including some adventures from Holmes's early days that he had only shared with me in recent months. Always very private in the past, he had become more open since Constance's death, talking about several of his earlier cases, such as that of the mysterious ritual of the Musgraves, as a way of distracting me from my recent bereavement.

I was pulled back from my wool-gathering by the arrival of the train in the station. No one spoke as we gathered our belongings and stepped out onto the platform. It was still raining steadily, and I pulled my coat tighter and settled my hat more firmly on my head.

Surrendering our tickets, we made our way outside and found one of the few carriages that would carry the three of us as well as the driver. "I'm afraid it's still a wee distance to the house," said MacDonald as we left the station.

There was no conversation during that miserable drive. Although it was April, my breath steamed in front of me, and occasionally a stray raindrop would work its way past my hat brim and down into my coat. It was hard to believe that only twenty-four hours earlier, it had been a beautiful spring day.

Finally, after I had lost track of time completely, the carriage turned, and the feel of the roadway changed. Looking up, I could see a large house, the features hidden in the mist and rain. It was two stories, and appeared to be in the shape of a shallow *U*, with the two wings on each side jutting toward us, and the wide base of the *U* set back in the middle. The carriage pulled to a stop across from the front door. The driver, who had not spoken throughout the entire journey, said in a gruff, little-used voice the only two words that I would hear him speak on the entire journey: "Briley House."

We had arrived at the scene of the crime.

". . . talking about several of his earlier cases, such as that of the mysterious ritual of the Musgraves, as a way of distracting me from my recent bereavement."

Chapter III
On The Scene

Holmes glanced up at the dark clouds, seemingly unaware of the spray finding its way under the bill of his fore-and-aft cap. "I don't believe that the weather will improve," he said, "so perhaps we should see where the body was discovered before things get any worse."

"As you say, Mr. Holmes," agreed MacDonald. "Driver, take us down toward the mere, where the dead man was found."

With a nod, the driver gigged the horse, but almost immediately MacDonald exclaimed, "Stop!" Before the carriage had finished rolling, he leapt down to the ground, gathered our bags awkwardly in both hands, and ran to the door of the house, speaking for just a moment to the servant who had thrown open the door at our arrival. The fellow took the bags, nodded, and went back inside, closing the door behind him. MacDonald returned to the carriage and climbed in. "Now you can proceed," he stated.

Settling awkwardly into his seat as the vehicle began to move forward once again, MacDonald stated, "I told the man at the door to find George Burton and have him meet us where the body was found. I thought it would save us a little time out in the elements if he gets there a bit faster."

"Excellent thinking," I said, burrowing deeper into my coat, thankful for its bulk.

We returned to the small road in front of the house. The lane soon straightened out, its ruts filled with water. An open yard was on either side of us, which in the distance sloped down to a stream, spanned by a stone bridge. There were trees growing there, with one quite a bit taller than the others, serving as something of a border between the grounds of the large house and the small cluster of cottages perched on a hill on the other side of the churning stream.

As we descended the hill and crossed the bridge, I could see more of the homes used by members of the estate community. They were solid, square structures, built of local stone, and each with windows that glowed with warm light against the cold wet day. The smell of coal smoke was in the air, only slightly dampened by the rain. I knew that on a day like this, the fireplaces in the cottages were not likely to be drawing well.

Approaching the houses, I could see that they were laid out in a strict grid arrangement, with narrow lanes running between each row. There were probably fifty or more of the little buildings, and for all their similarity, I could also spot individual touches, such as window boxes for

354

herbs and flowers, and doors painted in different colors. There would certainly be more obvious differences, and I would have seen them, if only the light were better. But the day was dark and seemed likely to stay that way.

Moving past the small cluster of houses, we left the road and continued on the slight slope down to where the stream appeared to curve back around the base of the hill. It widened, and while a clear movement of water could be seen drawing an open line down the center, the sides of the pond formed there were choked with reeds and other water grasses. A number of large trees grew along the perimeter of the mere, and off to our right, at the downstream end, was the carcass of one old giant elm that now lay on the ground, already sawn into several large pieces, its base and roots resting alongside a hole in the ground. There was a raw earthen line extending from that hole, back up the hill roughly parallel to our path down it, toward the houses now at our rear. This, then, was the path of the pipeline trench that had already been repaired.

The driver of the carriage was going slowly, in deference to the downward slope that we traversed, and the weight of a carriage with four grown men riding in it behind the single horse. He started bringing the animal to a stop well before our final destination. Setting the brake, he hopped off and walked to the horse's head. Taking her bridle, he rubbed her nose and made sure that she stayed in place while we stepped down.

Holmes darted ahead, looking into the hole, and then straightening up again. "It is as I feared," he said, gesturing to us when we joined him. The hole was filled with muddy water.

"Aye," agreed MacDonald. "There won't be anything to see in there for several days, and that's for sure."

"Then we will have to rely on your memory of what you saw on a brighter day," said Holmes, pulling his Inverness tighter as he finally appeared to acknowledge the weather.

MacDonald stepped to the lower rim of the hole, and gestured down. "You cannot tell it," he said, "but the trench contains a clay pipe of about one foot in diameter. This drains from the cottages up above, and into the lower end of the mere, where it is carried away by the stream.

"Of course, by the time I arrived, the body found here had already been removed. It seems that after the exposed leg was first seen, the hole was widened considerably, so that the workmen could gain access to the body. Dirt was removed from underneath as well, and also from the other side of the pipe, so it could be taken out gently, and without fear of a cave-in. Only after it was out did they realize the body was in a more sturdy condition than they had first anticipated. Both the hole *and* the body were more sturdy," MacDonald added.

There was a raw earthen line extending from that hole
back up the hill roughly parallel to our path down it . . . .

He gestured up the hill. "Right now, the fellow is up there, resting in an empty house. I had him left there, pending your examination, Mr. Holmes. It is locked, and seemed as good a place as any."

"Very good," said Holmes, glancing around. "And the tree? It was obviously growing at this location."

"Very near it, I'm told," nodded MacDonald, walking a step or two that way. "As you can see," he remarked, leaning over the stump, "the rings are quite defined, and easily count up to almost fifty. There are a few that are questionable on the outer side, near the bark, but it is certainly no older than that."

"I believe the rings are especially dark due to some aspect of the soil in this area," said a voice behind us.

We turned, to find a short fellow in his early thirties walking toward us. His face was hidden, as he was wearing very sturdy raingear, but almost immediately he pushed back his wide flat-brimmed hat, exposing a frank and open countenance. I had first thought that we had not heard him because of the masking sound of the rainfall, but I was to see later that he had a quiet step about him wherever he went.

"Inspector," he said, sticking out his hand toward MacDonald. "And this must be Mr. Holmes and Dr. Watson." He shook our hands as well, his grip warm and dry, surprising on this damp cold day.

"George Burton," he said, as a fresh gust of wind spattered raindrops horizontally at us. "I'm Mr. Briley's agent."

"It is good to meet you," said Holmes. "I agree with you regarding the apparent properties of the soil. One would expect something of the sort in a lowland area such as this near a mere. What little examination I can make of the soil layers that have been exposed in the walls of the diggings seem to confirm the peat-like nature." Holmes patted one of the great sections of the trunk. "This was a tall tree."

"It was," said Briley. "A fine old English elm. It could even be seen from certain windows in the main house. I hated to have it cut down, but in order to repair this pipe, it had to go.

"When we started repairs on the estate several months ago, one of the items high on our list was improving the drainage from the cottages. These pipes were installed in 1840, according to the estate books, when Mr. Briley first inherited the place from his father. At that time, he instituted a number of continuing improvements, including this project, in order to better the quality of life for his workers. Sadly, the working lifespan of the pipes have reached their end, for the workers living above were starting to report unsanitary backups in the line.

"We decided to tie onto the existing outfall location at the top of the hill, where the smaller pipes from the various cottages collect and combine to exit the site. Then, digging down alongside the existing pipe, we replaced as we went. This old tree wasn't exactly on top of the pipes, but it was right beside them, and it was close enough that it had to go.

"We had gotten this far," he said, gesturing along the earthen line going up the hill, showing where the pipe trench had been dug and refilled, "before we found the body, day before yesterday."

"And you were not here when it was found?" asked Holmes.

"Correct," replied Burton. "Even though this was a crucial part of the repair, I was required at the main house just then, to take care of another matter."

"Why was this a crucial part?" asked MacDonald.

"The steeper angle of the pipe running off the hill changes around this point and flattens as it moves toward the final outfall," said Burton. "I wanted to make sure that the turn was accomplished successfully so the slope would be correct from here on out to the mere."

"Why were you following the path of the original pipeline?" asked Holmes. "Why not just make a new trench?"

"Geometry, Mr. Holmes. Just plain, simple geometry. The shortest distance between two points is a straight line, and all that. We knew that we wanted to start at the existing junction of pipes at the top of the hill, nearly five hundred feet from here, and to have our outfall at its same location at the optimum point of discharge at the downstream side of the mere. From the top of the hill, we followed the exact straight-line path that was used when the line was originally installed. To have found an alternate way would have extended the work, since the shortest path was the one that was originally taken, and would also have possibly impeded the flow in the pipe by putting an unnecessary curve or bend into the path of the pipe."

"I see," said Holmes. "Have you studied engineering, Mr. Burton?"

"Some, Mr. Holmes. When I was younger, Mr. Briley took an interest in me and saw that I had some tutoring. However, much of what I know now is just from simple experience, with a little common sense, and a willingness to admit what I don't know, and then to ask questions until I find out."

"Admirable, indeed," replied Holmes. He pointed to the tree stump and projecting roots. "I would guess that the stump was pulled out by a sturdy team?"

"That's right. We hitched them to the stump after the rest of the tree was cut down. As you might imagine, roots getting into a pipeline are a major source of blockage, and it would do us no good to replace the line through here without trying to slow or eliminate a large part of the problem."

"Quite." Holmes seemed to think a moment, and then, changing the subject, he asked, "Is the fact that the body was missing the little finger of the right hand still secret?"

358

MacDonald looked at Burton, who replied, "I believe so. I was notified of the discovery by one of the laborers. Lambrick, the man in charge. He knew nothing at that time except that the body had been found. I sent Lambrick with word for the constable and the doctor, and then came here. The body was still mostly covered at that point. When it was finally dug out enough to be pulled from underneath the pipe, it was quickly wrapped in a tarp for examination elsewhere.

"I had asked for the doctor and the constable to be discreet as they made their way down here, and it seems that no one up in the cottages was aware that anything out of the ordinary was taking place. We moved the body, and it was only upon later examination that we discovered the missing finger. The laborers had not seen it, and the constable and the doctor agreed that the knowledge should be kept to ourselves.

"It was then that the implications were fully realized, and the Constable decided that we should contact Scotland Yard."

Holmes nodded, glanced toward the carriage, and then up the hillside. "As much as I hate to suggest it, I believe that we should walk back up the hill in order to examine the body. I am afraid that if we all try to ride in the carriage, the poor beast will never be able get its footing to pull us back up." He looked toward me. "Will your leg stand it, Watson?"

I raised my cane and gave it a shake. "Lead on. Anything to get us out of this infernal rain for a few moments."

Luckily, no one fell as we struggled back up that five-hundred feet of wet grass, with its gentle but slick slope, toward the cottages. There were a few times, however, when it was a close thing. Finally we reached the flatter parts around the buildings, and stopped to get our breaths for a moment. Then, Burton led off between the cottages until coming to a stop beside one of the shabbier structures, its windows dark. MacDonald stepped up and, fishing a large old-fashioned key from his pocket, unlocked the door. He moved back out of the way as we stepped inside.

Burton moved to the left and in moments had first one, and then a second, lantern alight. The interior of the room was undecorated, the only furniture being a large and heavy deal table placed in the center of the room, symmetrical with a cold stone fireplace. Heavy curtains were pulled across the window, keeping the figure on the table hidden from curious passers-by.

"This seemed like a good place to store the body," said MacDonald, gesturing toward the sheeted object resting on the table. "It was standing empty.

"It's one of several houses that are scheduled for renovations," said Burton, indicating with his glance the run-down condition of the place.

"We've left it untenanted after the most recent occupant departed, until we can make some repairs."

Holmes did not comment as he stepped quickly to the table. With a practiced flourish, he threw the sheet back to expose the body.

How to describe the horrid and macabre sight revealed there in that empty house, only poorly lit by the two flickering lanterns? It was the figure of a man, obviously, but twisted somewhat, and of a color that would not be natural, even when not seen in that nearly nonexistent light. Holmes grabbed one of the lanterns and swung it over the body. The shadows shifted crazily across the room, and for a minute I nearly felt myself dizzied by them, as the sudden shift made me reach out to grab the table, unsure of where I stood.

Holmes was leaning over the face of the corpse, shifting this way and that, looking directly at it from the front, then up from under the chin, or at either side into the ears. Moving closer myself, I saw that the fellow was incredibly well preserved, considering how long he had supposedly been buried. His hair, what there was left of it, seemed rather long in the old style, and lay in wet, dark, and lanky locks across his brow. His chin was firm, although his mouth sagged open, and his lips had receded, exposing teeth in rather bad condition. His nose had caved in, as would be expected, and of course his eyes, which were closed, were sunken as well.

"What would you estimate this man's age to have been at the time of his death, Watson?" Holmes asked.

I considered my answer for a moment. "As I'm sure you are aware," I finally answered, "there are a number of factors to take into account. However, my best conclusion at first glance would be that he was in his early twenties."

"I concur," said Holmes.

"Then this cannot be the body of Martin Briley's father, who died in 1840."

"Correct."

"Mr. Briley's father, Galton Briley, is buried in the family mausoleum," said Burton.

Holmes did not respond. Taking a blunt metal probe from his pocket, about five inches long, he attempted to push open one of the closed eyelids. Initially it refused to move, but then the upper lid slowly parted from the lower, revealing an empty cavity within.

"Mr. Holmes!" said MacDonald, his experience as a policeman clearly overcome by the instinctive revulsion against the death that all of us carry within us at some level.

"It was too much to hope for," said Holmes, pulling the probe away from the dead man's eye. "I wished to see if any of the eye remained. I had hoped to determine what color his eyes had been. It might have given us a clue as to his family relations."

"Yes, yes, indeed," said MacDonald, clearly embarrassed at slightly losing his professional composure. "I understand."

Holmes moved the lantern as he stepped along the table, examining the fellow from head to foot. He paid particular attention to the shoes of the dead man, before finally returning to the fellow's right hand, which I had wanted him to examine all along.

Gingerly picking up the hand, as if it might fall apart, he held it close to the lantern's light. After a moment, he said softly, "Watson? Your opinion, please."

I stepped around the table and leaned down to where he was directing. Ignoring my own revulsion, I took the hand, finding it much firmer than I would have imagined. I had assumed it would be like those that have been in traditional graves for any amount of time. These soften and liquefy as the decay process proceeds. On the other hand, drowning victims' flesh often transforms through the process of saponification into a soap-like material, as can also happen in the presence of some type of alkali that mixes with the fats and oils of the body. Perhaps the fact that this corpse had been preserved in an acidic element explained why the flesh was solid, even after all these years.

I had heard something of the bog mummies, as they are called, who have been pulled from peat in many locations across Europe and northern Britain over the years. Some of these had been incredibly well preserved, even after centuries, and occasionally the very expressions on their faces are still intact. The body that we were examining that night in the rain-soaked cottage was perhaps the most well-preserved of any that I had ever heard discussed. No doubt, that had something to do with the fact that it had only been buried for a period of fifty years or so.

Careful examination of the side of the hand, with its thumb and only three fingers, confirmed what Holmes had wanted me to see. There was no sign of a scar whatsoever where the little finger was missing. I was able to feel the internal bones adequately through the well-preserved skin enough to make a determination.

"Dissection is the only way to confirm for sure," I stated, "but my preliminary examination seems to suggest that the missing finger was not lost due to some misfortune, and that the man was born this way."

"Thank you, Watson," said Holmes. Straightening up, he turned to MacDonald. "Has he been examined underneath his clothing?"

"No, sir. When I decided to ask for your assistance, I left the body as I found it. I can tell you that there are no tears in the clothing, and no sign of any wounds passing through the clothing, such as would come from the use of a knife or gun. I believe that Dr. Watson will be able to confirm the cause of death if he looks at the back of the fellow's head."

"Nevertheless," said Holmes, "I would like to examine the clothing and the rest of the body. Gentlemen, if you please?"

I could tell that for just one instant, MacDonald wanted to suggest waiting for the official autopsy. However, his faith in Holmes overwhelmed his internal objections, and he stepped closer to the table, in order to facilitate Holmes's request. MacDonald and I both undressed the corpse, with difficulty, one piece of clothing at a time. It was stained and fragile, but still remarkably intact. Holmes peered at the various items closely under the lantern light as they came off. It was hard to believe that it was still only early afternoon outside. It was as dark as night, adding to the unpleasant aspects of the experience.

Burton did not help scrutinize the body, but rather stood to the side a few feet, near the second lantern by the fireplace. I did not blame him at all. This macabre situation was obviously something new to him, and certainly nothing that he would care to repeat.

Holmes silently completed his appraisal of the clothing, and then started with the body itself, again moving from head to toe, before asking us to rotate the man over and onto his stomach, so that the reverse side could be investigated as well. I followed along at Holmes's side, seeing what he saw, and hopefully observing what he observed. Concluding his examination at the back of the man's head, Holmes pressed the scalp with his fingers for a moment before motioning me to take over. I quickly found that to which MacDonald had referred. There was a large concavity there, nearly the size of a cricket ball, under the remains of the man's dark-looking hair. There was no indication of any broken skin. The wound would have been fatal, although I cannot say if it would have resulted in an immediate death. I stated as much to Holmes, who nodded.

"Conclusions, gentlemen?" he said. "Watson?"

"In the absence of any other information at this time, such as evidence of poisoning, I would expect that the cause of death was due to the obvious blunt trauma to the back of the head, located in the occipital region. Other bones, including the neck, appear to be intact, although only an autopsy can confirm some of this for sure. He appears to have been a thin fellow in his early twenties. Although his teeth are in bad shape, they do not appear to be worn enough to indicate that he was any older than that. The same for the soles of his feet. He grew up wearing shoes that were too tight, but there are not any calluses that might be on the feet of an older man. Or a working man, for that matter. Also, his hands are smooth, as near as I can determine, showing that he was not involved in manual labor, at least for some time immediately before his death.

"MacDonald?" said Holmes.

"Well, other than the wound on his head, and the missing finger, I'm not sure what else there is to see."

"Come, MacDonald, do not be too timid. Did you not observe anything of interest about his clothing?"

"No, Mr. Holmes. It seems like regular clothing that one might have expected to encounter in the 1830's and '40's."

"True, true, but there is more. The clothing appears to be homemade, and sturdy enough for common labor. The shoes are also very tough, and as Watson pointed out, they appear to have been too tight. In fact – "

He stopped, and held up a shoe against the bottom of the corpse's foot, using his other hand to straighten it against the sole of the shoe. " – these shoes do not fit at all." The foot, in spite of being buried for a half-century, still extended nearly an inch past the length of the shoe.

"Perhaps I misjudged earlier, Holmes," I said. "I had concluded that he grew up wearing shoes that were too tight, but perhaps I was just seeing the effect of his feet being forced into the smaller shoes over the last fifty-odd years."

"No, you were correct in your statement, Watson. His toes are naturally contorted from growing up in tight shoes throughout his formative years. However, one only has to observe the length of his overall foot, compared with the sole length of the shoes, to see that these are too small for him, much smaller than what he would have worn simply to cramp his toes.

"Granted, some shrinkage has occurred to the corpse over time, but not as much as one might expect, as it was buried in the preserving medium of the acidic peat, and therefore did not completely mummify."

After we had all observed the point that Holmes was making, he gently lowered the leg back to the table. "Clearly, the foot is too long for the shoe, or to put it another way, the shoes are too small for the feet. Thus, these shoes did not belong to this man, and he was not buried in his own shoes. And to extrapolate from this conclusion, these were not his clothes as well. This is confirmed by the fact that he does not appear to have done manual labor, as shown by his smooth hands and feet, while the clothes he is wearing *are* those of a laborer."

"So you think he was a gentleman, then?" interrupted Burton.

"It is quite possible," said Holmes.

"And he's missing a finger, like many of the Brileys. It wasn't cut off at some earlier date. You agree that he was born that way."

"That is true."

"Well, how could that be?" asked Burton. "I grew up here. I was taken in by Mr. Martin Briley as a boy, and I know all that there is to know about them. Mr. Briley never had any brothers or sisters. And he never had any cousins either. From 1840, when his father died, until now, he's been the last of the Brileys, and I believe that he will die that way."

"So you have no theory as to who this poor fellow might be?" asked Holmes.

"None in the world," replied Burton.

"Then we can expect nothing else from you about him then," said Holmes, rather abruptly. Thankfully, Burton did not seem to take offense.

Holmes walked to the foot of the table and grabbed the long fabric bundled there. As I lifted the lantern from the table, he hefted the sheet and started to pull it back over the body. Reaching the head, he began to lay it gently over the man's face before stopping himself. Pulling it back slightly, he leaned down and looked at the side of the man's head. "Watson, the lantern for a moment, if you please."

I edged it closer, trying to move it so that it wouldn't cast shadows from Holmes and his cap. He stared intently at the body's ear for a moment, and then stood and walked around to the other side. I followed and held the lantern while he repeated his actions. Then, having seen what he wanted to see, he stood and completed covering the now unclothed corpse.

"What did you notice, Mr. Holmes?" asked MacDonald.

"Hmm? Just a fact to document for later, Inspector. It may mean nothing, and then again, it may be a confirmation of sorts. And now," he said, gesturing toward the door, "let us return to the house, where we shall ask some questions, and possibly, I hope, find something hot to revive us."

"I can assure you of that, gentlemen," said Burton, leading us outside. We paused while MacDonald relocked the door, and then wound our way between the buildings until we found our waiting carriage, which had somehow made it back up the hillside. The rain seemed to have eased for a moment, but a cold wet wind was blowing, and the southwestern sky was filling with a new group of tall black clouds, spanning around to the north. As we moved past the lighted windows of the different cottages, I could see Holmes, looking at Burton with intense speculation, although Burton himself seemed completely oblivious to that fact.

As we were about to depart the collection of snug houses, Holmes suddenly reached out and grabbed Burton's shoulder. "Wait," he said. "Before we go back to the house, tell me where we can find the men who first discovered the body. Are they here, within these cottages?"

"I'm sure they're at the inn, back toward the village," replied Burton, signaling the carriage driver, who had started to slow, to move on. "You passed through it shortly before arriving at the house. I will send a message

364

down that you wish to speak to them later, after we have warmed ourselves for a while at the house."

"That will be satisfactory," replied Holmes, settling back against the wet seat.

Holmes seemed to be satisfied with some secret knowledge, but I could not think of anything that we had seen so far that would provide any answers whatsoever. However, this was not an unusual situation for me, and I was content with the understanding that all would eventually be revealed. While I pondered Holmes's apparent confidence, he happened to glance up, catching my attention. Spotting the familiar gleam in his eye, I knew that he had caught the scent, and the game was once again afoot.

Chapter IV
A Respite

There was no further conversation as we crossed the bridge over the stream, now even more noticeably swollen than when we had first passed this way, little more than an hour before. I foresaw that it would only continue to rise, as the rains from upstream collected and poured down in ever-increasing flows to join the channel. I began to ask Burton if the cottages were ever cut off from the rest of the estate by high water, but withheld the question, deciding that casual conversation while driving through the returning storm would be both unwise and unpleasant.

By the time we had reached the entrance to the house, the wind seemed to have shifted slightly, and held a cooler feel to it as well. I observed that Holmes seemed to be unaffected, as usual, but MacDonald and Burton had their hands thrust into their coat pockets, and the collars were pulled up around their necks, as was mine. Before we reached the door, it was thrown open by a man. He was small, not quite over five feet in height, but otherwise all was hidden as the warm welcome light from the hall spilled out behind him into the night-like darkness.

Stepping inside, we quickly divested ourselves of our outer attire, which the young man, as I could now see he was, gathered in his arms. Burton gave him quiet instructions about where to carry them in order to have them dried. I noticed that our traveling bags, both mine and Holmes's that had been carried in by MacDonald when we first arrived at the house, were lined up along the wall beneath an ornate mirror. Burton frowned. "I had planned to invite you gentlemen to stay with us here in the house for the night," he said. "I left instructions along those lines before I departed to meet you at the mere. I'm not sure why your bags haven't been taken upstairs."

"There is no need," began Holmes, but before he could continue, a voice interrupted from an archway at the back of the hall.

"I gave the instructions to keep the bags down here, Mr. Burton," said a woman, entering with a firm and purposeful step.

"Indeed, Mrs. Lynch. And by what authority did you go against my wishes?"

She stopped about ten feet in front of us. She was tall, well over five-and-a-half feet. Her height was accentuated by the way in which her hair was pulled up into what can only be described as a crown on her head. It was an iron grey, with streaks of white interestingly woven throughout.

366

There were no loose strands whatsoever, and her ears were completely exposed. She had a rather thin nose, and her mouth was a wide tight line, her lips pursed in irritation. Her hands were clasped loosely at waist level, in something of a prayerful repose, although there was nothing holy about her expression.

She wore no jewelry whatsoever, and her dress was black, in a style I had not seen in more than a decade. Her entire figure presented itself as that of a harsh schoolmistress, who was highly displeased with a rebellious student – in this case, Burton.

This displeasure found its expression and focus through her eyes, which were barely visible as she looked out beneath lowered lids. She took another step forward, changing the angle of the light when it hit her face as she looked at Burton, who was just slightly taller than she. I could suddenly see her face was lined with a fine mesh of countless lines and wrinkles that had not been visible just a moment before. Clearly, she was at least twenty years older than her early fifties, the age at which I had first placed her.

"The master has given you authority over the running of the estate, Mr. Burton," she said. "It does not extend to the household."

Burton did not back down in the least. When we had first entered the well-lit hallway, I had seen Burton clearly for the first time. As he had removed his rain apparel and stood in the light, I had concluded that he looked to be a friendly but capable individual, who naturally radiated the competence and leadership that would be required for his position as an estate agent. Now, when challenged by Mrs. Lynch, he retained his authority, but his good-natured manner disappeared.

"We will offer these men, who have come here to help us, the hospitality of the estate, Mrs. Lynch. The *entire* estate. The authority vested to me does not stop at the front door of this house, no matter how much you would like to wish it so."

"I do not believe the master would wish us to provide lodging for *policemen*," she sniffed.

"And I believe that you and I will go to the master and discuss it with him." He turned to us, clearly embarrassed, yet in control of the situation. "Gentlemen, if you will wait in this room?" He gestured through an open double door on the left side of the hall. "I understand Inspector MacDonald was in that room yesterday. In the meantime, Mrs. Lynch and I shall speak to Mr. Briley."

He turned back to her, and with a stiff wave of his arm, offered to let her go first toward some other part of the house. She stood without speaking for a moment, and then, without any physical signs of surrender, spoke in the same tone as before, saying, "There will be no need to discuss

367

this with the master at the present time, Mr. Burton. However, you can be sure I will be approaching him in the very near future to make sure there is a clear understanding of where the responsibilities of the estate start and where they end."

"I look forward to it," replied Burton. "And now, will you see about preparing rooms for these gentlemen? Also, we require food and drink. *Warm* food, if you please."

He turned toward us, gesturing again toward the room, clearly dismissing the older woman. "Gentlemen? If you wouldn't mind, we can go in and find seats by the fire."

He followed us in, and turned and shut both doors. Then, turning to face us, he visibly and almost comically relaxed, before letting a small grin cross his face.

"Whew," he said, "St. George versus the Dragon." He moved to a table holding a bottle containing what looked like brandy and some glasses. "I think we're safe in here now. For the moment, at least."

He opened the bottle, grabbed the first of the glasses, and started to pour. "Drinks, gentlemen? Mr. Holmes? Doctor? Inspector?"

With the tension released, I felt a smile come to my face, as MacDonald replied, "Well, I am on duty, I suppose, but I don't think anyone would mind if I had a restorative on a day like this."

"Here, here," I concurred, stepping forward to receive the second glass poured, after that given to MacDonald. "I can attest to the healing powers of brandy for these conditions."

Holmes remained silent while accepting his glass. Burton finished by pouring one for himself, and then raised it. "To the conqueror and his brave companions." He tipped up the glass, said softly, "Until next time," and turned to refill it.

MacDonald did not wait to be asked as he stuck out his glass as well. Holmes still held his, only one sip taken, while I considered my glass and decided not to have more on a quite empty stomach.

"There seems to be," Holmes began, "some tension in the house. I'm sure that I speak for Watson and MacDonald when I state that we do not wish to cause you any difficulties. We had always intended to stay at the inn in the village, should our investigation take longer than a day."

"Indeed," I added. "We don't want to force you to fight a battle before you need to."

"Do not worry, doctor. Disagreements with Mrs. Lynch occur one way or another on a nearly daily basis. I am quite comfortable with my understanding of my position on the estate, and where my limits are set."

"So you have the complete confidence of Mr. Briley, then?" asked Holmes, rather impolitely, to my mind.

"I believe that I do," said Burton, gesturing us toward the fire. We adjusted our seats so that each had access to the drying warmth, and then Burton continued. "I have been trained by Mr. Briley for this position, having been hand-picked, as it were, when I was just a lad, and I was long ago given to understand that my authority, when needed, also extended over Mrs. Lynch. As you said, doctor, I do pick my battles with her, but occasionally there *is* a battle that needs to be fought. She keeps an excellent household, there is no doubt about that, even if it is run too strictly for my taste. I certainly have no wish to interfere with the day-to-day workings of the place. In any case, I have my time well taken by the many tasks that call from outside the doors of the house."

"You say that you were hand-picked," said Holmes. "How exactly did that occur?"

Burton did not answer immediately, but instead, went and recharged his glass. He raised it with questioning eyes in our direction. Holmes and I shook our heads. MacDonald looked as if he dearly would like a third glass as well, but then reluctantly declined. Burton added a slight amount to his glass, and then returned to his seat.

"I was born and raised in the village, Mr. Holmes," he said. "It is a small place, and does not even really have a name, as it is not so much a village as a wide spot in the road on the way to Mr. Briley's estate."

Burton shifted and took another sip. "Mr. Briley owns the land and the buildings, the same as he does where the cottages are located. The village is made up of a number of houses and shops, used by the estate workers. There is an inn with a pub in the ground floor, where the men of the estate gather to socialize.

"The road which you traveled from the station at Leighton is generally only used by people who have estate business. It goes on through to Woburn, to the northwest, but as there is a more direct route, we rarely have any strangers passing through.

"As I said, I was born in the village. My father died before I was born, and my mother raised me alone and worked as a seamstress. Actually, she was the primary seamstress for the village. When quality work was needed, it was to my mother that the villagers turned.

"When I was ten years of age, in 1864, she caught a sudden illness, and within a few days, she was gone. Up until that time, I had given no thought to my future. I had worked as needed around our home, and had gone to school as was expected. We have always had an excellent school here, one of the finest around, started and financed by Mr. Briley."

"I have heard of it," said Holmes. "It is a model of how an estate owner who is willing to spend a little extra can reap much greater rewards

369

for his efforts. I believe he started it when he was a young man, soon after he inherited the estate."

"That is correct, Mr. Holmes. It was revolutionary at the time. There was certainly nothing else like it in England for many years. I understand he was initially heavily criticized, but the subsequent results more than silenced his detractors. And in any case, it was his land and his money, and he apparently did not care what anyone thought of him."

"And you were attending the school at the time of your mother's death?" I asked. "Were you even then being prepared for the running of the estate?"

"Not then, doctor," replied Burton. "In those days, I had no more than a vague awareness of Mr. Briley. There was some talk at the time of my mother's death that I would be accepted as an apprentice to one of the village craftsmen. That I might have become a blacksmith was a very strong possibility. But before a decision was made, Mr. Briley himself came to the neighbor's house where I had been staying since my mother's death.

"I had seen him before then, of course. He was not a large or imposing man, even in those days before age caught up with him, and there was certainly nothing frightening about him, in spite of his authority. But whenever he rode through town, people stopped and indicated their respect to him, doffing their caps or touching their foreheads. There was no irony to it, gentlemen. Mr. Briley has done a lot for this village, and there isn't anyone here who has not been touched in some way by his generosity or benevolence toward the community.

"The day Mr. Briley came to get me, I heard a horse stopping in the yard. Like the other children in that house, I ran to the windows and then to the door to see who it was.

"He was wearing a long cloak, and, it being a cold day, his face was bundled and hidden. Yet we knew who he was, if only from the fine strapping horse he was riding. He rode often in those days, and they said he had ridden even more in years past, before age started to overtake him.

"He was in his mid-forties then, and still a very vital and active manager of the estate. His gaze was always solemn, but his eyes could express amusement or approval, even as they could darken when he was displeased.

"He politely asked permission to enter, and of course it was given. He spoke for a moment or two to the owners of the house, in low tones. All of the children, myself included, started to scatter to the back rooms, as was the custom when adults wanted to discuss adult business. But my name was called, and I was told to stay.

370

"Returning cautiously to the main room, I found Mr. Briley, who was then uncloaked, sitting on a stool by the fire. He held a mug of something in his hands. The good woman of the house prodded me forward, where I stood while Mr. Briley peered intently, first at my face, and then up and down quickly, before again meeting my eyes with his frank and appraising gaze.

"'George,' he said, surprising me with his question, 'are you an intelligent young man?'

"I was not able to speak at first, until I felt someone nudge me from behind. As he asked it again, no doubt fearing I was not intelligent at all, I managed to reply, 'I believe I have my fair share, sir,' I said, all in a rush, and perhaps a bit impertinently, now that I think on it.

"He didn't seem to think there was anything forward at all about my answer. He nodded gravely, and said he wanted to make a proposal. 'I'm aware of your unfortunate loss,' he said. 'I believe I have a place for you, if you would like it. It means hard work, and a willingness to learn. I hear good things from your teacher. I think you're the right man for the job.'

"I thanked him, not knowing at that age how to take being called a man. I stammered something about arrangements having already been made for me to apprentice to the village blacksmith. I must have said it with a little bit of resigned despair, because it made Mr. Briley's eyes glimmer with amusement for the first time that afternoon.

"'You misunderstand me, George,' he interrupted. 'I want someone to learn how my estate works. If you come live with me, I'll show you. Someday, if you learn the lessons, if you learn my way of doing things, you'll be running the place.'

"As you can all imagine, it took me a few moments to get my mind settled about that. Of course, it would mean leaving the world I knew, but I was not wise enough at that time to realize that. The man and woman with whom I was staying started speaking over each other, complimenting Mr. Briley's generosity, while no doubt wondering why one of their own children was not picked.

"Whatever the reason, my belongings were gathered then and there, and I was put on the spare horse Mr. Briley had brought with him. There was no doubt that he had anticipated my acceptance of his offer. I rode with my new protector back to this house. Almost immediately my education began. Unfortunately, some of my practical lessons were learned thanks to Mrs. Lynch."

I expressed a sympathetic comment, and Burton nodded.

"Yes, you can imagine what that was like. She was the housekeeper then as well, and from the first time I crossed the threshold here, she let me know that she disagreed with Mr. Briley's decision to bring me in as his ward. Oh, it was never a direct statement. It was simply sly comments here and there, often to the staff when Mr. Briley was not present, but where I couldn't help but to overhear. It might have gotten the better of me, and rather quickly, if Mr. Briley hadn't gone out of his way to make me feel welcome.

"He quickly showed me that he had been serious about teaching me the running of the estate. He made sure I had my lessons, as much as I could take in without foundering. But he also took me with him each day, to the fields and tenant farms, and to the buildings and shops that he owns in the village, pointing out to me different things I would need to know. He showed me how things work, and why. And most importantly, he gave me a better understanding that all of his employees here are people, and not just faceless laborers that can be replaced as one would a worn-out cog in a machine.

"By the time I was sixteen, I nearly had my growth, and the estate workers would listen to me as if I were the master himself. Mr. Briley had always made it clear that I spoke for him, and he would back what I said. When I was eighteen, I went away for some specialized learning, just for a year or so, and when I returned, I settled in as before, handling the day-to-day affairs.

"Throughout that time, of course, I have had my difficulties with Mrs. Lynch. She's been the housekeeper here since Mr. Briley's father was alive – she is in her seventies now, but doesn't look a day older than when I first came to live here. Sometimes Mr. Briley will defer to her in matters of the household or staff, but he has never let her criticisms of me stand whatsoever.

"In addition, she has often made free with her opinions about Mr. Briley's good works in the village and on the estate, criticizing what she often claims were unnecessary expenses just for the sake of charity. Mr. Briley lets her have her say. I suppose he's known her for so long that he must, but he never lets what she says stop him from doing what he knows to be right."

At that moment, the doorway to the hall opened swiftly, as Mrs. Lynch herself stepped into the room. Her stance conveyed a hostile tension that led me to believe that she had been eavesdropping, and had heard Burton's frank statements concerning her. However, she intoned in an even voice, if unfriendly, "The food is ready, Mr. Burton. It's only shepherd's pie, which was to be for your dinner tonight, but it is no trouble to have it early for our *guests*."

Burton showed that he was aware of her ironic tone by flashing a suppressed grin to us. Standing, he gestured toward the hall. "I'm sorry,

372

gentlemen, for running on so. However, I suppose it helped pass the time while we dried out before the fire until the food was prepared."

At that moment, the doorway to the hall opened swiftly,
as Mrs. Lynch herself stepped into the room.

"Not at all, Mr. Burton," said MacDonald. "I myself rather enjoyed your tale. It's like something right out of a Dickens story."

Burton chuckled. "No doubt. However, I can assure you there is no person less like the old convict, Magwitch, than the good Mr. Briley." He seemed about to add something else, and then, with a smile, he stopped.

As we walked down the hall, Burton excused himself for a moment and spoke quietly to the young man who had let us in, and who was now loitering in a nearby doorway. Joining us, he explained, "I apologize, Mr. Holmes. I had forgotten I told you I would arrange to have the workmen who found the body meet us in the village. I've sent a message by Woods. The men should be at the inn a little later today in order to be questioned."

By this time, we were taking our seats in the nearby dining room. Mrs. Lynch stood off to the side, watching critically as a pretty maid offered cider to drink. I was surprised that a maid would be serving, but I decided that things were obviously run differently here in the Briley house.

In the center of the table was a shepherd's pie. Obviously we were not going to stand on ceremony, either because that was the custom of the house, or possibly because Mrs. Lynch was not going to provide any more hospitality than was required.

As we began to eat some of the excellent pie, Mrs. Lynch turned and silently left the room. The maid followed in her wake, and I happened to be looking up just as she glanced back and met Burton's eyes. His glance twinkled in her direction for just a moment, and I perceived the formation of a dimple on the girl's cheek before she vanished from the room. I surreptitiously looked toward Holmes and saw, unsurprisingly, that he had observed the small communication between the two as well.

MacDonald was helping himself to the food with heart-warming enthusiasm. "Ver' good," he muttered, his Scots burr becoming stronger as the victuals warmed him from within.

Taking a sip of the cider, Holmes stated, "I would enjoy it if you would tell us some more about Mr. Briley's good works. I have heard a little of him in London, of course, but he is renowned for being something of a recluse, especially in these later years. For instance, there was some talk several years ago of his name appearing on the birthday list, but he somehow managed to have it removed, without offending Her Majesty."

"That's correct," said Burton, reaching for some more of the cider, centered on the table in a pitcher. "Would anyone care for more?" he asked. MacDonald accepted, while Holmes and I declined. "We make do for ourselves much of the time here. That includes serving ourselves at meals. Mr. Briley, now an invalid, eats alone and does not have social events requiring staff members trained for such events. In fact, he has never gone in for that sort of thing, even when he was up and about, and running the place himself."

"How long has he been incapacitated?" I asked, reaching for another helping of the pie.

"It has been about seven years since he first started to withdraw more noticeably from the running of the estate, several years after I returned and assumed more of the daily responsibilities. Up until then, he was quite visible, both here and in the village, although I was carrying out most of the daily management by then. He was able to spend more time with his local charitable works, and the school."

"Ah, yes. Tell us more of the school," said Holmes.

"Quite," said Burton. "Years before I was born, probably not long after he inherited the estate from his father, Mr. Briley set up the village school, which at that time was unlike anything anywhere else in Britain. He hired several teachers, instead of one master for all of the students, and he personally reviewed their methods on a regular basis in order to make

374

sure they knew and understood their subjects, and also that they actually knew how to teach. Cruelty was never allowed. He made funds available for families so the children would not have to cease going to school in order to go to work to help provide for the family. He also established scholarships for promising village children, allowing many to continue into higher education. For those with less ability, he made certain they were well trained for jobs in the village or on the estate.

"Mr. Briley also hired a doctor soon after he came into his inheritance, paying the bills himself and making the man available to the whole village. In time, other doctors joined the first, and now there is a little hospital nearby, with free care for those who need it."

"Admirable," I said. "No wonder the man was offered a knighthood. Why did he refuse?"

"To be honest," responded Burton, "I've never really known. Mr. Briley's father had made a great deal of money when Mr. Briley was very young, and I've always had the impression that he did so in a rather ruthless manner. Sometimes, I've thought that Mr. Briley was trying to make up for his father's actions, which were fairly harsh, even for those rough days. On other occasions, I believe Mr. Briley had no wish to involve himself in the fripperies of the Court which might entangle him and take his time if he did accept a knighthood. He seemed to be more inclined to stay here, managing his properties and doing good works."

"And he never married?" I asked. "There was never a Mrs. Briley?"

"Never," replied Burton. "I understand that years ago, Mr. Briley had been living away from the estate in London for some time, and he only returned upon his father's death. I gather there was no good feeling between father and son in the later years of his father's life. As to what he did in the years when he was up in London, before his return, I have no knowledge. But I am certain he never married after he inherited the estate, nearly fifty years ago."

"And he had no brothers? No other family?" said MacDonald, wiping his mouth after pushing back his plate with a most satisfied sigh. He dropped the cloth with finality.

"No," said Burton, "at least none I've ever heard tell of. It has always been common knowledge in these parts that Mr. Briley was an only child, like his father before him."

"No heirs, eh?" said Holmes. I could tell that he wished to pull out his pipe, but was refraining. "Might I ask you a rather personal question?" Without waiting for a response, Holmes stated, "Are *you* his heir, Mr. Burton?"

Another man might have told Holmes to mind his own business, or to go to blazes, but Burton accepted the question with the open forthrightness that seemed to be his natural manner. "Honestly, Mr. Holmes, I do not know. There are many people who *believe* me to be the heir, and I *was* trained in order to run the place, but Mr. Briley has never once indicated to me one way or another who his heir is, or if he has even designated one. The estate is not entailed in any way, as it was all built on the funds obtained from the commerce of Mr. Briley's father, and to a degree that of his grandfather as well. Mr. Briley has been a careful steward, and has increased the assets of the estate many times over from the already vast amount he inherited from his father. I can tell you that because I have complete access to Mr. Briley's accounts, and his full confidence in carrying out the estate's business. But as to your question regarding an heir? As I said, I cannot tell you."

"I thank you for your willingness to answer my question. I cannot say whether or not it is of any relevance, but all knowledge is valuable, especially when trying to assemble a puzzle of this type."

I nearly snorted at this, as at times past Holmes has made some rather outrageous statements regarding the need to keep his brain-attic clear of unnecessary information. I believe that he knew what I was thinking in that moment, but he continued with this thought.

"Obviously, we have questions about Mr. Briley's family and heirs, as the body was found with the characteristic missing finger. Can you think of anyone you may have heard mentioned, or any name that you might have seen in a document, at any time, that could offer some clue as to who the dead man might have been?

"None, Mr. Holmes, none at all. And I assure you it has been weighing heavily on my mind since the body was found."

"I believe that Inspector MacDonald had a limited interview with Mr. Briley yesterday, but was unable to ascertain any specific facts relating to the investigation. Have you discussed it with him since then? Was he able to offer any theories? After all, the body has been here since the approximate time when he inherited the estate. I would think that the whole question would have some fascination for him."

"I have not spoken with him about the matter, gentlemen. Mr. Briley's health has been somewhat . . . fragile in the last year or so. When I saw how he reacted yesterday to the Inspector's questioning, I resolved not to pursue it on my own, unless it was first broached to me by Mr. Briley himself."

"He made it clear he did *not* want to talk to the likes of me," said MacDonald wryly.

"I understand, Mr. Burton," said Holmes. "However, I am very much afraid that we do not have the luxury of making that allowance again. I will also need to ask Mr. Briley some questions." Holmes pushed back his chair and stood, causing a small expression of surprise to widen Burton's eyes with the suddenness of the motion. "Is Mr. Briley available right now? I would like to begin questioning him as soon as possible."

A flat voice answered from the hall, growing louder as the speaker entered the room. "Mr. Briley is not available for visitors," said Mrs. Lynch. I wondered how long she had been standing in the hallway, lurking and listening. Surely we had not said anything objectionable?

"Mrs. Lynch," said the Inspector, also rising to his feet. "You cannot deny to us – "

"Mr. Burton will tell you that Mr. Briley always naps during the mid-afternoon, and cannot be disturbed now. Perhaps later, in a few hours, before dinner, you may have a few minutes of his time."

"I'm afraid I must concur, gentlemen. Mrs. Lynch is correct. Mr. Briley is almost certainly asleep right now, and will be for several more hours. As he ages, he tends to nap at regular intervals throughout the day. Although I am not certain of it, I believe he remains awake through parts of the night, reading, or sometimes just staring into the fire."

"He does, indeed, Mr. Burton," said Mrs. Lynch.

"If we are unable to see him now," Holmes said, "then so be it." He pulled his watch from his pocket and checked the time. "We shall proceed to the village and interview the laborers who found the body, assuming that they have assembled and made themselves available as requested. Will Mr. Briley be awake at five o'clock then, Mrs. Lynch?"

The thin line of her mouth became even thinner, as she said shortly, "He will."

Holmes did not say anything for a moment, as he stood at Mrs. Lynch's side, looking at her with a surprised interest that only I, who had known him for so many years, would recognize. He was docketing some fact, though I knew not what. Then, with a flash of satisfaction, he responded.

"Excellent. Then, gentlemen, I am afraid," said Holmes, moving toward the hall, "that I must request you to join me as we again throw ourselves to the mercy of the storm and make our way toward the village. As I recall, Mr. Burton, it is not a far walk?"

"Not far, but likely to be unpleasant on a day such as this. Shall I summon the carriage?"

"Let us take a vote. Inspector?"

MacDonald did not want to appear any less able than Holmes to face unpleasantness. "I can walk it," he said. Turning to me, he asked, "Doctor?"

Apparently I didn't want to appear any less able than Holmes, either. "Let us get it over with," I said, already dreading it.

"Excellent, then," said Holmes. "To our coats, and then a quick march to the . . . south, I should think!"

Chapter V
At The Inn

The less said of that trek to the village, the better. During that time of my life, in the spring of 1888, I was fairly well healed from the wounds that I had received at the Battle of Maiwand. Keeping up with Holmes during his investigations over the years had been the best therapy I could ask for. He was always aware of my limits, and he never asked of me any more than I was capable of providing. Still, I occasionally felt the twinges of my Afghan wound, especially on days such as that. Without seeing it, I knew the glass was falling, and the ill weather only promised to worsen as the day progressed.

After a trek that descended almost imperceptibly toward the village, we found ourselves turning a corner and suddenly facing the inn door. The entrance was well lit, and the sign hanging over the door, boldly proclaiming "The Ram and Lamb", was striking in its color and clarity. Burton saw me notice it, and said, as we were stepping through the door, "You'll find all the shops and businesses in the village are well kept, doctor. It's just another example of Mr. Briley's excellent stewardship."

"And yours, surely, at this point," I replied as MacDonald closed the door behind us.

We began to shed our coats, and Burton replied modestly, "I'm just carrying out Mr. Briley's wishes. He laid out the pattern years ago, and I simply make certain that nothing changes."

Hanging our coats and hats on handy pegs by the door, we turned to face the room. It was not large by any means, perhaps twenty feet deep, with stairs on the left wall, and a pair of doors in the back, one standing open to reveal another room, much like this one, filled with tables, and also well-lit by lanterns. It was certainly cleaner than most of the other rooms of this type that I had previously encountered. Down the right side of the room in which we stood was the bar, with an unexpectedly large selection of various bottles behind it, presenting many different and enticing colors and shapes.

There were nearly a dozen or so men in the place, most sitting at tables, but a couple of them leaned against the bar. One had his back to it, elbows propped there like someone from the American Wild West. A serving girl moved among the tables. Behind the bar was a large, chipper fellow sporting a trimmed military moustache very similar to my own. He was holding a cloth and talking to the man who was facing him.

Conversation softened as we entered, and everyone stopped to glance in our direction. Upon recognizing our companion, Mr. Burton, the men seemed to relax, and they returned to whatever their previous business had been. The hum of their voices rose to the original volume, and the warm sound of glasses being raised and replaced on tables resumed. A few of the men threw friendly hands up in our direction. Burton responded with a matching gesture.

As we waited for a moment, huddled near the door and already enjoying the warmth from the blaze in the fireplace across the room between the two doors, Burton stepped to one of the tables where three men sat. He spoke to them for a moment, gesturing our way, and then looking back over his shoulder at us when the other men did so as well.

While they spoke, I took a moment to look around the bar. It was extremely well kept for such a place, in as good a condition as any that I've seen in my travels. And the patrons appeared to be healthy and happy as well.

My attention was drawn to one old fellow, sitting at a table near the fireplace. His back was to the flames, which were doing a good job indeed of heating the room. I imagined the man would be very warm in the seat that he had chosen. He was slumped, with a hand resting on the table before him, near an empty glass. The flickering firelight behind him added a strange cast to his snow-white hair.

"He's seventy-five if he's a day," said Holmes softly. Knowing him as I did, I was not surprised that he had observed where I was looking.

"He's certainly earned a rest," I said. "He appears to be enjoying a well-deserved slumber."

"Oh, he's not asleep," said Holmes. "He's been watching us through lowered lids since we arrived. Ah, there! You see?"

While Holmes had been speaking, the serving girl had brought a refill to the old man. She set it on the table and removed his empty glass. Without changing his posture or the expression on his face whatsoever, which I had believed to be the typical nap of the elderly, he reached his hand toward the fresh beverage and brought it steadily to his lips.

Burton finished speaking with the men at the table and stepped back. The men stood, gathering their glasses, and Burton turned and walked a few steps to the right of the room, speaking now in a low voice to the bartender. The man nodded in a friendly way, and gestured with a glance toward the back room. Burton then motioned us forward, and we joined the group, all making our way out of the main room.

Burton waited until we had all passed him, and then followed us. This room also had a cheery fireplace, set immediately behind the one in the main room. There were several tables, one large enough to have a place for all of us. Burton asked what we would have to drink. MacDonald ordered whisky, Holmes and I brandy, while the three men wanted refills of beer. Burton left for just a moment to give the order to the tapster, and then returned, pulling the door behind him.

"While we wait, Mr. Burton," said Holmes, "would you mind introducing us?"

I knew that Holmes had no shyness about introducing himself, and he wanted the act to come from Burton, in order to have legitimacy and authority before these men. Burton then explained that both Holmes and I were criminal specialists down from London. I started to demur, but then decided not to confuse the issue.

Burton then introduced the large fellow in the middle, obviously regarded as the leader of the bunch, as Lambrick, while the older man to his right was Creed, and the fellow in his twenties on his left was Huggins.

Burton was explaining that the men had already been interviewed by MacDonald the previous day when the door reopened, and the man from the bar brought in our drinks. After distributing them, the fellow left, and Holmes began to speak.

"I'm aware that you were asked about finding the body in the trench yesterday by the Inspector. However, I beg of you to indulge me and repeat your story, trying to remember to tell it as fresh a manner as possible. Try not to think of it as you've previously repeated it, both to the authorities and to your friends, your family, and to the men out in the bar. I need you to see it as if it is new, so I may experience it through your eyes as if I were there."

The three men looked at one another, and then both seemed to defer to Lambrick, the large fellow in the middle. "Mr. Holmes, it was just another day. We had been working on digging that trench for nearly three weeks. I suppose you could say I was the foreman of the job, at least on times when Mr. Burton wasn't there. And you know we do a good job when you have to be away. Isn't that right, Mr. Burton?"

"Certainly. I have complete confidence in you," replied Burton.

"Tell me about that day," said Holmes. "What were the conditions? What time did you discover the body?"

"It was a sunny day, not too hot. It had rained some the day before, but not like what we're seeing today, and the ground wasn't too damp. It wasn't too long after our noontime meal," said Lambrick. "We had been pulling what was left of the tree out of the way in the morning, and then we kept digging to expose the pipe. We haven't always been digging down all the way to the old pipe, you understand. The old one was deep enough already that we had room to lay the new one near it, or on top of it, and still get a good fall so the flow would still go downhill."

"And why were you forced to dig deeper in this area?" asked Holmes.

"Well, we were at a point where the trench had turned less steep at the bottom of the hill and was starting to flatten out more as it neared the mere. Of course, we didn't want to go too deep, or we'd get into the groundwater. And then there was the tree. We had to dig down at that spot to make sure we got rid of the roots around there. Then we had to cut them back enough so they wouldn't interfere with the work."

"I see. And then you found the body. How did that occur?"

"It was Huggins what first saw it. He was digging on one side of the pipe and some of the dirt slid down, a big chunk, sudden-like, showing cloth. You tell him, Huggins."

The young fellow looked over at us, and then back at Lambrick. He took a long pull at his beer, wiped his sleeve across his mouth, stifled a belch, and said suddenly, "I swear to God I still wonder what'd happen if I'd've swung the pick right into him. I can almost feel it, d----d if I can't! Bloody nightmare stuff, by God!"

His sudden outburst caught us by surprise. I nearly laughed, and I could see the same expression in Holmes's face. MacDonald, on the other hand, scowled, and Burton looked mortified.

Lambrick glared at Huggins, and was about rebuke him, when Creed spoke, in a surprisingly even and educated voice.

"I believe, gentlemen," he said, "that I can answer your questions as well as my friends here. Incidentally, Mr. Holmes, perhaps you remember me? We met several years ago, when I was living out in Harrow Weald, where my people come from. You came to my place of employment, to ask us all some questions."

I saw Holmes's face flicker with recognition. "Ah, yes. Mr. Jeremiah Creed, the school teacher. And how is your brother? Still practicing law?"

Creed's expression saddened. "Unfortunately, Mr. Holmes, he perished in a fire the year after your visit. He was rescuing a child trapped in one of the rooms above 'The Red Boar,' where you and Dr. Watson had met with us on that dark afternoon."

I remembered the fellow now, although I'm not surprised that I didn't identify him at first. He had changed much since the early spring of 1883, when Holmes and I had become involved in a large, complex case that tested all our skills and had permanently cemented our friendship. I had made notes of the matter at the time, as best I could, but the convoluted path of the investigation had been almost more than I could follow, even after Holmes's lengthy explanations.

Mr. Creed had certainly changed in the five years since I had last seen him. I wanted to ask how he had made the unlikely journey from school teacher to laborer, digging trenches to lay pipes carrying away the waste from worker's cottages. As I recalled, he had given a very clear account of the tall landlady's actions, back in 1883, during the Affair of the Seven Silver Clocks. It will be recalled that Holmes, by postulating the existence of the *eighth* clock, was able to show to Inspector Gregson that the man from Trinity College had left the room *before* the explosion of the dynamite bomb, when he shouldn't have known to leave at all.

Creed took a sip of his beer, but unlike Huggins, he did not burst forth emotionally. Rather, he calmly explained that the collapse of dirt around the pipe had revealed the corpse's leg. "The left leg," he said, specifically. He went on to make clear that the body was lying in the direction of the pipe, rather than perpendicular to it, and completely under it as well. The head was resting toward the uphill side, and the feet in the direction of the mere.

"And after the body was first exposed, what did you all do?" asked Holmes. "Was there anyone else in the immediate vicinity, other than you three?"

"No, sir," said Creed. "When we first started digging, a few weeks ago, some of the village boys would hang around, curious about what we were doing. For that matter, so would some of the villagers and people who lived in the cottages, who would walk down when they had a free moment. But as the weeks progressed, the sight of digging down and connecting up yet another segment of pipe became boring for them. There was no one else there when we found the body."

"And Mr. Lambrick, was it you who summoned the authorities?"

"Yes, sir, it was. After we dug it out some more, I went to find Mr. Burton here. I didn't send Huggins because, well, he was right upset about the whole business, and also I didn't want him telling everyone he saw along the way, and leading back a hundred people as if they were going to look at the circus."

"After Mr. Burton arrived, did you resume removal of the body?"

"Well, Creed and Huggins did, under Mr. Burton's direction. I went to find the Constable and the Doctor. I was to make sure I didn't tell anyone what had been discovered, and also to see that no one saw me bringing them back, so that questions wouldn't be asked."

"And when you returned, was the body completely uncovered yet?"

"Not all the way, sir. It took at least another hour, because we had to scrape away around and under it, so that we didn't cause it any damage. It turned out to be sturdier than we first imagined."

"How long did it take you to get back with the other two men?"

"Not long at all," replied Lambrick. "When we got there, Mr. Burton explained the situation to them, and said he hoped to avoid a lot of gossip until we knew exactly what we had uncovered."

Holmes was silent for a moment, and then turned slightly, asking, "Mr. Creed, was there anything underneath the body or in the surrounding soil that might have provided a clue?"

Creed looked at Holmes frankly. "No, sir. We did look, of course, after the body was removed. After we dug some on its left side, I moved around to the other side and dug down there, so I was able to loosen it."

"On the body's right side?" said Holmes.

"Yes, sir. I wanted to loosen up the soil there, so when we pushed him toward his left, and the larger hole near where the tree had been, it would be easier to get him out. When it was finally time to remove the fellow, we carefully slid a tarp under him from the original hole, on his left side, and I pulled it up on the right. Then it was passed back through over the top of him, rubbing against the bottom side of the pipe, and the whole thing was pulled out that way. Then we finished wrapping him up, loaded him on the carriage, and the doctor took him back up to the cottages with Mr. Lambrick, who helped carry the body into an empty house there."

"That's right, sir," agreed Lambrick, attempting to look helpful as he glanced frequently toward Burton.

Huggins continued to contemplate the last half-inch of beer in his glass, and once, with a shudder, he muttered an unattached "By God!" to himself.

"Did you all comment on how well the body was preserved?" asked Holmes.

Lambrick nodded. "Yes, sir, we did. Mind you, we only saw his face and one of his hands, but they were tanned, like leather. Mr. Burton told us it was from soaking up the groundwater so near the mere. The earth there is almost like peat, and I've heard tell of other people found that way, up north. Mr. Burton said it's something that's in the water. It's tan . . . tan . . . ."

"Tannin," said Burton. "It's what makes the leaves turn brown in the fall. After the green colors fade away."

Lambrick nodded, and Holmes said, "Thank you, Mr. Burton." He had been leaning forward, his gaze taking in all three of the men in that hawk-like way. Lambrick, solid and middle-aged, had faced him with an open gaze, simply answering the questions as asked. Creed had sat forward, alert and watchful, his pose mimicking that of Holmes, although on a much smaller scale. And Huggins, almost still a boy, had attended at times, but on other occasions seemed to be lost in his own thoughts.

Holmes sat up straighter, indicating that the interview was at a close. "I thank you, gentlemen, for your time. I appreciate your willingness to meet here and discuss this matter, especially on a day such as this." He

384

looked toward MacDonald. "Do you have any further questions, Inspector?"

"No, Mr. Holmes. I spoke to these men yesterday, and their stories match what I heard then."

"Watson?" asked Holmes.

I simply shook my head. Holmes then stood, and we all followed. "Then, again, I thank you all."

"Not at all, sir. Just doing our duty," said Lambrick, with a nod toward Burton, who returned it. Then the three men moved toward the door. Creed reached it first, opened it, and stepped aside, allowing Burton, the older man, and the younger to precede him. As he started to follow, Holmes said, "Oh, Mr. Creed. Just another word, if you don't mind?"

Creed turned around, and did not seem surprised. He started to shut the door, but Holmes stopped him. "No need for that," he said. "Doctor Watson and the Inspector will wait for us in the other room."

Seeing as how we had been suddenly dismissed, MacDonald shared a look with me, where his amusement was revealed only by the smile in his eyes, and we walked out of the room. I started to close the door, but Holmes said, "Leave it, Watson. We will only be a moment."

MacDonald and I went out into the larger room. The conversation did not stop, but there was a perceptible decrease in volume. MacDonald went to the bar to order a wee dram, as he put it. I was sorely tempted to join him, as the pain in my leg continued to increase, even as the barometer was no doubt falling. In spite of the intensity of the storm we had we witnessed throughout the day, I had no doubt that things were going to get worse as night came on.

Burton stood at the side of the room, talking to Lambrick and Huggins. Several of the other men in the room cast their eyes toward them, but made no move to join the conversation. I watched the old man near the fireplace. He still looked as if he were collapsed in sleep, but now that I had been made aware of the situation, I could see he was watching everything very closely indeed through lowered lids.

Holmes and Creed walked back through the door. They stopped just this side of it, and Holmes offered his hand. "Again, Mr. Creed, I'm sorry to hear about the loss of your brother. He was a good man, and of great assistance to us."

"Thank you, Mr. Holmes," said Creed. "Your thoughts are much appreciated." Creed then joined Lambrick and Huggins, while Burton broke away to rejoin our party.

"Did you find out anything else from Creed, Mr. Holmes?" said MacDonald, softly so that none of the other men in the room could hear.

"I was simply expressing my condolences to Mr. Creed for the loss of his brother four years ago," Holmes replied, in an equally quiet tone.

"And I'm just going to grow wings and fly back to Briley House," whispered MacDonald, but with a good-natured smile. "Is it a secret, then?"

"Not at all," replied Holmes. "I just wanted to confirm that I had received the message that Mr. Creed was sending."

"Message?" murmured Burton. "What message?"

"That he *did* recognize that the body found showed the distinctive characteristic of the missing Briley finger. He was at great pains several times to point out that the left side of the body, with its whole hand, was first exposed, that *he* was the man on the right side who dug down and uncovered that segment, and that when the tarp was passed through and back, the right side was then covered before Lambrick or Huggins had a chance to see the malformed hand.

"Although he does know about the hand, and he recognizes the significance of it, I am certain he will not reveal anything to anyone here, or elsewhere, for that matter."

"And why not?" asked MacDonald. "Information like that would get drinks for someone all night long, at the very least."

"You forget that Watson and I have encountered Creed before, Inspector. While we only knew him for a short time, and certainly his circumstances have come down in the world since then, I believe him to be a man of better character than that. Also, he simply has an appreciation for knowledge, and is happy knowing something of the truth, without having a compulsion to reveal it.

"He told me that when the very first segment of the body was revealed, he recognized it as an old corpse. He understood the nature of peat mummification, and realized that perhaps he was seeing something along those lines. Then he perceived from design of the clothing, as well as the location of the body right underneath the pipe, that it was *not* one of the peat mummies such as those found in the northern climes, and that this body was more modern than that, though not recently buried. It was no great leap to decide that if a body was hidden in that way, it was probably related to a murder. Only when he saw the right hand did he realize the family connections that were implied."

MacDonald glanced over at Creed, who happened to be looking our way. Creed gave a nod, which MacDonald returned. The tall Inspector, who had still been holding his now-empty wee glass, set it on the bar and asked, "Well, Mr. Holmes, to whom can I guide you next?"

Holmes pulled out his watch. "I believe it's still more than an hour until Mr. Briley will be awake. Is that correct, Mr. Burton?"

Burton leaned over to see Holmes's watch, which Holmes turned to provide a better view. "That's right, Mr. Holmes. Although I would allow a little extra. He generally awakens at about the same time, but then he has tea with a little something before his dinner is brought in, a few hours later."

Holmes nodded. "Then I propose to spend some more time here, getting to know a few more of the locals. Watson, do you care to join me?"

I shook my head. I had been considering for a few minutes now that it would serve me well to get back to the house and get off my aching leg. I held up my cane and indicated that I would be returning with the others.

"Actually, doctor," said MacDonald, "if Mr. Holmes doesn't need anything from me right now, I have to arrange to have the body moved into Woburn for the autopsy."

"And I need to be checking on the cottages," said Burton. "If the rains continue, as it seems they will, they might be cut off by the stream later tonight, as has happened before and will happen again. They are only a few hundred yards from the main house, but it might as well be out on Lizard's Point at high tide when that stream gets up. I need to make sure that everyone will be all right if they can't get out for a day or so. One of the women is expecting, for instance, and it might be a good idea to move her up here to the village for the duration."

Holmes nodded, and rubbed his hands together. "So be it. I will plan on meeting you all back at the house at half past five. Barkeep! A glass of your beer." And with that, he turned away from us and stepped up to the counter, beginning an animated conversation with the ruddy man who placed a glass in front of him.

With an understanding smile shared between us all, we remaining three returned to the storm. We walked back up the grade toward the house, and luckily the wet wind was behind us. Had I realized when we made our way down to the village that the reverse journey would require much more effort, as it was all uphill, I might have voted to have the carriage hauled out after all. When we finally reached the house, Burton offered to go in with me, but I waved him off. He and MacDonald then turned and continued around the house toward the cottages and their various tasks. I did not envy them at all.

Chapter VI
An Overheard Conversation

I tried the knob of the great door, and found it to be unlocked. Stepping into the large entry hall of the main house, I then pushed the door shut behind me to find a silence that seemed almost other-worldly after the tumult outside. I was shedding my wet coat and hat when the lad who had greeted us earlier rushed up and took my things, apologizing that he had not known I was there. I relieved him of any responsibility, and asked if it would be possible to get a hot drink, preferably with something tipped into it. He assured me that he would be back very shortly with what I requested, and – with a not-so-subtle glance at the water puddled inside the front door, marking the site of my entrance, he walked off into another part of the house, while I stepped into the sitting room where we had tarried earlier, before being called in for our late lunch.

I settled into a comfortable chair, after determining that my outer coat had kept my clothing dry enough so as not to damage the fine old piece of furniture, and pushed my feet toward the fire. It occurred to me that, just as I had heard how Briley had done so much for the village and the estate workers, he had also kept a very nice home for himself, even though he now got to see very little of it, staying in one room as he did, living as an invalid and to my knowledge refusing to venture elsewhere. The fire in this room had been going when we had arrived earlier, and it was still going even now. In some houses, it would have been tempting for the room to be closed off until needed, and doubtless it now often went unused. I did not have the impression that a great number of visitors made their way to Briley House.

While I was pondering these thoughts, the lad, whose name I recalled was Woods, brought me a tall – and of more importance – *hot* toddy. "I hope this will do the trick, sir," he said. With a sip, I nodded with satisfied agreement.

"Exactly what the doctor ordered," I said. He grinned, and asked if there would be anything else. I thanked him and said no, and he departed. I was glad that in a house run by such a martinet as Mrs. Lynch, there was still some happiness. Perhaps I was misjudging her. After all, the well-run house was a testimony to her management, and a woman who had been in charge as she had been for over fifty years was bound to get set in her ways. The reasons for her resentment against Burton were unclear, since he seemed a very capable and likeable individual, but it must be remembered that she had probably been running the house for over a quarter-century before he appeared on the scene, and doubtless she had disliked having her routine disturbed.

I shook my head and took a sip of the drink. It was useless to speculate on these matters. They had no bearing on the investigation, and I was sure that by tomorrow, Holmes and I would have returned to London. While the matter of the man with the missing finger, buried under the pipe and probably some relative of the Briley family, was certainly interesting, I did not know what Holmes's efforts could possibly reveal after so much time.

As I sat before the fire, with the sound of the rain lashing against the windows, I slowly fell again into the mood that had trailed me like a black dog throughout the early months of that year. I was nearly thirty-six years old, and what was I doing with myself? I had returned from Maiwand with my health irretrievably shattered, or so I had believed. Many were the times when I had questioned where I would have ended up if I had not been introduced to Holmes by Stamford, my old dresser, on that New Year's Day of 1881. I might have, when realizing that I could no longer afford London, moved myself to the country, where I could have set out my shingle and found a way to start using my skills once again. Or more likely, I would have remained in London, pitying my situation, spending more money than I had, and drinking more than I ought, until I ended up like so many other unfortunate veterans that found their way to that Great Cesspool that is London, never to escape.

But that New Year's Day, and specifically the short trip to the Criterion, and then on to the chemical lab at St. Bart's, had been a memorable day indeed, and it had certainly made great changes in my life. It was not the first link in my life by any means, but it was an important one, and a solid one. It had been the link to which the rest of my life was inextricably attached. It was a strong link upon which to forge the rest of the chain, and I didn't regret the chain that followed at all. And yet, why was I so unsettled these last months? It was not simply grief for my dear departed wife. I was questioning my future. Was this my purpose? To accompany Holmes on his quests, with no further thoughts toward the next direction that my own life was to take?

All in all, I was certain that, whatever doubts I might be having, the meeting with Holmes on that day had probably saved my life. Sharing rooms on my limited and dwindling finances had certainly rescued me from penury and disgrace. Being under his watchful eye had quickly helped to limit my consumption of alcohol, which I was relieved to discover had not become a vile and uncontrollable habit. And most important of all, joining in Holmes's cases had given my mind something to focus upon, while the simple act of physical participation in the investigations had been better therapy for my wounds than anything else that might have occurred to me by way of my medical training. All of the unexpected summonses from Holmes at whatever ungodly hours had never left me time to think *"I cannot do this."* I had simply been expected to rise from my comfortable fireside chair and assist my friend, and I had. Truly, I was in debt to him.

I took another sip of the excellent restorative as a log settled, and decided that I had no regrets about my time in Baker Street, and the events of my subsequent marriage. My time with Constance had been precious, if short. I had known that there was something terribly unfair about her illness, and how it kept us apart for great periods while she and her mother traveled and sought both relief and a cure. Even during those times, my friendship with Holmes had provided a distraction, as I often returned to Baker Street to assist him in his adventures. I'm afraid that my practice was neglected during this time, but in all honesty, my heart was simply not in building it up when Constance was not there to share it with me. And when she was gone, I had no interest in it at all. Once again, the old rooms at 221b were a refuge that I gladly sought.

So that early part of 1888 had been a time of questioning myself. I was nearing middle age. Was this all that I was supposed to be? I was an army veteran, no longer fit for army service. I was a doctor who had built and then let go of a practice. I was a widower. And I was the friend, assistant, advisor, and Boswell (at least in one short published narrative) of the man who was doing more to modernize the practices of criminal investigation than possibly anyone else in the world.

In spite of my doubts, and questions as to whether I should move on, reopen a practice, possibly find another wife with whom to share my life, I had to admit to myself that I actually enjoyed my involvement in Holmes's cases, in a way that I had never felt while in practice. It was akin to the rush that one felt when in combat, without the deadly boredom that comes in between skirmishes. Perhaps, I thought, this present sensation of being unsettled is how Holmes feels between cases, when his restlessness threatens to overcome him, and he likens himself to a machine, racing and tearing itself apart, because it is not fixed up properly to accomplish its intended work.

God help me, I realized that deep down I was even enjoying the matter that had called us out on that terrible day in Bedfordshire. I tried to imagine spending the same day at my old practice, seeing a dozen patients, each with the same symptoms as those of the day before. The rain would be sliding down the windows, and the hiss of the gaslight would go on and on, relentless in its efforts to lull me to sleep. And the next day would be a variation of the same. Was that really what I seemed to be wishing for?

Of course, I terribly missed Constance, but even she had understood how I would anticipate a summons from Holmes, much like the reaction of a war horse when it hears the trumpets and senses the return to battle. She had understood it, and she had never begrudged it.

I drank the final sip of my drink, now cool on my tongue, and set the glass aside. I had reasoned my way through the black mood to the point where I was happy to be where I was, at least for now. The mood would return again throughout that spring, but with less and less power over me. And thankfully, Holmes and I would stay busy, pushing the problem further from my mind as the year passed.

But all of that was in the future. For now, I was simply grateful that I had recalled to myself that Holmes and I were doing important work. The warm drink and warmer fire had no doubt done their part to ease my troubled mind as well. I sank lower into the chair, considerably more at ease than when I had first placed myself there.

Some time later, a crack of thunder coincided with what could only be hail hitting the windows, and I pulled myself upright, surprised to find that I had fallen asleep. Looking at my watch, I saw I had been dozing for less than thirty minutes, and there was still a little time before we were to meet in order to speak with Mr. Briley in his chamber.

Standing and stretching before the fire, I looked to see that my empty glass was gone. Woods must have taken it while I slept. I did not want to return to my seat, and having nothing else to occupy me until my companions returned, I decided to explore the house.

Stepping out into the hallway, I glanced to my right, toward the heavy front door. I saw the water that had come in with me and had ended up on the floor was now gone. Woods had obviously removed more than my glass while I slept.

I walked to the other side of the hall and looked into an open door. This was another room, decorated very much like the one I had just departed. It had a cheery fire going as well, but the room was darker. On the far side was another open door where much stronger light was showing. I crossed the darkened room and passed through into a smaller sitting room, with furniture of a style from several generations past, but in excellent condition. A mantel clock of great age made tired little whirring sounds as a counterpoint to the rain on the windows, and I realized that I had not heard any further thunder or hail.

The room seemed to be more of a museum piece than a place that was actually used on a daily basis. I was reminded of the similar room that Holmes and I had visited while confirming the last clue relating to the lost mine of the Duchy of Lancaster. We had been summoned to that lonely house by our friend, Alton Peake, the spiritualist. It was he, as might be remembered, who had called to Holmes's attention the footprints left by the supposed apparition, trailing to the forgotten priest's hole where the varnished palimpsest had been discovered. While I did not always agree with Peake's sincere belief in the supernatural, I must praise him for being rightly suspicious of so many of the charlatans that he exposed when they tried to pass off their mummery to a gullible public.

As I left that room, returning to the central hallway, but deeper into the house and across from the dining room where we had eaten earlier, I heard raised voices. Upon closer approach, they seemed to be coming from beyond the dining room. I passed in, and making my way around the large table, already set with four places for dinner later that evening, I stepped into a darkened hallway. It ran from the dining room into a butler's pantry. The door to the pantry was partly shut, but I could clearly hear the angry and clipped tones of Mrs. Lynch and George Burton.

"It is really none of your business at all!" said Burton vehemently.

"It would not normally concern me," she replied, "except that the person in question is one of my maids, and I cannot – I *will not* – have anything like that going on my house!"

"Your house?" said Burton with incredulity. "I was under the impression that it was Mr. Briley's house. In each of the many ways he has taken me into his confidence, there has never been any mention in any of them that this was *your* house."

"I have run this house for longer than you can imagine, boy," said Mrs. Lynch with a menacing tone. "Nothing happens here without my knowledge or say so. Mr. Briley can do whatever he wants outside these walls. He can waste his money on that rabble in the village. He can build all the cottages he wants to shelter the workers. But what happens in this house is under *my* say-so. Mr. Briley understands that. He has understood it from the day he inherited it, and if you ask him, he will tell you so himself. You may have too much of your mother's blood in you to understand what you've seen in front of you from the day you got here, but I'm telling you as clearly as I can, this is *my* house, and if I intend to let a maid go for the good of running the place, I will!"

Burton was almost too angry to speak for a moment, and then he pulled himself in and replied in a very dangerous tone indeed. "You will never again speak of my mother, you evil crone. And as far as sending Lydia away, I can tell you it will do you no good at all. In fact, it will be a useful thing, in that my plans will simply be advanced. Lydia and I intend to marry, and if she is forced to leave, then we will simply marry all the sooner!"

392

"Marry! You would marry a *servant*, after you have been taken in by Mr. Briley and made his trusted ward? He won't stand for it. He would want you to marry someone of quality. Not a common – "

"Don't say it!" warned Burton. "Don't even say it, Mrs. Lynch, or I swear I'll have you out of here. You may have been here since you were a girl, and you seem to think that you will continue to stay here because you plan to live forever, but if you get in the way of my plans, I will see that you are put out of here immediately!"

"You wouldn't *dare!*" hissed Mrs. Lynch. "You don't even know what circumstances you're dealing with, boy. You should be grateful for the opportunity you have, and stop trying to rise above yourself before it is time."

"I can see that you fear what I've said, Mrs. Lynch. You know Mr. Briley will listen to me. Now I tell you, I could not care less if you continue to run this house the way you see fit until your last breath leaves your cruel body, no matter how much you seem to believe that will never happen. You do a good job here, and in spite of your sour disposition, the staff is actually content with you. I will put it to you simply: If you do not meddle in my affairs, then I will have no reason to conclude that you are my enemy, in spite of the way you have treated me since I came here as a boy. Now, I intend to marry Lydia, and if it needs to be sooner rather than later, so be it. So, tell me, Mrs. Lynch. Do we have an accord?"

From my hidden vantage point, I could not see either Burton or Mrs. Lynch, so I couldn't tell whether she nodded or rejected his question, but she gave no verbal indication either way to Burton's ultimatum. However, before any further conversation could continue, I heard the sound of the front door slamming. Quickly, before I could be discovered at my listening post, I eased backwards into the darkened hall and out through the dining room, where I spied my friends shedding their wet outer garments. Woods passed me from a different doorway at the back of the hall, coming from deeper within the house, going to their aid. In moments, Holmes, MacDonald, and I were all back in the sitting room, and Woods had gone to find hot drinks for the wet and weary men. I had indicated to Woods that I would like something else to drink as well. He had nodded as he departed, carrying the wet coats of my friends with him.

Before I knew it, Holmes had slipped past me, following Woods to the back of the house. MacDonald and I simply looked at one another for a moment or so before we heard footsteps returning. It was Holmes, briskly rubbing his hands together.

"Forgive me," he said. "It is a little habit of mine to identify the exits of whatever building I find myself in."

MacDonald nodded knowingly. "You never do a thing without a reason, I'm thinking," he said.

Holmes simply made the beginning of a grin, and then led us toward the chairs facing the fireplace. I had started to ask him what he had learned in the village, but he obviously saw the direction of my questions and warned me with a look not to broach that subject at present. I could tell, as only someone who knew Holmes well would be able, that he had discovered something of importance that added to his satisfaction, but he did not want to share it with the Inspector. I wondered what it could be, that Holmes would wish to exclude our friend. MacDonald, facing the fire with great contentment, did not see our exchange and was not aware what he had missed. He took the chair which I had occupied during my short nap, adjusted it closer to the warming blaze, and settled in with a sigh as his long legs stretched toward the restorative flames.

Soon Woods returned, distributing glasses all around. Holmes and MacDonald were each describing where they had been when the particularly nasty portion of the storm had passed overhead. Holmes had been walking back through the village, and had taken shelter in a convenient doorway when the hail came. MacDonald had been starting up from the cottages, and had actually seen the lightning strike that had been heralded by the thunder that had awakened me.

At that moment, Burton entered from the hallway, smiling and showing no signs of his recent conversation with Mrs. Lynch. "You actually saw the strike, Inspector?

"That's right," MacDonald replied. "It struck a large elm, standing very near the stone bridge that crosses the stream before one comes to the cottages."

"Did it have a bench underneath it?"

MacDonald nodded. "I did see a bench in the flash of light, before I was temporarily blinded."

"Then it's unfortunate indeed that the old elm of which you speak was the one that was hit. It was one of several English elms planted by Mr. Briley when he first inherited the estate. He always referred to it as a memoriam, I assume for his father. Many is the time Mr. Briley has sat on that bench at sunset, looking out over the cottages and the estate beyond. And I sat with him there numerous times as well while growing up."

"Well, I'm afraid it's done for," said MacDonald, rather heartlessly in my opinion, as he appeared not to notice Burton's sadness. "There were parts of the main trunk that looked like the sap within fair boiled and exploded!" MacDonald became caught up in his description as he relived the experience, the remembered sight vivid before his eyes. "Great chunks

394

blew out and fell to the ground, flames licking around them until the rains put them out. I've never seen anything like it!"

He finished and looked at each of us, as if expecting further comments, or perhaps a question. However, each of us was seeing it in our minds as well, and Burton sadly gave a short unconscious shake of his head. Finally, Holmes said quietly, *"Tempus fugit, mors venit."*

After another moment of reflection, Burton shook off his gloom and stated, "I came to let you know that Mr. Briley is awake, and will see us now."

"Excellent," said Holmes, setting aside his nearly untouched drink. MacDonald tipped his up, while mine, smaller than the one I'd had an hour or so earlier, was already gone.

We stepped across the hall, and moved toward the back of the house, passing through a doorway which I had not explored earlier. Turning right, we went along the base of the *U*-shaped building, and into a room where one of the wings turned toward the front. Knocking on the heavy door, Burton then opened it without waiting for a response and led us in to face the hostile glare of Mrs. Lynch, and the curious look from the old man sitting beside her.

Chapter VII
Interview With The Invalid

It was a corner room, square and stretching approximately forty feet in each direction. The ceiling was higher than rooms that I had seen in the rest of the house, and the walls had a cream-colored fabric on them, looking more yellow in the gaslight than they would have on a sunny day. I could see that daylight would make the room quite cheerful indeed, with windows spaced evenly on the outside walls. Between two of the windows was a full-length glass door, covered with a curtain, and leading outside.

To our right as we entered was a large desk, with neat stacks of papers on top. Comfortable furniture was placed in several locations around the room, resting on the unusual carpet, which was predominantly red, with yellow flower patterns and limbs crisscrossing it. It also had various sigil-looking designs concealed within the larger figures, and there were very randomly placed blue patterns which, to my eye, looked vaguely piscatorial.

Two of the four walls had a number of extravagantly built bookshelves, containing hundreds of volumes of various sizes and colors. I was curious as to what sort of titles a man such as Mr. Briley enjoyed.

A molding ran around the wall at the ceiling, from which suspended wires supported paintings of various sizes and shapes. One showed three men, standing on a dock and dressed in vaguely biblical-looking red cloaks, either pointing in accusation or offering a benevolent hand (I was not sure which) toward a man lying on the ground, while a crowd looked on as the background faded into mountains and clouds. Another couple of paintings, of similar style and color, showed large buildings against a bleak sky, with minute people carrying out their business in the foreground. A sizeable painting, in an apparent place of honor to the right of the fireplace, showed a middle-aged man staring out at the viewer, his figure centered and pictured from mid-torso. He had the high collar and coat of nearly a century earlier, and side-whiskers of a different and lighter shade than the thick hair on his head. His face was clean shaven, and his clothing was an odd greenish shade, matching the right side of the background, which faded to black on the left.

The most curious thing about the painting, aside from the stern and commanding look in the subject's eyes, was the right hand. The painter had captured the man in a three-quarter pose, partially turned to his left. Although the eyes stared straight out, the head itself was turned so that the right side was more exposed. This stance allowed for the man's right hand, resting on the back of a chair, to be in full view, thus exposing the characteristic missing little finger of the Brileys.

My attention was drawn back to the two individuals waiting for us as we entered the room, but not before I saw that something about the painting had captured Holmes's special interest.

Near the fireplace, in the unique bath chair which had been mentioned by MacDonald earlier, was Mr. Martin Briley himself, and I was saddened to see the condition in which we found him. He had obviously been a man of some strength once, in spite of Burton's earlier statement that he was not a large man. He still had a frame that appeared to have some width to his shoulders. However, an exact analysis of his build was not possible, as he was completely covered by several decorative blankets, except for his head. His white hair was thinning, and the skin around his eyes was red and puffy. Although he seemed to be quite enfeebled, he did not show signs of actual illness. And yet, there was the sense that he was not long for this world, and it wasn't just my medical training that caused me to have that feeling.

Standing beside him, as if she were Cerberus, was Mrs. Lynch, a scowl on her already stern face.

"Mr. Briley can see you for five minutes," she said in a clipped tone, brooking no disagreement. Holmes flicked a glance at her, and then dismissed her as he stepped forward into Briley's immediate view.

"Mr. Briley, my name is Sherlock Holmes. This is my friend, Dr. Watson, and I understand that you spoke to Inspector MacDonald yesterday."

Briley nodded. "I've heard much about you, sir," he said, his voice stronger than one would expect. "I would have enjoyed meeting you under different circumstances."

"As would I," replied Holmes. "I've heard a great deal about you, as well as the good works you have done over the years in this community."

"Ah, Mr. Holmes, I was simply carrying out my responsibilities. Paying a debt, if you will."

"A debt," Holmes asked. "A debt to whom?"

Mrs. Lynch's brow contracted into an irate set of lines as she glanced down at Briley, but he ignored her. "It isn't important, now, Mr. Holmes," he replied. "Suffice it to say, in my youth I contracted a quantity of debt, and I have been paying it down since then. As you can see, I don't have much longer to wait for what's coming to me, and anything that I've been able to accomplish since taking over the estate has nearly come to an end. At least for me. George here," he said, nodding his head at Burton, "will be left to carry on."

"Mr. Briley," said George, with honest worry in his face, "don't talk like that! You're just going through a rough patch, sir! You'll be back up to scratch in no time!"

Briley smiled and shook his head. "I don't think so, George. But not to worry, my boy. You've always had my full confidence. You'll do what's right."

Burton turned away for a moment, leaving an awkward silence. Mrs. Lynch took that opportunity to lean over and adjust the blankets at Briley's covered shoulders.

Holmes used the pause to walk over to the painting that had previously caught his interest and study it closer. He leaned in, reading the small brass plate affixed to the bottom of the frame. "Galton Briley?" he said, looking back over his shoulder toward Mr. Briley.

"That's right," said Briley. "Painted in about 1810, when he was in his early forties."

"So this was painted a generation before you inherited the estate?"

"Yes. I was born in 1820, and he died in 1840."

"And this is a Devis?" asked Holmes, looking back up at the painting, appearing to pay special attention to the stern gaze from the figure's eyes.

"Yes, Arthur William Devis. I believe he came down from London to paint it. It's one of his lesser known works."

Holmes looked around the room, and then turned back to Briley. "Did you never have your own portrait made?" he asked.

"Never, Mr. Holmes. I've really had no interest in memorializing myself."

"But surely you would have wanted to have your picture hanging with that of your ancestor?"

Briley closed his eyes and shook his head slightly, almost without awareness. "No, Mr. Holmes. I . . . did not feel a true connection with the elder Mr. Briley. He was already in his early fifties when I was born. My mother died when I was young. Later, when I was a young man, I did not agree with some of the harsh policies he used when running the estate. When I became the master here, I worked to correct many of the things I found objectionable. I suppose that I have spent my life doing that, in this little corner of the world."

"You should not speak of such things," said Mrs. Lynch. Briley simply closed his eyes and ignored her, while Burton looked angry that she should forget her place and offer an opinion. I was interested to observe the interactions between old Mr. Briley and the housekeeper, each having lived in this house for fifty-odd years. I wondered at how tangled and knotted their relationship had become over that half-century.

398

Holmes walked further around the room, moving over to the outside door and attempting to look out into the darkness. He pulled aside a curtain which hung over the glass door and leaned in for a moment before letting the curtain fall back. He continued along the window to the wall, easing through the narrow space behind Mr. Briley's chair and on around to the nearby shelves.

"I observe that you enjoy the works of Charles Dickens," he said, gesturing toward a set of green leather-bound volumes at eye level. "Most of the other shelves have a thin layer of dust, both on the volumes themselves and also on the thin exposed portion of the shelf in front of the books. However, these books show signs that they are actually used on a regular basis."

Briley smiled and nodded. "You are correct, Mr. Holmes. Long ago, I read most of the books you see around us. But as the years have gone on, I found that I kept returning to my favorite volumes, as if they were visits with old friends. I had first encountered the works of Mr. Dickens when I moved up to London for a few years, in the late 1830's. He was just beginning to write, and even then he was all the rage.

"I have always regretted that I wasn't there when *The Pickwick Papers* first appeared. I would have dearly loved to have been a part of the enthusiasm from the start. But I was there as its popularity grew, and I lined up with all the rest of them to get each new issue as it was published.

"During the time I lived there in London, it seemed that I encountered many people that were exactly like the characters in Dickens' books. Many years later, I was actually able to invite him down here for a visit."

"Dickens was here?" I interrupted. As someone who also enjoyed the works of one of the nation's finest storytellers, I was interested to think that I had been in some of the same rooms where he had visited.

Briley nodded. "I think he was interested in hearing about the conditions here on the estate, and what I was trying to accomplish for the people who lived and worked here. But all that I wanted to do was talk about one of his recent books that had meant so much to me. I wish that George could have met him, but it was just a few years before he moved into the house with us."

Holmes appeared to be deep in thought for just a moment, before asking, "Would that book that meant so much to you have been *Great Expectations,* perchance?"

Briley looked surprised, but answered, "Why, yes, Mr. Holmes. But how did you know?"

"Earlier today, Mr. Burton told us a short *précis* of the events leading to his move to this house, in 1864. If Mr. Dickens visited here just a few years before that time, and you discussed one of his recent books, then most likely it was *Great Expectations*, considered one of his more notable works, and published in 1860 through 1861. His next novel, *Our Mutual Friend*, appeared from 1864 to 1865, around the time that Mr. Burton would have come to live here. Clearly, that book appeared too late to be the one in question, and incidentally it was not nearly so well regarded."

"I am impressed, Mr. Holmes. You live up to your reputation. But then, after reading Dr. Watson's account last year, I expected nothing less from you."

Holmes raised his eyebrows. "You have read that – that is to say, you've read that publication?" he said, with slight distaste. He seemed taken aback, as the experience of meeting readers of my chronicles of his investigations was still a very new thing to him at that time.

"Why, yes," said Briley. "While I mainly read the works of Dickens for personal enjoyment, I still do try to stay current as well." He turned his head to me. "I enjoyed the story immensely, doctor. If you wouldn't mind, could I trouble you to autograph my copy?" He nodded his head toward a shelf behind me. "If you look on the third shelf up, near that set of the works of Poe, you will see it there."

I turned and walked to the specified shelf. The small volume was there, as he had said. I noticed that while most of the shelf was covered in the thin layer of dust previously mentioned by Holmes, a half-inch or so of width in front of the book in question was wiped away. Someone had already pulled this book out, and recently.

I removed the journal, last December's *Beeton's Christmas Annual*, and held it in my hand. While it contained a number of other stories as well, I noted that it fell open to the first page of my own small work published within, *A Study in Scarlet*. Stepping to the nearby desk, I leaned forward and wrote, "With Best Wishes, Dr. John H. Watson." Then, I stepped to the man's bath chair and held it toward him, pages open to show my signature.

He made no effort to extricate a hand from underneath the heavy blankets, instead craning his head forward in an attempt to better see the small volume. I leaned in so that he could read the inscription. He looked at it for a moment, and then smiled and nodded. Taking that as an indication that he was through with it, I replaced it on the shelf.

"Of course," Holmes said, "there was another indication that *Great Expectations* holds some special interest for you. Earlier, during a discussion of the good work you have done here, Mr. Burton had occasion to mention Magwitch, the doomed convict from the story. He then paused for just a moment, as if the thought had some additional remembrance or significance, or had caused him to perhaps make an association. Can you think of any reason why that might have been, Mr. Briley?"

Briley's face lost its pleasant expression for a fleeting instant, and he looked over at Burton. Standing to the side, Burton had a look of puzzled embarrassment. "As I recall," he said, "the subject of Dickens was mentioned obliquely, when the Inspector said that *my life* was like something out of a Dickens story. I said that Mr. Briley was nothing like Magwitch the convict, who funded poor Pip's rise in the world to the position of young gentleman. There was nothing more to it than that.

"Ah, well," said Holmes, "I now recall that it happened exactly the way that you said. I apologize if I've caused any confusion." He paused, and added, "Or discomfort." Holmes took another step or two, looking around the room before saying, "You have done very well for yourself here, Mr. Briley. I believe that if you did feel that you had some 'quantity of debt,' as you say, to repay, then you have accomplished what you set out to do with your life. You are spoken of very highly indeed."

"I don't care what anyone thinks of me," said Briley, looking up at Holmes with an odd expression. His tone had suddenly grown slightly surly, and his good-natured mood of a moment or two earlier seemed to have evaporated. "Surely, Mr. Holmes, you haven't waited to speak to me simply to express your opinion about the way I've managed the estate over the years. Do you not have questions about the poor fellow that was found under the pipe?"

"No, none at all," replied Holmes. "I believe that much of the matter is already clear to me." Suddenly, Holmes pivoted so that he was directly facing Briley. Taking a step toward him, he said, "However, I would like to ask, if I might be so bold, if I might shake your hand."

Briley's eyes opened wider, and he looked up at Holmes in surprise. Holmes thrust out his right hand over Briley's blanketed figure and held it there expectantly. After a long moment with no response, Briley's gaze dropped, and he shook his head.

"I'm sorry, Mr. Holmes, but I cannot."

Mrs. Lynch stepped forward, almost protectively. "In Mr. Briley's condition, he cannot be exposed to anything which might compromise his teetering health."

Briley raised his eyes toward Holmes for just an instant, and then dropped them again. "I'm sure that you will understand."

"Come, Mr. Briley," said Holmes, without acknowledging Mrs. Lynch's contribution. "You are a man well known and respected for all the good works that you have done. Certainly you can have no objection to shaking my hand. After all, our opportunities for doing so are dwindling."

Briley did not raise his head. "Please show them out, Mrs. Lynch," he murmured quietly.

401

"Certainly," she said, with pursed lips. "Gentlemen? This way."

Holmes dropped his hand. "Well, then, perhaps another time." He turned toward the door. MacDonald and I shared a glance, and I could see that MacDonald was slightly irritated with Holmes's behavior.

Burton, with a puzzled look, said, "Mr. Briley?" but Briley simply shook his head, closed his eyes, and seemed to be settling in for another nap. Burton stood for a short moment, and then turned to join us in the hall. Mrs. Lynch followed us out and pulled the door firmly shut behind her.

"Dinner will be served in just a few moments," she said. "We rarely have guests anymore, and I hope everything will be satisfactory." Her tone belied any graciousness that might have been in her words. She turned toward the rear of the house and left us standing there. As soon as she was gone, MacDonald spoke.

"I don't understand, Mr. Holmes," he said, his voice soft and his burr noticeably stronger. "I realize this is not the kind of case you usually consult upon, for Lestrade or some of the others, with a fresh corpse or life-and-death circumstances, but I thought it would be right up your alley. A body mysteriously murdered and buried before we were even born, with every indication that it is connected somehow to the family on whose estate it was found. That is just the kind of *outré* circumstance you are always telling me that you crave. And yet, when you get the chance to ask questions of the head of the household, who is old enough to have been around back when the murder was committed, who might have . . . might have . . . . " He lowered his voice even further, and said, "Forgive me Mr. Burton, but might have been *involved* in the murder, and you don't ask him *anything* of importance? Well, Mr. Holmes, I have to admit you've stumped me, and that's a fact."

Burton glared silently at MacDonald, while Holmes looked at him with a smile, and then to me. "And you, Watson? Are you 'stumped' as well?"

I considered my response for less than a heartbeat. "I *know* that this is exactly the type of investigation that you seek, Holmes. I have no question as to how you're handling things."

MacDonald quickly moved to make amends. "Well, I have no questions, as far as that goes. I have complete faith in you, Mr. Holmes. I don't think you would have come down here in this storm if you didn't want to follow up on this matter. And yet, I have to wonder at this missed opportunity."

"Perhaps it is a missed opportunity at that," replied Holmes. "We can't always play each hand with perfection, can we? If we did that, then where would be the challenge?"

402

MacDonald then had a new thought. "Perhaps you intend to question Mrs. Lynch, then? She's been around here fully as long as the old man. She can tell us a thing or two, I'll wager, and no mistaking it!"

Holmes shook his head. "Not yet. If the matter is still unclear, then we will speak to her about it tomorrow."

At that point, the gong was sounded, and Holmes turned toward the dining room. MacDonald and Burton shared a glance, and then both turned questioningly toward me. I raised an eyebrow in return, but could offer them no comfort. With that, Burton led us into the dining room.

Chapter VIII
A Quiet Dinner

The rain and wind outside should have given a cozy feeling to the meal, but instead, it simply seemed to add to the oppressiveness of the occasion. The food was served by the same girl who had brought our lunch. I now believed her to be Lydia, whom I had overheard being discussed by Burton and Mrs. Lynch. I looked to see if any communications passed between her and Burton, but she was quite subdued throughout the course of the meal.

The food was simple, but tasty and filling, and perfect for such a rainy night. It consisted of a hearty soup, followed by a joint of beef and roasted root vegetables. I certainly had no complaints, although I had been somewhat uneasy as to what Mrs. Lynch would provide, based on her attitude toward us all, and also because she had stated that the Shepherd's Pie from earlier in the day had been planned for the evening meal, implying that providing something for later would be a difficulty. I had been initially surprised that a residence the size of Briley House was able to function with such a small number of servants, all filling unexpected roles, but the place appeared to be run quite well. It was a testament to Mrs. Lynch, in spite of her noxious personality.

For the most part, the meal was quiet, with each of the four of us pondering our own thoughts. Burton informed us that the expectant mother had been successfully moved to the small village hospital. MacDonald tried to start a conversation, telling Burton about a case in which the three of us had been involved during the past January. It had begun on the morning after Holmes's birthday, and he had awakened in a contentious mood. Holmes normally did not acknowledge birthdays, and certainly did not celebrate them. However, he and Mrs. Hudson had conspired to try to make things a little more festive that year, in order to help me heal from the passing of Constance, little more than a week earlier. Never one for giving much weight to customs such as mourning, Holmes had tried to give me a reason to forget my sad circumstances, if only for one evening. As a result, we had both imbibed a little too much, alternating between periods of humor and morose reflection. It was after those events that MacDonald found us the next morning, to summon us to the site of a particularly grim murder.

MacDonald gamely tried to tell the story, revealing Holmes's amazing deductions regarding the coded message that Holmes had initially received from Professor Moriarty's informer, and the later significance of a missing dumbbell. However, MacDonald's narrative sputtered and died when he was trying to describe the significance of the corpse's condition, and its missing head, having been removed by a blast from a sawed-off American shot-gun. Realizing that this was a poor story for dinner, especially as he was telling this particular part while Lydia was serving dessert, he stopped altogether and simply focused on eating. I thought I saw a small smile twitch at the corner of Holmes's mouth, as he has always found humor in completely inappropriate circumstances, but I cannot be sure.

Finally, the mostly uncomfortable but perfectly edible meal came to a close, and we leaned back. Drinks were passed around for those that wanted them, and Holmes and MacDonald pulled out their pipes, with Burton's permission. MacDonald, now willing to speak again, said, "Tell us, Mr. Holmes, what did you learn when you stayed at the inn?"

Holmes pulled the pipe out of his mouth, and turned it to stare into the bowl. Satisfied that the leaf was evenly lit and burning well, he returned it and said, "We can be sure that, except for the perceptive Mr. Creed, no one else knows about the most interesting aspect of the discovered body, its missing finger, and thus the apparent connection to the Briley family. While others in the village are aware of the seeming age of the body, based on the clothing and the fact that it was found underneath the old pipe, they do not suspect anything else. And as I said, I am confident that Mr. Creed will not reveal what he knows."

"Well, that's a relief," said Burton. "I would hate to have any scandal attach itself to Mr. Briley. In his condition, he does not need to go through something of that sort. And in spite of the Inspector's comment," he added, glancing at MacDonald, "I cannot believe that he knows anything about this. He is too good of a man for that."

"I've heard nothing but confirmation today about what a boon he has been to this community," said Holmes. "Everyone feels lucky that he made the effort to be such a good steward over the years. One of the men I spoke to after you all left was the old man by the fireplace, Abner. He affirmed all of the good work Mr. Briley has done."

"Yes, old Abner Nelson," said Burton. "He's one of our local treasures, is Abner. Many was the time when I was a boy that he would make the effort to speak with me, or explain something I did not know. And this was both before and after I came to live with Mr. Briley. It made no difference to Abner. He was always willing to take an extra minute or two. I think a lot of him, and that's the truth."

Holmes nodded, and then said, "After I left the inn, I made my way to the doctor's office. He was kind enough to summon Constable

405

Timmons. I was able to determine to my own satisfaction that both of those men had nothing further to add, and in addition, they too will not reveal the connection of the body to the Briley family."

"I'm glad that the word hasn't gotten out about a possible family relation," said MacDonald.

"Yes, about that," said Holmes, shifting in his seat, and pulling himself a little straighter. He laid his pipe on the table and crossed his fingers on the cloth. "I would still like to be more certain in my mind about whether there is any possible family connection between the body and the Brileys. The missing finger seems an obvious link, but we can't get around the fact that there are no known legitimate or illegitimate heirs from either Mr. Briley's generation or that of his father, both men being only children. That's why I fear, Mr. Mac, that I'm going to need for you to run up to London and find the answer to these questions." He unlaced his fingers and reached into his coat, pulling out a folded set of small sheets, which I could see were covered with his fine, exact handwriting.

"Up to London, Mr. Holmes?" said MacDonald, his pipe clenched in his teeth, the end bobbing with each word. "When? Tonight? In this storm? Surely not!" There was a small throb of dismay in his voice.

"Yes, I'm afraid so. You just have time to make the last train. It is fortunate that you were able to eat before you have to leave." He handed the sheets to MacDonald, who took them and started to shuffle through each one, quickly reading the contents. "There are a series of specific questions to use when examining Briley's family connections, and who his blood kin might be, no matter how distant.

"I'll need you to go to Somerset House," continued Holmes. "You should be able to find someone to let you in, although it will be after hours, and then you can speak to a man named Dean, who is in some debt to me. He will be able to help you research the questions that I have. He has access to a number of records that, although not official, still provide a great deal of relevant information about unrecorded and less-than-legitimate family members." Picking up his pipe again, Holmes added, "Of course, you will be too late to return tonight, but we'll expect to see you in the morning."

"But . . . tonight, Mr. Holmes? In this storm?" asked MacDonald with a look of near-horror on his face. Truly, it was almost comical. When Holmes simply gave a sympathetic nod, MacDonald sighed and reached for the whisky bottle on the table. "Then at least," he said, "tell me you see a glimmer of light in this darkness."

Holmes smiled. "I do, Inspector, I do. There are some aspects that still need to be verified, but I believe that I have the correct thread in my grasp."

MacDonald nodded, and rubbed his large hand across his chin. "Any hints, then?" he asked.

Holmes thought for a moment. "As I have said," he then replied, "there is nothing new under the sun. This affair reminds me of a case that was rather similar, a matter that occurred in Nimes, thirty or so years ago."

"Quite before our time, then," said MacDonald, tipping up his glass for the last of his postprandial whisky. With a small cough, he set it back on the table, pushed back his chair, and stood. "Then I'd best be about it." As we stood as well, he waved us back, saying that there was no need to see him off, and that he knew the way to the door. With a resigned glimmer of humor in his eye, he added, "If you hadn't already had that list of questions prepared, Mr. Holmes, I might almost believe you were sending me on a wild goose chase as punishment for seeming to doubt you earlier."

Holmes smiled. "I assure you, Inspector, that the answers to those questions will have the utmost bearing on my final explanation of the case."

"Good enough, then, Mr. Holmes," said MacDonald, turning to go. In a moment, we heard the sounds of MacDonald summoning his coat and hat. Then, the front door slammed and he was gone.

We remained standing, as Burton explained that he must leave us as well. "I'm going to spend the night down at the cottages, in case there are any problems associated with the flooding. I've arranged for your rooms to be fully prepared by Mrs. Lynch. Is there anything else that I can do for you before I depart?"

"As a matter of fact," said Holmes, "do you happen to have a map or drawing of the layout of the estate? I'm interested in seeing a rather complete one, if it exists. Some of the features about the place that were described to me by the locals sound rather interesting, and I thought that I might while away part of the evening studying it, if possible."

"Certainly, Mr. Holmes," said Burton. He seemed puzzled, but by this time he was certainly learning that Holmes did not say or ask anything without a reason. Within just a moment, he had returned with the map. I could see that it was simply a well-handled sketch, with various locations around the estate generally labeled in the simplest terms. It was certainly not a document of any great antiquity.

(Later, after the events of that terrible night, I was able to make a copy of Burton's map, which is appended to this manuscript. – J.H.W.)

Holmes glanced at the drawing for a moment, and then folded it along the creases that already cut through the page. He placed it in a pocket, and then stood in silence for just a moment, his arms folded, and one hand raised to his chin, a finger tapping on his lips. Burton, not quite certain

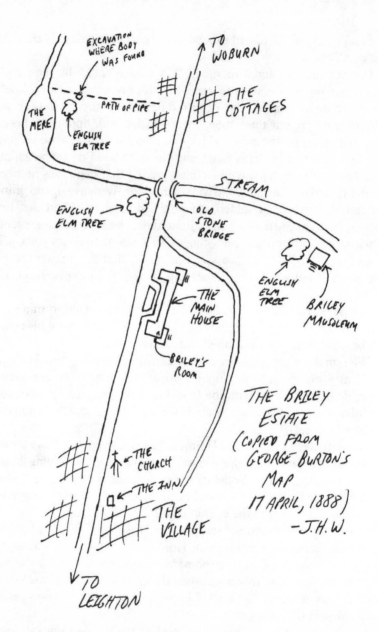

THE BRILEY
ESTATE
(COPIED FROM
GEORGE BURTON'S
MAP
17 APRIL, 1888)
—J.H.W.

what to think, glanced at me helplessly. I simply shook my head, a response that conveyed nothing at all.

Finally, Holmes seemed to come to a decision. "Mr. Burton, if I might have a word," he said. "Will you excuse us, Watson?"

I did not take any umbrage at my dismissal. I knew that Holmes, while often ignorant of some of the nuances of common social interaction, meant

408

no offense, and that if he felt the need for an action, there was a good reason for it. I made my way into the front sitting room, where I went to stand beside the fire.

Holmes and Burton talked for only five minutes or less before rejoining me. Burton seemed to be in a rather more tense state than he had been when I had last seen him. He stated again that he needed to go to the cottages, and apologized for leaving us so early. Then, with an anxious glance toward the back of the house, and good wishes all around, he departed for the night.

Holmes pulled the map back out from his pocket and glanced at it for just a moment, before appearing to see what he was looking for. Then, ringing the bell, he said, "Would you care to join me for a while as we smoke and discuss some things, Watson?" "Certainly," I replied, hoping that he would soon tell me the rest of the reasons why he had sent MacDonald to London.

Woods came in, and Holmes requested that we be shown to our rooms, as we were probably going to turn in. I was surprised, since it was still early. As we started to pass into the rear of the house, we encountered Mrs Lynch, standing like a guardian before the wing leading to Briley's room.

"Mr. Briley has gone to bed for the evening," she stated. "You won't be able to speak to him any further tonight."

Holmes smiled in his most charming manner and replied, "Not to worry, Mrs. Lynch. I can assure you that we will not be speaking any further to Mr. Briley during our stay, either tonight or at any other time."

Mrs. Lynch almost concealed her surprise, but not quite. She was speechless for just long enough to show that Holmes's statement had caught her off guard. No doubt she had been prepared to put up a strong argument in defense of Briley's time and health. I must admit that I, too, was not expecting to hear that we would have no further contact with the elderly invalid. Perhaps Holmes had learned enough already to explain who the mysterious dead man actually was, without further taxing the strength of the reclusive estate owner.

"Dr. Watson and I intend to turn in for the night," said Holmes, continuing as if Mrs. Lynch's awkward moment of silence had passed unnoticed. "The Inspector has returned to London, and tonight is definitely one that should be spent indoors, as I'm sure you will agree."

He cocked his head, drawing our attention to the shrieking storm, lashing rain into the nearby windows.

"Thank you again for your hospitality, Mrs. Lynch," added Holmes. "Being allowed to stay here in the house has aided our investigation substantially."

"I did not – " began Mrs. Lynch, and then she stopped herself, before beginning again. "That is to say, it was Mr. Burton's idea that you stay here instead of down to the inn. However, as you have indicated that you have no further need to disturb Mr. Briley, I do not see any objections."

"No need at all," replied Holmes agreeably.

Mrs. Lynch nodded, her lips tight with dislike for both of us. Holmes's charm obviously counted for naught with her, but that was no surprise at all. "Then I'll wish you both good night," she said, and turned back into the wing containing Mr. Briley's room without another word.

Woods led us back into the house, but instead of turning right toward Briley's corner room, we turned left where we immediately found a wide staircase. Going up, we were led into the left wing of the house, where Woods opened a door to a sitting room, joined on either side by two bedrooms, one for each of us. He asked if there was anything else that was required.

"I'm just curious," said Holmes. "Where do the other occupants of the house sleep?"

"There are very few other occupants at present," replied Woods. I had noticed that he had a certain forwardness about him that did not seem intimidated at all by either being in the presence of strangers, or the formality supposedly required by his position. "Mr. Burton sleeps in this wing, just down the hall. Mrs. Lynch has a corner room in the south wing, directly upstairs over Mr. Briley's room. The rest of the servants are either in the basement or near the kitchen."

"So Mrs. Lynch does not sleep with the servants?" said Holmes.

"No, sir. She's more like the lady of the house than a servant." Woods made this statement with the faintest hint of judgment. Holmes did not let it pass.

"Aren't you taking something of a chance, saying such things to total strangers? After all, you work under the direction of Mrs. Lynch. It would probably not be wise to get on her bad side."

"I'm not afraid," said Woods. "Mr. Burton knows how she is, and if she tried to get back at me, he would make sure that I still had a job in the village, even if she did get me moved out of the house. We've all seen how she tries to treat him, and how he stands up to her. She's been that way for years. Everyone around here knows just how far her power goes.

"And in any case," he added, "she can't live forever, and when my sister is the lady of the house, I'll be helping to run the estate myself, I expect, and then whatever Mrs. Lynch thinks won't matter at all."

"Your sister?" asked Holmes, but I interrupted.

"Of course, I should have seen it," I said. "Your sister – "

" – is the girl that has served our meals," finished Holmes. "I noticed the resemblance immediately, as I'm sure did Dr. Watson."

I had not. "Her name is Lydia," I added. "George Burton intends to marry her."

Holmes looked at me with amused surprise. "Clearly, we each have items to report to one another." Turning to Woods, he said, "That will be all, I think. And Woods?"

Woods, who had been reaching for the door, turned. "While your situation may seem protected at present, it would probably still be wise to avoid running afoul of Mrs. Lynch. I can assure you that it would not be wise to cross her."

Woods looked back in silence as these words sank in. Then, with a nod, he turned and left the room.

Holmes turned to me and said, "Let us sit and smoke for a while, Watson. We have time to discuss some things, before our investigation resumes."

Chapter IX
The Calm During The Storm

Holmes gestured toward the two armchairs located near the fire. I knew that he wished to use me as his sounding board, as he had so often in the past. By discussing the case with me, he would be able to arrange his thoughts in such a way as to order them from start to finish. Occasionally, I might ask a question which would reveal to him an aspect of the matter that might not have previously been considered.

After the travels of the day, the tramps through the rain, and the recent meal in the warm room downstairs, I wished that I was going to be dozing in front of the fire instead of discussing the case. Clearly, however, Holmes had something else planned for the night, and now was not the time to rest. We settled in, one on each side of the fire, mirroring our usual arrangement in the Baker Street sitting room. After taking time to prepare our pipes, we were at last ready to speak.

"I take it," said Holmes, "that you have gained some knowledge of Burton's plans for his future. I had noticed you were watching both him and the serving girl at dinner more closely than I would have expected, and certainly with more attention than you showed them during lunch."

I proceeded to relate the conversation that I had overheard before Holmes and MacDonald had arrived back at the house. In times past, I would have felt some hesitance and reluctance about eavesdropping as I had, as well as unhesitatingly reporting on what I had heard. However, I had long ago found that all was fair when conducting an inquiry with Holmes, and I also knew one might not realize which particular fact would be the key that would unlock the door, thus allowing Holmes to complete his case. Therefore, I always kept my eyes and ears open, and reported what I had learned as best as I could. It had paid off more often than not, especially during the recent events of the Shropshire House, and the wily counterfeiters who had ensconced themselves within it.

"I had suspected as much," said Holmes, "and it is well for Burton that it appears to be no secret. If Mrs. Lynch knows about and disapproves of it, you may be certain Briley knows about it as well. And since there seems to be no disappointment coming from that direction, one may assume Briley approves of the match. That is significant, since it is almost certain that Burton is the man's heir, in spite of there being no known written acknowledgement of the fact."

"And you believe Burton when he states that he does not *know* if he is the heir?"

"Provisionally."

"Is the lack of a written record regarding Briley's heir one of the facts that you confirmed while in the village this afternoon?"

"It was alluded to in an oblique fashion by several of the individuals that I encountered. At one point while I was at the inn, I managed to turn the conversation toward Burton. He is very well thought of, and I could not get any sense that anyone wishes him ill will. The story of his rescue as an orphan by Briley is well known, and there is no resentment associated with it at all. It is also common knowledge that Burton's cap is set on Lydia Woods, and the feeling is that it will be a fine match.

"She is a village girl, now in her early twenties, hired several years ago to work in the house. One of Briley's characteristics has been to provide places in service in his home for the young people of the area. Whatever one may say of Mrs. Lynch and her thorny disposition, she runs a smart household, and her staff is well-trained. If they decide to leave for other positions elsewhere, in London for instance, or at another country home, they are given excellent references."

I pulled on my pipe, which had reached that perfect point of fulmination, evenly lit and drawing well. As Holmes discussed Burton, I considered if this was the time to ask why he had pulled the young man aside after dinner. I chose to let the matter rest, realizing that Holmes would only share with me what had been discussed if and when he was ready.

After a moment or two of thought, I asked instead, "Will you not tell me the real reason for sending poor MacDonald back to London on such a night? I cannot conceive that you had such an urgent need of information regarding the Briley family that you couldn't have sent the man in the morning. Or you could have simply sent a wire to Dean in London, for that matter."

Holmes shook his head. "I assure you, Watson, that a quick trip to London is exactly what I needed from the Inspector. Of course, I intend to act before he returns, no matter what results he brings with him. What he discovers, however, may or may not help me to realize whether I've made the correct decision."

"So you have reached a solution to the matter?" I asked. "Was it from something that was conveyed to you this afternoon, after we left you in the village?"

"Actually, I had a fairly certain idea of the basic framework of the events that took place some fifty years ago before we ever left this house for the village."

"And are you ready to reveal the entire truth to me?" I asked.

Holmes smiled, shook his head, and said, "Not until I have answered all my questions to my own satisfaction." Then, he continued by saying, "My conversation with Abner, the old man by the fireplace, added a few additional brushstrokes of confirmation to the canvas, and the meeting with Mr. Briley after that fairly completed the picture. There is one other verification you and I must make tonight, Watson, just to sew up a loose end, or paint in the last corner, to complete my metaphor, and I apologize in advance, as it will certainly be unpleasant at best."

"And then, when the entire matter is clear to you, you may or may not share your results with MacDonald?" I asked. "It is, after all, his case, Holmes, and he summoned you here to provide assistance. Do you believe that you can suppress the truth of these events, whatever they turn out to be?"

He thought for a moment, letting his gaze drop reflectively toward the low fire. He seemed to be thinking carefully. Finally, he spoke, stating softly, "A quantity of debt, Watson, a quantity of debt."

"What?" I said. "That was what Briley said earlier. What does it mean?"

"Watson, have you read *Great Expectations*?" he asked.

I felt as if I was suddenly lost in high weeds, but I responded, "Yes, some years ago."

"What do you recall about it?"

"Well, it is the story of a young boy, Pip, who is the narrator of the tale. He lives in poverty, but has aspirations for something better. One day he helps an escaped convict named Magwitch. Then he becomes associated with a mad-woman named Miss Havisham, and falls in love with her adopted daughter, Estella."

My enthusiasm began to warm as I remembered more of the book. "Later, he is taken to London and made into a gentleman. He hopefully believes this has been done by Miss Havisham, but in fact it is due to the secret manipulations of the grateful convict, who in the intervening years was transported and subsequently made a fortune. Pip encounters Magwitch, who has returned secretly to London, and by that point he has gotten into debt from his extravagant lifestyle – "

"Your memory of the story is excellent," interrupted Holmes. "Having recalled that much, then you may remember that after young Pip moves to London, he uses the phrase 'a quantity of debt' to describe how he has begun to live with a buy-now and pay-later attitude. The lesson is, of course, that at some point, the debt must be paid.

"There have been times, Watson, especially when I was younger, when I felt upon looking back that my solution to one case or another may have caused more harm than good. I have occasionally dragged certain matters into the light of day that should have remained in darkness, because I was too interested in proving I was right, when I should have stepped back for a moment to consider the greater benefit of silence. I can assure you that later, when I had an opportunity to reflect upon my actions after the truth was irretrievably exposed, I regretted that I did not stay my hand.

"On those few occasions, I have caused more harm than good by revealing a solution in order to improve my reputation, or as a sop to my immediate vanity. My younger self was building up a quantity of debt I am sometimes forced to pay now by being more judicious with my conclusions. I have learned that occasionally justice should be tempered and dispensed in due moderation."

"And are you the person to decide?" I asked. "When it should be tempered?"

"Possibly. I have no official standing here, and my conclusions are my own. My perspective is from the outside looking in, so I do not see issues as one of the Yarders would. I can only try to balance the crime versus the greater good. And luckily, I have you, my friend, to help guide me at times as a moral compass."

"But surely, Holmes, when one considers murder versus some greater good . . . . " I let my voice trail off. I felt glad that he counted on me, but at the same time, I questioned whether I wanted to share any of the responsibility that he was taking upon his own soul.

Finally, after we had smoked in silence for some further minutes, he sighed and stated, "In this particular case, I must admit I'm not at all certain how justice can be exacted without punishing the innocent as well. That factor weighs on my decision."

"Do you feel that punishment is still possible for the crime we are now investigating, even after all the years that have passed since the poor fellow from the trench was murdered?"

"Yes, but I may have to reveal more of my cards than I would wish in order to force my opponent to do so as well."

"I believe that I am beginning to have a vague understanding of the direction that your thinking is leading, Holmes. After all, there have no doubt been many cases whereupon a man, wracked by guilt for the crime of murder, no matter how secretly he manages to hide it, then spends a lifetime trying to atone for it with good works. Do not forget that it was Briley who first mentioned the idea of 'a quantity of debt.' "

"My younger self was building up a quantity of debt I am sometimes forced to pay now by being more judicious with my conclusions."

"So you have fixed Mr. Briley as the murderer of the man buried beneath the pipe?"

"Is that not what you have implied?" I asked.

"I did not say so," said Holmes.

"But surely that would explain things? Fifty years ago, give or take, a man arrives who is somehow connected to the Briley family. Perhaps he was an illegitimate son, fathered by Mr. Briley's father. Let us say that he was older than Mr. Briley, and, in spite of his illegitimacy, he had some sort of document proving that he was the legitimate heir. Then, Mr. Briley, either with calculated cunning, or perhaps in a fit of rage, kills the visitor. He manages to hide the body until he can institute the installation of the pipe from the cottages down to the mere. Realizing it would be a perfect hiding place, he buries the body, where under almost any circumstances it would be unlikely ever to be excavated again. Little does he suspect that the nature of the soil there will mummify it, or that his ward, fifty years later, will take it upon himself as part of his duties while running the estate to make repairs in that same area, revealing the evidence of the long suppressed crime."

"And what if I tell you that, contrary to common belief now, I have it on good authority that the pipeline was actually begun by Mr. Briley's father, Galton, a month or so *before* the old man died and Martin Briley subsequently inherited the estate?"

"You learned this from Abner, I suppose?"

Holmes nodded. "Then it changes nothing," I said. "In fact, it makes it easier for Martin Briley to have done as I've described. After Briley killed the illegitimate visitor, he knew exactly where he could hide the body, since there was already open excavation taking place on the estate that he believed would never again be opened."

"It is an interesting theory, and there is much about it that fits the facts. And there is something else you have not thought of that, when viewed from your perspective, might tend to support the interpretation you have constructed. Do you see it?"

I thought for a moment, and then possibly longer, only drawn back to myself when some of the coal in the fireplace collapsed in upon itself. And then I spotted it.

"Mrs. Lynch!" I said. "Of course! If Mr. Briley *did* do the murder, somehow she knew about it, too, and has used it to blackmail him all these years, setting herself up as the queen of her little kingdom here in the house. Mr. Briley, feeling guilty for what he had done, has tried for the rest of his life to make up for his actions by being a benevolent figure to everyone under his influence, paying off his perceived quantity of debt. He has opposed Mrs. Lynch as he could, but only when truly necessary, picking his battles, but otherwise letting her act as if this were actually *her* home as much as his. In fact, she referred to it as *'my house'* when she was arguing with Burton!"

Holmes nodded. "That is certainly one way of looking at it," he said, "although I don't subscribe to that view. You are like a man riding on a train, looking over into a carriage traveling side-by-side on a parallel track. While some of the events occurring within it are clear for a moment, from your single fixed view, there is more to what is happening in the other carriage than you can possibly know for certain. And there is more to this matter than you are taking into account."

"Are you implying that there has been some illicit relationship between Martin Briley and Mrs. Lynch?"

"No, I'm certain that has not been the case."

"Then what, exactly, do you know that I do not, which prevents me from making an accurate assessment?"

"I know very little more, and some aspects must remain hidden at present, pending verification. I will tell some of it to you now, however. For instance, I have obtained information from old Abner, who is in his eighties, older than we first thought. He recalls certain facts relating to the events that occurred here at the time of the death of old Mr. Galton Briley.

But as I say, these facts only tend to confirm what I have already suspected. By the time we had set out for the inn this afternoon, you had also seen what I had seen. After I returned, you did not have the advantage of having heard Abner's story, but after we interviewed Mr. Briley in his chambers, you had at that point seen all of the physical evidence that I, myself, had witnessed as well."

"Seen, but not observed, apparently," I said, without rancor. I was far too used to that feeling to have any bitterness about it. "And is that why you chose not to ask Mr. Briley any questions? It was because you had already seen *and* observed enough to confirm your theories?"

"Exactly. I will confess that there was the case rather like this in Nimes, thirty or so years ago, that suggested itself soon after we examined the body. The exact date of that crime escapes me. I had thought of having MacDonald stop by our rooms to examine my indexes to confirm it, but I decided it would be wiser if he did not. Perhaps I should not have mentioned it to him at all, but in any case he seemed uninterested once he realized that it took place long ago.

"In spite of the fact that I cannot recall specifics of the matter, what I had observed here was enough to convince me that my supposition was correct, and that these events are laid out on lines of a similar course."

"And just so I'll be caught up," I said, "first will you now tell me what you learned from Abner?"

"With great pleasure, my dear Watson. It will help pass the time of this rainy evening until the next act of our drama."

He rose, threw another lump of coal on the fire, and returned to his seat. As he went again through the pipe-lighting ritual that I knew so well, I listened to the wind throwing sheets of water from the storm against the walls of the house. I pitied anyone out on a night such as this. Little did I anticipate what plans Holmes would propose when our quiet discussion was eventually completed.

"Old Abner is a beloved fixture in the village. He is enjoying a well-earned rest now, due to the charity and good works of Martin Briley, who has made certain that the old folks here are cared for in their later years. Abner has spent most of his life working in the estate stables, having started there when he was just a boy, back during the War of the Fifth Coalition."

I thought for a moment, as Holmes looked at me patiently. "If memory serves," I said, "that was in 1809, when we fought with Austria against Napoleon and his alliance with Bavaria."

"Very good, Watson."

"That makes Abner a very old man indeed."

"True. Abner told me that he was nine years old at the time he came to the stables, meaning he was born in 1800. As I said, the man is older than we initially thought, which says much for the restorative powers of country living, and he is still as sharp as a tack."

"Hold for just a moment, Holmes," I interrupted. "Are you not the man who chided me during the early days of our friendship by saying that a man's brain is like an empty attic, and only a fool takes in every sort of lumber, so that what might actually be useful to him must be crowded out? I believe you indicated that it was a mistake to believe that your brain-attic, as you called it, would stretch to hold every useless fact, and that eventually something of importance would be lost? You refused to acknowledge the Copernican Theory, for God's sake! How can you know about an obscure little war that was part of a series of other obscure little wars?"

Holmes's eyes glinted with a merry light. "We have surely established by now that I actually *do* believe that all knowledge might useful, at some point or other. The conversation that you recall, and which is now permanently and unfortunately memorialized in your publication of last winter, must have been on a day when I was feeling particularly querulous. I was certainly tweaking you, but you did not know me well enough then to realize it. And as far as knowing about the events of the Fifth Coalition, well, it is just possible that it *may* have had relevance in a previous case of mine, and perhaps I had an ancestor who fought in it."

I sat forward. "If it *was* one of your earlier cases, I would very much like to have a record of it for my notes."

"Ah, Watson, that would be a story for another time. For now, let us return to the matter before us, and the tale of Abner the Stable Hand."

Sadly realizing that he was not going to elaborate on that other case at the present time, and if I brought it up again at some future point he might not wish to discuss it, I released myself from its pull and settled back to resume our discussion of the venerable Abner.

"As I was saying, Abner was born in the village in 1800, and went to work in the house stables when he was nine years old. He recalls the events very clearly, even for a fellow of his age. In those days, Galton Briley was a hard man, intent on building his fortunes. And not long after Abner started his life's work in the stables, Galton Briley took a wife.

"Abner told me the estate was a much different place at that time. By then, Galton Briley was about forty years old, and had been living in this house where we are sheltering tonight for about twenty years, having built it in the very late 1700's. Upon the death of his father, the original founder of the fortune, Galton Briley had taken his father's money, made from a series of profitable shipping ventures, and had wisely invested it. This had allowed him to buy up a great deal of the land here. He eventually built a great estate, encompassing the village and a number of surrounding farms, stretching to the north almost to the lands around Woburn Abbey.

"Galton had found a girl in London and brought her back here. Abner remembers her as a sad young thing, quite a bit younger than her husband, less than half his age. Abner only recalls seeing her on rare occasions, but stated that she always appeared to have a grim cloud about her. She stayed inside most of the time, and there were no visitors to the house, ever.

"Even out in the stables, they were aware that Galton Briley's fortunes were increasing by leaps and bounds, and yet the Briley family had a marked unhappiness about it. This continued until 1820, more than a decade after Abner started working here. At that time, the house went through a period of subdued excitement, as the first and only child of Galton Briley was born. Abner recalls it was not celebrated as it ought to have been, due to both Galton Briley's grim disposition, as well as the fact that his wife was in ill health after the birth, a condition that plagued her until her death.

"Abner did not recall the exact date it occurred, but Martin Briley's mother died within a year or so of his birth. I was able, while returning from the village, to stop in and check the parish records, which confirmed that she passed in 1822."

"You made good use of your time," I said.

"Indeed. It was the church doorway in which I sheltered during the hail storm."

"When you described the incident earlier, when we were with MacDonald, I recall you did not mention that fact."

"You are correct. It would be wise to keep a close hand on our cards at present, as you will no doubt see later tonight, if all goes according to plan."

"So you expect this matter to be resolved this evening?"

"I do," replied Holmes.

"And getting MacDonald away and up to London is part of the plan."

"Yes. As I've implied, depending how the results of tonight's events turn out, it might do more harm than good for the officials to learn what we will find. But to return to Abner's story."

He pulled deeply on his pipe, and resumed. "Galton Briley was a hard man, but not necessarily a bad man, in the sense that he did not do evil just for the sake of evil. However, he assuredly was *not* considered a good man, and he was mostly interested in profit, often to the point of neglecting the people under his care. Abner did not fare too badly in his position, working so near the house. But some of the estate folk had a meager life indeed.

420

"You must remember that back in those days, the early decades of the century, very few people were rewarded with the type of lives that some of us are fortunate enough to have today. A roof over one's head and knowing where some – but not all – of your next meals were coming from was usually good enough. People did not tend to stray from their localities, or move off to London without a very good reason.

"And so, having set the scene, some of our more familiar characters start to take the stage. Abner related to me that there was a family in the village at this same time, a shiftless bunch that always maintained a rather unpleasant reputation. He was not sure about the exact date, but some years after he went to work in the stables, that family had a daughter. The family's name was Lynch."

Holmes paused, watching me to see if felt the need to comment, and I responded. "A daughter named Lynch. Is she somehow related to that most winning woman, Mrs. Lynch, who has graced us with her presence today?"

"The fact of the matter is, the woman we know as Mrs. Lynch is actually the same woman. She has never married."

"Never married?" I asked. "So like many housekeepers who never marry, she goes by the sobriquet of *Mrs.* as a badge of office."

"Precisely. I believe, from my conversation with Abner, that she gradually assumed that exact title over the years in order to avoid confusion and maintain her authority as the housekeeper. It seems that she is a piece of work, is our Mrs. Lynch, and she started on it early.

"Abner related to me that Mrs. Lynch, or Elizabeth, as she was known then, came to work in this house in around 1830, when he had been here over twenty years. By then he was a full-fledged member of the little family that comprised the staff, and he was in a position to watch as young Elizabeth started her steady rise to housekeeper. Abner was married by this point, and his wife worked in the house as well, so he was able to hear about the girl's steady progress.

"Elizabeth Lynch began as a scullery maid, and within just a couple of years, had risen to the unlikely position of head housekeeper, while just in her early twenties. Of course, the estate was scandalized, but she had been chosen by Galton Briley, and she had his authority behind her. One fine day the previous housekeeper was sent on her way, Elizabeth became Miss Lynch, and she began to run the house as it pleased her. Old Galton, then in his early sixties, simply sat back and let her.

"On some occasion after Miss Lynch had begun her long reign over the house, young Martin Briley departed from the scene. He had never been much involved with the estate during the entire time he was growing up, staying in the house, while his father went about and carried out the running of the place. There was never any sign that Martin was being trained to take over the management of either the estate or any of his father's other affairs. In the last years before Martin, while still a boy it seems, took himself off to London, there were rumors of bitter rows between him and his father in the house. Abner's wife told him what she knew, but it wasn't everything. All that Abner recalled was that one day, Martin Briley left for London, and his father started his slow decline, spending more and more time withdrawn in the house, while Miss Lynch expanded her influence.

"Over the years, as the generations came and went, the *Miss* became *Mrs.*, possibly as the newer and younger servants simply assumed that she had once been married. She must have allowed it, or perhaps seen its usefulness, as that is how she now refers to herself. Very few people other than Abner probably even recall any of her early history, or the fact that she has never been married. As for Abner's wife, she died while giving birth to their only child, along with the baby. He understandably had less interest in the doings of the house for quite some time after that point."

Holmes paused to stare at the fire for a moment, and then said, "And now we come to the most important part of the story. In the spring of 1840, nearly this time of year according to Abner, old Galton Briley, who had not been seen for months as he languished in this building, finally succumbed to old age. The odd thing is that, until Martin Briley showed up at the house, after having been gone for a number of years, the people of the estate did not even realize that the old man had died. Mrs. Lynch, as we shall now resume calling her, had prepared the body on her own, and had given her staff no indication whatsoever that anything was amiss.

"Abner recalls that one morning, there was simply an announcement from Mrs. Lynch that Martin Briley had returned to the estate, claiming his inheritance following the death of his father. Nothing had been seen or heard from Martin in several years, and suddenly he was back home, in the house, his arrival unnoticed by Abner or any of the staff.

"Abner stated that no one had any knowledge regarding Martin's activities in London. Oh, there had been rumors of wild living, debauchery, and extravagant use of his father's money over the past few years, but nothing was ever confirmed. And now the prodigal had returned.

"Mrs. Lynch gave everyone to understand that a private burial of the old man had already occurred in the family mausoleum, which had been built in the early 1820's, a year or so before the time of Martin Briley's mother's passing, in preparation for her impending death, as it was expected at the time that she would die earlier rather than later. No one was invited to pay their respects to Galton Briley. Mrs. Lynch related that an ancient clergyman from another village had been found to read a few words over the body, and the service, such as it was, had been attended solely by Mrs. Lynch before Martin Briley had been able to return. No subsequent memorial service was held in the church for any of the locals to attend, and truth be told, they had no interest in attending one.

"Thus, Galton Briley was laid to rest in the mausoleum, with his departed young wife, the only two occupants of the structure. And the only witness was Mrs. Lynch, the young housekeeper."

Holmes gave me a moment to digest what he had told me before continuing. "After the funeral, Martin Briley spent several months shut up in the house. Any instructions from him to the estate manager were conveyed by Mrs. Lynch. A number of cosmetic improvements were begun at that time, and they continued over the next several years, eventually making the house much more attractive and livable than it had been during the final years of Galton Briley's life."

"But," I asked, "how was Mrs. Lynch able to accomplish all this out without anyone questioning her?"

"You must remember that in those days, this was a much more remote area. There was no adequate law enforcement in existence. And Mrs. Lynch had spent several years building up her authority, as given to her by Galton Briley. Finally, the heir had returned to the house, and even though he wasn't seen for several months, Mrs. Lynch was presumably speaking for him when she provided direction to the estate manager and the staff.

"Finally, as the summer was turning to fall of 1840, Martin Briley began to emerge from his self-imposed hibernation. He started to take an interest in the affairs of the estate, which had been in the capable hands of the old estate manager hired years earlier by Galton. Martin apprenticed himself to the fellow, working to learn every aspect of the running of the place, and unafraid to get dirty as he did so. He began to make a number of substantial improvements to the living quarters of his tenants, and we've heard how over the years he also endeared himself to the locals with his progressive efforts toward maintaining good schools and medical care, and so on. He reversed a number of Galton Briley's oppressive conditions related to tenancy agreements as well."

"A quantity of debt," I said.

"Indeed. Interestingly, Martin Briley is now often credited with the plumbing improvements and the installation of the pipe where the body was discovered two days ago, but as I said, that was originally an improvement begun by the estate manager during Galton's final days, not because of any benevolent concern for the living conditions of the cottagers. Rather, it was due to the fact that whatever drainage system there was or was not in place before that time was leading to disease that was affecting the workers, and thus the prosperity of the estate as a whole."

I thought for a moment about what Holmes had related to me. Nothing in what he had said contradicted with my earlier theory, and I told him so. "Again, none of that negates my interpretation of what we have seen. An illegitimate Briley heir could have arrived, and Martin killed him to protect his inheritance. I had first believed that Mrs. Lynch gained her ascendance by blackmailing Martin, but I now see that she was already on her throne during Galton's lifetime. Whatever seamy arrangement had caused Galton to elevate her to the position of head housekeeper might not have been enough to influence Martin the same way. But if she had some hold over him in the form of knowledge about the murder he had committed, then that would be enough to assure that she would *continue* to maintain her position."

"Ah, Watson," said Holmes. "You are stubborn yet. But you are still not taking into account the things which you have seen today."

"Seen, but not observed," I said.

"Exactly."

I did not reply for a moment, and then asked, "And was there something in Abner's story which guided you toward the truth?"

"There is nothing definite that caused me to suddenly see these events with a new and unexpected clarity. As I mentioned, I already had a vague idea of what had occurred those many years ago. Abner simply helped me to focus some of the details, as did my examination of the information in the parish records."

An obvious thought occurred to me. "Holmes? Do you think that Mrs. Lynch had something to do with the death of old Galton Briley, those many years ago?"

He took his pipe from his mouth, and turned it so as to see into the bowl. The flame must have finally gone out, for he set it aside. "It is possible, Watson, and we may actually find out more about that part of the tale later tonight. However, it is incidental to the facts relating to the dead man found under the pipe. *That* is the question we can definitely answer. Although," he added, "I'm still of an uncertain mind as to what effect the answer will have. I cannot see a satisfactory solution, and I'm afraid we will have to let events run their course, once we nudge them into motion. And that, my friend, is a situation that is never the preferred option. Like a good solicitor, one should already know the answer before one asks the question. That way there will be no surprises."

He then stood up. "And sadly, Watson, you still haven't asked all of the right questions. But all will be made clear."

"Tell me, then, what is one of the questions that I should be asking?"

"Why, what I meant when I mentioned earlier that our discussion would pass some of the time until the next act of our drama. But now, there is no need to ask, for the curtain is about to rise. I believe that we have talked long enough that the household has settled, and all people with clear consciences, and a few without them as well, are now in for the night.

"Come, Watson, let us return to the storm. We have one more grim errand to perform, and then we shall have everything we need to present our case."

Chapter X
The Grim Errand

I had dreaded this moment, as I saw Holmes moving on silent feet toward the door to the hallway. I understood that he wished to move quietly, taking no chances of waking the house. He carefully opened the door and stepped out, expecting me to follow.

The hall was lit by a dim glow, where shadows could be avoided but not identified. Holmes moved like a cat, carefully placing each foot, in spite of the solid flooring which gave every indication that it would not creak or groan at an inopportune moment. I followed him as best I could, and I felt that I acquitted myself well, considering the aches in my leg that had been aggravated by the terrible weather.

Holmes led me to a set of back stairs at the left-hand side of the house, where the servants slept. On the ground floor, he unerringly found the alcove where our coats were hung. Woods had done his best to arrange them so that they would dry, but, as I had feared, they were still quite damp. I would be lucky to escape this particular adventure without a full-blown case of pneumonia. I feared that we were both heading for pesky spring colds, at best.

With a sigh, I followed Holmes out of a rear door, onto a stone-floored landing. I could sense more than see the rain drops dashing into the standing puddles all around us. "Leave the door on the latch," whispered Holmes, as he turned toward a set of steps leading down from the landing to the grounds below.

Away from the protection of the house, the wind found us. I clutched my coat tighter, wishing that I had dressed more for winter than spring. There was an iciness to the water that found its way under my hat and coat.

We were at least fifty yards from the house, as we traversed the wide sloping lawn at the rear, when Holmes paused and looked back. I turned as well, and saw that the massive structure standing above us was no more than a looming black shadow. However, to our left, at the base of the great house, a pair of rooms showed lights. One, on what would be the ground floor, and another one floor above it. The ground floor room appeared to have a door which opened onto a landing similar to the one that we had just used to exit the building.

"Mr. Briley's room," said Holmes with a gesture, "and that is Mrs. Lynch's there above him. It seems that neither can sleep tonight."

"Perhaps, as Mr. Briley's room is something of a sick chamber, a light is left burning throughout the night, in case he needs assistance."

"Possibly," said Holmes. "We shall see."

A thought occurred to me. "When you returned to the house this afternoon, you followed Woods into the back of the house. Was that when you determined where the rear entrance was located? And where our coats were being kept, as well?"

"Of course. As I told MacDonald, it has always been a habit of mine to identify the exits of whatever building in which I find myself."

"And the map you requested from Burton? Was it to locate our current destination?"

"Exactly, Watson. As for now, let us continue on our quest. What we have to do is not going to get any more pleasant by putting it off."

At that moment, lightning flashed, followed by a roll of thunder a few seconds later. "The storm is returning," said Holmes, needlessly.

"Then let us get this over with," I said. Gesturing, I added, "After you."

We set off down the rest of the gentle slope, stepping carefully so as not to lose our footing on the wet grass, or stride into some unseen depression. I had glanced at the map provided to Holmes earlier in the evening, and was starting to have an idea of our destination, although I could not yet understand the purpose.

We were now far enough away from the house that the lights from the bedrooms were no longer visible. There had been a few more flashes of lightning, but they were in the distance. However, the wind was blowing from that direction, and I knew the storm was steadily moving our way.

We were rounding a small copse that had been allowed to grow up through some ragged boulders when Holmes grabbed my arm and pulled me into the deeper shadows. For a moment I did not understand, and then I heard it as well. It was the sound of a carriage, making its way from our left, the direction of the stream and the cottages.

Gradually it came closer, the rhythm of the horses' hooves hitting the wet ground more felt than heard. I could see now that the carriage was rolling across a rough track that ran along the bottom of the hill. We had been about to cross it before Holmes stopped me, and I had not even realized it was there.

My eyes had finally adjusted to the night, especially after leaving the influence of the bedroom lights that we had turned and seen earlier, and now I could recognize details of the carriage. It was closed, with the driver sitting high on top, his hands gripping the reins as the horse moved steadily forward, but not too quickly. Just as it was passing in front of us, I recognized the driver. It was George Burton.

427

Sitting inside the carriage was another figure, with a pale face pressed to the window. Before I could recognize who it was, they were gone, down the track which undoubtedly led back in the direction of the village. The sounds faded away, and we were left with the familiar rain and wind once again.

"Holmes," I whispered, as if someone were out there to hear us, "what is he doing? He said he would spend the night down at the cottages, in case his help was needed should there be flooding. Do you suppose that there has been an emergency?"

"Perhaps," Holmes replied. "However, I fancy a somewhat different explanation, and I'm certain that all shall be made clear in the morning. I hope I am right, and that there still may be some sort of happy ending out of this whole nasty business. However, Burton's midnight ride does not affect in the least what we are doing right now. Pray, let us continue."

And with that, he stepped out and across the track without another word. I moved to catch up with him. We continued on down the gentle slope, and I knew from studying the map that if we kept going, we would eventually reach the stream at a location before it dropped and wound around the cottages and emptied through the mere. I believed, however, that we would reach our destination before we came to the stream, and in just a few more minutes, I was proved right.

We stopped on a low rise, near a wooded area that looked down on the water below us. It was simply a deeper black in the night around us, but I could hear the rush of the waters as they tumbled and lost elevation while speeding along the stream bed. Then my attention turned back to our goal. It was a small building, probably no more than twenty by twenty, and made of such white marble that it even seemed to shine weakly in the dark night. It was only a single story, with one heavily decorated metal door centered in the front wall. The corners of the small building were simulated Doric columns, incorporated within the walls, and supporting the gently sloped roof, also made of marble. A pair of Corinthian columns stood on either side of the door, and a small porch was reached by four very shallow marble steps.

Nearby was a lone tree, set apart from the others. It looked to be an elm, and at its base was a marble bench, consisting simply of a couple of side supports, and topped by a flat slab. In better weather, it would provide a lovely view out over the stream toward the cottages and farms.

Holmes did not see it that way. "A rather lonely spot," he said, stepping carefully up onto the porch, while fumbling under his Inverness coat for something. "Do be careful," he said. "These steps slope down from front to back, allowing water to pool along the risers. They also

428

appear to have settled in the years since the building was constructed, and they are quite slick."

I paid heed to his warning, and followed him onto the porch, where he was in the process of lighting a dark lantern. Then, with the opening narrowed to the thinnest possible slit, he bent and began to manipulate his splendid set of pick-locks into the mausoleum door.

I knew that any remonstrance I might make about what we were about to do would fall upon deaf ears. Holmes was on the track, like a hound that had taken the scent, and if he needed a fact to complete his case, then nothing would stand in his way. After some of the objectionable situations in which he and I had found ourselves over the years, such as the Dreadful Tragedy of the Powys Stone, I knew that there was almost nothing I could say which might dissuade him from his task. Even if, assuming that I was correct, that task involved desecration of a corpse.

It occurred to me, while Holmes worked on the lock, that I had not mentioned something that I had previously noticed. I explained how the dust had been disturbed in front of the copy of *Beeton's*, which had contained my own recently published story. "What do you think it means?" I asked.

"Possibly Mr. Briley simply refreshed his memory when it was announced that you and I would be arriving to make inquiries," he whispered, as he worked in darkness to feel the inner workings of the lock. "Or perhaps, he wanted to see what sort of opponents he might be facing." Then, with a triumphant but whispered, "A-ha!" Holmes straightened up and stepped back. The door had opened.

It had been but the work of a moment for Holmes to turn the lock in the heavy door. "Child's play," he muttered. "They think that just because it needs a great heavy key, it provides some extra protection. The larger the lock, the easier it is to feel the works."

He pushed the door open. The wind seemed to die at that moment, and a musty, yet not totally unpleasant, odor, reached us from the still air within. "It is ventilated," said Holmes. "There are often small gaps, you see designed between the walls
and the roof, to allow the building to breathe. Otherwise, the decay of the bodies within would be intolerable whenever the building had to be reentered."

He widened the opening a little further and stepped in. I followed, and pushed the door shut behind me, assuming that Holmes would want to expand the reach of the dark lantern without it being observed by someone on the outside, in the unlikely chance there actually was someone else out on such a night at that lonely location.

He pushed the door open. The wind seemed to die at
that moment, and a musty, yet not totally unpleasant,
odor, reached us from the still air within.

As the light exposed the room, Holmes reached up and pushed back
his fore-and-aft cap, allowing him to see around more clearly. It was a
square chamber, as might be expected from observing the shape of the
building from outside. There was only the one room, constructed of the
same white marble, and quite plain. Along the walls were several raised
platforms, or biers. Each of them was defined by ornate carvings along the

top edges, and on the corners were mounted round marble balls about the size of my fist.

Only two of the biers were being used. Side by side on the left wall, near the rear of the room, were two plain coffins, the black wood of each held together at the corners by sturdy ironwork. Holmes stepped over and held the dark lantern this way and that. "I believe the village had a unique blacksmith earlier in the century. Whoever built the metal supports of these coffins certainly knew what he was about."

He leaned forward and wiped a thumb across the small brass plaques at the end of each coffin. Then, gesturing with the lantern toward the one farthest back in the corner, he said, "This one is that of Martin Briley's mother, and was placed here twenty years before the other, that of Briley's father. Yet both were clearly made at about the same time. They been here more than half-a-century, and still the unusual iron work has kept them in wonderful structural condition."

"Somehow," I replied softly, "I doubt that discovering this fact is what we are here for."

"You are correct," said Holmes. "Examination of this ornate metalwork only means that we are delayed for an extra moment or two longer than we would have been otherwise. The blacksmith of old has affixed cunning latches on each coffin, which I must understand before we can open them and view the occupants."

It was as I had expected, although I did not know what he hoped to accomplish. However, this was not the first time that I had found myself in this situation, and I was prepared to help in any way that I could.

Holmes succeeded in opening the rear coffin. Raising the lid, he lifted the dark lantern to a better vantage, as he simultaneously moved a step in order to give me easier access, so as to view the terrible contents.

It was as one might expect. She, or what was left of her, rested peacefully on the rotted linen remains which lined the box, wearing the gown in which she had been entombed. She was on her back, staring upward into eternity, the bones of her arms loosely folded across her breast. As unpleasant as the sight was, I saw nothing abnormal, and said as much to Holmes.

"As I expected," he replied. "But it pays to make certain. Performing this task once is enough, as I'm sure you will agree, and I wanted to make certain there was nothing unusual about the contents of this coffin, as well as the other one that we came to see."

He lowered the lid and returned the unusual latch to its closed position. Then, walking around to the other side of Galton Briley's coffin, he repeated his actions of a moment earlier and raised that lid as well, uttering a small cry of satisfaction as he did so.

I stepped beside him, and could see that all was not as it should have been. The coffin contained the remains of a body, a figure taller than that of the woman's nearby. He was dressed in what was left of a suit of clothes of the style from over fifty years gone by. But, most unusually, the body was not lying flat on its back in the center of the coffin, staring upward as the woman's had been. Instead, it was rolled up onto its left side, facing the back wall of the coffin where the lid joined it by the long-ago blacksmith's hinges.

"Was this what you expected to find?" I asked.

"I wanted to confirm several things by the opening of this coffin. The shifting of the body answers one of my questions. Notice what is left of the linen lining underneath him."

"It appears to be pushed up against the man's back."

"Exactly. Even after all these years, it retains the flattening that occurred when something else was placed into the coffin beside Galton Briley's body. It would not have that appearance if the coffin had simply been tipped while being moved to the mausoleum or placed on the bier. At some point, this coffin was opened, the body was pushed up and rolled aside toward the back wall, and something was jammed in here for some amount of time, long enough to flatten the lining."

"Something like the body of the man found under the pipe?" I asked. "Are you suggesting that before the murdered man was placed under the pipe, he was put in this coffin for a time, long enough to have made an impression on the lining?"

"That is exactly what I believe happened. After the man was murdered, he was stored here until he could be moved to the trench excavation, where it was believed he would remain undiscovered forever."

"And is *this* what you hoped to discover?"

"Not specifically. What I wanted to absolutely ascertain first was whether this was actually Galton Briley in this coffin, and that he was *not* the body that was found in the trench."

"But we decided that the man found under the pipe was clearly younger. Galton Briley was an old man when he died."

"We did agree that the body was that of a young man, but we could not be absolutely certain based simply upon our limited examination, and also because of the mummified man's condition. The peat-like fluids that had leached into the body had darkened and wrinkled the skin, and leathered it. Also, what remained of the mummy's hair might have absorbed some of the tannic acid in the peat, giving us a false idea of a darker and younger color. No, an examination of this man's body, who had died at the same approximate time as that of the man in the trench, had to be done. Otherwise, there would still have been an element of uncertainty.

"But there is one other factor to consider, while we have the chance. This man's right hand, Watson. Look at his right hand."

Leaning past him at an awkward angle, I put my head closer, even as he moved the dark lantern to a more advantageous location. As the body had been rolled up to face the rear of the coffin, the right hand had dropped behind it, resting on the wrinkled linens. Of course, the flesh was gone, or what was left of it was too insignificant to recognize in the unnatural light of the lantern. But the bones were there. They had collapsed, but were lying neatly on the cloth. A quick examination and count confirmed that the body was a Briley.

"There are no little finger bones from this hand. I count twenty-four of the twenty-seven bones that should be here. There are no distal, intermediate, or proximal phalanges of the correct size, and at the metacarpophalangeal joint where the little finger would normally be attached, the end of the metacarpal bone is strangely deformed. It appears to be a natural deformity, and not due to some injury, I think that we are seeing the characteristic missing Briley finger, and we may conclude that this man was, in fact, Galton Briley."

"Very satisfactory, Watson," said Holmes. "Now, I think we can close this fellow up and let him return to his rest."

"But, Holmes," I said, "shouldn't we examine the remains while we have the chance, to see if there is any evidence that Galton Briley was murdered as well? After all, we may not have this opportunity again."

"I think not. If he were poisoned, there would be no way to know it at this point without further tests, and if he were stabbed, the only possibility of determining it is by a careful examination of the remaining bones, on the chance that the knife had possibly nicked one as it entered the body. As you can see, the skull seems to be intact, so there is no indication that this man died from a head wound, as did the man in the trench. No, Watson. Even if Galton Briley was murdered, it is incidental to our investigation. And there is every chance that if we discover the truth about the death of the man in the trench, a death that we believe to have been a murder, then any crime that might possibly be related to this man will most likely be revealed as well."

"Should we . . . turn him onto his back? As he undoubtedly was before he was pushed up into this position by whoever stored the other body here?"

Holmes shook his head. "Let us leave him as we found him, facing his wife. There is no indignity in that, I think, at this late date."

433

Holmes closed the lid and latched it. Stepping back, Holmes looked at the coffin for a moment, and then ran his hands along it. At the foot, he let them drop onto one of the decorative marble balls on the corner of the bier. It rolled loosely in his grip, and he took it off.

He bent to examine the corner where it had rested for so many years. There was some type of grout or mortar there, long dried, cupped in a shape to match the ball in Holmes's hand. He hefted it for a time or two, and then made a swinging motion with it, at about eye level. Then he nodded and turned to me.

"I believe this might be the murder weapon, my friend," he said, handing it to me. I examined it as well, guessing it to be about ten or twelve pounds. I ran my hand around its cold smoothness.

"It is certainly the right size," I said. "Was this something that you expected to find here as well?"

"Not at all," he replied, "but it does not raise any objections to my theoretical construct of the events of long ago."

"Why was he not left here?"

"There was always the possibility that the coffin might have been reopened, especially if someone came to question the odd events surrounding the death and burial of Galton Briley."

"But," I asked, "isn't it possible that the man in the trench died by accident? Couldn't he have fallen against the marble fixture? Stranger things have happened."

"Not likely, I think. Why else was so much trouble taken to hide him, in two different places? The logical conclusion is that he was murdered.

"In fact, I can imagine how it must have happened. The murdered man was lured here, where he was killed, and then immediately put into Galton Briley's coffin. It would have been easier to get the victim to come here himself, rather than trying to move a body here after the fact. What could have been more convenient for our murderer?

"What indeed," I said softly, replacing the marble ball back on its resting place.

Then, looking around for just a moment or two more in order to make sure that there was nothing else to be seen in the bare chamber, we turned and departed, narrowing the dark lantern's aperture nearly shut as we reached the door. Within minutes, we had departed, and the door was relocked as before.

"Well, Watson," said Holmes, as we both breathed deeply of the damp cool air as we stood on the porch. "We have a long uphill trek through darkness and rain back to the house. And then I believe that we might as well see an end to this matter. Are you game?"

"Yes," I said. "Let us have done with this," I said, and we set off.

The journey back was unpleasant, as might be imagined. The thunder still crashed intermittently in the distance, and the rain, which had been falling in straight, icy sheets, was now being whipped by the winds as the latest portion of the storm approached. It did not help that we were now climbing the hill while facing into the saturated breezes. When we finally reached a point on the hill close enough to see the house, I nearly gave a weak cheer. But I did not, because our desire was to return to the house in as discreet a manner as we had left it, and also because I could not have found the breath to do so in any case.

The house was in much the same condition as when we had departed, with one difference. Where before there had been two rooms with lights burning on the left rear side facing the back of the structure, now there was only one. The upper story window, which we understood to be that of Mrs. Lynch's room, was now dark. Only the ground floor room containing Martin Briley was still lit. The view of it had suddenly ruined my night vision, and all I could see now was the light spilling down the hill toward us. I looked down and could not even see my hands.

Holmes resumed the uphill trudge, but instead of turning toward the right, and the stairs that we had earlier used to exit the house, he angled to the left, and the brightly lit room. "Do you intend to have an immediate confrontation?" I asked.

"Yes," he replied. "Unless you would rather find dry clothing first."

I sighed. "Not at all. Let us continue. But did you not tell Mrs. Lynch that you had no further need to speak to Mr. Briley?"

"That is exactly correct," he replied, "I do not." He added nothing further.

We found the steps leading to the landing outside the door of Briley's room. Crossing the stones, Holmes led me to the door, and then paused. I stood beside him, feeling warm underneath my coat despite the damp and the rain. My shoes, of course, were soaked, but hopefully I would be able to do something about that sooner rather than later.

Holmes reached out for the handle of the door, and gently turned it. It moved freely and silently. Without opening the door, he murmured to me, "It seems that we are expected." Then, pushing the door open, he stepped in, and I followed.

A voice spoke to us, one that I recognized. "Come in, gentlemen, and warm yourself. It is a most terrible night to be out."

Chapter XI
The Unqualified Truth

Martin Briley was standing near the fireplace, looking more hearty than he had appeared several hours ago, when he was ensconced in his special bath chair by the fire. It was pushed off to the side now, piled with the blankets that had covered him from head to foot. He was beside one of a pair of fine chairs, between us and the fireplace. He was wrapped tightly in an expensive dressing gown, with his hands folded neatly in front of him.

I could see I had been right earlier, when I decided that he had, at some time in the past, been a much stronger physical figure than the one that now presented itself. His clothing, while well made, seemed to hang from him. The cut of his dressing gown across his shoulders appeared to be just a shade too wide, allowing the seams to sag where they would have been supported in years past by muscle. Earlier in the day, he had appeared to be near death's door. Now, he still had that door in sight, but he wasn't quite through it yet.

Beside him, on a small table between the two chairs, was a green book, shut with what appeared to be two envelopes protruding from the top edge. Next to it was a small bottle containing some warm-looking amber liquid and two snifters. A coal fire burned in the hearth, and I was very grateful for it indeed, as it had warmed the room to the point that it might have seemed uncomfortable after a long period, while just now it felt wonderful.

The portrait of Galton Briley still hung on the wall, of course, but its colors seemed darker and more melancholy without the little bit of daylight that had illuminated it earlier. I looked at it for a few seconds, trying to reconcile the hearty man painted in his forties, as he had been portrayed by the artist at the turn of the century, with those sad and disrupted remains that Holmes and I had examined less than a half-hour before.

The old man stepped back, and sank into the chair on his left, watching us as we approached. He smiled warmly, and I was reminded of all the good works that he had done in this part of the world through the long years. What set of circumstances could have occurred so ago that would have entangled such a benevolent fellow as this?

The rain rattled against the door and windows, and soon another round of thunder followed. I was conscious that my wet shoes were tracking moisture across the fine rugs lining the floor, but there was nothing to do about it now.

"I was expecting you," he said. "I left the door to the terrace unlocked, as well as the one to the hall, should you have wished to approach from either side. I suspected you might have something to ask that you didn't before. Possibly some questions to be discussed in confidence."

"Perhaps one or two," said Holmes. "Simply to clarify certain events. However, I believe that we have already been able to piece together enough of an idea of what has remained hidden for so long."

Briley nodded, watching from beneath lowered brows. His gaze was intent, but I perceived no menace from him. Slowly, he unfolded his hands in his lap. "Earlier today, Mr. Holmes, you asked if you could shake my hand. At the time I refused. It was then I realized for certain that you knew some, if not all, of the truth. My composure was quite shaken, and I reacted badly. Refusing to shake hands then has only delayed the inevitable, although it did give me a chance to arrange some things on my own terms. But now I am ready." He held out his right hand. "Mr. Holmes, do you still wish to shake my hand?"

Holmes smiled and looked at him for a moment. Then, without raising his own, he stepped slightly to the side, where he could get a better view of Briley's outstretched right hand. Briley, appearing to be puzzled, did not lower it as the awkward moment lengthened. Holmes then leaned in, looked closely, nodded once, and straightened.

"Perhaps some other time. But would you mind if, instead of shaking hands with me, that Dr. Watson had the honor?" He turned his head in my direction.

Puzzled, but finding no objection, I moved to Briley's side. Raising my own hand, I wondered what Holmes was hoping to accomplish by this unusual action. Briley, with a resigned look, as if he were crossing some personal Rubicon, reached out in my direction and clasped his hand to mine with the strength of a much younger man.

We held the grip for a second, and then I realized what it was that Holmes wanted me to find. A look of enlightened understanding must have passed across my face. Easing my hold on Briley's hand, I shifted my own fingers so as to hold his palm in the manner of a doctor examining a patient. Turning his hand onto its side, I leaned down and examined the outer edge.

"Holmes," I said. "There is a scar! A scar where the little finger should be!"

Briley pulled his hand away, not in a sudden and angry way, but simply as if he was tired of holding it up. He returned it to his lap, where he folded his left hand around it in a protective way.

I straightened up. "It is an old scar, with no obvious discoloration, at least that I can identify in this light. But there is a definite raised ridge of scarred tissue there." I turned away from Briley, whom I had been watching as I spoke. He continued to look toward Holmes. "Could it be a scar from some unrelated wound? At the site of the missing Briley little finger? Or did he perhaps – "

"Is that the confirmation that you needed, Mr. Holmes?" Briley asked, ignoring me completely.

"Yes, it is . . . Mr. Lynch."

Lynch! The name seemed to hang in the quiet room. Suddenly I began to have a better understanding of what must have taken place, those many years ago. But there was too much that was still unexplained, at least to me. And I had no idea what path Holmes had followed to reach his solution. He had referred to a similar case thirty or more years earlier in Nimes, but had that been enough to reveal the truth to him? Apparently Martin Briley, or rather, the man whom I had thought to *be* Martin Briley, was as puzzled as I was.

"I . . . I had come to believe that you knew the truth about the identity of the man found beneath the pipe, Mr. Holmes. But I was just as certain that you did *not* know the whole story. I was prepared to tell the entire tale, but I thought that parts of it would surprise you, including who I really am. Instead, you call me by a name that I have not used since 1840, revealing that you truly *do* know everything."

"Not quite," said Holmes. He pulled off his fore-and-aft, ran his long thin fingers through his hair, and began to divest himself of his wet Inverness. He looked around for an appropriate location to place it, but seeing nowhere to lay it except across the room's fine furniture, he finally deposited it carefully on the floor opposite the fireplace, near the door. Realizing that the room was becoming quite warm, and surprised at myself that I would find it to be so after being so cold and miserable just moments before, I removed my coat and hat as well. I placed them by Holmes's, as Briley – that is, Lynch – continued speaking.

"But how did you know?" he asked. "Of my true name, I mean."

"By the observation of your ears."

"My ears?" repeated Lynch.

"Yes. They have the unique characteristic of being small, and of having the outer rim, or *auricle*, shaped in something of a compression. It can be a family trait. I had happened to notice Mrs. Lynch's ears earlier today, when we were first introduced to her, and I observed the formation of her ears at that time. I had happened to be thinking of ears a littler earlier in the afternoon, as I will explain in a moment. Later, when we were brought in here to speak to you, I found that your ears presented the same shape. There is no doubt that *she* is the person that she has always claimed to be, Elizabeth Lynch. This is confirmed by the testimony of an old man in the village, who has known her for her whole life. Therefore, if you have the Lynch ear, and you are *not* a Briley, it follows that you must be a Lynch."

"But . . . this is incredible, Mr. Holmes," said Lynch.

Holmes ignored him, and instead took a step to the side, gesturing toward the painting of Galton Briley, hanging on the wall. "Furthermore, having noticed the similarity between your ears and those of Mrs. Lynch, and thus confirming that this inherited family characteristic indicated a blood relation between you and her, I next wanted to satisfy my doubts regarding your legitimacy as the true heir to the Briley family. We were fortunate enough to find Galton Briley's portrait, making the job quite a bit easier. Examining the right ear shown on the painting's subject indicated to me that, along with not sharing the characteristic Briley finger, which I did not know at the time, you also do not have the Briley ear."

I stepped to the painting and saw that he was correct. The careful representation, so accurate in detail from fingernails to eyebrows, also presented a clear image of the right side of Galton Briley's face. The figure was turned into a three-quarter view, so that his right hand, with its missing finger, presented itself, along with the man's right ear. It was not a small ear at all, and looked nothing like that of the man seated nearby. Rather, the rim was flared, and once noticed, could not be ignored.

"But Holmes," I asked. "How do you know that this ear in the painting is a characteristic of the Briley family? It might simply be that Galton Briley's ear had that particular shape, with no correspondence to the ears of any his other relations."

"I know that it is another shared characteristic of the Brileys, because we have seen another such ear much like it elsewhere today," he replied.

I thought for a moment. "Someone in the village?" I asked.

"No, Watson. We have seen a very similar ear on the body of the man found in the trench. Though it was quite mummified, his ear still retains the same shape as that shown in the painting. I noticed how well it was preserved when we examined the body, but gave it no more thought at the time, simply cataloging my observations as a part of my general examination. It was merely a curiosity.

"Later, when we were introduced to Mr. Lynch here, in his guise as the Briley heir, I compared his ear to my recollection of the dead man's. Obviously, they did not match. We had already decided that the man in the trench was a Briley, based on the fact that his missing finger seemed to have occurred naturally, with no signs of a corresponding injury. This knowledge was augmented when I saw that the ear in the painting of a genuine Briley *did* match that of the dead man. When I had an opportunity to observe Mr. Lynch's ear, it did not match *either* of the Briley ears.

"In any case, by the time we were allowed to interview Mr. Lynch, I already had some hint as to the identity of both the dead man and Mr. Lynch."

"And may I ask how, Mr. Holmes?" said Lynch.

"Certainly. My knowledge of past crimes is extensive, and it has often been of some use to me. I must admit I was aware of a matter with many similarities to this one that took place decades ago, in France. There was a family much like the Brileys, with a widowed father and an estranged son. When the old man died, an imposter took the place of the heir. Years later, the true son's body was found, and all was revealed.

"While I do not yet know the specifics of how events in *this* location played out, all those years ago, I feel certain that the unfortunate dead man in the trench is not some illegitimate child of Galton Briley, as Watson has theorized, or perhaps an unknown cousin. Rather, he is in fact *Martin Briley, the true and actual heir*, who was murdered and hidden upon his return to the village at the time of his father's death. At that point, you, with the connivance of your sister, took his place, and have held it to this day."

"His sister?" I said. "Then Mrs. Lynch is his sister?"

"Exactly. I do not know how she came to her position as housekeeper under old Galton Briley, while still very young, and the squalid disagreeable details are probably unimportant at this late date. However, when the old man died, and it was time for his son Martin to return from London, his murder was arranged. Mr. Lynch, here, who had moved away long before as well, returned and took Martin's place. Does that cover the basic facts, Mr. Lynch?"

"Yes." He swallowed, and repeated, "Yes, it does. But there are aspects of the matter that you do not yet know. And I will explain them to you. But first, tell me how you knew these things before you even entered this room? I could tell that you suspected the truth when you came in here, before I refused to shake your hand. Comparing my ear to that of Galton Briley in the painting was only an afterthought. How did you come to discover that Elizabeth is my sister? I have heard of your reputation before you ever walked through our door, but I still want to hear how you knew!"

"Today in the village," replied Holmes, "I spoke at length with an old man, formerly of the stables, named Abner." Lynch nodded in recognition, and Holmes continued. "As he told me, he is probably the only person left within miles who is old enough to remember the long-ago days when Mrs. Lynch, then known as *Miss* Lynch, or simply Elizabeth, came to work in the house. One of the other facts that he mentioned in passing was that she had come from a poor family, always barely scrabbling by, and often living on charity due to the actions of her shiftless father."

Lynch winced at this statement, but Holmes continued. "One thing that Abner mentioned was that young Elizabeth Lynch had been the older of two children, the younger being a brother, who had fled the area while still in his teens after a particularly brutal beating by the siblings' father, during one of his many drunken episodes. Abner seemed to attach no more significance to this event.

"On the way back to the house from the village, I paused at the church to examine the parish records and confirmed the existence of this brother, one Peter Lynch, born in 1821. That would be you, would it not, Mr. Lynch?"

Lynch simply nodded, and then closed his eyes. "It has been most of my life since I last saw my brute of a father, and still the memory of him affects me, as you can see."

Holmes nodded. "Further confirmation of your relation to Mrs. Lynch came when we were introduced late this afternoon. At the same time I became aware that you did not have the Briley ear, I saw that you *did* possess the same ear type as Mrs. Lynch, which I had already chanced to particularly notice earlier in the day."

Lynch pondered this for a moment, and then seized on an aspect of Holmes's statement. "But why had you noticed my sister's ear before that?"

"Because, I had seen a very similar ear earlier this afternoon, before we were even introduced to Mrs. Lynch."

I had caught up by that point, and I blurted, "Burton! George Burton has that type of ear!"

"Very good, Watson! Very good, indeed! When we examined the mummified body in the cottage, I remarked to myself on the exceptionally well-preserved condition of the ear, along with the rest of the fellow. With ears still on my mind, I idly glanced at other ears as we began our journey back to the house, and in doing so, I cataloged Burton's ear type, comparing it to MacDonald's and Watson's, both of whose I had observed and classified years ago. Then I thought no more about it until we reached the house. I confess that I was astonished to see that Mrs. Lynch had the same type of ear as Burton's. They were obviously related, but I saw no indication of any acknowledgement of the fact between them. In truth, they seemed to be warily hostile of one another.

"Then, when Burton told us the story of his adoption into the household, I began to piece together a possible connection to you, Mr. Lynch. After all, it seemed unlikely that you would adopt a village orphan to be your apparent heir for no obvious reason. It was far more likely that

441

there was some hidden relation between the two of you, however unknown. It only took an observation of your own ears, showing the same family characteristic, to confirm it. George Burton is a Lynch, as well."

In spite of the number of times I had been exposed to Holmes's gifts, I could not suppress a soft, "Amazing."

"Not at all, Watson," said Holmes. "As I told you, by that time you had seen all that I had seen, the ears of both the living and the dead. Abner's story simply filled in confirming details. The family traits had been observable before that conversation. However," he added charitably, "I am sure that you would have eventually reached the same conclusion yourself, having now been exposed to my methods for so long."

I was pleased by Holmes's faith in me, but I doubted that his belief that I would have puzzled it out would actually have come to fruition. A thought occurred to me. "Mrs. Lynch is unlikely to be Burton's mother, as there is no indication that she has ever had a child. Therefore, that means that – "

"Yes, doctor. It means that I am George Burton's father," said Lynch quietly. "His mother was a new widow when we met, and it was true love between us, although she would not let me acknowledge it. She felt ashamed of us. She pretended that the boy was the child of her recently deceased husband, although we both knew differently, and the villagers believed her. I managed to find a way to get money to them as George grew. And then she died, and I was able to take him in, although I never revealed the truth, as doing so would destroy my beloved's reputation, as well as the love the boy felt for his dead mother."

"The conclusion that Burton is your son was quite easy to theorize," said Holmes, "considering how Burton was brought here after the death of his mother for no apparent reason, in your guise of Martin Briley, and trained to one day take over the estate."

"But not legitimately," I stated. "After all, it is *not* actually this man's estate to pass on." I gestured toward Lynch. "It does not matter whether or not Burton is Lynch's heir, or that Burton has been trained since childhood to run the place. Neither is a Briley. The estate should go to the true heirs of the Briley family."

"My research in the parish records suggested that there are no true heirs, Watson. And Abner believes that there were no illegitimate ones, either. He is certain that such a thing would have been a well known fact in those days. Just to make certain, I have MacDonald in London tracking down the last verification. But in any case, I'm sure that the Briley line died out with the true Martin Briley, forty-eight years ago."

"And so this man has gotten away with murder for half a century!" I cried.

442

"In his case, Watson, I feel safe to say that the accurate description of the situation is that he has gotten away with *covering up a murder*, since he did not commit the actual crime itself. Am I right about that, as well, Mr. Lynch?"

Lynch nodded. "I see that you understand everything. But how do you know that? Did Abner suspect something for all these years? Did we leave some clue, perhaps on the body, unseen at the time but obvious under your examination, that told you the whole story?"

"It was simply a matter of the timing. From what I understand, your sister had lived in the house for several years up to the time of Galton Briley's death. She was conniving enough to have made herself the housekeeper while still nearly a girl. I believe that it was her planning behind all of this. I don't think that you, living away from here in the years leading up to old Galton Briley's death, could have adequately contrived such an event from a distance.

"However, your sister *was* living in the house, knowledgeable at each hour of how Galton Briley was sinking, and aware that Martin Briley was being called home, returning after several years as a near stranger to his father and the village. Finally, she was the kind of sister who, according to Abner, had always tried to protect her younger brother. This protection extended to the point of killing in order to allow her brother to assume a life of luxury."

"Mrs. Lynch," I breathed. "She was the murderer."

"Yes," said Lynch. "It was my sister who did the deed." He shifted in the chair, and then he began to cough, a racking, deep cough that seemed to tear at him from inside out. His face reddened, and tears fell involuntarily from his clenched eyes. I had nearly forgotten that he was as ill as all that, as we had found him standing when we arrived, and out of his sick chair.

I rushed to his side and supported him while the coughing eased. As he sat back and caught his breath, I turned to the small table beside him, took the stopper from the oddly shaped bottle containing the amber liquid, and poured a finger or two into the glass snifter beside it. Handing it to him, I said, "Here, drink this. It will help."

"Thank you, doctor," he said, straightening up and adjusting his dressing gown. "Your kindness toward an old man is much appreciated." He held the glass in his right hand, but did not drink.

"You are correct in your suppositions, Mr. Holmes," he said. "I knew when George told me that the Inspector was bringing you here, time was probably starting to run out.

"I believe," he said, "that you should know the true story of what happened in the spring of 1840, when Galton Briley's iron constitution began to fail, and my sister saw a way to not only preserve her position within the household, but find a place for her baby brother as well, back here in the village of his birth, instead of surrounded by the terrible dangers of London. Sometimes I wish I had never answered her summons!" He shook his head. "What might have been, but for the formation of that first link on that one memorable day?"

"What might have been, but for the formation of that first link on that one memorable day?"

Chapter XII
The Old Man's Tale

As the storm grew outside, Lynch tried to make himself more comfortable. He shifted in his chair, and gently set the glass back on the small table beside him, untouched. Then the old man began his tale. The thunder increased as the rain lashed at the windows, but we did not hear it, as we were drawn back into those long ago days before either Holmes or I were born.

"I'm from this village," began Lynch, "born not a mile from where we are now. And you cannot imagine a more different set of circumstances. It was in a little house there, and it still stands, although many were the times when I was younger, after I had obtained the money and influence that came from the Briley estate, that I thought about having it knocked down. Instead, I made sure it was one of the best-kept homes around, and that the children living there never had to go through what I did. Pray to God no child ever should, but I know that they will. Even with access to the Briley fortune, there was only so much I could do.

"As you said, Mr. Holmes, I was born in 1821, a year after the true Martin Briley. My father brought my mother and my sister here before I was born. My sister was very young then. My father had been employed by the East India company in his youth, but he would never speak of it, save with a bitter jibe or a sneer, so we learned not to bring the subject up. Therefore, I never learned much else about my antecedents. I have no knowledge of where my father met my mother, or where she came from. And having discussed it with my sister when we were younger, I know that she is as ignorant as I am.

"In any case, here my father brought his family, and here I was born. He worked as a hand in the fields, but somehow he was knowledgeable enough about things that mattered that he was given a position of greater responsibility, and thus a small house. In those days, Galton Briley managed things quite differently than I have, and the houses at times were little better than wind-breaks with poorly fitted roofs. I recall many a night when it seemed that the inside of our little house was colder than the outside, as the cracks and crannies seemed to focus the wind into a living thing with a vengeance against me.

"My father must have been a successful man at some time in the past, because he was always well spoken, and never crude. Sadly, it was this ability which allowed him to aim his bitter tongue at each member of his

445

family with the accuracy of an Italian *stiletto*. And when he was drinking, matters became so much worse. As time went on, he drank more and more. No doubt it is a story you've heard many times before, but it is where mine begins, and where I started on the long road to end up here, tonight.

"I know that you gentlemen don't want to hear a list of every one of my father's torments upon his own family, and it's not relevant to our discussion. Suffice it to say, as time went on, my mother weakened, and was less and less able to defend her children. My father tended to save special attention to me, as I was the boy, and he seemed to expect something from me that I was not able to provide. It fell to my sister, nine years my senior, to defend and shield me when my mother could not. She did the best that she could, but it could not help but to transform her into the hard, cold, and mistrustful woman she is today. The kind of woman who would have no hesitation about taking what she felt that she deserved, and being quite ruthless about it.

"When I was about fourteen, my mother died, leaving us with only our father for a parent. He had become even more unpleasant as the years and the drink affected him. At that time, I was already finding work in the village, as old Mr. Briley certainly did not provide any schools for the local children. My sister had already gone to work in this very house, and as such no longer lived at home. It was just me and my father in the little house now, and he turned his full bitterness upon me.

"My sister was worried more than she would ever admit, and a few months after our mother died, she finally urged me to be away from here, rather than take anything else off of my father. I believe she was also worried that, as I reached my full growth, I would some day turn on my father and in anger do something which I would either regret, which wasn't likely, or perhaps commit some act against him that would lead to my arrest. I must admit, when she explained I would need to leave and break ties from this area completely, I was greatly intrigued by the idea. We both knew that if I stayed, I would never be completely free of my father. I decided I would go to London.

"As I said, I believe my father must have been a successful man at some time in the past. He was also an educated man, and in spite of my many grievances against him, I must be thankful that he saw to it that I learned to read. This allowed me to find my way to other areas of learning, and I soon taught myself enough to know how much I did *not* know. I have pursued knowledge from the time that I was small, and when I went to London, I managed to find a situation in a school, perhaps the best place I could have landed at the time.

"Of course, I was not a student. Rather, I was a young man of all work. But I did manage to teach myself the basics of mathematics, and also get my first exposure to literature and philosophy, reading books that were left unused and unopened by the students. The owners of the school were good, kind-hearted people, nothing like characters that might be portrayed in a Dickens novel. I was very satisfied, and believed that staying there would comprise the rest of my life. At that age, I had no true idea about how long a life can really be. And then, after I had lived there for several years, my sister wrote to say that Mr. Galton Briley's death was imminent, and that I needed to hurry home immediately.

"I had no idea why I should be present for such an event. I had only seen old Mr. Briley in the village on a handful of occasions, and had certainly never actually met him. His death would mean nothing to me. Yet, my sister urged me to come home, and how could I refuse her?

"We had remained in touch during the years I was up to London. We wrote on a regular basis, and she was always very encouraging when I would describe the things I was learning, or relate some of the added responsibilities I was taking on at the school. She had always sent money, and over time the amounts increased. Long before she had been elevated from her earlier position to that of head housekeeper, but I understood that the less I knew about her methods, the better.

"So having decided to obey my sister's command, I traveled back here from London. It was raining when I arrived in the village. This was before there were trains. I had ridden in coaches all day, and found it very wearying. My sister had given me specific instructions about which routes and times I should travel. I learned later that this was intentional, as my traveling companion was also someone who was returning to this village after a long time away. He had made his plans known to my sister in her position as the housekeeper, thus allowing her to be certain that I would be journeying with him. Of course, I'm referring to Martin Briley, coming home for the impending death of his father.

"Martin was a year older than I was, and had left for London following a disagreement with his father as well, although it was a year or so before I departed. By that time, we had both been gone for a number of years. Quite frankly, I did not recognize him as we rode the coaches, as he had changed considerably, and as he was more drunk than not throughout the entire day. There was no conversation between us that would have provided any opportunity to realize that we had this village in common. When we eventually reached the village, we were traveling by ourselves.

"We were met at the inn by my sister, who was driving a carriage. She had always been strong and independent, and did not worry at all about anyone's opinion of her. I would guess that people might have thought it unusual for a woman to be driving in that day and age. They still do now sometimes, I suppose. But when I saw her there, I was not surprised at all.

"She nodded to me in her reserved way, for she has never been an affectionate person, and then spoke to Martin Briley, telling him that the carriage was ready for him. She rushed him into it before anyone took notice of us. Martin climbed in, without seeming to give it any thought when she ascended to the driver's bench. I joined her there, and I don't think Martin even realized that the same man who had been traveling with him all day was going on with him to his family's estate.

"I wanted to ask my sister why she had summoned me, and I also wanted to ascertain what the chances were that we might encounter my father. But I held my tongue, not wanting to have any conversation in front of Martin, although it was doubtful that he would have cared anyway, as he seemed to have finally passed out from his day of drinking.

"As we drove onto the estate, my sister took the side road that runs down and behind the house, rather than along the main road leading past the front door, and then so on to the cottages. Again, I wanted to ask her questions, but I refrained, trusting her as I always had. Even when she brought the horse to a stop at the Briley mausoleum, overlooking the stream and the fields beyond, I kept my thoughts to myself.

"My sister climbed down and went to the side of the carriage. She reached inside and shook Briley until he awoke. 'We're here,' she said. 'I knew you'd want to see your father as soon as you could.' I thought I understood why we had come to the mausoleum, to see the dead body of Galton Briley, but I believed my sister's handling of the situation seemed to be in very poor taste, and was unnecessarily cruel to Martin Briley as well, no matter what sort of wastrel he appeared to have turned out to be.

"As he dropped to the ground, Briley looked to be waking up, but he still staggered with every step as my sister led him to the mausoleum door. The building was much newer then, of course, as it had only been built when Galton Briley's wife was slowly approaching her death. They say he loved his wife, as cold as he was. When she was ill, he built the mausoleum to honor her, and when she died, he had a matching coffin built for himself to lie beside her.

"We reached the mausoleum door, which was unlocked, and my sister pushed it open and led Martin inside. I followed, dreading what I thought was about to happen, and having no idea what my sister had actually planned.

"For I had believed that she simply intended to lead Martin to his father's coffin as a way of letting him know that the old man had died. I had thought it heartless, but I did not intervene. Even as we stepped closer to the coffin, with its lid open, I could not stop myself from following. The chamber was lit by several lanterns, and the hellish yellows and reds from the flames, as reflected by the cold marble walls, sent a thrill of terror through me. I did not want to see what was in that coffin, and yet I could not turn away.

"My sister led Martin Briley right to the side of the ornate box, and then left him, stepping away for just a moment. I moved closer, and was just able to see the ghastly form of Galton Briley lying there, when Martin opened his mouth, the beginnings of a wail on his lips, as the full realization fell upon him. It was at that moment that my sister pushed me roughly aside. She stepped behind Martin Briley, and swung her arm into his head. I could see that she held a round object, which I later learned was a decorative marble fixture from the tomb. Briley's cry stopped abruptly, and he sank to the floor, a horrible soft moan leaking from his dying lungs.

"I was aghast at what my sister had done. She stood looking at Martin for a moment, before straightening herself with a determined shake and replacing the marble fixture. And then she turned to me and spoke.

"'I have always tried to protect you, and to make a better life for you. This you know to be true. And even now, you must trust me. I will tell you this. I have had to sacrifice much to achieve the position I now hold, and I will never speak – even to you! – of what I have had to do. But you must understand that Galton Briley was an evil man. An *evil* man! I have *known* his evil. And before he departed for London, Martin Briley, the son, was evil as well. I have managed to stay informed, through his father, of Martin's rakish and wanton life, and he was not fit to live, anymore than his father. That is all I will tell you. You must trust me. But for now, help me get him into the coffin with his accursed father.'

"I know how the body of Martin Briley was found by the workmen under the pipe a few days ago. That was where it was eventually hidden, some days later, with the belief that it would never be found. But initially, we put the body into the coffin of Galton Briley. The old man had died a few days before my return to the village, and the funeral – such as it was – had already been conducted. My sister had managed everything, including what information was given out relating to the return of Martin Briley. She had told everyone who cared, and I'm sure that there were very few, that she had sent for him, but he was not going to be able to make it back home in time to see his father laid to rest. However, he would be expected at some unknown point in the future, to claim his inheritance.

"She had also sent a message to Martin Briley, telling him that his father was only sick, and not yet dead. She made the specific arrangements for his travels so that she would know exactly when he was entering her web. Such was the fear of her around the estate, even then, that she had no problem at all fixing things exactly as she wanted them. For she had conceived a plan, a bold plan indeed, and she meant to bring it to fruition.

"And so we concealed Martin's body in the coffin. Before that, however, my sister had me change clothes with him, so I would be wearing those of the dead man. I was moving as if in a fog, still shocked by my sister's actions, and willing to trust her as she had asked, but her request did not make sense to me at first. Later, I learned that she wanted to make sure that if I were unexpectedly seen after we left the mausoleum, I would be mistakenly recognized by my better clothing as the wealthy heir. But that was beyond my understanding in that moment. All I knew then was that my sister had committed a murder, and I was wearing a dead man's clothing that was too big for me.

"After wrestling Martin into my clothes, we lifted him up and rolled him into the coffin, holding up his father's body to make room. To this day, I'm not certain if my sister's blow actually killed Martin Briley immediately, or if he died later, sealed in his father's coffin, shoved up against his father's corpse.

"After we put the body into the coffin and shut the lid, my sister pulled me down beside her on one of the empty platforms, built for nonexistent members of the Briley family that would now never occupy them. The line was extinct. Even then, we knew that. It had always been common knowledge that Galton Briley had no living relatives, near or distant, except for his son. There were no heirs. And so, my sister explained, she had decided to make *me the heir!*

"She laid it all out quite succinctly. No one in the village had seen me in a number of years, and in the meantime I had grown and filled out. I did not look anything like the boy that I had been. I walked upright with a certain amount of pride now, reflecting the inner man I had constructed. No one would recognize me. And most of all, our father was dead, and he could certainly never tell anyone that I had returned.

"I was surprised at the death of my father, and more than a little suspicious about it, but my sister explained without emotion that he had passed not long after my departure, and she did not want to burden me, far away in London, with any thoughts wasted in his direction. After my initial surprise, I realized she was correct. I was better off without him in every respect.

"But I asked her, how would I fool everyone into thinking that I was Martin Briley, the long lost prodigal son? My sister had considered that as well. She believed he had been gone long enough so that few would remember him very clearly. The household staff had completely changed by this point, never lasting too long in the presence of both Galton Briley and my sister. As an adult, I now superficially resembled Martin Briley,

450

enough to fool anyone who might need to have dealings with me. There was only one thing that needed to be done, in order to carry off the impersonation . . . .

"My sister has always been a hard woman, and she needed to be, in order to do what must be done. In many ways, I was the weak one. I've long suspected, although she kept her word and never discussed it, that old Galton Briley was carried off before his time. I even believe, deep down, that my sister visited her form of justice upon our father. And she knew what had to be done to finish changing me into Martin Briley. I never would have been able to face it on my own. My sister gave me the strength and the courage. The last thing we did that night, in the hellish light of the mausoleum, was to complete the transformation.

"In her preparations for Martin Briley's arrival, my sister had also brought some other necessary supplies with her to the mausoleum. Holding my gaze, giving me strength to do what we had to do, she laid my hand across the empty platform where we sat, resting it upon fresh linens, as we had tried to make the conditions there as clean as possible. I bit down on a wooden dowel, wrapped in rags, and closed my eyes. The last thing I saw, before the incredible pain took me, was my sister raising the hatchet, already looking bloody in the reddish lantern light, over my extended little finger."

He paused for a moment, swallowing once or twice with the memory, still fresh after these many years. I shook my head, as if to chase away the dreadful picture that he had painted. I glanced over at Holmes, who was staring intently at our host, his pipe clenched in his teeth. I realized that I had been completely unaware that he had lit it.

"While I was unconscious," continued Lynch, "my sister poured whisky liberally over the wound, making sure that it came into contact with all the raw and affected areas. Beforehand, she had also poured it over the hatchet blade as well. By the time I was coming around, she was nearly finished bandaging my hand.

"The pain was unbearable, but somehow I made it back to the carriage, which she drove back to the house. No one saw us, as had been planned and arranged by my sister. She got me inside, and put me to bed in Galton Briley's room. And for the next three weeks, she nursed me, scouring out the infection that tried to take root in my hand, and helping me through the fever. She had told the staff that Martin Briley had returned, but was in a state of near death from his debauched London lifestyle. She was helping me to recover, so that I could take over the running of the estate.

"During the weeks that I was in bed, there had only been one visitor, the old man who was Galton Briley's attorney and man of business. It

451

seems that he had never known Martin Briley very well at all, but did know about his reputation. It was no surprise to him that I was recovering in bed all that time. Later, when I was able to get up and about, I met with him in this very room, bundled up much as you found me today, feigning that I had a chill and could not shake his hand. He believed it all, and happily entrusted me with the care and keeping of Galton Briley's fortune, which turned out to be sizably more than either I or my sister had believed.

"Sometime during my recovery, Elizabeth went alone to the mausoleum, and moved the body to what was supposed to be its final resting place. My sister has always been very strong. The installation of the pipe was already proceeding, and she believed that Martin Briley would never be found there. She reopened a portion of the trench where work had already been completed, and placed him there. I'm told that something in the soil has preserved him. I can only say I am grateful that I don't have to look upon him. At least not in this life.

"There were so many ways my sister's plan could have gone wrong. We could have been seen when we arrived at the village, or going to and from the mausoleum. We might have been questioned when she helped me into the house. She could have been discovered when she moved and buried the body.

"Later, perhaps some crony of Martin Briley's might have come down from London. We were careful to pay any of Martin's debts that appeared, before questions could be asked. Eventually, his London creditors must have been appeased, because we heard no more from them.

"I was careful never to go to London, so that I wouldn't run into anyone that either knew me from the old days, or any of Martin's dubious associates. As the years went by, I stayed here, although I would dearly have loved to get back there, and perhaps visit some of the locations memorialized in my favorite books. But the habit was ingrained by then, and there was always something to do here at home.

"When I first assumed Martin's place, I was especially worried that the villagers might recognize me, but they seemed to accept my new identity. Perhaps I had changed enough while I was gone that no one here knew me any longer. I had certainly never had any friends while I was growing up, and there was no real school then to attend. Possibly the locals were just happy to have someone at the estate who was interested in seeing to their welfare for a change, and they didn't question the situation too closely. In any case, I was careful to wear work gloves for a number of years until I was sure that my scar would pass unnoticed.

"The rest of my story passes quickly, as does a life when viewed from the wrong end. I assumed the role of Martin Briley, but I vowed that I would not live like he would have lived. I well remembered my

452

experiences as a poor mistreated village boy, and I made every effort to improve the lives of those that fell within my sphere. I started the schools, and made improvements where I could, as you have probably heard. Often my sister opposed me, saying I was just wasting the money, but I had to do it. After all, how else could I justify what we had done, if not to do something good with it? I had built up a quantity of debt, and it had to be repaid, even if it took the rest of my life. And it has.

"I don't know how Martin Briley would have lived his life here, had he gotten the chance. I suspect that he would have been dead within a year, all on his own. But circumstances had placed me in a position to do some good, and so I tried to do so. I hadn't planned anyone's murder, but I had helped to conceal one, and I must try to make amends.

"Of course, my sister never married. She has been content to live in this house, under the title of housekeeper, as if it were her own. And in a way, it has been. She paid a dear price for it, even more than I did. I believe she paid her very soul. Well, we are both old now, and we will soon find out.

"I expected that I would remain as alone as she, devoting my life to what service I could find around here. But then I met George's mother, and life changed for me.

"It was not long after she was widowed. She was a seamstress in the village, and I was riding by one night in a storm when I was thrown from my horse. She saw what happened and took me in. That night, there was just an innocent conversation lasting only a few minutes. But my heart was touched in a way that had never happened before. I found excuses to return, always being very discreet, and before long I knew she loved me as well. However, she quickly determined that she was bearing my child. Of that, there was no doubt.

"I wanted to marry her then. She would not, stating that the village would be able to work out the truth of her shame in the matter. I offered to run away with her, leave everything, including the debt that I had taken on, in order to go somewhere that we could start new lives, but she wouldn't hear of it. She would not let me leave my responsibilities here. She gave everyone to understand that she was carrying the child of her recently deceased husband. She refused to have any further dealings with me, claiming it was for the best. I believe now that, at the bottom of it all, she was too ashamed of dishonoring her late husband's memory to ever allow us to be together. Completely inexperienced in the ways of the heart, I retreated to this house, a heartbroken man. And so, my son was born, while I sat up here brooding, and going through the empty motions of my life.

"I followed the boy's progress, and made opportunities for both him and his mother as I could. When she suddenly died, I realized that I had still been hoping for some miraculous reconciliation, even after all those empty years. For days I kept to myself, afraid to even show the staff any of my complete and total grief. And then I emerged, informing my sister that I intended to take the boy in, even if I could not reveal to him that I was actually his father without shaming his mother's memory.

"My sister fought me, more than she ever did on any of the many instances when trying to convince me to stop spending money on the countryside. But I was adamant. I went and got him, and brought him back here, and there is not a day that goes by when I don't see his mother's beautiful face looking back at me from his.

"I think that I have been a good father to him, even if he does not know that I am. I have trained him to be a skillful manager, and a good man. Years ago, I placed several benches around the estate, where I could sit at the end of a day's work and think. Many have been the evenings when George was smaller, when he would sit with me on one of the benches, and lean against me for warmth as the sun dropped beneath the horizon. And my arm has curled around him, my own son, and I have felt fulfilled more than at any other time in my life.

"A couple of these benches are under special trees. Soon after I took over the estate, I planted three English elms at certain locations on the property. I placed them so that at some time or another, every day, I would see at least one of them from wherever I was working and be reminded of what I had helped my sister to do, and what my payment was. The trees were in honor of the Brileys, an unspoken acknowledgement of what I was trying to accomplish with their resources. One of the trees was a specific memorial to the man I had replaced, planted where he was secretly buried. I didn't put a bench under that tree. As lovely as that spot is, I couldn't bear to sit that close to the body that I knew was hidden there. That was the tree George pulled down a few days ago without my knowledge, when he was repairing the pipe leading to the mere.

"The second memorial tree is down by the mausoleum, by a bench looking out over the farms. You cannot tell it now, but the top of that tree can be seen from here in the house on a clear day. The third tree was near the stone bridge, where I would see it whenever I went to the cottages, which used to be a daily occurrence. I understand that lightning struck it today, killing it. Perhaps it is a sign, now that everything has come crashing down. I had really come to believe the old crimes would not be discovered, not at this late date. I had hoped that my penance would have paid the price, but as the old saying goes, murder will out."

454

We were all quiet for a few moments, thinking about what had been said, and listening to the sounds of the wind. Lynch reached up, adjusted the filled glass slightly to a different position on the small table, and then let his hand rest gently on the book there.

Finally, Holmes said, "Thank you, Mr. Lynch, for an illuminating account of the history of the matter. You have filled in the gaps in my understanding quite adequately. Sadly, I've heard nothing that relieves me of my dilemma."

"Dilemma?" I asked. "Holmes, what can you mean?"

"I think that I understand, doctor," said Lynch. "Mr. Holmes does not know whether or not to reveal the truth to the authorities. Am I correct?"

Holmes nodded. "Indeed. There is no doubt that you have performed a lifetime of good service here in the village, paying your 'quantity of debt,' as Mr. Dickens put it in your favorite book."

Lynch's eyes widened, as he realized that Holmes had indeed recognized where the quote originated. "If it were just you that still survived," said Holmes, "I would not be facing such a decision. But there is still a murderer who profits from what she has done, possibly a murderer several times over, and I do not think that even your years of penance can satisfy justice. And yet, if I reveal the truth about your sister, it cannot fail but to undo the work that you yourself have done.

"If it is revealed that you are not Martin Briley, the estate will pass from your control. Your careful plan to groom George Burton, who is a good man and suited for the position, will fail, and the estate will be broken up into whatever manner the courts see fit. An heir to the Brileys will be found, no matter how distant, and quite possibly inappropriate, such a person turns out to be. And this village, and its schools, and the workers and families who are tied to it, may all be hurt."

Holmes turned and paced a step or two, before shifting back toward Lynch. "I, too, have a quantity of debt. To myself. I want to believe that it would be better to allow you to live out the rest of your life doing good, rather than undo all that you have accomplished. Exposing you would exact a heavy price. And yet, there is the question of your sister."

"We, my sister and I, are both old now, Mr. Holmes," said Lynch. "These things have a way of taking care of themselves."

Holmes looked at him silently for a long moment. Then, Lynch tapped the book beside him and said, "I can tell from some of your perceptive comments that you must have read and know the works of Dickens, Mr. Holmes."

This apparent *non sequitur* seemed to take Holmes aback for just a moment. "In spite of Doctor Watson's early assessment of my limits, in which he stated that my knowledge of literature was 'nil,' I do have a passing acquaintance with one of our greatest writers."

"And you know *Great Expectations*? I must confess, the works of Dickens have been my particular favorites over the years, but this book has been of special comfort to me, as you will have perceived. I believe that you can understand why."

"Hmm. The story of a boy who rises from his humble beginnings to a better life," answered Holmes.

"And perhaps," I added, "the similar parallel of Burton being raised to a higher position, as was Pip, because his benefactor is actually a criminal."

Lynch seemed to wince slightly at my description, but he nodded. "There is another quote in the book that has always meant a great deal to me. 'I have been bent and broken, but – I hope – into a better shape.' "

Holmes replied, "I, too, recall a different passage in the volume which I have found applicable. 'Take nothing on its looks; take everything on evidence. There's no better rule.' "

Lynch nodded in agreement. "You do not disappoint, Mr. Holmes. And I would hope that the evidence that you have seen, and what I've tried to do with my bent and broken life, and the better shape that I tried to accomplish, would be enough."

"But Holmes," I interrupted. "We cannot allow a murderer to go unpunished!" I cried. "I agree that Lynch has worked for a lifetime to make up his part of the debt, and there is little doubt that if the Briley family had continued to run the estate, the lives of countless people would not be as well off as they are now. And yet, there must be a way – we must *find* a way – to punish the wicked!."

The door to the hall flew open at this statement, and Mrs. Lynch, who had obviously been listening for some unknown length of time, stepped in. "Wicked?" she cried. The flickering fire light only served to illuminate the madness flashing in the deadly eyes of the old woman advancing upon us. "You dare to call me *wicked*? I *saw* wickedness! I was *touched* by wickedness! The wicked have already *been* punished!"

Chapter XIII
Bent and Broken

"Sister," said Lynch, rising unsteadily from his chair. "Elizabeth," he said, in a softer tone. Then he nearly sagged for a moment, and I started toward his side, but he straightened and waved me back. His sister, also seeing his momentary failure, seemed to forget her rage for an instant, and a look of concern crossed her features. It occurred to me that she had been taking care of him, one way or another, for his whole life, and the small matter of being revealed to be a murderer, probably three times over, if not more, was not enough to turn her from her path.

She took several steps toward him before stopping, separated from him now by only a few feet. She was still dressed in the same dark clothing as earlier in the day, and she had obviously not been to bed. Seeing that Lynch was all right, she turned a glance toward Holmes, and then me. As her earlier rage quickly returned, her breathing became more ragged, and the whites of her eyes were quite visible as she looked back and forth from her brother to the both of us, standing to her right.

"What have you done?" she hissed at Lynch, taking another step toward him. "What have you told them? They never needed to know *anything*. It was fifty years ago! No one would ever have been able to figure it out!"

She rocked in place for a second, as if the violence within her was seeking a place to escape. "Elizabeth," began Lynch, but she spoke over him, her sibilant tones stabbing like knives.

"I would have thought of a way to silence them," she said. "I just needed more time! I could have put something in their food." Lynch raised a shaking hand and covered his eyes.

She turned to Holmes and me, facing us straight on as her expression darkened even further, if that were possible. "I didn't do it just to have the house or the lands. You have to understand that. I could have had them anyway. I had the old man wrapped around my finger. He wanted to *marry me!* My God, he believed that I wanted to marry him as well. But he was *evil*! He was the devil himself. His poor wife had found that out on her own, years earlier, before I was ever here. It put her into an early grave. And his son was going to be the same way. I could tell. No, it wasn't about the house. It was more than that. I had to put a stop to it. I had to put a stop to him. To both of them, father *and* son. For what they had both done! For what they had both done *to me!*"

457

Her strained voice trailed into a thin shriek, which coincided with a loud clap of thunder, followed almost immediately by a flash of lightning. She began to shake, and then gave a great sob before relapsing into near silence, the only sound being a high, thin, keening sound, which would have been barely audible, even if the storm outside was not displaying such renewed violence. Her arms hung straight to her sides, and her shoulders were rounded and sagging. It was terrible to behold. But it only lasted for the briefest of moments, and then she stopped it, as if throwing a curtain shut against the daylight. As quick as that, her outburst was gone, and the same Mrs. Lynch of earlier in the day was with us again, albeit a Mrs. Lynch now teetering on the edge of a homicidal rage toward the two meddlesome visitors who had helped to reveal her secret.

Lynch took a step or two toward her, and folded her into his arms. She resisted at first, and it was as if he were trying to bend a tree with his puny grasp. Then, little by little, she leaned into him, almost imperceptibly. He guided her into the second chair, on the other side of the small table from where he had been sitting. Feeling the seat of the chair behind her knees, she finally collapsed without any resistance. Slowly the emotions of a moment ago returned, and her face contorted into a terrifying rictus of agony, and her eyes were squeezed shut as tears began to flow down her lined cheeks. She was muttering something now, but too low to understand. Whatever it was, it seemed to be the same phrase, over and over again, until it ceased to sound like words at all.

Lynch reached for the glass on the table that I had filled for him earlier, when he seemed to be tearing himself apart while coughing. He had held the glass then for a while, before eventually setting it untouched upon the table. Now, he picked it up and held it to her lips. He was bent awkwardly, stroking her hair and murmuring to her softly, seeming finally to break the spell of grief and anger which held her. She took a sip of the liquid, and then another.

Pulling the glass away, Lynch turned slightly and refilled it, before bringing it back to her lips again. She drank it all at once this time, closing her eyes and grimacing as the burn of it moved down her throat. Lynch then filled the glass a third time, and placed it in his sister's hand. He had to grip her fingers around it for a moment before she seemed to comprehend that he wanted her to take it. Finally, she grasped and held it. While Lynch turned and filled the second glass, she took another sip, and then lowered her hand and the glass, now half empty, back to her lap. She continued to weep, but with less emotion than before.

Lynch moved over to his chair, turned and sat down with a sigh. He raised the glass to his lips and took the smallest of sips, before stating, "I expect that last bolt of lightning took out the third memorial tree, the one

458

down by the mausoleum. It would only be fitting that now, here at the end, all three of them would go down. The first when the body was found, and then the second by the bridge while you were investigating, and now the last." He coughed slightly, and winced in the slightest way. "Have you seen it? The tree by the mausoleum?"

I nodded, and Holmes said, "Only in the darkness, I'm afraid. We were down there tonight, just before we returned to the house and began our chat with you.

Lynch raised his eyebrows. "You were down there? Down at the mausoleum? And did you go in?"

Holmes nodded, and Lynch continued. "Well, I'm sure you needed to see for yourself whatever it was that you required in order to answer all of your questions. But it really was a wasted trip, you know. I was waiting here, prepared for you. I had unlocked the terrace door in case getting past my sister in the house proved to be too difficult.

"As I said, I knew earlier today that you had figured out the truth. I thought that you would come in soon after dinner. I was prepared to speak with you, and then we would have summoned my sister." More softly, he said, "Instead, she found her way in here on her own. It has always been her way to take the initiative."

He glanced at Mrs. Lynch, who was holding the third glass of liquid loosely, and staring at the floor in front of her. She was starting to sag in the chair, and she hadn't made any attempt to drink any more from the glass.

Lynch started to raise his own glass back to his lips, and then he decided to speak instead. "There is a place in *Great Expectations*," he said, tapping a finger on the back of the green leather-bound book beside him, "when Pip says, 'In a word, I was too cowardly to do what I knew to be right as I had been too cowardly to avoid doing what I knew to be wrong.' That day, many years ago, when my sister committed a murder in front of my very eyes, I was a coward. I would like to think that tonight, I have finally been able to do what had to be done."

Holmes was watching him intently. Suddenly, I understood why. And, God help me, I simply watched as well, as Lynch raised his glass and drank the rest of the contents.

Beside him, his sister had seemed to settle lower in her seat. Her fingers opened, and the glass that she had loosely grasped dropped from her hand, fell, and rolled away, spilling the last unconsumed drops onto the fine rug beneath her. She made a small moan, and my trance was broken as I rushed to her side. A quick examination revealed the truth. "She's dead, Holmes," I whispered.

I stood and took a step back. Lynch was setting his glass onto the small table, obviously taking care to avoid looking at his sister. He then picked up his copy of *Great Expectations* from the tabletop and grasped it to his chest with his thin fingers. "You will have noticed, Mr. Holmes," he said, "that this volume contains two bookmarks." He tilted the book, so that we could see both of the envelopes pressed within it. "This evening, while I waited for you and Dr. Watson to arrive, I wrote a couple of documents, now here in this book. Since then, I have been revisiting some of my favorite passages."

He winced again, and then made a sharp little gasp, as if he had been pricked with a pin. I could see that even with only one glass of the liquid in him, unlike the nearly three that he had given to his sister, he was not long for this world. "One of these envelopes contains my will. It names my son, George, as my heir. I will tell you that the document does *not* explain that I am his father. As much as I have wanted to tell him the truth, it is now too late, and it would be far too terrible a burden to reveal to him at this point, and tell him that everything he has believed has been a lie.

"The other envelope contains a complete confession of the events that we have discussed tonight, signed and dated. I have been careful to explain everything, with no attempt at making any excuses whatsoever. It is a fair and balanced account, and should it be read, it will no doubt relate all the facts to whomever reads it, including whichever distant Briley relation that is found to take over the estate.

"I leave it to you, Mr. Holmes, and to you too, Dr. Watson, to decide what to do. Throw one or the other – or both or neither! I shall be beyond caring soon – into the fire. In moments it won't matter to me one way or the other." He coughed, louder this time, and twisted to the side in the chair, trying to find some relief.

Holmes said nothing for a moment. Then stepping forward, he leaned toward the dying man, making sure that Lynch could see him. "You should know what George is doing tonight."

Lynch, whose gaze was already fading, pulled himself back for a moment and focused on Holmes. "What?" he said. "What is George doing?"

"He has arranged to be married. On this very night, to Lydia Woods. He has been considering it for quite a while, as you know. It is also common knowledge in the village, where I talked to several people who knew about it. Her family knows, including her brother. Your sister had been becoming ever more objectionable about George's feelings toward the girl, not wanting your heir to marry a simple maid. George believed that Mrs. Lynch was eventually going to do something to irretrievably complicate matters if things kept going on as they have been.

"Finally, I took him aside tonight and revealed that I suspected his plans, and encouraged him to go ahead. It would serve to keep him out of the house, should he find a reason to interrupt our investigation and subsequent conversation. And at the very least, he needed to cement his happiness in case tonight's outcome should have any unpleasant ramifications.

"He did not want to do it without you. He agonized over the decision before I finally convinced him. Earlier, Watson and I saw him driving the carriage with Lydia inside, on their way to meet the minister, with whom he had earlier made arrangements. He intends to return here in the morning to surprise you with the happy news."

Lynch smiled, a forced and hideous smile, considering the pain that he seemed to be suffering, but a sincere smile nonetheless. "George married. I'm very glad to hear it. Very glad indeed." He roused himself one last time, and looked up at Holmes. "It is something else, then, for you to take into your considerations, Mr. Holmes," he said.

Lynch held Holmes's eyes for a moment, than weakly raised his right hand. Holmes, sensing the unspoken question, took a step forward and clasped it, shaking it now when he had declined to do so earlier. Then, Lynch released his grip and rested his head on the back of the chair, closing his eyes. Folding both hands around the old book, he breathed, "Decide well, Mr. Holmes." Then, with a sigh, his soul passed from his body and he entered eternity.

We were left with the sound of the crackling fire and the terrible storm passing without. After what seemed like several long moments, I breathed softly, "My God."

Holmes, who had been as silent as I, seemed to return to himself. "Yes," he replied softly. He swallowed, and said again, with slightly more volume, "Yes."

He stepped forward and, raising a hand, closed the old man's eyes. Then, after a slight hesitation, he pulled the book from Lynch's hands. Letting it fall open, he retrieved the two envelopes, one labeled "Last Will and Testament" and the other marked "My Confession." He started to shut the book, and then shifted it closer to his eyes as he studied something with renewed focus. Then he glanced at me, and said, "There is a marked passage. Shall I read it aloud?"

I nodded, and he began. " *'That was a memorable day to me, for it made great changes in me. But it is the same with any life. Imagine one selected day struck out of it, and think how different its course would have been. Pause you who read this, and think for a moment of the long chain of iron or gold, of thorns or flowers, that would never have bound you, but for the formation of the first link on one memorable day.'* "

He stood silently as we both thought of the words, and how they related to the life of Peter Lynch and that day so long ago when he had returned home at his sister's request, only to find that fate had thrust him onto a most unimaginable path. Certainly he had pondered that one unique day a number of times, and the marked passage in his favorite book had certainly resonated all the more for him.

But surely, I thought, it is the same with anyone, as was the point of the author. The day Martin Briley had returned home had been such a day for him, when his destiny was altered. Or when the Lynches' father had brought his family to Bedfordshire. Or when old Galton Briley had allowed Elizabeth Lynch into his house as a scullery maid. Was that the day that had forged the first links in the long chain of events leading to the deaths of the two old siblings in front of us? Truly, everyone could look back at a hundred days, nay a thousand, in his or her own life and find where a different path was taken than the one that had been expected or hoped for. And yet, not all paths followed the route of the one that fate had laid out for Peter Lynch, known now for nearly a half-century as Martin Briley.

Holmes may have been thinking some of the same thoughts. His gaze was quite far away, and then he seemed to bring his focus back to the scene in front of us. He closed the book, and then opened one of the unsealed envelopes and pulled out a couple of sheets, covered in even, old-fashioned copperplate. He read for a moment, and then passed the pages to me. "The will," he said, unnecessarily. He was apparently more shaken than I had believed. I glanced at it quickly, and then reread it more slowly. It did not take long.

"Everything to George Burton," I said. "With no other explanation of any sort."

"It seems to be completely legal," said Holmes.

"And the confession?" I asked, nodding toward the other envelope. Without a word, Holmes removed it and started reading, passing each page to me as he completed it. There were considerably more sheets than the two comprising the will, with each written in the same careful handwriting. It took us several long minutes to read the thing completely through. In the meantime, the two Lynches, brother and sister, both bound in death as in life by their secrets, sat in their chairs, almost expectantly as if to see what our decision would be.

Finally, I finished the last sheet and handed it back to Holmes. He folded it neatly with the rest of the confession, and placed it back in its own envelope. "Written exactly as he told it," Holmes said. "I see no reason to doubt its veracity."

"Neither do I."

"Then – ?" asked Holmes, holding up both of the envelopes, his eyebrows raised.

I nodded toward one of them, and Holmes agreed. He tucked that one back into the green book, and then stepped to the fireplace. He leaned down and carefully placed the other envelope onto the coals, making sure that it did not fall behind the grate for possible later discovery. We had seen that sort of thing happen before. This was one document that we wanted to make certain had been destroyed.

We both watched as it began to spark around the edges, and then smoke and blacken. It took several minutes, during which time it seemed that it might not burn at all, but rather simply char and curl. However, it finally burst into flame, and in just a moment, it was fully ablaze. Holmes took the poker, and carefully broke up the remaining leaves into ash. The document was gone.

Holmes walked over and locked the outside door. Then he replaced the green leather book and the document that it held on the shelf, in the open space with the rest of the Dickens collection. He did not push it all the way in, but it was not obvious that it was pulled out, either. He and I retrieved our coats and hats from the floor. We gave another look back at the two old figures sitting in their chairs, separated by the small table. Holmes frowned, and then seemed to reach a decision, saying, "Just one more thing."

He walked over to the table and picked up the bottle of unknown liquid, which we now knew to be a potent killer. He removed the stopper and cautiously sniffed, before shaking his head. "There is nothing that I can tell this way. There is no odor. Only a chemical test would reveal the truth." He stepped to the fireplace. "I don't suppose that it matters in any case. Probably Lynch obtained this and held it in reserve for quite a while, in the eventuality that he ended up requiring such a drastic solution."

He bent by the flames and poured some of the liquid onto the fire. It sizzled and steamed, and then it was gone. The fire quickly returned where the liquid had been poured. Holmes held up the bottle, and I could see that there were now only a few drops remaining. "It is enough for the police to analyze, if they so choose, but not enough to remain and cause further mischief."

He put the stopper back in the bottle and stepped to the small table, between the two bodies. Then he placed the bottle conspicuously on Mrs. Lynch's side of the table, instead of where it had previously rested by her brother. He took a moment to feel in the pocket of Lynch's dressing gown, before pulling out a key, which he proceeded to transfer to the pocket of Mrs. Lynch's dress. Then, seemingly satisfied, he rejoined me at the door, and we stepped softly into the hall.

The house was silent, and the sounds of the storm were muted this deep into the house. Pulling the door shut, Holmes retrieved his picklocks from a pocket, and then he bent and locked the door.

We rehung our coats and hats where we had found them, and relocked the door to the terrace. Holmes motioned that I should precede him, and we crept upstairs to our rooms. There, we both found the same seats that we had occupied some hours earlier and sat down to smoke. There was no conversation. None was needed. We would not be sleeping this night, as we waited for the grim discovery to be made in the morning.

Chapter XIV
The New Day

Sometime around dawn, both Holmes and I roused ourselves from our respective chairs to prepare for the day. As I had expected, neither of us had slept. I had stopped smoking long before Holmes, of course. He often spent many a night with his pipe, wrestling with a problem until he had shaped it into a structure that he could comprehend. I suspect that often his "three-pipe problems" stretched until they were four, five, or even six pipes.

The storm had ended during the early hours of the morning, and when the sun rose, it revealed a bright spring day, washed clean and alive. Even from our window, I could see that the gardens and flower beds close to the house showed fresh new growth. The window was on the side of the house facing in the direction of the cottages. Down the long slope in that direction, it was obvious that the stream was up, and part of the old bridge was under water, cutting off the collection of tiny homes from the rest of the estate.

Beside it, caught in the muddy water and forcing it to swirl as it flowed past, was the shattered wreckage of one of the elms that Peter Lynch had planted as a memorial and a reminder to himself. MacDonald's description of the night before had been accurate. It looked as if the lightning had caused the upper portions of the tree to explode.

As I turned away from the window, one of the maids brought in hot water. She was surprised, I think, to find us already up. It occurred to Holmes to turn and muss the beds, so as to appear that we had actually slept. After a shave and a fresh shirt and collar, I felt ready to face what we both knew was coming. Holmes managed to look refreshed, as he had always displayed a certain cat-like cleanliness, except on those many occasions when he was forced to undertake a filthy disguise. Except for some circles under his eyes, giving them a slight bruised look, one would never believe that he had been up all night. I was certain that I did not look nearly so well.

We eventually started down to breakfast. Before reaching the stairs, Holmes pulled me over to one of the back windows, looking out on the rear grounds of the house. I could see the slope that we had traversed in the darkness the night before, the narrow track passing from left to right, and the copse where we had momentarily hidden while Burton's carriage had passed us. Past the track was the mausoleum, shining brightly in the

465

clear morning light. Beside it was the wreckage of a great tree, destroyed in the storm. It looked as if it had been struck in the middle by lightning. As the top half had fallen away, part of it had remained attached to the trunk below, pulling the whole thing out of the waterlogged ground. It had fallen, just missing the mausoleum, but completely destroying the marble bench beside it. One of the same marble benches, according to Peter Lynch, that he and his son had used.

"He was right," Holmes said softly. "The storm did take the third and final tree, there at the end of it all."

We made our way downstairs, and Holmes contrived to lead us by the room where Lynch and his sister were waiting to be discovered. So far, the door was undisturbed, and we passed on into the dining room, where we found that breakfast had been laid.

Several of the servants were whispering as we served ourselves, and I gathered that they were puzzled by Mrs. Lynch's absence, as well as Lydia's. I made an effort to appear oblivious to their huddled conversations, instead concentrating on eating my breakfast. Holmes had gotten some food as well, and he ate it with machine-like precision. I almost believe that he only ate so that the servants clearing the table would not have reason to comment on the guest who partook of nothing, which might have seemed suspicious in some way.

We had nearly finished that joyless meal when there was a commotion at the front of the house. Before we could rise and determine its source, we heard quick footsteps coming down the hallway to the dining room. Turning in my chair, I was in time to see a beaming George Burton enter, with his glowing bride clinging to his arm. I reminded myself that I was supposed to know nothing of the tragedy waiting to be discovered across the hall, and of how I should react when I heard Burton's good news.

"We did it, Mr. Holmes! We were married last night!" One of the serving girls clearing the table audibly gasped, and Lydia looked her way. Their eyes locked, and Lydia smiled, dimples appearing on her cheeks. The young maid could not help herself, and a smile broke on her face as well. Setting down the dishes, she dashed from the room to the back of the house, barely able to contain herself. We could hear her calling the news to the staff before she ever reached them.

Holmes and I moved around the table, offering our most sincere congratulations. I was happy for Burton, and glad that Holmes had encouraged him to go ahead and wed his true love. She would give him strength for the trial that was lying ahead of them both.

Burton was still explaining the events of the night before, how he had arranged with the local clergyman to perform the ceremony after having gotten the license weeks earlier, and how he had put Lydia into the closed carriage and driven her from the cottages, where she lived with her parents, and over the bridge, which was even then starting to flood. They had gone on to the church, where they were married before Lydia's parents, who had arrived ahead of time to make preparations, and their friends in the village. His only regret, said Burton, was that his protector and mentor, Mr. Martin Briley, had not been able to attend. However, he knew that the old man was too ill, and the wedding could not wait any longer. He was sure that Mr. Briley would understand. Holmes glanced at me quickly, and then away, before we might give anything away.

While we were still talking with the Burton newlyweds, we heard the front door open and close. There were muted conversations in the front hall, and then footsteps, as Woods led Inspector MacDonald into our presence. Woods was beaming, and he caught his sister's eye, and then mine as well, before he turned and left the room.

"I took the early train," he said, looking at us all, one at a time. His gaze lingered on the Burtons, and especially young Lydia's tight grip on her new husband's arm. "And have I missed something?" he asked.

Burton quickly explained that he and Lydia had gotten married the night before. I could see that his natural policeman's suspicions were aroused, but he seemed to accept that Burton had simply been driven to wed his bride by Mrs. Lynch's constant interfering, and the belief that she might do something to cause more trouble if matters were not taken in hand.

At the mention of Mrs. Lynch's name, one of the girls stepped forward hesitantly, and said, "Excuse me, gentlemen? And . . . and . . . Mrs. Burton," she said hesitantly, with the hint of a small giggle. Lydia beamed back at her. "About Mrs. Lynch. It seems that . . . well, we can't *find her*," the girl blurted out. "We've looked everywhere. She's always the first one up, but not today. She didn't answer any of the knocks at her room, and finally Polly was brave enough to open the door. Her bed hasn't been slept in. There's only one place left to look.

"We already tried it, and the door to Mr. Briley's room is locked. We can't check in there," she continued, rather helplessly. "Usually Mrs. Lynch takes care of the master, with our help, but today no one has been in there. There is no answer when we knock, and the door is locked," she repeated. "That door is never locked. We even tried to see in from the outside windows, but the curtains are blocking our view. I hate to ask, but . . . Mr. Burton? Sirs? Can you check to see if Mrs. Lynch is in there with Mr. Briley?"

There is little need to elaborate on what happened next. A key was eventually found for the door, after some little trouble. Holmes made no effort to offer the use of his skills or his lock-picking devices. Finally the door was opened, and the bodies of the two old people were found. Burton had previously sent his wife to wait with the staff, but she was called back to her husband's side when he had to be led away after seeing the silent remains of the closest thing to a father that he'd ever had.

Holmes made cursory glances around the room, but left most of the inspection to MacDonald. The Inspector spent a long time looking at the two figures by the fire, now long since burned out. Finally, he said, "What do you think, Mr. Holmes?" He gestured toward the table, the two glasses, and the bottle beside the old housekeeper. Holmes, who had given the arrangement a passing look when we entered the room, was then over by the desk.

"Hmm?" he asked, his hand pushed into an open drawer. "What do you mean?"

"The glasses, of course," said MacDonald. "Do you think that it's poison?"

"Oh, certainly," replied Holmes in an off-hand manner. "I should certainly have it tested, but I would expect that it is a quick-acting alkaloid, probably derived from the juice of a berry or plant, and easily disguised in the liquor."

"But what of the placement of the bottle?" MacDonald said. "Do you agree that Mrs. Lynch has done this thing? She had the key to the room in her pocket, indicating that she was the one who locked the door. The bottle is clearly on her side of the table. It seems obvious she must have poured something for old Mr. Briley, and then when he had drunk it, she poured one for herself, set the bottle on the table beside her, and drank hers off as well."

"So it would appear," said Holmes.

"But why? Why would she kill him after all these years?"

"No doubt there was something about the discovery of the body in the trench that forced her hand," replied my friend. "We may never know at this point, nearly fifty years after the original crime, exactly what happened, or what she feared might be revealed."

MacDonald eyed Holmes shrewdly. "It seems to me that you appear unnaturally disinterested, Mr. Holmes." He stepped closer to my friend, saying. "I've seen you crawl around the scene of a crime on your stomach looking for clues. You must admit that you barely glanced at the two corpses."

"It was obvious from the time that we walked into the room that the two had been poisoned, undoubtedly when one had the other drink unknowingly, and then the murderer drank the deadly liquid as well. It was apparent that the bottle was by Mrs. Lynch. Thus, the conclusion must be that she did the deed, rather than Mr. Briley."

MacDonald continued to look at Holmes, who met his gaze without looking away. Finally, MacDonald looked back toward the bodies and said, "I spoke with your friend, Dean, last night. He confirmed that there are no other Briley heirs to speak of. The line is as moribund as can be imagined. This man here is truly the last of the Briley's."

He sighed, and continued, "There are absolutely no Briley heirs anywhere to be found. We might find a cousin thirteen-times removed, *if* we advertise from John o' Groats to Beachy Head, and *if* we bring in the Royal College of Arms to help us, but that would be the *only* way another Briley would be found."

"Dear me," said Holmes. "Then to whom shall the estate pass?"

"It will be up to the Crown, I expect," said MacDonald. He turned and walked over to the desk, where he shuffled half-heartedly through some of the papers there. Then, he turned back to us. "There was one other thing, however."

Holmes raised his eyebrows. "Really? And what would that be?"

"Before I departed from your friend, Dean, I thought to ask him if he'd heard of anything similar to this crime in Nimes, several decades ago."

"Indeed," replied Holmes. "And what did he say."

"He said it sounded familiar to him, but he couldn't recall the details."

"How unfortunate."

"But," added MacDonald, "he did recall where he could find them. It took him less than ten minutes. Interesting case, that." He waited for Holmes to inquire, but when nothing was forthcoming, he continued. "It seems that a body was found, hidden on an estate. It was discovered that it was actually the heir to the family fortune, murdered many years before. He had been killed by the man who had taken his place, living a life of luxury ever since."

"Ah, yes, now I recall some of the details," said Holmes.

"I'm sure that you do," said MacDonald, wryly. "The difference between that case and this one was that the man who took over the dead man's identity in Nimes was a true villain in every sense of the word. Quite a different man, according to Dean, than someone like poor Mr. Briley, here, for instance."

"Yes," said Holmes. "From all that we've heard, Mr. Briley spent a lifetime doing good works. The area will miss him greatly."

"That is true. It is unfortunate, indeed, that there is no will which might, for instance, pass on the estate to that fine young Mr. Burton."

"Hmm, yes, about that," said Holmes, turning away from MacDonald and toward the shelves. "I did notice something a moment ago. Now let me see . . . ."

He stepped to the section containing the green leather-bound books and peered closely at them, without touching them. Then, he said, "MacDonald, a moment, if you don't mind."

MacDonald joined him, but not before glancing my way with a gaze that suspiciously seemed to indicate that he was enjoying this game. "What is it, Mr. Holmes?"

"If you will observe, Mr. Mac, these are the Dickens books that we saw yesterday, when we interviewed Mr. Briley in this room. At the time, I pointed out that they seemed to be special favorites, as they were the only ones where there was no dust on the shelf."

"Yes, I recall it."

"I can assure you that when I looked at the books yesterday, all of them were pushed fully into the shelf. Now, as you can see, one of them is pulled slightly out."

"True," said MacDonald. *Great Expectations.*"

"Exactly," said Holmes. "If you would do the honors?" he indicated.

MacDonald reached up and pulled out the book. He laid it flat on his large palm, and it fell open, revealing the envelope hidden within. "It's the will," he breathed. Then he looked startled for a second before his gaze shot toward Holmes. He started to say something, and then stopped himself.

We stepped over toward the desk. I was happy to let MacDonald precede me, since he didn't know what it said, while I did. Holmes reached across and lifted the envelope off the opened book. He pulled out the two handwritten sheets, and held them so MacDonald could read them over his shoulder.

"So the young man *does* inherit everything," MacDonald said. "No surprise, from what I've heard. And on the day after his wedding, too." Holmes handed MacDonald the will and the envelope. MacDonald looked at them, thoughtful for a moment, and then his natural suspicions took over. "You don't think that George Burton might have had something to do with this, do you?" He waved his arm back toward the bodies. "After all, the timing is quite fortuitous for him."

"Not at all," replied Holmes. "I'm sure that he was spending his wedding night at the inn, and it can easily be verified. No," he continued, nodding his head toward the bodies, "as you said, the evidence indicates that Mrs. Lynch did the deed, for whatever reason. We, all of us, may never know what happened here."

MacDonald walked back over to the chairs containing the old figures, placing the will in his coat pocket as he did so. He leaned down toward Lynch's body, reached out, and picked up the dead man's right hand. He turned it this way and that, examining the outer edge where the little finger should have been. Then, with a deep sigh, he let it drop back onto the dead man's lap.

Inspector MacDonald stood for the longest time, his arms akimbo on his hips. Finally, he shook his head and said, "I've known you for a while now, Mr. Holmes," he said, without facing us. "I want you to know that I trust you. I really do. Your wordplay of a moment ago, about *all of us* may never know the truth, did not pass unnoticed. You may be right that, for now, *all of us* might not know, but I hope that someday *all of us* will. In the meantime, I will continue to trust you."

He turned then, and looked at us, as we both waited expressionless as to what he was going to say. He gave another long sigh, and then a smile. "So, gentleman, and I think that you'll agree with me, this case is closed. And after all, what could anyone really expect us to discover about a fifty-year old mummy from the days of our grandparents, anyway? And regarding these other recent events, what has happened in this room is . . . unfortunate. But that's all it is. Unfortunate.

"But," he added, "I have the wee feeling that this could have been a very complicated mess indeed, more than I know. So I'm thankful for your presence here, Mr. Holmes. I'm certain that, somehow, I owe you a debt."

Holmes's eyes widened, almost imperceptibly, at MacDonald's unknowing word choice.

"And now," MacDonald said, moving toward the door, "shall we go see about arranging to have these people removed, and setting things right as fast as we can, so that new young family can get on with their lives?"

We took our leave soon after. MacDonald chose to stay behind, to tie up any loose ends. Before we departed, Burton managed to meet with us with his new bride at his side, in the sitting room, where he had told us his story the afternoon before. His grief was apparent, and it had only started to sink in that he was now the master of the estate.

"Thank you for coming down, Mr. Holmes," he said. "Inspector MacDonald told me how you found the will hidden in one of Mr. Briley's books. I'm – that is, *we* are in your debt. I can't begin to tell you how difficult matters would have been after his . . . his death, if the estate wasn't settled. I had come to believe that Mr. Briley was preparing me to take the place over after his death, but I was never certain. And I was not prepared for it to be this way, gaining the estate by the actions of Mrs. Lynch."

Holmes glanced my way, noting that I had also heard Burton's statement, which, in spite of his ignorance, was completely accurate.

471

Burton now had the estate through Mrs. Lynch's long-ago efforts, when she placed her brother Peter in Martin Briley's place.

"It is certainly due to what she did that the estate has passed to you," Holmes agreed. "I'm sorry that we couldn't tell you more about the body that was found under the pipe. It has been my experience that some old secrets are never revealed."

MacDonald cleared his throat, but Burton did not appear to notice. It seemed to me that Holmes was walking a little too close to the edge with his cleverly ambiguous but truthful statements.

"Nevertheless," said Burton, "I am very grateful that you were here, if only because you convinced me that it was time to marry Lydia." His hand, which had enclosed her smaller one, seemed to hold tighter as he spoke. "I don't know how I would face this without her at my side." He paused to gain control of himself, and then said, "If there is ever anything that I can do for you . . . ."

"There is one thing that I would request, if it would not be too bold," said Holmes. After I heard what he wanted, I thought that *had* been too bold, and had asked for too much, but Burton did not seem to believe so. Perhaps, if he hadn't been in shock, he would have objected. In any case, he went and retrieved the item, which he placed into Holmes's hands. And then we departed.

Later, on the train back to London, I looked at Holmes, and he understood my unspoken question. "Lynch had taken it on himself to punish his sister, as a final act of courage to make up for his lack of it all those years ago, on the day that Martin Briley was murdered." he said, "He did it in his characteristic way, attempting to repay his quantity of debt by doing the deed so that he could take the blame. If I had left the bottle beside *him*, then MacDonald, and more importantly, young Burton, would have believed that Peter Lynch was the one who poured the final poisoned drink, and then we would have either had to reveal why he felt the need to do it, or left Burton with a doubt about the man who had been like a father to him, and in fact *was* his father. In the end, I did not want to have Lynch take that blame, in spite of the fact that it was true.

"Lynch knew as well as I did the choice that I faced. I could either let both him and his sister go, to live out the rest of their lives unpunished until old age took them, with their secret intact, or I could bring them both down together in order to serve justice. It is possible, perhaps even likely, that, if revealed, Mrs. Lynch might have taken all the blame to save her brother, but it was not certain.

"Lynch knew my dilemma. He had accomplished so much good over his lifetime, paying back his debt, and if it were revealed that he was *not* a Briley, all the effort that he had invested in order to train Burton to carry

472

on his good works would have been wasted. Granted, the estate might have gone on just as successfully as before, but then again, it probably would not have. If nothing else, the story of the long-ago murder would have permanently attached itself to the place.

"I mentioned earlier that at times I've built up my own quantity of debt. Useful phrase, that. Lynch chose to assume the burden of the choice from me and take matters into his own hands as his final payment.

"But even after the deed was done, I did not want Mrs. Lynch to get away blameless from that crime as well, as she had from the murder of Martin Briley, as well as her likely involvement in the deaths of Galton Briley and her own father. And who knows how many more there have been over the years, as she protected both the secret and also her brother?

"It is truly a tragedy, I suppose, that she felt forced into murder all those years ago, and who knows what evils she endured before she was driven to that point? But murder it was, or rather, murders they were, no matter the root causes. It took a lifetime, but in the end, she faced justice, at the hand of her brother."

We rode on in silence for a while longer. Despite the tragedy that we had just uncovered, into which we had been propelled only a day earlier, I felt somehow strangely renewed. Perhaps it was seeing how Lydia had already been such a source of strength for her new husband as he grieved for the old man – they would be fine. Or possibly it was simply looking out of the carriage window as the train rocked back to London, and seeing all of the new spring growth, shining in the mid-morning sun, and washed clean by the storms of recent days. In any case, my mood was one of careful optimism, and it felt as if it must be nurtured, like a tiny spark being encouraged into a flame, or perhaps more fitting on this beautiful spring day, like a tiny seedling into a flower. It was a strange feeling, because I still missed my dear Constance, but perhaps I was also starting to move on.

Holmes had been looking at the item which Burton had given him, just before we departed. It was Lynch's copy of *Great Expectations,* the worn green leather open across Holmes's lap. " *'Pause you who read this, '* " he said, the underlined passage clearly marked in the bright morning sunlight spilling across the yellowed sheet, " *'and think for a moment of the long chain of iron or gold, of thorns or flowers, that would never have bound you, but for the formation of the first link on one memorable day.'* "

He closed the book, and said, "So, are you still considering finding another practice, and moving out of Baker Street?"

I chuckled, and said, "Did you deduce that the question has been on my mind of late?" Before he could respond, I said, "Never mind. By this

473

time, your powers do not surprise me any longer." Then I dropped my eyes as my amusement fell away, and I was silent for a while. Holmes sat quietly, patiently awaiting my answer. Finally, I replied, "Move out?" I cleared my throat, and said in a firmer voice, "No, I do not believe so."

There was more that I wanted to say. That I did not want to face the emptiness of another practice without my wife by my side, with the long hours of work broken by longer hours of loneliness until the next new day began. That I enjoyed the work that Holmes and I did, and found value and reward in it, and that I had finally come to understand that, even if my role was not luminous in and of itself, I could be a conductor of light. Perhaps most of all, I had my own quantity of debt to pay.

I did not realize at the time what the rest of that year would hold. We would meet many more people who needed Holmes's help, and he would provide it, with my assistance. I would continue to aid him in his ever-escalating battle with Professor Moriarty. That fall, I would meet Holmes's brother, Mycroft, for the first time. After the events at the Briley house, I was certain to notice that Mycroft and his brother Sherlock did, indeed, share the same type of ears.

Not long after meeting Mycroft, Holmes and I would become involved in the most trying and convoluted investigation our partnership would ever face, that of the Ripper Murders and the events ever after associated with the vile alleys of Whitechapel. Holmes and I had never faced a more serious crisis as that one, when that evil cabal of madmen united under the flag of death to terrorize a city. They worked together from all levels of society, threatening to engulf us. I cannot imagine any other way that the matter could have been resolved, except by Holmes and me, working in harness together. If I had been back in practice by that point, as I had considered just a day before, all might have been lost, including the British Empire!

But most importantly, that same autumn, I would meet someone who would heal my devastated heart. In the course of one of Holmes's investigations, I would encounter his client, the woman who would become my new wife, Mary Morstan. And if I had gone back into the lonely practice that I had been considering only a day before, I would have forged a completely different set of links on my chain, and my path and hers might never have crossed at all.

So my answer to Holmes, "I do not believe so," was the only reply that I gave. He nodded and took out his pipe. Really, nothing further needed to be said. He scratched a match and puffed until a comfortable flame was evenly burning across the tobacco. I shifted in my seat, and turned back toward the window. After a while, I was excited to see the outskirts of the great metropolis come rolling into view. We were nearly home.

And with any luck, we would not have to wait long for our next adventure to begin.

About the Author

David Marcum plays *The Game* with deadly seriousness. He first discovered Sherlock Holmes in 1975 at the age of ten, and since that time, he has collected, read, and chronologicized literally thousands of traditional Holmes pastiches in the form of novels, short stories, radio and television episodes, movies and scripts, comics, fan-fiction, and unpublished manuscripts. He is the author of over eighty Sherlockian pastiches, some published in anthologies and magazines such as *The Strand*, and others collected in his own books, *The Papers of Sherlock Holmes*, *Sherlock Holmes and A Quantity of Debt*, and *Sherlock Holmes – Tangled Skeins*. He has edited almost sixty books, including several dozen traditional Sherlockian anthologies, such as the ongoing series *The MX Book of New Sherlock Holmes Stories*, which he created in 2015. This collection is now up to 27 volumes, with more in preparation.

He was responsible for bringing back August Derleth's Solar Pons for a new generation, first with his collection of authorized Pons stories, *The Papers of Solar Pons*, and then by editing the reissued authorized versions of the original Pons books, and then volumes of new Pons adventures. He has done the same for the adventures of Dr. Thorndyke, and has plans for similar projects in the future. He has contributed numerous essays to various publications, and is a member of a number of Sherlockian groups and Scions. His irregular Sherlockian blog, *A Seventeen Step Program*, addresses various topics related to his favorite book friends (as his son used to call them when he was small), and can be found at *http://17stepprogram.blogspot.com/*

He is a licensed Civil Engineer, living in Tennessee with his wife and son. Since the age of nineteen, he has worn a deerstalker as his regular-and-only hat. In 2013, he and his deerstalker were finally able make his first trip-of-a-lifetime Holmes Pilgrimage to England, with return Pilgrimages in 2015 and 2016, where you may have spotted him. If you ever run into him and his deerstalker out and about, feel free to say hello!

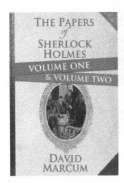 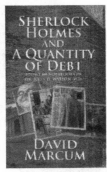 

480

Edited by David Marcum
from MX Publishing
The MX Book of New Sherlock Holmes Stories
(MX Publishing, 2015-)

"This is the finest volume of Sherlockian fiction I have ever read, and I have read, literally, thousands." – Philip K. Jones

"Beyond Impressive . . . This is a splendid venture for a great cause!"
– Roger Johnson, Editor, *The Sherlock Holmes Journal*,
The Sherlock Holmes Society of London

<u>In Preparation</u>
Part XXXI (and XXXII and XXXIII?) – 2022 Annual

. . . and more to come!

Edited by David Marcum
from MX Publishing
The MX Book of New Sherlock Holmes Stories
(MX Publishing, 2015-   )

<u>*Publishers Weekly*</u> says:

Part VI: *The traditional pastiche is alive and well . . . .*

Part VII: *Sherlockians eager for faithful-to-the-canon plots and characters will be delighted.*

Part VIII: *The imagination of the contributors in coming up with variations on the volume's theme is matched by their ingenious resolutions.*

Part IX: *The 18 stories . . . will satisfy fans of Conan Doyle's originals. Sherlockians will rejoice that more volumes are on the way.*

Part X: *. . . new Sherlock Holmes adventures of consistently high quality.*

Part XI: *. . . an essential volume for Sherlock Holmes fans.*

Part XII: *. . . continues to amaze with the number of high-quality pastiches.*

Part XIII: *. . . Amazingly, Marcum has found 22 superb pastiches . . . This is more catnip for fans of stories faithful to Conan Doyle's original*

Part XIV: *. . . this standout anthology of 21 short stories written in the spirit of Conan Doyle's originals.*

Part XV: *Stories pitting Sherlock Holmes against seemingly supernatural phenomena highlight Marcum's 15th anthology of superior short pastiches.*

Part XVI: *Marcum has once again done fans of Conan Doyle's originals a service.*

Part XVII: *This is yet another impressive array of new but traditional Holmes stories.*

Part XVIII: *Sherlockians will again be grateful to Marcum and MX for high-quality new Holmes tales.*

Part XIX: *Inventive plots and intriguing explorations of aspects of Dr. Watson's life and beliefs lift the 24 pastiches in Marcum's impressive 19th Sherlock Holmes anthology*

Part XX: *Marcum's reserve of high-quality new Holmes exploits seems endless.*

Part XXI: *This is another must-have for Sherlockians.*

Part XXII: *Marcum's superlative 22nd Sherlock Holmes pastiche anthology features 21 short stories that successfully emulate the spirit of Conan Doyle's originals while expanding on the canon's tantalizing references to mysteries Dr. Watson never got around to chronicling.*

Part XXIII: *Marcum's well of talented authors able to mimic the feel of The Canon seems bottomless.*

Part XXIV: *Marcum's expertise at selecting high-quality pastiches remains impressive.*

Part XXV: *The variety of plots is matched by the contributors' skills. Once again, those who relish traditional Holmes stories will be delighted.*

Edited by David Marcum
from MX Publishing
The MX Book of New Sherlock Holmes Stories
(MX Publishing, 2015-   )

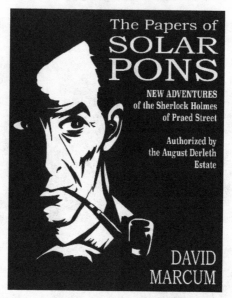

Edited by David Marcum
from Belanger Books

Holmes Away From Home:
Adventures from The Great Hiatus
Volumes I and II

Sherlock Holmes:
Adventures Beyond the Canon
Volumes I, II, and III

Sherlock Holmes: Before Baker Street

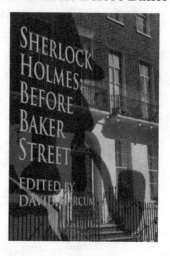

Sherlock Holmes and Doctor Watson:
The Early Adventures
Volumes I, II, and III

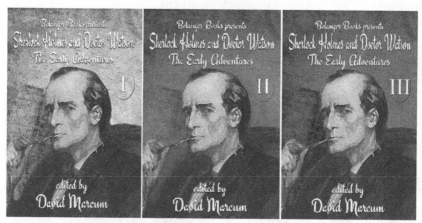

486

Edited by David Marcum
from MX Publishing

Imagination Theatre's Sherlock Holmes

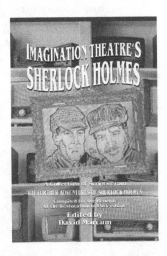

The Further Adventures of Sherlock Holmes:
The Complete Jim French Imagination Theatre Scripts

Edited by David Marcum
from MX Publishing

Sherlock Holmes in Montague Street
by Arthur Morrison
Sherlock Holmes's Early Investigations
Originally published as Martin Hewitt Adventures

Complete Hardcover Edition and Three-volume Paperback Edition

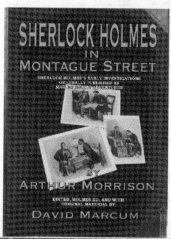

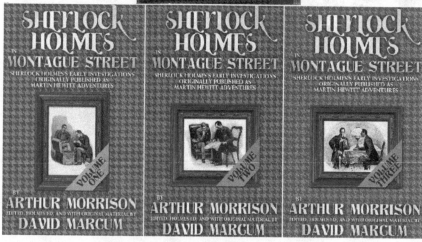

Edited by David Marcum
from MX Publishing

The Complete Dr. Thorndyke
by R. Austin Freeman
Volumes I-IX

Hardcover and Paperback

A Proof Reader's Adventures of Sherlock Holmes
by Nick Dunn-Meynell

Hardcover and Paperback

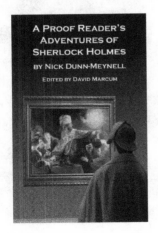

Edited by David Marcum
from Belanger Books

The Complete Solar Pons
by August Derleth

8-volume Paperback Edition

4-volume Hardcover Edition

Edited by David Marcum
from Belanger Books

The New Adventures of Solar Pons

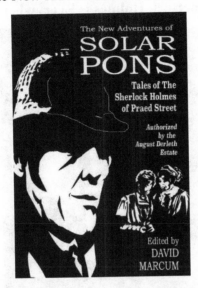

The Meeting of the Minds:
The Cases of Sherlock Holmes and Solar Pons

Edited by David Marcum,
Derrick Belanger, and Sonia Fetherston
from Belanger Books

Sherlock Holmes is Everywhere!

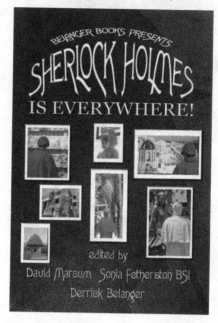

MX Publishing

MX Publishing is the world's largest specialist Sherlock Holmes publisher, with over five-hundred titles and over two-hundred authors creating the latest in Sherlock Holmes fiction and non-fiction

The catalogue includes several award winning books, and over two-hundred-and-fifty have been converted into audio.

MX Publishing also has one of the largest communities of Holmes fans on Facebook, with regular contributions from dozens of authors.

www.mxpublishing.com

@mxpublishing on Facebook, Twitter and Instagram

CPSIA information can be obtained
at www.ICGtesting.com
Printed in the USA
LVHW101116260322
714399LV00030B/250/J

9 781787 058996